FLOWERS
by COLOUR

A Complete Guide to over 1000
Popular Garden Flowers

GENERAL EDITOR
Mary Moody

HORTICULTURAL CONSULTANTS
Kenneth A. Beckett, VMM
Ruth Rogers Clausen

MEREHURST PRESS
LONDON

Published 1990 in Great Britain by
Merehurst Press
Ferry House, 51/57 Lacy Road
Putney, London SW15 1PR

By arrangement with Weldon Russell Pty Ltd

Produced by Weldon Russell Pty Ltd
372 Eastern Valley Way
Willoughby NSW 2068 Australia

A member of the Weldon International Group
of Companies

Horticultural Consultants: Kenneth A. Beckett, VMM,
Ruth Rogers Clausen

Contributors: Joyce Beaumont, Cert. Hort., Cert. Land
Design; Kaye Healey; Cheryl Maddocks, Cert. Hort.; Peggy
Muntz, Assoc. Dip. Hort., MAIH; Graeme Purdy; Lorna
Rose, Assoc. Dip. Hort., MAIH; Harold Wilkes, BA,
FRHS, FAIH, Cert. Hort., past president AIH, FICM.

Principal Photographers: Nan Barbour, Gillian Beckett,
Stirling Macoboy, Lorna Rose

Project Co-ordinator: Christine Mackinnon

Editor: Shirley Jones

Design Concept: Warren Penney

Designers: Christie & Eckermann Art Design Studio,
Catherine Martin,   Kathie Baxter Smith

First published 1990

ISBN 1 85391 123 2

Typeset by Savage Type Pty Ltd, Brisbane, Qld, Australia
Produced by Mandarin Offset, Hong Kong
Printed in Hong Kong

A KEVIN WELDON PRODUCTION

ACKNOWLEDGMENTS

Weldon Russell Pty Ltd would like to thank the following people for their
assistance in the production of this book:

Picture research: Joanna Collard; Jane Lewis; Rosemary Wilkinson

Horticultural advisers: Ross Bond; Tony Rodd; Jan Wilson

Photographers: Adelaide Botanic Gardens; Heather Angel; Ardea London Ltd;
Australian Picture Library; A–Z Collection; Bay Books; Ross Bond; Eric
Crichton; Garden Picture Library; Pamela Harper; Shirley Jones; Tania
Midgley; Photos Horticultural; Pamela Polglase; Graeme Purdy; Tony Rodd;
Royal Botanic Gardens, Melbourne; Don Schofield; Harry Smith Collection;
Smith Polunim Collection; Peter Valder; Weldon Trannies.

Front cover: left to right; top to bottom
Hydrangea macrophylla
Thunbergia grandiflora
Ceratostigma willmottianum
Ranunculus asiaticus
Narcissus (daffodil)
Laburnum anagyroides
Dahlia
Zinnia elegans
Rosa 'Bloomfield Courage'

Endpapers:
Wisteria and *Rhododendrons*, Nooroo,
Mt Wilson, N.S.W.

Page 1:
Cottage garden, Sissinghurst, U.K.

Page 2:
Iris germanica 'Amethyst Flame'

CONTENTS

Rosa 'Cecile Brunner'

HOW TO USE THIS BOOK

This book has been divided into five color groups: orange-red, pink, purple-blue, white and yellow. Each color group is further divided into six plant types: annuals, bulbs, climbers, perennials, shrubs and trees. Within each of these groups entries are listed alphabetically by botanical name. A comprehensive Index of Botanical Names will help you to locate the entry within these major groupings.

If you are unsure of the botanical name of the plant species refer to the Index of Common Names. Where a plant is known by more than one botanical name refer to the Index of Synonyms.

Sample entry
All entries in the book contain the following information.

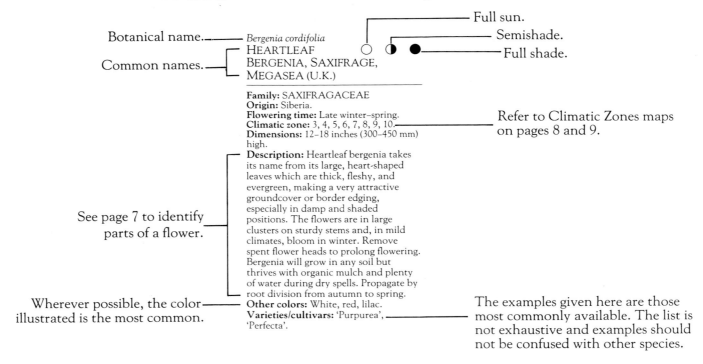

Botanical name. — *Bergenia cordifolia*

Common names. — HEARTLEAF BERGENIA, SAXIFRAGE, MEGASEA (U.K.)

Full sun.
Semishade.
Full shade.

Family: SAXIFRAGACEAE
Origin: Siberia.
Flowering time: Late winter–spring.
Climatic zone: 3, 4, 5, 6, 7, 8, 9, 10.
Dimensions: 12–18 inches (300–450 mm) high.

Refer to Climatic Zones maps on pages 8 and 9.

See page 7 to identify parts of a flower.

Description: Heartleaf bergenia takes its name from its large, heart-shaped leaves which are thick, fleshy, and evergreen, making a very attractive groundcover or border edging, especially in damp and shaded positions. The flowers are in large clusters on sturdy stems and, in mild climates, bloom in winter. Remove spent flower heads to prolong flowering. Bergenia will grow in any soil but thrives with organic mulch and plenty of water during dry spells. Propagate by root division from autumn to spring.

Wherever possible, the color illustrated is the most common.

Other colors: White, red, lilac.
Varieties/cultivars: 'Purpurea', 'Perfecta'.

The examples given here are those most commonly available. The list is not exhaustive and examples should not be confused with other species.

Parts of a flower
To enable you to plan your garden using color every entry is illustrated. To help identify the parts of a flower and their distinguishing features, see the diagrams on page 7.

Glossary
The glossary on page 298 explains many of the horticultural terms readers may not be familiar with and defines some of the more general descriptive terms; for example,

Raceme: a group of flowers arranged along an unbranched stem, each floret having a distinct stalk.

Climatic zones
Each entry lists the climatic zones in which the flowers can be grown. The climatic zones are outlined on the maps on pages 8 and 9. These maps are based on average annual minimum temperatures provided by the United States Department of Agriculture (U.S.D.A.). Regions indicated by the dark areas on the maps on page 9 are, in most cases, suitable for growing plants from zones 8, 9 and 10. Each zone covers a large area and does not take into account changes in altitude, varying rainfall, soil conditions or microclimates. Therefore the zonings should be used as a guide only, with the understanding that most species will adapt to slighter warmer (one zone above) or slightly cooler (one zone below) conditions than those listed. Readers should check with their local garden center to ensure that species are suited to cultivation in a specific area.

Using color in your garden
Before consulting the individual entries in this book, it will be helpful to read the 'Introduction to Using Color in Your Garden'. Color is one of the most striking

elements in a garden and can reflect happiness and vitality, create peace and harmony or result in disarray and discord. It is, therefore, important to understand the effects that color can have when planning your garden.

The introduction explains briefly the symbolism of color, which factors affect the appearance of color, how to use color when designing your garden; for example, how to accentuate space, how to complement the environment, and how to establish particular types of gardens, such as a cottage garden, a rockery, or a more formal garden.

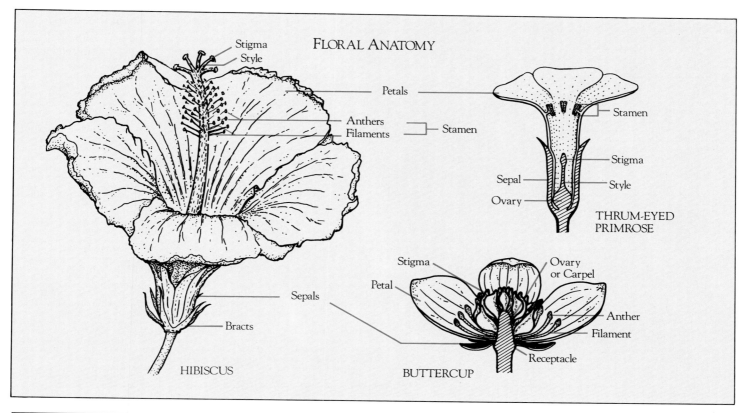

FLORAL ANATOMY

Stigma
Style
Petals
Anthers
Filaments
Stamen
Sepals
Bracts
HIBISCUS

Petals
Stamen
Stigma
Sepal
Style
Ovary
THRUM-EYED PRIMROSE

Stigma
Petal
Ovary or Carpel
Anther
Filament
Receptacle
BUTTERCUP

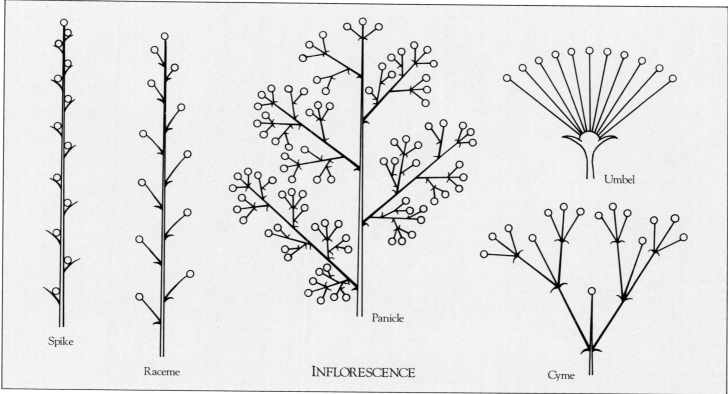

Spike

Raceme

INFLORESCENCE

Panicle

Umbel

Cyme

7

Climatic (U.S.D.A) Zones

	F°		approx. C°
ZONE 1	Below −50°		Below −46°
ZONE 2	−50° to −40°		−46° to −40°
ZONE 3	−40° to −30°		−40° to −34°
ZONE 4	−30° to −20°		−34° to −29°
ZONE 5	−20° to −10°		−29° to −23°

	F°		approx. C°
ZONE 6	−10° to 0°		−23° to −18°
ZONE 7	0° to 10°		−18° to −12°
ZONE 8	10° to 20°		−12° to −7°
ZONE 9	20° to 30°		−7° to −1°
ZONE 10	30° to 40°		−1° to 4°

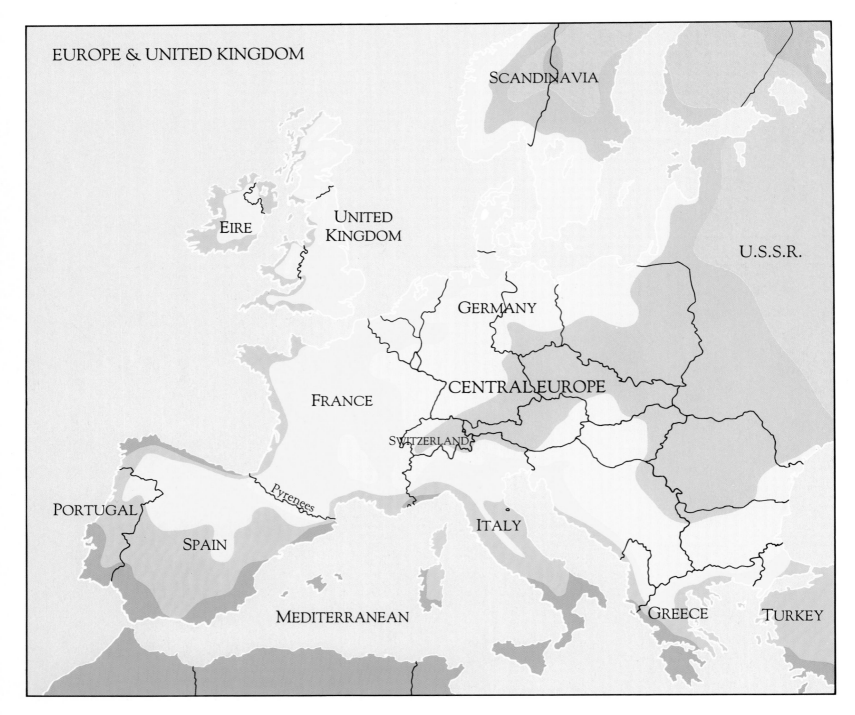

EUROPE & UNITED KINGDOM

SCANDINAVIA

EIRE

UNITED KINGDOM

U.S.S.R.

GERMANY

CENTRAL EUROPE

FRANCE

SWITZERLAND

Pyrenees

PORTUGAL

SPAIN

ITALY

GREECE

TURKEY

MEDITERRANEAN

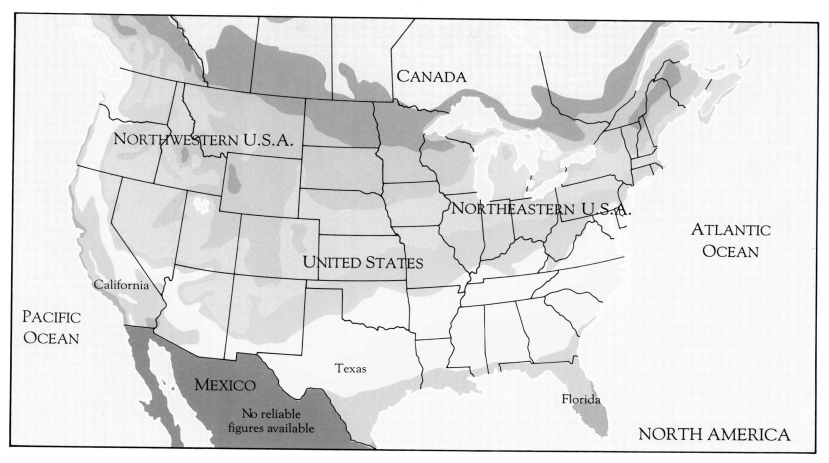

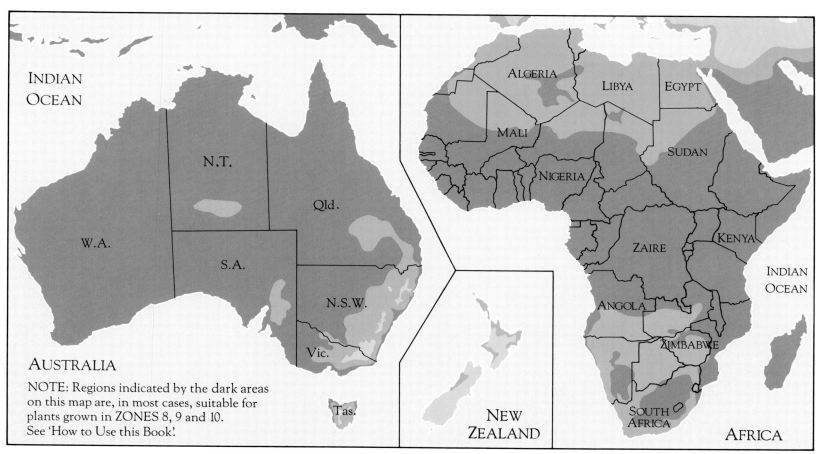

9

INTRODUCTION TO USING COLOR IN YOUR GARDEN

N o other feature in the garden is as important as color. We use color to shape the garden, to create a mood, to add interest, to impose an effect of distance and to create a particular atmosphere in a particular space. Color can be used in many different ways, sometimes to establish a natural effect, sometimes to establish a personal touch.

Color has always had symbolic significance. Bright, vivid colors suggest happiness and vitality. They tend to excite responses and to lead the eye from one area to another in the landscape. Subdued and cool colors suggest reflection and contemplation and can be used to produce a relaxing and peaceful effect.

Flower color is the most striking of the elements used in designing gardens and is often the least understood. We can't really say that gardens are an extension of nature and that therefore all colors 'go' together. In the same way as we can have a clash of color in the garments we wear, we can also have a clash of color in the garden. It is therefore important to understand how color works and how it can be used to create different effects and moods when we are planning a garden.

What is Color?

We have special color receptors in the retina of the eye that react to the wavelength of light. The brain interprets this as color. Unreflected daylight appears more or less white. White light is a combination of all the colors of the spectrum, that is, of the rainbow. If the surface of an object reflects back all wavelengths of light reaching it, the object appears to be white. If the pigment at the surface absorbs all wavelengths except green, then that object appears green.

White Strictly speaking, white is not a color in itself, but a combination of all the other colors of the rainbow. White is a symbol of purity and peace. Because it is light and delicate, it reduces the intensity of adjacent colors and is often used to soften them or to blend in with them.

Yellow One of the brightest of the colors, yellow suggests cheerfulness and liveliness. It has strong associations with the sun and energy and in primitive cultures was used to portray sunlight and signify divine glory. Yellow is associated with emotions such as jealousy and treachery and denotes cowardice. In the garden, yellow can be used to lighten dark corners.

Green Green is the most common color in the landscape. Like blue, it is regarded more as a passive than an active color and suggests contemplative moods. In the environment, green is associated with freshness. Because there are so many different shades of green in nature, it never becomes a boring or dominant color. Green, like yellow, is associated with jealousy.

Because color plays such a very important part in the design of the modern garden, we tend to forget that in earlier times color was not considered at all when gardens were planned. We tend to forget, too, that until recently few ordinary people in the Western world had gardens attached to their houses, although there were possibly cottage gardens around the smaller homes. Most gardens were in public parks, or attached to the larger manor houses or the chateaux and castles of the period. These gardens depended for their effect on the use of form and mass, the three-dimensional shapes of trees, shrubs and small hedges being used in the spatial layout of the grounds. This is particularly the case with the Renaissance gardens. When the gardens at Versailles were designed, the added flower color within the specially landscaped layout was coincidental to the architecture.

Color was not consciously introduced into the design of gardens until the eighteenth century. William Chambers in England is said to have been the first person to plant an area in flowers of the same color.

The use of form and symmetry for effect.

The primary colors

Red, yellow and blue are described as the primary colors, because by mixing one or more of these colors in different proportions, all the other colors can be produced. The color wheel shown illustrates the relationship between colors. The three larger segments show the primary colors of light. Adjacent to each primary color are shades of its secondary color.

Symbolism of color

Red   Red is a popular color in the garden. In early times, peoples such as North American Indians colored their totem poles red, the early African tribes used red clay to fashion their figurines and the Australian Aborigines used red in their rock paintings to contrast with the vegetation. Red symbolises anger, passion, danger and strife. In the garden, the color red draws the eye and is often used to call attention to a specific area. Large expanses of red, however, are tiring to look at.

Pink   Pink is a softer, gentler color than red but, like it, signifies warmth and welcome. It is a color that is affected by adjacent colors and is therefore considered to be neutral. It shows up well at dusk in the half-light and is seen to best effect against silver and gray foliage. Mixing different tones of pink gives the illusion of distance, the colors softening into a gentle blur.

Purple   This color is associated with royalty and the church. Monarchs, and cardinals who can be regarded as 'princes' of the church, both wore purple for ceremonial robes. To Christians, purple symbolizes penitence and celibacy and suggests moods of resignation, melancholia and affliction.

Blue   Blue is the classical symbol of serenity, coolness and passivity, and is often used to suggest loneliness. Because blue does not force its presence upon the eye, it is often used to create an effect of distance and to suggest spaciousness. It can be used as a unifying element in the landscape.

Factors Affecting the Appearance of Color

Many different factors can affect the color of a flower. These fall into three categories: the effects of different sorts of light; the treatment the plants receive; and the actual characteristics of the plants themselves.

Natural phenomena and conditions

Distance affects the appearance of a color. The further away from the viewer a color is, the less impact it has. If a flowering tree, such as a crab apple, is to be viewed from the kitchen window, for example, then it should be planted fairly close to it. The further away it is from this viewing point, the more likely its color is to become diffused by lights and shadows and thus to lose its effect.

Sunlight and shade

The angle of the sun, the humidity, the amount of cloud cover and the temperature will all, separately or together, have an effect on the color of flowers. In regions like Florida, the Mediterranean and the tropical areas of Australia, the light is very much more intense than in the cooler temperate regions of the northern hemisphere, like Britain. This strong light tends to wash out color. The degree of shade will also affect plant color, very vivid colors being softened by shade. Shade can also affect flowers in another way. Flowers such as agapanthus are normally grown in full sun. They will grow in shaded areas, but may not flower so prolifically. Because of this, the flowers do not form such a mass of color and lose much of their visual impact.

Geographical location

Because temperature affects the way we see color, a particular flower will have a different intensity of color in different geographical zones. In warm temperate zones, such as Florida, plants may flower for a longer period than in colder zones, but the color may be less intense. Conversely, in colder climates, as in Britain, for example, the flowering period may be short, but the color more intense.

Intensity of light

We must realize that the quality of the light differs in different parts of the world. In the northern hemisphere, the light is soft, while in the Mediterranean regions, it is brighter, producing harsh contrasts and throwing dark shadows. Time of day also affects light intensity and the way we see color. In the early morning and at dusk, pastel colors appear more vivid than at noon. Colors such as red are difficult to discern in the late evening, but white flowers will shine like beacons. The warm colors such as reds, oranges and yellows have a tendency to appear closer to the viewer than the cooler colors like green and blue.

Treatment

Types of soil

Soil conditions will affect flower color. It is often important to know the pH of the soil (how acid or alkaline it is), but the degree of acidity or alkalinity can be easily controlled by digging in certain substances such as peat or lime, which means that gardeners can adjust soil conditions to suit the plants they want to grow.

The pH of the soil will often affect the color of particular flowers. Hydrangeas, for example, have blue flowers if the soil is acid, and pink flowers if it is alkaline. This is why gardeners add lime to the soil if they want hydrangeas to retain their pink color.

Methods of propagation

The way in which a plant propagates itself may influence its color. A nursery may sell seedlings of pink forget-me-nots. If a gardener plants these near blue-flowering forget-me-nots, the two species may be cross-pollinated. The seeds produced by the pink flowers as the result of this cross-fertilization will produce seedlings that have blue flowers, not pink.

A similar situation can arise with plants that are cultivars. If seeds are taken from an orange-flowering nasturtium cultivar, for instance, there is no guarantee that the seedlings produced will have flowers of the same color as the plant they came from.

Pruning

Pruning can be used to help rectify color 'errors', as, for example, when a plant of a particular color has been inadvertently grown where its color clashes with its neighbors. Heavy pruning can prevent it from flowering until it can be transplanted to a more appropriate position in the garden. In some instances, pruning is used to stop the plants from flowering altogether. In Japan, azaleas are grown purely for their foliage, and have to be constantly pruned so that they do not flower.

Plant characteristics

Shape

The form or shape of a plant will also affect the appearance of its color. The arrangements of its branches, the thickness of its foliage, its shape, will all affect how much light penetrates it. This in turn affects how intense the color of the leaves and flowers appears to the eye. The angles of the branches and stems throw certain shadows that also affect color intensity. Height and width are further factors in the way we see the color of a plant. Flowers growing thickly on a low-growing, spreading plant appear much more vivid and colorful than flowers borne here and there on a tall tree high above the line of sight.

The arrangement of flowers on a plant will intensify or weaken the effect of their color. Dogwood flowers prolifically along the full length of the branches. This makes it appear a much more colorful tree than one like horse chestnut, which bears flowers at the ends of the branches only.

Texture

The texture of the parts of a plant will alter the appearance of color. If both leaves and petals are finely textured, their color appears softer and less intense than in those plants that have dark, glossy leaves and vivid, bold flowers. Dark, glossy surfaces reflect more light than rough-textured ones. This makes the shiny surfaces appear lighter in color than the rough-textured ones that are not so highly reflective. On the other hand, the light reflected from shiny surfaces can make colors round about appear more intense. The dark, glossy leaves of the evergreen magnolia reflect light onto the flowers, which intensifies their whiteness.

There is a strong link between color and texture in plants. Soft pastel colors are associated with fine texture, and bright, vivid colors with coarse textures.

Use of Color in Designing a Garden

We can produce many different effects in the garden by careful use of color. By itself it does little to enhance an area. It is the way it is used, and its association with the other elements in garden design such as line, unity, symmetry, shape and texture, that give color its effect. It is important to have some overall plan or theme. Psychologists have demonstrated that both our physical and mental well-being can be influenced by color. A disorganized and chaotic mass of color in the garden can produce an unsettling and disturbing effect; well-planned use of color can give a sense of peace and calm.

Color composition

There are three types of color composition that we can employ when designing a garden — (a) the use of one color only; (b) the use of complementary colors; (c) or the use of a variety of colors.

Tone of one color.

A variegated color composition.

(a) In a monochromatic composition, we use only the one color, or tones of it, throughout the garden. An example of this is a silver and white garden, using plants that have white flowers and plants that have silver foliage.

(b) Here the dominant color chosen is one of the primary ones, and other flowers grown for accent are mixtures of its opposite, or complementary color. If, for example, in a perennial border we grow yellow flowers as the dominant ones, the others in the mixture would be shades of mauves and violets.

(c) In this type of composition, colors are used at random to create a colorful picture. The cottage garden is a good example of such a composition.

Use of Color to Create Special Effects

Creating the effect of space

When designing a garden, the distance at which particular plants will be viewed is an important consideration. Careful use of color can alter perspective. If, for instance, you wish to make a long, narrow space appear shorter, flowers of warm, solid colors like reds and oranges, planted at the far end of the space, can foreshorten it. Alternatively, the cooler, more subdued colors like greens and blues, appropriately used, can appear to extend it.

Color should not be regarded as merely a decorative medium. It can be used to shape the landscape, enrich the view and disguise unwanted elements. It can be used to produce a relaxing, peaceful atmosphere or a vibrant, busy atmosphere.

Scale

Gardens should be designed so that their scale is appropriate for the size of the grounds they occupy and the size of the buildings they complement. A garden surrounding a two-storey home will need some taller shrubs and trees in it and perhaps a high wall or fence, if it is not to appear too small for the area. As many of today's gardens are small, color can be used to make them appear larger.

Color can be used also to break up areas that appear too solid. If the garden has a boundary wall that is often in shadow, placing pale-colored plants nearby will make the area appear less solid, and this illusion can be heightened by adding a strongly colored mass in the foreground.

Complementary colors.

Color can be used to break up areas that appear too solid.

Use of color in the natural background area enhances the garden.

Background color

The background to a garden may be within the garden itself, or it may lie outside it. It can be composed of trees, shrubs, a neighboring house wall, or features in a neighboring garden or in adjoining open, natural areas. We need to establish whether we wish the background to appear either further back or further forward. This naturally depends on the size of the garden and the spaces within it. In some circumstances, a neutral tone acts as a foil for the range of colors in the foreground. Sometimes it is necessary to plant subdued colors in the background to create an illusion of distance, or finely textured plants can be grown there for the same effect.

Color as accent

An accent color is one that highlights certain areas in the garden. We often wish to draw attention to a particular section of the garden. This can be done by the dramatic use of color. Flowers with a strong, vibrant color can be planted

and a contrasting range of flowers, either in the complementary color or of an entirely different color, planted alongside. The strong, bright colors attract the eye and draw attention to the area. The eye will be drawn from one section of bright color to the next, creating a sense of movement through the garden. Often accent color can be used to induce a sense of excitement or happiness, but if it is overused it will tend to have the opposite effect and defeat its purpose.

Color harmony

Strategic use of color is an important way of achieving harmony in the garden. The intimate areas of the garden should harmonize with one another and the whole garden should also harmonize with the surrounding landscape to avoid a sense of confusion. Restricting the number of colors used will create not only harmony, but a sense of calm as well.

One way of balancing color and creating harmony is to use shadow and the foliage of plants as neutralizing agents to subdue color. Interspersing white flowers and gray or green foliage between color masses tones down the brightness of the masses.

Another way of achieving harmony is to use a sequence of color to give a sense of continuity and to draw the eye in a calm and orderly manner through the garden space. The sequence could move gradually from dark tones of a particular color, through to medium and then light creating a rhythmic pattern of color. Sharp breaks in the visual link will upset this sequential effect.

Cut flowers

Many people use their gardens as a source of cut flowers. Choosing to plant flowers whose colors will harmonize with the different rooms to be decorated and whose blooms, when cut, last well indoors can give the gardener a keen sense of enjoyment.

Accent color draws attention to a particular section of the garden.

Planning the Garden

The seasons

Different flowers are produced at different seasons and gardens can be planned around these seasonal changes. In the milder climates where winter flowerers grow well, we can plan the garden so that there are always some flowers in bloom creating areas of color. Seasons, however, are not always consistent. Variations in temperature and rainfall can result in flowers being produced either earlier or later than normal and in some cases the flowering period can be foreshortened or brought to a sudden conclusion. Nature can prove to be very perverse and we must make allowances for this.

Climate

Climate is, of course, closely connected to geographic location. The color of a flower which is blooming in the snow appears very different from that same flower blooming against a different background. Helleborus and crocus look

Color and neutral foliage are used to create harmony.

far more striking flowering in the snow than in areas where it does not snow. Climate also determines, to a large extent, the length of the flowering period. In England, forsythia is recognized as the first of the spring flowering shrubs, while in Australia it is a winter flowerer. When planning a garden we must take climate into account and choose only those plants which will show to best advantage in our own particular geographic location.

Color to Complement the Environment

The manufactured environment

We must consider the color and texture of the hard landscape elements when we select plants that are going to grow near them. We must choose plants that harmonize with such things as paving surfaces, the texture of a wall, and the nearby garden furniture. Often it is not possible to change materials or the manufactured structures in the garden when desired, and in this case plants can be carefully selected so that the colors neither highlight the undesirable structure, nor clash with it.

Surrounding architecture

When choosing color schemes, the architectural style of the surrounding buildings and the age of the garden are both important considerations. If we want to make a faithful reconstruction of an earlier-style garden, then we will select those species of plant that were available at that particular time. If we merely wish to approximate the style, we will select colors that suit the color scheme of the building, rather than attempt a faithful restoration. This is adaptation rather than restoration. Because of the large number of hybrids on sale today, there is a much greater range of color to choose from than there was in earlier times.

Surrounding landscape

When planning a garden, the surrounding environment

A color scheme to suit the surrounding buildings.

A cottage garden — a place of relaxation.

must be given careful consideration. This is particularly important where a garden adjoins a natural landscape, when flowers should be chosen, not only for their color, but also to harmonize with the landscape. There is an overwhelming desire today to grow the rare and exotic plants, simply because they *are* rare and exotic, rather than to choose what is appropriate for the landscape. If the garden has no natural landscape surrounding it, the choice of flowers is not so important.

Types of Gardens

The cottage garden

A cottage garden is one that provides the owner with all his or her needs in the way of flowers and vegetables. Usually, the space is limited, so plants are crowded together. Vegetables, herbs, fruit trees and flowers are mixed in together, and there is always something ready for picking, whether it is flowers or fruit. The nature of the layout makes this type of garden a happy place to be in; it is not only productive, but also provides a place of relaxation and recreation for the owner-gardener.

The formal garden

The formal garden is characterized by a strong emphasis on line, on symmetry in layout and on the shape of the plants used. It reflects the architectural style of the buildings it encompasses by, perhaps, using plant species that were characteristic of that particular era. The layout is stylized and the plants are set out so that they follow the lines of the paths. The old-fashioned rose garden is a good example of a formal garden.

The wild garden

The wild garden can be simply part of an undisturbed natural environment, or it can be created to simulate such an environment. Regeneration occurs because the plants seed themselves naturally. In general, the plants are massed

A formal garden — the emphasis is on line and symmetry.

A wild garden — plants are massed and grow at random.

and grow at random with no concern for neatness of the garden, the beds are not clearly defined and it is the trees and their canopies that determine the layout. The wild garden, like a wilderness, is a place to lose yourself in.

The rockery

The rockery originated from the gardener's desire to grow the rare and fragile alpine plants. Today, rocks are often brought into the garden to make a suitable environment for such plants. In a garden where there are changes in level, you can retain soil with the aid of rocks, and grow suitable plants in the space between them. If you are lucky enough to have a garden which has natural rock areas in it, it is important not to remove them. Design the garden around them, rather than digging them up to make a rock garden.

•   •   •   •   •

There are numerous different styles of garden, usually designed to suit the style of the architecture, the size of the grounds and individual taste. Today we place great emphasis on color in the design of the garden.

Color should not be regarded as merely a decorative medium. It can be used to shape the landscape, to enrich the view and to disguise unwanted elements. With proper thought and planning it is possible to use color to achieve many different effects in the garden and to produce many different sorts of atmosphere from the relaxing and peaceful to the vibrant and busy. By discriminating use of color, we can make our gardens functional and aesthetic retreats from the hurly-burly of the modern world.

JAN WILSON

A rockery — a place for rare or fragile plants, or to utilize different levels in the garden.

ORANGE·RED FLOWERS

Alonsoa warscewiczii
MASK FLOWER ○

Family: SCROPHULARIACEAE
Origin: Peru.
Flowering time: Summer.
Climatic zone: 6, 7, 8, 9, 10.
Dimensions: Up to 2 feet (600 mm) high.
Description: This subtropical plant produces its small, individual flowers in terminal racemes. It is usually well-branched which shows off its bright, flat flowers, whose petals curl slightly outwards at the extremities. Mask flower may be grown in any well-drained soil, outdoors as an annual or in a greenhouse.
Varieties/cultivars: There is a compact form A. *compacta* growing to 12 inches (300 mm) high.

Alonsoa warscewiczii

Amaranthus caudatus
KISS-ME-OVER-THE-GARDEN-GATE (U.S.A.), ○
LOVE-LIES-BLEEDING (U.K.),
TASSEL-FLOWER

Family: AMARANTHACEAE
Origin: Tropical Africa, South America.
Flowering time: Summer.
Climatic zone: 6, 7, 8, 9, 10.
Dimensions: Up to 3 feet (1 meter) high.
Description: This tall, annual plant is eye-catching with its minute, red flowers clustered in dense, pendant tails which are sometimes more than 15 inches (400 mm) long. Grow in any well-drained garden soil but add compost or well-rotted manure prior to planting. Best suited to large spaces where it can be displayed as a feature. It needs plenty of sunshine.
Varieties/cultivars: 'Viridis' (green flowers).

Amaranthus caudatus

Amaranthus tricolor

Amaranthus tricolor
JOSEPH'S-COAT, ○
FOUNTAIN PLANT

Family: AMARANTHACEAE
Origin: Tropical Africa.
Flowering time: Summer.
Climatic zone: 9, 10.
Dimensions: Up to 4 feet (over 1 meter) high.
Description: Joseph's-coat, as its name indicates, has multi-colored foliage which is most striking in massed plantings. The flowers are red and, although tiny, appear in dense spike-like clusters hidden among the foliage which is flushed or striped with many shades of yellow, orange, and red. Protect from snails while seedlings are young, and water well during hot weather.
Varieties/cultivars: 'Splendens' (red foliage, red flowers), var. *salicifolius* (narrow leaves).

Antirrhinum majus
COMMON SNAPDRAGON, ○
TOAD'S MOUTH

Family: SCROPHULARIACEAE
Origin: Southwestern Europe.
Flowering time: Late summer–autumn.
Climatic zone: 6, 7, 8, 9, 10.
Dimensions: Up to 3 feet (1 meter) high.
Description: Snapdragon is usually classed as an annual, but may persist as a short-lived perennial. Its tall stems, well-clothed with foliage, are topped by racemes of showy, tubular flowers. The strong stems and long-lasting flowers make snapdragon ideal for tall floral arrangements. Although old-fashioned, it is still popular in the garden because of its height and versatility. The dwarf varieties available in segregated or mixed colors make it an excellent massing or border flower. Plant seedlings in an open, sunny position in moderately rich and well-drained soil.
Other colors: White, cream, yellow, pink, purple.
Varieties/cultivars: 'Tetraploid', 'Guardsman', 'Floral Carpet' (dwarf), 'Little Darling' (semidwarf).

Antirrhinum majus

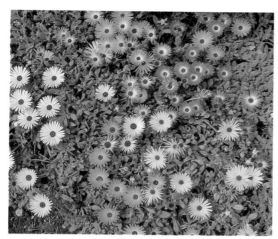

Dorotheanthus bellidiformis

Dorotheanthus bellidiformis syn.
Mesembryanthemum criniflorum
LIVINGSTONE DAISY ○

Family: AIZOACEAE
Origin: South Africa.
Flowering time: Early summer–autumn.
Climatic zone: 6, 7, 8, 9, 10.
Dimensions: Up to 3 inches (75 mm)
high.
Description: A dwarf plant,
Livingstone daisy is frost-tender,
preferring warmer weather. It has
succulent foliage, a mat-forming habit,
and short, spreading, flat, daisy-like
flowers up to 2 inches (50 mm) in
diameter. The original flower was rosy-
red with white centers but the plant is
now available in mauve, orange, and
yellow, usually with a ring of white near
the center. The colors are iridescent and
the flowers make an excellent annual
border in hot, dry climates. In dull or
wet conditions, they will close, as they
also do at night. It tolerates poor, dry
soil, but prefers a well-drained, sunny
site.
Other colors: See Description.
Varieties/cultivars: 'El Cerrito'.

Eschscholzia californica
CALIFORNIAN POPPY ○

Family: PAPAVERACEAE
Origin: United States (west coast).
Flowering time: Summer–autumn.
Climatic zone: 6, 7, 8, 9, 10.
Dimensions: Up to 12 inches (300 mm)
high.
Description: Californian poppy, the
official floral emblem of California, is a
hardy annual or short-lived perennial
that seeds prolifically, so it is wise to
locate it where it can spread without
interference. The brilliant open flowers,

Eschscholzia californica

which are complemented by the fine,
fern-like, gray-green foliage, fold at
dusk, but make a vivid show in strong
sunlight. They are not suitable for
indoor decoration. The plant tolerates a
wide range of soils, but dislikes
continued dampness.
Other colors: Creamy-white, yellow,
gold, pink.
Varieties/cultivars: Among many
varieties are 'Alba', 'Crocea', 'Rosea',
'Mission Bells', 'Ballerina', 'Double
Mixed'.

Mirabilis jalapa
FOUR-O'CLOCK, ◑
MARVEL-OF-PERU

Family: NYCTAGINACEAE
Origin: Central South America.
Flowering time: Summer.
Climatic zone: 6, 7, 8, 9, 10.
Dimensions: Up to 3 feet (1 meter) high.
Description: This is a perennial plant

Mirabilis jalapa

which may be grown as an annual. It is
soft-wooded, of bushy habit, and
produces terminal flowers. It is called
four-o'clock because its flowers open in
the late afternoon and may even remain
open through the night. The fragrant
flowers, which cover the outside of the
plant, are tubular and flare out to about
1 inch (25 mm) across. They seed
prolifically. The foliage is easily bruised
but recovers quickly from damage. Plant
in full sun, in light, well-drained soil.
Water regularly or they will droop in
hot weather. Feed monthly from spring
through summer.
Other colors: Pink, white, yellow.

Papaver nudicaule

Papaver nudicaule
ICELAND POPPY ○

Family: PAPAVERACEAE
Origin: Sub-arctic region in Europe, Asia,
North America.
Flowering time: Late winter–early spring.
Climatic zone: 5, 6, 7, 8, 9, 10.
Dimensions: Between 10 and 18 inches
(250–450 mm) high.
Description: Iceland poppies make a
distinctive floral display, with their cup-
shaped flowers on naked, hairy stems.
They like a sunny aspect where they are
protected from the wind. The showy,
papery flowers emanate from pairs of
boat-shaped, hairy sepals. Poppies are
very suitable for mass planting as well as
for harvesting as cut flowers. They may
be picked in bud to open later indoors.
Iceland poppies prefer cool climates and
light, well-drained soil. The plants
should be sustained on complete
fertilizer, but should not be allowed to
produce flowers too early.
Other colors: White, cream, yellow,
pink.
Varieties/cultivars: 'Spring Song',
'Coonara', 'Artists Glory', 'Rimfire'.

Papaver rhoeas

Papaver rhoeas
FLANDERS POPPY, SHIRLEY OR CORN POPPY (U.K.) ○

Family: PAPAVERACEAE
Origin: Europe, Asia.
Flowering time: Summer.
Climatic zone: 4, 5, 6, 7, 8, 9, 10.
Dimensions: Up to 3 feet (1 meter) high.
Description: This is the common European poppy, seen often among the fields of wheat (corn) in Europe where it is regarded as a weed. In cultivation, it becomes a hardy, colorful annual with wiry stems and sparse foliage. The short-lived flowers are borne singly at the top of each stem well above the foliage; they are mostly single red, with very noticeable black stamens. Removing the spent blooms encourages flowering. Shirley poppies like full sun, rich soil, and good drainage. Seed may be sown directly into the ground after adequate preparation. They are best displayed in the landscape as a mass planting or at the back of a perennial border.
Other colors: White, pink, and bicolors.

Penstemon x *gloxinioides*
PENSTEMON ○ ◑

Family: SCROPHULARIACEAE
Origin: Hybrid.
Flowering time: Spring–summer.
Climatic zone: 5, 6, 7, 8, 9, 10.
Dimensions: Up to 3 feet (1 meter) high.
Description: Penstemon is a hardy perennial which may be grown as an annual. It produces several sturdy stems from the base, with flowers covering the terminal racemes. The plant is stiff and erect and lends charm to the cottage garden. As a vase flower, it is long-lasting and because of its long stems, is a favorite in large flower arrangements and bouquets. Penstemons require full sun or at least four hours of sunlight daily. They may be propagated by cuttings in late summer. Penstemon prefers a loose, gravelly soil with excellent drainage. Ensure there is some wind protection.
Other colors: Pink, mauve, blue, white.

Penstemon x *gloxinioides*

Salpiglossis sinuata
PAINTED-TONGUE (U.K.), VELVET TRUMPET FLOWER ○

Family: SOLANACEAE
Origin: Chile, Peru.
Flowering time: Summer.
Climatic zone: 4, 5, 6, 7, 8, 9, 10.
Dimensions: Up to 2 feet (600 mm) high.
Description: This is a hardy annual which grows into a many-branched, rather slender plant, bearing brightly-colored flowers each 2 inches (50 mm) in diameter. Most colors have a herringbone marking on the petal, but this is not as noticeable with the reds and purples. Its profusion of blooms makes *Salpiglossis* ideal for cutting and indoor use. Good drainage is important as root rot is a problem. Add plenty of well-rotted compost to the ground prior to planting.
Other colors: Yellow, mauve, cream.

Salvia splendens

Salvia splendens
SCARLET SAGE ○ ◑

Family: LABIATAE
Origin: Brazil.
Flowering time: Summer, autumn, winter.
Climatic zone: 4, 5, 6, 7, 8, 9, 10.
Dimensions: Up to 2 feet (600 mm) high.
Description: *Salvias*, with their strong, upright, shrubby growth habit, provide a vivid display of scarlet flowers. They are best used in borders or in association with perennials where a focal point is required. *Salvias* flower about four months after sowing and in cool climates require a heated glasshouse for germination. They need a sunny location and are tolerant of a wide range of soils.
Other colors: White, pink, dark-purple.
Varieties/cultivars: 'Blaze of Fire', 'Salmon Pigmy', 'White Fire', 'Purple Blaze', 'Tom Thumb' (dwarf).

Salpiglossis sinuata cultivar

Senecio x *hybridus* cultivar

Senecio x *hybridus*
CINERARIA ◑

Family: COMPOSITAE
Origin: Hybrid.
Flowering time: Late winter–spring.
Climatic zone: 9, 10.
Dimensions: Up to 3 feet (1 meter) high.
Description: Cineraria is a perennial, but is best grown as an annual. It is slow to develop from seed, but the floral display makes the wait worthwhile. The flower clusters are up to 12 inches (300 mm) across and are composed of numerous daisy-like flowers, about 2 inches (50 mm) wide, many having a white circle towards the center. The color range, though wide, does not include yellow or gold. The plant requires protection from full sun, frosts, and strong wind. Apart from its use as a mass bedding display, cineraria may be potted to provide vivid color indoors. This is especially so in cold climates where it does best under glass.
Other colors: Brown, pink, blue, purple, bicolors.
Varieties/cultivars: 'Stellata', 'Multiflora', 'Californian Giant', 'Grandiflora Nana', 'Prized Mixed', 'Exhibition', 'Berliner Market'.

Ursinia anthemoides
DILL LEAF ○

Family: COMPOSITAE
Origin: South Africa.
Flowering time: Summer.
Climatic zone: 4, 5, 6, 7, 8, 9, 10.
Dimensions: Up to 12 inches (300 mm) high.
Description: This charming low-

Ursinia anthemoides

growing annual is similar to arcotis, except for its delightfully fine, feathery foliage. The flowers are prolific and daisy-like, with purple centers and bright yellow-orange petals. Seeds for this annual should be sown in late winter or spring in average soil with good drainage. In cold climates, sow under glass. Over-rich soil encourages foliage production at the expense of flowers. Choose a sunny position and water daily until germination, which is usually rapid. When established, the plants require little or no maintenance. Dill leaf is an excellent border specimen.
Other colors: Various shades of orange.
Varieties/cultivars: Some hybrid forms.

Zinnia elegans
ZINNIA ○

Family: COMPOSITAE
Origin: Mexico.
Flowering time: Summer.
Climatic zone: 5, 6, 7, 8, 9, 10.
Dimensions: Up to 2½ feet (750 mm) high.
Description: Zinnias prefer a warm, sheltered position in the garden, where they can enjoy full sun and protection

Zinnia elegans cultivar

from the wind. Their tall, erect stems with clasping foliage can often be brittle. The showy, single or double, daisy-like flowers, which are about 4 inches (100 mm) across, make a striking display in the garden as well as being suitable for cutting. Zinnias take twelve weeks to flower from seed and in cooler climates should be sown later than in warmer ones. The plants are subject to fungal diseases in unusually wet periods.
Other colors: White, yellow, rose-pink, apricot, lavender, purple.
Varieties/cultivars: Many cultivars available including 'Happy Talk' (unusual petals), 'Envy' (lime-green), 'Lilliput' (2½ inches (30 mm) wide — pompom), 'Thumbelina' (dwarf).

Zinnia haageana 'Dazzler'

Zinnia haageana
PERSIAN CARPET, ○
MEXICAN ZINNIA (U.S.A.),
CHIPPENDALE DAISY

Family: COMPOSITAE
Origin: Mexico.
Flowering time: Summer.
Climatic zone: 5, 6, 7, 8, 9, 10.
Dimensions: Up to 2 feet (600 mm) high.
Description: This is a warm-climate bedding plant, producing masses of flowers above deep-green, spear-shaped leaves. The blooms are 2½ inches (60 mm) wide and the layers of ray florets are bright red, with yellow to orange tips. Since the stems are soft, the flowers are not suitable for floral work. The plant flowers for over three months in the garden. Moderately rich soils and shelter from winds are essential.
Other colors: Bicolors.
Varieties/cultivars: 'Old Mexico', 'Persian Carpet', 'Dazzler'.

Canna indica

Canna indica
INDIAN-SHOT, CANNA ○

Family: CANNACEAE
Origin: Central and South America.
Flowering time: Summer.
Climatic zone: 9, 10.
Dimensions: Up to 5 feet (approx. 2 meters) high.
Description: Indian-Shot was first introduced into Europe in 1846 by a French consular agent who planted his "souvenirs" in a garden near Paris. The leaves of this versatile plant were formerly used for wrapping food and its seeds for ammunition and rosary beads. Often seen gracing public parks, it makes a lofty statement amidst lower shrubs. Indian-Shot forms a lush backdrop against a wall and with its small tubular flowers looks especially effective with the foreground planted with zinnia and salvia. It prefers fertile, deep soil in full sun and should be watered regularly. It is one parent of many popular garden hybrids known as *Canna* x *generalis*.

Crocosmia masonorum

Crocosmia masonorum
MONTBRETIA (U.K.), GOLDEN SWAN ○

Family: IRIDACEAE
Origin: South Africa.
Flowering time: Summer.
Climatic zone: 7, 8, 9.
Dimensions: Up to 4 feet (approx. 1 meter) high.
Description: As the common name "golden swan" suggests, this plant has a graceful, arching quality. Its stems of bright orange flowers bend like the neck of a bird. It is a good companion plant with *Gladiolus* as its foliage and growth habit are similar, and they require the same conditions — full sunlight and a well-drained position in deeply prepared soil. The flowers are ideal for cut flower arrangements.

Dahlia hybrids

Dahlia hybrids
DAHLIA ○

Family: COMPOSITAE
Origin: Hybrid.
Flowering time: Summer–autumn.
Climatic zone: 3, 4, 5, 6, 7, 8, 9, 10.
Dimensions: Up to 6 feet (2 meters) high.
Description: Dahlias, which were cultivated by the Aztecs, were introduced into Europe in 1789. A favorite of the Empress Josephine of France, these members of the daisy family were reserved for the royal gardens. Grow them in large beds with their sisters, aster and chrysanthemum, and use the dwarf varieties for borders. Dahlias are much favored by florists during their flowering season. They prefer moist soil, well-dug and fertilized. These sun worshippers were termed "water-pipe" by the Mexicans.
Other colors: Red, orange, pink, purple, white, yellow.
Varieties/cultivars: Single, anemone flowered, collerette, paeony flowered, decorative, ball, pompom, cactus and semi-cactus.

Gloriosa rothschildiana
CLIMBING LILY, GLORY LILY ◐

Family: LILIACEAE
Origin: Tropical Africa.
Flowering time: Spring–summer, northern hemisphere; spring–autumn, southern hemisphere.
Climatic zone: 9, 10.
Dimensions: Up to 5 feet (approx. 2 meters) high.
Description: This is a spectacular lily, which climbs using fingertip tendrils at the tops of its leaves. The bright yellow and red flame-like petals turning to orange and claret curve backwards while the flower stalk itself arches down. A tropical plant, it needs plenty of water and leaf mold. A well-drained but moisture-retaining potting mix is beneficial. Plant it as a backdrop to orchids or train it along a trellis or wall that is partially shaded and protected from the winds. Prune it to ground level when the plant dies back.

Gloriosa rothschildiana

Haemanthus multiflorus

Haemanthus multiflorus
FIREBALL LILY, BLOOD LILY, SCARLET STARBURST (U.S.A.)

Family: AMARYLLIDACEAE
Origin: Tropical and southern Africa.
Flowering time: Spring–summer.
Climatic zone: 9.
Dimensions: Up to 18 inches (450 mm) high.
Description: This exotic member of the amaryllis family has broad leaves and deep-red flowers, followed by scarlet berries. Unable to withstand frost, it is best grown in clumps, in warm but shady nooks. In colder climates, it prefers greenhouse conditions. Ginger lily (*Hedychium gardnerianum*) can be used as a companion for color accent and perfume. The neck of the bulb should be planted just below the surface of well-drained soil. Flower spikes last for one to two weeks.
Other colors: White, orange.

Hippeastrum puniceum
BARBADOS LILY, GIANT AMARYLLIS

Family: AMARYLLIDACEAE
Origin: South America.
Flowering time: Spring, northern hemisphere; spring–summer, southern hemisphere.
Climatic zone: 9,10.
Dimensions: Up to 3 feet (1 meter) high.
Description: These exotic specimens

make ideal pot plants. Up to three or four red trumpet-like blooms are borne on long stems, the strap-like leaves appearing after the flowers. In tropical climates they can be grown outdoors, but in cooler climates they must be grown indoors near a sunny window. The bulb should be two-thirds buried in potting mixture and moved into the sunlight when it sprouts. Feed monthly with weak liquid fertilizer. This lily may be induced to flower in mid-winter.
Other colors: White, purple, orange.

Hippeastrum puniceum

Lachenalia aloides
CAPE COWSLIP, SOLDIERS

Family: LILIACEAE
Origin: South Africa.
Flowering time: Spring.
Climatic zone: 9, 10.
Dimensions: 9–12 inches (225–300 mm) high.
Description: When these hardy plants are mass-planted, their bright flowers look like marching soldiers. Because of their size, lachenalias are especially suited to borders and rock gardens, providing good cut flowers which retain their color even after drying. The foliage is spotted at the base and attractive. The plants may also be grown in pots or hanging baskets and like a seaside environment. Lachenalias attract birds and are almost disease- and pest-free. They grow in any good garden loam. In very cold climates, a greenhouse environment is preferred.
Other colors: Red, orange, white, blue, pink.

Lachenalia aloides

Lapeirousia cruenta syn. Anomatheca cruenta
FLAME FREESIA, PAINTED PETALS (U.S.A.)

Family: IRIDACEAE
Origin: South Africa.
Flowering time: Late spring–summer, northern hemisphere; spring, southern hemisphere.
Climatic zone: 9, 10.
Dimensions: Up to 10 inches (250 mm) high.
Description: These pretty ornamental flowers look well in rock gardens and as pot plants and provide good blooms for cut floral arrangements. Grow them in pots of sandy soil or well-drained pockets in sheltered or warm situations. In cold climates, they prefer a greenhouse. The bright coral-red blooms on long spikes will flower for extensive periods. They resemble miniature gladioli and plants will often self-sow. Divide the bulbs every few years to prevent overcrowding. If placed in a woodland setting, they can be allowed to naturalize.
Other colors: Blue-purple, yellow, white.

Lapeirousia cruenta

Lilium pardalinum

Lilium pardalinum
PANTHER OR LEOPARD LILY ◑

Family: LILIACEAE
Origin: California.
Flowering time: Summer, northern hemisphere; spring–summer, southern hemisphere.
Climatic zone: 7, 8, 9, 10.
Dimensions: 4–6 feet (1.2–2 meters) high.
Description: Belonging to the Turk's Cap group, one of the two main groups of *Lilium*, this is an erect bulb with red and yellow drooping waxy flowers. The tips of the spotted petals curve back almost to the stem. This quick-growing lily bears flowers for many weeks. It does not like being overcrowded nor being disturbed once it is established, but tolerates groundcovers because they give protection to its roots. It is best planted as a feature on its own. Water well.
Other colors: Purple.

Schizostylis coccinea
KAFFIR LILY (U.K.), ○
CRIMSON FLAG, RIVER LILY

Family: IRIDACEAE
Origin: South Africa.
Flowering time: Autumn.
Climatic zone: 8, 9.
Dimensions: Up to 2 feet (600 mm) high.
Description: Renowned for its long spikes of four to six crimson, star-shaped flowers, this lily is a vigorous grower. The flower spikes last well in floral

arrangements. It can be grown successfully outdoors in northern Europe and North America though it cannot tolerate severe winters, and likes positions in or near shallow water, which makes it an ideal ornamental pond plant. A site protected from winds but affording full sun is preferable. It may be propagated by seed or root division.
Other colors: Pink.
Varieties/cultivars: 'Mrs Hegarty', 'Viscountess Byng', 'Major'.

Schizostylis coccinea 'Major'

Sparaxis tricolor
HARLEQUIN FLOWER ○
(U.K.), VELVET FLOWER

Family: IRIDACEAE
Origin: South Africa.
Flowering time: Summer.
Climatic zone: 6, 7, 8, 9.
Dimensions: Up to 18 inches (450 mm) high.
Description: The name *sparaxis* comes from the Greek for "torn" and refers to the torn spathe , or pair of bracts, that encloses the flowers of this species. Several flowers grow on each stem. Borders, large tubs, or indoor containers are all suitable for this sun-loving plant. It will grow successfully in partial shade, but the flowers close in dull weather. Ordinary garden soil mixed with compost gives good results. Protect from frost by lifting the corms when they die down in autumn. Plant again in spring.
Other colors: Red, orange, pink, white.

Sparaxis tricolor

Sprekelia formosissima
AZTEC LILY (U.S.A.), ○ ◑
JACOBEAN LILY (U.K.)

Family: AMARYLLIDACEAE
Origin: Mexico.
Flowering time: Summer.
Climatic zone: 9, 10.
Dimensions: Up to 12 inches (300 mm) high.
Description: These striking crimson flowers resemble fleur-de-lys, the deep-green, ribbon-like leaves developing as the flower dies. The plant was introduced into Europe by the German botanist, von Sprekelsen, in the 18th century. It can be grown in pots or the greenhouse and brought indoors for flowering. If grown in the garden it merits a feature position. Plant the bulbs in light fertile soil mixed with compost, with the neck just below ground level.

Sprekelia formosissima

Tulipa hybrid cultivars

Tritonia crocata
BLAZING STAR (U.K.), ○
WEATHERCOCK, MONTBRETIA
(U.K., U.S.A.)

Other common names: FLAME
FREESIA
Family: IRIDACEAE
Origin: South Africa.
Flowering time: Spring–summer.
Climatic zone: 9.
Dimensions: Up to 18 inches (450 mm)
high.
Description: A showy herbaceous
perennial, *Tritonia* bears orange or
yellow, bell-shaped flowers for several
weeks. Suited to pot-planting, borders
or massed plantings with freesias or
other bulbs. It is called *Tritonia*,
meaning weathercock, because of the
variable directions of the stamens.
Although there are about fifty species,
this is the only one commonly
cultivated. A hardy grower, it likes a
sunny situation in ordinary garden soil
and should be treated like its near
relative, the gladiolus. In cold climates,
a greenhouse environment is preferred.
Other colors: Red, pink, yellow.

Tritonia crocata

Tulipa hybrid cultivars
TULIP ○

Family: LILIACEAE
Origin: Turkey.
Flowering time: Spring.
Climatic zone: 5, 6, 7, 8, 9.
Dimensions: 6–30 inches (150–750 mm)
high.
Description: The tulip was first
introduced into Europe in 1554 by the
Austrian Ambassador to the Sultan of
Turkey. By 1634 the tulip craze had
swept the Netherlands. Fortunes were
made and lost and rare bulbs
commanded high prices. Tulips provide
magnificent color in massed plantings.
In cooler climates they can be grown
indoors in pots and make pretty
window displays. Bulbs should be grown
in slightly alkaline, rich, well-drained
soil. They respond well to fertilizing and
are sensitive to windy areas.
Other colors: Red, white, pink, yellow.

Vallota speciosa
SCARBOROUGH LILY, ○
GEORGE LILY

Family: AMARYLLIDACEAE
Origin: South Africa.
Flowering time: Summer.
Climatic zone: 9, 10.
Dimensions: Up to 2 feet (600 mm) high.
Description: Clusters of scarlet,
trumpet-shaped blooms accompany
leaves up to 2 feet (600 mm) long.
Planting the lily in clumps with white
amaryllis provides dramatic contrast. It
is well-suited to pot-planting or in
garden beds where full sun is available.
In colder climates, the protection of a
greenhouse or warm window sill is
necessary. It thrives in deeply dug, well-
drained soil which has been fertilized.
Other colors: White.
Varieties/cultivars: *V. alba*.

Vallota speciosa

Berberidopsis corallina
CHILEAN CORAL VINE, CORAL PLANT (U.K.) ○

Family: FLACOURTIACEAE
Origin: Coastal forests of Chile.
Flowering time: Summer.
Climatic zone: 8, 9.
Description: The leaves of this scrambling, twining shrub are oblong, 2–3 inches long (50–70 mm), glossy dark-green, and sharply-toothed. Crimson rounded flowers hang in drooping clusters, and are followed by small berries. It is not an easy plant to grow, but it will do best in a cool, lime-free soil with protection from wind and frost. Severe winters can damage or kill it. Unless trained onto a trellis or frame, this evergreen plant will grow as a sprawling mound.

Berberidopsis corallina

Bougainvillea x buttiana 'Scarlet O'Hara' syn. 'San Diego' (U.S.A.)
BOUGAINVILLEA ○

Family: NYCTAGINACEAE
Origin: Hybrid.
Flowering time: Summer.
Climatic zone: 9, 10.
Description: This is one of the most spectacular tropical vines in cultivation, its vivid color being due to the three prominent bracts that surround the small, insignificant flowers. The strong branches have sharp spines. The plant requires sun, heat, and good drainage. Do not overwater. Hard pruning is necessary to control the size of the vine and to promote flowering. Although an evergreen in warm climates, it can become semideciduous or deciduous in

Bougainvillea x buttiana

cooler zones, but only the mature plant can withstand even moderate cold. Usually grown on a sunny wall, bougainvillea can be kept in pots if limited in size, and it can also be trained to a "standard" tree shape.

Campsis grandiflora syn. C. chinensis
TRUMPET VINE, TRUMPET CREEPER (U.K.) ○

Family: BIGNONIACEAE
Origin: China.
Flowering time: Summer.
Climatic zone: 7, 8, 9.
Description: Sprays of brilliant orange-red, trumpet-shaped flowers open out to five rounded lobes. *Campsis* is a strong, deciduous vine with heavy, woody growth, and with aerial rootlets which cling to rough surfaces. In hot climates, hard pruning in winter will promote new vigorous growth for the following year. In cooler climates, pruning is unnecessary. Grow in full sun and give average watering to produce a quick-growing vine. It can withstand salty winds and is a good choice for coastal areas.

Campsis radicans
COMMON TRUMPET CREEPER ○

Family: BIGNONIACEAE
Origin: Southeastern United States.
Flowering time: Midsummer–late summer.
Climatic zone: 5, 6, 7, 8, 9.
Description: A larger and more vigorous vine than *Campsis grandiflora*, this plant will quickly cover a brick, stone, or timber wall. Its attractive foliage has nine to eleven toothed leaflets, and flowers are 3 inch (75 mm) long, orange tubes. Use it for large-scale effects, and quick summer screens, but keep it under control as it can become top-heavy. A cold winter can kill the stem tips, but new growth appears quickly in spring.
Other colors: Yellow.
Varieties/cultivars: 'Flava'.

Campsis grandiflora

Campsis radicans

Clerodendrum splendens
GLORY-BOWER ○ ◐

Family: VERBENACEAE
Origin: Tropical West Africa.
Flowering time: Spring and autumn.
Climatic zone: 9, 10.
Description: Scarlet flowers hang in large clusters on this evergreen shrubby scrambler. Shiny, corrugated, leathery leaves up to 6 inches (150 mm) long give it an attractive appearance. It may be short-lived if not given good drainage

and protection from the wind. To grow as a climber, it will need to be tied and trained to a trellis or wire frame, but can be grown as a mounded shrub. Use it where a light vine is required; it will not become large or invasive. In cold climates, a greenhouse is necessary.

Distictis buccinatoria syn. *Phaedranthus buccinatorius*
MEXICAN BLOOD ○ ◐ TRUMPET, BLOOD-RED TRUMPET VINE

Family: BIGNONIACEAE
Origin: Mexico.
Flowering time: Bursts of flower throughout the year.

Clerodendrum splendens

Distictis buccinatoria

Climatic zone: 9, 10.
Description: The trumpet-shaped, waxy flowers, 4 inches (100 mm) long, have flaring lobes. They are crimson red, with a scarlet sheen and an orange-yellow throat, and are conspicuous because they stand out beyond the foliage. This is a very vigorous vine with rough, leathery, oval leaflets, and needs annual pruning to keep it under control. It will attach itself by tendrils to walls, fences, and sheds. For a quick-growing, dense, evergreen cover, this is a good choice, especially with the added bonus of spectacular flowers. In a cold climate, a greenhouse environment is essential.

Eccremocarpus scaber

Eccremocarpus scaber
CHILEAN GLORY ○ FLOWER

Family: BIGNONIACEAE
Origin: Chile.
Flowering time: Late summer and early autumn.
Climatic zone: 8, 9.
Dimensions: Up to 10 feet (3 meters) high.
Description: This charming climber is rather delicate in appearance, with dainty foliage and bright orange-red, tubular flowers. By no means a vigorous grower, it requires a deep, rich, and well-drained soil, and a sunny, open position. Encourage the young plant to grow on a trellis, and water and feed it frequently, especially during summer. In cool climates, where frosts are a problem, it can be grown as an annual.
Other colors: Yellow, carmine.
Varieties/cultivars: *E. s. aureus*, *E. s. carmineus*.

Kennedia rubicunda

Kennedia rubicunda
DUSKY CORAL PEA ○

Family: LEGUMINOSAE
Origin: Eastern Australia.
Flowering time: Spring and early summer.
Climatic zone: 9, 10.
Description: An excellent evergreen plant for a quick screen on a fence or trellis, the dusky coral pea is also a very good groundcover. It needs sun and warmth, and once established is drought-tolerant. The oval leaves are in groups of three, tough and leathery, with the new growth an interesting silky brown. The red pea-shaped flowers hang down, usually in pairs, and are 1½ inches (40 mm) long. This is a hardy and vigorous vine, but not invasive.

Lapageria rosea
CHILEAN BELLFLOWER, ○
CHILE-BELLS

Family: PHILESIACEAE
Origin: Chile.
Flowering time: Late spring–autumn.

Lapageria rosea

Climatic zone: 8, 9.
Description: One of the most strikingly beautiful flowers, the Chilean bellflower is a highly prized climbing plant for cool districts. A cool mountain zone with rich soil is its preference. The roots should be well mulched to retain moisture and keep an even temperature. The growth is slender, never dense, and the vine needs support to grow up against a wall. Given the right conditions, this is a beautiful plant with trumpet-shaped, waxy flowers, 2 inches (50 mm) long. It is the national flower of Chile.
Other colors: White.
Varieties/cultivars: *L. r.* var. *albiflora.*

Lathyrus grandiflorus
TWO-FLOWERED PEA, ○
EVERLASTING PEA

Family: LEGUMINOSAE
Origin: Southern Europe.
Flowering time: Midsummer.

Lathyrus grandiflorus

Climatic zone: 7, 8, 9.
Description: With smaller leaves than *L. latifolius,* but larger flowers, this hardy, herbaceous, climbing perennial is a popular plant for cut flowers. It is easily grown and long-lived if given adequate water and fertilizer. After it dies down each year, a good mulch over the roots is advisable, and it will produce new shoots from the root clump in spring. It prefers cool conditions, but a sunny position. The flowers, although not fragrant, are charming and useful in floral arrangements.

Lonicera sempervirens
TRUMPET ○ ◑ ●
HONEYSUCKLE,
CORAL HONEYSUCKLE

Family: CAPRIFOLIACEAE
Origin: Southeastern United States.
Flowering time: Summer.
Climatic zone: 7, 8, 9.
Description: This robust, fast-growing climber is evergreen in mild climates, and will tolerate a shady position. Rich orange-scarlet flowers with yellow inside appear at the ends of branchlets, usually in groups of six. The upper leaves are joined in pairs. The flowers are not fragrant but are large, 2 inches (50 mm) long, and rich in color. Good soil and cool roots will result in a handsome vine which should be thinned out occasionally. A support should be provided for its twining habit.
Other colors: Yellow.
Varieties/cultivars: 'Sulphurea'.

Lonicera sempervirens

Manettia bicolor

tendril-climbers. It was believed that features of the flower were representations of the suffering of Jesus Christ. The red passionflower has shiny, wide scarlet petals, 4 inches (100 mm) across. The very free-blooming habit in summer makes it desirable as a cover over pergolas or on fences or, in a cooler climate, it can be grown in large pots and brought indoors in the winter months. It may not flower until two or three years old, but removing old wood in the winter will promote flowering.

Pyrostegia venusta

Manettia bicolor syn. *M. inflata*
FIRECRACKER PLANT, ○ ◐
FIRECRACKER FLOWER (U.K.)

Family: RUBIACEAE
Origin: Paraguay, Uruguay.
Flowering time: Spring, summer, autumn.
Climatic zone: 9, 10.
Description: An evergreen, small, dainty twiner, *Manettia* is an easily managed little plant. The 1 inch (25 mm) long, waxy, tubular flowers are yellow-tipped, and the lower half is covered with bright scarlet bristles. The flowers give a delightful sprinkling of color for many months. It is useful as cover for pillars, and to produce light shade over pergolas. Rich soil and a sheltered position are preferred, and it can be grown among shrubs for protection from cool winters. In cold climates, a greenhouse environment is essential.

Passiflora coccinea
RED PASSIONFLOWER (U.K.), ○
SCARLET PASSIONFLOWER

Family: PASSIFLORACEAE
Origin: Venezuela–Brazil.
Flowering time: Summer.
Climatic zone: 9, 10.
Description: The startlingly beautiful flowers gave the name to this genus of

Pyrostegia venusta
FLAME VINE, ○ ◐
FLAMING TRUMPET, APRICOT
BELLS

Other common names: GOLDEN SHOWER
Family: BIGNONIACEAE
Origin: Brazil, Paraguay.
Flowering time: Winter, spring.
Climatic zone: 9, 10.
Description: In full flower, the flame vine has clusters of slender-tubed flowers hanging like a dense curtain from a woody, evergreen vine. It is an exceptionally vigorous grower, and will cover high walls or roof tops. It produces its best growth when planted in a very sunny position. A strong support is necessary, as new growth drapes over the previous growth, and eventually the vine becomes very thick and dense. It will tolerate wind and mild frost when established, and is improved with regular watering. Adaptable to a greenhouse in cooler areas.

Passiflora coccinea

Quisqualis indica

as a good groundcover, even in fairly poor soil. As it has a habit of taking root from the stems which are in contact with the soil, it can spread over a wide area. It is often grafted to a tall standard to produce a weeping standard rose. The flowers, which are single, deep-red with white centers and yellow stamens, and are about 1½ inches (40 mm) across, hang in clusters.

Rosa 'Bloomfield Courage'

Quisqualis indica
RANGOON CREEPER ○ ◑

Family: COMBRETACEAE
Origin: Burma to the Philippines and New Guinea.
Flowering time: Summer.
Climatic zone: 9, 10.
Description: The slender, dainty flower tubes of the rangoon creeper are 3 inches (75 mm) long, and change from white to pink and crimson. The delicious and unusual fragrance resembles apricots, and is very pervasive at night. Support is needed to train this shrubby vine up over a wall or fence, and it can make climbing stems up to 3 feet (1 meter) long each year. Although it will tolerate some shade, a warm protected site is best. Plant it near an open window to gain the benefit of its distinctive perfume.

Rosa 'Albertine'
ALBERTINE ROSE ○

Family: ROSACEAE
Origin: Cultivar.
Flowering time: Summer.
Climatic zone: 5, 6, 7, 8, 9.
Description: Grown as a rather lax shrub, or trained as a climber, this popular rose has loosely double, large, and richly-fragrant, coppery-pink blooms. The flowers are in clusters of six to ten, and are carried on upright stems

6 inches (150 mm) above the prostrate branches. It is a very useful plant as a groundcover, to cover low walls, or to train up pillars. It is sufficiently vigorous to train up house walls and even over sheds or out-house buildings. Prune after flowering.

Rosa 'Albertine'

Rosa 'Bloomfield Courage'
BLOOMFIELD COURAGE ○

Family: ROSACEAE
Origin: Cultivar.
Flowering time: Midsummer.
Climatic zone: 5, 6, 7, 8, 9.
Description: A trailing plant which can grow stems 10 to 12 feet (3 to 4 meters) long in one season, this rose can be used

Rosa 'Excelsa'
EXCELSA ROSE ○

Family: ROSACEAE
Origin: Cultivar.
Flowering time: Spring.
Climatic zone: 6, 7, 8, 9.
Description: The small, bright crimson flowers on this supple-stemmed climber are double, and produced in great abundance in springtime. It will grow up to 12 to 15 feet (4 to 5 meters), and is often grafted onto the top of a tall stem to create a weeping standard rose. It also

Rosa 'Excelsa'

makes an excellent groundcover, or can be grown over a tree stump, or low wall, or trained up a post or pillar. Pruning in the winter is needed to remove old wood and selectively shorten some of the branches.

Tecomaria capensis
CAPE HONEYSUCKLE ◯ ◐

Family: BIGNONIACEAE
Origin: South Africa.
Flowering time: Autumn and winter.
Climatic zone: 9, 10.
Description: Best used as a clipped hedge, this *Tecomaria* is a rambling, scrambling, shrubby plant with evergreen foliage. It is easily grown in warm districts, but needs to be controlled. New growth comes from the base each year, so the width increases quite significantly. It can be used to cover a bank, or be trained up through a wire frame as a free-standing hedge, or supported against a fence or wall. The orange flowers are prolific, but are reduced with regular clipping.
Other colors: Orange-yellow, pink, yellow.

Tecomaria capensis

Thunbergia alata
ORANGE CLOCK VINE, ◯
BLACK-EYED SUSAN VINE
(U.S.A.)

Family: ACANTHACEAE
Origin: Tropical Africa.
Flowering time: Late summer–autumn.
Climatic zone: 5, 6, 7, 8, 9, 10.
Description: This well-known twining perennial vine has toothed, triangular

Thunbergia alata

leaves on little winged stems. The slender stems and light appearance are deceptive. It is able to cover a shed or a sloping bank very quickly. The funnel-shaped orange flowers are a colorful addition to a dreary corner. It is easily kept under control if grown as an annual (especially in cooler districts). It prefers a sunny position and foliage will be thicker and more attractive if adequate water is provided.
Other colors: Creamy-yellow, white.

Tropaeolum speciosum
FLAME CREEPER ◯

Family: TROPAEOLACEAE
Origin: Chilean Andes.
Flowering time: Summer.

Tropaeolum speciosum

Climatic zone: 7, 8, 9, 10.
Description: From five to seven leaflets make up the small circular leaves of this climbing perennial herb. The fleshy tubers produce new growth each year. The curious-looking flowers have a scarlet spur and yellow petals, and look like little, tailed balloons. This is a very pretty summer-flowering twiner, and should have support to hold it in place. Wire frames can be used, which will be quickly covered, or it can be grown in a hanging basket for summer display. In cold areas, it will flower in spring under glass.

Tropaeolum tricolorum

Tropaeolum tricolorum
CLIMBING NASTURTIUM, ◯
TRICOLORED INDIAN CRESS

Family: TROPAEOLACEAE
Origin: Chile.
Flowering time: Spring–summer.
Climatic zone: 9.
Description: Unusual, beautiful flowers appear on this herbaceous climbing perennial. It has a fast-growing habit, with the fleshy roots producing new growth in the spring. The flowers are about 1½ inches (40 mm) wide with little "stemmed" petals which give an open, delicate appearance. They are vivid scarlet with yellow at the base. The vine itself likes the sun, but the roots should be kept cool and moist, and protected from temperature changes. Neutral to acid soil is essential. Severe winters can kill this plant.

Alstroemeria aurantiaca

Alstroemeria aurantiaca
PERUVIAN LILY, ○ ◑
CHILEAN LILY

Family: ALSTROEMERIACEAE
Origin: South America.
Flowering time: Summer.
Climatic zone: 8, 9.
Dimensions: Up to 3 feet (1 meter) high.
Description: Although the Peruvian lily is quite hardy, it is both drought- and frost-susceptible, and requires well-drained, moist soil and shelter. Its showy flowers are valued as pot specimens and for cut flower arrangements. It can be naturalized under trees or grown in cool greenhouse conditions, but it is best in an open, sunny, sheltered site. Propagate it from root division in autumn after the rapid root increase of summer, or propagate from seed. Peruvian lily is a handsome companion for agapanthus and scabiosa in a sheltered border.
Other colors: Pink, yellow.
Varieties/cultivars: 'Dover Orange', 'Moerhaim Orange', 'Lutea'.

Anigozanthos manglesii
KANGAROO-PAW ○

Family: HAEMODORACEAE
Origin: Western Australia.
Flowering time: Late spring–summer.
Climatic zone: 9.
Dimensions: Up to 6 feet (2 meters) high.
Description: *A. manglesii* is an easy species of kangaroo paw to grow. Although

it is susceptible to cold, high humidity, and fungal disease, it is worth growing for its unusual and exotically colored flowers and its red woolly stems. It prefers sandy, well-drained soil and requires manure and plenty of water in spring. With its narrow strap-like foliage and interesting flowers it makes an impressive show. It is a good cut flower, fresh or dried.
Other colors: Yellow, green, pink.

Anigozanthos manglesii

Aquilegia canadensis
COMMON ○ ◑
COLUMBINE, CANADIAN
COLUMBINE (U.K.)

Family: RANUNCULACEAE
Origin: North America.
Flowering time: Early summer.

Climatic zone: 3, 4, 5, 6, 7, 8, 9.
Dimensions: Up to 18 inches (450 mm) high.
Description: Aquilegias are one of the loveliest of perennials for the spring border. *C. canadensis* has yellow petals with red sepals and spurs and looks well planted with the strong blue of *cynoglossum* and the white of *Anemone sylvestris*. It prefers a well-drained, sandy loam and liquid fertilizer during its growth period. In hot climates a semi-shaded aspect is preferable and plants will be short-lived if allowed to become waterlogged. It self-sows modestly in cold climates and is a good cut flower.

Aquilegia hybrids
COLUMBINE ○ ◑

Family: RANUNCULACEAE
Origin: U.K.
Flowering time: Early summer.
Climatic zone: 3, 4, 5, 6, 7, 8.

Aquilegia hybrids

Aquilegia canadensis

Dimensions: Up to 2½ feet (750 mm) high.

Description: Aquilegias come in myriad colors and in single and double varieties. Their foliage is dainty and rather like coarse maidenhair fern. The taller cultivars are most suited to the herbaceous border and the smaller ones for rockeries. Some aquilegias are propagated by root division in spring; others are best left to self-sow, which they do profusely in cool, moist conditions. They are frost-resistant, but drought-susceptible, and are best grown in well-drained, sandy loam. They look attractive if left to naturalize under deciduous trees, and are good as cut flowers.

Other colors: Pink, blue, white, yellow, purple.

Varieties/cultivars: 'Snow Queen', 'Nora Barlow', 'McKana Hybrids', 'Laudham Strain'.

Astilbe x *arendsii*
ASTILBE, FALSE SPIREA

Family: SAXIFRAGACEAE
Origin: Hybrid.
Flowering time: Summer.
Climatic zone: 4, 5, 6, 7, 8, 9.
Dimensions: Up to 4 feet (approx. 1 meter) high.
Description: Astilbes are seen at their best in partial shade. Naturalized under trees and beside ponds they are spectacular. However, they will grow in the herbaceous border provided they have rich, moist soil. Their foliage is as pretty as their feathery flowers and often has a coppery-pink tinge. The

Astilbe x *arendsii*

plants are best propagated from root division in autumn and early spring. Astilbes are heavy feeders, so fertilize well in spring and summer. Cut back in autumn and divide every three years. They are a showy cut flower.

Other colors: White, pink.

Varieties/cultivars: 'Feuer', 'Bressingham Charm'.

Astilbe x *crispa*
GOATSBEARD

Family: SAXIFRAGACEAE
Origin: Hybrid.
Flowering time: Summer.
Climatic zone: 5.
Dimensions: Up to 10 inches (250 mm) high.
Description: *Astilbe* x *crispa*, with its salmon-pink, feathery flowers, is an excellent choice for rockeries, especially those surrounding small ponds. It is also lovely when grown edging pathways beneath established deciduous trees. Its requirements are moist soil and semishade. As plants reproduce rapidly, division every few years is advisable. Propagate from root division in autumn and early spring.

Varieties/cultivars: 'Perkeo', 'Peter Pan', 'Gnome', and several others.

Astilbe x *crispa*

Centaurea dealbata 'Steenbergii'
WILD CORNFLOWER

Family: COMPOSITAE
Origin: Caucasus.
Flowering time: Summer.
Climatic zone: 4, 5, 6, 7, 8.
Dimensions: Up to 3 feet (900 mm) high.
Description: *Centaurea dealbata* 'Steenbergii' is valuable in the herbaceous border, both for its foliage and its flowers. Its leaves are lobed and silvery-white on the underside, and its thistle-like flowers are a rich crimson.

Centaurea dealbata 'Steenbergii'

The plant looks showy when grown with *Lavandula angustifolia* and *Catananche caerulea*. It requires a light, dry but fertile soil, and may need to be staked. Propagate it by root division in spring or sow in autumn or spring. As a cut flower, it forms a splash of color indoors.

Other colors: Pink, purple.

Centranthus ruber
RED VALERIAN (U.K.), JUPITER'S BEARD

Family: VALERIANACEAE
Origin: Mediterranean region.
Flowering time: Summer.
Climatic zone: 7, 8, 9.
Dimensions: 2–3 feet (600–900 mm) high.
Description: Red valerian is an herbaceous perennial which grows pleasantly bushy. It thrives in any well-drained soil and needs little attention apart from the cutting back of spent flowers. Often used for dry situations where other plants do not do well, it self-sows profusely and can become a problem if not contained. Propagate it from seed in spring or soft tip cuttings. Red valerian looks well planted with *Veronica spicata* and *Iberis sempervirens*, and is a good cut flower.

Centranthus ruber

Clivia miniata

Clivia miniata
KAFFIR LILY

Family: AMARYLLIDACEAE
Origin: South Africa.
Flowering time: Spring.
Climatic zone: 9, 10.
Dimensions: 1½–2 feet (450–600 mm) high.
Description: The Kaffir lily can be naturalized beneath large trees. With shelter from hot summer sun and winter frosts, good drainage, and plenty of compost, it will reward you with a dazzling floral display in spring. In cold climates it needs to be grown under glass. This is followed by a crop of deep crimson berries from late summer into winter. It needs to be kept moist in spring and summer, but needs drier conditions in autumn and winter. Propagation is by root division after spring flowering. Large clumps provide a showy effect. It is an excellent cut flower and pot specimen.
Varieties/cultivars: 'Grandiflora'.

Dianthus deltoides
MAIDEN PINK ○

Family: CARYOPHYLLACEAE
Origin: Europe.
Flowering time: Late spring.
Climatic zone: 4, 5, 6, 7, 8, 9.
Dimensions: Up to 10 inches (250 mm) high.
Description: Maiden pink, with its spreading habit and neat mat-like appearance, makes an excellent groundcover, border edging, and rockery plant. It requires very well-drained alkaline soil and good air

Dianthus deltoides

circulation, so do not mulch. Propagation is by cuttings in late summer, root division or seed in spring. Extend flowering by cutting back spent flowers and prune the flowering stems in autumn. As long as they do not crowd it out, it looks lovely grown with *Bellis perennis*, *Myosotis scorpioides* and *Cerastium tomentosum*. This is an excellent cut flower.
Other colors: Pink, white with crimson eye.
Varieties/cultivars: 'Albus' and some others.

Euphorbia griffithii 'Fireglow'

Euphorbia griffithii 'Fireglow'
FIREGLOW ○ ◑

Family: EUPHORBIACEAE
Origin: Cultivar.
Flowering time: Early summer.
Climatic zone: 5, 6, 7, 8, 9.
Dimensions: Up to 3 feet (1 meter) high.

Description: Fireglow is one of the hardier euphorbias. It is perennial, with attractive veined foliage, and produces masses of rich orange flowers for about 2 months in early summer. The color is actually in the bracts, not the petals. It prefers semishade and is easy to grow in any moderately fertile, well-drained soil. Propagation is by cuttings or root division. Care should be taken to avoid contact with the sticky, milky substance exuded by all euphorbias when cut. At best it is an irritant, at worst poisonous.

Gaillardia x *grandiflora*
BLANKET FLOWER ○

Family: COMPOSITAE
Origin: Hybrid.
Flowering time: Summer.
Climatic zone: 4, 5, 6, 7, 8, 9.
Dimensions: 1–3 feet (300–900 mm) high.
Description: Gaillardias come in dazzling shades of red and yellow and are particularly showy if planted en masse. They tend to get a bit untidy, so if this is a problem, choose the more compact dwarf variety, 'Goblin'. They are fussy about soil in that they need it to be exceptionally well-drained in autumn and winter. Any summer dryness can be counteracted with mulch. Liquid manure is beneficial at the budding stage. Propagation is by root division in autumn or spring. Gaillardias are good cut flowers.
Other colors: Yellow, deep crimson, bicolors.
Varieties/cultivars: 'Burgundy', 'Copper Beauty', 'Dazzler', 'Yellow Queen'.

Gaillardia x *grandiflora*

Gazania x *hybrida*

Gazania x *hybrida*
GAZANIA, TREASURE FLOWER ○

Family: COMPOSITAE
Origin: Hybrid.
Flowering time: Summer.
Climatic zone: 8, 9, 10.
Dimensions: Up to 12 inches (300 mm) high.
Description: Gazanias are available in trailing and clumping varieties, the trailing form being especially useful in rockery and terraced situations. They prefer light (even poor), well-drained soil in full sun and benefit from a dressing of blood and bone in spring. Propagation is by stem cuttings or seedlings in autumn. Gazanias are salt-resistant, so are good in coastal areas, but they are very frost-susceptible and in frost-prone regions should be lifted and stored over winter. The flowers, with their habit of closing in the late afternoon, have no value when picked.
Other colors: White, cream, yellow, pink, green.
Varieties/cultivars: 'Freddie', 'Sunbeam'.

Geum quellyon syn. *G. chiloense*
AVENS ○ ◑

Family: ROSACEAE
Origin: Chile.
Flowering time: Summer.

Geum quellyon 'Prince of Orange'

Climatic zone: 5, 6.
Dimensions: Up to 2 feet (600 mm) high.
Description: This is a charming old fashioned perennial with pinnate, hairy, coarsely toothed leaves and tall stems topped by panicles of brilliant red flowers. Ideal as part of an herbaceous border, it can be grown successfully in any moderately rich soil with good drainage, and will propagate easily from seed.
Other colors: Yellow, orange.
Varieties/cultivars: 'Lady Stratheden', 'Mrs. Bradshaw', 'Prince of Orange', 'Red Wings', 'Starkers Magnificent'.

Heuchera sanguinea

Heuchera sanguinea
CORAL BELLS ○ ◑

Family: SAXIFRAGACEAE
Origin: Southwestern United States, Mexico.

Flowering time: Summer.
Climatic zone: 4, 5, 6, 7, 8, 9.
Dimensions: Up to 2 feet (600 mm) high.
Description: In 1885, several plants of coral bells survived a journey from Mexico to England and were later hybridized. *H. sanguinea* is at home in shaded rock gardens. Mix it in with white primula and dark-blue campanula in borders. Mulched, well-drained soil encourages it to flower freely.
Varieties/cultivars: Many cultivars are available.

Kniphofia uvaria and hybrids
RED-HOT-POKER, TORCH LILY ○

Family: LILIACEAE
Origin: Hybrid.
Flowering time: Spring–autumn.
Climatic zone: 6, 7, 8, 9.
Dimensions: 2–4 feet high.
Description: Red-hot-pokers, with their brightly colored, torch-like flowers erupting from large clumps of grass-like foliage, make handsome specimen plants and are a showy feature in the summer border. They need well-drained, sandy loam with the addition of compost or animal manure. Mulch to protect the crown from freezing in cold climates and to retain moisture during the flowering season. Propagation is by root division in late winter or early spring.
Other colors: Yellow (without *uvaria*).
Varieties/cultivars: 'Yellow Hammer', 'Buttercup', 'Mount Etna', 'Royal Standard' (all of hybrid origin).

Kniphofia uvaria

Lobelia cardinalis
CARDINAL FLOWER ○ ◑

Family: LOBELIACEAE
Origin: Eastern North America.
Flowering time: Summer.
Climatic zone: 4, 5, 6, 7, 8, 9.
Dimensions: 3–6 feet (1–2 meters) high.
Description: The cardinal flower is suitable for both the sheltered border and the cottage garden. It is sun-tolerant but will also grow in partial shade. It needs constantly moist, well-mulched, and well-drained soil, and in colder climates protection against prolonged cold and damp is essential. It can be propagated by root division and cuttings in spring. Cardinal flower looks well planted with *Artemesia lactiflora* and *Astilbe arendsii*. Its flowers are short-lived.
Other colors: White.
Varieties/cultivars: 'Alba', 'Angel Song', 'Arabella's Vision', 'Twilight Zone'.

Lobelia cardinalis

Lobelia laxiflora
PEACH-LEAVED LOBELIA, TORCH LOBELIA ○

Family: LOBELIACEAE
Origin: Arizona to Mexico and Colombia.
Flowering time: Summer.
Climatic zone: 9, 10.
Dimensions: From 3 feet (1 meter) high.
Description: This is a tall, shrubby

Lobelia laxiflora

member of the genus *Lobelia* with a spread equal to its height. Place it among other sun-loving, evergreen shrubs or near a wall where it will be protected from frosts. Do not plant it near gross feeders, as it likes rich, moist, well-drained soil. The red and yellow flowers, 1 inch (30 mm) across, are in terminal leafy spikes. Propagation is by seed or cuttings.

Lupinus 'Russell Hybrid'
RUSSELL HYBRID LUPIN ○ ◑

Family: LEGUMINOSAE
Origin: Hybrids.
Flowering time: Summer.
Climatic zone: 5, 6, 7, 8, 9.
Dimensions: 3 feet (1 meter) high.
Description: Lupins are among the showiest of the herbaceous perennials. They form handsome clumps, their gray-green foliage a perfect backdrop for their own abundantly colored blooms

Lupinus 'Russell Hybrid'

and for companion plantings of *Papaver orientale*, *Phlox paniculata*, *Penstemon gloxinioides*, and *Baptista australis*. They prefer a light, neutral, sandy soil and plenty of water. Propagate them from seed sown direct in autumn or by division in early spring. Lupins are good cut flowers.
Other colors: White, cream, yellow, pink, blue, lilac, purple.
Varieties/cultivars: 'Betty Astell', 'Lilac Time', 'Fireglow', 'Gladys Cooper'.

Lychnis chalcedonica

Lychnis chalcedonica
MALTESE-CROSS ○ ◑

Family: CARYOPHYLLACEAE
Origin: Northern Russia.
Flowering time: Summer.
Climatic zone: 4, 5, 6, 7, 8.
Dimensions: Up to 3 feet (1 meter) high.
Description: *Lychnis chalcedonica* adds vibrant color to the herbaceous border or cottage garden. It is hardy, a prolific seeder, and looks very well planted with the blues and purples of some varieties of salvia, and *Nepeta x faassenii*, offset by splashes of white from *Achillea*. It thrives in any well-drained, moist soil, but appreciates extra mulch and water in spring and summer. Propagation is by seed in spring or by division in late winter. Regular picking keeps the plant under control and prolongs flowering.
Other colors: White, rose-pink.
Varieties/cultivars: 'Alba', 'Flora Plena'.

Monarda didyma

Monarda didyma
BEE BALM, OSWEGO ○ ◑
TEA

Family: LABIATAE
Origin: North America.
Flowering time: Summer.
Climatic zone: 4, 5, 6, 7, 8, 9.
Dimensions: 2–3 feet (up to 1 meter) high.
Description: *Monarda didyma* is a delight. Its colors are superb, its fragrance overwhelming, attracting bees and butterflies in profusion. It looks as well in the herbaceous border as the herb garden, particularly if care is taken with color combinations. It requires only average, well-drained soil, but benefits from good mulching and plenty of water in dry conditions, especially if planted in full sun. Its leaves can be used for potpourri. Propagate from seed or by division in spring. It is susceptible to powdery mildew.
Other colors: White, pink, mauve, purple.
Varieties/cultivars: 'Blue Stocking', 'Cambridge Scarlet', 'Snow Maiden', 'Croftway Pink'.

Paeonia officinalis 'Rubra Plena'
COMMON PEONY ○ ◑

Family: PAEONIACEAE
Origin: Cultivar.
Flowering time: Late spring.
Climatic zone: 5, 6, 7, 8, 9.
Dimensions: Up to 3 feet (1 meter) high.
Description: Once established, peonies will grow for decades in the cool-climate garden. They require well-drained, deep, fertile soil, enriched with plenty of animal manure, and ample water during the flowering period. They also need

protection from strong winds and, in warmer areas, extra shade. Propagation is by tuber division in early autumn, but take care to disturb established clumps as little as possible. Prune by removing spent flower stems when foliage yellows. Picked at the bud stage, peonies are excellent cut flowers.

Paeonia officinalis 'Rubra Plena'

Papaver orientale
ORIENTAL POPPY ○

Family: PAPAVERACEAE
Origin: Southwestern Asia.
Flowering time: Early summer.
Climatic zone: 4, 5, 6, 7, 8, 9.
Dimensions: 3–4 feet (approx. 1 meter) high.
Description: The oriental poppy is a long-time favorite for the herbaceous border and cottage garden. Its large, open blooms, often darkly blotched at the base, come in dazzling colors and more than compensate for its foliage, which becomes very untidy after flowering. This is best disguised by surrounding poppies with perennials like *Stokesia laevis*, *Veronica virginica*, and *Anemone* x *hybrida*. Oriental poppy

Papaver orientale 'Harvest Moon'

requires well-drained, deep loam with a good dressing of manure in early spring. Propagation is by division in spring or by seed. It is a good cut flower.
Other colors: Pink, rose, white, yellow.
Varieties/cultivars: 'China Boy', 'Mrs Perry', 'Grossfurst', 'Perry's White', 'Princess Victoria Louise', 'Harvest Moon'.

Pelargonium x *domesticum*
MARTHA WASHINGTON ○
GERANIUM (U.S.A.), REGAL OR
SHOW GERANIUM (U.K.)

Family: GERANIACEAE
Origin: Hybrids.
Flowering time: Spring–summer.
Climatic zone: 9, 10.
Dimensions: 18 inches (450 mm) high.
Description: *Pelargonium* x *domesticum* is larger in habit than *P.* x *hortorum* and has a shorter flowering season. Its foliage is evergreen and pleasantly aromatic when bruised, and its flowers are deeply colored and ruffled. In the northern hemisphere, it is often grown as a showy greenhouse pot specimen. It requires well-drained, light soil with a dressing of complete fertilizer in late winter to encourage flowering. Do not overwater. It is susceptible to frost and fungal disease. Remove spent flowers to prolong blooming.
Other colors: White, pink, mauve, purple.
Varieties/cultivars: 'Axminster', 'Mrs G. Morf', 'Hula', 'Carefree', 'Annie Hawkins'.

Pelargonium x *domesticum*

Pelargonium x *hortorum*
ZONAL GERANIUM ○

Family: GERANIACEAE
Origin: Hybrids.
Flowering time: Late spring–autumn.
Climatic zone: 9, 10.
Dimensions: 6 inches–3 feet (450 mm–1 meter) high.
Description: *Pelargonium* x *hortorum* is a shrubby evergreen perennial, valuable for its variable foliage as well as its flowers, which come in single, semidouble and double form. It likes well-drained, neutral, light soil and dislikes excess water. Water only in dry weather. To keep the plant thick and encourage flowering, prune regularly. Propagation is by cuttings in summer in cold climates, and year-round elsewhere. It is a good cut flower, but is susceptible to frost and fungal disease.
Other colors: White, pink, salmon, mauve.
Varieties/cultivars: 'Dagata', 'Rubin', 'Highland Queen', 'Henri Joignot'.

Pelargonium x *hortorum*

Penstemon barbatus
BEARDLIP PENSTEMON, ○
PENSTEMON (U.K.)

Family: SCROPHULARIACEAE
Origin: South western United States, Mexico.
Flowering time: Summer–autumn.
Climatic zone: 4.
Dimensions: 2–3 feet (600–900 mm) high.
Description: Beardlip penstemon, formerly known as *Chelone barbatus*, takes its name from its flowers' bearded

Penstemon barbatus

throat and lip. The species appears in several colors, but the scarlet-flowered one is the most popular. It is not particularly hardy and requires well-drained, fertile soil and shelter from wind. Excess water in winter will kill it. Propagation is from cuttings in late summer or seed sown under glass in spring. The plant needs hard pruning to ground level in spring, just as new growth begins. Beardlip penstemon is good for planting on wild, sheltered slopes.
Other colors: Pink, purple, lavender.
Varieties/cultivars: 'Carnea'.

Penstemon x *gloxinioides* 'Firebird'
PENSTEMON, ○ ◑
GLOXINIA PENSTEMON

Family: SCROPHULARIACEAE
Origin: Hybrid.
Flowering time: Summer–autumn.

Penstemon x *gloxinioides* 'Firebird'

Climatic zone: 8, 9.
Dimensions: 2 feet (600 mm) high.
Description: *Penstemon* x *gloxinioides* 'Firebird' is similar to *P. barbatus*, but its flower is larger and unbearded, and it flowers more abundantly. Well-drained soil and a sheltered position are necessary for good growth, and it benefits from winter mulching. Partial shade will give the plant a longer life and weekly application of soluble fertilizer will extend its flowering. It is at its best in the herbaceous border with perennials like *Anthemis sancti-johannis*, *Helenium autumnale* and *Lavandula stoechas*.

Pentas lanceolata

Pentas lanceolata
EGYPTIAN STAR- ○ ◑
CLUSTER

Family: RUBIACEAE
Origin: East Africa–southern Arabia.
Flowering time: Summer.
Climatic zone: 9, 10.
Dimensions: 2–5 feet (600–1500 mm) high.
Description: *Pentas lanceolata* is ideal for the sunny subtropical garden, preferring wet summers, warm winters, and no frost. In cooler climates, it can be grown under greenhouse conditions and it lends itself to pot cultivation. It requires well-drained, sandy soil with the addition of plenty of organic mulch. It is fast-growing, with a shrubby habit. To keep its shape and induce constant flowering, prune it lightly and regularly. Propagation is from seed or, more commonly, from tip cuttings taken in spring to autumn and grown in humid conditions.
Other colors: White, pink, rose, lilac.
Varieties/cultivars: 'Coccinea'.

Physalis alkekengi syn. *P. franchetii*
BLADDER CHERRY, CHINESE LANTERN (U.K.)

Family: SOLANACEAE
Origin: Southeastern Europe–Japan.
Flowering time: Summer–autumn.
Climatic zone: 3, 4, 5, 6, 7, 8, 9, 10.
Dimensions: Up to 2 feet (600 mm) high.
Description: *Physalis* is a hardy, creeping perennial, grown largely for its showy, berry-bearing calyx that becomes brightly colored and inflated after flowering. It requires well-drained soil and plenty of summer water. Because of its creeping habit, it can be useful as a groundcover, particularly the dwarf cultivar 'Nana'. Propagation is by seed or by root division in autumn or early spring. The dried calyces make handsome winter decoration and the berries are edible.
Varieties/cultivars: 'Gigantea', 'Orbiculare', 'Monstrosa', 'Nana'.

Physalis alkekengi

Potentilla atrosanguinea
RUBY CINQUEFOIL

Family: ROSACEAE
Origin: Himalayas.
Flowering time: Summer, northern hemisphere; spring, southern hemisphere.
Climatic zone: 5, 6, 7, 8, 9.
Dimensions: Up to 18 inches (450 mm) high.
Description: A very useful plant for a small garden, ruby cinquefoil is compact and colorful, its strawberry-like blooms flowering for many months. It looks effective in a border, when complementing *Gypsophila* and *Alyssum*. This pretty perennial will thrive in moderately moist soil of average

Potentilla atrosanguinea

fertility, providing it has full sun. This reason alone makes it a good choice for small, suburban gardens. Propagate it by division or seed in spring.
Other colors: Yellow.
Varieties/cultivars: 'Gibson's Scarlet', 'California'.

Potentilla nepalensis
NEPAL CINQUEFOIL

Family: ROSACEAE
Origin: Himalayas.
Flowering time: Summer, northern hemisphere; spring, southern hemisphere.
Climatic zone: 5, 6, 7, 8, 9.
Dimensions: Up to 18 inches (450 mm) high.
Description: This is a tufted herbaceous perennial which is a good front of border plant. The deep-green, serrated leaves accompany rose-red flowers with darker centers. It will flower profusely for many months during the spring or summer. Plant it in a border among phlox and primula for a pretty, cottage-garden look. It will flourish in ordinary soil in full sun, and

is a good choice in a garden where the soil has been neglected.
Varieties/cultivars: 'Miss Wilmott', 'Roxana'.

Potentilla nepalensis 'Roxana'

Verbena x *hybrida*
ROSE VERVAIN, COMMON VERBENA (U.K.)

Family: VERBENACEAE
Origin: Hybrid.
Flowering time: Summer–autumn.
Climatic zone: 9, 10.
Dimensions: Up to 2 feet (600 mm) high.
Description: This pretty, spreading, border or groundcover plant will bloom for long periods. Densely packed flower heads set amid dark-green leaves give an effective display. There are many named varieties in a wide choice of colors. Usually grown as an annual, verbena will develop a compact habit if new shoots are pinched out. Remove dead flower heads to prolong the blooming period. Lower growing varieties look attractive, spilling over rock edges or walls. Grow the plant from seed or cutting.
Varieties/cultivars: 'Lawrence Johnston'.

Verbena x *hybrida* 'Lawrence Johnston'

Bauhinia galpinii syn. *B. punctata*
RED BAUHINIA (U.S.A.), ○
ORCHID TREE, BUTTERFLY
TREE

Family: LEGUMINOSAE
Origin: Tropical Africa.
Flowering time: Summer.
Climatic zone: 9, 10.
Dimensions: 6 feet (2 meters) high.
Description: During summer this shrub
is a mass of brick-red flowers. The mid-
green leaves have the appearance of a
butterfly, hence the common name. For
best results grow red bauhinia in a well-
drained acid soil. A mulch of cow
manure or a handful of complete plant
food applied around the tree in early
spring will ensure a good flower display.
After flowering, the shrub is covered in
masses of brown pea-like pods the seeds
from which can be used for
propagation.

Bauhinia galpinii

Begonia x *corallina*

Begonia x *corallina*
CORAL BEGONIA ○ ◐

Family: BEGONIACEAE
Origin: Hybrid.
Flowering time: Spring–autumn.
Climatic zone: 9, 10.
Dimensions: 8–10 feet (2–3 meters) high.
Description: A pretty free-flowering
shrub having coral-red flowers and
attractive foliage, coral begonia is an
ideal shrub for a herbaceous garden. It
can also be grown in a large tub on a
patio or verandah. In cold climates, a
greenhouse is required. A sheltered
position is a must. Its main requirement
is a well-drained soil that is enriched
with animal manure or compost.

Other colors: Pink, white.

Calliandra tweedii
RED TASSEL FLOWER, ○ ◐
FLAME BUSH, RED
POWDERPUFF

Family: LEGUMINOSAE
Origin: Brazil.
Flowering time: Summer and again in
autumn.
Climatic zone: 9, 10.
Dimensions: 6 feet (2 meters) high.
Description: This dense shrub is
covered in numerous short branches
and finely divided dark-green, fern-like
foliage. The large rich-red flowers have
a pompom-like appearance. Red tassel
flower prefers a well-drained soil, but is
adaptable to other soil types. Apply a
mulch of manure or compost in spring.
Where summers are hot keep well-
watered. In cold climates a glasshouse is
required. Prune, if necessary, after
flowering has finished in autumn. This
shrub makes an ideal feature plant.

Calliandra tweedii

Callistemon citrinus 'Endeavour'

Callistemon citrinus 'Endeavour'
CRIMSON BOTTLEBRUSH ○ ◑

Family: MYRTACEAE
Origin: Cultivar.
Flowering time: Spring.
Climatic zone: 9, 10.
Dimensions: 5 feet (approx. 2 meters) high.
Description: A hardy shrub in milder climates, crimson bottlebrush thrives in a wide range of soil types including sandy loam, clay and wet, soggy soil. Large, crimson, bottlebrush-like flowers cover it in spring. Pruning should be carried out if necessary as soon as the flowers fade and before new growth develops. Fertilize around the shrub with either an organic mixture or a mulch of cow manure. Crimson bottlebrush may be used in a shrub border or on its own as a specimen plant.

Callistemon citrinus 'Western Glory'

Callistemon citrinus 'Western Glory'
BOTTLEBRUSH ○

Family: MYRTACEAE
Origin: Cultivar.

Flowering time: Spring–summer.
Climatic zone: 9, 10.
Dimensions: 6–13 feet (2–4 meters) high.
Description: This bushy, medium-sized shrub, which has large spikes of deep mauve-pink flowers, can be used as a specimen shrub or screen plant in a warm climate garden. The flowers last quite well when picked and brought indoors for decoration. This bottlebrush will grow in any well-drained garden soil. Mulch around the base with cow manure or compost in spring. This will not only feed the plant, but keep the soil moist. Water well during summer.

Callistemon viminalis
WEEPING OR DROOPING BOTTLEBRUSH ○ ◑

Family: MYRTACEAE
Origin: Eastern Australia.
Flowering time: Summer and again in autumn.
Climatic zone: 9.
Dimensions: 20 feet (6 meters) high.
Description: An outstanding feature plant, this large shrub has an attractive weeping habit and during spring and autumn is covered in a profusion of bright-red flower spikes. The new leaf growth is an attractive bronze color.

Callistemon viminalis

Weeping bottlebrush is tolerant of most soils and makes an excellent screen plant. It prefers a mild climate but will tolerate some frost. Organic fertilizer applied in late spring and plenty of summer water speeds growth. It makes an excellent cut flower.
Varieties/cultivars: 'Captain Cook', 'Hannah Ray', 'Gawler', 'King's Park Special'.

Calycanthus floridus

Calycanthus floridus
COMMON SWEET SHRUB (U.S.A.), CAROLINA ALLSPICE (U.K.), STRAWBERRY SHRUB ○ ◑

Family: CALYCANTHACEAE
Origin: North America.
Flowering time: Spring–summer.
Climatic zone: 5, 6, 7, 8, 9.
Dimensions: 8–10 feet (2–3 meters) high.
Description: This is a hardy, deciduous shrub which prefers a position in partial shade, though in cold climates full sun is necessary to ensure flowering. When flowering, it is covered in attractive reddish-brown flowers. The soil should be rich and well-drained with compost or leaf mold added to it each other spring. Pruning out the old wood after flowering has finished helps to maintain this shrub's atttractive appearance. Common sweet shrub looks delightful when planted in a shrub border next to white flowering shrubs.

SHRUBS

Cantua buxifolia
FLOWER-OF-THE-INCAS   ○ ◑

Family: POLEMONIACEAE
Origin: Peru.
Flowering time: Spring–summer.
Climatic zone: 9, 10.
Dimensions: 6–10 feet (2–3 meters) high.
Description: A sparse, evergreen shrub, *Cantua buxifolia* has beautiful pendulous clusters of bright-rose or pale-red funnel-shaped flowers with an elongated tube. For best results, plant it in well-drained soil enriched with well-rotted compost or leaf mold. It requires at least half-sun and some protection from heavy frosts. In cooler climates, plant *Cantua buxifolia* against a warm sunny wall. Do not prune — this will ruin its shape.

Cestrum fasciculatum 'Newellii'

organic matter such as compost or manure. A good soil will ensure quick growth. It can be easily propagated from cuttings taken in autumn or winter. In colder areas it can be grown on a sunny wall or in a conservatory.

Cantua buxifolia

Cestrum fasciculatum 'Newellii'
RED CESTRUM   ○

Family: SOLANACEAE
Origin: Cultivar.
Flowering time: Spring–summer.
Climatic zone: 7, 8, 9.
Dimensions: 6–8 feet (2–3 meters) high.
Description: 'Newellii' is a seedling variant. The spectacular, bright orange-red, pitcher-shaped tubular flowers cover it in spring and summer. Grow it at the back of a shrub border or among other screening shrubs. The soil should be well-drained but enriched with

Chaenomeles japonica
DWARF FLOWERING QUINCE, JAPONICA, JAPANESE QUINCE (U.K.)   ○ ◑ ●

Family: ROSACEAE
Origin: Japan.
Flowering time: Spring.
Climatic zone: 5, 6, 7, 8.
Dimensions: 3 feet (1 meter) high.
Description: Dwarf flowering quince is a low, spiny, deciduous shrub that spreads wider than its height. Bright orange-red flowers cover the plant before the leaves appear or just as they unfold. The hard, round apple-shaped yellow fruits are delightfully fragrant and make excellent jam or jelly. It is a very hardy shrub which will tolerate full shade or sun, and will thrive in any free-draining garden soil. It can be grown in city conditions, as it is tolerant of pollution. It is often used in hedges or in a shrub border.
Varieties/cultivars: 'Alpina'.

Chaenomeles japonica

Chaenomeles speciosa

JAPONICA, ○ ◑ ●
COMMON FLOWERING QUINCE
(U.S.A.), FLOWERING OR
JAPANESE QUINCE (U.K.)

Family: ROSACEAE
Origin: China.
Flowering time: Spring.
Climatic zone: 5, 6, 7, 8.
Dimensions: 6–10 feet (2–3 meters) high.
Description: A delightful deciduous shrub, flowering quince has a wide, spreading, rounded habit with dark, glossy green foliage. When grown in milder climates it is only partly deciduous. The 2-inch (50 mm) wide flowers are scarlet to blood-red. Yellowish-green fruit, which makes excellent jam, follows the flowers. This hardy shrub will grow in any soil type as long as it is well-drained. Mulching with manure or compost in late winter ensures a good flower display.
Other colors: Deep crimson, pink and white, pink, white, orange, buff-coral, creamy-salmon, orange-red, creamy-apricot.
Varieties/cultivars: Numerous cultivars have been developed from this species.

Chorizema cordatum

HEART-LEAF FLAME ○ ◑
PEA, FLAME PEA, CORAL PEA

Family: LEGUMINOSAE
Origin: Western Australia.
Flowering time: Late spring and summer.

Chaenomeles speciosa 'Umbilicata'

Climatic zone: 9, 10.
Dimensions: 3–6 feet (1–2 meters) high.
Description: An attractive low-growing shrub, flame pea is used in rockeries as a specimen plant in hot climates. In colder areas, a greenhouse may be necessary. The small red and orange pea-shaped flowers, which are very bright, attractive, and abundant, cover the plant for nearly six months. The leaves are heart-shaped. Its main requirement is a well-drained, sandy soil. It is frost- and drought-resistant. Flame pea is easily propagated from seed, but these should be soaked in water that is near boiling point before they are sown.

Cytisus scoparius 'Crimson King'

COMMON BROOM ○

Family: LEGUMINOSAE
Origin: Hybrid.
Flowering time: Spring.
Climatic zone: 6, 7, 8, 9.
Dimensions: 4–9 feet (1–3 meters) high.
Description: 'Crimson King', a cultivar of *Cytisus scoparius* has magnificent true red flowers. It is extremely easy to cultivate, but prefers a well-drained soil. In warmer climates, pruning it back by at least half its height after flowering ensures a thicker shrub. In cool areas, pruning should be limited to avoid dieback. This is an ideal plant for a shrub or perennial border and looks magnificent if planted near white flowering plants. It is easily propagated from cuttings taken in early spring.

Chorizema cordatum

Cytisus scoparius 'Crimson King'

Euphorbia milii

Euphorbia milii
CROWN-OF-THORNS ○

Family: EUPHORBIACEAE
Origin: Madagascar.
Flowering time: Summer.
Climatic zone: 9, 10.
Dimensions: 3 feet (1 meter) high.
Description: Crown-of-thorns is a spiny, succulent shrub with brown, almost leafless stems and long, straight, tapering spines. The leaves are very sparse and appear at the ends of branches. The flowers themselves are inconspicuous but are surrounded by showy, bright scarlet bracts. In warm climates, the best location for the crown-of-thorns is in a large rockery or against a wall. A greenhouse location is essential in cold climates. Its needs are a hot position and a well-drained soil.

Feijoa sellowiana
FEIJOA, PINEAPPLE ○
GUAVA (U.S.A.), FRUIT SALAD
TREE

Family: MYRTACEAE
Origin: Brazil.
Flowering time: Summer.
Climatic zone: 8, 9, 10.
Dimensions: 5–20 feet (2–6 meters) high.
Description: This attractive ornamental shrub is grown for its crimson-and-white flowers and edible fruit. The leaves are gray-green with a white, felty underside. The dark-green fragrant fruits ripen in winter and, when mature, fall on the ground. They can be eaten raw or used in jam. Feijoa likes a well-drained soil but requires ample summer water for good fruit production. The fragrant petals can be eaten and look delightful sprinkled over the top of a salad. Not suited to areas where winters are severe.
Varieties/cultivars: 'Variegata', 'Gigantea', 'Coolidgei'.

Fuchsia magellanica
MAGELLAN ○ ◑ ●
FUCHSIA, COMMON FUCHSIA
(U.K.)

Family: ONAGRACEAE
Origin: Southern Chile, Argentina.
Flowering time: Summer–autumn.
Climatic zone: 7, 8, 9.
Dimensions: 6–10 feet (2–3 meters) high.
Description: This is a free-flowering shrub with long, arching branches and an abundance of pendant flowers. The

Fuchsia magellanica 'Gracilis'

flower sepals are bright crimson and the petals are purplish-blue. It can be used in a shrub border or as a hedge plant. The nodding flowers are very rich in honey, making this a valuable bird-attracting plant in the garden. It is easily propagated from cuttings taken in late summer or spring. For best results plant in a rich, free-draining soil.
Other colors: Scarlet and deep violet; white and mauve; white and pink.
Varieties/cultivars: 'Alba', 'Riccardo, 'Variegata', 'Gracilis'.

Hibiscus schizopetalus
FRINGED HIBISCUS, ○
JAPANESE HIBISCUS

Family: MALVACEAE
Origin: Tropical East Africa.
Flowering time: Spring–summer.
Climatic zone: 9, 10.
Dimensions: 5–10 feet (approx. 1½–3 meters) high.
Description: Fringed hibiscus is a pretty shrub with slender stems which usually require supporting. The orange-red pendant flowers have fringed, backward curving petals with long stamens projecting beyond them. Fringed hibiscus requires a warm, sheltered position and a rich, well-drained soil. It can be trained on a wall or trellis. In spring cut away any

Feijoa sellowiana

Hibiscus schizopetalus

unwanted growth, and shorten the stems and branches to within 5 inches (125 mm) of the base. It can be grown in a large pot or tub. In cool climates, it grows best in a greenhouse.

Lechenaultia formosa
LECHENAULTIA

Family: GOODENIACEAE
Origin: Western Australia.
Flowering time: Spring and summer.
Climatic zone: 9.
Dimensions: 11 inches (300 mm) high.
Description: This prostrate shrub is covered in small grayish-green leaves and an abundance of vermilion-red flowers in spring. It is variable in form and also flower color which can vary from white, yellow, pink, rose to any combination of these. Its main

Lechenaultia formosa 'Scarlet O'Hara'

requirement is an extremely well-drained sandy soil. A rockery, especially one on a sloping site, is an ideal position, but in cooler climates a greenhouse is necessary.
Other colors: See description.
Varieties/cultivars: 'Scarlet O'Hara'.

Leonotis leonurus
LION'S EAR

Family: LABIATAE
Origin: South Africa.
Flowering time: Late summer–autumn.
Climatic zone: 9, 10.

Leonotis leonurus

Dimensions: 4–7 feet (approx. 1–2 meters) high.
Description: *Leonotis* is a pretty, square-stemmed plant with downy, dull-green leaves and showy spikes of orange-scarlet flowers. The name *Leonotis*, from *leon* (lion) and *otos* (ear), was given because the flower looks like a lion's ear. This fast-growing plant thrives in well-drained soil. A mulch of manure or compost in spring will ensure good flower production. Pruning can be carried out if required after the flowers have finished.

Leucospermum reflexum
ROCKET PINCUSHION

Family: PROTEACEAE
Origin: South Africa.
Flowering time: Spring.
Climatic zone: 9.
Dimensions: 6–10 feet (2–3 meters) high.
Description: This eye-catching shrub has downy, bluish-gray leaves and large orange-red flowerheads about 4 inches (100 mm) across. Good drainage is essential for the plant's success. It should not be planted where there is a heavy clay subsoil, as the excessive moisture retained will eventually rot the roots, causing plant collapse. During wet spring weather the new shoots will often rot and collapse. This is not a disease and does not occur when the weather is dry and hot.

Leucospermum reflexum.

Mussaenda frondosa
MUSSAENDA ○

Family: RUBIACEAE
Origin: Tropical Africa, Asia, Pacific islands.
Flowering time: Summer.
Climatic zone: 9, 10.
Dimensions: 3–6 feet (1–2 meters) high.
Description: The orange-yellow flowers of this shrub are actually quite inconspicuous, but they are surrounded by large white bracts which stay on the plant for a long time after the flowers have fallen. The combination of the soft-green leaves and the white bracts is very striking. Mussaenda thrives in warm coastal districts where the soil is free-draining. Plant it in a shrub border or use as a specimen plant. In colder climates, a greenhouse location is necessary. Feed it in early spring and water well during the summer months.

Mussaenda frondosa

Odontonema strictum syn.
Thyrsacanthus, Justicia coccinea
RED JUSTICIA, FIERY SPIKE ○

Family: ACANTHACEAE
Origin: Tropical America.
Flowering time: Autumn.

Odontonema strictum

Climatic zone: 9, 10.
Dimensions: 8 feet (2–3 meters) high.
Description: A favorite plant for hot-climate gardens, it has large, glossy green leaves and spectacular scarlet flowers which open irregularly. It is often grown on patios in a large pot. Red justicia's main cultivation requirements are a rich soil, preferably with leaf mold added, and ample summer water. It is easily propagated from spring cuttings.

Protea grandiceps

Protea spp.
PROTEA ○

Family: PROTEACEAE
Origin: South Africa.
Flowering time: Depends on the species, but generally winter.
Climatic zone: 9, 10.
Dimensions: 2–10 feet (approx. 1–3 meters) high.
Description: There are many species of proteas. The flowers of *Protea pulchra* vary from deep ruby-red to salmon and pink. *Protea neriifolia* 'Taylors Surprise' has brilliant salmon-red flowers and *Protea nana* is renowned for its bright rosy-crimson to orange-red flowers. Proteas strongly resent over-rich soils and thrive in rather poor slightly acid soil that contains a lot of rubble or sand. Add sulfur to the soil if it is too alkaline. Avoid using phosphates. Do not overwater.
Other colors: Pink, white, green, cream.

Punica granatum
POMEGRANATE ○

Family: PUNICACEAE
Origin: Southwest Asia.
Flowering time: Summer.
Climatic zone: 8, 9.
Dimensions: 10–20 feet (3–6 meters) high.
Description: The new spring leaves of this large deciduous shrub are coppery in color before changing to a deep, shiny green. In autumn they turn a bright yellow. The orange-red flowers have a wrinkled appearance. The fruit needs a long hot summer before it develops properly. Pomegranate's main requirements are a hot position and a well-drained soil. It can be grown very successfully in large pots or tubs, or against a sunny wall. Feed with a complete plant food in spring.
Other colors: Scarlet-red, ruby-red, reddish-salmon.
Varieties/cultivars: 'Pleniflora', 'Spanish Ruby', 'Nana', 'Nana Plena', 'De Regina', 'Albo-plena'.

Punica granatum

Rhododendron x *gandavense*

Rhododendron x *gandavense*
GHENT AZALEA, ○ ◑ DECIDUOUS AZALEA, MOLLIS AZALEA

Family: ERICACEAE
Origin: Hybrid.
Flowering time: Spring.
Climatic zone: 6, 7, 8, 9.
Dimensions: 5 feet (approx. 2 meters) high.
Description: This is a mixed race of hybrids, the result of crossing between *R. luteum* and several other species. Many are in the orange-red color range. The flowers are lightly perfumed and the shrub is slightly more twiggy than other deciduous azaleas. Ghent azaleas like a cool, acid soil which has been enriched with organic matter, preferably peat. They will grow in full sun in cool climates, but in temperate climates prefer partial shade.
Other colors: Pink, yellow.
Varieties/cultivars: There are numerous cultivars throughout the world.

Rhododendron Knap Hill

Rhododendron Knap Hill
DECIDUOUS AZALEA ○ ◑

Family: ERICACEAE
Origin: Hybrid.
Flowering time: Spring.
Climatic zone: 6, 7, 8, 9.
Dimensions: 3–9 feet (1–3 meters) high.
Description: Knap Hill hybrids originated in England in the early 1900s. They are valued for their orange-red color range. The leaves color in autumn before they drop. They like cool to cold climates and will grow in full sun in colder climates but perform just as well or better in dappled shade. A mulch of leaf mold or cow manure, applied around the base of the shrubs in spring, will keep the shallow roots moist and cool during summer.
Other colors: Yellow, gold, orange, scarlet, pink, white.
Varieties/cultivars: Numerous cultivars are available throughout the world.

Telopea speciosissima
NEW SOUTH WALES ○ ◑ WARATAH

Family: PROTEACEAE
Origin: Australia (N.S.W.).
Flowering time: Spring.
Climatic zone: 9, 10.
Dimensions: 10 feet (3 meters) high.
Description: Very large, red flowers (3–6 inches, 80–150 mm in diameter) appear on this shrub during spring. The flowers are followed by long brown pods. Waratahs tend to respond to cultivation provided that the soil is acid and rainfall high. They always look more magnificent in a garden than in the wild. For best results feed only with organic fertilizers and prune rather hard to shape them after flowering. Waratahs attract birds to the garden as well as making superb feature plants. Keep well watered during summer.
Varieties/cultivars: 'Braidwood Brilliant'.

Telopea speciosissima

Brachychiton acerifolium
ILLAWARRA FLAME TREE, ◯
FLAME BOTTLE TREE (U.K.)

Family: STERCULIACEAE
Origin: Eastern Australia (coastal slopes).
Flowering time: Late spring–early summer.
Climatic zone: 9, 10.
Dimensions: 35–45 feet (11–14 meters) high.
Description: This tree is erratic in its flowering habit, but the blooms, which appear as a cloud of scarlet on bare wood, are a sight worth waiting for. Sometimes only one side of the tree will produce flowers. Good flowering seems to follow a dryish winter. It is mostly evergreen, but is deciduous on the flowering branches. The Illawarra flame tree flourishes in warm, coastal districts and is a popular garden tree. It does not suffer from any special pest or disease problems.

Brachychiton acerifolium

Callistemon viminalis 'Hannah Ray'
BOTTLEBRUSH ◯

Family: MYRTACEAE
Origin: Cultivar
Flowering time: Spring and autumn, southern hemisphere; summer, northern hemisphere.
Climatic zone: 8, 9, 10.
Dimensions: 13 feet (4 meters) high x 6 feet (2 meters) wide.
Description: A cultivar of the weeping bottlebrush, this delightful, small,

Callistemon viminalis 'Hannah Ray'

evergreen tree flowers for long periods and, like most bottlebrushes, will grow in very variable soil conditions, from poorly drained to well drained. Its long, brush-like, crimson flowers attract honey-eating birds. Young foliage is a pink color which later turns to green. Sawflies, which in some areas cluster on leaves and branches in warmer months, may be removed by hand.

Ceratonia siliqua
CAROB BEAN, LOCUST ◯

Family: CAESALPINACEAE
Origin: Eastern Mediterranean.
Flowering time: Spring, northern hemisphere; spring–autumn, southern hemisphere.
Climatic zone: 6, 7, 8, 9.
Dimensions: 15–30 feet (5–10 meters) high.
Description: This compact-growing tree is grown chiefly for the generous shade it affords in hot climates, and for the edible beans which follow the flowers in autumn, and which St. John

Ceratonia siliqua

the Baptist is believed to have eaten in the wilderness. Although slow growing in its native lands, it is more vigorous in cultivation. The leaves are dark green and leathery in texture, while the reddish flowers appear in small clusters close to the branches. Ideal for growing in hot and dry conditions, well-drained soil produces the best results. A male and female plant are required to produce the edible pods.

Crataegus laevigata 'Paulii' syn.
C. oxyacantha 'Paul's Scarlet'
DOUBLE RED HAWTHORN, ◯
MIDLAND HAWTHORN (U.K.),
SCARLET THORN

Family: ROSACEAE
Origin: Cultivar
Flowering time: Spring–early summer.
Climatic zone: 5, 6, 7, 8, 9.
Dimensions: 16–20 feet (5–6 meters) high.
Description: A hardy little tree-cum-shrub, English hawthorn is smothered in gorgeous scarlet flowers in spring. Often used in the landscape as a hedge, the leaves turn yellow in autumn, and its dense, thorny growth gives protection even in winter when the leaves have dropped. It prefers a limestone soil, performs best in a cool climate, and is problem-free.

Crataegus laevigata 'Paulii'

Delonix regia
ROYAL POINCIANA ◯
(U.S.A.), PEACOCK FLOWER,
FLAME TREE

Other common names:
FLAMBOYANT TREE
Family: CAESALPINACEAE
Origin: Madagascar.
Flowering time: Summer.
Climatic zone: 9, 10.

Delonix regia

Dimensions: 40–50 feet (12–15 meters) high x 50–65 feet (15–20 meters) wide.
Description: Flamboyant by name, flamboyant by nature, *Delonix regia* flowers only in the warmest of climates or in a warm microclimate, when suddenly the whole canopy of the tree is covered in showy bunches of red flowers. Grown as a beautiful shade tree, the canopy often spreads to twice the width of the height. Leaves are similar to those of the blue-flowering jacaranda — lacy and bright green, almost evergreen. This tree is widely planted in Florida and tropical towns in Australia.
Other colors: Cream (rare).

Erythrina x *sykesii* syn. *E. indica*,
E. variegata
COMMON CORAL TREE, ○
SYKES'S CORAL TREE (U.K.)

Family: LEGUMINOSAE
Origin: Hybrid.
Flowering time: Late winter–early spring, northern hemisphere; mid-winter–late spring, southern hemisphere.
Climatic zone: 9, 10.
Dimensions: 40–60 feet (12–18 meters) high.
Description: Belonging to a large genus of over 100 species, the common coral tree is a familiar sight in both northern and southern hemispheres. Its brilliant red flowers are a welcome sight in winter as they appear on bare branches, the leaves following later. Sharp, fat prickles cover trunk and branches. A tree of generous proportions, with a wide canopy and a short trunk, it flourishes

in coastal districts. It is often planted as a shade tree in large gardens, and in parks and car parks. It may also be grown in pots in a frost-free greenhouse though it does not flower in containers.
Other colors: White.
Varieties/cultivars: 'Alba', var. *orientalis*.

Erythrina x *sykesii*

Eucalyptus ficifolia
RED-FLOWERING GUM, ○
SCARLET-FLOWERING GUM

Family: MYRTACEAE
Origin: Western Australia (southern coast).
Flowering time: Summer, northern

Eucalyptus ficifolia

hemisphere; late spring–summer, southern hemisphere.
Climatic zone: 9, 10.
Dimensions: 15–40 feet (8–12 meters) high.
Description: If planted in full sun with excellent drainage, this small tree will reward you with masses of fluffy, red flowers each year. Large gum nuts (the fruits), which follow, hang on the tree for a long time, and can be used as dried arrangements for the house. One of the most popular small eucalypts, it has found its way into coastal gardens of both hemispheres. It needs a sheltered position and mild winter climate.
Other colors: Color is variable.

Eucalyptus leucoxylon 'Rosea'
WHITE IRONBARK ○

Family: MYRTACEAE
Origin: Cultivar.
Flowering time: Winter–late spring.
Climatic zone: 9, 10.
Dimensions: 30–45 feet (10–15 meters) high.
Description: White ironbark, which is a winter-flowerer, is popular in many home gardens and parks for its abundant, pretty rose-pink flowers and contrasting handsome bark. Its long-stalked buds with their pointed caps which are found in groups of three, make the tree readily identifiable. Although the bark is mainly smooth and yellowish, the tree is nevertheless classed as an ironbark rather than a smoothbark, because of the fibrous, persistent bark near the base. A medium-sized eucalypt, white ironbark adapts well to most soils and conditions.

Eucalyptus leucoxylon 'Rosea'

Euphorbia pulcherrima

Malus 'Profusion'

yearling. It belongs to a group of *M. niedzwetkyana* hybrids. Like most crab apples it is very hardy and is happy in most soils, given adequate humus. Mass-plant it or use along a driveway or pathway for a spectacular display of flower color in spring, and of brilliant crab apples in autumn.

Metrosideros excelsa
POHUTUKAWA (N.Z.), NEW ○
ZEALAND CHRISTMAS TREE

Family: MYRTACEAE
Origin: New Zealand.
Flowering time: Summer, northern hemisphere; late spring–summer, southern hemisphere.
Climatic zone: 9, 10.
Dimensions: 30–60 feet (10–18 meters) high.
Description: *Metrosideros* is very much at home clinging to soil at the beach edge. This evergreen revels in salt-laden, windy, and exposed sites, and sports eye-catching, fluffy red flowers in time for Christmas in the southern hemisphere. It requires a cool, prolonged

Metrosideros excelsa

Euphorbia pulcherrima
CHRISTMAS STAR, ○
POINSETTIA (U.K.)

Other common names: MEXICAN FLAMELEAF
Family: EUPHORBIACEAE
Origin: Tropical Mexico and Central America.
Flowering time: Winter–spring, northern hemisphere; late autumn–late spring, southern hemisphere.
Climatic zone: 9, 10.
Dimensions: 10–12 feet (3–4 meters) high.
Description: Brilliant red bracts surround the insignificant flowers of this world-popular plant. Grown outdoors, it needs a warm, sheltered position. Short days and long dark nights are necessary for good flowering. Commercial growers simulate these conditions in glasshouses to produce flowers over a very long period. Plant potted specimens outdoors in warm climates when the flowers have died.

Cut back most of the stem after flowering and tip-prune a few weeks after new shoots appear. The stems are brittle and the milky sap is poisonous.
Other colors: Cream, pale pink.
Varieties/cultivars: 'Henrietta Eck', 'Annette Hegge' (dwarf).

Malus 'Profusion'
ORNAMENTAL CRAB ○
APPLE, RED CRAB APPLE,
FLOWERING CRAB APPLE (U.K.)

Family: ROSACEAE
Origin: Hybrid.
Flowering time: Early summer.
Climatic zone: 4, 5, 6, 7, 8, 9.
Dimensions: 6–20 feet (2–6 meters) high.
Description: As its name suggests, this delightful, small crab apple is one of the most free-flowering of all the crab apples, producing flowers when just a

winter to flower well, and needs plenty of space to develop a wide crown from the short, stout trunk. It makes a good hedge or windbreak and will stand heavy pruning. Grow new plants from cuttings or seed.
Other colors: Creamy yellow.
Varieties/cultivars: 'Aurea'.

Prunus campanulata
TAIWAN CHERRY, BELL- ○
FLOWER CHERRY, FORMOSAN
CHERRY

Family: ROSACEAE
Origin: Taiwan and Ryuku Archipelago.
Flowering time: Late winter–early spring.
Climatic zone: 9.
Dimensions: 20–30 feet (6–8 meters) high.
Description: Pretty, carmine, bell-shaped flowers hang in small clusters from this deciduous, ornamental tree before the leaves appear. One of the reddest-flowered cherries, it is for a warm climate only. It is seldom grown in areas with late frosts, which damage the blossom and foliage. Its single trunk and wide canopy make for a splendid garden tree under which can be grown plants that enjoy dappled shade in summer and sun in winter.

Prunus campanulata

Prunus persica 'Magnifica'
DOUBLE RED-FLOWERING ○
PEACH

Family: ROSACEAE
Origin: Cultivar.
Flowering time: Spring.
Climatic zone: 5, 6, 7, 8, 9.
Dimensions: 10–20 feet (3–6 meters) high.
Description: One of the best red-flowering cultivars, this tree comes into blossom in late spring. It has large, double, bright rosy-red flowers. In wet climates the disease peach leaf curl is a

Prunus persica 'Magnifica'

problem. Spray with bordeaux mixture each spring when flower buds swell or color up, to kill over-wintering fungus, or prune back the branches to about half their length immediately after flowering. Plant this tree to provide a canopy of color over spring-flowering shrubs and perennials.

Spathodea campanulata
WEST AFRICAN TULIP ○
TREE, FOUNTAIN TREE,
FLAME-OF-THE-FOREST

Family: BIGNONIACEAE
Origin: West Africa.
Flowering time: Early spring–late summer.
Climatic zone: 9, 10.
Dimensions: 30–60 feet (9–18 meters) high.
Description: Bold in every way, this tree will take your breath away at first sight. Handsome, evergreen, compound

Spathodea campanulata

leaves support the magnificent, scarlet-orange flowers that are borne in spikes just above them. The display lasts a long time as flowers open one after the other instead of en masse. The tree develops a broad dome. It thrives in warm coastal areas, but should be protected from strong, salt-laden winds. Plant it in fertile soil with good drainage. It can be easily grown from seed sown in spring in the glasshouse.

Stenocarpus sinuatus

Stenocarpus sinuatus
QUEENSLAND FIREWHEEL ○
TREE

Family: PROTEACEAE
Origin: Australia (Queensland and N.S.W.).
Flowering time: Early autumn–mid-winter, southern hemisphere.
Climatic zone: 8, 9, 10.
Dimensions: 30–100 feet (10–30 meters) high.
Description: Not grown nearly as much as it deserves in Australia, it is often planted as a street tree in California, where it is well appreciated. Beautiful and interesting at every stage of its development, there is no other flower quite like this one, aptly described as a "wheel". The "spokes", or flower buds, arranged around a central hub, split open to expose the golden stamens within. A slow-growing, slender tree, it reaches in cultivation only half the height it attains in its native habitat. This evergreen can be grown in warm areas only.

PINK FLOWERS

Agrostemma githago
CORN COCKLE ○

Family: CARYOPHYLLACEAE
Origin: Mediterranean region.
Flowering time: Summer.
Climatic zone: 3, 4, 5, 6, 7, 8, 9.
Dimensions: Up to 3 feet (1 meter) high.
Description: This is an erect, slender plant with narrow, grayish, hairy foliage. The rosy pink to magenta-colored flowers are on single stems and open flat to 2 inches (50 mm) wide. The corn cockle is still considered to be a weed in grain-growing areas where its flowers are prominent in the fields. In cultivation it is hardy, but it is of no use in floral work, as the flower folds towards evening. It needs a sunny, well-drained position.
Other colors: White, rose-purple, lilac-pink.
Varieties/cultivars: 'Milas' (flowers are 3 inches (75 mm) wide, 'Purple Queen'.

Agrostemma githago

Begonia semperflorens
WAX BEGONIA ○

Family: BEGONIACEAE
Origin: Brazil.
Flowering time:
Spring–summer–autumn.
Climatic zone: 4, 5, 6, 7, 8, 9, 10.
Dimensions: Up to 12 inches (300 mm) high.
Description: This is a tender summer annual or perennial which flowers continuously in warmth. The flowers, though small — up to 1 inch (25 mm) wide — are produced in clusters on a stiff, succulent stem. Begonias are used for borders or massed bedding with contrasting colors of foliage and flowers. The leaves may be deep bronze to bright green according to variety. Plant in rich, well-drained soil, but allow soil to dry out a little between waterings.
Other colors: White, red.
Varieties/cultivars: 'Thousand Wonders', 'Comet'.

Begonia semperflorens

Bellis perennis
COMMON OR LAWN DAISY, ENGLISH DAISY ◑

Family: COMPOSITAE
Origin: Europe–western Asia.
Flowering time: Spring–summer.
Climatic zone: 6, 7, 8, 9.
Dimensions: Up to 4 inches (100 mm) high.
Description: This is the original daisy. The flowers are up to 1 inch (25 mm) wide, and are double in form. They are formed on a single stem and protrude from the basal leaves, which are shiny green and in the form of a rosette. The plant may be used as an attractive edging in cooler gardens. It will not stand continued hot sun. Although usually grown as an annual, it may be perennial. Rich, moist soil conditions are essential for success.
Other colors: White, rosy-red.
Varieties/cultivars: 'Montrosa' (larger heads of flowers, red), 'Rosea' (rose-pink), 'Prolifera' (secondary heads on the stem).

Callistephus chinensis
CHINA ASTER ○

Family: COMPOSITAE
Origin: China, Japan.
Flowering time: Summer–early autumn.
Climatic zone: 4, 5, 6, 7, 8, 9.
Dimensions: Up to 2 feet (600 mm) high.
Description: This is one of the best garden plants for floral art. The stiff stems may branch to form up to six flowers on each. The flowers, up to 5 inches (125 mm) wide, are many-petaled and double. The plant is subject to wilt which may weaken it considerably and suddenly. For healthy asters, ensure

Bellis perennis cultivar

that soil is light and sandy. Add lime if pH levels are acid.
Other colors: White, blue, violet.
Varieties/cultivars: 'Princess' (larger than average flowers), 'King' (more branches), 'Seven Dwarfs' (low variety).

Callistephus chinensis

Celosia cristata
CRESTED CELOSIA ○

Family: AMARANTHACEAE
Origin: Tropical Asia.
Flowering time: Summer.
Climatic zone: 5, 6, 7, 8, 9, 10.
Dimensions: Up to 2 feet (600 mm) high.
Description: This erect plant forms

Celosia cristata

upright flowers which look like woolly feathers in terminal spikes. Their vibrant colors make them a good summer annual for hot and dry conditions. The leaves may also be variegated in red and gold colors. The flowers, in their crested shape, may be up to 6 inches (150 mm) wide and brilliant in color. They are very suitable for large displays in parks. Celosia thrives in rich, well-drained soil that is kept constantly moist.
Other colors: Yellow, orange, red, and occasionally, white and purple.
Varieties/cultivars: 'Forest Fire', 'Golden Triumph' 'Fairy Fountain' (dwarf, mixed colors, 12 inches (300 mm) high).

Clarkia unguiculata

Clarkia unguiculata syn. *Clarkia elegans*
CLARKIA (U.K.), GARLAND ○ FLOWER

Family: ONAGRACEAE
Origin: California.
Flowering time: Summer.
Climatic zone: 4, 5, 6, 7, 8, 9, 10.
Dimensions: Up to 2 feet (600 mm) high.
Description: This erect, hardy annual produces many flowers on stiff stems. The rose-pink flowers have four petals, widening at the outer edge, and up to 2 inches (50 mm) across when open. The cut flowers are good for indoor

decoration. Excellent for poor, sandy soils — in fact, avoid using too much humus as flowers will be overwhelmed by foliage.
Other colors: Red, lavender, salmon, purple.
Varieties/cultivars: Single and double cultivars available.

Cleome hassleriana syn. *C. pungens*, *C. spinosa*
SPIDER FLOWER ○

Family: CAPPARIDACEAE
Origin: West Indies, Brazil–Argentina.
Flowering time: Summer.
Climatic zone: 4, 5, 6, 7, 8, 9, 10.
Dimensions: Up to 5 feet (1–1½ meters) high.
Description: In the right climate, this annual can be a commanding background to lower-growing annuals. The long, clawed petals, and extended stamens of the flowers, give them their spider-like appearance. The flowers are clustered to form large heads up to 5 inches (125 mm) across, in pale pink, almost white colors, with overtones of deeper pink and mauve. Cleome is a good flower for large, open areas such as parks and needs plenty of space, as each plant is quite wide. Warm conditions are essential. Water well.

Cleome hassleriana

Clarkia amoena
GODETIA

Family: ONAGRACEAE
Origin: Western North America, Chile.
Flowering time: Summer.
Climatic zone: 4, 5, 6, 7, 8, 9.
Dimensions: Up to 2 feet (600 mm) high.
Description: A delightful annual from California, previously classified as Godetia, this plant has graceful spikes of showy, pale pink or lavender to white flowers, measuring 2 inches (50 mm) across. Foliage is lance-shaped and toothed. The slender, erect habit of this annual makes it an ideal cut flower or useful pot plant for a cool greenhouse. Plant it in an open, sunny position in well-drained, humus-rich soil and ensure adequate water during spring growth and the summer flowering period.

Clarkia amoena

Cosmos bipinnatus
COMMON OR GARDEN COSMOS

Family: COMPOSITAE
Origin: Mexico.
Flowering time: Summer–autumn.

Cosmos bipinnatus

Climatic zone: 4, 5, 6, 7, 8, 9, 10.
Dimensions: Up to 6 feet (2 meters) high.
Description: Cosmos is a tall annual, well suited as a background in a cottage garden. The plant produces many flowers which are suitable for use indoors. The foliage is fern-like, providing an attractive background for the flowers, which are flat, open, and up to 2½ inches (65 mm) wide with yellow centers. Cosmos will thrive in most soils, preferring light, dry conditions.
Other colors: Red, white, deep mauve.
Varieties/cultivars: 'Mammoth Single', 'Bright-lights' (double flowers), 'Alba'.

Dianthus chinensis syn. *D. sinensis*
CHINA PINK, INDIAN PINK

Family: CARYOPHYLLACEAE
Origin: Eastern Asia.
Flowering time: Summer–autumn in cooler climates.
Climatic zone: 6, 7, 8, 9, 10.
Dimensions: Up to 18 inches (450 mm) high.
Description: This is a semi-hardy annual or short-lived perennial and may behave as a biennial. The semi-double flowers, which are up to 2 inches (50 mm) wide, have attractive, tooth-edged petals. They may be on single stems or loosely clustered and are only faintly fragrant. A neutral to limey soil is important and it should also be light, sandy and well-drained.
Other colors: White, lilac, red.
Varieties/cultivars: *D. c.* var. *Heddewigii*

Dianthus chinensis var. *Heddewigii*

Gomphrena globosa
GLOBE AMARANTH

Family: AMARANTHACEAE
Origin: Tropical Asia.
Flowering time: Midsummer–early autumn.
Climatic zone: 4, 5, 6, 7, 8, 9, 10.
Dimensions: Up to 18 inches (450 mm) high.
Description: This very low-growing, dense, annual plant likes a warm, dry climate. It is tough and needs no special soil conditions. It has a rounded, bushy habit, the flowers borne on slender stalks that protrude slightly from the edge of the foliage. The tight, clover-like flower heads are up to 1 inch (25 mm) in diameter. When cut, the flowers last well and are suitable for small arrangements and posies; they also dry well. Mulch in summer.
Other colors: Red, white, orange, purple. Variegated flowers are sometimes seen.
Varieties/cultivars: 'Rubra'.

Gomphrena globosa

Impatiens balsamina
COMMON OR GARDEN BALSAM

Family: BALSAMINACEAE
Origin: India–Malaya.
Flowering time: Summer.
Climatic zone: 4, 5, 6, 7, 8, 9, 10.
Dimensions: Up to 12 inches (300 mm) high.
Description: This is a tender annual that thrives in warm shade. The stiff stems are somewhat brittle and may easily suffer wind damage. The flowers are single or double and up to 2 inches (50 mm) wide. They are long-lasting on the plant and quickly replaced, but they have no value as a cut flower. Choose a good fertile soil that does not dry out and pinch back to encourage more bushy growth.

Other colors: Scarlet, yellow, white, purple. May be occasionally striped.
Varieties/cultivars: Double-flowered types are often called 'Camellia-flowered'.

Impatiens balsamina cultivar

Impatiens walleriana
BUSY LIZZY, PATIEN LUCY, SULTANA

Family: BALSAMINACEAE
Origin: Tanzania, Mozambique.
Flowering time: Warm months, but may flower all year.
Climatic zone: 5, 6, 7, 8, 9, 10.
Dimensions: Up to 2 feet (600 mm) high.
Description: This brittle-stemmed perennial is often grown as an annual. It thrives in warm, shaded areas where it is possible for it to flower most of the year. The flowers are up to 2 inches (50 mm) wide on single stems, and open flat. They have four petals, which are broad at the edge and curve slightly downwards. It is possible to use this plant for tubs and baskets and also to bring it indoors as a house plant. Water well in hot weather, and mulch with well-rotted compost for good results.
Other colors: Red, purple, orange, white.
Varieties/cultivars: There are double forms, also 'Nana' (dwarf-growing), and 'Variegata' (foliage variegated white).

Impatiens walleriana cultivar

Lathyrus odoratus cultivar

Lathyrus odoratus
SWEET PEA ○

Family: LEGUMINOSAE
Origin: Southern Italy, Sicily.
Flowering time: Summer–early autumn.
Climatic zone: 6, 7, 8, 9, 10.
Dimensions: Climbing plant to 6 feet (2 m) high.
Description: The sweet pea, with its delightful fragrance, is one of the most popular of plants, both for background planting in the garden and as a cut flower for floral use. Up to seven of the large, pea-like blooms, which are about 2 inches (50 mm) wide, are borne on a long, stiff stem. They appear in various shades of both bright and subtle colors. Being a tendril-climber, sweet pea needs the support of wires, strings, or a lattice. Add lime, and blood and bone to the soil prior to planting, and water well until plants are established.
Other colors: White, purple, red.
Varieties/cultivars: There are many cultivars of the above, some with large flowers, and very long stems. 'Bijou' is a dwarf variety, also used for bedding. Some varieties are early flowering and heat resistant.

Lavatera trimestris
ANNUAL MALLOW ○

Family: MALVACEAE
Origin: Mediterranean region, Portugal.
Flowering time: Early spring–autumn.
Climatic zone: 4, 5, 6, 7, 8, 9, 10.

Dimensions: Up to 3 feet (1 meter) tall.
Description: This plant likes well-drained soil and flowers best in the cooler months in a warm climate. The leaves are slightly hairy and almost round in shape with clear, ribbed veins. The flowers, which are mostly solitary on the outside of the plant, are as large as the leaf — up to 4 inches (100 mm) wide — and open flat.
Other colors: Shades of red and white.
Varieties/cultivars: 'Loveliness' (satiny, rose-pink), 'Splendens' (rose-red and occasionally white), 'Silver Cup'.

Lavateria trimestris 'Silver Cup'

Linaria maroccana

Linaria maroccana
TOADFLAX, BABY SNAPDRAGON, FAIRY FLAX ○

Family: SCROPHULARIACEAE
Origin: Morocco.
Flowering time: Spring.
Climatic zone: 6, 7, 8, 9, 10.
Dimensions: 12–18 inches (300–450 mm) high.
Description: This low-growing annual is mostly used as a border plant near other low-growing annuals. It should be densely planted to make a show of the delicate, small flowers, which are about 1 inch (25 mm) long and ½ inch (15 mm) wide and look like miniature snapdragons with a long spur. They are found only in soft, pastel shades and most of them have a yellow-spotted throat. Any well-drained soil will suffice, but take care not to overwater.
Other colors: Red, purple, and occasionally dark-blue.
Varieties/cultivars: 'Excelsior', 'Fairy Bouquet' (dwarf).

Linum grandiflorum
SCARLET FLAX ○

Family: LINACEAE
Origin: North Africa.
Flowering time: Summer.
Climatic zone: 6, 7, 8, 9, 10.
Dimensions: Up to 18 inches (450 mm) tall.

Description: This is a slender and gracefully erect plant, which is very tolerant and produces wide, open flowers at the stem tips. It may grow in poor soil but prefers a moderately fertile one and will flower throughout the season. It will not persist in extremes of heat. Flowers are up to 1½ inches (40 mm) wide.
Other colors: Scarlet, purple, red.
Varieties/cultivars: 'Coccineum' (scarlet), 'Caeruleum' (bluish-purple), 'Roseum' (rose pink), 'Rubrum' (deep-red).

Linum grandiflorum

Lunaria annua
HONESTY, MOONWORT, ◑ MOONEYPLANT

Other common names:
SATINFLOWER, PENNY FLOWER, SILVER DOLLAR
Family: CRUCIFERAE
Origin: Mediterranean region.
Flowering time: Spring–summer.
Climatic zone: 7, 8, 9, 10.
Dimensions: Up to 3 feet (900 mm) high.
Description: Although this plant is grown principally for its dried seed casing, it does bear an attractive head of small purplish-pink flowers. When these flowers fall and the seed pods appear, it presents quite a different appearance. The seed pods are flat, broadly oval to almost circular, 1½–2½ inches (40–60 mm) long. When ripe, the walls of the pod fall away to reveal a central silvery membrane which glows with a pearly lustre. In this silvery pearly form, the plant lasts indefinitely indoors and is an excellent decoration. Most soils are suitable providing drainage is adequate.
Other colors: White.
Varieties/cultivars: 'Alba', 'Variegata'.

Lunaria annua

Malcolmia maritima
VIRGINIA STOCK ○

Family: CRUCIFERAE
Origin: Greece, Albania.
Flowering time: Early summer–autumn.
Climatic zone: 6, 7, 8, 9, 10.
Dimensions: Up to 10 inches (250 mm) high.
Description: Virginia stock is a hardy annual for cool to warm climates. The plant is low-growing and bushy which makes it ideal as an annual border for taller annuals and perennials. It is a good bedding plant for massing between shrubs. The flowers, which are only ¾ inch (19 mm) wide, are found in clusters in terminal racemes. Their sweet

Malcolmia maritima

fragrance is reminiscent of stock.
Matures quickly if planted in a warm,
sunny position, in rich, well-drained
soil.
Other colors: Red, purple, white.

Matthiola incana
STOCK, BROMPTON
STOCK, GILLYFLOWER ◯

Family: CRUCIFERAE
Origin: Mediterranean region.
Flowering time: Spring.
Climatic zone: 7, 8, 9.
Dimensions: Up to 2½ feet (750 mm)
high.
Description: Stock is much sought
after. With its excellent, lasting
qualities, good color range, and
delightful fragrance, it is ideal for floral
decoration. Varieties produce long (up
to 18 inches (450 mm)) stems of tight,
either single or double flowers. The
single flowers have the stronger
perfume, but the doubles are more
showy. Individual flowers are only
1 inch (25 mm) wide but there are many
of them on strong upright stems. The
plant may be grown as either an annual
or a biennial. The soil should be
enriched with lime and plenty of
organic matter before planting. Water
well for good results.
Other colors: White, yellow, purple,
red.

Varieties/cultivars: 'Perfection', 'Hi-
double' (Trisomic), 'Giant Column' (tall
heads of flowers), 'Austral' (slightly
dwarf to 18 inches (450 mm)), 'Dwarf'
(up to 12 inches (300 mm) high).

Matthiola incana cultivar

Petunia x *hybrida*
PETUNIA ◯

Family: SOLANACEAE
Origin: Hybrid.
Flowering time: Summer.
Climatic zone: 6, 7, 8, 9, 10.
Dimensions: Up to 18 inches (450 mm)
high.
Description: The petunia in any one of
its many forms is the most universally
known and widely used annual in the
world. It is an asset anywhere with
bright summer colors in all shades. The
flowers are up to 4 inches (100 mm)
wide, rather flat, but sometimes fringed
and frilled on the edges. They are often
striped in lines from the center or in
contrasting-colored circles. They may
also have contrasting vein markings.
The plants have soft stems and may
trail, which makes them attractive in
hanging baskets or bowls in good
sunlight. Fertile soil and a sunny
position are essential.
Other colors: All colours, including
white, yellow, and mixtures of these.
Varieties/cultivars: 'Bonanza',
'Dazzler', 'Color Parade', 'Giant
Victorious', 'Fringed', and many others.

Petunia x *hybrida* cultivar

63

Phlox drummondii
ANNUAL PHLOX,
DRUMMOND PHLOX, TEXAN
PRIDE

Family: POLEMONIACEAE
Origin: Texas.
Flowering time: Summer.
Climatic zone: 6, 7, 8, 9, 10.
Dimensions: Up to 18 inches (450 mm) high.
Description: This is a popular summer annual which grows readily in sunny situations. The separate flowers are up to 1½ inches (35 mm) wide and make a vivid show because they are closely clustered. All colors are available as well as fringed bicolors or contrasting centers. Generally phlox is not used as a cut flower, but lasts well enough to be used in small posies or bowls. Light, dry, and well-drained soils give the best results. Take care not to overwater.
Other colors: All colors and mixtures.
Varieties/cultivars: 'Compact' (dwarf form), 'Twinkle' (star-like), 'Bright Eyes', 'Derwent'.

Phlox drummondii

Portulaca grandiflora
ROSE MOSS, SUN MOSS,
WAX PINK

Other common names: SUN PLANT, GARDEN PORTULACA
Family: PORTULACACEAE
Origin: Brazil–Argentina.
Flowering time: Midsummer.
Climatic zone: 6, 7, 8, 9, 10.
Dimensions: Up to 5 inches (125 mm) high.
Description: Portulacas have soft, succulent stems and a trailing habit, and can be used as groundcover or a border. The flowers, which are about 1½ inches (35 mm) wide, and may be single or double, are borne on short stems and are found in bright, clear colors with, occasionally, tiny, contrasting-colored centers. They open in the heat of the day and close at night or in cloudy conditions. Portulacas prefer hot, dry climates.
Other colors: White, yellow, red, purple.
Varieties/cultivars: 'Sunglow', 'Sunnybank'.

Portulaca grandiflora cultivar

Schizanthus pinnatus
BUTTERFLY FLOWER,
POOR MAN'S ORCHID

Family: SOLANACEAE
Origin: Chile.
Flowering time: Spring–summer.
Climatic zone: 7, 8, 9.
Dimensions: Up to 3 feet (approx. 1 meter) high.
Description: This lovely, soft-stemmed plant forms an erect, dense, compact mass of pale-green foliage which is ferny in appearance and attractive. It prefers a cool, sheltered position and produces masses of small flowers up to 1 inch (25 mm) wide in pastel tonings with vein-like markings and a contrasting-colored rim. The flowers have an upper and lower lip shaped like a small orchid. They are very decorative in hanging baskets, but are not ideal for picking. Plant in semishade in rich, moist, and well-drained soil. Pinch back new growth to encourage more blooms. Depending on the climate, this plant suits either a summer garden bed or a greenhouse.
Other colors: White, red, mauve, cream.
Varieties/cultivars: 'Dwarf Bouquet', 'Giant Hybrid', 'Hit Parade'.

Silene pendula
NODDING CATCHFLY

Family: CARYOPHYLLACEAE
Origin: Mediterranean region–Caucasus, southern U.S.S.R.
Flowering time: Summer.
Climatic zone: 6, 7, 8, 9.
Dimensions: Up to 18 inches (300 mm) high.
Description: This hardy annual is not freely grown. It forms a bushy, densely-leaved plant which bears clusters of small flowers up to 1 inch (25 mm) wide.

Schizanthus pinnatus

The flower heads are not dense and although delicate in appearance, they are hardy. Can be grown successfully in a wide range of soils, providing drainage is good.

Other colors: Carmine, occasionally white.

Varieties/cultivars: 'Ruberrima Bonnettii', 'Compacta'.

Viola x *wittrockiana* cultivar

Silene pendula

Viola x *wittrockiana*
PANSY, HEARTSEASE, LADIES' DELIGHT ○

Family: VIOLACEAE
Origin: Hybrid.
Flowering time: Spring–winter.
Climatic zone: 6, 7, 8, 9.
Dimensions: Up to 9 inches (225 mm) high.
Description: Pansies are one of the best known of the annual, flowering plants. The foliage spreads to about 12 inches (30 mm) wide, from which single-stemmed flowers appear face-up. They are available in all shades, in separate colors or with contrasting marks and veining. The flat flowers have four petals in opposite, overlapping pairs. They are suitable for posies or small vases and bloom for a long period. Pansies often have a very velvety texture, and prefer semishaded conditions and a moderately rich, moist soil.

Other colors: Purple, blue, maroon, red, yellow, orange, white.

Varieties/cultivars: 'Can Can', 'Roggli', 'Swiss Giants', 'Jumbo'.

Xeranthemum annuum
EVERLASTING, ANNUAL ○
EVERLASTING, IMMORTELLE

Family: COMPOSITAE
Origin: Southeastern–central Europe.
Flowering time: Summer.
Climatic zone: 7, 8, 9, 10.
Dimensions: Up to 2 feet (600 mm) high.
Description: This very hardy annual will grow in poor soil, produce many single-stemmed flowers typically daisy-like in shape, but with shiny, papery petals and a firm seed center. The flowers cover the bushes although, individually, they are only up to 1½ inches (40 mm) wide. They are very useful as cut flowers and dry well also.

Other colors: White, mauve, purple.

Varieties/cultivars: 'Ligulosum'.

Xeranthemum annuum

Cyclamen neapolitanum

Amaryllis belladonna

Amaryllis belladonna
BELLADONNA LILY, NAKED LADY ○

Family: AMARYLLIDACEAE
Origin: South Africa.
Flowering time: Summer–autumn.
Climatic zone: 8, 9, 10.
Dimensions: Up to 3 feet (1 meter) high.
Description: Named after a shepherdess in Greek mythology, this legendary plant has numerous fragrant trumpet-shaped flowers borne on long stems. Strap-shaped leaves usually appear after the plant blooms. If left undisturbed in a sheltered position, bulbs will multiply and give a massed display. It is suitable for borders along a gravel drive or against sunny fences. Cut flowers add elegance indoors. Water well when buds appear. Belladonna lily can be cultivated in pots for indoor display.
Varieties/cultivars: 'Rubra'.

Anemone nemorosa
WOOD ANEMONE, FAIRY'S ◑ WINDFLOWER

Family: RANUNCULACEAE
Origin: Europe including U.K.
Flowering time: Spring.
Climatic zone: 5, 6, 7, 8.

Anemone nemorosa

Dimensions: Up to 12 inches (300 mm) high.
Description: This pretty, pink perennial is a delightful flower to associate with ferns and primroses and will spread rapidly in woodland settings. The flowers are solitary with 6 sepals. Moist soil in a protected position suits it best. It will do well near water features in the garden.
Other colors: Blue, white.
Varieties/cultivars: 'Wilkes white', 'Flore Pleno'.

Cyclamen neapolitanum syn. *C. hederifolium*
ROCK CYCLAMEN, ◑ COMMON CYCLAMEN (U.K.), SOWBREAD

Family: PRIMULACEAE
Origin: Southern Europe.
Flowering time: Late summer–autumn.
Climatic zone: 7, 8, 9.
Dimensions: Up to 4 inches (100 mm) high.
Description: Rock cyclamen, with its unusual rose or white petals turned backwards to resemble shuttlecocks, was used in ancient times as an ingredient in love potions. Most of the flowers are produced before the deep green and silver leaves fully expand, the first flowers appearing in late summer before any leaf shows. This cyclamen will flower for up to eight weeks. A pretty addition to a fernery it can also be grown indoors in pots. Use fertilizer sparingly. Some bulbs have been known to produce for over 100 years. Allow it to colonize in light shade beneath trees or in garden pockets. Avoid excessive use of water.
Other colors: White, purple, red.

Lilium rubellum
LILY ○

Family: LILIACEAE
Origin: Japan.
Flowering time: Early–midsummer.
Climatic zone: 6, 7, 8, 9.
Dimensions: Up to 2 feet (600 mm) high.
Description: This oriental hybrid produces clusters of fragrant, pink flowers. It can be planted among herbaceous perennials or in lightly wooded areas. Water settings can be enhanced by including it among stones or pebbles. Adaptable to most good,

well-drained soils, it prefers an open sunny position. Light frosts will not affect it adversely, but it is sensitive to drought and excessive feeding. Large tubs of lilies look particularly effective at the entrance to a house or by the gate.

Lilium rubellum

Nerine bowdenii
SPIDER LILY ○

Family: AMARYLLIDACEAE
Origin: South Africa.
Flowering time: Autumn.
Climatic zone: 7, 8, 9.
Dimensions: Up to 18 inches (450 mm) high.
Description: A hardy grower with eight or more tubular flowers produced on long stems, spider lily is ideally suited for planting in rock gardens, near water, in tubs on patios or verandahs. The graceful spider-like flowers enhance trees when grown at their base. After bulbs have been planted they should be left undisturbed for several years until clumps form. They benefit from an application of general fertilizer in spring. Maintain adequate moisture.
Other colors: Red.
Varieties/cultivars: 'Pink Beauty', 'Hera', 'Fenwick's Variety'.

Nerine bowdenii

Oxalis adenophylla
MOUNTAIN SOURSOP, WOOD SORREL (U.S.A.), ◑ OXALIS

Family: OXALIDACEAE
Origin: Chile and Argentina.
Flowering time: Summer, outdoors; winter, indoors.
Climatic zone: 8, 9.
Dimensions: Up to 4 inches (100 mm) high.
Description: *Oxalis* is often overlooked as a garden flower because of its weed reputation. *O. adenophylla* is not a weed, but a pretty, long-flowering perennial adaptable to rock gardens, pot culture, and window boxes. Softly colored, gray-green crinkled leaves accompany pale lilac/pink flowers. Although termed wood sorrel, this is not one for making soup from. Like many of the 800 species of *Oxalis*, this plant has a sour juice when extracted. Grow it in a cool situation in neutral or slightly alkaline soil. It can be grown indoors in winter.
Other colors: Red, purple, yellow, white.

Oxalis adenophylla

Primula malacoides
FAIRY PRIMROSE ◑

Family: PRIMULACEAE
Origin: China.
Flowering time: Spring.
Climatic zone: 8.
Dimensions: Up to 18 inches (450 mm) high.
Description: Associated with the arrival of spring, this plant will thrive in wooded situations or in the vicinity of water gardens and is a versatile plant for pots, edges, borders, rock gardens, and window boxes. *P. malacoides* flowers in various shades of rose and lavender to pure white. It prefers a moist, cool position with some sun. In colder

climates, a greenhouse is essential. Propagation is by seed or division.
Other colors: White, red, purple.

Primula malacoides

Rhodohypoxis baurii
ROSE GRASS ○

Family: HYPOXIDACEAE
Origin: South Africa.
Flowering time: Spring–summer.
Climatic zone: 8, 9.
Dimensions: Up to 4 inches (100 mm) high.
Description: A rhizomatous, herbaceous perennial, rose grass derived its botanical name from the Greek 'rhodon' meaning rose. The tufted foliage is hairy and masses of rose-colored flowers show pale undersides. This small, slow-growing plant is an attractive rock garden addition. A sheltered, sunny site is best. The corm-like rhizome should be located in lime-free and moist, well-drained garden soil. An easy plant to look after, it is seldom attacked by garden pests.
Other colors: White.
Varieties/cultivars: 'Apple Blossom', 'Platypetala'.

Rhodohypoxis baurii

Antigonon leptopus
CORAL VINE, CORALLITA, MOUNTAIN ROSE ○ ◑

Other common names: QUEEN'S WREATH
Family: POLYGONACEAE
Origin: Mexico.
Flowering time: Mid-summer–autumn.
Climatic zone: 9, 10.
Description: Fast-growing, *Antigonon* climbs trees, fences, or trellises by attaching itself with small, strong tendrils. Flower sprays are numerous and make a spectacular display in summer. Treat it as a perennial in cooler districts, or in very hot zones where it may burn if planted in a windy exposed position. It can be used as a groundcover for sloping banks or sunny hillsides, or as a cover over a pergola. The arrow or heart-shaped leaves are an attractive addition to the bright floral display.
Other colors: White, red.

Antigonon leptopus

Bauhinia corymbosa
CLIMBING BAUHINIA ○

Family: LEGUMINOSAE
Origin: South East Asia.
Flowering time: Spring and autumn.
Climatic zone: 9, 10.
Description: Orchid-like flowers with red stamens appear on this evergreen plant in spring and autumn. The typical *Bauhinia* leaves, folded in half, are small and dainty and have reddish, hairy stems. A warm and sunny spot with rich soil will help this rather slow-developing vine to reach maximum growth. Some support will be necessary to train this sprawling plant as a climber. A warm climate plant, it needs full sun, good drainage, and a protected position. It is well worth growing for its attractive appearance all year.

Bauhinia corymbosa

Clematis montana 'Rubens'
PINK ANEMONE CLEMATIS (U.S.A.), TRAVELLER'S JOY ○ ◑

Family: RANUNCULACEAE
Origin: Himalayas – western China.
Flowering time: Spring–summer.
Climatic zone: 5, 6, 7, 8, 9.
Description: Pink anemone clematis has a dainty, fragrant flower with four petals in the shape of a cross. The flowers are rose-pink, fading to light pink, and are about 2 inches (50 mm) across. This deciduous vine is thin-stemmed and needs support during its spring–summer growing period when it is covered with a mass of blooms. In cold climates it flowers in early summer. It likes a warm sunny position, but does not like direct sun on the soil over the roots. Protect it by putting plenty of compost round its roots. It is best left unpruned, but if pruning is necessary, remove unwanted stems during the growing season.

Lonicera x *americana*
HONEYSUCKLE ○

Family: CAPRIFOLIACEAE
Origin: Hybrid.
Flowering time: Summer.
Climatic zone: 7, 8, 9.
Description: A vigorous, deciduous climber, this honeysuckle has large clusters of fragrant, yellowish-white flowers that are tinged with pink when in bud. Leaves are broad, and pointed at the tip. May be pruned after flowering, or in winter, to prevent it from becoming too prolific. Well-drained, moist soil and a sunny or partially shaded position give best results.

Lonicera x *americana*

Clematis montana 'Rubens'

Mandevilla sanderi
BRAZILIAN JASMINE, ○ ◑
DIPLADENIA (Aust.), CHILEAN
JASMINE (U.K.)

Family: APOCYNACEAE
Origin: Brazil.
Flowering time: Almost all year.
Climatic zone: 9, 10.
Description: Unlike the white *Mandevilla*, this beautiful little vine does not have fragrant flowers, but its clear pink, 3-inch (75-mm) blooms continue nearly all year provided conditions are warm enough. Grow as a tub plant with a trellis or wire support, or train over a lattice or trellis. Protect it from harsh sun, and provide rich soil and ample water for a delightful patio plant. In very warm zones, Brazilian jasmine can be grown in full shade, but filtered light is best. In cool areas, it does well as a greenhouse or house plant.

Mandevilla splendens

Mandevilla sanderi

Mandevilla splendens syn. *Dipladenia splendens*
CHILEAN JASMINE ○ ◑

Family: APOCYNACEAE
Origin: Southeastern Brazil.
Flowering time: Most of the year.
Climatic zone: 9, 10.
Description: Magnificent, clear pink flowers are scattered over this lovely vine almost all year long in warm climates. In cooler areas, a greenhouse is often necessary. It is evergreen, and although it will reach 20 feet (6 meters) if grown in the best position in the ground, it is usually treated as a container plant for patios. Twining stems will climb on to a trellis or wire support. A slender pole or frame is required for container growing, or it can be pruned to a low shrubby shape. Protect it from harsh sun and give regular water and deep compost for best results.

Pandorea jasminoides 'Rosea'
BOWER OF BEAUTY, ○ ◑
BOWER PLANT

Family: BIGNONIACEAE
Origin: Cultivar.
Flowering time: Summer–autumn.
Climatic zone: 9, 10.
Description: An evergreen, quick-growing climber, *Pandorea* has attractive, glossy, compound leaves with five to nine leaflets. The trumpet-shaped flowers are 2 inches (50 mm) long, and are pinkish-white streaked with pink or red inside the throat. Protect it from strong winds and give it adequate support for maximum cover over a fence, or train it to climb up a pillar. It is not tolerant of cold or frost, so in colder areas a greenhouse is required. It does best with regular watering and good soil. The shiny leaves make it a handsome plant when the flowers have finished.

Pandorea jasminoides 'Rosea'

Pelargonium peltatum cultivar

Pelargonium peltatum
IVY GERANIUM, IVY-LEAVED GERANIUM (U.K.) ○ ◑

Family: GERANIACEAE
Origin: Eastern South Africa.
Flowering time: All year.
Climatic zone: All zones.
Description: Widely grown for its continual flowering habit and range of brightly colored flowers, the ivy geranium can tolerate sunny conditions, or partial shade. It is treated as an annual in cold districts, when it is grown just for the summer months. It can be used in hanging baskets, window boxes, pots, tubs, or can be tied to and trained up a lattice or wire frame to cover a fence or wall. The ivy-like, pointed, five-lobed leaves are shiny and attractive and ivy geranium is one of the most adaptable and versatile light trailing plants.
Other colors: White, red, purple.
Varieties/cultivars: Many including 'Amethyst', 'Galilee', 'Gardenia', 'Gloire d'Orleans', 'The Pearl'.

Podranea ricasoliana
PORT ST. JOHN CREEPER, ○
PINK TECOMA

Family: BIGNONIACEAE
Origin: South Africa.
Flowering time: Summer.
Climatic zone: 9, 10.
Description: The flowers appear above

the leaves on this lovely climber, and almost cover the plant. It is evergreen with glossy deep-green leaves divided into seven to eleven leaflets. The flowers are trumpet-shaped, 2 inches (50 mm) long, with rounded lobes, and are produced in large clusters. Support is needed to hold the plant against a wall or fence, or it can be allowed to grow into a wide, flowing shrub which will "lean" against a fence. It is tolerant of wind and will withstand a light frost, but in cold climates a greenhouse is essential.

Rosa 'Cecile Brunner'
PINK CLIMBING ROSE, ○
CLIMBING CECILE BRUNNER
(U.K.)

Family: ROSACEAE
Origin: Hybrid.
Flowering time: Summer.
Climatic zone: 5, 6, 7, 8, 9.
Description: The beautifully shaped shell-pink miniature flowers of 'Cecile Brunner' are often found among the red-colored new growth of the leaves. The plant has a tendency to be shrubby, but it can reach up to 15 feet (5 meters) or more. Give it plenty of room to spread, as the bright green foliage is attractive and will disguise an ugly corner. Even when it has become wide and thick, it still has a rather open, airy appearance. The flowers have a light, delicate fragrance.

Rosa 'Cecile Brunner'

Podranea ricasoliana

Rosa 'Dorothy Perkins'

Wisteria floribunda 'Rosea'
PINK WISTERIA ○

Family: LEGUMINOSAE
Origin: Cultivar.
Flowering time: Late spring–early summer.
Climatic zone: 4, 5, 6, 7, 8, 9.
Description: 'Rosea' is the pink form of the commonly grown Japanese wisteria. Superbly fragrant, pea flowers hang in profusion in long sprays. The flowers open progressively from the base to the tip of the spray. It differs from the Chinese wisteria in the number of leaflets (fifteen to nineteen), and in its longer flower sprays. It usually blooms a few weeks later. It is best grown over a pergola where its spectacular beauty can be seen to advantage. It needs pruning during the summer growing season, and shaping during the winter.

Rosa 'Dorothy Perkins'
PINK CLIMBING ROSE,
PINK RAMBLER (U.K.) ○

Family: ROSACEAE
Origin: Hybrid.
Flowering time: Summer.
Climatic zone: 5, 6, 7, 8, 9.
Description: This is a beautiful little rose which has lost some popularity, due to its short blooming period and susceptibility to mildew. The non-recurrent flowers are small, dainty, double, and rosette-like. Bright pink, slightly fragrant, they are produced prolifically during early summer. Because of its vigorous growth and long, arching habit, it is often used for grafting onto a tall stem to create a weeping standard rose. The tiny buds are favorites for old-fashioned posies or small flower arrangements.

vine an unusual climber. It has a vigorous twining habit, and dark-green pinnate leaves with prominent veins. The flowers are borne in drooping clusters, and are bell-shaped. Fairly humid conditions are preferred, so it is most successful in hotter climates. In other areas, a greenhouse may be necessary. It is a very showy climber on a fence or trellis in a semishaded position.

Wisteria floribunda 'Rosea'

Tecomanthe hillii
PINK TRUMPET VINE ◑

Family: BIGNONIACEAE
Origin: Australia (Northeastern coast).
Flowering time: Summer.
Climatic zone: 9, 10.
Description: Rosy flowers marked with purplish lines make the pink trumpet

Tecomanthe hillii

Acanthus mollis 'Latifolius'

Acanthus mollis 'Latifolius'
BEAR'S-BREECH, OYSTER PLANT ○ ◑ ●

Family: ACANTHACEAE
Origin: Cultivar.
Flowering time: Summer.
Climatic zone: 6, 7, 8, 9.
Dimensions: Up to 4½ feet (over 1 meter) high.
Description: *Acanthus mollis* is much desired as a border and specimen plant, both for its handsome, deeply-cut and glossy foliage and its showy flowers on spikes up to 18 inches (450 mm) long. Given a sheltered, sunny position, it flowers profusely and likes a moderately rich, well-drained loam. *Acanthus* is slow to establish but forms a large clump once settled. It is propagated by seed sown in spring, or by root division in autumn or spring. Prune it by removing spent flowers and leaves. It attracts snails.
Other colors: White, lilac, purple.

Alcea rosea syn. *Althaea rosea*
HOLLYHOCK ○

Family: MALVACEAE
Origin: Eastern Mediterranean region.
Flowering time: Summer.
Climatic zone: 4, 5, 6, 7, 8, 9.
Dimensions: 5–9 feet (2–3 meters) high.
Description: Hollyhocks are at their best when grown as a backdrop to a profuse summer border, and given the shelter and support of a wall. They will stand sentinel to delphiniums, foxgloves, zinnias, rudbeckias, and all the other dazzling blooms of summer. They require fairly rich, well-drained

soil, and plenty of water in dry periods. Short-lived, they are often treated as biennials. To promote longer life, remove flower stalks at the base as soon as the flowers fade. Hollyhocks are subject to attack by red spider and rust. They are attractive in mixed flower arrangements.
Other colors: White, purple, red, yellow.
Varieties/cultivars: 'Chater's Improved', 'Summer Carnival', 'Begonia Flowered'.

Alcea rosea

Antennaria dioica
CAT'S FOOT, PUSSY TOES ○ (U.S.A.), MOUNTAIN EVERLASTING

Family: COMPOSITAE
Origin: Eurasia.
Flowering time: Late spring.
Climatic zone: 4, 5, 6, 7, 8.
Dimensions: Up to 6 inches (150 mm) high.

Antennaria dioica

Description: *Antennaria dioica* is a useful mat-forming rockery plant because of its creeping, fast-growing habit. Its flowers are small, tubular and borne in terminal clusters, and the foliage is tufted and woolly in appearance. Although the plant grows as well in rich, moist soils as in dry, sandy conditions, it nevertheless needs good drainage. It is propagated by seed in autumn or spring or by division and looks well planted with *Achillea x lewisii* (King Edward). It has no particular value as a cut flower.
Other colors: White, rose-red.
Varieties/cultivars: 'Minima', 'Rosea', 'Rubra'.

Armeria pseudarmeria

Armeria pseudarmeria
THRIFT, PLANTAIN ○ THRIFT

Family: PLUMBAGINACEAE
Origin: Portugal.
Flowering time: Summer.
Climatic zone: 6, 7, 8, 9.
Dimensions: 1½–2 feet (450–600 mm) high.
Description: Plantain thrift is a relatively tall variety of *Armeria* and is therefore more useful in the herbaceous border than the lower-growing common thrift, *A. maritima*. With its round flower heads borne on stiff stalks and its grass-like, tufted foliage, it is easy to grow in most soils, but thrives in well-drained, sandy loam. Removing spent blooms prolongs flowering. Easily propagated by division of clumps in autumn, plantain thrift makes a long-lasting pot specimen in cool conditions and is a good cut flower.
Other colors: White, red.
Varieties/cultivars: 'Bees Ruby'.

Aster novae-angliae

Aster novae-angliae
NEW ENGLAND ASTER ○
(U.S.A.), MICHAELMAS DAISY
(U.K.), EASTER DAISY (Aust.)

Family: COMPOSITAE
Origin: Eastern North America.
Flowering time: Late summer–autumn.
Climatic zone: 4, 5, 6, 7, 8, 9.
Dimensions: 3–5 feet (nearly 2 meters) high.
Description: *Aster novae-angliae* brings a wonderful splash of color to the autumn garden. It is equally lovely as a late-flowerer in the summer border or grown in the smaller space of a city garden. Its foliage is dense and grayish-green; the flowers are large, and clustered on strong, hairy stems. It prefers well-mulched, moist, fertile soil that is well-drained and benefits from complete fertilizer in spring and summer. It has an unhappy habit of closing at night. Use it as a cut flower in indoor decorating.
Other colors: Blue, purple.
Varieties/cultivars: 'Alma Potschke', 'Barr's Pink', 'Harrington Pink', 'Ryecroft Purple'.

Aster novi-belgii 'Patricia Ballard'
NEW YORK ASTER (U.S.A.), ○
MICHAELMAS DAISY (U.K.),
EASTER DAISY (Aust.)

Family: COMPOSITAE
Origin: Cultivar.
Flowering time: Late summer–autumn.
Climatic zone: 5, 6, 7, 8, 9.
Dimensions: Up to 3 feet (900 mm) high.
Description: What color the New York aster brings to the autumn garden! Plant

Aster novi-belgii 'Patricia Ballard'

it against a backdrop of autumn leaves and scarlet berry colors and highlight it by the white of the Japanese windflower. It prefers well-composted, moist, and well-drained soil. Fertilizer in spring and summer, and plenty of water in dry periods are essential. Prune it by cutting spent flower stems to ground level. New York aster provides good cut flowers.

Astrantia maxima

Astrantia maxima syn. *A. helleborifolia*
MASTERWORT ○ ◑

Family: UMBELLIFERAE
Origin: Caucasus, Turkey.
Flowering time: Summer.
Climatic zone: 4, 5, 6, 7, 8, 9.
Dimensions: Up to 2 feet (600 mm) high.
Description: Masterwort, with its tall stems, numerous delicate flowers, and interesting foliage, is best suited to wild or cottage gardens. The flowers may be cut and dried for use in floral arrangements. Any ordinary garden soil suits masterwort, but it needs adequate water in summer. Propagate it by root division or by seed.

Aubrieta deltoidea
FALSE ROCK CRESS, ○ ◑
AUBRIETA (U.K.)

Family: CRUCIFERAE
Origin: Southern Greece, Sicily.
Flowering time: Spring–early summer.
Climatic zone: 5, 6, 7, 8, 9.
Dimensions: Up to 6 inches (150 mm) high.
Description: Aubrieta is a cheerful, profusely flowering rockery or border-edging plant. Its flowers appear in loose clusters, held above the foliage. They come in both single and double forms. Its grayish-green, downy leaves form a spreading mat which can be invasive if not trimmed back. Propagation is by seed sown in spring or by cuttings. Well-drained, light soil is required for best results where summers are mild.
Other colors: Mauve, lilac, purple, blue, white.
Varieties/cultivars: Several cultivars include 'Borsch's White', 'Gloriosa', 'Greencourt Purple', 'Mrs. Rodewald', 'Purple Gem', 'Variegata'.

Aubrieta deltoidea cultivar

Begonia x *semperflorens-cultorum*

Bergenia cordifolia hybrid cultivar

Begonia x *semperflorens-cultorum* syn.
B. *semperflorens*, B. *cucculata* var.
hookeri
WAX BEGONIA ◑

Family: BEGONIACEAE
Origin: Hybrid.
Flowering time: Summer.
Climatic zone: 3, 4, 5, 6, 7, 8, 9, 10.
Dimensions: Up to 18 inches (450 mm)
high.
Description: A useful perennial with
fleshy foliage and showy clusters of pink
flowers, *Begonia* requires a rich, moist
soil and semishaded conditions.
Protection from summer midday sun is
essential. Often grown as a summer
bedding plant among annuals and other
perennials, it likes plenty of water
during summer and several applications
of liquid plant food to encourage good
flower production. It is not difficult to
propagate from stem or leaf cuttings in
spring or summer, or raise from seed.
Other colors: Red, pink, white, doubles
and singles, bronze and purple foliage.
Varieties/cultivars: Many cultivars are
available including 'Carmen',
'Flamingo', 'Galaxy', 'Indian Maid',
'Linda', 'Organdy'.

Bergenia cordifolia
HEARTLEAF ○ ◑ ●
BERGENIA, SAXIFRAGE,
MEGASEA (U.K.)

Family: SAXIFRAGACEAE
Origin: Siberia.
Flowering time: Late winter–spring.
Climatic zone: 3, 4, 5, 6, 7, 8, 9, 10.
Dimensions: 12–18 inches (300–450 mm)
high.

Description: Heartleaf bergenia takes
its name from its large, heart-shaped
leaves which are thick, fleshy, and
evergreen, making a very attractive
groundcover or border edging,
especially in damp and shaded
positions. The flowers are in large
clusters on sturdy stems and, in mild
climates, bloom in winter. Remove
spent flower heads to prolong flowering.
Bergenia will grow in any soil but
thrives with organic mulch and plenty
of water during dry spells. Propagate by
root division from autumn to spring.
Other colors: White, red, lilac.
Varieties/cultivars: 'Purpurea',
'Perfecta'.

Bergenia x *schmidtii*

Bergenia x *schmidtii*
BERGENIA, ○ ◑
MEGASEA

Family: SAXIFRAGACEAE
Origin: Hybrid.
Flowering time: Late winter–late spring.

Climatic zone: 4, 5, 6, 7, 8, 9.
Dimensions: 9–18 inches (225–450 mm)
high.
Description: This useful and hardy
perennial has large, thick, almost
leathery leaves and a showy display of
pink flowers borne in nodding flower
heads. It really thrives in moderately
rich and well-drained soil, but can
survive in less favorable conditions,
including rocky and poor soils. Plant it
in light shade, or in full sun if moisture
is provided.

Centaurea hypoleuca 'John Coutts'

Centaurea hypoleuca 'John Coutts'
PINK CORNFLOWER ○

Family: COMPOSITAE
Origin: Cultivar.
Flowering time: Summer.
Climatic zone: 4, 5, 6, 7, 8, 9.
Dimensions: 1½–2 feet (450–600 mm)
high.
Description: The pink cornflower, with
its deep rose-colored and fringed ray
flowers, looks stunning in a massed
border display. Its lobed leaves, green
on the surface and whitish underneath,
are also attractive. It prefers dry, well-
drained soil and an open position.
Propagate by dividing established
clumps in autumn or spring. The cut
flowers are attractive in floral
decorations.

Chelone lyonii
PINK TURTLEHEAD ◑

Family: SCROPHULARIACEAE
Origin: Southeastern United States.
Flowering time: Summer–autumn.
Climatic zone: 4, 5, 6, 7, 8, 9.

Dimensions: Up to 3 feet (1 meter) high.
Description: *C. lyonii* is most desirable in the summer garden for both its dark, glossy foliage, and its slightly hooded, rosy-pink flowers borne on a terminal spike. It prefers partial shade and moist, humus-enriched soil. Propagate it from seed sown in spring or root division in autumn or spring.

Chelone lyonii

Coronilla varia
CROWN VETCH

Family: LEGUMINOSAE
Origin: Central and southern Europe.
Flowering time: Summer.
Climatic zone: 4, 5, 6, 7, 8, 9, 10.
Dimensions: Up to 18 inches (450 mm) high.
Description: This sprawling perennial can be invasive in the garden. It is ideal as a groundcover for steep, sunny banks or in borders. The long tricolored flowers of pink, rose, and white are pea-shaped. These dense clusters are most attractive against their ferny foliage which closes up at night. Fast-growing, crown vetch will cover mounds or building rubble and control erosion if the soil is dry. Propagation is by seed.
Varieties/cultivars: 'Aurea', 'Penngift'.

Coronilla varia

Darmera peltata syn. *Peltiphyllum peltatum, Saxifraga peltatum*
UMBRELLA PLANT, INDIAN RHUBARB

Family: SAXIFRAGACEAE
Origin: California, Oregon.
Flowering time: Spring.
Climatic zone: 6, 7, 8, 9.
Dimensions: Up to 4 feet (over 1 meter) high.
Description: This moisture-loving perennial has pale pink flowers that form clusters on sturdy stems about 2 feet (600 mm) high. The leaves are lotus-like and borne at the top of stems growing between 3 and 4 feet (approx. 1 meter) high. It is a suitable plant for moist areas beside ponds or streams but, because it can become very invasive, it is unsuitable for small gardens. The Californian Indians ate the peeled leaf stalks, hence the name "Indian rhubarb". Propagate it by root division or seed.
Other colors: White.
Varieties/cultivars: 'Nanum' (dwarf).

Darmera peltata

Dianthus barbatus

Dianthus barbatus
SWEET WILLIAM ○

Family: CARYOPHYLLACEAE
Origin: Southern Europe and
Mediterranean region.
Flowering time: Summer.
Climatic zone: 6, 7, 8, 9.
Dimensions: Up to 16 inches (400 mm)
high.
Description: Once known as the divine
flower of Jupiter and Zeus, this
perennial will bloom for six to ten
weeks. Sweetly scented flowers are single
or double and occur in a variety of
colors. It is suitable for borders, edges,
or potted on garden steps and decks.
Related to the carnation and pinks
family, *Dianthus* likes an open sunny
position in sandy loam. Generous
colorful heads will result from an
application of lime and compost when
planting.
Other colors: Red, purple, white.
Varieties/cultivars: 'Giant white',
'Dunnets dark crimson', Dwarf mixed.

Dianthus caryophyllus
CARNATION, CLOVE ○
PINK

Family: CARYOPHYLLACEAE
Origin: Central Europe.
Flowering time: Summer.
Climatic zone: 7, 8, 9.
Dimensions: Up to 2 feet (600 mm) high.
Description: *Dianthus caryophyllus*,
known and used as a garland flower
from the time of the Norman conquest,
and referred to as "the divine flower" by
the ancient Greeks, is the parent of
modern carnations. Commonly referred
to now as "the perpetual", carnation is
a perennial with multi-petaled flowers,
that blooms all year round. A wide
choice of colors is available. There are

Dianthus caryophyllus hybrid

also border carnations available, which
flower only once a year and have a
bushier growth than the perpetuals.
Plant carnations in light, sandy soil
mixed with compost and lime. Stakes
are required for support when plants
grow tall. Carnations dislike wet,
sunless winters so need a greenhouse
environment in these areas.
Other colors: Red, yellow, white.
Varieties/cultivars: 'Dwarf Pygmy
Mixed', 'Enfant de Nice', 'Giant
Chabaud'.

Dianthus plumarius
COMMON PINK, GRASS ○
PINK, COTTAGE PINK

Family: CARYOPHYLLACEAE
Origin: Eastern and central Europe.
Flowering time: Early summer.
Climatic zone: 5, 6, 7, 8, 9.

Dianthus plumarius

Dimensions: Up to 18 inches (450 mm)
high.
Description: *D. plumarius* is thought to
be the parent of the old-fashioned and
modern pinks. Similar to carnations in
their foliage, pinks have simpler flowers
and share a wide color range. Use them
as borders in beds of carnations or sweet
William. Their fragrant perfume adds an
old-fashioned touch to gardens. Plant
cuttings in light, sandy soil mixed with
compost and lime. Provide them with a
sunny position protected from wind,
and water regularly. They make pretty
posies indoors.
Other colors: White, red, purple.

Dianthus x allwoodii
ALLWOOD PINK ○

Family: CARYOPHYLLACEAE
Origin: Hybrid.
Flowering time: Spring–summer.
Climatic zone: 7, 8, 9.
Dimensions: Up to 18 inches (450 mm)
high.
Description: Allwood pink is a hybrid
whose flowers are fringed or plain-
petaled and can be single, double, or
semidouble. The petals spray outwards
in a delicate formation from their
tubular base, and are found in shades of
pink, red and white, or combinations of
these. Planted in front of delphiniums,
they produce a cottage garden effect.
Allwood pink is easy to grow in any
garden soil, but requires good drainage.
Alkaline soil, provided with additional
humus, gives best results. Prolong the
flowering period by removing spent
flowers.
Other colors: White, red.
Varieties/cultivars: 'Doris', 'Lilian',
'Robin', 'Timothy'.

Dianthus x *allwoodii* 'Doris'

Dicentra eximia 'Bountiful'

Dicentra spectabilis

Dicentra eximia
FRINGED BLEEDING HEART, WILD BLEEDING HEART

Family: FUMARIACEAE
Origin: Eastern United States.
Flowering time: Spring–summer.
Climatic zone: 3, 4, 5, 6, 7, 8, 9, 10.
Dimensions: Approx. 12 inches (300 mm) high.
Description: Fern-like foliage and rose-purple, heart-shaped blooms that bees love make this a useful border perennial. *D. eximia* is equally at home in sun or shade, providing the soil is moist. It is a good choice for corners of the garden needing a little color. Open borders, ferneries, and rock gardens will also suit it if the soil is rich, moist, and has had humus added. Propagate by root division in early spring.
Other colors: White, red.
Varieties/cultivars: 'Alba', 'Luxuriant', 'Bountiful'.

Dicentra spectabilis
COMMON BLEEDING-HEART, DUTCHMAN'S BREECHES

Family: FUMARIACEAE
Origin: Japan, Korea, China.
Flowering time: Spring–early summer.
Climatic zone: 3, 4, 5, 6, 7, 8, 9.
Dimensions: Up to 2 feet (600 mm) high.
Description: The outstandingly elegant, heart-shaped flowers droop from arching, horizontal stems. White petals glisten at the tip of each "heart" like tears. A Japanese-style garden would suit this plant to perfection. Feature *D. spectabilis* against a cool rock wall where it will not have to compete to show its splendor. It should be planted in light sun or shade in cool, rich, well-drained soil, and protected

from slugs. Lifted plants can easily be grown in a warm greenhouse.
Other colors: White.
Varieties/cultivars: 'Alba'.

Digitalis x *mertonensis*

Digitalis x *mertonensis*
MERTON FOXGLOVE

Family: SCROPHULARIACEAE
Origin: Hybrid.
Flowering time: Summer.
Climatic zone: 6, 7, 8, 9, 10.
Dimensions: Up to 3 feet (1 meter) high.
Description: This hybrid of *D. purpurea* is a favorite of bees and smaller insects which shelter in the drooping, rose-pink blooms. Foxglove forms a good backdrop for beds of annuals, and looks well with most cottage garden favorites. This hybrid requires frequent division in spring to maintain its perennial character. An easy plant to grow in ordinary well-drained garden soil, it benefits from an application of compost in spring.

Dodecatheon meadia
COMMON SHOOTING STAR

Family: PRIMULACEAE
Origin: Eastern United States.
Flowering time: Spring–early summer.
Climatic zone: 4, 5, 6, 7, 8, 9.
Dimensions: Up to 18 inches (450 mm) high.
Description: A member of the primrose family, *D. meadia* has up to twenty rose-purple, reflexed flowers resembling shooting-stars. The yellow or purple anthers form a dart-like tip, giving the blooms their starry appearance. The foliage dies down when flowering has finished. The plant is suited to wild gardens, rock gardens, and shaded borders, and is easily grown in rich, sandy soil with plenty of organic matter. Good drainage is needed, as is moisture during the growing season. Propagate this plant by division or seed.
Other colors: Red, purple, white.
Varieties/cultivars: 'Album'.

Dodecatheon meadia

Eremurus robustus

Eremurus robustus
FOXTAIL LILY, DESERT CANDLES ○

Family: LILIACEAE
Origin: Turkestan.
Flowering time: Summer.
Climatic zone: 7, 8, 9.
Dimensions: Up to 10 feet (3 meters) high.
Description: This lofty plant, with soft-pink, closely packed flowers borne on long spikes, is a stately herbaceous perennial which can be companion-planted with delphiniums and irises. The leaves of some species of this lily are eaten in Afghanistan as a vegetable. The tubers are octopus-shaped and need to be planted 6–8 inches (150–200 mm) deep, resting on sand. Well-drained soil in an open, sunny position suits this spectacular plant best.

Filipendula palmata syn. *F. multijuga*
SIBERIAN MEADOWSWEET ◑

Family: ROSACEAE
Origin: Siberia.
Flowering time: Summer.
Climatic zone: 4, 5, 6, 7, 8, 9.
Dimensions: Up to 2½ feet (750 mm) high.
Description: A graceful perennial with large seven-lobed leaves and showy flat heads of pinkish-purple flowers. A useful addition to a mixed floral border, it has a spreading habit and requires plenty of space to give a good display. Likes moderately rich, moist soil. Can be propagated either by division, or from seed. It benefits from an application of compost in the spring.

Filipendula palmata syn. *F. multijuga*

Filipendula rubra 'Venusta'

Filipendula rubra
QUEEN-OF-THE-PRAIRIE ◑

Family: ROSACEAE
Origin: Eastern United States.
Flowering time: Summer.
Climatic zone: 3, 4, 5, 6, 7, 8, 9.
Dimensions: Up to 5 feet (approx. 2 meters) high.
Description: Peach-pink flowers form airy clusters on this tall, feathery border plant. Related to the rose, it needs plenty of space in a shaded part of the garden. Plant it in filtered sun under large trees or among ferns and orchids.

F. rubra looks attractive planted behind pink and white peonies in a bed. It is easy to grow in very moist garden soil, especially if humus has been added to help retain moisture. Propagate it by division of the clumps in early spring.
Other colors: Deep pink.
Varieties/cultivars: 'Venusta'.

Geranium x *magnificum*
CRANESBILL ○ ◑

Family: GERANIACEAE
Origin: Hybrid.
Flowering time: Summer.
Climatic zone: 4, 5, 6, 7, 8, 9.
Dimensions: Up to 2 feet (600 mm) high.
Description: A most successful cross between *G. ibericum* and *G. platypetalum*, this clump-forming perennial is superior to either of its parents. The wide and deeply-lobed foliage grows vigorously, while the showy violet flowers have reddish stems and bloom in profusion, measuring 1½ inches (30 mm) in diameter. It likes well-drained, moderately-rich soil and can be incorporated into a mixed bed of perennials, or grown in a large container.

Geranium x *magnificum*

Geranium psilostemon

Geranium psilostemon
ARMENIAN CRANESBILL ○ ◖

Family: GERANIACEAE
Origin: Turkey, Caucasus.
Flowering time: Spring–summer.
Climatic zone: 5, 6, 7, 8, 9.
Dimensions: Up to 3 feet (900 mm) high.
Description: With its brilliant magenta flowers, black-spotted at the base, and its deeply-lobed leaves, Armenian cranesbill makes an eye-catching border plant. It forms large clumps in full sun, and also looks well placed among other herbaceous perennials against a stone wall, or along pathways, or in woodland areas. It flowers freely in any light, well-drained soil, in full sun where summers are cool, but appreciates partial shade in hot areas. Propagate it by seed, cuttings, or division.
Other colors: Blue-purple.

Geranium sanguineum
BLOODY CRANESBILL ○ ◖

Family: GERANIACEAE
Origin: Europe, western Asia.
Flowering time: Spring–summer.
Climatic zone: 4, 5, 6, 7, 8, 9, 10.
Dimensions: Up to 18 inches (450 mm) high.
Description: An invaluable and highly adaptable plant, with flowers ranging from pale pink to reddish-purple, bloody cranesbill will tolerate full sun even in hot, dry summers. It is a good choice for open borders and sloping sites, and can also be planted among large boulders, on mounds, and in rock garden pockets. Grow it in fertile, well-

Geranium sanguineum

drained soil, mulch and water it well in summer, and give it fertilizer. Its dwarf variety, *G. sanguineum* var. *lancastrense*, forms flat carpets of large, rosy flowers.
Other colors: White, purplish-red.
Varieties/cultivars: 'Album', 'Shepherd's warning', G. s. var. *lancastrense*.

Gypsophila repens 'Rosea'
CREEPING BABY'S ○
BREATH, FAIRY GRASS

Family: CARYOPHYLLACEAE
Origin: Central and southern European mountains.
Flowering time: Spring–summer.
Climatic zone: 3, 4, 5, 6, 7, 8, 9.
Dimensions: Up to 8 inches (200 mm) high.
Description: Dense mats of this dainty-flowered creeper soften sloping sites. The masses of pale pink flowers bloom profusely throughout spring and summer. It is an effective groundcover grown near paved areas or cascading over walls. Plant it in fertile, well-

Gypsophila repens 'Rosea'

drained soil in a sunny position and water regularly. Apply complete fertilizer in spring and trim after flowering. Gathered in bunches, creeping baby's breath is excellent for small floral arrangements.
Other colors: White.

Helleborus orientalis
LENTEN ROSE, HELLEBORE ◑

Family: RANUNCULACEAE
Origin: Greece, Turkey.
Flowering time: Late winter–spring.
Climatic zone: 4, 5, 6, 7, 8, 9.
Dimensions: Approx. 18 inches (450 mm) high.
Description: The hellebores, whose name is derived from the Greek "elein" (to injure) and "bora" (food), have been known and used since ancient times. Although the plants are poisonous, they have been used medicinally. Lenten rose is the easiest species of *Helleborus* to grow and is a popular addition to gardens. Each stem carries several cup-shaped flowers, often speckled inside. The plant grows well among trees or shrubs as a low-maintenance groundcover. Moist soil is essential.
Other colors: Pale yellow, white, green, red, maroon.
Varieties/cultivars: Several cultivars are available.

Helleborus orientalis

Heterocentron elegans syn. *Schizocentron elegans, Heeria elegans*
SPANISH SHAWL ◑

Family: MELASTOMATACEAE
Origin: Mexico, Guatemala, Honduras.
Flowering time: Summer.
Climatic zone: 9, 10.
Dimensions: Up to 2 inches (50 mm) high.
Description: This perennial is shy of the sun despite its tropical origins. The stems are prostrate, with trailing or cascading branches which can reach out to 3 feet (1 meter) across. Oval or heart-

Heterocentron elegans

shaped, bright green leaves accompany profuse pink flowers. Needing filtered sunlight, spanish shawl is a groundcover suited to shady edges, near ferns or in cool rock garden pockets. It prefers rich, moist, well-drained soil in a protected position. Propagation is by seed or root division. It is susceptible to drought and frost.

Incarvillea delavayi

Incarvillea delavayi
HARDY GLOXINIA, PRIDE OF CHINA ○

Family: BIGNONIACEAE
Origin: China.
Flowering time: Summer.
Climatic zone: 5, 6, 7, 8, 9.
Dimensions: Up to 2 feet (600 mm) high.
Description: This is a showy perennial with large clusters of flared, trumpet-shaped flowers. Its bright purplish-pink blooms have yellow throats and together with the fern-like leaves make a good display in a sunny position in a temperate garden. It grows well in borders, rock gardens, or pots. Light soils suit it best and it needs good drainage or the roots will rot. Although it is easily propagated by seed, the seedlings take about two years to flower. In colder zones, provide winter protection. Apply a complete fertilizer in late winter.

Liatris spicata

Liatris spicata
GAY FEATHER, BLAZING STAR ○

Family: COMPOSITAE
Origin: Eastern and central United States.
Flowering time: Summer–autumn.
Climatic zone: 3, 4, 5, 6, 7, 8, 9.
Dimensions: Up to 5 feet (approx. 2 meters) high.
Description: This herbaceous perennial produces tall spikes of rose-lilac flowers like fluffy feather dusters; the grass-like leaves grow in tufts. A quick-growing plant, gay feather is ideal for a mixed border and looks attractive with *Dianthus* x *allwoodii* in the foreground. It likes an open, sunny position and light or ordinary garden soil. Water it regularly and apply a complete fertilizer in spring. Cut it back after flowering. This plant is seldom attacked by pests or diseases.
Varieties/cultivars: *L. s. montana*, *L. s. m.* 'Kobold'.

Lychnis coronaria

Lychnis coronaria
ROSE CAMPION, DUSTY MILLER ○ ◑

Family: CARYOPHYLLACEAE
Origin: Southern Europe.
Flowering time: Summer.
Climatic zone: 4, 5, 6, 7, 8, 9.
Dimensions: Up to 2 feet (600 mm) high.
Description: Rose campion has wheel-like, cerise-pink flowers on pale stems. The foliage has fine, silvery hairs. A gray groundcover can be created by removing the flowers. It is a good, but short-lived, border plant, the seedlings flowering within a year. Growing either as a biennial or perennial, it likes alkaline, moist, well-drained soil and a position in sun or partial shade.
Other colors: White.
Varieties/cultivars: 'Alba', 'Abbotswood Rose', *L. c.* var. *oculata*.

Lychnis viscaria syn. *Viscaria vulgaris*
GERMAN CATCHFLY ○

Family: CARYOPHYLLACEAE
Origin: Europe.
Flowering time: Spring–summer.
Climatic zone: 4, 5, 6, 7, 8, 9.
Dimensions: Up to 18 inches (450 mm) high.
Description: The purplish-pink flowers form in clusters on top of the sticky stems that have given the common name, German catchfly, to this plant. The stickiness protects the plants from

insects, particularly ants. It likes moist, sandy soil, and an open position. Propagate it by division in autumn or by sowing seed in spring. Double-flowered varieties are available.
Other colors: White, red, purple.
Varieties/cultivars: 'Splendens', 'Splendens Plena', 'Alba', 'Zulu'.

Lychnis viscaria

Lythrum salicaria

Lythrum salicaria
PURPLE LOOSESTRIFE ○ ◑

Family: LYTHRACEAE
Origin: Asia, Europe, North Africa.
Flowering time: Summer.
Climatic zone: 3, 4, 5, 6, 7, 8, 9.
Dimensions: Up to 4 feet (over 1 meter) high.

Description: The name *Lythrum* is from the Greek word for "blood", alluding to the color of the flowers. These are vibrant magenta-pink and borne in whorls around the stems, the leaves being willow-like. Marsh-loving, it is ideal planted beside ponds, near streams, or in damp places in the garden, but it also flowers freely in ground that is not especially wet. A valuable and widely grown plant, it has been used for tanning leather and in treating dysentery and blindness. *L. salicaria* may be invasive, but the cultivars are not.
Other colors: Red, violet.
Varieties/cultivars: 'Happy', 'Robert', 'Dropmore Purple', 'Firecandle', 'Morden's Gleam', 'Morden's Pink', 'Purple Spires'.

Malva alcea 'Fastigiata'

Malva alcea
MALLOW, HOLLYHOCK MALLOW ○ ◑

Family: MALVACEAE
Origin: Europe.
Flowering time: Summer–autumn.
Climatic zone: 5, 6, 7, 8, 9.
Dimensions: Up to 4 feet (over 1 meter) high.
Description: The flowers of hollyhock mallow are a delicate pink, and the downy, heart-shaped leaves add to the plant's ornamental value in borders and beds. Related to the hibiscus, which is also a member of the mallow family, *M. alcea* is like a smaller version of this flower, which is probably why some consider it to be inferior. Flowers are borne in terminal spikes, and occur in great profusion. It is easy to grow in any garden soil, but prefers it dry. Propagate by dividing it in spring.
Other colors: Purple.
Varieties/cultivars: 'Fastigiata'.

Malva moschata
MUSK MALLOW, MUSK ROSE

Family: MALVACEAE
Origin: Europe, North Africa.
Flowering time: Summer–autumn.
Climatic zone: 4, 5, 6, 7, 8, 9, 10.
Dimensions: Up to 3 feet (1 meter) high.
Description: The handsome pink flowers of musk mallow appear mostly at the top of the stems. Its leaves emit a musky fragrance when bruised. Musk mallow makes an attractive ornamental border plant among hollyhocks and lupins in cottage gardens. Drought-tolerant, it does well in most soils, but prefers a well-drained position. Propagate it from seed in spring. Musk mallow has medicinal properties.
Other colors: White.
Varieties/cultivars: 'Alba'.

Malva moschata

Oenothera speciosa
SHOWY PRIMROSE, EVENING PRIMROSE

Family: ONAGRACEAE
Origin: Southern United States, Mexico.
Flowering time: Summer.
Climatic zone: 5, 6, 7, 8, 9.
Dimensions: Up to 18 inches (450 mm) high.
Description: Like most evening primroses, showy primrose has flowers that open during the day. They are shallowly basin-shaped and fragrant,

Oenothera speciosa

fading to a soft rose color, and look attractive at the front of a border or in a large rock garden. Because of its spreading habit, the plant is a good choice for a wild garden and is easy to grow in a sunny spot, in sandy or loamy soil.

Paeonia officinalis
COMMON PEONY

Family: PAEONIACEAE
Origin: Southern Europe.
Flowering time: Early summer.
Climatic zone: 3, 4, 5, 6, 7, 8, 9.
Dimensions: Up to 3 feet (1 meter) high.
Description: An extremely hardy perennial, common peony grows well

only in frosty areas, but needs a position where the early morning sun will not damage the flowers after frost. The solitary, crimson flowers are saucer-shaped with yellow stamens and red filaments. It grows well in fertile, well-drained soil and must be well-watered in dry weather. A plant known to the ancients, peony was said to cure lunacy, nightmares, and nervous disorders. Ideal for low maintenance gardens, they are also excellent cut flowers.
Other colors: Red, white.
Varieties/cultivars: 'Rubra Plena', 'Alba Plena'.

Phlox subulata
GROUND PINK, MOSS PINK, MOSS PHLOX (U.K.)

Family: POLEMONIACEAE
Origin: Northeastern United States.
Flowering time: Late spring, northern hemisphere; summer, southern hemisphere.
Climatic zone: 3, 4, 5, 6, 7, 8.
Dimensions: Up to 6 inches (150 mm) high.
Description: Introduced into England in the early part of the eighteenth century, ground pink is an old, easy-to-grow favorite. An evergreen creeper, it forms a thick carpet and produces dense flowers which are ¾ inch (20 mm) wide with slightly notched petals. A profuse flowerer, this alpine phlox suits rock

Paeonia officinalis

Phlox subulata 'Alexander's Surprise'

long borders beside driveways and paths, or near fruit trees to attract the bees. It likes moist soil in a shaded position, although where summers are cool it will grow in full sun.

Polygonum bistorta 'Superbum'

Polygonum capitatum

gardens and sloping sites and looks attractive planted to give a spill-over effect over rocks or down stone walls. It prefers average, well-drained garden soil. Prune the stems severely after flowering to promote denser growth. Propagate it from seeds, cuttings or division of the roots.
Other colors: White, red, lavender-blue.
Varieties/cultivars: 'Alba', 'Brilliant', 'Temiscaming', 'G. F. Wilson', 'Alexander's Surprise', 'Oakington Blue Eyes', 'Red Wings', 'White Delight'.

Plectranthus Sp.
CANDLE PLANT ◑ ●

Family: LABIATAE
Origin: South Africa.
Flowering time: Autumn.

Plectranthus Sp.

Climatic zone: 9, 10.
Dimensions: Up to 2 feet (600 mm) high.
Description: This plant is a most useful groundcover for shady areas, where its long branches frequently send down roots at each leaf node. The profuse spires of flowers are pale mauve when they open, fading to white, and the attractive, oval leaves are green above and deep-purple on the underside. Candle plant does not tolerate dry conditions, growing best in moist soil with plenty of leaf mold. It propagates very easily from cuttings and makes a fine hanging basket, house, or greenhouse plant.

Polygonum bistorta 'Superbum'
COMMON EUROPEAN ○ ◑ BISTORT, EASTER LEDGES, SNAKEWEED (U.S.A.)

Family: POLYGONACEAE
Origin: Cultivar.
Flowering time: Summer.
Climatic zone: 3, 4, 5, 6, 7, 8, 9.
Dimensions: Up to 3 feet (1 meter) high.
Description: The pink flowers of this perennial appear in dense, robust spikes about 6 inches (150 mm) long, on stems well above the foliage. Its large, paddle-like leaves make it a handsome plant even when not in flower. Given the right position, it may bloom twice during the summer. Mass-plant it in

Polygonum capitatum
FLEECE FLOWER, ○ ● JAPANESE KNOT-FLOWER

Family: POLYGONACEAE
Origin: Himalayas.
Flowering time: Spring–autumn.
Climatic zone: 9, 10.
Dimensions: Up to 6 inches (150 mm) high.
Description: This vigorous and quick-growing perennial has attractive, pink, globular flowers and dark-green leaves with V-shaped bands. Its low, spreading habit makes it a useful groundcover, but pruning may be necessary to control its spread. An easy-to-grow plant, it is tolerant of a wide range of soils and conditions and is seldom bothered by pests or diseases. Plant cuttings or seed in full sun or shade.

Primula japonica

Primula japonica
JAPANESE PRIMROSE ◑

Family: PRIMULACEAE
Origin: Japan.
Flowering time: Late spring–early summer.
Climatic zone: 5, 6, 7, 8, 9.
Dimensions: Up to 16 inches (400 mm) high.
Description: Primula has strong stems bearing whorled tiers of glistening flowers which look spectacular mass-planted under trees or around shrubs. A moisture-lover, it grows well near ponds and streams and in damp and partially shady problem areas in the garden. Plant it in humus-enriched soil and provide constant moisture. It does not like hot, dry summers. *Astilbe* species, which need similar conditions, make ideal companion plants.
Other colors: White, red, purple, lavender.
Varieties/cultivars: 'Miller's Crimson', 'Postford's White'.

Prunella grandiflora 'Rosea'
SELF-HEAL, HEART-OF- ○ ◑ THE-EARTH (U.S.A.), LARGE-FLOWERED SELF-HEAL (U.K.)

Family: LABIATAE
Origin: Cultivar.
Flowering time: Summer.
Climatic zone: 5, 6, 7, 8, 9.
Dimensions: Up to 12 inches (300 mm) high.
Description: A member of the mint family, self-heal is said to heal wounds, and cure headaches and sore throats. The parent species has been a common pasture plant in Europe and U.K. for centuries. The two-lipped tubular flowers appear in dense spikes on erect stems well above the foliage. It appreciates damp and shady places in rock or wild gardens. A hardy perennial, it thrives in full sun in cool climates, but in warmer areas it needs partial shade. Plant it in moist, humus-enriched soil. Propagate by division.

Prunella grandiflora 'Rosea'

Saponaria ocymoides
ROCK SOAPWORT ○

Family: CARYOPHYLLACEAE
Origin: Central and southern Europe.
Flowering time: Spring–summer.
Climatic zone: 3, 4, 5, 6, 7, 8.
Dimensions: Up to 8 inches (200 mm) high.
Description: With its masses of bright, showy flowers growing in loose clusters, this vigorous alpine rock plant looks graceful near steps or trailing over edges or rock walls. Rock soapwort thrives in a sunny position, in sandy soil with good drainage. It can be propagated from cuttings, from seed in early spring, or by division of rootstock in early spring or autumn. 'Rubra Compacta' has deeper pink flowers and a more compact form.
Other colors: Red, white.
Varieties/cultivars: 'Alba', 'Rubra', 'Rubra Compacta', 'Splendens'.

Saponaria officinalis
BOUNCING BET, ○ SOAPWORT

Family: CARYOPHYLLACEAE
Origin: Europe, Asia.
Flowering time: Summer.
Climatic zone: 3, 4, 5, 6, 7, 8, 9.
Dimensions: Up to 3 feet (1 meter) high.
Description: With its bright pink clusters of flowers often borne in profusion, soapwort is well suited to both wild and cottage gardens. Grow it in sandy, well-drained soil; in moist, fertile soil it tends to be invasive, so choose a position where its growth can be checked if necessary. Soapwort gets its name from the fact that if its leaves are bruised and swished in water, they form a lather. It was used in ancient times as a soap and also for its medicinal properties.
Other colors: Red, white.
Varieties/cultivars: 'Rubra Plena', 'Rosea Plena', 'Alba Plena'.

Saponaria ocymoides

Saponaria officinalis 'Rosea Plena'

Saxifraga moschata 'Peter Pan'

Saxifraga moschata and hybrids
MOSSY ○ ◑ ●
SAXIFRAGE

Family: SAXIFRAGACEAE
Origin: Southern Spain, Italy, Balkans.
Flowering time: Spring.
Climatic zone: 3, 4, 5, 6, 7, 8.
Dimensions: Up to 6 inches (150 mm)
high.
Description: Mossy saxifrage is a quick-
growing perennial which forms a low
mound and is ideal in rock garden
pockets, in courtyards, or under trees
and shrubs. The leaves are fan-shaped
and deeply lobed; the flowers are only
½–1 inch (12–24 mm) wide. There are
several cultivars, some of which are
hybrids with allied species. Many of
these perennials prefer positions either
shaded from midday sun or in complete
shade. Moist, gritty soil with lime suits
them best. Propagate them by seed, root
division or cuttings.
Other colors: Scarlet, yellow, white.
Varieties/cultivars: 'Cloth of Gold',
'Triumph', 'Peter Pan'.

Scabiosa caucasica
PINCUSHION FLOWER, ○
COMMON SCABIOUS, BORDER
SCABIOUS

Family: DIPSACACEAE
Origin: Caucasus.
Flowering time: Summer, northern
hemisphere; spring–summer, southern
hemisphere.
Climatic zone: 4, 5, 6, 7, 8, 9.
Dimensions: Up to 2½ feet (750 mm)
high.

Scabiosa caucasica

Description: Introduced into Britain in
1591, pincushion flower blooms for a
long time and the cut flowers are
excellent in floral arrangements. The
flowers are flat, 2–3 inches (50–70 mm)
wide, and similar to the daisy in
appearance. Grow it in a border in full
sun, in well-drained, limy soil. It resents
being moved; if this is necessary, move
it in the spring. Propagate it by root
division in winter. If the plants become
sickly try another cultivar.
Other colors: Lavender, lavender-blue,
white.
Varieties/cultivars: 'Moorheim Blue',
'Bressingham White', 'Loddon White',
'Clive Greaves', 'Miss Willmott'.

Sedum maximum 'Atropurpureum'
ICE PLANT, GREAT ○ ◑
STONECROP

Family: CRASSULACEAE
Origin: Cultivar.
Flowering time: Summer–autumn.
Climatic zone: 4, 5, 6, 7, 8, 9, 10.
Dimensions: Up to 2 feet (600 mm) high.
Description: The spectacular flowers
and foliage make this a good plant in a
border or rock garden. The thick, fleshy
leaves, green at first and turning a deep

claret color later, look dramatic with the
pink flowers. Plant it where this effect
will brighten a bare part of the garden
in autumn. It is easy to grow if it has
good drainage, particularly in winter.
For best results, plant it in average soil,
in sun or partial shade.

Sedum maximum 'Atropurpureum'

Sedum spectabile

Sedum spectabile 'Autumn Joy'

Sedum spectabile
LIVE-FOR-EVER,
SHOWY STONECROP (U.S.A.),
ICE PLANT (U.K.)

Family: CRASSULACEAE
Origin: Korea–central China.
Flowering time: Late summer–autumn.
Climatic zone: 4, 5, 6, 7, 8, 9, 10.
Dimensions: Up to 2 feet (600 mm) high.
Description: Much loved by butterflies and bees, ice plant is grown for its showy, plate-like heads of starry, pink flowers, borne in clusters on sturdy stems. The oval, succulent leaves help the plant withstand long dry periods. Good drainage is necessary, particularly in winter, for robust, freely blooming plants. An excellent plant in a border or rock garden, it is easy to grow in average soil, in either sun or partial shade. Apply complete fertilizer in spring and propagate by seed, division, cuttings, or from the leaves themselves.
Other colors: Red, rose-salmon, white.
Varieties/cultivars: 'Brilliant', 'Meteor', 'Autumn Joy', 'Iceberg', 'September Ruby', 'Stardust', 'Variegatum'.

Sedum spectabile 'Autumn Joy'
WILD THYME,
MOTHER OF THYME

Family: CRASSULACEAE
Origin: Cultivar.
Flowering time: Summer.
Climatic zone: 4, 5, 6, 7, 8, 9, 10.
Dimensions: Up to 2 feet (600 mm) high.
Description: The salmon-pink aging to rusty-red flowers of this plant form in clusters resembling broccoli heads. Bees

and butterflies love them. A compact perennial which is ideally suited to borders, it is easy to grow in average soil. Good drainage is essential, particularly in winter. Propagation is by division, cuttings, or leaves.

Sidalcea malviflora
CHECKERBLOOM,
PRAIRIE MALLOW

Family: MALVACEAE
Origin: Oregon–California, Mexico.
Flowering time: Summer.
Climatic zone: 5, 6, 7, 8, 9, 10.
Dimensions: Up to 3 feet (1 meter) high.
Description: This graceful, long-flowering, herbaceous perennial has spikes of pink flowers resembling a small hollyhock. The spikes may need staking if the plant becomes too tall. Fast-

Sidalcea malviflora

growing, it is a good choice for wild or cottage gardens and in sunny, slightly unruly gardens is a good companion plant for delphiniums and gypsophila. Easily grown in average, well-drained soil with some moisture, it likes full sun in colder climates and partial shade in hot areas. Propagate it by seed or root division.
Other colors: Red.
Varieties/cultivars: 'Loveliness', 'Brilliant', 'Croftway Red', 'Sussex Beauty', 'William Smith', 'Rose Green', 'Elsie Heugh'.

Thalictrum aquilegifolium
KING-OF-THE-
MEADOW, COLUMBINE
MEADOWRUE

Family: RANUNCULACEAE
Origin: Eastern and central Europe–northern Asia.
Flowering time: Early summer, northern hemisphere; spring, southern hemisphere.
Climatic zone: 5, 6, 7, 8, 9, 10.
Dimensions: Up to 3 feet (1 meter) high.
Description: With its fluffy heads of tassel-like, pink flowers and decorative ferny foliage, king-of-the-meadow makes a handsome border plant. It is unusual in that the male and female flowers bloom on separate plants, the male being the more showy. King-of-the-meadow provides a good foil for larger-flowered plants. Easy to grow in moist, well-drained soil enriched with humus, it needs shade in hot summers. Water regularly, protect it from the wind, and apply complete fertilizer in late winter.
Other colors: White, purple, mauve.

Thalictrum aquilegifolium

Thalictrum delavayi

Thalictrum delavayi syn.
T. dipterocarpum
MEADOWRUE, ○ ◑
LAVENDER SHOWER

Family: RANUNCULACEAE
Origin: Western China.
Flowering time: Summer, northern
hemisphere; spring, southern hemisphere.
Climatic zone: 5, 6, 7, 8, 9.
Dimensions: Up to 5 feet (over 1 meter)
high.
Description: The delicate branching
stems of this meadowrue produce
numerous gracefully hanging, mauve-
pink blooms with yellow anthers. The
ferny foliage resembles maidenhair,
giving the plant a delicate, oriental look.
It forms a good backdrop to annuals or
among other perennials. For best
results, mulch the plant annually with
compost or well-rotted manure. Care is
needed when cultivating the soil around
the plant, as new growth, which
emerges near the parent plant, may be
easily severed. It is easy to grow in
moist, well-drained soil and should be
divided in early spring.
Other colors: White, rose-purple,
mauve.
Varieties/cultivars: 'Album', 'Purple
Cloud', 'Hewitt's Double'.

Thymus praecox arcticus syn. *T. drucei*

MOTHER OF THYME, ○ ◑
WILD THYME

Family: LABIATAE
Origin: Europe.
Flowering time: Spring–summer.
Climatic zone: 4, 5, 6, 7, 8, 9.
Dimensions: Up to 4 inches (100 mm)
high.
Description: Mother of thyme is a
prostrate, evergreen groundcover. One

of the carpet-forming thymes, it is very
useful in the rock garden and needs
little attention. It can also be placed
among paving stones and around paths,
emitting a pungent aroma when walked
on. The flowers are two-lipped, small,
and tubular, appearing in terminal
spikes. Plant it in fertile, sandy soil and
prune if it becomes invasive. It is
propagated by root division or cuttings.
This herb can be used in cooking.
Other colors: White, red.
Varieties/cultivars: 'Albus',
'Coccineus', 'Annie Hall', 'Pink Chintz'.

Thymus praecox arcticus

Tradescantia x *andersoniana* syn.
T. virginiana
WIDOW'S TEARS, ○ ◑
COMMON SPIDERWORT

Family: COMMELINACEAE
Origin: Hybrid.
Flowering time: Spring–summer.
Climatic zone: 5, 6, 7, 8, 9.

Tradescantia x *andersoniana* 'Carmine
Glow'

Dimensions: Up to 2 feet (600 mm) high.
Description: Related to the American
wandering Jew, this free-flowering
perennial produces attractive clumps.
The blooming period is long, though
the flowers themselves are short-lived.
The clumps may become untidy unless
pruned in autumn. Plant it in well-
drained soil, in partial shade in hotter
areas, and in full sun in cooler climates.
Divide it in spring.
Other colors: Many colors.
Varieties/cultivars: Great variety of
cultivars available.

Valeriana officinalis

Valeriana officinalis
COMMON VALERIAN ○

Family: VALERIANACEAE
Origin: Europe, Asia.
Flowering time: Summer.
Climatic zone: 5, 6, 7, 8, 9.
Dimensions: Up to 4 feet (approx.
1 meter) high.
Description: Valerian is an ancient
plant with medicinal uses. The aromatic
roots have a great attraction for cats.
A good border plant, it produces
numerous pink flowers in fragrant
clusters. It may be prey to aphids. Easy
to grow, it prefers very moist, well-
drained soil in full sun. Propagate it by
seed or division.
Other colors: White, lavender.

Abelia schumannii

Abelia schumannii
SCHUMANN'S ABELIA

Family: CAPRIFOLIACEAE
Origin: Western China.
Flowering time: Summer–autumn.
Climatic zone: 7, 8, 9.
Dimensions: 4–6 feet (1–2 meters) high.
Description: In the northern hemisphere, Schumann's abelia is semi-deciduous but in the southern hemisphere it is evergreen. The new leaves are purplish at first, changing later to a mid-green. Attractive rosy-pink flowers cover the plant for a long period. Plant it in a shrub border or use as a screen plant. Mulch with manure or feed with a complete plant food in early spring. It is not fussy about soil type, but it needs a well-drained position.

Abelia x grandiflora
GLOSSY ABELIA

Family: CAPRIFOLIACEAE
Origin: Hybrid.
Flowering time: Summer–autumn.
Climatic zone: 6, 7, 8, 9.
Dimensions: 3–6 feet (1–2 meters) high.
Description: A fast-growing semi-evergreen shrub, glossy abelia is widely used as a hedge or screen plant. It

Abelia x grandiflora

carries its pink and white flowers over a long period; after these have fallen the reddish-brown calyxes remain attractive for months. The leaves are dark-green and glossy. The shrub will grow in any type of free-draining soil in a sheltered site. It can be pruned after flowering if required. Cut back into the old wood so that new arching branches can be formed.
Varieties/cultivars: 'Prostrata'.

Abutilon 'Tunisia'

Abutilon 'Tunisia'
CHINESE LANTERN, FLOWERING MAPLE (U.K.)

Family: MALVACEAE
Origin: Cultivar.
Flowering time: Summer.
Climatic zone: 9, 10.
Dimensions: 4–6 feet (1–2 meters) high.
Description: Chinese lantern is a spectacular shrub having large, fuchsia-pink flowers similar in appearance to the old-fashioned hollyhock. Prune it back to at least two-thirds of the current year's growth each winter to maintain bushy growth. Fertilize in spring with a complete plant food or mulch around the plant with manure or compost. Ample summer water is required. Chinese lantern makes an excellent background shrub for a perennial border or can be used as a feature plant. It can also be grown in a large tub.

Andromeda polifolia
BOG ROSEMARY

Family: ERICACEAE
Origin: Europe, northern Asia, North America.
Flowering time: Spring–summer.
Climatic zone: 2, 3, 4, 5, 6, 7.

Andromeda polifolia

Dimensions: 12 inches (300 mm) high.
Description: This is an extremely pretty shrub having clusters of delicate, urn-shaped, pale-pink flowers. As the common name suggests, it will only grow in moist and cool soil which must be acidic. Adding peat to the soil and using it as a mulch around the shrub provides perfect conditions. Summer heat and dry soil will kill the plant. It may become straggly with age, but this can be overcome by an occasional heavy pruning after flowering has finished.

Bauera rubioides
DOG ROSE, RIVER ROSE, WIRY BAUERA

Family: BAUERACEAE
Origin: Australia.
Flowering time: Spring–summer.
Climatic zone: 9.
Dimensions: 3 feet (900 mm) high.
Description: This semi-prostrate, heath-like shrub, with its small, dainty, pale-pink flowers, blooms for a long period. Dog rose will grow in full sun, but prefers a shaded position and damp, acidic, well-drained soil. A mulch of leaf

Bauera rubioides

mold around the plant will keep the soil moist and cool. This delicate shrub is suited to a cottage garden or rockery, but in cold climates, it needs to be grown under glass. Fertilize in spring with manure, compost or organic fertilizer. Dog rose does not appreciate artificial fertilizers.

Boronia floribunda
PINK BORONIA

Family: RUTACEAE
Origin: Australia (N.S.W.).
Flowering time: Spring.
Climatic zone: 9.
Dimensions: 3 feet (900 mm) high.
Description: Pink boronia is a very free-flowering, small shrub, bearing fragrant, pale-pink, star-like flowers. The small leaves are a soft, light-green. Plant it near a doorway or window so that the strong fragrance can be appreciated. In very cold areas, it needs to be grown under glass. The main requirements of pink boronia are good drainage and a sandy soil. Apply a heavy mulch of leaf litter under which the surface roots can remain cool. Feed in spring with well-rotted compost, cow manure, or an organic fertilizer.

Boronia floribunda

Callistemon citrinus 'Pink Clusters'
BOTTLEBRUSH

Family: MYRTACEAE
Origin: Cultivar.
Flowering time: Spring.
Climatic zone: 9, 10.
Dimensions: 10–11 feet (3–4 meters) high.
Description: This pretty cultivar has very light-green young leaves which turn darker as they age. The pink flower spikes are 3 inches (80 mm) long.

Callistemon citrinus 'Pink Clusters'

Although the main flowering period is spring, there are always one or two flowers on the shrub throughout the year. Use in the garden as a specimen shrub or at the back of a shrub border. A warm climate plant, crimson bottlebrush likes well-drained soil. Mulch with manure or compost in spring, or feed with blood and bone.

Calluna vulgaris and cultivars
HEATHER

Family: ERICACEAE
Origin: Europe, Asia Minor.
Flowering time: Depends on the cultivar but always summer–autumn.
Climatic zone: 5, 6, 7, 8, 9.
Dimensions: 18 inches (450 mm) high. Height of cultivars differs.
Description: Many varieties of heather are cultivated in gardens, and vary in their shades of pink, flowering time, and habit. The flowers are valued for indoor decoration. They are all easily-grown

Calluna vulgaris 'Anne Marie'

plants, tolerant of lime-free soils and even, moist positions. Although tolerant of some shade, they flower better in full sun. Pruning, if necessary, can be carried out after flowering finishes. Heather combines well with old-fashioned plants in a cottage garden scheme.
Other colors: Red, white, mauve, purple, crimson.
Varieties/cultivars: There are many different cultivars throughout the world.

Camellia japonica 'Drama Girl'

Camellia japonica and cultivars
JAPANESE CAMELLIA, COMMON CAMELLIA

Family: THEACEAE
Origin: China, Korea, Japan.
Flowering time: Winter–spring.
Climatic zone: 7, 8, 9.
Dimensions: 20 feet (6.0 meters) high.
Description: There are hundreds of different cultivars of this plant in every shade of pink imaginable. Flower shape includes single, double, semi-double, and formal double. The leaves are a shiny dark-green. Camellias like moist, but free-draining, acid soil. The root systems are shallow, so mulch around the plant with peat or leaf mold to encourage acid conditions and to keep the soil damp. Lack of water, especially during summer, will cause the buds to drop.
Other colors: Many different shades of pink, red and white, and combinations of these.
Varieties/cultivars: There are many different cultivars throughout the world.

Camellia sasanqua 'Plantation Pink'

Camellia sasanqua cultivars
SASANQUA ○ ◑
CAMELLIA

Family: THEACEAE
Origin: Japan.
Flowering time: Autumn–spring.
Climatic zone: 7, 8, 9.
Dimensions: 6–10 feet (2–3 meters) high.
Description: A similar-looking plant to
Camellia japonica, *C. sasanqua* is hardier
and has a more open habit. There are
several cultivars of this plant in various
shades of pink. In cold areas it requires
protection near a wall, but as it ages it
becomes more tolerant of cold. The soil
should be acidic and moist but free-
draining. A mulch is essential to protect
the surface roots. Use pine leaves, peat,
or leaf mold.
Other colors: Color range is from white
through to red with combinations of
these.
Varieties/cultivars: There are several
different cultivars throughout the
world.

Cercis chinensis
CHINESE REDBUD (U.S.A.), ○
CHINESE JUDAS TREE (U.K.)

Family: LEGUMINOSAE
Origin: China.
Flowering time: Spring.
Climatic zone: 7, 8, 9.
Dimensions: 15 feet (5 meters) high.
Description: Chinese redbud is a
pretty, deciduous shrub with large
round, but pointed, glossy green leaves.
In spring it is clothed in clusters of
bright pink flowers. Although it is a
hardy shrub which is easily grown
under average conditions, it does not
transplant readily. The soil should be

well-drained and mulched every spring
with manure or compost, or
alternatively fed with a small amount of
complete plant food. Pruning is not
necessary.

Cercis chinensis

Cotinus coggyria
VENETIAN SUMACH ○ ◑
(U.S.A.), SMOKE TREE (U.K.),
SMOKEBUSH

Family: ANACARDIACEAE
Origin: Central and southern Europe.
Flowering time: Summer.
Climatic zone: 5, 6, 7, 8, 9.
Dimensions: 10–15 feet (3–5 meters) high.
Description: A pretty, deciduous
shrub, smoke tree is grown for its lovely
autumn color and profusion of fawny-
pink feathery flower-stalks which
eventually turn a smoky-gray. The
flower stalks persist for months and
actually do look like clouds of smoke.
Smoke tree is easy to grow in any
ordinary garden soil that is not too rich
or moist.
Other colors: Purple. The leaves of
some cultivars are also purple or red.
Varieties/cultivars: 'Purpureus', 'Royal
Purple', 'Foliis Purpureis', 'Flame'.

Cotinus coggyria

Dais cotinifolia

Dais cotinifolia
POMPOM TREE ○

Family: THYMELAEACEAE
Origin: South Africa.
Flowering time: Spring.
Climatic zone: 9, 10.
Dimensions: 10–20 feet (3–6 meters) high.
Description: The bark of this shrub is
the strongest fiber known to the
Africans who use it as a thread. The
whole bush is covered for at least a
month in attractive pompom-like heads
of pinkish-lilac flowers measuring about
2 inches (50 mm) across. The smooth
leaves are a bluish-green. Plant in a well-
drained soil that is enriched annually
with cow manure or compost. Pruning,
if necessary, can be carried out after
flowering.

Daphne cneorum

Daphne cneorum
ROSE DAPHNE (U.S.A.), ○ ◑
GARLAND FLOWER (U.K.)

Family: THYMELIACEAE
Origin: Central and southern Europe.
Flowering time: Spring.
Climatic zone: 4, 5, 6, 7, 8.

Dimensions: 12 inches (300 mm) high.
Description: Garland flower is a popular plant on account of its fragrant, rose-pink flowers which are borne in clusters on prostrate branches. It is an ideal shrub for a rock garden or as a border to a large shrubbery. Garland flower requires a cool, lime-free soil which must be friable and well-drained. Before planting, dig in copious amounts of leaf mold or peat. Do not use chemical fertilizers. A mulch of leaf mold or cow manure annually will suffice and will not harm the plant.
Other colors: White.
Varieties/cultivars: 'Eximea', 'Alba', 'Variegata', 'Major'.

Deutzia scabra 'Flore Pleno'
SNOWFLOWER

Family: SAXIFRAGACEAE
Origin: Cultivar.
Flowering time: Summer.
Climatic zone: 5, 6, 7, 8, 9.
Dimensions: Up to 6 feet (2 meters) high.
Description: This pretty, deciduous shrub has a compact shape with arching branches of dull green foliage, and abundant clusters of white flowers that are suffused with rose-purple on the outside. Adaptable to a wide range of soils and conditions, this shrub benefits from a light pruning after flowering to maintain its shape. It makes an excellent addition to a cottage garden.

Deutzia scabra 'Flore Pleno'

Erica canaliculata
TREE HEATH, PURPLE HEATH

Family: ERICACEAE
Origin: South Africa.
Flowering time: Late winter–early summer.
Climatic zone: 8, 9, 10.
Dimensions: 4–6 feet (1–2 meters) high.
Description: A hardy shrub which, in flower, becomes entirely covered in pale pink or white bells. It forms a neat bush and looks most delightful when planted at the back of a perennial border. Since an acid soil is essential for success, dig in copious amounts of peat or leaf mold, and add a handful of sulfur before planting. Tree heath is easily propagated from self-rooted layers or late summer cuttings.

Erica canaliculata

Erica carnea and cultivars
HEATH, SPRING HEATH, WINTER HEATH

Family: ERICACEAE
Origin: Central Europe.
Flowering time: Winter–spring. Different cultivars flower at different times during this period.
Climatic zone: 5, 6, 7, 8, 9.
Dimensions: 8–12 inches (200–300 mm) high and twice this wide.
Description: The delightful urn-shaped, rosy-red flowers are about 3 inches (75 mm) long, but there are innumerable cultivars available in a wide range of shades. Cultivars can be planted so that one of them is in flower from late autumn to late spring. *Erica carnea* and its cultivars prefer an acid soil, too much lime can actually retard

growth. Bush mold, decayed oak leaves, or peat worked into the soil will provide the desired conditions. Heath makes an ideal cut flower.
Other colors: A wide range through the white-pink-purple spectrum.
Varieties/cultivars: Numerous cultivars have been developed from this species.

Erica carnea cultivars

Erica vagans 'Mrs D. F. Maxwell'

Erica vagans
CORNISH HEATH

Family: ERICACEAE
Origin: Southwestern Europe.
Flowering time: Summer–autumn.
Climatic zone: 6, 7, 8, 9.
Dimensions: 1–3 feet (300–900 mm) high.
Description: A small, hardy shrub which produces an abundance of purplish-pink flowers, Cornish heath can be used in a rockery or in the front of a shrub border. The main requirements for healthy growth are an acid, well-drained but moist soil. This can be provided by digging leaf mold or peat into the soil before planting and by sprinkling a handful of sulfur around the plant. Picking the flowers for indoor decoration helps to keep the bush more compact.
Other colors: White, shades of pink and red.
Varieties/cultivars: There are numerous cultivars of this shrub.

Erica tetralix 'Con Underwood'

Erica tetralix and cultivars
CROSS-LEAVED HEATH

Family: ERICACEAE
Origin: Northern and western Europe.
Flowering time: Summer–autumn.
Climatic zone: 6, 7, 8, 9.
Dimensions: 12–18 inches (300–450 mm) high.
Description: *Erica tetralix* has dainty, urn-shaped, soft-pink flowers and grayish-green foliage. There are several different cultivars and many of them are in different shades of pink. An acid, moist soil is essential for success with this plant. Add peat or leaf mold to the soil when planting, or as a mulch to provide the necessary acidity. A handful of sulfur sprinkled around the plant is also beneficial. This is an ideal shrub for a rockery. It also makes a pretty groundcover.
Other colors: White, shades of pink and red.
Varieties/cultivars: There are numerous cultivars of this shrub.

Erica x *darleyensis*
DARLEY HEATH

Family: ERICACEAE
Origin: Hybrid.
Flowering time: Winter–spring.
Climatic zone: 6, 7, 8, 9.
Dimensions: 4 feet (approx. 1 meter) high.
Description: When in flower this hardy hybrid, with its compact, cushion-like habit, is smothered with numerous small, rosy-pink bells. It looks like a natural companion when planted with *Erica carnea*. It is as lime-tolerant as *E. carnea*, but thrives when mulched

with leaf mold or peat. Plant it in a cottage garden or use at the front of a shrub border. The cut flowers last for a long time indoors.
Other colors: Magenta, red, white, shades of pink.
Varieties/cultivars: There are several cultivars of this species.

Erica x *darleyensis* 'Darley Dale'

Fuchsia x *hybrida*
FUCHSIA

Family: ONAGRACEAE
Origin: Hybrids.
Flowering time: Spring, summer, autumn.
Climatic zone: 7, 8, 9, 10.
Dimensions: 2 feet (600 mm) high.
Description: There are hundreds of different cultivars of fuchsias throughout the world, many of them in the pink color range. These delightful plants will flower freely for many months. When cut back severely in autumn in cooler areas, they will burst forth with new shoots the following spring. Fuchsias like a rich, well-drained soil. A mulch of manure or a handful of complete plant food in early spring will

Fuchsia x *hybrida*

ensure a good flower display. They are very suited to pot culture.
Other colors: Red, purple, blue, white, violet, and combinations of these.
Varieties/cultivars: Numerous cultivars are available.

Grevillea rosmarinifolia

Grevillea rosmarinifolia
ROSEMARY GREVILLEA

Family: PROTEACEAE
Origin: Eastern Australia.
Flowering time: Throughout the year.
Climatic zone: 9, 10.
Dimensions: 4 feet (approx. 2 meters) high.
Description: This pretty shrub has thin green leaves and flowers which vary from red to creamy pink mainly in spring and summer. Some flowers remain throughout the year. Plant rosemary grevillea where it can be seen from a window, as it is very attractive to birds. It can be heavily pruned to make a formal hedge if required. It requires a greenhouse environment in cool climates. Its main requirements are a well-drained soil and applications of organic fertilizer. Propagation can be carried out from cuttings taken in early spring.
Other colors: Red and dark pink.
Varieties/cultivars: 'Jenkinsii', 'Olympic Flame'.

Hibiscus rosa-sinensis cultivars
ROSE-OF-CHINA, CHINESE HIBISCUS

Family: MALVACEAE
Origin: Southern China.
Flowering time: Spring–summer.

Hibiscus rosa-sinensis

Justicia carnea

Kalmia latifolia

Kolkwitzia amabilis

Lantana camara

Climatic zone: 9, 10.
Dimensions: 6–10 feet (2–3 meters) high.
Description: This is a beautiful flowering shrub with literally hundreds of different cultivars, many of which grow in various shades of pink. They make beautiful feature plants or can be grown in a shrub border. In cool climates, a greenhouse environment is essential. Bushes should be pruned back to near half height each winter to maintain a good shape and to produce a better display of flowers the following year. A well-drained soil and regular applications of plant food during spring and summer are their main requirements.
Other colors: White, orange, red.
Varieties/cultivars: There are numerous cultivars.

Justicia carnea
PINK JACOBINIA, ○ ◑
BRAZILIAN-PLUME FLOWER,
KING'S-CROWN

Other common names: PINK ACANTHUS
Family: ACANTHACEAE
Origin: Brazil.
Flowering time: Summer–autumn.
Climatic zone: 9, 10.
Dimensions: 5 feet (approx. 2 meters) high.
Description: Pink jacobinia has large, deeply veined, dark-green leaves and big cone-shaped flower heads. Each flower head consists of many rosy-pink flowers. It is a fast-growing shrub which becomes straggly and unattractive unless it is drastically pruned every spring. It is often grown as an indoor plant. For best results, plant in a rich, well-drained soil and feed every spring with a complete plant food. It is easily propagated from early spring cuttings.

Kalmia latifolia.
MOUNTAIN LAUREL, ◑
CALICO BUSH

Family: ERICACEAE
Origin: Eastern North America.
Flowering time: Summer.
Climatic zone: 4, 5, 6, 7, 8, 9.
Dimensions: 7–15 feet (2–5 meters) high.
Description: This is one of the most beautiful and valued evergreen shrubs for a cold-climate garden. The delightful shell-pink, saucer-shaped flowers are crinkled at the edges. An acid, lime-free soil is an essential requirement. It will not grow in heavy clay soils nor in areas which have hot, dry summers. Plant it in soil that has been heavily enriched with leaf mold or peat and apply a mulch of this around the shrub.

Kolkwitzia amabilis
BEAUTYBUSH ○

Family: CAPRIFOLIACEAE
Origin: Western China.
Flowering time: Spring–summer.
Climatic zone: 5, 6, 7, 8, 9.
Dimensions: 8–12 feet (2.4–4 meters) high.
Description: Beautybush is an extremely attractive, erect shrub. The bell-like flowers are pink with a yellow throat. It is useful for a cottage garden. Although not fussy about soil type, it appreciates a handful of complete plant food sprinkled around its base in late winter. Do not prune unless absolutely necessary. Pruning will not only spoil the shape but will prevent flowering for a season as flowers are produced on the previous year's growth.

Lantana camara
COMMON LANTANA, ○
RED SAGE, YELLOW SAGE (U.K.)

Family: VERBENACEAE
Origin: Tropical America.
Flowering time: Summer–autumn, but in warmer climates there are some flowers on the shrub throughout the year.
Climatic zone: 9, 10.
Dimensions: 3 feet (1 meter) high.
Description: A prickly-stemmed shrub, lantana has dull-green, strangely-scented leaves which are rough to the touch. It is valued for its yellow flowers ageing to red or white which stay on the plant for a long period. The flowers are followed by shining black, berry-like seeds that are relished by birds. It will thrive when planted near the coast or in areas that experience drought. Grow common lantana in a sandy, free-draining soil. It needs to be pruned in spring to prevent legginess.
Other colors: White, cream, lilac, orange yellow.
Varieties/cultivars: There are several cultivars throughout the world.

Leptospermum scoparium and cultivars
TEA TREE, MANUKA ○ ◑

Family: MYRTACEAE
Origin: Australia, New Zealand.
Flowering time: Spring–summer.
Climatic zone: 8, 9, 10.
Dimensions: 3–6 feet (1–2 meters) high, depending on the cultivar.
Description: Tea trees are attractive evergreen shrubs bearing white, red, or pink flowers. They are very suited to coastal planting as the majority of them often thrive where not much else will grow. All the cultivars of leptospermum like a slightly acid soil of a sandy nature, and an open sunny position, but they can become accustomed to dappled shade. Prune lightly after flowering if they become too straggly. The cut flowers are pretty indoors.
Other colors: Various shades of white, red, pink.
Varieties/cultivars: Numerous cultivars are available.

Leptospermum scoparium 'Sunraysia'

Lonicera tatarica
TATARIAN ○ ◑
HONEYSUCKLE

Family: CAPRIFOLIACEAE
Origin: Central Asia, Russia.
Flowering time: Spring.
Climatic zone: 4, 5, 6, 7, 8.
Dimensions: 8–10 feet (2–3 meters) high.
Description: An old-fashioned, bushy honeysuckle which has multitudes of fragrant, soft-pink flowers during spring, followed by red berries. This species is variable and the flowers are often rich pink. The leaves are oval. It makes an ideal background shrub in a cottage garden. If it becomes too leggy it can be pruned after flowering has finished.

Lonicera tatarica

Tatarian honeysuckle is not fussy about soil type as long as the drainage is good.
Other colors: White, red.
Varieties/cultivars: 'Alba', 'Arnold Red', 'Hack's Red', 'Sibirica'.

Luculia gratissima
LUCULIA, PINK SIVA ○ ◑

Family: RUBIACEAE
Origin: Himalayas, India.
Flowering time: Late autumn–late winter.
Climatic zone: 9, 10.
Dimensions: 4–6 feet (1–2 meters) high.
Description: Luculia is one of the most beautiful winter-flowering shrubs. Fragrant clusters of soft-pink flowers cover the bush. The large leaves are light-green with a slightly downy underside. Plant near a window or door where the beautiful fragrance can be appreciated. Luculia flowers last well when picked and brought indoors. A well-drained soil and ample summer water are essential. Prune moderately after flowering — severe pruning can lead to the death of the plant.

Luculia gratissima

Melaleuca decussata
TOTEM POLES, ○ ◑
CROSS-LEAVED HONEY-MYRTLE

Family: MYRTACEAE
Origin: Australia (S.A., Vic.).
Flowering time: Spring–summer.
Climatic zone: 9, 10.
Dimensions: 6–11 feet (2–4 meters) high.
Description: This rounded shrub, with fine, stiff, narrow gray-green leaves, has mauve-pink bottlebrush-like flowers that quickly fade to white. They are very attractive to birds. It is an adaptable shrub which will survive wet or dry conditions. *Melaleuca* can be used as a specimen shrub or as a windbreak or hedge. Feed annually with cow manure or compost. Alternatively, apply a handful of blood and bone around the plant in spring.

Melaleuca decussata

Nerium oleander and cultivars
OLEANDER, ROSE-BAY ○
(U.S.A.)

Family: APOCYNACEAE
Origin: Southern Europe, North Africa, Japan.
Flowering time: Summer–autumn.
Climatic zone: 9, 10.
Dimensions: 4–15 feet (1–5 meters) high.
Description: Oleander is an extremely hardy shrub which will tolerate heat, drought, and salt. However, in cool climates, it needs to be grown under glass. The large, open-faced pink or white flowers stay on the plant throughout summer. There are few shrubs which flower for so long a period. The dark-green leaves are in pairs or whorls of three around the stem. All parts of this plant are poisonous, so keep children and pets from eating it. Do not burn the leaves. The many cultivars of this plant have

Nerium oleander

become much more popular than the species itself.

Other colors: White, yellow, buff, red.
Varieties/cultivars: Several cultivars have been developed throughout the world.

Paeonia suffruticosa and cultivars
TREE PEONY, MOUNTAIN PEONY (U.S.A.)

○ ◑

Family: PAEONIACEAE
Origin: China.
Flowering time: Early summer.
Climatic zone: 6, 7, 8, 9.
Dimensions: Up to 6 feet (2 meters) high.
Description: The tree peony and its cultivars are among the finest of all spring-flowering shrubs. The large, shaggy-petalled flower heads are 6–8 inches (150–200 mm) wide. Flower color of the species is pink to white, each petal having a maroon splash at the base. Whilst tree peony and its cultivars are frost-hardy, the new growth is susceptible to late-spring frosts so it should be given protection. Tree peonies grow best in a neutral to acid,

Paeonia suffruticosa

humus-rich soil, with shelter from strong winds.

Other colors: White, red.
Varieties/cultivars: 'Godaishu', 'Hodai', 'Kumagai', 'Sakurajishi', 'Taiyo'.

Pimelea ferruginea

Pimelea ferruginea
PINK RICE FLOWER

○ ◑

Family: THYMELAEACEAE
Origin: Western Australia.
Flowering time: Late spring – summer.
Climatic zone: 9, 10.
Dimensions: 1–3 feet (100–900 mm) high.
Description: A neat, rounded shrub with small, glossy green leaves, pink rice flower has a profusion of pink flowers borne in terminal heads during spring. It is an ideal plant for use in a rockery. Salt-tolerant, it is a useful shrub for beachside planting. It likes a well-drained soil. Very little fertilizer or pruning is required to maintain this shrub.

Protea cynaroides

Protea cynaroides
GIANT PROTEA, KING PROTEA (U.K.)

○

Family: PROTEACEAE
Origin: South Africa.
Flowering time: Winter–summer.

Climatic zone: 9, 10.
Dimensions: 2–6 feet (1–2 meters) high.
Description: Giant protea is the most spectacular of all the proteas. The beautiful flower heads of soft silvery pink are 8–12 inches (200–300 mm) across. In the right position the shrub will flower for nine months of the year. In some cold areas, a greenhouse is required. All proteas strongly resent over-rich soils and will thrive in rather poor, slightly acid soil that contains a lot of rubble or sand. Add sulfur to the soil if it is too alkaline. Avoid using phosphates. Do not overwater.

Protea neriifolia

Protea neriifolia
OLEANDER-LEAF PROTEA

○

Family: PROTEACEAE
Origin: South Africa.
Flowering time: Spring–winter.
Climatic zone: 9, 10.
Dimensions: 4–6 feet (1–2 meters) high.
Description: One of the most popular proteas, *P. neriifolia* has deep rose-pink flowers 5 inches (125 mm) long and 3 inches (75 mm) wide. The tips of the petals are black and furry. The long leaves are a soft green. Grow proteas in soil that is not too rich. A poor, slightly acid soil that contains a lot of rubble or sand is ideal. Add sulfur to the soil if it is too alkaline. Avoid using phosphates. Do not overwater, especially in winter. A greenhouse may be necessary in cold climates.

Other colors: Salmon-red.
Varieties/cultivars: 'Taylors Surprise', 'Snow Crest'.

Rhaphiolepis x *delacourii*
PINK INDIAN HAWTHORN   ○

Family: ROSACEAE
Origin: Hybrid.
Flowering time: Spring and autumn.
Climatic zone: 8, 9.
Dimensions: 6 feet (2 meters) high.
Description: This is a charming shrub which has a neat rounded habit and glossy-green leaves. The rose-pink flowers are borne in terminal branching clusters. Pink Indian hawthorn is a slow-growing shrub, but a worthwhile addition to the garden. It is used for hedges and in shrub borders. It is not fussy about soil type, but appreciates a handful of complete plant food around its base in late winter.
Other colors: Crimson.
Varieties/cultivars: 'Coates Crimson'.

Rhaphiolepis x *delacourii*

Rhododendron indicum
INDIAN AZALEA   ○ ◑

Family: ERICACEAE
Origin: Southern Japan.
Flowering time: Winter–spring.
Climatic zone: 8, 9.
Dimensions: 3–8 feet (1–2 meters) high.
Description: This species is the origin of most of the garden forms developed by hybridizing with the allied species. It is a small, dense, evergreen bush. The funnel-shaped flowers are single or in pairs. There are hundreds of different cultivars, many of which are in the pink color range. Indian azaleas require an acid, well-drained soil enriched with leaf mold or compost. Mulching around the plant is also important as the roots are very shallow.
Other colors: White, red, orange, purple.
Varieties/cultivars: There are numerous cultivars of this species.

Rhododendron indicum 'Alphonse Andersen'

Rhododendron Kurume Group
KURUME AZALEA   ○ ◑

Family: ERICACEAE
Origin: Japan.
Flowering time: Spring.
Climatic zone: 6, 7, 8.
Dimensions: Can reach 4 feet (over 1 meter) high.
Description: Kurume azaleas originated from the Kurume province in Japan so they can withstand more cold than *R. indicum*. They are evergreen, with small, rounded leaves. Although the flowers are smaller than other azaleas, they are produced in such profusion that they completely cover the bush. Plant in an acid, well-drained soil which has been enriched with leaf mold or compost. Mulching around the base of the plant is important, as the roots are very shallow.
Other colors: Orange, red, purple, white.
Varieties/cultivars: There are numerous hybrids and varieties of this species.

Rhododendron Kurume Group 'Fairy Queen'

Rhododendron spp.
RHODODENDRON,   ○ ◑
AZALEA

Family: ERICACEAE
Origin: Japan, China, Himalayas, Burma.
Flowering time: Winter–spring.
Climatic zone: 5, 6, 7, 8, 9.
Dimensions: 1–10 feet (up to 3 meters) high.
Description: The genus rhododendron is one of the largest, numbering over 800 species, which range from tiny, prostrate plants to large shrubs. The flowers vary through the whole color spectrum. The majority of the species like a sheltered position and an acid, well-drained soil that has been enriched with leaf mold or compost. A mulch around the shallow, fibrous roots is essential to keep them cool and moist.
Other colors: White, red, yellow, purple, blue.
Varieties/cultivars: There are numerous cultivars.

Rhododendron spp.

Ribes sanguineum
FLOWERING   ○ ◑
CURRANT (U.K.), AMERICAN
CURRANT

Family: GROSSULARIACEAE
Origin: Western North America.
Flowering time: Spring.
Climatic zone: 6, 7, 8.
Dimensions: 5–12 feet (2–4 meters) high.
Description: An ornamental and pretty, deciduous shrub, flowering currant can be used as a feature shrub or in a shrub border of a cottage garden. During spring it is covered in hanging flower heads, 3–4 inches (75–100 mm) long, of rosy-pink flowers which are followed by black berries with a waxy, white patina which makes them look gray from a distance. The leaves have a characteristically pungent smell. Flowering currant is an easily grown

Ribes sanguineum

shrub, thriving in any soil. Prune after flowering. It can be propagated from layering, cuttings, or seeds.
Other colors: White, red, crimson.
Varieties/cultivars: 'King Edward VII', 'Splendens', 'Album', 'Albescens', 'Carneum'.

Robinia kelseyi
ALLEGHENY MOSS LOCUST (U.S.A.)

○ ◑

Family: LEGUMINOSAE
Origin: South Allegheny Mountains (U.S.A.).
Flowering time: Spring, southern hemisphere; summer, northern hemisphere.
Climatic zone: 6, 7, 8, 9.
Dimensions: 8–10 feet (2–3 meters) high.
Description: This graceful shrub or small tree with slender branches and elegant foliage has slightly fragrant rose-pink flowers hanging in clusters. Allegheny moss locust makes a perfect feature shrub. A sheltered position is essential as the branches are very brittle and easily broken by wind. It is excellent in dry, inland areas, as it will withstand near-drought conditions.

Robinia kelseyi

Rondeletia amoena
YELLOW-THROAT RONDELETIA

○ ◑

Family: RUBIACEAE
Origin: West Indies.
Flowering time: Summer.
Climatic zone: 9, 10.
Dimensions: 6-10 feet (2–3 meters) high.
Description: Yellow-throat rondeletia is a bushy evergreen shrub, with large, handsome, rather leathery leaves. The salmon-pink, fragrant, tubular flowers are borne in terminal clusters and have a golden beard at the throat. It is useful as a screen or feature shrub, and will grow in any well-drained garden soil. However, in cold climates it grows best in a greenhouse. Prune, if required, to just above the lower leaves on the branches as the flowers finish.

Rondeletia amoena

Spiraea japonica
JAPANESE SPIRAEA, PINK MAY

○ ◑

Family: ROSACEAE
Origin: Japan.
Flowering time: Summer.
Climatic zone: 5, 6, 7, 8, 9.

Spiraea japonica 'Ruberrima'

Dimensions: 4-6 feet (1–2 meters) high.
Description: This hardy deciduous shrub, valued for its flattened heads of pink flowers, is a popular landscape or feature plant. Japanese spiraea is easily grown in any type of garden soil as long as it is well-drained. Removing some of the older, less productive branches at the base each year after flowering will encourage the growth of new, vigorous wood. The cut flowers last well indoors.
Other colors: Red, white, crimson.
Varieties/cultivars: 'Alpina', 'Atrosanguinea', 'Bullata', 'Fastigiata', 'Little Princess', 'Ruberrima', var. *albiflora*.

Weigela florida cultivar

Weigela florida and cultivars
WEIGELA, APPLE BLOSSOM (U.S.A.)

○ ◑

Family: CAPRIFOLIACEAE
Origin: Japan, Korea, northern China.
Flowering time: Spring–summer.
Climatic zone: 5, 6, 7, 8, 9.
Dimensions: 7–10 feet (2–3 meters) high.
Description: This is a pretty, deciduous shrub with cane-like branches covered in funnel-shaped, rose-pink flowers which are pale-pink inside. There are many attractive hybrids of this plant. Weigela will grow in any garden soil and should be pruned only after flowering has finished as flowers are borne on the current season's growth. Grow in a shrub border or as a feature plant.
Other colors: White, red, crimson, rosy-crimson.
Varieties/cultivars: There are numerous varieties throughout the world.

Aesculus x *carnea* 'Briottii' syn. *A. rubicunda*
RED HORSE CHESTNUT ○

Family: SAPINDACEAE
Origin: Hybrid.
Flowering time: Late spring–early summer.
Climatic zone: 4, 5, 6, 7, 8, 9.
Dimensions: Up to 40 feet (13 meters) high.
Description: This strikingly beautiful horse chestnut tree has an attractive rounded shape and a profusion of large heads of deep pink blooms during its flowering period. It can be grown from seed, and should be planted where there is plenty of space to allow its shape to develop. Like most horse chestnuts it is quite slow growing, and unless rich, moist soil is provided the foliage will burn and growth will be retarded.

Aesculus x *carnea* 'Briottii'

Albizia julibrissin
MIMOSA TREE (U.S.A.), ○
PERSIAN SILK TREE

Family: LEGUMINOSAE
Origin: Western Asia–Japan.
Flowering time: Late spring–early summer.
Climatic zone: 9, 10.
Dimensions: 16–20 feet (5–6 meters) high x 25–27 feet (7–8 meters) wide.
Description: Soft, feathery green leaves combined with pretty, fluffy, pink-and-cream flowers belie the toughness of this small, deciduous tree. Once established, it thrives in hot, dry areas, in light sandy soils. Typical of the Leguminosae family, it closes its leaves at night to conserve moisture. A fast grower, it is particularly suitable to plant in a new garden as a screen or splendid shade

tree. Much smaller and bushier is *A. j.* 'Rosea'. Both are easily grown from seed.
Other colors: White.
Varieties/cultivars: 'Alba', 'Rosea'.

Albizia julibrissin

Bauhinia x *blakeana*
HONG KONG ORCHID ○
TREE, BUTTERFLY TREE

Family: LEGUMINOSAE
Origin: Hybrid.
Flowering time: Winter, northern hemisphere; late summer–late spring, southern hemisphere.
Climatic zone: 9, 10.
Dimensions: 15–25 feet (5–7 meters) high.
Description: Floral emblem of Hong Kong, this tree deserves that honor, for there are not many months when it is not actually producing flowers. An evergreen, growing almost as wide as it does high, it produces a dense, leafy canopy offering welcome shade in hot climates. The fragrant and exotic orchid-like flowers do not produce the bean pods common to its genus (which can look rather messy), for it is a sterile hybrid. Grow it from cuttings. Prune to shape it while young and prune after each flush of flowers. Hong Kong orchid tree grows well in California and Florida.

Bauhinia x *blakeana*

Bixa orellana
LIPSTICK TREE, ○
ANNATTO TREE

Family: BIXACEAE
Origin: Tropical America.
Flowering time: Summer.
Climatic zone: 9, 10.
Dimensions: 10–30 feet (3–10 meters) high.
Description: An evergreen tree for very warm climates only, bixa is normally bushy in habit but can be trained by careful pruning into a single-stemmed, small tree. Quick-growing, it makes a handsome screen or hedging plant. The flowers form at the tips of branches, and are followed by red-brown spiny fruit. To enjoy summer-long fragrant flowering, trim after the fruits deteriorate, then allow new buds to form. Water well in dry weather. Bixa can be grown from seed.

Bixa orellana

Brachychiton discolor
QUEENSLAND LACEBARK, ○
PINK FLAME TREE (U.K.), HAT
TREE

Other common names: WHITE KURRAJONG (Aust.)
Family: STERCULIACEAE
Origin: Australia (northern N.S.W., Queensland, and Northern Territory coastal regions).
Flowering time: Late spring–early autumn.

Climatic zone: 9, 10.
Dimensions: 20–65 feet (6–20 meters) high.
Description: The Queensland lacebark is widely grown as a shade tree in hot, dryish climates, including California, South Africa, and the Mediterranean. Although normally evergreen, it loses some leaves in cooler regions. The leaves are variable in shape, smooth above and woolly beneath. In a good year, the flowers are spectacular and when they fall, forming a carpet beneath the tree, they create a picture of mirrored beauty. Lacebark prefers deep soils and high rainfall. It is commonly planted as a street tree.

Brachychiton discolor

Calodendrum capense
CAPE CHESTNUT ○

Family: RUTACEAE
Origin: South Africa (coast to tropics).
Flowering time: Late spring–mid-summer in southern hemisphere.
Climatic zone: 8, 9, 10.
Dimensions: 30–45 feet (9–15 meters) high.
Description: An extremely beautiful and adaptable tree, Cape chestnut grows in a range of climates from warm temperate to tropical. Sprays of highly perfumed, mottled pink flowers that cover the canopy seem to be orchid look-alikes. Because it is slow to flower from seed, it is best grown as a grafted plant. Given a good start in fertile soil, it grows fairly quickly, but slows down later, seldom reaching more than 30 feet (10 meters) in the garden. It needs plenty of water in dry weather. Cape chestnut is evergreen in warm climates, but semideciduous in frost areas.

Calodendrum capense

Camellia reticulata and cultivars
NET VEIN CAMELLIA, ○ ◑
NETTED CAMELLIA

Family: THEACEAE
Origin: Yunnan, western China.
Flowering time: Late autumn and early spring, southern hemisphere; spring, northern hemisphere.
Climatic zone: 8, 9.
Dimensions: 6–35 feet (2–10 meters) high.
Description: Really a large shrub, *Camellia reticulata* grows to tree proportions in the wild. Its flowers are larger than other camellias and very free-forming, and although its growth is not as compact as in C. *japonica*, the new cultivars are producing denser

Camellia reticulata cultivar

growth. Easily grown in tubs or for use as tall, background plants, reticulatas are long-lived, requiring only good drainage and a fairly acid soil. Like all camellias and azaleas, their roots are shallow-surfaced, so constant mulching is very beneficial. Reticulatas perform well in full sun, protected from winds.
Other colors: Red, coral, crimson, dark purple-red, white.
Varieties/cultivars: 'Pagoda', 'Letitia', 'Buddha', 'Franci L', 'Howard Asper', 'Purple Gown', 'Tali Queen'.

Cercis canadensis

Cercis canadensis
EASTERN REDBUD, ○ ◑
AMERICAN JUDAS TREE (U.K.)

Family: LEGUMINOSAE
Origin: Southeastern Canada, eastern United States, northeastern Mexico.
Flowering time: Spring.
Climatic zone: 4, 5, 6, 7, 8, 9.
Dimensions: 20–40 feet (6–12 meters) high.
Description: Related to the Judas tree, with similar, but heart-shaped leaves and narrower growth habit, the eastern redbud is a beautiful feature of the spring landscape in the eastern and central states of America. One of the first trees to bloom after winter, numerous clusters of stemless flowers are borne on mature branches, often coming straight out of the wood. It quickly grows into a small, round-headed tree in cultivation. Although not fussy as to soil, it must have good drainage and plenty of water in dry, hot summers. It is deciduous.
Other colors: White.
Varieties/cultivars: 'Alba', 'Plena'.

Cercis siliquastrum
JUDAS TREE, LOVE TREE (U.S.A.) ○

Family: LEGUMINOSAE
Origin: Southern Europe, western Asia.
Flowering time: Early–late spring.
Climatic zone: 7, 8, 9.
Dimensions: 20–30 feet (6–9 meters) high.
Description: This was the tree from which Judas Iscariot supposedly hanged himself after betraying Christ. Like all *Cercis* species, it grows into a delightful small tree, smothering itself with rosy-colored blossom in spring. Typical of the genus, the pea-shaped flowers appear on all parts of the bare wood, even straight out of the trunk. The leaves are kidney-shaped. Most adaptable, it will flourish in heat and drought, is resistant to light frost and will grow in coastal gardens. It is deciduous.
Other colors: White.
Varieties/cultivars: 'Alba'.

Cercis siliquastrum

Cornus florida 'Rubra'
PINK-FLOWERING DOGWOOD ○ ◑

Family: CORNACEAE
Origin: Cultivar.
Flowering time: Spring.
Climatic zone: 5, 6, 7, 8, 9.
Dimensions: 13–40 feet (4–12 meters) high.
Description: Pink-flowering dogwood is one of the most beautiful sights of spring when it flowers on bare wood from upturned twigs. The actual flowers are small and greenish in color, surrounded by four, showy, rosy-pink bracts. A second treat arrives with autumn as the scarlet-colored fruit ripens and the leaves become crimson. Happiest in cool, moist climates, it develops into a

Cornus florida 'Rubra'

small, wide-canopied tree. It needs excellent drainage in acid soil but must not be allowed to dry out. Mulch regularly.

Dombeya x *cayeuxii*
MEXICAN ROSE, PINK BALL DOMBEYA, CAPE WEDDING FLOWER ○

Family: BYTTNERIACEAE
Origin: Hybrid.
Flowering time: Late autumn–spring.
Climatic zone: 9, 10.
Dimensions: 15–30 feet (4–9 meters) high.
Description: The parents of this hybrid are *D. burgessiae* and *D. wallichii*. The hanging clusters of shell-pink flowers are somewhat like those of a viburnum and the leaves are poplar-shaped and large. A good fill-in plant for a warm corner position or background situation, it develops a shrubby growth habit. It is easily grown from cuttings in spring and is widespread in many climates including those of Florida, India, Africa, and Australia.

Dombeya x *cayeuxii*

Eucalyptus caesia

Eucalyptus caesia
GUNGUNNA, GUNGURRU ○ (Aust.)

Family: MYRTACEAE
Origin: Southwestern Western Australia.
Flowering time: Winter–mid-spring in southern hemisphere.
Climatic zone: 9, 10.
Dimensions: Up to 27 feet (8 meters) high.
Description: One of the most delightful small eucalypts, it develops an open, somewhat sprawling, tree-like habit when cultivated. It is admired for the showy stamens of the flowers which appear on branches covered in a whitish waxy patina. Very decorative, mealy-covered, urn-shaped gumnuts form later which hang for months, and make interesting indoor dried arrangements. Gungunna will not tolerate bad drainage or a prolonged humid atmosphere. Grown from seed, it should be pruned lightly for more compact growth.
Varieties/cultivars: 'Silver Princess'.

Magnolia campbellii
CHINESE TULIP TREE, PINK TULIP TREE, CAMPBELL MAGNOLIA ○

Family: MAGNOLIACEAE
Origin: Himalayas.
Flowering time: Spring.
Climatic zone: 7, 8, 9.
Dimensions: 40–160 feet (12–50 meters) high.
Description: Probably seen at its

maximum height only in its native habitat, the Chinese tulip tree is very slow-maturing, and takes about 12–15 years to come into flower. Plant it for your children to enjoy! Its maximum height in the U.K. is 60 feet (18 meters). The flowers sit on bare wood and are large, pink, and waxy. Large velvety leaves follow, their color in autumn complementing the spikes of scarlet seeds. This tree grows best in frost-free areas.

Other colors: White, purple.
Varieties/cultivars: M. *c.* var. *mollicomata*.

Magnolia campbellii

Malus floribunda
JAPANESE CRAB APPLE ○

Family: ROSACEAE
Origin: Japan, China.
Flowering time: Spring.
Climatic zone: 5, 6, 7, 8, 9.
Dimensions: 16–25 feet (5–7 meters) high.

Malus floribunda

Description: Although some crab apples are inclined to bloom only every two years, M. *floribunda* is renowned for its reliability in flowering every year. The backs of the petals are a rosy color and the insides white — which produces a delightful sight when rosy buds are opening among already-opened, white flowers. Beautiful fruits, yellow with a reddish flush, develop in autumn, although in the U.K. this species fruits poorly and the very small 'apples' are not usually brightly colored. The crab apple prefers a moist climate with long winters. Protect it from strong winds but allow it plenty of root space.

Other colors: Purplish-red.
Varieties/cultivars: 'Gibb's Golden Gage', 'Indian Magic', 'Indian Summer', 'Liset', 'Makamik', 'Mary Potter', 'Robinson'.

Malus ioensis 'Plena'
PRAIRIE CRAB (U.S.A.), ○
BECHTEL CRAB APPLE

Family: ROSACEAE
Origin: Cultivar.
Flowering time: Late spring–early summer.
Climatic zone: 2, 3, 4, 5, 6, 7, 8, 9.
Dimensions: 20–30 feet (6–9 meters) high.
Description: This is arguably the most beautiful of the flowering crab apples, but is not a strong grower. M. *ioensis* 'Plena' is a double-flowered bud-mutant (that is, produced by a mutation in one of the buds) of M. *ioensis*, discovered by Bechtel, an Illinois nurseryman.

Malus ioensis 'Plena'

Flowers are abundant and sweetly perfumed, opening later than those of most crab apples, which is useful if you want to prolong spring flowering. Fruit is seldom seen, but the leaves color in autumn to vivid shades of yellow, orange, and crimson. It can be susceptible to juniper rust.

Malus spectabilis 'Plena'

Malus spectabilis 'Plena'
CHINESE CRAB APPLE, ○
DOUBLE FLOWERED CHINESE
CRAB APPLE

Family: ROSACEAE
Origin: Cultivar.
Flowering time: Mid–late spring.
Climatic zone: 4, 5, 6, 7, 8, 9.
Dimensions: 16–30 feet (5–9 meters) high.
Description: This is possibly a natural hybrid of Chinese origin. It is unknown as a native tree growing in the wild. Flowers of M. *s.* 'Plena' are semidouble, rose-pink when in bud, opening to blush-pink, then fading to white. They are faintly perfumed. Its beauty when flowering, plus its vigorous growth habit, make this tree a valuable addition to any cool, moist, elevated garden in regions with longish winters. A row of crab apples lining a driveway or footpath, in blossom or in fruit, is a breathtaking sight.

Malus x *purpurea* 'Eleyi'
PURPLE CRAB APPLE ○

Family: ROSACEAE
Origin: Hybrid.
Flowering time: Late spring.
Climatic zone: 4, 5, 6, 7, 8, 9.
Dimensions: 20–25 feet (6–7 meters) high.
Description: Flowers of M. x *p*. 'Eleyi' are a pretty rosy-magenta in bud, opening to a paler shade. Purplish-red fruits persist into late autumn. It is a deciduous tree. Trees and shrubs with reddish to purplish leaves are best used with discretion for they can easily dominate a garden landscape. *Malus* x *p*. 'Eleyi', can be beautifully integrated with plants that have silvery-gray foliage. Try planting it with willow-leaved pear (*Pyrus salicifolia*) as did Vita Sackville-West in her famous White Garden at Sissinghurst. For best results, plant in well-drained, rich soil and mulch annually with well-rotted compost or manure. Water well in summer.

Malus x *purpurea* 'Eleyi'

Prunus mume 'Geisha'
JAPANESE APRICOT ○

Family: ROSACEAE
Origin: Cultivar.
Flowering time: Early–late spring, northern hemisphere; winter, southern hemisphere.
Climatic zone: 7, 8, 9.
Dimensions: 20–27 feet (6–8 meters) high.

Description: The semidouble, rosy-red flowers of P. m. 'Geisha' appear in clusters on one- and two-year-old wood in winter or spring. Being on very short stalks, they appear as solid branches of color. The small, deciduous tree, which develops a broadly rounded crown, is ideal for planting bulbs beneath. Plant it against a warm wall in cold areas.

Prunus mume 'Geisha'

Prunus persica
PEACH, WILD PEACH ○

Family: ROSACEAE
Origin: China.
Flowering time: Spring.
Climatic zone: 5, 6, 7, 8, 9.
Dimensions: 10–25 feet (3–7 meters) high.
Description: Many varieties have been bred from this species, first found growing in the wild in China. Rose-pink flowers appear, followed by round, edible fruits. Unfortunately the tree is subject to borer attack and peach leaf curl (a fungus disease). In parts of Australia the fruit is attacked by fruit fly, and must be treated as the fruit begin to ripen. Keep the tree vigorous by regular feeding and watering, and spray the leaves with a fungicide at bud-swell stage. If you only want flowers, it is advisable to grow one of the many cultivars.
Other colors: White, rosy-red, white-and-red stripes.

Varieties/cultivars: 'Alba Plena', 'Alba Plena Pendula', 'Foliis Rubis', 'Klara Mayer', 'Lilian Burrows', 'Magnifica', 'Rosea Plena', 'Versicolor'.

Prunus persica

Prunus 'Amanogawa' syn. *P. serrulata erecta*
JAPANESE FLOWERING ○
CHERRY

Family: ROSACEAE
Origin: Hybrid.
Flowering time: Late spring, northern hemisphere; mid–late spring, southern hemisphere.
Climatic zone: 5, 6, 7, 8, 9.
Dimensions: 13–20 feet (4–6 meters) high.
Description: Unlike most Japanese flowering cherries, which either spread their branches wide to form a flattened crown or develop a broad vase shape, P. 'Amanogawa' develops into a narrow, upright form. Given its narrow habit, this cherry is best used as a background tree or in a narrow space. Semidouble, blush-pink, fragrant flowers appear in erect clusters on this deciduous tree. Do not prune it. Cherries, badly pruned, can die from producing excess gum.

Prunus 'Amanogawa'

Prunus serrulata 'Shimidsu Sakura'
JAPANESE FLOWERING CHERRY ○

Family: ROSACEAE
Origin: Cultivar.
Flowering time: Mid–late spring.
Climatic zone: 5, 6, 7, 8, 9.
Dimensions: 10–13 feet (3–4 meters) high.
Description: Pink buds opening to pure white, hanging clusters of flowers adorn this small, deciduous tree from mid- to late spring. Considered one of the most beautiful of the flowering cherries, it develops wide-spreading, gracefully arching branches to form a broad, flattened crown. Green leaves color brilliantly in autumn. It prefers a cool, moist climate on elevated soils.

Prunus serrulata 'Shimidsu Sakura'

Prunus subhirtella

Prunus subhirtella and cultivars
HIGAN CHERRY, ROSEBUD CHERRY ○

Family: ROSACEAE
Origin: Hybrid.
Flowering time: Spring.
Climatic zone: 6, 7, 8, 9.
Dimensions: 20–30 feet (6–9 meters) high.
Description: The tiny, pink flowers of the natural hybrid *P. subhirtella* are not as beautiful as in the cultivated varieties. Slender branches carry small, green leaves which color well in autumn and then drop. As with all flowering cherries, avoid pruning, but if it becomes necessary prune in summer. For showier flowers and smaller growth, plant the cultivars.
Other colors: Deep to light pink, single and double.
Varieties/cultivars: 'Pendula', 'Pendula Rosea', 'Pendula Rubra', 'Autumnalis', 'Fukubana'.

Prunus subhirtella 'Autumnalis'

Prunus subhirtella 'Autumnalis'
WINTER SPRING, WINTER CHERRY (U.K.) ○

Family: ROSACEAE
Origin: Cultivar.
Flowering time: Autumn, winter, spring.
Climatic zone: 6, 7, 8, 9.
Dimensions: 20–30 feet (6–9 meters) high.

Description: Other cherries may be much more showy, displaying beautiful, hanging clusters of flowers, but this cultivar has the advantage of flowering over an extended period. In a mild winter it can begin to flower in autumn and continue intermittently into spring. The modest clusters of flowers cling to small shoots that grow straight out of the trunk. As with all deciduous cherries, it performs best in a cool, moist climate.

Prunus subhirtella 'Pendula Rosea'

Prunus subhirtella 'Pendula Rosea'
WEEPING CHERRY, SPRING CHERRY ○

Family: ROSACEAE
Origin: Cultivar.
Flowering time: Spring, northern hemisphere; late spring, southern hemisphere.
Climatic zone: 6, 7, 8, 9.
Dimensions: 6–10 feet (2–3 meters) high.
Description: Fountains of delightful, dainty, pink, single flowers cascade from the canopy of this weeping small tree each spring. They are a rich pink when in bud, fading later to blush pink. Beautiful, slender, arching branches give the tree the appearance of a miniature weeping willow. It can provide an avenue of color, or be grown as an individual against a background of evergreen trees. Often grown as a small standard, this tree makes an ideal specimen in a small garden. Very little pruning is necessary.

Prunus x *amygdalo-persica* 'Pollardii'
FLOWERING ALMOND ○

Family: ROSACEAE
Origin: Hybrid.
Flowering time: Spring, southern hemisphere.
Climatic zone: 6, 7, 8, 9.
Dimensions: 10–20 feet (3–6 meters) high.
Description: A cross between a peach and an almond, this Australian-raised hybrid quickly grows into a robust, small tree. Single, soft rose-pink flowers appear in profusion each spring, well before the leaves unfurl. If cut while still in bud, the flowers will open indoors, lasting a week in water. It is reasonably resistant to the peach leaf curl which attacks so many flowering peaches. Fruits are almond-shaped. The green leaves do not produce good autumn coloring.

Prunus x *amygdalo-persica* 'Pollardii'

Prunus x *blireana*
DOUBLE ROSE CHERRY, ○
FLOWERING CHERRY PLUM

Family: ROSACEAE
Origin: Hybrid.
Flowering time: Spring, northern hemisphere; early spring, southern hemisphere.
Climatic zone: 6, 7, 8, 9.
Dimensions: 8–17 feet (2–5 meters) high.
Description: Flowering cherry plum is a cross between *P. cerasifera* 'Atropurpurea' and *P. mume* 'Alphandii'. It is a small, compact, deciduous tree, bearing semidouble, rose-pink, fragrant flowers. These appear en masse and are much in

Prunus x *blireana*

demand for use in floral art and as an indoor cut flower. The tree has coppery-purple leaves, and as with all trees and shrubs with reddish leaves, in a small garden it may overpower other plants. In a larger setting, plant as an avenue.
Other colors: Pale pink flowers, pale reddish-purple leaves.
Varieties/cultivars: 'Moseri'.

Prunus x *yedoensis*
JAPANESE FLOWERING ○
CHERRY, YOSHINO CHERRY

Family: ROSACEAE
Origin: Hybrid.
Flowering time: Spring, northern hemisphere.
Climatic zone: 6, 7, 8, 9.

Prunus x *yedoensis*

Dimensions: 27–40 feet (8–12 meters) high.
Description: This beautiful deciduous tree has long been cultivated in Japan and is the principal park and street cherry tree grown in that country. Thought to be a cross between *P. subhirtella* and *P. speciosa*, it has a short main trunk, and forms a flattish, broad-domed shape. Almond-scented, blush-pink flowers appear in profusion each spring. Ideal for cool and temperate climates, it thrives in well-drained, moderately rich soil that is well watered in summer. Incorporate plenty of well-rotted compost prior to planting.
Other colors: White, pale pink.
Varieties/cultivars: 'Ivensii', 'Shidare Yoshino', 'Akebono'.

Rhododendron arboreum

Rhododendron arboreum
TREE ○ ◑
RHODODENDRON

Family: ERICACEAE
Origin: Himalayas.
Flowering time: Mid-winter–spring, northern hemisphere.
Climatic zone: 8, 9.
Dimensions: 20–50 feet (6–15 meters) high.
Description: Parent to many sturdy hybrids, this tall species rhododendron was first discovered in the Himalayas in 1820 and is the first known tree rhododendron. It injected a rich, red color into the breeding program. Regal-looking flower clusters open atop rosettes of handsome, evergreen leaves which droop down at flowering time to display the blooms. It prefers a cool, moist climate and acid soils, and needs regular mulching.
Other colors: White.
Varieties/cultivars: 'Blood Red', 'Roseum', 'Sir Charles Lemon', 'Cornubia', 'Gill's Triumph', 'Glory of Penjerrick'.

Robinia hispida
ROSE ACACIA (U.K.), BRISTLY LOCUST, MOSS LOCUST ○

Family: LEGUMINOSAE
Origin: Southeastern United States.
Flowering time: Late spring, northern hemisphere; early summer, southern hemisphere.
Climatic zone: 5, 6, 7, 8, 9.
Dimensions: 4–7 feet (1–2 meters) high.
Description: Although really a shrub, *R. hispida* is often grafted onto the standard rootstock of *R. pseudoacacia*, to form a small tree. Fragrant, pea-shaped flowers of a charming rose-pink color hang in clusters, partly hidden by the green, fern-like foliage. Plant where its slightly drooping branches can hang over a wall to best display the flowers. If grown as a shrub, it tends to sucker, but does not outgrow its welcome. As its stems are very brittle, if grown on a standard, plant it in a wind-protected spot, preferably against a sunny wall. Buy grafted stock, or propagate shrubs from suckers or root cuttings.
Varieties/cultivars: var. *macrophylla* 'Superba'.

Robinia hispida 'Macrophylla'

Tamarix aphylla
ATHEL TREE, EVERGREEN TAMARISK ○

Family: TAMARICACEAE
Origin: India, northwest Africa, eastern Mediterranean.
Flowering time: Late summer–early autumn.
Climatic zone: 8, 9.

Dimensions: 30–40 feet (10–12 meters) high.
Description: This tree has tiny whitish pink flowers which appear along slender ½ inch (12 mm) spikes in summer. It is valuable for its ability to survive under hot, dry conditions. An evergreen, it is a perfect specimen for the hot and arid places in Australia, Africa, and the U.S.A. Once established, it can withstand the heat and a rainfall of less than 5 inches (125 mm) per year. It is also a useful tree for seaside planting, withstanding salt-laden winds and providing shelter for less hardy plants. Good drainage is essential. It resents being moved.

Tamarix aphylla

Tamarix parviflora
TAMARISK ○

Family: TAMARICACEAE
Origin: Yugoslavia, Greece, Turkey, Crete.
Flowering time: Spring.
Climatic zone: 6, 7, 8, 9.
Dimensions: 10–15 feet (3–5 meters) high.
Description: All tamarisks are useful plants in low rainfall areas. *T. parviflora*, although not showy, is a picture in spring when masses of tiny, pale-pink flowers festoon the fine, bare branches. These are followed by feathery foliage. An excellent plant to use in a subtle landscape design, it provides shelter for less hardy plants in a seaside location or in a hot, dry situation. Good drainage is essential and if not provided, plants can become infested by borer. With its open, irregular shape and no main trunk, it is shrub-like in appearance.

Tamarix parviflora

Virgilia capensis syn. *V. oroboides*
KEURBOOM, ○ ◑ VIRGILA

Family: LEGUMINOSAE
Origin: South Africa.
Flowering time: Spring–early summer.
Climatic zone: 9, 10.
Dimensions: 27–33 feet (8–10 meters) high.
Description: One of the fastest-growing trees in cultivation, it enjoys a good but brief life, often dying after about fifteen years. Like fast-growing wattles, it makes a good "nurse" plant, protecting slower-growing species close by and filling in areas where privacy is needed. It is an erect evergreen that lives longer in cool rather than hot areas and prefers light, well-drained soils with adequate water in hot summers. Trim the plant back each year to keep it more compact and vigorous.

Virgilia capensis

PURPLE-BLUE FLOWERS

Ageratum houstonianum
COMMON AGERATUM, FLOSSFLOWER ○ ◑

Family: COMPOSITAE
Origin: Mexico.
Flowering time: Summer–autumn.
Climatic zone: 5, 6, 7, 8, 9, 10.
Dimensions: 18 inches (450 mm) high.
Description: The flower heads are borne in dense terminal clusters of many flowers, each one of which is ¼ inch (6 mm) in diameter, but the entire head is up to 2 inches (50 mm) wide and looks like a single flower. The flower heads, which are mainly blue to lavender, are soft and fluffy and, especially in the dwarf varieties, can cover the top of the plant. Ageratum makes an excellent border plant because of its contrasting color and dense habit. The taller types can be cut and last well indoors. Sow seedlings in spring in any well-drained soil.
Other colors: Pink, white.
Varieties/cultivars: 'Blue Angel', 'Lilac Angel', 'Blue Blazer', 'White Angel', 'Blue Mink'.

Ageratum houstonianum 'Blue Mink'

Borago officinalis
BORAGE, TALEWORT ○ ◑

Family: BORAGINACEAE
Origin: Mediterranean region.
Flowering time: Summer.
Climatic zone: 4, 5, 6, 7, 8, 9, 10.
Dimensions: Up to 2 feet (600 mm) high.
Description: This is a plant grown principally as a culinary herb. Both the leaves and the very attractive soft-blue flowers may be used as a garnish or to flavor drinks. It is a quick-growing annual with stiff but soft, hairy, gray-green foliage. The flowers form in a terminal head up to ¼ inch (18 mm) wide, and are also hairy, giving the plant a soft, clouded appearance. Bees are attracted to the flowers which may be crystallized, used in potpourri, or as a cake decoration; the leaves may be shredded and used in salads. Plant in full sun or semishade in moderately rich, well-drained soil.
Other colors: Purple, white.

Borago officinalis

Centaurea cyanus

Centaurea cyanus
CORNFLOWER, ○ ◑ BLUEBOTTLE, BLUE BONNETS

Other common names: BATCHELOR'S-BUTTON, RAGGED SAILOR
Family: COMPOSITAE
Origin: Southern and eastern Europe.
Flowering time: Summer–autumn.
Climatic zone: 5, 6, 7, 8, 9.
Dimensions: Up to 2 feet (600 mm) high.
Description: A very useful floral plant, grown as an annual, it has bright blue flowers on stiff upright stems which make it ideal for florist work. The flowers are up to 1½ inches (40 mm) wide in a tight head. It is hardy and flowers best in early summer before it is too hot. It is not a leafy plant but produces many flower stems. Choose a sunny or lightly shaded position and ensure that the soil is light but rich with organic matter. Water well while buds are forming.
Other colors: White, lavender, pink.
Varieties/cultivars: 'Alba'.

Consolida orientalis syn. *Delphinium orientale*
LARKSPUR ○

Family: RANUNCULACEAE
Origin: Southern Europe–western Asia, North Africa.
Flowering time: Summer.
Climatic zone: 5, 6, 7, 8, 9.
Dimensions: Up to 3 feet (1 meter) high.
Description: With its tall, strong-stemmed, many-flowered spikes, this larkspur is an attractive garden plant. It is a favorite with florists for use as background in floral arrangements with its even, blue flowers. Flower spikes are up to 12 inches (300 mm) long and covered in small blooms 1½ inches (30 mm) wide. It is excellent for bedding as a background to other shorter annuals. Although hardy, it does not tolerate hot, dry conditions. For a good display sow seeds or seedlings in clumps in slightly alkaline soil — add lime if the soil is acid. Feed weekly while buds are forming.
Other colors: Violet, pink, white.
Varieties/cultivars: 'Rainbow' mixed may produce other colors.

Consolida orientalis

Delphinium consolida syn. *Consolida regalis*

DELPHINIUM

Family: RANUNCULACEAE
Origin: Southern and central Europe–western Asia.
Flowering time: Summer–autumn.
Climatic zone: 5, 6, 7, 8, 9.
Dimensions: Up to 7 feet (2 meters) high.
Description: The majestic tall flower spikes of this Delphinium species make it the most-prized of these useful perennials. The flowers are soft and blue/purple in color, while the kidney-shaped foliage is mid green. Ideal for an old-fashioned flower garden, it should be positioned towards the back. Plant in deep, rich and slightly alkaline soil and provide some shelter from strong winds as the tall flower spikes are prone to collapse if not protected.
Other colors: Pink, mauve, lilac, white.

Delphinium consolida

Eustoma grandiflorum syn. *Lisianthus russellianus*

LISIANTHUS, PRAIRIE GENTIAN

Family: GENTIANACEAE
Origin: Central southern United States.
Flowering time: Summer.
Climatic zone: 6, 7, 8, 9.
Dimensions: Up to 3 feet (1 meter) high.
Description: This flower is shaped like an upturned bell, flaring at the edges and blotched at the base, being some 2 inches (50 mm) wide. It is long-lasting

as a cut flower, and useful as an indoor flowering pot plant in a well-lit situation. The foliage is pale-green, dull, and not impressive. It is hardy, tolerating a wide range of conditions.
Other colors: White, pink, lavender, dark purple.
Varieties/cultivars: 'Yodel Pink', 'Yodel Blue', 'Yodel White' (all compact to 18 inches (450 mm) high).

Eustoma grandiflorum

Exacum affine

PERSIAN VIOLET

Family: GENTIANACEAE
Origin: South Yemen.
Flowering time: Spring–autumn.
Climatic zone: 9, 10.
Dimensions: Up to 10 inches (250 mm) high.
Description: This is a low-growing, compact plant, suitable for borders in sheltered areas in warm climates. It needs partial shade because the stems and leaves are tender and will not tolerate frost. The tiny flowers, lavender with yellow centers, are about ½ inch (13 mm) wide and cover the plant profusely. They have a sweet perfume. Its compact habit makes it an ideal plant for small containers. It will live and flower indoors or under shelter in good light for three to four months. It does not like to be overwatered. It is a short-lived perennial usually grown as an annual. It is well-suited to a greenhouse in cold climates.
Other colors: White, pink.

Exacum affine

Limonium sinuatum

Limonium sinuatum

STATICE, SEA LAVENDER, SEA PINK

Family: PLUMBAGINACEAE
Origin: Mediterranean region–Portugal.
Flowering time: Spring–summer.
Climatic zone: 6, 7, 8, 9, 10.
Dimensions: Up to 18 inches (450 mm) high.
Description: Its strong, wiry stems and many-colored flowers, added to its lasting qualities when picked, make statice popular with florists and for indoor arrangements. The tiny flowers are only ⅜ inch (9 mm) wide, but are tightly clustered to give good color. They are dry and papery when in full bloom and are borne on winged branches. The plant is biennial but is mostly grown as an annual. The foliage is in a rosette at the base of the plant and of minor importance. Valued for its tolerance to low rainfall and also to seaspray, it is excellent in both seaside and country gardens. Apply a general fertilizer when buds are forming, to encourage a good floral display.
Other colors: Dark-red, yellow, pink, white.

Lobelia erinus
COMMON LOBELIA, EDGING LOBELIA ○

Family: LOBELIACEAE
Origin: South Africa.
Flowering time: All seasons, excluding frost.
Climatic zone: 5, 6, 7, 8, 9, 10.
Dimensions: Up to 6 inches (150 mm) high.
Description: This is a wiry-stemmed bushy plant but some types have a trailing habit. Although short in stature with small flowers, it gives a mass of color when in bloom. Individual flowers, which are barely ½ inch (13 mm) wide, are deep-blue and often have a white eye. When grown with multicolored annuals, their rich color forms a vivid contrast. The stems are slender but when the plants are grown closely together they form a continuous color border. The trailing varieties are used effectively in hanging baskets in cool but light situations. Best results are obtained if planted in rich, moist soil.
Other colors: Pale blue, white, purple, red, cream.
Varieties/cultivars: 'String of Pearls' (mixed variety), 'Basket Lobelia' (trailing).

Lobelia erinus

Lupinus hartwegii
LUPIN, ANNUAL LUPIN, HAIRY LUPIN ○

Family: LEGUMINOSAE
Origin: Mexico.
Flowering time: Summer–autumn.
Climatic zone: 7, 8, 9.
Dimensions: Up to 2½ feet (750 mm) high.
Description: This is a tall, upright, strong-growing annual, with a long flowering period. The foliage is compact and stiff and produces flower stems up to 18 inches (450 mm) high, making lupin an ideal cut flower. The long-lasting flowers are about 1 inch (25 mm) long and cover the stems densely in pastel shades of blue, pink, and white. All the foliage and the flowers are covered with soft, silky hairs. A fertile, moist soil ensures best results. Full sun and good drainage are essential.
Varieties/cultivars: 'Pixie' (dwarf form, growing 8 inches (200 mm) high).

Lupinus hartwegii

Nemophila menziesii

Nemophila menziesii
BABY-BLUE-EYES ◑

Family: HYDROPHYLLACEAE
Origin: California.
Flowering time: Summer.
Climatic zone: 5, 6, 7, 8, 9.
Dimensions: Up to 8 inches (200 mm).
Description: While this plant grows only to a low height, it spreads well and has dainty fern-like foliage. On the tips of the stems are many bright blue flowers with white centers, saucer-like in shape, up to 1½ inches (40 mm) wide. The outstanding blue with white shows prominently in the garden when baby-blue-eyes is planted closely in groups. It is not suitable for picking, but is attractive in hanging baskets in a cool situation.
Other colors: White, blue-margined white, and brownish-purple margined white.
Varieties/cultivars: 'Alba', 'Peter Blue' (veined purple), 'Crambeoides', 'Atomaria', 'Disoidalis'.

Nierembergia hippomanica
CUPFLOWER ○ ◑

Family: SOLANACEAE
Origin: Argentina.
Flowering time: Summer–autumn.
Climatic zone: 6, 7, 8, 9, 10.
Dimensions: Up to 15 inches (380 mm) high.
Description: This plant is usually grown as an annual, but is a shrubby perennial in mild winters. It is hardy and withstands strong sunlight. The flowers though small, up to 1 inch (25 mm) wide, are numerous and tightly packed. They are shaped like a tiny cup, yellow in the center and violet on the rim. Cupflower is useful for hanging baskets, but has no picking value. Easy to cultivate in a wide range of soils and conditions, in full sun or semishade.
Varieties/cultivars: 'Violacea', 'Purple Robe'.

Nierembergia hippomanica

Nigella damascena
LOVE-IN-A-MIST,
DEVIL-IN-THE-BUSH, WILD
FENNEL

Family: RANUNCULACEAE
Origin: Southern Europe, North Africa.
Flowering time: Summer–autumn.
Climatic zone: 5, 6, 7, 8, 9.
Dimensions: Up to 18 inches (450 mm) high.
Description: Bright green, lace-like foliage gives an attractive background to the small flowers scattered on the surface. The flowers may be white, light blue, rose-pink, mauve, or purple, and are up to 1½ inches (40 mm) wide. Both the flowers and the globe-shaped dried seed pods keep well when cut. The plant is hardy and has a long flowering season. Choose a sunny position and ensure that soil is well-drained.

Nigella damascena

Salvia patens
GENTIAN SAGE

Family: LABIATAE
Origin: Mexico.
Flowering time: Summer.
Climatic zone: 5, 6, 7, 8, 9, 10.
Dimensions: Up to 3 feet (1 meter) high.
Description: This is a hardy plant usually grown as an annual, but may persist as a perennial especially if old flower heads are cut back. The flower spike is upright and protrudes from the foliage, which is dull green and hairy. When grown closely, 12 inches (300 mm) apart, the plant makes an attractive hedge or background for other annuals. Flowers are bright blue,

up to 3 inches (75 mm) long, and flower spikes are up to 12 inches (300 mm) long. Plant in a sunny but sheltered position and enrich the soil with plenty of well-rotted manure or compost prior to planting.
Other colors: White.
Varieties/cultivars: 'Alba'.

Salvia patens

Torenia fournieri
WISHBONE
FLOWER, BLUEWINGS

Family: SCROPHULARIACEAE
Origin: Vietnam.
Flowering time: Summer.
Climatic zone: 6, 7, 8, 9.
Dimensions: Up to 12 inches (300 mm) high.
Description: These low-growing, rather tender plants need to be grown closely together to give a massed border effect. The flowers are 1½ inches (35 mm) long and 1 inch (25 mm) wide with four petals, three of them purple and the largest pale blue, all with yellow spots in the throat. They are attractive in hanging baskets but no use as a cut flower. Warm, humid conditions and a

rich, moist soil are essential. In the right climate it can be grown in full sun or shade.
Other colors: White, also with yellow spots in the throat.
Varieties/cultivars: 'Alba'.

Torenia fournieri

Viola tricolor
JOHNNY-JUMP-UP,
PANSY, HEARTSEASE

Family: VIOLACEAE
Origin: Europe, Asia.
Flowering time: Spring–autumn.
Climatic zone: 6, 7, 8, 9.
Dimensions: Up to 12 inches (300 mm) high.
Description: *Viola tricolor* is the true wild species pansy which varies in size and color. One plant produces many tiny flowers in two tones of blue to purple, often bicolored. Flowers are usually borne singly and are from ¾ inch (19 mm) to 4 inches (100 mm) wide. It is useful for planting over naturalized bulbs and also in pots and baskets. Rich, moist soil and a sunny to semishaded position are ideal for pansies.

Viola tricolor

Allium aflatunense

Allium aflatunense
ORNAMENTAL ONION   ○ ◑

Family: LILIACEAE
Origin: Central Asia–China.
Flowering time: Spring.
Climatic zone: 6, 7, 8.
Dimensions: Up to 2½ feet (750 mm) high.
Description: This plant, which belongs to the leek, chive, garlic and shallot family, produces large, beautiful flowers. It is one of the larger varieties and can be featured in mixed borders naturalized in grass, woodland and rock gardens. This Asian variety produces large round heads of purple star-like flowers and has attractive strap-like leaves. Clumps can be lifted and divided in early autumn.

Anemone coronaria
WINDFLOWER,   ○ ◑ ●
POPPY-FLOWERED ANEMONE

Family: RANUNCULACEAE
Origin: Mediterranean.
Flowering time: Spring.
Climatic zone: 8, 9.
Dimensions: Up to 18 inches (450 mm) high.
Description: During the Crusades, soil

Anemone coronaria 'St. Brigid'

from the Holy Land was taken to Pisa as ship's ballast to bury dead soldiers. The following spring, the area was carpeted with anemones. The flowers were called "blood drops of Christ" and spread across Europe. These anemones will grow abundantly in full sun or partial shade. Provide well-drained sandy soil rich in humus. Both single and double blooms are available and look pretty in borders or massed under trees.
Other colors: Red, white, mauve, yellow.
Varieties/cultivars: 'St. Brigid'.

Babiana stricta
BABOON FLOWER (U.K.),   ○
BABOONROOT, WINE CUPS

Family: IRIDACEAE
Origin: South Africa.
Flowering time: Spring.

Babiana stricta

Climatic zone: 9, 10.
Dimensions: Up to 8 inches (200 mm) high.
Description: These plants were named by early settlers to South Africa when they discovered baboons eating the corms. The plants produce about six purple flowers, not unlike freesias, on each stem. They are well-suited to growing in pots, tubs, or window boxes. This species will adapt equally well to naturalizing in woodlands and lawns. Full sun is needed and successful growth depends on the bulbs being planted deeply in sandy soil. The same procedure applies if planting in pots. A greenhouse environment is necessary in cold climates.
Other colors: Mauve, cream, red, white, yellow.

Chionodoxa luciliae

Chionodoxa luciliae
GLORY-OF-THE-SNOW   ◑

Family: LILIACEAE
Origin: Turkey.
Flowering time: Spring.
Climatic zone: 4, 5, 6, 7, 8, 9.
Dimensions: Up to 6 inches (150 mm) high.
Description: This small, colorful bulb is at its best when clustered under deciduous trees and shrubs. It is one of the early flowers of spring, hence the common name, glory-of-the-snow. Naturalize it in wooded areas or rock gardens. This plant will tolerate shade and can be grown indoors in pots or window boxes. Plant in well-drained soil mixed with organic matter. Apply fertilizer when flowering has finished. This flower is a good choice for a blue garden.
Other colors: Pink and white.
Varieties/cultivars: 'Rosea', 'Zwanenburg', 'Pink giant'.

Colchicum cilicicum 'Byzantinum'

Crocus tommasinianus

Crocus tommasinianus
WINTER CROCUS ○

Family: IRIDACEAE
Origin: Yugoslavia–Hungary.
Flowering time: Winter–spring.
Climatic zone: 5, 6, 7, 8, 9.
Dimensions: Up to 5 inches (130 mm) high.
Description: Affectionately known as "Tommies" by many gardeners, these crocus pop up everywhere, even among pebbles. Landscape usage is very flexible. They can be planted in rock gardens, borders, and pots. Although easy to grow, these crocus do like definite cold in winter. Provide light- to medium-rich soil in a sunny open position. If naturalizing in a lawn, do not mow once buds emerge from the soil.
Varieties/cultivars: 'Whitewell purple', 'Ruby giant'.

Colchicum cilicicum 'Byzantinum'
AUTUMN CROCUS ◑

Family: LILIACEAE
Origin: Cultivar.
Flowering time: Autumn.
Climatic zone: 4, 5, 6, 7, 8, 9.
Dimensions: Up to 12 inches (300 mm) high.
Description: Autumn crocus are best planted in a nook by themselves with a groundcover. The funnel-shaped flowers of rose-pink and purple shoot out of the ground without any leaves. Their lush, coarse foliage appears in spring. Crocus prefer well-composted, well-drained soil. This perennial will flourish in an open sunny situation. To divide the plants, lift and move them while they are dormant before flowering. Replant immediately, as the root growth is active at that time. As it is a woodland species, it should not be allowed to dry out too much.
Other colors: White, pink, purple.

Crocus speciosus
AUTUMN CROCUS ◑

Family: IRIDACEAE
Origin: Turkey, Iran, Crimea, Caucasus.
Flowering time: Autumn.
Climatic zone: 5, 6, 7, 8, 9.
Dimensions: Up to 6 inches (150 mm) high.
Description: This is an easily grown corm producing violet flowers. Naturalize in grassy areas or under trees. This plant is also adaptable to rock gardens and pot-planting. As with most corms, it looks best when massed generously, rather than used as a small feature. There are many other species available offering a good color selection. Plant in organic mulch in well-drained soil. Water regularly from when flowers first appear to when the leaves die back. Fertilize weekly during the growing period.
Other colors: White, lavender, blue, yellow.

Crocus speciosus

Crocus vernus 'Enchantress'

corms. Mainly used as a potted specimen it does well in a warm but not hot position. It must be grown under glass in colder climates. Fragrant strains are available and there is a wide choice of colors. Grow in pots of gritty compost with leaf mold and add pieces of chalk or limestone in the drainage area. Excessive temperatures will lead to failure. This species needs plenty of light (though not more than four hours of direct sunlight per day) and a slightly moist atmosphere and does not tolerate high temperatures. Wet soil will cause the buds and leaf base to rot.
Other colors: White, pink, purple, red.
Varieties/cultivars: Many cultivars are available.

Dierama pulcherrimum

Crocus vernus and cultivars
DUTCH CROCUS, SPRING CROCUS ○ ◑

Family: IRIDACEAE
Origin: Mediterranean region.
Flowering time: Spring.
Climatic zone: 3, 4, 5, 6, 7, 8, 9.
Dimensions: Up to 8 inches (200 mm) high.
Description: Originally the purple or white crocus found growing wild on alpine slopes, it is now cultivated to produce free-flowering bulbs. It can be planted in clumps in lawns, under trees, and in beds or window boxes. It looks attractive indoors in blue delft pots to accentuate the "Dutch touch". For selective planting, grow it in rock walls, gravel pathways, or between paving stones. Crocus is not very particular about soil types, but needs good drainage. A sunny location is necessary in cold climates to open the flowers, but in hot areas, filtered sun is best.
Other colors: Pale lilac, mauve, white, deep purple, golden-yellow.
Varieties/cultivars: 'Yellow Giant', 'Dutch Yellow', 'Negro Boy', 'Striped Beauty', 'Haarlem Gem', 'Enchantress'.

Cyclamen persicum

Cyclamen persicum
FLORIST'S CYCLAMEN, COMMON CYCLAMEN ◑

Family: PRIMULACEAE
Origin: Eastern Mediterranean.
Flowering time: Winter–spring.
Climatic zone: 9.
Dimensions: Up to 12 inches (300 mm) high.
Description: This plant needs special attention if grown from seed or tuber-

Dierama pulcherrimum
WANDFLOWER, FAIRY FISHING ROD, FAIRY BELLS ○ ◑

Family: IRIDACEAE
Origin: South Africa.
Flowering time: Spring–summer.
Climatic zone: 8, 9.
Dimensions: Up to 5 feet (approx. 2 meters) high.
Description: A delightful plant, it has long fishing-rod stems which arch with the weight of hanging flowers. The graceful, arching growth merits a front row position in a border. The fairy quality of this flower enhances cottage gardens. A hardy grower, it requires sun in temperate climates but needs shade in the tropics. The soil should be moist, fertile, and well-drained.
Other colors: White, pink, purple, red.
Varieties/cultivars: 'Blackbird', 'Jay', 'Kingfisher'.

Hyacinthus orientalis

Endymion hispanicus hybrid

Endymion hispanicus and hybrids syn.
Scilla hispanica, S. campanulata
SPANISH BLUEBELL, GIANT BLUEBELL ◑

Family: LILIACEAE
Origin: Spain and Portugal–central Italy.
Flowering time: Spring.
Climatic zone: 5, 6, 7, 8, 9.
Dimensions: Up to 18 inches (450 mm) high.
Description: Bluebells look pretty planted in borders, edges, rock gardens or under deciduous trees and shrubs. They blend well with lily-of-the-valley and a carpet of alyssum. They will naturalize rapidly if planted in woodland settings. Bluebells can also be grown in containers indoors. Plant the bulbs in autumn in deep, fertile soil in a lightly shaded or sunny position. Water regularly in winter and spring but keep them dry once foliage turns yellow.
Other colors: Pink, white.

Fritillaria meleagris
SNAKE'S-HEAD FRITILLARY (U.K.), BLOODY WARRIOR, LEOPARD LILY ○

Other common names: CHECKERED LILY, GUINEA FLOWER
Family: LILIACEAE
Origin: U.K., central Europe, Scandinavia.
Flowering time: Spring.
Climatic zone: 4, 5, 6, 7, 8, 9.
Dimensions: Up to 18 inches (450 mm) high.
Description: This is an old-fashioned favorite that lasts for years and is easy to grow. It looks well in rock gardens. The solitary and delicate bell-shaped flower belies its fierce common names. Leopard lily is a corruption of leper lily, so-named because the flower resembled the warning bell of lepers. The checkered bells add a distinctive contrast to a garden. Plant in deep humus-rich soil, in a sunny position. It is native to damp European meadows.
Other colors: Orange, white, green, purple, yellow.
Varieties/cultivars: 'Alba'.

Fritillaria meleagris

Hyacinthus orientalis
DUTCH HYACINTH, COMMON HYACINTH ○

Family: LILIACEAE
Origin: Mediterranean region.
Flowering time: Winter–spring.
Climatic zone: 5, 6, 7, 8, 9.
Dimensions: Up to 18 inches (450 mm) high.
Description: Hyacinths are best suited to formal settings because of their stiff stems and dense flower spikes. They have heavily perfumed, waxy, bell-shaped flowers and do well indoors. They can also be grown most effectively if planted in groups in the garden. They can be susceptible to fungal conditions in soil that is too wet, the bulbs becoming soft and rotten. All garden hyacinths are derived from *H. orientalis*. Some varieties have double blooms. For an exotic touch they can be grown indoors in water in special hyacinth glasses.
Other colors: White, yellow, pink, mauve, purple.
Varieties/cultivars: *H. o. albulus*.

Ipheion uniflorum
TRITELEIA, SPRING STARFLOWER ◑

Family: LILIACEAE
Origin: Peru.
Flowering time: Spring–summer.
Climatic zone: 7, 8, 9.
Dimensions: Up to 8 inches (200 mm) high.
Description: *Ipheion* is well suited to massing at the front of borders or rock gardens. This prolific plant produces numerous solitary flowers. The perfumed blooms are funnel-shaped, with white, pale mauve, or lilac petals. The grassy leaves emit a faint onion-like odor when pressed. *Ipheion* multiplies rapidly in a sunny position in well-drained soil. Bulbs should be left undisturbed for several years until clumps form. They will flower for up to eight weeks and need little attention.

Ipheion uniflorum

Iris reticulata

Iris reticulata
SPANISH IRIS ○

Family: IRIDACEAE
Origin: Central Turkey, Caucasus, Iran, Iraq.
Flowering time: Spring.
Climatic zone: 6, 7, 8, 9.
Dimensions: Up to 18 inches (450 mm) high.
Description: Spanish iris is a violet-scented beauty with grassy leaves and deep-blue or purple flowers. In some areas it is best grown in a cool greenhouse. It is suitable for rock gardens, the front of borders and will grow well in pots. Iris likes sandy light soil in a sunny position protected from wind. The best results are achieved if bulbs are lifted after flowering. They should be stored in dry sand. It is important to keep the bulbs as dry as possible during their dormant period.
Other colors: Yellow.
Varieties/cultivars: There are many cultivars available.

Iris xiphioides
ENGLISH IRIS ○

Family: IRIDACEAE
Origin: Spain, the Pyrenees.
Flowering time: Spring–summer.

Iris xiphioides

Climatic zone: 6, 7, 8, 9.
Dimensions: Up to 18 inches (450 mm) high.
Description: Early botanists thought that this plant was an English native. Although it flourished for centuries near Bristol, it had been brought from Spain by merchant seamen. It blooms in various shades of blue, except for one white form. This blue and gold beauty makes a colorful addition to the rose garden and flowers for up to eight weeks. Iris, which was named after the goddess of the rainbow, is an excellent cut flower. It requires cool, moist soil in a sunny area protected from strong wind.

Iris xiphium
SPANISH IRIS ○

Family: IRIDACEAE
Origin: Spain, Portugal, southern France.
Flowering time: Early summer.
Climatic zone: 6, 7, 8, 9.
Dimensions: Up to 2 feet (600 mm) high.
Description: *I. xiphium* is a parent of the dutch iris. The flowers have petals the standards and falls of which are often of different colors. Use it in borders or in a sunny corner against a fence or trellis. Their eye-catching beauty makes them ideal for indoor floral arrangements and ornamental pot plants. Plant in fertile soil using plenty of organic matter and protect from winds.
Other colors: White, yellow, orange, bronze.
Varieties/cultivars: Several cultivars are available.

Iris xiphium 'Franz Hals'

Muscari armeniacum

Muscari armeniacum
GRAPE HYACINTH ◑

Family: LILIACEAE
Origin: Asia Minor.
Flowering time: Spring.
Climatic zone: 4, 5, 6, 7, 8, 9.
Dimensions: Up to 8 inches (200 mm) high.
Description: The dense heads of rich blue fragrant flowers suit borders and edges. Several varieties of these grape-shaped flowers are available. They make good companions for yellow violas and white primula. They will readily naturalize when planted in grass or lightly wooded areas, and are good plants for potting indoors. Cultivate in well-rotted compost and water regularly.
Other colors: Mauve, white.
Varieties/cultivars: 'Blue spike', 'Cantab'.

Puschkinia scilloides
STRIPED SQUILL ○ ◑

Family: LILIACEAE
Origin: Eastern Turkey, Caucasus, Lebanon.
Flowering time: Spring.
Climatic zone: 4, 5, 6, 7, 8, 9.
Dimensions: Up to 6 inches (150 mm) high.

Puschkinia scilloides

Description: These dainty powder-blue flowers with deep-blue stripes blend well with violas and rock garden plants. They need to be placed where they complement other plants, as they are not very showy on their own. Easy to grow in sandy soil enriched with humus, they will take full sun or partial shade. The bulbs need not be disturbed for several years. If flowering diminishes, they will need to be relocated in new soil.

Scilla bifolia
BLUEBELL, TWIN-LEAF SQUILL

Family: LILIACEAE
Origin: Southern Europe–Turkey.
Flowering time: Spring.
Climatic zone: 5, 6, 7, 8, 9.
Dimensions: Up to 6 inches (150 mm) high.
Description: These hardy bulbs are adaptable to most cool soils and positions. *Scillas* are good carpet plants in beds of early-flowering tulips. They are easy to grow, will rapidly increase, and are suitable for borders, edges, pots, and in clumps under deciduous trees.

Scilla bifolia

Plant in rich, sandy soil in sun or partial shade. They will benefit from an occasional top dressing of good soil or old manure. Divide small bulblets from older bulbs in autumn to accelerate their spread.

Scilla peruviana
CUBAN LILY, PERUVIAN SCILLA, PERUVIAN LILY (U.K.)

Family: LILIACEAE
Origin: Southern Europe.
Flowering time: Early summer.
Climatic zone: 8, 9.

Scilla peruviana

Dimensions: Up to 18 inches (450 mm) high.
Description: Cuban lily is a showy bulb featuring clusters of fifty or more flowers. It can be massed in beds, planted as a backdrop to annuals, or used as a border along fences, and as an edge between garden beds. This species is easy to grow in rich, sandy soil in sun or partial shade. Divide the bulbs for extra plantings in autumn. At this time, they will also benefit from an occasional top dressing of old manure or good soil.

Scilla sibirica
SIBERIAN SCILLA, SPRING SQUILL (U.K.)

Family: LILIACEAE
Origin: Turkey, Iran, Caucasus.
Flowering time: Spring.
Climatic zone: 3, 4, 5, 6, 7, 8.
Dimensions: Up to 6 inches (150 mm) high.
Description: As its origins suggest, this dainty species is hardy. The deep-blue, drooping flowers produce three to five blooms to a stem. *Scilla* is ideal for rock gardens or planted under azaleas and camellias. Intersperse it with other bulbs where it can form a carpet. If rich, sandy soil is provided, it will rapidly increase. Top dress with good soil, compost, or old manure. Divide the plant when dormant to cover a large area quickly.
Varieties/cultivars: 'Spring Beauty', 'Atrocaerulea'.

Scilla sibirica

Akebia quinata

Clematis x *jackmanii*
CLEMATIS, LARGE-FLOWERED CLEMATIS ○

Family: RANUNCULACEAE
Origin: Hybrid.
Flowering time: Summer.
Climatic zone: 5, 6, 7, 8, 9.
Description: One of the early hybrids of this magnificent genus, this clematis has a profusion of 4–5 inch (100–125 mm), rich purple flowers. Later hybrids have larger, but not as many, flowers. Rich soil, full sun, and cool roots are the requirements for these vines. This one flowers on new season's growth, so severe pruning is necessary in the winter, or when leaves drop. Lime

Clematis x *jackmanii*

Akebia quinata
AKEBIA, FIVE-LEAFED AKEBIA ○ ◑

Family: LARDIZABALACEAE
Origin: China, Korea, Japan.
Flowering time: Spring.
Climatic zone: 4, 5, 6, 7, 8, 9.
Description: Akebia's unusual purplish-brown flowers are often the subject of much comment. They appear in spring on short stems, are often freely produced, and are quite fragrant. This is a fast-growing vine, but not invasive. The attractive leaves, in clusters of five, make a handsome cover for fences or pergolas, and it will tolerate a shady position. It is evergreen in warm zones. If it becomes too thick or unmanageable, cut it back to a few small, branching canes, and it will soon become green and dense again.

Clematis 'Barbara Jackman'
BARBARA JACKMAN CLEMATIS, LARGE-FLOWERED CLEMATIS ○

Family: RANUNCULACEAE
Origin: Cultivar.
Flowering time: Early summer.
Climatic zone: 5, 6, 7, 8, 9.
Description: A popular cultivar, this clematis has purple flowers, not as dark as those of *C.* x *jackmanii*, and about

4–5 inches (100–125 mm) across. Clematis needs plenty of compost and protection from heat around the roots. It can be grown beside a sheltering shrub, and if grown in pots or large containers, needs a climbing support and a deep mulch as well as shade for the containers to prevent the whole root system from becoming overheated.

Clematis 'Barbara Jackman'

may be needed in the soil, as it is not tolerant of very acid soil.
Varieties/cultivars: Many, including 'Rubra', 'Henry', 'Mrs Cholmondeley', 'The President'.

Clytostoma callistegioides
VIOLET TRUMPET VINE, ARGENTINE TRUMPET VINE ○ ◑

Family: BIGNONIACEAE
Origin: Brazil, Argentina.
Flowering time: Late spring–summer.
Climatic zone: 9, 10.
Description: Lavender streaked with violet is the color of the large funnel-shaped flowers, which appear in pairs at the ends of long, drooping stems. Although evergreen, this strong-growing climber may be semideciduous in cooler zones. Tendrils help it to climb a fence or a wall, but some support is required. A sunny position with rich soil and regular watering suits this very attractive and colorful vine, but it will also tolerate a semishaded site, as long as it is a warm one. A greenhouse is necessary for cold climates.

Clytostoma callistegioides

Cobaea scandens
CUP-AND-SAUCER VINE, CUP-AND-SAUCER CREEPER (U.K.), CATHEDRAL BELLS ◑

Family: POLEMONIACEAE
Origin: Mexico–northern Chile.
Flowering time: Spring, summer, autumn.
Climatic zone: 5, 6, 7, 8, 9, 10.
Description: *Cobaea* is a fast-growing, vigorous climber with most unusual

Cobaea scandens

flowers. They are large and bell-shaped, up to 2 inches (50 mm) long, opening yellow-green and changing to purple. They have a slight resemblance to a cup sitting on a saucer. A branched tendril at the end of the group of leaflets is the means of support to hold this vine against a wall. Grow it in a warm, semishady position and protect it from wind. It needs good soil, deep mulch, and regular watering. It can be grown as an annual.

Distictis laxiflora
VANILLA TRUMPET VINE ○

Family: BIGNONIACEAE
Origin: Mexico.
Flowering time: Most of the year.
Climatic zone: 9, 10.
Description: Less rampant than many of the trumpet vines, *Distictis laxiflora* has two or three leaflets, the leaves giving this evergreen climber an attractive appearance for the short time that the flowers are not present. The

Distictis laxiflora

flowers are vanilla-scented and about 3½ inches (80 mm) long. They open as a violet color and fade to lavender and white. This is a hot climate plant and needs a greenhouse in colder areas.

Hardenbergia comptoniana
LILAC VINE (U.S.A.), ○ ◑ WILD SARSAPARILLA, NATIVE WISTERIA (Aust.)

Family: LEGUMINOSAE
Origin: Western Australia.
Flowering time: Late winter–spring.
Climatic zone: 9.
Description: Violet-blue pea-flowers are massed in graceful sprays on this evergreen climber. Grow it over a low mesh fence, or trail it over the wall of a raised garden bed. It is an easily controlled vine, growing to about 10 feet (3 meters), or a groundcover, when it grows quite flat and spreading. Choose a sunny, well-drained position with minimum water. A wire frame in a container makes a good base for a pillar shape, but it can be trained into any shape. A warm climate plant, it needs to be grown under glass in other areas.

Hardenbergia comptoniana

Hardenbergia violacea

Hardenbergia violacea
PURPLE CORAL PEA, ○
NATIVE SARSAPARILLA (Aust.),
WILD SARSAPARILLA

Family: LEGUMINOSAE
Origin: Eastern and southern Australia.
Flowering time: Spring.
Climatic zone: 9.
Description: Masses of small purple-blue flowers on slender, wiry stems make a glorious display in spring. This twining vine has long, oval, and pointed leaves, and will endure harsh, dry conditions. Plant it in full sun in well-drained soil. It will be happy to creep over banks and trees, or it can be trained as a vine. The denser and coarser texture of this species makes it more tolerant of wind and very sunny positions than the lilac vine, and it is faster growing.
Other colors: White, pink.

Ipomoea purpurea
MORNING GLORY ○ ◑

Family: CONVOLVULACEAE
Origin: Tropical America.
Flowering time: Summer.
Climatic zone: 4, 5, 6, 7, 8, 9, 10.
Description: A vigorous, twining climber, morning glory has broadly ovate leaves and large open purple flowers that bloom in profusion during summer. Easy to cultivate in a wide range of soils and conditions, it can become a pest in warmer climates as it tends to take a stranglehold on the garden. In cooler climates treat as an annual planting in spring after the

Ipomoea purpurea

chance of frost has passed. Young shoots can be trained to cover a trellis or column.
Other colors: Pink, blue.

Ipomoea tricolor
MORNING GLORY ○

Family: CONVOLVULACEAE
Origin: Tropical America.
Flowering time: Summer–autumn.
Climatic zone: 4, 5, 6, 7, 8, 9, 10.
Description: This is the popular morning glory cultivated as an annual in gardens all over the world. In warm zones it is a perennial climber. The flower buds are red and open to large, purplish-blue blooms 4 inches (100 mm) across. It is an excellent plant for climbing fences, or growing over arches,

or in pots on a terrace or patio. Kept restricted in root space, there is a tendency for earlier flowering. The flowers last only one day, fading to a lighter color in the afternoon.
Other colors: Scarlet, white.
Varieties/cultivars: 'Heavenly Blue', 'Alba', 'Rose Marie', 'Scarlet O'Hara'.

Kennedia nigricans
BLACK CORAL PEA ○ ◑

Family: LEGUMINOSAE
Origin: Western Australia.
Flowering time: Summer.
Climatic zone: 9, 10.
Description: A vigorous evergreen twiner, *Kennedia nigricans* has black-purple flowers with a yellow blotch on the top petal. They are most unusual and distinctive, and are followed by flat, hairy pods. The vine is tolerant of a shady position, but prefers a warm site with very good drainage. Being quite

Kennedia nigricans

Ipomoea tricolor

drought-tolerant when established, it is worth growing in an awkward spot to give a good fence cover or groundcover. A hot climate plant, it needs greenhouse protection in colder areas.

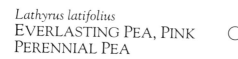
Lathyrus latifolius

Lonicera japonica var. *repens*

Passiflora caerulea

Petrea volubilis

Lathyrus latifolius
EVERLASTING PEA, PINK PERENNIAL PEA ○

Family: LEGUMINOSAE
Origin: Southern Europe.
Flowering time: Summer.
Climatic zone: 5, 6, 7, 8, 9.
Description: Many new shoots come from the base of this perennial climber each year. It is happy in most conditions, including windy sites near the sea, and will grow up to 10 feet (3 meters) high. The large attractive sprays of flowers are held on long, upright stems. The vine looks beautiful trained over a summerhouse, porch, or trellis, but needs a sunny position. Although quick-growing, it is not featured as often as it deserves. Mulch well and prune off all old growth at the end of summer.

Lonicera japonica var. *repens* syn. *L. j.* var. *flexuosa, L. j.* 'Purpurea'
JAPANESE HONEYSUCKLE ○ ◑

Family: CAPRIFOLIACEAE
Origin: Japan, China, Korea.
Flowering time: Summer.
Climatic zone: 6, 7, 8, 9.
Description: The white flowers of this well-known climber are tinged with purple on the outside. An evergreen or semideciduous, this Japanese honeysuckle has highly fragrant flowers which appear in summer, growing in pairs. A vigorous vine, it can quickly cover a fence, and should be planted in a warm, sheltered position. It will tolerate quite cool conditions if grown under trees or given some protection from frost. It does not seem to be fussy about soil, and will thrive almost anywhere.

Passiflora caerulea
BLUE-CROWN PASSION FLOWER, BLUE PASSION FLOWER, COMMON PASSION FLOWER (U.K.) ○ ◑

Family: PASSIFLORACEAE
Origin: Western and central South America.
Flowering time: Summer.
Climatic zone: 8, 9.
Description: This is the best *Passiflora* for growing in frosty districts, although it is happy in warm areas. A slender, but strong-growing vine, which will quickly climb up a tree or over a fence, it needs either plenty of space, or regular pruning. The flowers are white with a central fringe of blue, white, and purple, and are followed by orange-colored fruit which is not edible. This species was often used as root stock on which the edible types of passionfruit were grafted.

Petrea volubilis
QUEEN'S WREATH, PURPLE WREATH ○

Family: VERBENACEAE
Origin: Mexico–Panama, West Indies.
Flowering time: Winter–spring.
Climatic zone: 9, 10.
Description: Rough, brittle leaves on this wiry-stemmed twiner contrast with the beauty of the rich-colored, five-lobed petals. The lilac calyx remains on the plant for a long time and finally falls, spinning like a tiny top. A hot climate is necessary for this evergreen vine. Rich soil and ample water will give best foliage. It is a delightful climber which is easy to control and will never be invasive. It can combine with another light climber with white flowers, to give a two-colored effect.

Phaseolus caracalla

Phaseolus caracalla syn. *Vigna caracalla*
SNAIL FLOWER, CORKSCREW FLOWER

Family: LEGUMINOSAE
Origin: Tropical South America.
Flowering time: Spring or summer.
Climatic zone: 5, 6, 7, 8, 9, 10.
Description: This relative of the scarlet runner bean is an equally vigorous grower and has masses of curious flowers with a delightful fragrance. The flowers are coiled like snails and fleshy, with creamy, purple colors. Quick-growing, this deciduous twiner can be pruned back to ground level in late autumn and will soon cover a fence in the following spring. It does best in rich soil and prefers a sheltered position. The dense, lush foliage needs a wire support to help it attain an upright growth. In cooler climates, it is best grown as an annual.

Sollya heterophylla
AUSTRALIAN BLUEBELL CREEPER

Family: PITTOSPORACEAE
Origin: Western Australia.
Flowering time: Summer–autumn.
Climatic zone: 9.
Description: This vine's slender twining stems will gradually cover a fence without ever becoming a problem. Clusters of tiny, bell-shaped, bright-blue flowers hang in delicate little sprays in spring and summer, and are followed by purple berries. Tolerant of semishade, it is a good groundcover, or will twine around a post or pergola. Best foliage is obtained when it is given sheltered conditions, with ample water and good drainage. The narrow, glossy green leaves are attractive, and make this evergreen vine a good choice for container-growing. In cold climates, it will grow well in a greenhouse.
Other colors: Pink, white.

Sollya heterophylla

Thunbergia grandiflora
SKY FLOWER, CLOCK VINE, BLUE TRUMPET VINE

Family: ACANTHACEAE
Origin: Northern India–southern China.
Flowering time: Summer, autumn.

Thunbergia grandiflora

Climatic zone: 9, 10.
Description: Rough, toothed leaves cover this woody twiner with vigorous growth. The bell-shaped flowers, 2 inches or more across (50–60 mm), are a clear periwinkle blue with a white throat. The flowers are single, appear in the leaf axils, and are slightly pendant. This is a showy, robust climber which needs good soil and adequate summer water to look its best. It is not tolerant of frost, although if grown in a sheltered position it will survive quite cool conditions. A greenhouse is ideal for cooler zones.

Wisteria floribunda

Wisteria floribunda syn. *W. multijuga*
JAPANESE WISTERIA

Family: LEGUMINOSAE
Origin: Japan.
Flowering time: Early summer.
Climatic zone: 4, 5, 6, 7, 8, 9.
Description: The fragrant pea-shaped flowers on this lovely vine appear at the same time as the new leaves. The flower sprays are in shades of violet-blue, and hang in clusters 18 inches (450 mm) long. The display lasts longer than in other species as the flowers at the base of the spray open first, followed gradually by those nearer the tip. The attractive, glossy leaves are made up of between thirteen and nineteen leaflets. It is a vigorous climber and needs a strong support for the dense canopy produced in the summer time.
Varieties/cultivars: 'Rosea', 'Violacea Plena', 'Macrobotrys', 'Alba'.

Wisteria floribunda 'Macrobotrys'

Wisteria floribunda 'Macrobotrys' syn. *W. multijuga*
JAPANESE WISTERIA, LONG JAPANESE WISTERIA ○

Family: LEGUMINOSAE
Origin: Cultivar.
Flowering time: Spring–early summer.
Climatic zone: 5, 6, 7, 8, 9.
Description: Honey-scented violet-purple flowers hang in enormous sprays, up to 3 feet (900 mm) long, on this tall-climbing woody vine. Each flower is about 1 inch (25 mm) long. They appear either before or with the glossy green leaves which have thirteen to nineteen leaflets. The flowering season is very short, and flowers are followed by long, soft-green, velvety pods. For an eye-catching display, grow this wisteria over a tall pergola, or arbor, which the blossoms can cascade down. Water well during flowering to hold the blossoms.

Wisteria floribunda 'Violacea Plena'
DOUBLE JAPANESE WISTERIA ○

Family: LEGUMINOSAE
Origin: Cultivar.
Flowering time: Spring.
Climatic zone: 5, 6, 7, 8, 9.
Description: Both the flowering and the growth habit distinguish this cultivar from its parent plant. The small, tight, flower clusters hang in sprays 6–8 inches (150–200 mm) long,

but they are double flowers and held in a fairly tightly packed group. The dense, bushy growth is more shrub-like, and can be trained into a shrub or small tree if pruned during summer. It will need support on which to climb when used as a vine. Loamy acid soil is best, with plenty of water at flowering time.

Wisteria floribunda 'Violacea Plena'

Wisteria sinensis
CHINESE WISTERIA ○ ◑

Family: LEGUMINOSAE
Origin: China.
Flowering time: Spring–early summer.
Climatic zone: 5, 6, 7, 8, 9.
Description: This wisteria is an early spring favorite. The slightly fragrant, lilac flowers are in drooping clusters from 8–12 inches (200–300 mm) in length, and tend to open nearly the full length of the cluster at one time. A very vigorous deciduous vine, it will develop a trunk like a tree, but with constant pruning in summer it can be trained as a weeping standard tree, or it can become a gnarled-trunked shrub. Velvety, bean-like pods are attractive decoration among the leaves when the flowers are finished.
Other colors: White.
Varieties/cultivars: *Wisteria sinensis* 'Alba'.

Wisteria sinensis

Aconitum carmichaelii

Aconitum carmichaelii syn. *A. fischeri*
AZURE MONKSHOOD ◑

Family: RANUNCULACEAE
Origin: Eastern Asia.
Flowering time: Late summer–autumn.
Climatic zone: 3, 4, 5, 6, 7, 8, 9.
Dimensions: Up to 4 feet (approx.
1 meter) high.
Description: Azure monkshood is one
of the most popular of the garden
monkshoods. The dramatic blue hoods
of the flowers extend into a spur-like
visor and are borne on long stems.
These may need staking. A showy
border plant, it needs a position in
partial shade and does not like to be
disturbed. Plant it in rich, moist, well-
drained soil. As the juice is highly
poisonous, it is not wise to plant
monkshood in a garden used by small
children.

Aconitum napellus
COMMON MONKSHOOD ◑

Family: RANUNCULACEAE
Origin: Europe, Asia.
Flowering time: Summer.
Climatic zone: 3, 4, 5, 6, 7, 8, 9.
Dimensions: Up to 5 feet (approx.
2 meters) high.
Description: Common monkshood has
brilliant green foliage and tall spikes of
helmet-like flowers in a rich violet-blue.
It is a useful cottage garden plant, and
suitable as a background border. It
grows best in cool-climate gardens, in
deep, rich, moist soil that has adequate
drainage. The foliage dies back in
winter. Despite the fact that all parts of
the plant are poisonous, common

monkshood was regarded as a valuable
ingredient in medieval potions.
Other colors: White, pink.
Varieties/cultivars: 'Album',
'Carneum'.

Aconitum napellus

Aconitum x *bicolor*
HYBRID ○ ◑
MONKSHOOD, WOLFBANE

Family: RANUNCULACEAE
Origin: Hybrid.
Flowering time: Summer.
Climatic zone: 3, 4, 5, 6, 7, 8, 9.
Dimensions: 3–4 feet (approx. 1 meter)
high.
Description: This dramatic old-
fashioned favorite gives a wonderful
display of violet-blue and white, helmet-
shaped flowers that are borne in a

Aconitum x *bicolor*

terminal raceme. The foliage is mid-
green in color. Ideal for an herbaceous
border, monkshood should be grown in
semishade in rich, moist soil with good
drainage. The plant may require staking
when it reaches its full height.
Other colors: Deeper violet blue, blue
and white.

Adenophora confusa
LADYBELLS ○ ◑

Family: CAMPANULACEAE
Origin: Eastern Asia.
Flowering time: Mid–late summer.
Climatic zone: 4, 5, 6, 7, 8, 9.
Dimensions: Up to 3 feet (1 meter) high.
Description: Ladybells is a charming
plant with tall, slender stems and large,
dark-purple, bell-shaped flowers,
measuring up to ¾ inch (18 mm) in
length. Plant it in either full sun or
semishade in well-drained, moderately
rich soil. It can even be grown in rather
poor soils providing there is adequate
moisture and good drainage. It makes a
very pretty addition to a mixed bed of
summer-flowering annuals and
perennials.

Adenophora confusa

Agapanthus praecox syn. *A. umbellatus*
AGAPANTHUS, ○ ◑
AFRICAN LILY, BLUE AFRICAN
LILY

Family: AMARYLLIDACEAE
Origin: South Africa.
Flowering time: Summer.

Amsonia tabernaemontana

Agapanthus praecox

Climatic zone: 8, 9.
Dimensions: 2–3 feet (600–900 mm) high.
Description: Agapanthus is a useful and hardy specimen, which looks most attractive as a border or background plant. It forms a large clump of strap-like leaves and produces tall stems in summer, topped by large, globular flower heads in various shades of blue to purple. Full sun or semishade suits it best, and it will grow in most soil conditions providing reasonable drainage is provided. The clumps can be divided during winter to produce new plants.
Other colors: White.
Varieties/cultivars: Many varieties and cultivars are available.

plant, it is attractive in rock gardens, under large trees, or between pavers. Plant it in a sunny or semishaded position and water regularly. It will tolerate poor and heavy soils. Cut back the dead flower heads. Propagate it by its free-rooting stems or by seed in spring. An infusion of the plant was used for centuries to cure coughs, bruises and hemorrhages.
Other colors: White, pink.
Varieties/cultivars: 'Burgundy Glow', 'Alba', 'Atropurpurea', 'Delight', 'Multicolor', 'Pink Elf', 'Variegata'.

Amsonia tabernaemontana
BLUE STAR, WILLOW AMSONIA

Family: APOCYNACEAE
Origin: Central and eastern United States.
Flowering time: Summer.
Climatic zone: 4, 5, 6, 7, 8, 9.
Dimensions: Up to 2 feet (600 mm) high.
Description: The very pale, small, star-like flowers of this perennial form in clusters at the top of the tall, leaved stems. It is suited to partially shaded or sunny herbaceous borders and in the right position will become quite bushy. If growth is sparse and open, cut back the plant to half its size to encourage denser growth. It looks attractive planted with campanulas; *C. lactiflora* 'Alba' complements it well. Blue star is easy to grow in any moist, ordinary garden soil and can be propagated by division in spring or autumn. It is often sold as *A. salicifolia*.

Ajuga reptans
COMMON BLUE BUGLEWEED, BUGLE, COMMON BUGLE

Family: LABIATAE
Origin: Europe–Southwestern Asia.
Flowering time: Spring–summer.
Climatic zone: 4, 5, 6, 7, 8, 9.
Dimensions: 8–12 inches (200–300 mm) high.
Description: This is a spreading perennial groundcover with oval, dark-green leaves and spikes of blue flowers. Cultivars have variegated cream, pink, and burgundy foliage. A quick-growing

Ajuga reptans

Anchusa azurea

Anchusa azurea syn. *A. italica*
ITALIAN BUGLOSS ○

Family: BORAGINACEAE
Origin: Caucasus–central Europe.
Flowering time: Late spring–early summer.
Climatic zone: 4, 5, 6, 7.
Dimensions: 3–5 feet (approx. 1–2 meters) high.
Description: This delightful wild plant is a relative of the herb borage, and has lance-shaped, gray-green foliage and small, round, bright blue flowers. It likes an open, sunny position and can be grown in a wide range of soils, as long as drainage is good and water is provided during hot summer weather.
Varieties/cultivars: 'Loddon Royalist', 'Morning Glory'.

Aquilegia caerulea
ROCKY MOUNTAIN ○ ◑
COLUMBINE

Family: RANUNCULACEAE
Origin: Rocky Mountains, North America.
Flowering time: Late spring–early summer.
Climatic zone: 4, 5, 6, 7, 8, 9.
Dimensions: Up to 2 feet (600 mm) high.
Description: *A. caerulea*, with its soft lavender-blue and creamy white blooms, is the state flower of Colorado. Plant it in sun or partial shade and leave undisturbed so that the seeds drop and colonies form. Moist soils that neither dry out in summer nor become waterlogged in winter suit it best.

Arisaema triphyllum

Arisaema triphyllum
JACK-IN-THE-PULPIT, ◑ ●
INDIAN TURNIP

Family: ARACEAE
Origin: North America.
Flowering time: Spring–summer.
Climatic zone: 4, 5, 6, 7, 8, 9.
Dimensions: Up to 2½ feet (750 mm) high.
Description: A cool fernery or rock garden is the ideal position for *Arisaema*, with its purplish-green hooded spathe. Plant it in rich, moist humus soil in a sheltered, partially shaded site, and give it plenty of water in summer. Propagate by offsets or by seed. The North American Indians used the turnip-shaped, acrid root to cure headaches, and also as a contraceptive.
Varieties/cultivars: *A. t. stewardsonii*, *A. t. zebrinum*.

Aster thomsonii
ASTER, THOMSON'S ○
ASTER (U.K.)

Family: COMPOSITAE
Origin: Western Himalayas.
Flowering time: Summer–autumn.
Climatic zone: 7, 8, 9.
Dimensions: Up to 2 feet (600 mm) high.
Description: This is one of the lavender-blue group of asters which has produced many hybrids. The daisy-like flowers are profuse and the almost heart-shaped leaves are serrated. Plant it in sunny, open borders where the soil will not dry out during the growing season. Protect it from wind and stake it if necessary. This is a good plant for cut

Aquilegia caerulea

Aster thomsonii 'Nana'

floral arrangements. The dwarf form, 'Nana', grows to a height of about 15 inches (375 mm).
Varieties/cultivars: 'Nana'.

Aster x *frikartii*
ASTER ○

Family: COMPOSITAE
Origin: Hybrid.
Flowering time: Summer–autumn.
Climatic zone: 5, 6, 7, 8, 9.
Dimensions: Up to 3 feet (1 meter) high.
Description: These vibrant lavender-blue daisies with yellow centers provide a constant source of flowers for floral

arrangements. A fragrant perennial plant that is well suited to cottage gardens, it will grow quite quickly into an attractive clump. Plant it in full sun along pathways and low fences or beside a front gate. It likes fertile, well-drained soil, and may be prone to mildew in humid areas.

Astilbe chinensis 'Pumila'
ASTILBE, DWARF FALSE GOATSBEARD ◑

Family: SAXIFRAGACEAE
Origin: Cultivar.
Flowering time: Summer.
Climatic zone: 4, 5, 6, 7, 8, 9.

Astilbe chinensis 'Pumila'

Aster x *frikartii*

Dimensions: Up to 12 inches (300 mm) high.
Description: This handsome perennial is a good choice for the front of borders. The densely clustered, mauve-pink flowers and attractive foliage contrast well with white daisies or silver-gray artemisia. 'Pumila' tolerates drier soils than other astilbes and, being a gross feeder, needs an extra application of fertilizer during summer. Easy to grow in any ordinary, moist garden soil, it reproduces quickly and should either be given plenty of space to spread or be divided every three years.

Astilbe taquetii 'Superba'

Astilbe taquetii 'Superba'
ASTILBE, FALSE GOATSBEARD ◑

Family: SAXIFRAGACEAE
Origin: Cultivar.
Flowering time: Late summer.
Climatic zone: 5, 6, 7, 8, 9.
Dimensions: Up to 4 feet (approx. 1 meter) high.
Description: Long, feathery spikes of magenta or reddish-purple flowers accompany bronze-green foliage. A single plume may have hundreds of florets and the overall effect is spectacular. 'Superba' suits borders and rock gardens and particularly the surrounds of rock pools. A deep, rich, moisture-retaining soil with a liberal application of humus is the ideal environment for it. This cultivar is more drought-tolerant than some strains.

Baptisia australis

Baptisia australis syn. *B. exaltata*
WILD INDIGO, FALSE
INDIGO

Family: LEGUMINOSAE
Origin: Eastern United States.
Flowering time: Spring–summer,
northern hemisphere; summer, southern
hemisphere.
Climatic zone: 4, 5, 6, 7, 8, 9.
Dimensions: Up to 5 feet (over 1 meter)
high.
Description: Wild indigo has numerous
deep purplish-blue, pea-like flowers
borne in terminal racemes These are
followed by attractive seed pods.
Resembling lupins, they are attractive in
indoor floral arrangements. The plant
likes an open, sunny position in sandy
loam which has had compost added,
and is useful for the drier parts of
borders or in wild gardens. Cut it back
after flowering. This plant was used in
ancient times to cure infections.

Brunnera macrophylla syn. *Anchusa
myosotidiflora*
SIBERIAN BUGLOSS
(U.S.A.), FORGET-ME-NOT (U.K.),
ANCHUSA (U.K.)

Family: BORAGINACEAE
Origin: Western Caucasus.
Flowering time: Spring.
Climatic zone: 4, 5, 6, 7, 8, 9.
Dimensions: Up to 18 inches (450 mm)
high.

Description: The branching, starry,
blue flowers of Siberian bugloss
resemble forget-me-nots. A member of
the borage family, this woodland species
has rough, heart-shaped leaves and
hairy stems. Grow it in open woodland
areas, under trees and shrubs, or in
borders. Tolerant of soil types, it can
survive in dry, shady positions, but
prefers partial shade in moist soil.
Varieties/cultivars: 'Variegata'.

Brunnera macrophylla

Campanula carpatica
CARPATHIAN
HAREBELL

Family: CAMPANULACEAE
Origin: Carpathian mountains.
Flowering time: Spring–summer.
Climatic zone: 4, 5, 6, 7, 8, 9.

Dimensions: Up to 12 inches (300 mm)
high.
Description: Carpathian harebell
grows in clumps. The large (2 inches
(50 mm) wide), deep-blue flowers are
bell-shaped and the leaves are oval. A
quick-growing plant, it is useful for
groundcover in rock gardens or on
sloping sites. Plant it in fertile, moist soil
protected from summer sun and water it
liberally. Propagate it by division or
from cuttings.
Other colors: Many shades from white
to sky-blue.
Varieties/cultivars: 'Loddon Fairy',
'Riverslea', 'White Star'.

Campanula cochleariifolia syn.
C. pusilla
BELLFLOWER

Family: CAMPANULACEAE
Origin: European mountains.
Flowering time: Summer.

Campanula cochleariifolia

Campanula carpatica

Climatic zone: 6, 7, 8, 9.
Dimensions: Up to 6 inches (150 mm) high.
Description: This is another easy-to-grow campanula which is useful for edging beds or planting in rock garden pockets. The solitary, drooping bells appear in great profusion during summer. In larger areas such as sloping sites, plant several different varieties and colors of campanula together to form an effective display. It likes moist, fertile soil protected from summer sun. It is propagated by division or seed.
Other colors: White.
Varieties/cultivars: 'Alba', 'Oakington Blue', 'Miranda'.

Campanula garganica

Campanula garganica
BELLFLOWER ○ ◑

Family: CAMPANULACEAE
Origin: Italy, Greece.
Flowering time: Summer–autumn, northern hemisphere; spring–autumn, southern hemisphere.
Climatic zone: 5, 6, 7, 8, 9.
Dimensions: Up to 4 inches (100 mm) high.
Description: This sprawling, low-growing evergreen is often grown in rock gardens or as a groundcover. Wheel-shaped flowers are borne on long, slender stems, and the leaves are kidney-shaped and coarsely toothed. Flowering begins early in the season and may continue in a sporadic fashion until autumn. Plant it in partial shade in warmer climates, and in full sun in cooler zones. Ordinary garden soil is suitable, but this plant benefits from the addition of compost. Do not allow the soil to dry out.

Campanula glomerata

Campanula glomerata
CLUSTERED ○ ◑
BELLFLOWER, DANESBLOOD
BELLFLOWER

Family: CAMPANULACEAE
Origin: Europe–western Asia.
Flowering time: Summer.
Climatic zone: 3, 4, 5, 6, 7, 8, 9.
Dimensions: Up to 3 feet (1 meter) high.
Description: This is one of the taller types of *Campanula*. The individual funnel-shaped blooms are rich violet, large, and showy. They form in clusters at the top of stems that are about 1–2 feet (300–600 mm) high and are suitable for floral arrangements. *C. glomerata* is useful in shaded rockeries and is also popular in a border. It grows well in ordinary garden soil. A double-flowered form is available and a variety with deep-violet flowers growing in large clusters.
Other colors: White, violet.
Varieties/cultivars: Several varieties and cultivars are available including *C. g.* var. *dahurica*.

Campanula latifolia
GIANT BELLFLOWER ○ ◑

Family: CAMPANULACEAE
Origin: Europe–western Asia, Siberia.
Flowering time: Summer.
Climatic zone: 4, 5, 6, 7, 8.
Dimensions: Up to 4 feet (approx. 1 meter) high.
Description: Now growing widely across Europe to the mountains of Kashmir, giant bellflower, with its numerous, showy, violet-colored bell-shaped flowers, makes a fine border plant once established. Self-seeding, it will create a good summer display if

allowed to colonize. Although tall, giant bellflower seldom requires staking. It is at home in shady, moist areas but, depending on the climate, will grow in a sunny or semishaded position, in ordinary garden soil. The cultivar 'Macrantha' has purple flowers that are wider than those of giant bellflower.
Other colors: White.
Varieties/cultivars: 'Alba', 'Brantwood', 'Macrantha'.

Campanula latifolia

Campanula medium

Campanula medium
CANTERBURY-BELLS ○

Family: CAMPANULACEAE
Origin: Southern Europe.
Flowering time: Summer.
Climatic zone: 7, 8, 9.
Dimensions: Up to 3 feet (1 meter) high.
Description: These flowers are said to have been named in honor of St. Thomas à Becket because they resemble the horse bells used by pilgrims visiting his shrine at Canterbury Cathedral. A hardy, quick-growing biennial with blue bell-shaped flowers, they make an excellent border plant that will flower from six to nine weeks. Plant the seeds in soil mixed with fertilizer and compost. An application of lime will benefit growth. It likes a sunny position sheltered from wind.
Other colors: White, pink, mauve.
Varieties/cultivars: *C. m. calycanthema*.

Campanula persicifolia

Campanula persicifolia
PEACH-LEAVED ○ ◐
BELLFLOWER

Family: CAMPANULACEAE
Origin: Europe, Asia.
Flowering time: Summer.
Climatic zone: 4, 5, 6, 7, 8, 9.
Dimensions: Up to 3 feet (1 meter) high.
Description: Once used medicinally, this evergreen, perennial border plant produces excellent blue, bell-shaped flowers suitable for cutting. Remove spent blooms to encourage a second flowering. It likes moist, ordinary garden soil and a position in partial shade or full sun, depending upon the climate.
Other colors: White.
Varieties/cultivars: 'Alba'.

Campanula poscharskyana
SERBIAN ○ ◐
BELLFLOWER

Family: CAMPANULACEAE
Origin: Western Yugoslavia.
Flowering time: Summer–autumn.
Climatic zone: 4, 5, 6, 7, 8, 9.
Dimensions: Up to 6 inches (150 mm) high.
Description: Serbian bellflower produces masses of lilac flowers which create a dense carpet of color. Its sprawling habit makes it a good choice for a sloping site or a well-drained rock garden; it is also suited to wild gardens,

Campanula poscharskyana

where it can ramble unhindered. One of the easier campanulas to grow, it is drought-resistant. Plant it in ordinary garden soil in sun or partial shade.
Varieties/cultivars: 'E. K. Toogood'.

Campanula portenschlagiana syn.
C. muralis
DALMATIAN ○ ◐
BELLFLOWER

Family: CAMPANULACEAE
Origin: Yugoslavia.
Flowering time: Spring–summer.
Climatic zone: 5, 6, 7, 8, 9.
Dimensions: Up to 6 inches (150 mm) high.
Description: This little alpine is easier to grow than many other campanulas. The deep bluish-purple, bell-shaped flowers look attractive in rock garden pockets, in rock walls, or edging garden beds. Woodland drifts are also suitable sites for this plant. Its masses of dark-green, heart-shaped leaves make it a good groundcover, but the foliage may be susceptible to slugs. Plant in well-drained, gritty soil in sun or partial shade.
Other colors: White.

Campanula portenschlagiana

Campanula rotundifolia
HAREBELL OF ENGLAND, ○
BLUEBELL OF SCOTLAND

Family: CAMPANULACEAE
Origin: Northern temperate and arctic regions.
Flowering time: Summer.
Climatic zone: 3, 4, 5, 6, 7, 8, 9.
Dimensions: Up to 12 inches (300 mm) high.
Description: One of the more easily grown alpine campanulas, harebell is not unlike *C. cochleariifolia* in form. The nodding bells of bright blue flowers grow in a loose cluster on thread-like stems. It is best planted in open areas, and in wild gardens, or shrubberies, where it will quickly establish itself and self-seed. This little sun-lover is at home in the Scottish Highlands, where it grows wild.
Other colors: White.
Varieties/cultivars: 'Alba'.

Campanula rotundifolia

Catananche caerulea
CUPID'S-DART, BLUE ○
SUCCORY

Family: COMPOSITAE
Origin: Portugal–Italy.
Flowering time: Summer.
Climatic zone: 6, 7, 8, 9, 10.
Dimensions: Up to 2 feet (600 mm) high.
Description: A romantic flower, as its common name implies, cupid's dart was once used as an ingredient in love potions. A cornflower-like plant, the mauve heads are protected by silver, papery bracts. The leaves are hairy. Apart from its garden value, the flowers, which rustle when touched, are

Catananche caerulea

and needs only average, well-drained soil. It looks attractive at the front of a cottage garden border. Propagate it by root division in spring. It is a good cut flower for mixed spring arrangements.
Other colors: White, pink, red.
Varieties/cultivars: 'Alba', 'Rosea', 'Rubra'.

Cheiranthus mutabilis

excellent for dried floral arrangements. A drought-tolerant plant, it is easy to grow in a sunny position in ordinary garden soil, but good drainage is essential, and wet soil in winter may kill it.

Centaurea montana
MOUNTAIN BLUET, ○
PERENNIAL CORNFLOWER,
MOUNTAIN CORNFLOWER (U.K.)

Other common names: KNAPWEED (U.K.)
Family: COMPOSITAE
Origin: European mountains.
Flowering time: Mid-spring–early summer.
Climatic zone: 3, 4, 5, 6, 7, 8, 9.
Dimensions: 1½–2 feet (450–600 mm) high.
Description: Mountain bluet is one of the most popular of the perennial *Centaurea* species. Its flowers are thistle-like, with large, deeply fringed, marginal florets. It has a long blooming period,

Centaurea montana

Cheiranthus mutabilis
WALLFLOWER, ○
CHANGEABLE WALLFLOWER

Family: CRUCIFERAE
Origin: Canary Islands, Madeira.
Flowering time: Late spring–early summer.
Climatic zone: 8, 9.
Dimensions: Up to 12 inches (300 mm) high.
Description: A perennial cousin of the commonly grown wallflower, this species has attractive gray-green foliage and masses of slightly fragrant flowers which open yellow but age lilac-purple. It likes full sun, and soil that is either neutral or slightly alkaline, with excellent drainage. Take care not to overwater. Feed it well during summer to extend the flowering season.
Varieties/cultivars: *C. m.* var. *variegatus.*

Clematis heracleifolia

Clematis heracleifolia
TUBE CLEMATIS

Family: RANUNCULACEAE
Origin: China.
Flowering time: Summer.
Climatic zone: 4, 5, 6, 7, 8, 9.
Dimensions: Up to 4 feet (approx.
1 meter) high.
Description: This is a woody-based
clematis suited to the herbaceous
border. The blue, narrowly bell-shaped
flowers resemble the hyacinth and are
fragrant. It likes full sun to partial shade
and moist, fertile soil, which should not
be allowed to become either too wet or
too dry. If the soil is light and sandy,
apply peat moss, compost, or leaf mold
generously before planting. It is
advisable to mulch in spring.
Varieties/cultivars: 'Wyevale',
'Davidiana'.

Convolvulus sabatius syn.
C. mauritanicus
GROUND MORNING
GLORY (U.S.A.), BINDWEED

Family: CONVOLVULACEAE
Origin: North Africa.
Flowering time: Summer.
Climatic zone: 8, 9, 10.
Dimensions: Up to 12 inches (300 mm)
high.
Description: This perennial, evergreen,
trailing plant has widely funnel-shaped,
satiny, violet or blue flowers with white
throats. It is an attractive basket plant
for a greenhouse or a rambler in
sheltered rock gardens, and looks
particularly effective spilling over rock

walls. Plant it as rooted cuttings in
ordinary garden soil mixed with
compost and a complete fertilizer and
water it well.
Other colors: Pink.

Convolvulus sabatius

Cynoglossum nervosum

Cynoglossum nervosum
GREAT HOUND'S TONGUE
BLUE HOUND'S TONGUE

Family: BORAGINACEAE
Origin: Himalayas.
Flowering time: Summer.
Climatic zone: 5, 6, 7, 8, 9.
Dimensions: Up to 2 feet (600 mm) high.
Description: The small, intensely blue
flowers of this hound's tongue are borne
on tall, branching stems and resemble
forget-me-nots. The long, thin, hairy
leaves easily identify it as a member of
the borage family. Use it in borders or
rock gardens where the soil is not very
rich, as very fertile soil may cause the
stems to fall over. This is a plant which
will thrive in full sun and average, well-
drained soil. Propagate it by division or
seed in spring.

Delphinium elatum hybrids
DELPHINIUM, CANDLE
LARKSPUR

Family: RANUNCULACEAE
Origin: Hybrids.
Flowering time: Summer, northern
hemisphere; spring–summer, southern
hemisphere.
Climatic zone: 4, 5, 6, 7, 8, 9.
Dimensions: Up to 6 feet (2 meters) high.
Description: The name *Delphinium*
comes from the Greek word for
"dolphin" which the flower buds were
thought to resemble. The stately,
candle-like flowers on their tall stems
make these hybrids most striking in a
border. Grow them in moist soil in full
sun, and fertilize them regularly. Protect
them from the wind, staking if
necessary. They are susceptible to pests
and mildew and the juice of the plants
is poisonous.
Other colors: Red, pink, white, cream.
Varieties/cultivars: Many hybrid
cultivars are available.

Delphinium elatum

Dianella caerulea
FLAX LILY

Family: LILIACEAE
Origin: Eastern and southern Australia.
Flowering time: Early spring and
summer.
Climatic zone: 9, 10.
Dimensions: Up to 4 feet (approx.
1 meter) high.
Description: This is an attractive,

Dianella caerulea

Erinus alpinus

fibrous-rooted perennial which spreads by means of underground rhizomes. The foliage appears at various intervals and is tough and flax-like. The flowers are up to ½ inch (12 mm) wide, starry, six-petaled and blue or whitish with a central cone of yellow stamens, carried in large, airy panicles. They are followed by pretty, deep-blue berries. Flax lily can be grown in most soils and conditions, but must be watered well in summer. The rhizomes can be easily divided to create new plants.

Digitalis purpurea
COMMON FOXGLOVE ◑

Family: SCROPHULARIACEAE
Origin: Western Europe and U.K.
Flowering time: Spring–summer.
Climatic zone: 5, 6, 7, 8, 9.
Dimensions: Up to 4 feet (approx. 2 meters) high.
Description: Foxglove is a good choice for a high backdrop to a border. It likes shade and blends well with ferns and campanulas. Although loved by cottage gardeners, it is considered a noxious weed in some countries. This plant possesses an important medicinal compound, digitalin, which is extracted from the leaves and used for certain

heart conditions. In the past, herbalists prescribed foxglove for fevers and liver complaints. With its masses of bell-shaped flowers, this biennial will bloom for six to ten weeks. Plant it in a shady position in humus-rich soil.
Other colors: Yellow, white, pink, red, purple.
Varieties/cultivars: 'Alba', 'Excelsior', 'Shirley'.

Echinops ritro 'Veitch's Blue'

Echinops ritro
GLOBE THISTLE ○

Family: COMPOSITAE
Origin: Eastern Europe–western Asia.
Flowering time: Summer.
Climatic zone: 3, 4, 5, 6, 7, 8, 9, 10.
Dimensions: Up to 4 feet (approx. 1 meter) high.
Description: This is a handsome, old-world, thistle-like plant which is useful in hardy borders. The blue flowers and the white, woolly foliage can be cut and used in dried floral arrangements. A bold and showy plant, it associates well with phlox in the garden, but needs plenty of space and a moderately sunny position. It prefers ordinary garden soil and may need to be staked if the soil is too moist or fertile. Propagate by division or seed.
Varieties/cultivars: 'Taplow Blue', 'Veitch's Blue'.

rock garden pockets it will form a close-tufted, evergreen mound. Starry, rosy-purple flowers are borne in profusion on terminal sprays. Mix the seed with moist loam or peat and place it in cracks of walls or rocks to germinate. Well-drained soil in full sun or half-shade will ensure good results.
Other colors: White, pink.
Varieties/cultivars: *E. a.* var. *albus*, 'Dr. Hanaele', 'Mrs. Boyle'.

Eryngium x zabelii
ZABEL ERYNGO, SEA ○
HOLLY (U.K.)

Family: UMBELLIFERAE
Origin: Hybrids.
Flowering time: Summer.
Climatic zone: 6, 7, 8, 9.
Dimensions: Up to 2½ feet (750 mm) high.
Description: These hybrids are thistle-like plants with blue flowers. The flowers can be dried for use in floral arrangements. Plant them in well-drained, sandy soil that is moderately fertile, and provide plenty of space for growth. They are difficult to transplant. In ancient times they had many medicinal uses.

Digitalis purpurea

Erinus alpinus
SUMMER STARWORT, ○ ◑
FAIRY FOXGLOVE (U.K.)

Family: SCROPHULARIACEAE
Origin: European Alps, Pyrenees.
Flowering time: Spring–summer.
Climatic zone: 3, 4, 5, 6, 7, 8, 9.
Dimensions: Up to 6 inches (150 mm) high.
Description: Rock crevices or confined spaces in a wall are ideal environments for this little alpine. When planted in

Eryngium x *zabelii*

Gentiana acaulis syn. *G. excisa*
STEMLESS GENTIAN, ○ ◑
TRUMPET GENTIAN (U.K.)

Family: GENTIANIACEAE
Origin: European mountains.
Flowering time: Spring.
Climatic zone: 5, 6, 7, 8, 9.
Dimensions: Up to 4 inches (100 mm) high.
Description: This is one of the best known of the gentians that grow in the alpine meadows in Europe, and needs similar conditions if it is to thrive in the garden. If the environment is right and not too warm, stemless gentian produces a glorious carpet of vivid blue flowers that enhance garden edges and rock garden pockets, or it can be planted in drifts. It needs cool, moist, light, well-drained soil. If it produces leaves but no flowers, it needs to be moved to a warmer position.

Gentiana acaulis

Gentiana asclepiadea
WILLOW GENTIAN ◑ ●

Family: GENTIANIACEAE
Origin: European Alps, Apennines.
Flowering time: Late summer–autumn.
Climatic zone: 5, 6, 7, 8, 9.
Dimensions: Up to 2 feet (600 mm) high.
Description: One of the more reliable and easy-to-grow perennial gentians, it produces flowers of a deep purple-blue, which bloom year after year on long arching stems. Planted in shaded borders or in rock gardens, willow gentian will freely reproduce from seed. It is best grown in acid, humus-rich soil that is kept moist and cool, emulating the mountain conditions of its native

habitat. As a rule, gentians do not appreciate root disturbance so a thriving colony should be left alone.
Other colors: White.
Varieties/cultivars: *G. a.* var. *alba.*

Gentiana asclepiadea

Hesperis matronalis
DAME'S ROCKET, ○ ◑
DAME'S VIOLET

Family: CRUCIFERAE
Origin: Europe–central Asia.
Flowering time: Summer.
Climatic zone: 5, 6, 7, 8, 9.
Dimensions: Up to 3 feet (1 meter) high.
Description: Known to cooks as "garden rocket", the acrid leaves are eaten like cress in salads in some countries. The purple, mauve or lilac-

Hesperis matronalis

purple flowers resemble phlox, and have a lovely fragrance which is given out only at night. In modern gardens, it is a short-lived perennial and needs to be replaced with seedlings. It likes moist, well-drained soil and is longer lived in poorer soils.
Other colors: White.
Varieties/cultivars: 'Alba'.

Hosta fortunei
FORTUNE'S PLANTAIN ◑
LILY, PLANTAIN LILY

Family: LILIACEAE
Origin: Japan.
Flowering time: Summer.
Climatic zone: 3, 4, 5, 6, 7, 8, 9.
Dimensions: Up to 2 feet (600 mm) high.
Description: This spectacular plant has striking foliage and handsome spikes of mauve or violet flowers. This lily is ideal for special positions where fine foliage effects are desired — stone planter boxes, by a garden seat, in shady borders, or reflected in a water feature. The clumps will improve with age and should be left undisturbed. Plant it in rich humus soil that does not dry out. Avoid full sun as it may burn the leaves. Divide in spring to propagate it. Cultivars differ in the markings and color of foliage.
Other colors: White.
Varieties/cultivars: 'Aurea-marginata', 'Albopicta'.

Hosta fortunei

Hosta sieboldiana

Hosta sieboldiana
SIEBOLD PLANTAIN LILY, PLANTAIN LILY

Family: LILIACEAE
Origin: Japan.
Flowering time: Summer.
Climatic zone: 3, 4, 5, 6, 7, 8, 9.
Dimensions: Up to 18 inches (750 mm) high.
Description: The large, striking leaves which seem almost to be stitched or quilted are an outstanding feature of this lily. The lilac flowers with deeper stripes rise on a slender stem that is generally shorter than the foliage. Place this plant in a key position near a water feature, flanking shady steps, or beside a garden seat. In summer it prefers cool, moist soil, but wet soil in winter may damage the leaves. It is susceptible to slugs and snails.

Hosta ventricosa
BLUE PLANTAIN LILY, PLANTAIN LILY

Family: LILIACEAE
Origin: Eastern Asia.
Flowering time: Late summer.
Climatic zone: 3, 4, 5, 6, 7, 8, 9.
Dimensions: Up to 3 feet (1 meter) high.
Description: One of the plantain lily family, it is usually grown for its spectacular foliage. Common in old-fashioned gardens and easy to grow, *H. ventricosa* has long, heart-shaped leaves, and deep-violet, funnel-shaped flowers occurring in loose, terminal clusters. This is a drought- and frost-tender perennial suited to borders. It prefers shade, and soil that is moist in summer. Increase it by division in spring or autumn.

Hosta ventricosa

Iris germanica
TALL BEARDED IRIS

Family: IRIDACEAE
Origin: Southern Europe.
Flowering time: Summer, northern hemisphere; spring, southern hemisphere.
Climatic zone: 4, 5, 6, 7, 8, 9.
Dimensions: Up to 2½ feet (750 mm) high.
Description: This is one of the species from which most bearded irises have

Iris germanica 'Velvet Vista'

been bred. Tall, it is best suited to growing in separate beds or in groups among shrubs. The flowers are deep purple with a yellow beard and a pretty effect can be achieved by planting it in a circular bed or as a backdrop along a sunny wall. It likes very well-drained, fertile soil mixed with plenty of organic matter, and protection from wind. Water it freely during its growing period.
Other colors: Orange with yellow, cream.
Varieties/cultivars: 'Ola Kala', 'Rippling Waters', 'Starshine', 'Velvet Vista'.

Iris kaempferi 'Garry Gallant'

Iris kaempferi syn. I. ensata
JAPANESE WATER IRIS, JAPANESE IRIS

Family: IRIDACEAE
Origin: Japan, China.
Flowering time: Spring.
Climatic zone: 5, 6, 7, 8, 9.
Dimensions: Up to 3 feet (1 meter) high.
Description: This moisture-loving iris is well suited to waterside planting. Some of the cultivars are very colorful, some double-flowered, blotched, stippled, or striped. It makes a good companion plant with primula in a damp border that is free of lime. Plant it at the water's edge, but not below the water surface. Japanese iris will also grow well in ordinary garden soil, providing it has plenty of moisture throughout the growing season. It will die back completely during winter, when dead leaves should be removed.
Other colors: White, pink, red.
Varieties/cultivars: Several cultivars are available.

Iris pumila

Iris pumila
DWARF BEARDED IRIS ○

Family: IRIDACEAE
Origin: Central Europe–Turkey, southern U.S.S.R.
Flowering time: Spring.
Climatic zone: 4, 5, 6, 7, 8, 9.
Dimensions: Up to 8 inches (200 mm) high.
Description: This broad-leafed dwarf iris flowers earlier than the taller flag irises, and looks most effective planted in rock garden pockets or massed at the front of borders. It is short-stemmed and the leaves grow longer after the plant has flowered. Most of the dwarf bearded irises are cultivars and a good selection of colors is available. Irises rarely need mulching. Propagate by division. They are prone to iris borer.
Other colors: White, yellow.
Varieties/cultivars: 'Blue Denim', 'Pogo'.

Iris sibirica
SIBERIAN IRIS ○ ◑

Family: IRIDACEAE
Origin: Central Europe–Lake Baikal, U.S.S.R.
Flowering time: Summer.
Climatic zone: 4, 5, 6, 7, 8, 9.
Dimensions: Up to 4 feet (approx. 1 meter) high.
Description: The parent species of several cultivars and hybrids, *I. sibirica* is a moisture-lover which will form large clumps at the edge of ponds. The flowers are lilac-blue to blue-purple with a purple-veined, white basal patch. It

grows best in slightly moist soil but will still do well in conditions that are less than ideal.
Other colors: White, pearly-gray.
Varieties/cultivars: 'Caesar', 'Caesar's Brother', 'White Swirl', 'Snow Queen', 'Mrs Rowe', 'Perry's Blue', 'Cambridge Blue'.

Iris sibirica 'Cambridge Blue'

Jasione perennis
SHEPHERD'S ○ ◑
SCABIOUS (U.S.A.), SHEEP'S-BIT (U.K.)

Family: CAMPANULACEAE
Origin: Europe.
Flowering time: Spring–summer.

Climatic zone: 6, 7, 8.
Dimensions: Up to 12 inches (300 mm) high.
Description: This low-growing perennial is ideally suited to sunny rock garden pockets. It has a dense rosette of leaves and lilac-blue flower heads composed of many tiny florets which resemble pincushions. The heads are borne on erect stems. Plant it in winter in light, open soil in a sunny or semishaded position. Apply complete fertilizer in early spring and propagate it by root division in winter.

Limonium latifolium
BORDER SEA LAVENDER ○

Family: PLUMBAGINACEAE
Origin: Southeastern Europe–U.S.S.R.
Flowering time: Summer–autumn.
Climatic zone: 4, 5, 6, 7, 8, 9, 10.
Dimensions: Up to 2 feet (600 mm) high.

Limonium latifolium

Jasione perennis

Description: This member of the plumbago family is resistant to salt spray. It has rosettes of large leaves topped by long stems packed with masses of deep lavender-blue flowers. Bunches may be gathered and dried for semipermanent floral arrangements. It is easy to grow in sunny positions in light, sandy, moist soil, and is a good choice for the gardens of holiday houses which cannot be constantly maintained.
Varieties/cultivars: 'Violetta', 'Chilwell Beauty'.

Linum perenne syn. *L. sibiricum*
PERENNIAL FLAX ○

Family: LINACEAE
Origin: Europe.
Flowering time: Summer.
Climatic zone: 6, 7, 8, 9.
Dimensions: Up to 2 feet (600 mm) high.
Description: Perennial flax is a hardy border plant with gray-green leaves and clusters of pale blue, saucer-shaped flowers. The roots generally throw up numerous stems. It likes ordinary, well-drained soil, a sunny position, and regular watering. Apply a complete fertilizer in spring. Propagate it by seed in spring.

Linum perenne

Lobelia x *gerardii*
LOBELIA ○

Family: CAMPANULACEAE
Origin: Hybrid.
Flowering time: Summer.
Climatic zone: 5, 6, 7, 8, 9, 10.
Dimensions: Up to 3 feet (1 meter) high.
Description: This is a less commonly

Lobelia x *gerardii*

grown hybrid Lobelia, whose ancestry is uncertain due to back-breeding. In general it is a robust plant with leafy stems and a striking display of violet-purple flowers appearing in terminal racemes. The flowering period is spread over many weeks as the axillary branches are later to bloom. It prefers moderately rich and well-drained soil, with a good mulch of organic matter to protect the roots in winter. Makes a beautiful cut flower.
Other colors: Pink.
Varieties/cultivars: 'Surprise'.

Mazus reptans
TEAT FLOWER ○

Family: SCROPHULARIACEAE
Origin: Himalayas.
Flowering time: Spring.
Climatic zone: 6, 7, 8, 9.
Dimensions: Up to 9 inches (225 mm) high.
Description: This low-growing perennial forms a dense carpet and is well suited to sloping sites and rock gardens. Plant several close together near large rocks where the prostrate stems can form mats. The flowers are light purplish-blue with white, yellow and purple markings on the lower lips. It adapts to most soil types, but likes a moist soil and an open, sunny position. It is frost-resistant, but susceptible to drought.

Mazus reptans

Meconopsis betonicifolia syn. *M. baileyi*
HIMALAYAN BLUE ○ ◑
POPPY, TIBETAN POPPY

Family: PAPAVERACEAE
Origin: Himalayas.
Flowering time: Early summer.
Climatic zone: 6, 7, 8, 9.
Dimensions: Up to 4 feet (approx. 1 meter) high.
Description: The satiny, rich-blue, poppy-like flowers of Tibetan poppy are borne in groups of three or four at the tops of strong, slim stems. A cold-climate species, this herbaceous perennial from the Himalayan mountains needs deep, cool, fertile, moist soil in semishade or full sun. Protect it from the wind, water it regularly, and apply a complete fertilizer in the spring. Propagation is by seed in autumn.

Meconopsis betonicifolia

Mertensia virginica

Mertensia virginica
VIRGINIA BLUEBELLS ◑

Family: BORAGINACEAE
Origin: Central eastern and southeastern United States.
Flowering time: Late spring.
Climatic zone: 4, 5, 6, 7, 8, 9.
Dimensions: Up to 18 inches (450 mm) high.
Description: This pretty perennial has pale blue-green foliage and long, tubular, purple-blue flowers in drooping clusters. It needs cool soil that is rich in organic matter and that is kept moist, especially in the warm weather when the foliage dies back after flowering. Mulch the soil well with rotted compost.
Other colors: White, pink.
Varieties/cultivars: 'Alba', 'Rubra'.

Myosotis sylvatica
FORGET-ME-NOT ◑

Family: BORAGINACEAE
Origin: Europe.
Flowering time: Spring.
Climatic zone: 5, 6, 7, 8, 9.
Dimensions: Up to 12 inches (300 mm) high.

Myosotis sylvatica 'Royal Blue'

Description: This bushy biennial makes a good indoor winter pot plant. If using in borders it will spread rapidly and needs to be checked. It is best used with spring bulbs in pots, and under deciduous trees and shrubs where it will self-sow many seedlings each season. Cottage gardens are an ideal environment for it. Forget-me-not will grow in ordinary garden soil and thrives in rich, limed, sandy loam.
Varieties/cultivars: 'Royal Blue'.

Nepeta x *faassenii*
CATMINT ○

Family: LABIATAE
Origin: Hybrid.
Flowering time: Summer.
Climatic zone: 4, 5, 6, 7, 8, 9, 10.
Dimensions: Up to 18 inches (450 mm) high.

Nepeta x *faassenii*

Description: When the leaves of catmint are bruised, the aroma has a curious fascination for some cats, who chew the plant, roll on it, and eventually become quite intoxicated. This useful edging plant has aromatic spikes of small, mauve flowers and silver-gray leaves. It likes warm, sandy, well-drained soil and is easily grown and propagated from seeds in spring or by root division.

Omphalodes verna
CREEPING FORGET-ME-NOT, BLUE-EYED MARY ●

Family: BORAGINACEAE
Origin: Central southern Europe.
Flowering time: Spring.
Climatic zone: 5, 6, 7, 8, 9.
Dimensions: Up to 8 inches (200 mm) high.
Description: Creeping forget-me-not forms a clearblue groundcover when planted in woodland or under large trees and shrubs. The erect stems bear clusters of forget-me-not-like flowers in loose sprays. The plant thrives in neutral or slightly alkaline soil, provided it is cool, moist, and well-drained, and enriched with organic matter. It likes full shade and in the right position will flower for several months. Propagation is by seed in spring or by root division in spring or autumn.
Other colors: White.
Varieties/cultivars: 'Alba'.

Omphalodes verna

Perovskia atriplicifolia

Perovskia atriplicifolia
AZURE SAGE ○

Family: LABIATAE
Origin: Western Himalayas, Afghanistan.
Flowering time: Summer.
Climatic zone: 6, 7, 8, 9, 10.
Dimensions: Up to 5 feet (approx.
2 meters) high.
Description: Although this plant is a
member of the mint family, it has a
strong, sage-like aroma when bruised.
With its attractive blue flowers it makes
a good companion plant with globe
thistle in an open border. In full sun it
forms a very attractive, upright plant,
but in shaded situations it is inclined to
sprawl. Cut it back to ground level each
spring to promote strong new growth
and good flowering. Azure sage is easy
to grow in well-drained soil and is
propagated by cuttings in late summer.

Platycodon grandiflorus
BALLOON FLOWER, ○
CHINESE BELLFLOWER (U.S.A.)

Family: CAMPANULACEAE
Origin: Eastern Asia.
Flowering time: Late summer.
Climatic zone: 4, 5, 6, 7, 8, 9.
Dimensions: Up to 3 feet (1 meter) high.
Description: This compact, clump-
forming, herbaceous plant sends up
numerous leafy flower stems. The
balloon-like buds open to form wide,
cup-shaped flowers. It is an easy plant to
grow provided it has a sunny position in
an enriched, loamy soil. It makes an

Platycodon grandiflorus

attractive picture when planted in
combination with fuchsias. Propagation
is either by division or from seed in
spring.
Other colors: White, pink.
Varieties/cultivars: 'Mariesii', 'Mother
of Pearl', 'Capri'.

Platycodon grandiflorus 'Mariesii'
DWARF BALLOON ○
FLOWER

Family: CAMPANULACEAE
Origin: Cultivar.
Flowering time: Summer.
Climatic zone: 4, 5, 6, 7, 8, 9.
Dimensions: Up to 18 inches (450 mm)
high.
Description: This smaller growing
cultivar of *Platycodon grandiflorus* was
introduced into England from Japan
and is now the form of balloon flower
most widely grown in gardens. It is a
vigorous perennial, forming quite large
clumps after two or three years. The
flowers last well both on the plant and
when picked. It is easily propagated by

Platycodon grandiflorus 'Mariesii'

lifting the clumps after a few years and
carefully dividing them, replanting the
separated pieces immediately.
Other colors: White.

Polemonium caeruleum
JACOB'S-LADDER ○ ◑

Family: POLEMONIACEAE
Origin: Northern hemisphere.
Flowering time: Summer.
Climatic zone: 4, 5, 6, 7, 8, 9.
Dimensions: 2–3 feet (600–900 mm) high.
Description: The neatly divided leaflets, arranged in opposite pairs resembling the rungs of a ladder, give this plant its common name. The blooms are arranged in loose clusters of small, silky, bell-shaped flowers, with prominent orange stamens. It is an easily grown plant, though often short-lived unless divided in spring and replanted. Alternatively, it can be easily increased by seed.
Other colors: White.
Varieties/cultivars: 'Richardsonii', 'Dawn Flight', 'Sapphire'.

Polemonium caeruleum

Polemonium reptans
DWARF JACOB'S- ○ ◑
LADDER, CREEPING
POLEMONIUM

Family: POLEMONIACEAE
Origin: Eastern United States.
Flowering time: Spring–summer.
Climatic zone: 4, 5, 6, 7, 8, 9.
Dimensions: 8–12 inches (200–300 mm) high.
Description: This is an early flowering species which has branching stems and leaves divided into six or seven pairs. The pendant, cup-shaped flowers are carried in loose terminal clusters. This

Polemonium reptans

plant has a spreading rather than creeping habit, and prefers rich and moist well-drained soils and a protected position. It is frost-resistant but sensitive to drought. It can be propagated by seed or division.

Pulmonaria officinalis
LUNGWORT, SPOTTED ◑ ●
DOG, SOLDIERS AND SAILORS
(U.K.)

Family: BORAGINACEAE
Origin: Central Europe.
Flowering time: Spring.
Climatic zone: 4, 5, 6, 7, 8, 9.
Dimensions: Up to 12 inches (300 mm) high.

Description: The tubular flowers of this species are purple-pink at first but become shades of purple and then violet-blue as they mature. The large, bristly, heart-shaped leaves are irregularly spotted with white and were thought by ancient herbalists to cure spots on the lung. This plant is not particular about soil type, but prefers moist conditions. It is usually propagated by division in late winter.
Other colors: White.

Pulsatilla vulgaris syn. *Anemone pulsatilla*
PASQUE FLOWER ○ ◑

Family: RANUNCULACEAE
Origin: Europe and western U.S.S.R.
Flowering time: Spring.

Pulsatilla vulgaris

Pulmonaria officinalis

Climatic zone: 3, 4, 5, 6, 7, 8, 9.
Dimensions: 8–12 inches (200–300 mm) high.
Description: Pasque flower is an attractive rock garden plant with ferny leaves and nodding flowers on erect, hairy stems. Its common name was given because it comes into bloom round about Easter in the northern hemisphere. Well-drained garden soil suits it best and it is propagated by seed.
Other colors: Pink, mauve.

Salvia farinacea 'Blue Bedder'

Salvia farinacea
MEALY-CUP SAGE

Family: LABIATAE
Origin: Texas, New Mexico.
Flowering time: Summer–early autumn.
Climatic zone: 7, 8, 9.
Dimensions: 3–4 feet (approx. 1 meter) high.
Description: A slightly frost-tender member of the salvia genus, this species makes an excellent display in the summer border. The flowers are borne on long, graceful spikes, somewhat resembling lavender but much larger, and the aromatic leaves are long and narrow. Propagate the plant by division, or sow the seeds in spring. It is advisable to plant out in the garden after the risk of frost has passed
Other colors: White.
Varieties/cultivars: 'Blue Bedder', 'Alba'.

Salvia officinalis

Salvia officinalis and cultivars
COMMON SAGE

Family: LABIATAE
Origin: Southern Europe.
Flowering time: Summer.
Climatic zone: 6, 7, 8, 9.
Dimensions: Up to 3 feet (1 meter) high.
Description: Common sage has strongly aromatic, gray-green leaves and bluish-purple flowers. It has been cultivated for centuries as a culinary herb. The cultivar 'Purpurascens' is commonly called purple-leafed sage because both new stems and foliage are suffused with purple. 'Tricolor' is very distinctive with its gray-green leaves splashed with creamy white and suffused with purple and pink. Sage will grow in any free-draining garden soil. The leaves can be used fresh for cooking and in salads, or picked and dried for later use.
Other colors: White.
Varieties/cultivars: 'Alba', 'Icterina', 'Purpurascens', 'Tricolor'.

Salvia pratensis
MEADOW CLARY

Family: LABIATAE
Origin: Europe and North Africa.
Flowering time: Summer.
Climatic zone: 5, 6, 7, 8, 9.
Dimensions: 2–3 feet (approx. 1 meter) high.
Description: This sturdy plant forms a good basal clump of leaves below long spikes of violet-blue flowers. The leaves, slightly spotted with red, are rather coarse and the flower stems are square in shape. Like most members of the salvia genus, it prefers warm and dryish conditions and does not tolerate heavy

frosts. It should be cut back after flowering and can be propagated from cuttings.
Other colors: White, pink.
Varieties/cultivars: 'Baumgartenii', *S. p. tenorii.*

Salvia pratensis

Salvia x *superba*

Salvia x *superba*
VIOLET SAGE

Family: LABIATAE
Origin: Hybrid.
Flowering time: Summer–early autumn.
Climatic zone: 5, 6, 7, 8, 9.
Dimensions: 2–3 feet (up to 1 meter) high.
Description: The violet-red bracts which surround the crimson-purple flowers of this species persist after the flowers themselves have finished, providing a long and colorful display. The small, green leaves on the upright stems are aromatic. It is a useful plant for a mixed border and the flowers are excellent for cutting and drying. It grows well in ordinary garden soil and can be propagated by seed.
Varieties/cultivars: 'Lubeca', 'East Friesland'.

Stachys byzantina syn. *S. lanata*,
S. olympica
LAMB'S EARS, LAMBS' ○ ◑
TONGUES, DONKEY'S EARS
(U.S.A.)

Family: LABIATAE
Origin: Southwestern Asia–Turkey.
Flowering time: Summer.
Climatic zone: 5, 6, 7, 8, 9.
Dimensions: Up to 18 inches (450 mm)
high.
Description: This is an excellent
groundcover with its dense mats of
woolly, gray leaves. It thrives in full sun
or part shade and often succeeds in poor
soil. The spikes of small purple flowers
are half-hidden by silver bracts.
Propagation is by division.
Varieties/cultivars: 'Silver Carpet'
(non-flowering), 'Cotton Boll'.

Stachys byzantina

Stachys macrantha syn. *S. grandiflora*,
Betonica macrantha
BIG BETONY (U.S.A.), ○ ◑
GRAND WOUNDWORT (U.K.)

Family: LABIATAE
Origin: The Caucasus.
Flowering time: Summer.
Climatic zone: 4, 5, 6, 7, 8, 9.
Dimensions: Up to 2 feet (600 mm) high.
Description: The dark-green, downy
leaves of this plant have an unusual
wrinkled or corrugated appearance.
From the dense clumps of leaves, erect
flower stems emerge with three or four
whorls of hooded blooms of a purplish-
mauve color. Garden forms exist which
have deeper and richer violet flowers
and there are also those with pink and
white blooms. It is easily propagated by

Stachys macrantha

division in early spring. Plant in well-
drained soil.
Other colors: Pink, white
Varieties/cultivars: 'Superba',
'Robusta'.

Stokesia laevis
STOKES' ASTER ○ ◑

Family: COMPOSITAE
Origin: Southeastern United States.
Flowering time: Summer–autumn.
Climatic zone: 5, 6, 7, 8, 9.
Dimensions: 18 inches (450 mm) high.
Description: From a basal rosette of
plain, green leaves, the flower stems
emerge with a cornflower-like bloom set
off by a collar of green leaves (or bracts).
The blue flowers can often be up to 4

inches (100 mm) across with paler
centers. They last well on the plant and
are also good for picking. The plants
thrive in any good, well-drained soil,
and are usually propagated by division
in late winter.
Other colors: Pink, white.
Varieties/cultivars: 'Blue Star', 'Alba',
'Rosea'.

Teucrium fruticans
MINT GERMANDER, ○ ◑
SHRUBBY GERMANDER

Family: LABIATAE
Origin: Western Mediterranean region
and Portugal.
Flowering time: Summer–autumn.
Climatic zone: 8, 9, 10.
Dimensions: 4 to 7 feet (1–2 meters) high.

Teucrium fruticans

Stokesia laevis

Description: Mint germander is an easily cultivated, evergreen shrub with attractive gray-green oval leaves, slightly curled at the edges. It flowers over a long period. It is a dense shrub and can be clipped to shape, making it ideal for hedges. A quick grower in any good garden soil, even the slightly alkaline, it is also useful for seaside planting, tolerating warm, dry conditions. In cooler areas, it grows well against a sunny wall, or in a container on a patio. It can be propagated from cuttings taken in late summer, or from seed.

Teucrium marum

Teucrium marum syn. *Micromeria corsica*
CATNIP, CAT THYME ○

Family: LABIATAE
Origin: Yugoslavia and Mediterranean islands.
Flowering time: Summer.
Climatic zone: 7, 8, 9, 10.
Dimensions: 6–12 inches (150–300 mm) high.
Description: This is an adaptable plant, growing well in most types of soil providing it is well-drained. It is frost-resistant and will tolerate drought. The gray-green, oval leaves on wiry stems have an aromatic odor. It can sometimes be an unfortunate addition to a garden as cats are said to be inordinately fond of it, tearing it to pieces and rolling on its neighbors! It can be grown in a rockery and propagated by seed or cuttings.

Tricyrtis formosana

Tricyrtis formosana
TOAD LILY ◐ ●

Family: LILIACEAE
Origin: Taiwan.
Flowering time: Early autumn.
Climatic zone: 5, 6, 7, 8, 9.
Dimensions: 2–3 feet (600–900 mm) high.
Description: Toad lilies, so called because of their spotted flowers, have shiny, dark leaves and upright flower stems that branch into heads of mauve-white flowers having yellow, purple-spotted throats. Grow them in a soil that does not dry out and that contains plenty of organic matter. They do well in a shady position, although a little dappled sunshine will hasten the development of flowers. Propagation is by seeds or offsets.
Other colors: Reddish-purple.
Varieties/cultivars: *T. f. stolonifera*.

Veronica austriaca teucrium
SPEEDWELL, BLUE ○ ◐
SPEEDWELL, HUNGARIAN
SPEEDWELL (U.S.A.)

Family: SCROPHULARIACEAE
Origin: Europe.
Flowering time: Summer.
Climatic zone: 4, 5, 6, 7, 8, 9.
Dimensions: 1–2 feet (300–600 mm) high.
Description: This charming perennial has slender spikes of lavender-blue flowers and narrow, deep-green leaves on slender stems. A useful plant for borders or rockeries, it likes a sunny or semishaded position and a fertile, well-drained soil. Cut it back in autumn to encourage strong growth the following spring, and divide clumps every four years to produce new, healthy plants.

Feed it with a liquid fertilizer in spring to encourage good flower production.
Other colors: Various shades of blue.
Varieties/cultivars: 'Blue Fountain', 'Crater Lake Blue', 'Trehane', 'Pavane', 'Shirley Blue', 'Knallblau'.

Veronica austriaca teucrium 'Knallblau'

Veronica spicata

Veronica spicata
SPIKE SPEEDWELL, ○ ◐
CAT'S TAIL SPEEDWELL (U.K.)

Family: SCROPHULARIACEAE
Origin: Europe and Asia.
Flowering time: Summer–early autumn.
Climatic zone: 4, 5, 6, 7, 8, 9.
Dimensions: 18 inches (450 mm) high.
Description: This is a valuable plant for the front of a border as it makes a fine display. It forms a compact tussock of leaves from which arise the numerous dense spikes of flowers. It is easy to grow in most soil types, provided they are well-drained. Over the years it has been successfully crossed with other species to produce many attractive garden varieties. The best method of propagation is by division.
Other colors: Pink, white.
Varieties/cultivars: 'Sarabande', 'Icicle', 'Blue Fox', 'Red Fox', 'Blue Peter', 'Snow White'.

Veronica spicata var incana

Veronica spicata var. *incana* syn. *V incana* ○
GRAY SPIKE SPEEDWELL (U.K.),
WOOLLY SPEEDWELL (U.S.A.)

Family: SCROPHULARIACEAE
Origin: Northern Asia and U.S.S.R.
Flowering time: Summer.
Climatic zone: 4, 5, 6, 7, 8, 9.
Dimensions: 12–18 inches (300–450 mm) high.
Description: Gray speedwell is a more-or-less evergreen plant that is easy to grow in average garden soil provided it receives ample sunshine. The deep blue flowers are carried in terminal spikes, and the leaves are silvery-gray and slightly toothed. This plant makes a

Vinca minor

good show in the garden and has a long flowering period. The best method of propagation is by division, either in autumn or in spring.
Other colors: Pink.
Varieties/cultivars: 'Barcarolle', 'Minuet'.

Vinca minor
LESSER PERIWINKLE ◐ ●
(U.K.), RUNNING MYRTLE

Family: APOCYNACEAE
Origin: Europe and western Asia.
Flowering time: Spring–summer.
Climatic zone: 5, 6, 7, 8, 9.
Dimensions: Prostrate to 4 inches (100 mm) high.
Description: A hardy, trailing plant with small, dark-green, shiny leaves, dwarf periwinkle spreads rapidly over the soil surface, rooting at every node to form new plants. This is a most useful plant for covering the ground in shaded areas under trees. The flower color is somewhat variable, but always in shades of blue, purple, and white. There are several cultivars, including two with variegated foliage. It is easily propagated by simply cutting the rooted stems and planting them elsewhere. Vinca grows well in most well-drained soils.
Other colors: Pink, white.
Varieties/cultivars: 'Alba', 'Bowles Variety', 'Rosea'.

Viola cornuta

Viola cornuta
HORNED VIOLET ◐ ●

Family: VIOLACEAE
Origin: Pyrenees.
Flowering time: Late spring–autumn.
Climatic zone: 5, 6, 7, 8, 9.
Dimensions: Up to 8 inches (200 mm) high.
Description: This dainty little edging or rock garden plant is a short-lived perennial which prefers a semishaded position in ordinary garden soil. The evergreen leaves form a compact tuft and violet-colored flowers are held on long stalks. The flowering period can be prolonged if the dead flowers are removed regularly. Once established, this viola will spread well to form an attractive groundcover. It is closely related to pansies and violets.
Other colors: White.

Viola hederacea
WILD VIOLET, ◐ ●
AUSTRALIAN NATIVE VIOLET,
IVY-LEAVED VIOLET

Family: VIOLACEAE
Origin: Southeastern Australia.
Flowering time: Spring–autumn.
Climatic zone: 8, 9, 10.
Dimensions: Prostrate to 4 inches (100 mm) high.
Description: This dense mat-forming plant with kidney-shaped leaves spreads on long runners that bind the soil or cascade over banks. A good groundcover plant for either sandy or clay soils, it prefers a moist and semisheltered position. One plant will cover up to 1 square yard

Viola hederacea

(approximately 1 square meter) of soil. It is tolerant of some frost and snow provided that winters are not too severe. It is also moderately tolerant of limy soil.
Other colors: White.
Varieties/cultivars: 'Baby Blue'.

Viola labradorica 'Purpurea'
LABRADOR VIOLET

Family: VIOLACEAE
Origin: Cultivar.
Flowering time: Spring–summer.
Climatic zone: 3, 4, 5, 6, 7, 8, 9.
Dimensions: 4 inches (100 mm) high.
Description: This little violet is an attractive groundcover all year round due to the deep purple-green of its leaves. It makes a useful color contrast in the garden, especially if near plants with lime-yellow foliage. The flowers are a pretty lavender-blue, but without any perfume. It spreads easily in most soils, rooting at the nodes, and is usually propagated by division during autumn or winter.

Viola labradorica 'Purpurea'

Viola odorata

Viola odorata
COMMON VIOLET, SWEET VIOLET (U.K.)

Family: VIOLACEAE
Origin: Europe, North Africa, Asia.
Climatic zone: 6, 7, 8, 9.
Dimensions: 6 inches (150 mm) high.
Description: For the size of this little perennial, the flowers are relatively large, being up to 1 inch (25 mm) across. Their perfume is sweet and quite strong. The plant spreads by runners and it can be divided in autumn and spring. It often self-sows. It is an easily grown groundcover, which likes moist, moderately rich soil. There are now many garden forms.
Other colors: White, pink, apricot.
Varieties/cultivars: 'Marie Louise', 'Princess of Wales', 'Czar', 'Royal Robe'.

Wahlenbergia gloriosa
ROYAL BLUEBELL

Family: CAMPANULACEAE
Origin: Southeastern Australia.
Flowering time: Late spring–summer.
Climatic zone: 8, 9.

Dimensions: Prostrate, spreading up to 3 sq. feet (1 sq. meter).
Description: This is a very showy creeper which spreads quite rapidly by suckering. It is a hardy, frost-resistant plant although it does not withstand severe winters. It grows best in a loamy soil with plenty of moisture. It looks spectacular when mass-planted, but it can also be grown successfully and looks attractive in a tub or large pot. Its flower is the floral emblem of the Australian Capital Territory.

Wahlenbergia gloriosa

Brunfelsia australis

Brunfelsia calycina

Description: A large shrub with gracefully arching branches bearing long, narrow leaves, fountain buddleia produces an abundance of fragrant, lilac-purple flowers that weigh the branches down. Pruning, if required, should be carried out after flowering has finished, as flowers appear on the previous year's growth. Fountain buddleia is popular in cottage gardens and makes a good screen plant. It will grow in any well-drained garden soil. Apply a handful of complete plant food in early spring.
Other colors: Mauve-pink.
Varieties/cultivars: 'Argentea', 'Hever Castle'.

Brunfelsia australis syn. *B. latifolia*
YESTERDAY-TODAY- ○ ◑
AND-TOMORROW

Family: SOLANACEAE
Origin: Central America.
Flowering time: Spring–summer.
Climatic zone: 9, 10.
Dimensions: 3–6 feet (1–2 meters) high.
Description: The common name is derived from the flowers which, over a period of three days, change from violet-blue, fading to lavender and eventually to white. The phlox-like flowers are very fragrant and the leaves are grayish-green. In cold climates, yesterday-today-and-tomorrow is grown in greenhouses or indoors. It likes a warm, sheltered position and benefits from a light pruning after flowering. Feed in early spring with a complete plant food.

Brunfelsia calycina
DWARF BRUNFELSIA, ○ ◑
YESTERDAY-TODAY-AND-
TOMORROW

Family: SOLANACEAE
Origin: South America.
Flowering time: Spring–summer.
Climatic zone: 9, 10.
Dimensions: 3–4 feet (approx. 1 meter) high.
Description: Compact, with slender, semi-glossy green foliage, dwarf brunfelsia makes a pretty feature shrub. The fragrant violet flowers virtually cover the plant and fade to white as they age. The shrub requires a warm, sheltered position and well-drained soil. A mulch of manure or compost in

spring will feed it and keep the roots moist. A light pruning after flowering encourages more compact growth.
Varieties/cultivars: 'Eximea', *B. c.* var. *floribunda*.

Buddleia alternifolia
FOUNTAIN BUDDLEIA, ○ ◑
ALTERNATE-LEAFED
BUDDLEIA

Family: LOGANIACEAE
Origin: China.
Flowering time: Early summer.
Climatic zone: 5, 6, 7, 8, 9.
Dimensions: 10–20 feet (3–6 meters).

Buddleia alternifolia

Buddleia davidii

Buddleia davidii
BUTTERFLY BUSH, ○ ◑
BUDDLEIA

Family: LOGANIACEAE
Origin: China.
Flowering time: Summer.
Climatic zone: 5, 6, 7, 8, 9.
Dimensions: 10 feet (3 meters) high.
Description: Butterfly bush is a very worthy addition to gardens because of its hardiness, attractiveness to butterflies, and its tolerance of a wide range of soils, temperatures, and environments. Its rapid growth makes it useful for screen plantings. The gray-green foliage is attractive and complements the mauve spikes of the flower heads. Pruning in winter is essential to control the shape of the bush.
Other colors: Rich red-purple, white.
Varieties/cultivars: 'Royal Red', 'White Bouquet', 'Ile de France'.

Callicarpa bodinieri var. *giraldii*

Callicarpa bodinieri var. *giraldii*
CHINESE BEAUTYBERRY, BEAUTY BERRY (U.K.) ○

Family: VERBENACEAE
Origin: Western China.
Flowering time: Summer.
Climatic zone: 6, 7, 8, 9.
Dimensions: 6 feet (2 meters) high.
Description: This is a handsome shrub valued for its downy foliage and rosy-lilac flowers, which are followed by clusters of shining bluish-lilac fruits. Use it as a background plant for a shrub border. Easily grown, Chinese beautyberry will thrive in any well-drained soil that does not dry out. A sunny aspect is essential. Pruning is not necessary unless the plant becomes straggly, when it can be cut back heavily in late winter. Chinese beautyberry can be propagated from cuttings or seed.

Calluna vulgaris
LING, HEATHER, SCOTCH HEATHER ○ ◑

Family: ERICACEAE
Origin: Europe, western Asia, Morocco, the Azores.
Flowering time: Spring and summer.
Climatic zone: 5, 6, 7, 8, 9.
Dimensions: 12 inches (450 mm) high.
Description: Heather is loved for its evergreen foliage and profusion of small, bell-like, purplish-pink, nodding flowers and is a good shrub to use in front of borders or as a groundcover in a small

Calluna vulgaris

garden. It will grow in poor soil as long as it is well-drained and acidic. Cultivate around the plant with care as the roots are very close to the surface. A mulch of leaf mold or peat is beneficial. Pruning can be carried out after flowering to keep the plants compact.
Other colors: White, mauve, crimson, pink.
Varieties/cultivars: There are numerous cultivars of heather throughout the world.

Caryopteris incana
BLUEBEARD, BLUE SPIRAEA (U.K.) ○

Family: VERBENACEAE
Origin: Japan, Korea, China.
Flowering time: Late summer–autumn.

Caryopteris incana

Climatic zone: 5, 6, 7, 8, 9.
Dimensions: 3 feet (1 meter) high.
Description: This small shrub has an abundance of grayish-green, aromatic leaves. The axillary clusters of violet-blue flowers appear at the tips of the shoots. A valued shrub because it flowers when few other blue-flowering shrubs are in bloom, bluebeard will thrive in a moisture-retentive but well-drained loamy soil. Because flowers are produced on the new wood, prune during winter.

Caryopteris x *clandonensis*

Caryopteris x *clandonensis*
BLUEBEARD, BLUE SPIRAEA (U.K.) ○

Family: VERBENACEAE
Origin: Hybrid.
Flowering time: Summer–autumn.
Climatic zone: 5, 6, 7, 8, 9.
Dimensions: 2 feet (600 mm) high.
Description: This pretty plant is also known as *Caryopteris* x *clandonensis* 'Arthur Simmonds' after the man who first raised it. The bright blue flowers appear among the aromatic, dull green, downy foliage. A hardy shrub, it will grow in almost any soil and is an ideal subject for mass-planting. Pruning during winter will encourage more flowers the next season. Apply mulch, manure, compost, or a handful of complete plant food in early spring.
Other colors: Lilac-blue.
Varieties/cultivars: 'Ferndown', 'Heavenly Blue', 'Blue Mist', 'Kew Blue'.

Ceanothus 'Pacific Beauty'

Ceanothus cultivars
CALIFORNIA LILAC, ○
WILD LILAC (U.S.A.),
BUCKBRUSH (U.S.A.)

Family: RHAMNACEAE
Origin: Cultivars.
Flowering time: Spring–summer.
Climatic zone: 7, 8, 9.
Dimensions: 3–12 feet (1–4 meters) high,
depending on the cultivar.
Description: There are many different
cultivars of *Ceanothus* in a wide variety
of shades of blue. Varying in size from
small, prostrate plants to vigorous, tall
shrubs, when in bloom, they are almost
entirely covered with flowers. These
showy plants will thrive in any well-
drained soil, and are excellent shrubs for
seaside plantings. Prune after flowering
has finished.
Other colors: Lavender, violet and
various shades of blue.
Varieties/cultivars: There are
numerous cultivars of *Ceanothus*.

Ceanothus impressus
CEANOTHUS, ○
CALIFORNIAN LILAC, SANTA
BARBARA CEANOTHUS

Other common names: WILD LILAC
(U.S.A.), BUCKBRUSH (U.S.A.)
Family: RHAMNACEAE
Origin: California.
Flowering time: Spring.
Climatic zone: 8, 9.
Dimensions: 6–10 feet (2–3 meters) high.
Description: *Ceanothus impressus* is a
dense, compact shrub, which, during
spring, is completely covered in deep-

blue flowers. The impressed vein pattern
of the foliage is distinctive, dark green
marked with pale green. Use ceanothus
in a shrub border or as a feature plant.
It is semideciduous in colder climates,
but tends to remain evergreen in
temperate climates. Plant it in well-
drained soil and feed with a complete
plant food during spring. It can be
pruned when it has finished flowering.

Ceanothus impressus

Ceanothus thyrsiflorus var. repens
CREEPING BLUE ○ ◑
BLOSSOM, CALIFORNIAN
LILAC, SANTA BARBARA
CEANOTHUS

Other common names: WILD LILAC
(U.S.A.), BUCKBRUSH (U.S.A.)
Family: RHAMNACEAE
Origin: California.
Flowering time: Summer.
Climatic zone: 8, 9.
Dimensions: 3 feet (900 mm) high.
Description: This shrub, prostrate
when young and then gradually
building up into a mound-shaped bush,
produces generous quantities of sky-blue
flowers. Use creeping blue blossom in
the front of a shrub border or in a
rockery. Plant it in well-drained soil that
is enriched annually with manure or
compost or, alternatively, apply a

Ceanothus thyrsiflorus var. repens

handful of complete plant food.
Pruning, if necessary, should be done
just after flowering. The plant is easily
propagated from cuttings taken in early
spring or late summer.

Ceanothus x veitchianus
CALIFORNIA LILAC, ○
WILD LILAC (U.S.A.),
BUCKBRUSH (U.S.A.)

Family: RHAMNACEAE
Origin: Hybrid.
Flowering time: Early summer.
Climatic zone: 7, 8, 9.
Dimensions: 10 feet (3 meters) high.
Description: An evergreen hybrid,

Ceanothus x veitchianus

California lilac forms a bushy, many-branched shrub with small oval leaves and clusters of deep-blue flowers. The flowers appear at the tips of the branches towards the end of the previous year's growth. Plant California lilac in a sheltered position, as it has a tendency to produce growth quickly during the first couple of years and then die off equally quickly if it is damaged by prolonged frost.

Ceratostigma griffithii

Ceratostigma willmottianum

Climatic zone: 8, 9.
Dimensions: 2–3 feet (600–900 mm) high, 3–4 feet (approx. 1 meter) wide.
Description: Ceratostigma is a loose, open bush with distinctive sharp-angled stems. Red autumn foliage and bright

blue tubular flowers make a colorful show for a large part of the year. It can be used at the front of a border or as an informal low hedge. It is hardy and tolerates a wide range of soils. Annual pruning is required.

Cistus x *purpureus*
PURPLE ROCK ROSE, ○
ORCHID ROCK ROSE,
SUNROSE (U.K.)

Family: CISTACEAE
Origin: Hybrid.
Flowering time: Summer.
Climatic zone: 8, 9, 10.
Dimensions: 3–4 feet (over 1 meter) high.
Description: The showy purple flowers of purple rock rose have a darker blotch on each petal and a yellow "eye". The gray-green leaves are nearly stalkless. It is an ideal plant for the seaside and hot, dry areas, but will grow in cool areas if given a warm position and well-drained soil. It will not tolerate overwet soil or severe frost. During spring, feed it with a complete plant food.

Ceratostigma griffithii
CERATOSTIGMA, ○
BURMESE PLUMBAGO,
HARDY PLUMBAGO (U.K.)

Family: PLUMBAGINACEAE
Origin: Himalayas, Burma.
Flowering time: Summer.
Climatic zone: 8, 9.
Dimensions: 2 feet (600 mm) high.
Description: A beautiful shrub, ceratostigma makes a delightful, hardy feature shrub, producing an abundance of deep-blue flowers over a long period. The leaves often turn conspicuously red in autumn. It likes full sun, a sheltered site, and a well-drained soil, and during spring should be mulched with manure or compost. Alternatively, apply a handful of complete plant food. Regular feeding will ensure a good flower display. Propagation can be carried out easily from cuttings or by root division.

Ceratostigma willmottianum
CERATOSTIGMA, ○
CHINESE PLUMBAGO,
HARDY PLUMBAGO (U.K.)

Family: PLUMBAGINACEAE
Origin: Western China.
Flowering time: Late summer.

Cistus x *purpureus*

SHRUBS

Daboecia cantabrica

Daboecia cantabrica and cultivars
IRISH HEATH, ST. DABEOC'S HEATH, CONNEMARA HEATH

Family: ERICACEAE
Origin: Western Europe.
Flowering time: Early summer–early autumn.
Climatic zone: 5, 6, 7, 8.
Dimensions: 12–18 inches (300–450 mm) high.
Description: These low-growing shrubs are popular for their long flowering period. There are several cultivars in various shades of purple, which can be used in rockeries or mass-planted. They thrive in cold climates in a free-draining, acidic soil. To ensure that the soil is acid, mulch around the plants with peat to a depth of about 1 foot (300 mm). Irish heath are easily propagated from seed or autumn cuttings.
Other colors: White, rich pink.
Varieties/cultivars: There are several cultivars of this shrub.

Daphne mezereum
DAPHNE, FEBRUARY DAPHNE, MEZEREON (U.K.)

Family: THYMELAEACEAE
Origin: Central and southern Europe, Asia Minor, Siberia.
Flowering time: Spring.
Climatic zone: 5, 6, 7, 8.
Dimensions: 3 feet (1 meter) high.
Description: A deciduous shrub, daphne is loved for its sweet-smelling, purple-red flowers. These cover the

previous year's shoots and are followed by scarlet fruits, which are poisonous. Daphne's survival seems to depend on a cold winter. It likes a well-drained, alkaline soil. Daphne does not like chemical fertilizers — a mulch of cow manure or leaf mold annually will suffice.
Other colors: White, rose-pink.
Varieties/cultivars: 'Alba', 'Grandiflora', 'Rosea'.

Daphne mezereum

Daphne odora
DAPHNE

Family: THYMELAEACEAE
Origin: China.
Flowering time: Late winter–spring.
Climatic zone: 7, 8, 9.
Dimensions: 3 feet (900 mm) high x 4 feet (approx. 1 meter) wide.
Description: Daphne, though often difficult to grow, is worthy of a place in the garden because of its wonderful perfume. These small, evergreen, compact bushes require special conditions of good drainage and rich, crumbly, slightly acidic soils. At their flowering peak, the bushes are covered with dense heads of up to thirty star-shaped flowers which are rose-purple in bud and paler within. They are happy growing in association with rhododendrons or in containers as a focal point.
Other colors: Pink, white.
Varieties/cultivars: 'Alba', 'Aureomarginata', 'Rubra'.

Daphne odora

Disanthus cercidifolius
DISANTHUS

Family: HAMAMELIDACEAE
Origin: Japan, South-east China.
Flowering time: Autumn.
Climatic zone: 5, 6, 7, 8, 9.
Dimensions: 6–10 feet (2–3 meters) high.
Description: This large and beautiful deciduous shrub has slender branches and heart-shaped, thick leaves which turn from green to glorious shades of red and orange in autumn. The dark purple flowers have thin, spidery petals and are borne in pairs on short stalks. Best grown in cool, moist, and slightly acid soil, it should be located in a sheltered position and pruned lightly to keep the growth habit dense.

Disanthus cercidifolius

Echium fastuosum

Echium fastuosum
VIPER'S BUGLOSS, PRIDE OF MADEIRA (U.K.) ○

Family: BORAGINACEAE
Origin: Canary Islands.
Flowering time: Spring–summer.
Climatic zone: 9, 10.
Dimensions: 4 feet (approx. 1 meter) high.
Description: Viper's bugloss is a soft-wooded shrub which is sometimes classed as a woody perennial. The dense branches bear a great profusion of lance-shaped, gray-green, hairy leaves. These develop central spikes up to 12 inches (300 mm) long, tightly packed with long-stamened, blue or purple flowers. Viper's bugloss will thrive near the seaside in a hot, sunny position. It needs a well-drained soil and tends to flower more profusely in poor and fairly dry soils. Cut off the older rosettes after flowering.

Eupatorium megalophyllum
SHRUB AGERATUM, ○ ◑ MIST FLOWER, EUPATORIUM (U.K.)

Family: COMPOSITAE
Origin: Southern Mexico.
Flowering time: Late spring.

Eupatorium megalophyllum

Climatic zone: 9, 10.
Dimensions: 6 feet (2 meters) high.
Description: Eupatorium requires temperatures above 32°F (0°C) and consequently is not commonly seen in northern hemisphere gardens. The plant looks like an overgrown ageratum, but is distinguished from it by its furry foliage with dense clusters of mauve flowers in late spring. The size of eupatoriums gives scale to a shrub border. They are an attractive companion plant to rondeletias.

Felicia amelloides
BLUE MARGUERITE, ○ BLUE DAISY, AGATHAEA, FELICIA

Family: COMPOSITAE
Origin: South Africa.
Flowering time: Early summer and intermittently through into autumn.
Climatic zone: 9, 10.
Dimensions: 20 inches (500 mm) high.
Description: This is a hardy, evergreen shrub with a compact form which becomes covered with a profusion of bright blue, daisy-like flowers with yellow centers. It is a very useful fill-in plant, and will complement a perennial border. It likes full sun and good drainage, and a moderate pruning after flowering helps maintain its shape. It differs from *F. angustifolia*, its near relative, in its leaf arrangement.

Felicia amelloides

Felicia angustifolia

Hebe speciosa 'La Seduisante'

Felicia angustifolia
FELICIA (U.K.), ◯ ◑
KINGFISHER DAISY

Family: COMPOSITAE
Origin: South Africa.
Flowering time: Spring.
Climatic zone: 9, 10.
Dimensions: 3 feet (1 meter) high.
Description: A very free-flowering
small shrub, felicia has daisy-like, light-
purple flowers which cover the bright
green foliage for a few weeks during
spring. Because of its spreading and
trailing habit, it makes a good
groundcover or rockery plant. It is a
hardy plant which will thrive in any
well-drained garden soil. A light
pruning after flowering encourages more
flowers the following season. Feed in
early spring with a handful of complete
plant food.

Hebe hulkeana
NEW ZEALAND LILAC, ◯ ◑
VERONICA

Family: SCROPHULARIACEAE
Origin: New Zealand.
Flowering time: Spring–summer.
Climatic zone: 8, 9.
Dimensions: 3 feet (1 meter) high.
Description: This is one of the most
beautiful species of *Hebe* in cultivation.
It is a small shrub, with a loose, open

growth and glossy green leaves. It bears
large clusters of delicate, lilac-blue
flowers. It is easily grown in any type of
soil, but dislikes drying out during
summer. A mulch of manure or
compost will keep the soil moist, as well
as providing food. New Zealand lilac
may need pruning every second winter
to maintain a good shape.

Hebe hulkeana

Hebe speciosa 'La Seduisante'
SPEEDWELL HEBE, ◯ ◑
SHRUBBY VERONICA (U.K.)

Family: SCROPHULARIACEAE
Origin: Cultivar.
Flowering time: Summer.
Climatic zone: 8, 9.
Dimensions: 3 feet (1 meter) high.
Description: This French cultivar has
bright rosy-purple flowers, and
interesting, dark-green leaves that are
purple underneath. It makes a lovely
feature plant as it looks attractive even
when not in flower. Mulch around the
plant with manure or compost to
prevent the shallow roots from drying
out during summer. It can be pruned
after flowering if it loses its shape.

Hebe x *andersonii*
SPEEDWELL HEBE, ◯ ◑
SHRUBBY VERONICA (U.K.)

Family: SCROPHULARIACEAE
Origin: Hybrid.
Flowering time: Summer–autumn.

Hebe x *andersonii*

Climatic zone: 8, 9.
Dimensions: 4–6 feet (1–2 meters) high.
Description: This vigorous shrub has leaves 4–6 inches (100–150 mm) long and 5-inch (125-mm) long spikes of soft lavender-blue flowers which fade to white. There is also a variegated form which has creamy-white margins along the leaves. It is a fast-growing shrub which makes an excellent screen plant. Before planting, enrich the soil with manure or compost and mulch around it to protect the shallow roots. Speedwell hebe can be lightly pruned after flowering to encourage a denser habit.
Varieties/cultivars: Cultivars include 'Variegata', 'Anne Pimm'.

Hebe x *andersonii* 'Anne Pimm'
SPEEDWELL HEBE, ○ ◑
SHRUBBY VERONICA (U.K.)

Family: SCROPHULARIACEAE
Origin: Hybrid.
Flowering time: Summer–autumn.
Climatic zone: 8, 9.
Dimensions: 4–6 feet (1–2 meters) high.
Description: This vigorous shrub has leaves 4–6 inches (100–150 cm) long, mid-green and flushed with reddish-purple underneath when young. The soft lavender-purple flowers are borne on long spikes, making a most attractive display over many weeks. It is a fast-growing shrub, which makes an excellent screen plant. Incorporate plenty of compost into the soil prior to planting, and mulch well to protect the shallow roots. Lightly prune after flowering to encourage a denser habit.

Hebe x *franciscana* 'Blue Gem'

Hebe x *franciscana* 'Blue Gem'
SPEEDWELL HEBE, ○ ◑
SHRUBBY VERONICA (U.K.)

Family: SCROPHULARIACEAE
Origin: Cultivar.
Flowering time: Summer.
Climatic zone: 8, 9.
Dimensions: 3 feet (1 meter) high.
Description: This compact shrub produces dense racemes of bright blue flowers. It is one of the hardiest hebes, and its resistance to salt-laden winds makes it a popular shrub for seaside plantings. It is often used for low hedges. Plant it in soil that has been enriched with manure or compost. This will provide food as well as keep the soil moist. It can be pruned to shape during winter.

Heliotropium arborescens
CHERRY-PIE, ○ ◑
HELIOTROPE

Family: BORAGINACEAE
Origin: Peru.
Flowering time: Spring–summer.

Climatic zone: 9, 10.
Dimensions: 6 feet (2 meters) high.
Description: Cherry-pie is a pretty shrub with wrinkled, hairy leaves and branched spikes crowded with fragrant, violet or lilac flowers. Powerfully scented, these flowers are used in the manufacture of perfume. It will adapt to any well-drained soil and should be fed in spring with a handful of complete plant food. Water it well during the summer months.

Hebe x *andersonii* 'Anne Pimm'

Heliotropium arborescens

Hibiscus syriacus

Hibiscus syriacus
ROSE-OF-SHARON, SYRIAN HIBISCUS, MALLOW ○

Other common names: BLUE HIBISCUS
Family: MALVACEAE
Origin: Eastern Asia.
Flowering time: Late summer–autumn.
Climatic zone: 5, 6, 7, 8, 9.
Dimensions: 8 feet (over 2 meters) high.
Description: A hardy, deciduous shrub, rose-of-Sharon is valued for its late summer and autumn flowers, which vary greatly in color. Although predominantly blue and purple, there are often two or more shades in the same flower. One of its common names is Syrian hibiscus, but it has never been found growing wild in that country.
Other colors: Red, white, rose, carmine, pink.
Varieties/cultivars: There are numerous varieties throughout the world.

Hovea chorizemifolia
HOLLY-LEAF HOVEA ◑ ●

Family: LEGUMINOSAE
Origin: Western Australia.
Flowering time: Spring.
Climatic zone: 9.
Dimensions: 22 inches (600 mm) high.
Description: An erect, sparsely branched, small shrub with holly-like leaves and deep-purple pea flowers, this very pretty shrub is not often found in cultivation. It needs excellent drainage

and some overhead shade to grow successfully. The roots must be kept cool with a mulch of leaf litter or well-rotted compost. It can be easily propagated from seed.

Hovea chorizemifolia

Hydrangea macrophylla and cultivars
COMMON HYDRANGEA, BIGLEAF HYDRANGEA (U.S.A.), FLORIST'S HYDRANGEA (U.K.) ○ ◑ ●

Other common names: HORTENSIA (U.S.A.)
Family: HYDRANGEACEAE
Origin: Japan.

Flowering time: Spring–summer.
Climatic zone: 7, 8, 9, 10.
Dimensions: 3–6 feet (1–2 meters) high.
Description: Hydrangeas are popular plants because of their hardy nature and beautiful flower colors; the various shades of blue available depend on the cultivar. The color of the flower generally depends on the soil. An alkaline soil produces pink flowers while an acid soil produces blue flowers. To maintain the blue color of the flowers add aluminum sulfate annually to the soil (1 tablespoon per square meter), or keep the soil mulched with peat moss or oak leaves.
Other colors: Pink, red, mauve.
Varieties/cultivars: There are numerous cultivars throughout the world.

Indigofera australis
AUSTRALIAN INDIGO ○ ◑ ●

Family: LEGUMINOSAE
Origin: Australia.
Flowering time: Spring.
Climatic zone: 9, 10.
Dimensions: 6 feet (2 meters) high.
Description: This open, spreading plant, which grows to 6 feet (2 meters) wide, is covered in sprays of purple, pea-like flowers in spring. Australian indigo

Hydrangea macrophylla

Indigofera australis

flowers just as well in full sun as in the shade, and will grow in most soils except those which are very wet. Prune it after the flowers have finished, to maintain a good shape. It is easily propagated from seed or cuttings.
Varieties/cultivars: 'Signata'.

Lavandula angustifolia syn.
L. officinalis, L. spica, L. vera
ENGLISH LAVENDER,
COMMON LAVENDER (U.K.)

Family: LABIATAE
Origin: Mediterranean region.
Flowering time: Summer.
Climatic zone: 6, 7, 8, 9.

Dimensions: 3 feet (1 meter) high.
Description: What garden is complete without the fragrance of lavender? The beautiful lavender-blue spikes of flowers attract bees to the garden and the leaves have a similar scent to the flowers. Plant it along the side of a path where the perfume can be appreciated. English lavender will thrive in a sandy soil and is a handy shrub for seaside gardens. Prune it after flowering to maintain a compact shape. It is easily propagated from cuttings taken in late summer.
Other colors: Pink, white, violet.
Varieties/cultivars: There are several varieties of this shrub.

Lavandula dentata
FRENCH LAVENDER,
SPANISH LAVENDER,
TOOTHED LAVENDER

Family: LABIATAE
Origin: Spain and Balearic Islands.
Flowering time: Summer.
Climatic zone: 8, 9.
Dimensions: 3 feet (1 meter) high.
Description: *Lavandula dentata* is a popular, hardy, garden plant, grown for its silvery leaves and its wonderful perfume. It is distinguished by a gray, toothed leaf and a mauve spike of aromatic flowers, both of which are used for potpourri. It is tolerant of a wide range of soils, providing drainage is good, and grows well near the sea. Pruning is essential to maintain its shape and prevent it from becoming woody. Lavender requires full sun.

Lavandula dentata

Lavandula stoechas
FRENCH LAVENDER,
TOPPED LAVENDER

Family: LABIATAE
Origin: Mediterranean region, Portugal.
Flowering time: Summer.
Climatic zone: 7, 8, 9.
Dimensions: Up to 2 feet (600 mm) high.
Description: This is a small, intensely aromatic shrub with narrow, grayish-green leaves. The dark-purple flowers are borne in dense, terminal heads. It can be used as a low, fragrant hedge along the side of a path or as a border around a cottage garden. The main requirements of French lavender are a warm, sunny position and a sandy, well-drained soil. Cutting off the flower heads when the flowers have finished will keep it more compact in shape.

Lavandula angustifolia

Lavandula stoechas

Lavatera maritima

Lithospermum diffusum

Lavatera maritima
SHRUBBY MALLOW, FRENCH MALLOW, SEA MALLOW (U.K.)

Family: MALVACEAE
Origin: Southern France.
Flowering time: Summer–autumn.
Climatic zone: 8, 9.
Dimensions: 4–6 feet (up to 2 meters) high.
Description: This elegant shrub has unusual grayish, downy stems and leaves. The large saucer-shaped flowers are pale lilac with purple veins and eye, and remain on the plant for a long period. It makes an ideal feature shrub, but to be grown successfully it must be given a warm, sheltered position, preferably against a wall. Mulch it annually with well-rotted manure or compost or apply a handful of complete plant food.

Lechenaultia biloba
BLUE LECHENAULTIA

Family: GOODENIACEAE
Origin: Western Australia.
Flowering time: Spring.
Climatic zone: 9, 10.
Dimensions: 16 inches (400 mm) high.
Description: This straggly plant, though short-lived in cultivation, is most desirable because of its intense blue flowers. It needs excellent drainage to survive, and is best used in the garden trailing over rocks or walls, or as an informal groundcover.
Varieties/cultivars: 'White Flash'.

Lechenaultia biloba

Lithospermum diffusum
LITHOSPERMUM, HEAVENLY BLUE

Family: BORAGINACEAE
Origin: Southern Europe.
Flowering time: Spring–summer.
Climatic zone: 8, 9.
Dimensions: 3–4 inches (75–100 mm) high.
Description: This prostrate shrub forms a large mat which becomes covered in lovely blue flowers. It is valued for its long flowering period, and for its usefulness as a rockery plant and a groundcover. Old plants tend to die out in bad winters, especially in poorly drained soils, but if they are cut back a little after flowering they seem to be more durable. Add peat or leaf mold to the soil to keep it acidic, as lithospermum dislikes lime.
Other colors: White.
Varieties/cultivars: 'Album', 'Grace Ward', 'Heavenly Blue'.

Mackaya bella
MACKAYA

Family: ACANTHACEAE
Origin: South Africa.
Flowering time: Summer.
Climatic zone: 9, 10.
Dimensions: 4–6 feet (approx. 1–2 meters) high.
Description: An extremely pretty shrub, mackaya is valued for its 5-inch-long (125 mm), oblong leaves and large, spotted, lilac flowers. It makes an elegant feature shrub in warm climates. It is not fussy about soil type, but likes a sheltered position. Feed it in early spring by mulching with manure or compost, or, alternatively, apply a handful of complete plant food. Propagation is carried out from cuttings taken in early spring.

Mackaya bella

Oxypetalum caeruleum

Michelia figo
PORT WINE MAGNOLIA, ○ ◑
BANANA SHRUB (U.K.),
FRUIT SALAD MAGNOLIA

Family: MAGNOLIACEAE
Origin: China.
Flowering time: Spring–summer.
Climatic zone: 9, 10.
Dimensions: 10–15 feet (3–5 meters) high.
Description: An attractive, evergreen shrub, port wine magnolia has a neat, rounded appearance. The young shoots are brown and hairy, and the elliptic, dark-green leaves are smooth and shiny. The purplish-colored flowers, initially enclosed in brown bracts, are strongly scented, emitting their perfume throughout the garden. This is a perfect shrub to plant near a doorway or window so that the perfume can be appreciated. It is easy to grow and its main requirement is a neutral to acid soil that does not dry out.

Plumbago auriculata

Oxypetalum caeruleum
TWEEDIA ○

Family: ASCLEPIADACEAE
Origin: South America, West Indies.
Flowering time: Summer–autumn.
Climatic zone: 9, 10.
Dimensions: 3 feet (1 meter) or more high.
Description: This is a weak-stemmed, small, spreading sub-shrub with grayish-green leaves which are covered in a soft down. The terminal clusters of starry, sky-blue flowers cover the plant from summer to autumn, but in warm climates there are generally flowers on the plant throughout the year. It is pretty planted in the sunny foreground of shrubberies, or included in an annual or perennial garden. Tweedia is a short-lived plant, but it is easily raised from seed or cuttings.

Plumbago auriculata syn. *P. capensis*
CAPE LEADWORT, ○
PLUMBAGO (U.K.)

Family: PLUMBAGINACEAE
Origin: South Africa.
Flowering time: Early summer–autumn.
Climatic zone: 9, 10.
Dimensions: 4–8 feet (approx. 1–2 meters) high.
Description: A slender-stemmed, rambling shrub with neat, evergreen leaves and large trusses of sky-blue, phlox-like flowers, plumbago is a favorite in warm climate gardens. It clambers over other shrubs, makes attractive hedges, sprawls down banks, or becomes a good wall shrub. Given a sunny position with no frost, plumbago will flower off and on throughout the year. Plant it in a well-drained soil, enriched with manure or compost.

Michelia figo

SHRUBS

Polygala myrtifolia var. *grandiflora*

Polygala myrtifolia var. *grandiflora*
BLUE CAPS, MILKWORT (U.K.) ○ ◑

Family: POLYGALACEAE
Origin: South Africa.
Flowering time: Winter–autumn.
Climatic zone: 9, 10.
Dimensions: 4–8 feet (approx. 1–2 meters) high.
Description: The prolonged flowering period of this shrub is its greatest asset. The rich-purple, "sweet pea" like flowers are produced in clusters near the end of the shoots. It will tolerate dappled shade, but under these conditions flowers only for short periods. Blue caps will thrive in any soil type. It should be fed during early spring with a complete plant food. Pruning during this season will encourage more compact growth.

Prostanthera rotundifolia
ROUND-LEAF MINTBUSH, MINTBUSH (U.K.) ○

Family: LABIATAE
Origin: Eastern Australia.
Flowering time: Spring.
Climatic zone: 9.
Dimensions: 6 feet (2 meters) high.
Description: This outstanding but fairly short-lived shrub is covered in heavy masses of purple flowers during spring. The leaves are small and round.

Prostanthera rotundifolia

Use it as a specimen shrub, or as a background shrub in herbaceous borders. The main requirement of the round-leaf mintbush is perfect drainage. Light pruning after flowering will keep it more compact.

Rosmarinus lavandulaceus
PROSTRATE ROSEMARY ○

Family: LABIATAE
Origin: Southern Spain, North Africa.
Flowering time: Spring–summer.
Climatic zone: 9, 10.
Dimensions: 1 foot (300 mm) high.
Description: This evergreen shrub forms a large, dense, mat which

becomes thickly studded with clusters of blue, fragrant flowers. The green leaves have a pale downy underside and are very fragrant. Prostrate rosemary should be planted along the tops of walls or banks where it can cascade down the side. It needs a mild winter climate and does not tolerate frosts. It is a useful plant for seaside gardens.

Rosmarinus lavandulaceus

Rosmarinus officinalis
COMMON ROSEMARY ○

Family: LABIATAE
Origin: Mediterranean coastal regions.
Flowering time: Late spring–early summer.
Climatic zone: 7, 8, 9, 10.
Dimensions: 3–6 feet (1–2 meters) tall.
Description: Rosemary, though more commonly known for its culinary and medicinal uses, is a worthwhile addition

Rosmarinus officinalis

to a garden because of its dark-green foliage and delicate lavender flowers. This plant requires heavy pruning to prevent bare woody growth. It makes a very suitable hedging plant.
Varieties/cultivars: 'Blue Lagoon'.

Strobilanthes anisophyllus

Strobilanthes anisophyllus
GOLDFUSSIA   ○   ◑

Family: ACANTHACEAE
Origin: South East Asia.
Flowering time: Summer–autumn.
Climatic zone: 8, 9, 10.
Dimensions: 2–3 feet (up to 1 meter) high.
Description: A bushy shrub, goldfussia produces an abundance of purple, narrow, lance-shaped leaves. The small groups of long, tubular, lavender flowers with bell-shaped mouths appear between the leaves and stems. In colder climates it is often grown as an indoor plant. Best results are achieved if this shrub is given well-drained soil and regular spring applications of plant food.

Syringa vulgaris 'Charles Joly'
COMMON LILAC,   ○
EUROPEAN LILAC, ENGLISH LILAC

Family: OLEACEAE
Origin: Cultivar.
Flowering time: Late spring–early summer.

Syringa vulgaris 'Charles Joly'

Climatic zone: 4, 5, 6, 7, 8.
Dimensions: 4–10 feet (1–3 meters) high.
Description: Lilac is loved for its highly perfumed flowers. There is probably no other shrub or tree that has given rise to so many cultivars as *Syringa vulgaris*, the parent of 'Charles Joly'. 'Charles Joly' has dark purplish-red flowers which appear later in spring than most other lilac varieties. During winter, cut the tops of the more vigorous stems to produce side shoots, as this new growth carries next season's flowers. Lilac likes a slightly limy, well-drained soil.

Tibouchina urvilleana
LASIANDRA, GLORY BUSH   ○
(U.K.), SPIDER FLOWER

Other common names: PRINCESS FLOWER (U.S.A.)
Family: MELASTOMATACEAE
Origin: Tropical America.
Flowering time: Summer–autumn.
Climatic zone: 9, 10.
Dimensions: 4–15 feet (approx. 1–5 meters) high.
Description: A handsome but straggly shrub, glory bush has very showy, large, vivid purple flowers and large velvety leaves. Its shape can be improved by pruning after flowering. Pinching the new shoots will also promote a denser bush. Even though glory bush needs full sun, its roots must be kept cool. This can be achieved by placing a mulch of leaf litter, compost, or manure around the base in late winter and again in early summer. Neutral to acid soil is essential for rich-green leaves and free-flowering.

Tibouchina urvilleana

Bauhinia variegata

Jacaranda mimosifolia
JACARANDA, FERN TREE ○

Family: BIGNONIACEAE
Origin: Northwestern Argentina.
Flowering time: Late spring.
Climatic zone: 9, 10.
Dimensions: 40–50 feet (12–15 meters) high.
Description: One of the loveliest trees of all time, jacarandas in flower, in a good year, are a breathtaking sight. A whole street planted in jacarandas appears misty blue. The drier the winter, the better they flower. Jacarandas develop a broad dome of lacy, soft green-colored leaves which, although deciduous, can remain on the tree until late winter. Given full sun and good drainage, jacarandas add immense charm to any garden in warm areas. They are excellent shade trees.

Lagerstroemia indica 'Heliotrope Beauty'

Lagerstroemia indica
CREPE MYRTLE ○

Family: LYTHRACEAE
Origin: India, South East Asia, China.
Flowering time: Late summer–early autumn.
Climatic zone: 9, 10.
Dimensions: 20–30 feet (6–9 meters) high.
Description: Many cultivars have been bred from the species, often much

Bauhinia variegata
BUTTERFLY TREE, ORCHID ○
TREE, MOUNTAIN EBONY

Family: CAESALPINACEAE
Origin: Pakistan–Burma, China.
Flowering time: Spring, northern hemisphere; mid-spring–early summer and intermittently autumn, southern hemisphere.
Climatic zone: 9, 10.
Dimensions: 16–27 feet (5–8 meters) high.
Description: Bauhinias are easily identified by their showy, orchid-like flowers and bilobed leaves. *Variegata* in this case refers to the mixed streaks of color in the flowers which are about 2 inches (50 mm) across and usually rosy-purple, but the colors vary somewhat when the plant is grown from seed. The tree grows in warm districts. If cultivated in cooler climates, it develops a rather straggly canopy and becomes semideciduous. It enjoys rich, well-drained soils and a position in full sun, protected from cold or salty winds.
Other colors: White.
Varieties/cultivars: B. v. var. *candida*.

Jacaranda mimosifolia

smaller in habit. *L. indica* is a charming, deciduous tree, happiest in warm-climate gardens. Clusters of crinkly flowers are liberally borne in summer, lingering into autumn. When the leaves have dropped, the beautiful mottled bark is revealed. Many people spoil the tree's natural, graceful, spreading shape by severe pruning in the winter. In humid areas some pruning is necessary, though, for powdery mildew attacks the leaves if the tree is not pruned or treated each year.

Other colors: White, pink, lavender, red, bicolors.

Varieties/cultivars: 'Eavsii', 'Heliotrope Beauty', 'Matthewsii', 'Newmannii', 'Petites' (Californian series).

Melia azedarach var. *australasica*
WHITE CEDAR, CHINABERRY ○

Family: MELIACEAE
Origin: Orient, South East Asia, Australia.
Flowering time: Mid–late spring, southern hemisphere.
Climatic zone: 9, 10.
Dimensions: 30–50 feet (10–15 meters) high.
Description: Rapid adaptability to a wide range of soils and climates has made this species a very popular garden tree. The woolly sprays of flowers are lilac in color, followed by oval, orange-yellow berries during winter. This variety has naturalized on much of the east coast of Australia, from N.S.W. to Queensland, and is in cultivation in many other parts of the country. The main species has adapted to many areas of the United States and is relatively pest-free. In coastal parts of Australia, however, this particular variety, which is deciduous, is attacked by white cedar caterpillars in autumn, which can be controlled by trapping them at night in a hessian bag wrapped around the tree trunk.

Paulownia tomentosa syn. *P. imperialis*
EMPRESS OR PRINCESS ○ TREE, ROYAL PAULOWNIA, FORTUNE'S PAULOWNIA

Other common names: MOUNTAIN JACARANDA
Family: BIGNONIACEAE
Origin: Central China, Korea.
Flowering time: Spring, southern and northern hemispheres.
Climatic zone: 7, 8, 9.
Dimensions: 50 feet (15 meters) high.
Description: This beautiful, deciduous tree, named after a Russian princess, has a single trunk with a broad, spreading crown. Large, heart-shaped leaves are covered in downy hairs. The trumpet-like flowers, borne in upright clusters, are violet-blue, paling to white at the base which is marked with violet and yellowish streaks and spots. Severe winters may damage dormant flower buds. Easily grown from seed, paulownia likes a well-drained soil with ample water in summer. This tree is often mistaken for catalpa, a close relative.

Paulownia tomentosa

Melia azedarach

WHITE FLOWERS

Asperula odorata syn. *Galium odoratum*
WOODRUFF ○ ◐ ●

Family: RUBIACEAE
Origin: Caucasus.
Flowering time: Spring–summer.
Climatic zone: 6, 7, 8, 9, 10.
Dimensions: Up to 12 inches (300 mm) high.
Description: This leafy plant sprawls and is useful for filling gaps among shrubs and perennials. As an annual it also has its own place in summer beds and borders. The masses of tiny, tubular, white flowers are ⅜ inch (9 mm) long and borne in tight, terminal clusters. Beneath each flower is a leafy bract which persists after the flower has died. In hot climates, woodruff prefers shade and ample moisture, but in general it is hardy. The flowers are not suitable for floral work.

Asperula odorata

Chrysanthemum parthenium syn. *Matricaria eximia*
FEVERFEW, MAYWEED ○ ◐

Family: COMPOSITAE
Origin: Southeastern Europe–Caucasus.
Flowering time: Summer–autumn.
Climatic zone: 4, 5, 6, 7, 8, 9.
Dimensions: Up to 3 feet (1 meter) high.
Description: Small, white daisy-like flowers cover this plant in profusion. It is useful for floral work and flowers for many weeks in cooler climates. *Chrysanthemum parthenium* is a herb which can be used as an insect repellant and medicinally for headaches. It is excellent as a border for a vegetable garden. Good soil preparation is vital. Add some dolomite, well-rotted cow manure, and an all-purpose fertilizer

prior to planting. Best results when planted in full sun.
Varieties/cultivars: 'Golden Feather', 'White Stars', 'Selaginoides', 'Aureum'.

Chrysanthemum parthenium

Euphorbia marginata
SNOW-ON-THE-MOUNTAIN, GHOSTWEED ○ ◐

Family: EUPHORBIACEAE
Origin: Central United States.
Flowering time: Summer.
Climatic zone: 6, 7, 8, 9.
Dimensions: Up to 3 feet (1 meter) high.
Description: This plant forms a good background hedge for lower annuals, or a tall border for a shrubbery. The flowers are tiny, up to ¼ inch (7 mm) and greenish white. They are almost concealed by clusters of showy, white and green bracts. The lower leaves are bright green; those nearing the top are white-margined. Snow-on-the-mountain is a very decorative plant and in much demand for floral work. Valued for its ease of cultivation in a wide range of soils and conditions, in either full sun or partial shade.

Gypsophila elegans

Gypsophila elegans
ANNUAL BABY'S BREATH ○

Family: CARYOPHYLLACEAE
Origin: Caucasus, Iran, Turkey.
Flowering time: Summer–autumn.
Climatic zone: 4, 5, 6, 7, 8, 9.
Dimensions: Up to 18 inches (450 mm) high.
Description: Although this rather slim annual has a delicate appearance, it is

Euphorbia marginata

tough. Its stems are stiff and upright and the leaves are small and sparse. The tiny flowers (¼ inch (6 mm) wide) which appear on many-branched stems are usually white and move with the lightest wind. Baby's breath is very popular with florists for use in bunches of mixed flowers and table decorations. It lasts well and is grown as a hardy annual. Well-drained, slightly alkaline soil is preferred. After the first flush of flowers fade, trim back to allow new blooms to be produced.
Other colors: Rose, purple, pink.
Varieties/cultivars: 'Carminea', 'Grandiflora Alba', 'Purpurea', 'Rosea'.

Iberis umbellata
GLOBE CANDYTUFT, ANNUAL CANDYTUFT ○

Family: CRUCIFERAE
Origin: Mediterranean region.
Flowering time: Summer–autumn.
Climatic zone: 5, 6, 7, 8, 9.
Dimensions: Up to 16 inches (400 mm) high.
Description: This is an erect, many-branched annual which prefers cool but sunny climates. The flower clusters, which are up to 2 inches (50 mm) wide, are carried just above the foliage, often in abundance. They are shaped like a pincushion and may be cut for decoration. Plant in full sun in any moderately rich, well-drained soil.
Other colors: Pink, mauve, violet, purple-red.
Varieties/cultivars: 'Atropurpurea', 'Cardinal', 'Lavender', 'Lilac', 'Rosea'.

Iberis umbellata

Lobularia maritima syn. *Alyssum maritimum*
SWEET ALYSSUM ○ ◑

Family: CRUCIFERAE
Origin: Mediterranean region.
Flowering time: Spring–autumn.
Climatic zone: 5, 6, 7, 8, 9.
Dimensions: Up to 6 inches (150 mm) high.
Description: This low-growing annual is very popular with gardeners because it grows easily, readily produces viable seeds, and thus may persist for many years. The small plants grow closely together to form a continuous edging of color. The flowers, though tiny, form tight clusters, and have a honeyed perfume that attracts bees. It is excellent for window boxes or hanging baskets. This adaptable annual can be grown in virtually any well-drained soil, thriving in full sun or partial shade.
Other colors: Pink, purple.
Varieties/cultivars: 'Rosie O'Day', 'Royal carpet'.

Lobularia maritima

Moluccella laevis
BELLS-OF-IRELAND, MOLUCCA BALM, SHELL-FLOWER ○ ◑

Family: LABIATAE
Origin: Turkey–Syria.
Flowering time: Summer–autumn.
Climatic zone: 6, 7, 8, 9, 10.
Dimensions: Up to 2 feet (600 mm) high.
Description: The tiny flowers of this plant are ½ inch (6 mm) wide and are enclosed in cup or shell-shaped, bright green calyces which form conspicuous spikes. The profusion of the flower spikes is a feature of the plant, which is prized by florists and home decorators. Plant in spring in moderately rich soil, and water and feed sparingly during the main growing period.

Moluccella laevis

Nicotiana alata
FLOWERING TOBACCO ◑

Family: SOLANACEAE
Origin: South America.
Flowering time: Spring, summer, autumn.
Climatic zone: 6, 7, 8, 9, 10.
Dimensions: Up to 3 feet (1 meter) high.
Description: This soft-foliaged short-lived perennial grown as an annual forms an ideal background in cottage gardens and perennial borders. It produces many stems about 12 inches (300 mm) long, terminating in fragrant, outward-pointing flowers. These are tubular, up to 4 inches (100 mm) long, and about 2 inches (50 mm) wide at the mouth. Flowering tobacco seeds readily. This fragrant annual likes average garden soil with good drainage.
Other colors: Cream-yellow, rose-red, green, pink, maroon, purple.
Varieties/cultivars: 'Nana' (dwarf form to 18 inches (450 mm) high), 'Rubelle' (red).

Nicotiana alata

Allium triquestrum

Convallaria majalis

Allium triquestrum
TRIQUESTROUS GARLIC

Family: ALLIACEAE
Origin: Mediterranean region.
Flowering time: Spring.
Climatic zone: 8, 9, 10.
Dimensions: Up to 18 inches (450 mm) high.
Description: Numerous small, white flowers which occur in terminal umbels create a pretty spring display. The stem is erect, while the slender mid-green foliage is linear. Adaptable to most soils, it prefers a protected, sunny position and requires regular watering in summer if the conditions are hot and dry. Pretty in a cottage garden landscape, or as a potted specimen on a sunny verandah or balcony.

Cardiocrinum giganteum
GIANT LILY

Family: LILIACEAE
Origin: Himalayas, southeastern Tibet.
Flowering time: Summer.
Climatic zone: 7, 8, 9.
Dimensions: Up to 10 feet (3 meters) high.
Description: Giant lily is a magnificent plant for a damp position in an open

woodland area. The tall, robust stem produces many drooping, long, white flowers, like those of a trumpet lily. Because of its heart-shaped leaves, and the size of the plant, it merits a special place in the garden. The bulbs usually take more than a year to settle down before they flower; it takes five to seven years from seeding to flowering. After flowering, the main bulb dies, but produces small offset bulbs which can be lifted.

Cardiocrinum giganteum

Convallaria majalis
LILY-OF-THE-VALLEY

Family: LILIACEAE
Origin: Northern temperate zone.
Flowering time: Spring.
Climatic zone: 4, 5, 6, 7, 8.
Dimensions: 6–8 inches (150–200 mm) high.
Description: Lily-of-the-valley is a favorite with many gardeners because of its sweet perfume. The delicate, waxy, bell-shaped flowers appear with the broad leaves, and the foliage persists through the summer. It likes a rich soil full of humus and, once established, should not be disturbed for a number of years until the clump becomes overcrowded. In good conditions, the flowers are followed by scarlet berries. The rhizomes should be planted in early winter.
Other colors: Pink, beige.
Varieties/cultivars: 'Everest', 'Fortune's Giant', 'Variegata'.

Crinum x *powellii* 'Album'
CRINUM

Family: AMARYLLIDACEAE
Origin: Hybrid.
Flowering time: Summer.
Climatic zone: 8, 9.
Dimensions: Up to 4 feet (1.2 meters) high.

Description: A tender hybrid, crinum produces six to eight large white flowers on each long stem. This handsome plant is a rich feeder and needs plenty of water. Suited to water landscapes near ponds, among ferns and trees, it can be temperamental if moved and may not flower for a season after being lifted. If left alone it will produce a clump of striking-looking flowers. Propagate from the offset bulbs which will take two to three years to flower. Crimum also does well grown in pots in a greenhouse.
Other colors: Pink.

Crinum x powellii 'Album'

Crocus biflorus
SCOTCH CROCUS

Family: IRIDACEAE
Origin: Italy – Caucasus and Iran.
Flowering time: Spring.
Climatic zone: 5, 6, 7, 8, 9.
Dimensions: Up to 4 inches (100 mm) high.
Description: Scotch crocus is a pretty addition to the rock garden. The closed, white petals of the flower are striped in purple and open to reveal the delicate, yellow-throated center. When flowering in small clumps it resembles a bouquet. Plant it near gates and pathways where visitors can admire its beauty. It may be naturalized in lawns, which should not be mown until the foliage dies down. This species needs a cold winter.
Other colors: Violet, blue.
Varieties/cultivars: *C. b. adamii, C. b. weldonii.*

Crocus biflorus weldonii

Crocus niveus
AUTUMN CROCUS,
CROCUS (U.K.)

Family: IRIDACEAE
Origin: Southern Greece.
Flowering time: Autumn.
Climatic zone: 6, 7, 8, 9.
Dimensions: Up to 6 inches (150 mm) high.

Crocus niveus

Description: Autumn crocus provides delicate color in a bare season. Emerging from light groundcovers, its delicacy is accentuated. It is a useful addition to herb gardens which often die back in autumn. Plant in a sunny spot with warm, well-drained soil where it can self-sow, naturalize it in lawns, but do not mow the grass until the foliage dies back. Definite cold is required in winter.
Other colors: Pale lilac.

Erythronium dens-canis 'White Splendour'

Erythronium dens-canis 'White Splendour'
DOG-TOOTH VIOLET

Family: LILIACEAE
Origin: Cultivar.
Flowering time: Spring.
Climatic zone: 5, 6, 7, 8.
Dimensions: Up to 6 inches (150 mm) high.
Description: Called "dog-tooth" because of its small, tooth-shaped bulb, this violet will flower for up to three weeks. Plant it in rock garden pockets and at the front of shady borders. A beautiful and graceful specimen, it is quite hardy and adapts to woodlands and wet areas. If planted in open positions, it will multiply rapidly. Clumps need to be divided every three to four years. It can be grown successfully indoors in containers and should be watered well.

Erythronium revolutum 'White Beauty'
COAST FAWN LILY, AMERICAN TROUT-LILY, DOG-TOOTH VIOLET (U.K.)

Family: LILIACEAE
Origin: California.
Flowering time: Spring.
Climatic zone: 6, 7, 8, 9.
Dimensions: Up to 6 inches (150 mm) high.
Description: This is one of the finest trout-lilies from America, with its cream flowers accompanying faintly mottled foliage. It establishes itself well in a damp position. Plant it in rock gardens or at the front of shaded borders. When planted in open places it may increase very quickly. Avoid transplanting it as *Erythronium* does not like being moved. Indoor cultivation in pots is possible if it is given rich, moist soil and is well maintained.
Other colors: Pink.

Erythronium revolutum 'White Beauty'

Eucharis grandiflora
AMAZON LILY

Family: AMARYLLIDACEAE
Origin: South America.
Flowering time: Spring–summer.
Climatic zone: 9, 10.
Dimensions: Up to 2 feet (600 mm) high.
Description: "Eucharis" is Greek for pleasing or graceful, a word which describes the beauty of these fragrant white flowers. Four to six snow-white blooms, up to 5 inches (120 mm) across, droop from a long stem. Amazon lily is a glasshouse plant in temperate areas, but can be grown outdoors in semishade in warmer zones. The easiest and most effective way to grow this plant is by planting several bulbs together in a large pot. The bulbs need a constant mild temperature and frequent watering.

Freesia x *hybrida*

Freesia x *hybrida*
FREESIA

Family: IRIDACEAE
Origin: Hybrid.
Flowering time: Spring–late summer, northern hemisphere; spring, southern hemisphere.
Climatic zone: 9, 10.
Dimensions: Up to 2 feet (600 mm) high.
Description: Freesias are highly popular flowers especially for the cut-flower market. Most of the present-day hybrids have been derived from *F. refracta* and *F. armstrongii*. The highly perfumed, trumpet-shaped flowers open successively in branched spikes. Greenhouse cultivation is preferable in very cold climates. Outdoors they can be naturalized in grass and wooded areas or planted in pots and window boxes. Freesias have been heavily

hybridized, but the older cultivars seem to have a stronger scent. Many colors are available.
Other colors: Yellow, orange, pink, blue.
Varieties/cultivars: 'Snow Queen', 'Orange Favourite', 'Pink Giant', 'Sapphire'.

Galanthus elwesii
GIANT SNOWDROP

Family: AMARYLLIDACEAE
Origin: Western Turkey.
Flowering time: Winter–spring.
Climatic zone: 4, 5, 6, 7, 8.
Dimensions: Up to 8 inches (200 mm) high.

Galanthus elwesii

Eucharis grandiflora

Description: *G. elwesii* is one of the largest flowers in the genus. The white drops have green patches at the base and tip and two wing-like petals on either side. Naturalize them in wooded areas, under trees, in rock gardens, and in pots. They prefer partial shade and cool, slightly moist soil with a mulch of well-rotted manure or compost in autumn.

Galanthus nivalis
SNOWDROP

Family: AMARYLLIDACEAE
Origin: Europe and western Asia.
Flowering time: Winter.
Climatic zone: 4, 5, 6, 7, 8.
Dimensions: 4–8 inches (100–200 mm) tall.
Description: The common snowdrop is one of the earliest bulbs to bloom, its delicate, bell-shaped flowers appearing in mid-winter. The pure white petals are tipped with bright green. Snowdrop prefers cool, moist soil, and should be planted in shade, except in the coldest districts where partial sun is of some benefit to open the flowers. It looks best when grown in clumps scattered through beds and borders, or when allowed to naturalize at the base of trees or in the lawn.
Varieties/cultivars: 'Atkinsii', 'S. Arnott'.

Galanthus nivalis

Galtonia candicans
SUMMER HYACINTH (U.K.), CAPE HYACINTH

Family: LILIACEAE
Origin: South Africa.
Flowering time: Summer.
Climatic zone: 7, 8, 9.
Dimensions: Up to 4 feet (approx. 1 meter) high.

Galtonia candicans

Description: Summer hyacinth has numerous showy, fragrant, bell-shaped, white flowers on a single stem. It is well-suited to herbaceous borders and seaside gardens, especially with red-hot-pokers or agapanthus as companions. Plant the bulbs in well-rotted compost about 6 inches (150 mm) deep, in a sunny, open position protected from wind, and water regularly during spring and summer. The plants can be propagated by offsets from the bulbs in late winter, and should not be lifted until they become crowded.

Leucojum aestivum
GIANT SNOWFLAKE, SUMMER SNOWFLAKE (U.K.)

Family: AMARYLLIDACEAE
Origin: Europe.
Flowering time: Spring.
Climatic zone: 4, 5, 6, 7, 8.
Dimensions: Up to 2 feet (600 mm) high.
Description: *Leucojum*, from the Greek for "white violet", probably alludes to the perfume of the giant snowflake. The nodding, bell-like, white blooms, with a green spot near the apex, appear in clusters of between two and five to a stem. Plant between shrubs, in borders among ferns, in rock gardens, or under deciduous trees. A sunny, moist position is best. The bulbs should be planted in very moist soil with plenty of compost and leaf mold. Giant snowflake can be grown indoors in containers.
Varieties/cultivars: 'Gravetye'.

Leucojum aestivum 'Gravetye'

Leucojum vernum
SPRING SNOWFLAKE (U.K.), SNOWFLAKE

Family: AMARYLLIDACEAE
Origin: Southern Europe.
Flowering time: Late winter–early spring.
Climatic zone: 4, 5, 6, 7, 8.
Dimensions: 6–10 inches (150–250 mm) high.
Description: The dainty quality of this plant belies its hardiness. Similar to its sister *L. aestivum*, it is suitable for growing in rock gardens, under deciduous trees, or in containers indoors. The large, usually solitary, fragrant blooms bear a yellow or green spot at the apex of each petal. Like *L. aestivum*, it too has a preference for a damp location. Plant it in humus-rich, sandy, well-drained soil. Once planted, the bulbs need not be disturbed for several years. Propagate by separating offset bulbs when the plant is dormant.

Leucojum vernum

Lilium auratum

Lilium auratum
GOLDEN-RAYED LILY ◑

Family: LILIACEAE
Origin: Japan.
Flowering time: Summer.
Climatic zone: 7, 8, 9.
Dimensions: Up to 5 feet (approx. 2 meters) high.
Description: This lily created a sensation when introduced into Europe from Japan in the mid-19th century. The spectacular flowers can measure up to 12 inches (300 mm) across, and sometimes individual stems will bear 20–30 buds. The large, white, fragrant flowers have golden bands from throat to petal edge and have purplish-red flecks. Give this lily a special place of its own. It likes acid to neutral, not alkaline soil, but is not easy to keep growing for more than a few years.
Other colors: Yellow, orange, red, pink, purple.

Lilium candidum
MADONNA LILY (U.K.), ○ ◑
ANNUNCIATION LILY

Family: LILIACEAE
Origin: Mediterranean region.
Flowering time: Summer.
Climatic zone: 7, 8, 9.

Dimensions: Up to 4 feet (approx. 1 meter) high.
Description: This elegant lily is sweetly perfumed. Grown by the Cretans and Egyptians, it was portrayed on vases and other artifacts around 1750 BC. It was popular in monasteries in the Middle Ages, and in Renaissance art was associated with the Virgin, as the name Madonna lily suggests. The immaculate white flowers are carried on long stems, and it prefers to be undisturbed once it is established. This lovely lily merits a special place of its own in the garden. It can also be planted among herbaceous perennials. It requires plenty of moisture.

Lilium candidum

Lilium formosanum

Lilium formosanum
FORMOSAN LILY ○

Family: LILIACEAE
Origin: Taiwan.
Flowering time: Summer–autumn.
Climatic zone: 7, 8, 9.
Dimensions: Up to 7 feet (approx. 2 meters) high.

Description: This is a tender species susceptible to virus disease. Cultivated in the Orient, it is best grown in a greenhouse environment or among ferns in a sheltered position. If planted close to a house, the fragrance from the trumpet-shaped flowers will waft in through open windows. The long, white blooms are stained purplish-red on the outside and grow horizontally from the top of leafy stems. Most lilies benefit from a light groundcover to shade their roots. This also protects new shoots as they emerge from the soil.

Lilium longiflorum

Lilium longiflorum
TRUMPET LILY, EASTER ◑
LILY

Family: LILIACEAE
Origin: Japan.
Flowering time: Summer.
Climatic zone: 8, 9.
Dimensions: Up to 3 feet (1 meter) high.
Description: These traditional white, trumpet-shaped lilies are used extensively in garden landscapes. They are popular with the cut-flower trade and for church floral decorations. Providing they are not overcrowded, they associate well with other herbaceous perennials. At no time should the bulbs be allowed to dry out. Sun and shade are required in equal amounts, so plant them against a garden wall which receives early morning sun and afternoon shade. Trumpet lilies can also be cultivated in well-drained pots which are kept well watered.
Varieties/cultivars: *L. l.* var. *eximium*.

Lilium regale 'Album'

Lilium regale
REGAL LILY ◯

Family: LILIACEAE
Origin: Western China.
Flowering time: Summer.
Climatic zone: 5, 6, 7, 8, 9.
Dimensions: 3–6 feet (1–2 meters) high.
Description: A popular lily discovered in China by E. H. Wilson in 1904, these fragrant funnel-shaped flowers have rose-purple markings on the outside, with a white throat blending to yellow. The large flower clusters are extremely useful for garden display. Use as a majestic backdrop to a lower front bed and border, but do not overcrowd them. *L. regale* is quite hardy and should be grown in full sun in moist but well-drained soil. It becomes soft if overfed.
Varieties/cultivars: 'Album'.

Lilium speciosum var. *album*

Lilium speciosum var. *album*
JAPANESE LILY, PINK ◯ ◑
TIGER LILY

Family: LILIACEAE
Origin: Japan.
Flowering time: Summer–autumn.
Climatic zone: 7, 8, 9.
Dimensions: 3–5 feet (1–1.5 meters) high.
Description: The long stems of this lily carry 6–10 white flowers with strongly-reflexed petals with crimson spots. The large, drooping flowers are 4–6 inches (100–150 mm) across, and are perfumed. Plant Japanese lily in clumps in full sun or partial shade in leafy glades near trees. It may also be cultivated in large, movable tubs. If the position is too hot, move the tub to a cooler area in summer. This exotic, fragrant lily enhances any garden setting. Keep the soil it is in moist and well-drained.

Narcissus poeticus
POET'S NARCISSUS ◯ ◑

Family: AMARYLLIDACEAE
Origin: Spain–Greece.
Flowering time: Spring.
Climatic zone: 5, 6, 7, 8, 9.
Dimensions: Up to 18 inches (450 mm) high.
Description: *Narcissus poeticus* is named after the mythological youth who fell in love with his own reflection in a pool and became a flower. Fragrant, starry white blooms blend well with early-flowering perennials. Grow the bulbs at random under trees and in wild

Narcissus poeticus 'Actaea'

gardens. The cut flowers are excellent for use indoors where their perfume lingers. Bulbs will grow in full sun or part shade. Plant in light, crumbly, well-drained soil to which has been added some compost. Water regularly during the growing period and fertilize when buds appear.
Other colors: Yellow.
Varieties/cultivars: 'Actaea', 'Queen of Narcissi'.

Narcissus tazetta 'Paper White'

Narcissus tazetta 'Paper White'
WHITE NARCISSUS ◯ ◑

Family: AMARYLLIDACEAE
Origin: Cultivar.
Flowering time: Later winter–early spring.
Climatic zone: 7, 8, 9.
Dimensions: 18 inches (450 mm) high.
Description: An exquisite member of the polyanthus narcissus group, white narcissus has star-like flowers with pure white petals. It flowers quite early, bringing life to the garden before the main flush of spring. The best results are achieved by planting the bulbs in autumn in deep, rich, well-drained soil, and by making sure that the ground is lightly damp — never wet — during the cool winter. Choose a sunny position, except in warmer climates where the shade of a deciduous tree is beneficial. Never cut back the greenery after flowering, and remember to divide the clumps every four years. Often grown indoors in cool climates.
Varieties/cultivars: 'Paper White Grandiflora'.

Ornithogalum thyrsoides
WONDER FLOWER, CHINCHERINCHEE (U.K.) ○

Family: LILIACEAE
Origin: South Africa.
Flowering time: Summer.
Climatic zone: 9, 10.
Dimensions: Up to 18 inches (450 mm) high.
Description: Wonder flower is a splendid bloomer, producing masses of cream or yellow buds opening from the base of the conical head. When cut it will last for several weeks even without water. Cultivate it as a border plant, in a cool greenhouse, or in pots on sunny window ledges. This species is tender and needs good drainage to prevent rot. Use a compost of sandy loam and leaf mold, and water well once the plant is established. Give it fertilizer when the buds appear.

Ornithogalum thyrsoides

Ornithogalum umbellatum

Ornithogalum umbellatum
STAR-OF-BETHLEHEM ○

Family: LILIACEAE
Origin: Europe, U.K., North Africa.
Flowering time: Late spring–early summer.
Climatic zone: 5, 6, 7, 8.
Dimensions: Up to 8 inches (200 mm) high.
Description: A seemingly delicate, but quite hardy, little perennial, star-of-Bethlehem will spread rapidly when naturalized. The flowers, twelve to twenty in a cluster, open late in the morning and close late in the afternoon.

A pretty effect can be achieved by planting it under trees or shrubs or in a wild garden. Considered in parts of North America as an invasive garden pest, it is used by some herbalists as a remedy for sadness or depression. Allow it free range in an open, sunny area.

Polianthes tuberosa
TUBEROSE ○

Family: AGAVACEAE
Origin: Central America.
Flowering time: Summer–autumn.
Climatic zone: 9, 10.
Dimensions: Up to 3 feet (1 meter) high.
Description: Tuberose is easy to grow where the summers are long and warm. A favorite with brides for bouquets and headdresses, it is also cultivated widely in France for the perfume industry. The exquisite fragrance is produced from white, single or double flowers. Plant tuberose in the garden in rich soil near open windows and doors. The tubers will not flower in the second year and are usually discarded after flowering.

Offsets can be planted when frosts have finished. This is a good pot plant for greenhouses in colder climates.
Varieties/cultivars: 'The Pearl' (double).

Polianthes tuberosa 'The Pearl'

Watsonia hybrids
BUGLE LILY ○

Family: IRIDACEAE
Origin: South Africa.
Flowering time: Summer–autumn, northern hemisphere; spring–summer, southern hemisphere.
Climatic zone: 9, 10.
Dimensions: Up to 6 feet (2 meters) high.
Description: A colorful and showy plant for high borders and wild gardens, *Watsonia* thrives in warmer areas, but dislikes the cold. Like its relative the *Gladiolus*, it will form clumps and is easy to grow in the right environment. It appreciates plenty of water and sun, and rich, but well-drained soil. Popular as cut flowers, *Watsonia* hybrids offer a profusion of colors. Deciduous and evergreen hybrids are available, the former being the hardier as they can be lifted and rested. *Watsonia* is a good greenhouse plant in cold climates.
Other colors: Red, orange, pink, purple.

Watsonia hybrids

Zantedeschia aethiopica
ARUM LILY (U.K.), LILY OF THE NILE ○

Family: ARACEAE
Origin: South Africa.
Flowering time: Spring–late summer, northern hemisphere; summer, southern hemisphere.
Climatic zone: 9, 10.
Dimensions: Up to 4 feet (approx. 1 meter) high.
Description: This perennial water-plant

Zantedeschia aethiopica

is suited to ponds, marshy areas, and damp sites in the garden. It was called "pig lily" by the early settlers in South Africa when they found porcupines (which they called pigs) eating the fleshy roots. The flower, because of its interesting bracts, is widely cultivated

for the cut flower market, and is often seen in church floral arrangements. Plant arum lily tubers in permanently damp soil or in very shallow water. It needs generous feeding and will flower profusely.

Zephyranthes candida
WIND FLOWER (U.K.), ○ ◐ RAIN LILY, ZEPHYR LILY

Family: AMARYLLIDACEAE
Origin: Argentina, Uruguay.
Flowering time: Autumn.
Climatic zone: 8, 9, 10.
Dimensions: Up to 12 inches (300 mm) high.
Description: This dainty perennial looks like a crocus. When massed in rock gardens and edges the white, star-like flowers provide a showy display, and planted in a warm, sheltered border against a wall the plant will multiply rapidly. Suited to pot-planting in temperate climates, it needs well-drained soil enriched with organic matter. Water well during the flowering period and apply a complete fertilizer when buds first appear.

Zephyranthes candida

Aristolochia elegans
CALICO DUTCHMAN'S PIPE

○ ◑ ●

Family: ARISTOLOCHIACEAE
Origin: Brazil.
Flowering time: Summer.
Climatic zone: 7, 8, 9, 10.
Description: A most attractive evergreen vine that can grow to 10 feet (3 meters) in the right conditions. The woody, twining stems are covered with large, heart-shaped leaves while the reddish-purple flowers are marked with white and yellow. The vine also carries interesting fruit, in basket-like pods. Plant in a sheltered, semi-shaded position in rich, moist soil with plenty of organic matter added. Will not withstand frost, or drought conditions.

Beaumontia grandiflora

Aristolochia elegans

Beaumontia grandiflora
HERALD'S-TRUMPET, EASTER-LILY VINE

○ ◑

Family: APOCYNACEAE
Origin: India.
Flowering time: Spring.
Climatic zone: 9, 10.
Description: An arching, semi-twining, evergreen vine, *Beaumontia* will spread to 30 feet (10 meters). Its large, dark-green leaves are smooth and shiny, and its white, fragrant, trumpet-shaped flowers, 5 inches (125 mm) long, somewhat resemble Easter lilies. Prune after flowering to promote new shoots. The flowering shoots grow on old wood, so avoid removing all old wood. It appreciates deep, rich soil and plenty of fertilizer. A warm wall with strong support for climbing is the most suitable position.

Clematis armandii
EVERGREEN CLEMATIS, ARMAND CLEMATIS

○ ◑

Family: RANUNCULACEAE
Origin: Central and western China.
Flowering time: Spring.
Climatic zone: 7, 8, 9.
Description: One of the most beautiful, evergreen, flowering climbers, this clematis has the same requirements as other woodland plants. It needs deep, rich soil, shaded from the sun, but is able to take hot sunny conditions on the upper canopy. Severe winters will kill it. The pure white flowers, 2 inches (50 mm) across, are clustered three to a stalk. They are perfumed with a fragrance like honey and almonds, and gradually change color from white to rose-pink. As the blooms are on old wood, prune lightly after flowering, and when the vine becomes too dense, prune out old and dead wood.
Varieties/cultivars: 'Apple Blossom' (rose pink), 'Snowdrift' (white).

Clematis armandii 'Snowdrift'

Clematis montana
ANEMONE CLEMATIS ○ ◑

Family: RANUNCULACEAE
Origin: Himalayas, China.
Flowering time: Spring.
Climatic zone: 5, 6, 7, 8, 9.
Description: Vigorous, hardy, and easy to grow, anemone clematis blooms magnificently in early spring. The flowers are white when they open and change to delicate pink. Prune the vine after flowering, as flowers appear on old wood. For heavy pruning, selectively remove some branches to thin out the vine and reduce its overall size. This lovely deciduous climber tolerates warmer conditions than most clematis, but prefers cool or mountain climates. Plant it where the roots will remain in shade, but where it can reach up to the sun.
Varieties/cultivars: 'Rubens' (rose pink), 'Tetrarose' (rose pink, more vigorous than 'Rubens').

Clematis montana

Clerodendrum thomsonae
BLEEDING-HEART VINE ○

Family: VERBENACEAE
Origin: Tropical West Africa.
Flowering time: Summer.
Climatic zone: 9, 10.
Description: This eye-catching flower is a crimson tube encased in a large, white calyx with very long white stamens. The blooms hang in forking clusters from this delicate, evergreen vine, which requires frost-free conditions and a warm, sheltered, humid position. Suitable for container growing, it can be grown successfully as an indoor plant. Prune regularly to obtain a compact plant. Feed and water it well until it is established, then reduce the feeding and watering to mature the wood and induce flowering.

Clerodendrum thomsonae

Hoya australis
AUSTRALIAN WAX PLANT, PORCELAIN FLOWER (U.S.A.) ◑

Family: ASCLEPIADACEAE
Origin: Northern and eastern Australia.
Flowering time: Summer.
Climatic zone: 9, 10.
Description: The very fragrant, long-stalked, waxy-white flowers of *H. australis* form a dome-shaped cluster about 4 inches (100 mm) across. The leaves are thick, textured, and look attractive all year round. This strong-growing vine climbs by twining stems and can be trained onto a frame. It makes a good pot plant, but needs support and requires a warm, moist, shaded position.

Hoya australis

Hoya carnosa
COMMON WAX PLANT, WAXFLOWER ○ ◑

Family: ASCLEPIADACEAE
Origin: Southern China–northern Australia.
Flowering time: Early summer–autumn.
Climatic zone: 9, 10.
Description: Common wax plant is one of the most highly prized of small climbing plants. It twines by using aerial roots. Its fleshy, waxy leaves hang sparsely from the firm stems of this lovely vine which has fragrant star-shaped waxy, white flowers with deep-pink centers. As the flowers emerge from the same stalk each year, cutting or pruning will reduce the blooms for the following year. It thrives in a pot in a sunny or shady position, but must have well-drained soil, and does not seem to mind being in a too-small container.
Varieties/cultivars: Variegated form.

Hoya carnosa

Hydrangea petiolaris syn. *H. anomala* var. *petiolaris*
CLIMBING HYDRANGEA ○ ◐

Family: SAXIFRAGACEAE
Origin: Japan, Taiwan.
Flowering time: Summer.
Climatic zone: 5, 6, 7, 8, 9.
Description: Climbing hydrangea is a vigorous, deciduous vine which grows well only in cooler climates. Its flat, white flowers are borne on long stems and form clusters about 6–10 inches (150–250 mm) across. The attractive, heart-shaped leaves are 2–4 inches (50–100 mm) wide. A sturdy climber, the vine attaches itself to upright surfaces by aerial rootlets, but grown without support, it can be trained as a shrub if pruned annually to remove the long stems.

Hydrangea petiolaris

Jasminum grandiflorum
SPANISH JASMINE ○ ◐

Family: OLEACEAE
Origin: South East Asia.
Flowering time: Spring, summer, autumn.
Climatic zone: 7, 8, 9.
Description: Spanish jasmine grows very rapidly. The leaves are made up of five to seven leaflets, and the large, single flowers, which are intensely fragrant, are pink in the bud and open to white. Although each flower lasts only a short time, the vine bears flowers for several months. The long, arching branches can be cut to maintain a shrubby growth, or can be retained and trained onto walls or pergolas. Spanish jasmine always has a light, open, lacy appearance.

Jasminum grandiflorum

Jasminum nitidum syn. *J. ilicifolium*
ANGEL-WING JASMINE, STAR JASMINE (U.K.) ○ ◐

Family: OLEACEAE
Origin: South Pacific.
Flowering time: Spring, summer.
Climatic zone: 9, 10.
Description: Angel-wing jasmine's windmill-like, fragrant white flowers are 1 to 1½ inches (25–40 mm) long, and are grouped in small sprays. The buds have a purplish color, and open out to bright-white, flat-topped flowers. With its attractive, glossy leaves this evergreen vine makes a good specimen for a container plant. It can be grown as a shrub or a climber, but it will need to be trained if it is to climb up a post or over a wall. Suited to warm conditions only, it is attractive all year round.

Jasminum polyanthum
PINK JASMINE, CHINESE JASMINE, SWEET-SCENTED JASMINE ○ ◐

Family: OLEACEAE
Origin: Western China.
Flowering time: Early spring–late summer.
Climatic zone: 8, 9, 10.
Description: Grown in sun or shade this jasmine can become invasive if not kept under control. The pink buds open to white flowers in a great burst in the springtime, giving out an exceptionally pervasive perfume. This magnificent display lasts for about a month. A vigorous climber, pink jasmine will build up a thick layer of dense, twiggy growth, with new foliage appearing on the surface. A strong support is necessary and, occasionally, very hard pruning. Branches will take root where they make contact with the soil. It will not survive severe winters.

Jasminum polyanthum

Jasminum nitidum

Jasminum sambac

Mandevilla laxa syn. *M. suaveolens*
CHILEAN JASMINE, ◯ ◗
HUG ME TIGHT, MANDEVILLA

Family: APOCYNACEAE
Origin: Bolivia, Argentina, Peru.
Flowering time: Summer.
Climatic zone: 8, 9.
Description: A vigorous grower in warm climates, Chilean jasmine prefers the shelter of surrounding foliage in cooler climates, and will happily use shrubs or trees to climb through or up to get to the sun. It also grows well on a sheltered wall. The white, intensely fragrant flowers are funnel-shaped and appear in sprays during summer. They tend to be at the tops of the long, arching, slender branches. The vine is widely grown in mild climates, but needs to have its size or spread reduced if it is to be kept under control. Rich, sandy loam and regular water are essential. It cannot withstand severe winters.

Jasminum sambac
ARABIAN JASMINE, ◯ ◗
PIKAKE

Family: OLEACEAE
Origin: India.
Flowering time: Spring, summer, autumn.
Climatic zone: 9, 10.
Description: An evergreen, shrubby vine up to 8 feet (2.4 meters) high, this is a very versatile plant. With support and training it can grow as a climber or it can be pruned to form a compact shrub, and is also excellent as a container plant. The white, intensely-perfumed flowers appear in tight clusters at the ends of branchlets, and are used for the flavoring in jasmine tea. The leaves are shiny, pointed and very decorative. Jasmine has a long flowering period, but can only be grown in warm conditions.
Varieties/cultivars: 'Grand Duke of Tuscany'.

Lonicera japonica 'Halliana'
HALL'S ◯ ◗
HONEYSUCKLE, JAPANESE
HONEYSUCKLE

Family: CAPRIFOLIACEAE
Origin: Cultivar.
Flowering time: Spring and summer.
Climatic zone: 4, 5, 6, 7, 8, 9.

Description: This honeysuckle has white flowers which turn yellow as they age. They are very fragrant and their nectar is enjoyed by both birds and children! It is a very quick-growing vine, and will cover a fence or a shed in one good growing season. It needs to be controlled, or it will find its way to the top of adjoining trees. Its evergreen habit makes it useful for the quick disguising of old sheds.

Mandevilla laxa

Lonicera japonica 'Halliana'

Pandorea jasminoides
BOWER PLANT, BOWER-OF-BEAUTY ○ ◐

Family: BIGNONIACEAE
Origin: Australia (Queensland, N.S.W.).
Flowering time: Summer–autumn.
Climatic zone: 9, 10.
Description: An attractive, fast-growing, evergreen climber, this *Pandorea* will tolerate coastal conditions or cooler inland conditions. It is a very useful, versatile climber, and produces a mass of trumpet-shaped white flowers with pink throats, standing out from the shiny, dark-green leaves. Protection from strong wind and frost will be needed, but in a sheltered position it will withstand occasional cold nights. Good soil and summer water give best results.
Varieties/cultivars: 'Rosea' (pink), 'Alba' (pure white).

Pandorea jasminoides

Pandorea pandorana
WONGA-WONGA VINE ○ ◐ ●

Family: BIGNONIACEAE
Origin: Southern and eastern Australia–New Guinea.
Flowering time: Throughout the year.
Climatic zone: 9, 10.
Description: Small, cream flowers with purple or maroon-striped throats are produced in abundance on this shiny, evergreen vine. The foliage is attractive all year, and the vine is fast-growing. Rich soil will help it become established, and it is happy in either a sunny or shady position. Pruning is advisable after flowering to tidy up the branchlets, and to induce further compact growth.

Without support the vine can become a sprawling shrub, but needs pruning if a rounded shape is required. A warm climate plant, it cannot tolerate frost.

Pandorea pandorana

Passiflora edulus
PASSION FRUIT, PURPLE GRANADILLA, PASSION FLOWER ○

Family: PASSIFLORACEAE
Origin: Brazil–northern Argentina.
Flowering time: Summer.
Climatic zone: 9, 10.
Description: Passion fruit's attractive white and green flowers with a purple zoned center are partially hidden by the dense foliage. The flowers are followed by thick-skinned, purple fruit which is edible, and which falls to the ground when ripe. Tolerant of occasional very light frost only, this very quick-growing vine can be used for covering fences, pergolas, or be trained through lattice or wire frames. Excellent drainage and regular summer watering will produce good fruit. Passion fruit is often a relatively short-lived vine.
Varieties/cultivars: *P. e.* var. *flavicarpa* (yellowish fruits).

Passiflora edulus

Polygonum aubertii syn. *Fallopia aubertii*
SILVER FLEECE VINE, SILVER LACE VINE, RUSSIAN VINE (U.K.) ○

Family: POLYGONACEAE
Origin: Western China–Tibet.
Flowering time: Late summer.
Climatic zone: 4, 5, 6, 7, 8, 9.
Description: A rapid grower, silver lace vine can quickly cover an area of 100 square feet (9 square meters), with its heart-shaped, glossy leaves. It is covered with masses of small, creamy-white flowers in long sprays in summer. Grow it to provide quick cover for fences or arbors, or as groundcover. It is not fussy about soil, and is tolerant of coastal conditions. Although it is evergreen in mild climates, it may be deciduous in cooler areas. Prune it hard to control its size; it can become invasive.

Polygonum aubertii

Rosa banksiae 'Alba Plena'
BANKS' ROSE, LADY BANKS' ROSE, BANKSIA ROSE ○
(Aust.)

Family: ROSACEAE
Origin: Cultivar.
Flowering time: Summer.
Climatic zone: 8, 9.
Description: Double, white flowers cover this popular, thornless rose in summer. It is a vigorous plant, resistant to many of the diseases that plague most

roses. In a sheltered position on a sunny wall this old favorite will grow in quite cool climates. Prune old growth regularly to help reduce the many stems rising from the base, and make the vine easier to control. If space permits, allow it to flow, sprawl, and climb to fill a wide space.

Rosa banksiae 'Alba Plena'

Rosa laevigata
CHEROKEE ROSE ○

Family: ROSACEAE
Origin: China.
Flowering time: Summer.
Climatic zone: 7, 8, 9.
Description: The single, fragrant, white flowers of this beautiful old rose grow up to 5 inches (125 mm) wide, have prominent yellow stamens, and are followed by bright red hips. Although this rose was common in the temperate zones of China, surprisingly, it was found in the southern states of the United States, where it is now the state flower of Georgia. Trained up a pillar, or over a pergola, this delightful rose will be evergreen in mild climates. It is not tolerant of cold zones.

Rosa laevigata

Rosa wichuraiana

Rosa wichuraiana
MEMORIAL ROSE ○

Family: ROSACEAE
Origin: Japan, China, Korea, Taiwan.
Flowering time: Summer.
Climatic zone: 6, 7, 8, 9.
Description: This nearly prostrate, semi-evergreen, rambler has long, horizontal branches and can be trained as an upright vine. Individual, fragrant flowers are 2 inches (50 mm) across and are held in clusters above the foliage.

Train it over old trees, or stumps, or use it to cover sloping banks. Because the branches root if left in contact with soil, the vine makes a good groundcover.
Varieties/cultivars: Many hybrid cultivars have been developed from this hardy plant.

Solanum jasminoides, 'Album'
POTATO CREEPER, ○
POTATO VINE, JASMINE
NIGHTSHADE (U.K.)

Family: SOLANACEAE
Origin: Cultivar.
Flowering time: Summer–autumn.
Climatic zone: 8, 9.
Description: The potato creeper is a quick-growing, evergreen climber, popular in warm climates. It is not fussy about soil, but requires a warm, sunny position. Severe winters will kill it. The dainty foliage and clusters of white flowers make a delightful contrast with the stems which become strong and woody over the years. Some support is needed to help the vine climb a wall or fence, or it can be trailed over a low wall or fence. Try it as a container plant, either spilling over the edges, or trained up a slender frame.

Solanum jasminoides, 'Album'

179

Stephanotis floribunda

Flowering time: Summer–autumn.
Climatic zone: 9, 10.
Description: This white variety of the skyflower is perhaps not quite so vigorous a grower as *Thunbergia grandiflora*, but it will cover a fence or pergola and give good shade. The flowers are slightly drooping, and hang singly or in small clusters. An attractive, evergreen vine, it needs a sheltered position protected from wind and frost if grown in cooler climates. In hot, inland districts, a semishaded position is tolerated. Prune gently to reduce the size; heavy pruning will result in few flowers the following year.

Trachelospermum asiaticum
JAPANESE STAR ◯ ◑ ●
JASMINE

Family: APOCYNACEAE
Origin: Japan, Korea.
Flowering time: Summer.
Climatic zone: 8, 9.
Description: Creamy-yellow flowers and smaller, darker leaves distinguish this vine from the Chinese star jasmine. Generally it is a tidier vine, more easily held to a flat surface. The sweetly-scented flowers appear for several months, but not in such profusion as on the Chinese jasmine. Although it is a vigorous climber, it is slow to start, and needs well-drained, rich soil, with regular watering in summer. Tolerant of cool conditions, it will withstand quite heavy shade. However, it cannot withstand severe winters.

Stephanotis floribunda
MADAGASCAR ◯ ◑
JASMINE, CHAPLET FLOWER,
CLUSTERED WAXFLOWER

Family: ASCLEPIADACEAE
Origin: Madagascar.
Flowering time: Late spring–early autumn.
Climatic zone: 9, 10.
Description: The delightful fragrance of this beautiful trumpet-shaped flower has made it a highly prized bloom for floral arrangements, especially wedding bouquets. The flowers hang in clusters of eight to ten from late spring to early autumn. Rich, free-draining soil is required and although the roots should be in a shady, cool position, the vine needs to be able to climb up in the sunlight. This is a light climber which will enhance an archway or patio, or can be grown in a container. In cool climates, this makes a good house or greenhouse plant.

Thunbergia grandiflora 'Alba'

Thunbergia grandiflora 'Alba'
BENGAL CLOCK ◯ ◑
VINE, SKYFLOWER, TRUMPET
VINE (U.K.)

Family: ACANTHACEAE
Origin: Cultivar.

Trachelospermum asiaticum

Trachelospermum jasminoides
STAR JASMINE, ○ ◐ ●
CHINESE STAR JASMINE,
CONFEDERATE JASMINE

Family: APOCYNACEAE
Origin: Southern China, Japan.
Flowering time: Spring, early summer.
Climatic zone: 9.
Description: Wiry stems with their milky sap will develop into a sturdy trunk after many years. The very fragrant, star-shaped flowers are borne in profusion during spring and early summer. Glossy dark-green foliage makes an excellent background for the bright white blossoms. Support is necessary to grow this vine as a climber, but it will enhance a wall or fence, and is also excellent as a groundcover, a spill-over, or pruned to a small shrub. It can also be trained up a slender pole as a container plant. In cool climates, a greenhouse is preferred.
Varieties/cultivars: 'Variegatum' (variegated leaf color).

Trachelospermum jasminoides

Wisteria floribunda 'Alba' syn.
W. f. 'Longissima Alba'
JAPANESE WISTERIA ○

Family: LEGUMINOSAE
Origin: Cultivar.
Flowering time: Early summer.
Climatic zone: 4, 5, 6, 7, 8, 9.
Description: The clusters of white flowers on this vigorous, deciduous vine appear at the same time as the early leaves. The flowers begin opening at the base of the cluster and gradually continue opening towards the tip, thus prolonging the blooming period, but not making quite such a spectacular display as those of *W. floribunda*. Developing a dense canopy, it will quickly cover a pergola, fence, or wall, or it can be trained up the face of a building. Regular pruning is required during the summer to remove long, arching branches, and to restrict the overall size.

Wisteria floribunda 'Alba'

Wisteria sinensis 'Alba'
CHINESE WISTERIA ○

Family: LEGUMINOSAE
Origin: Cultivar.
Flowering time: Late spring.
Climatic zone: 5, 6, 7, 8, 9.
Description: The white flowers of Chinese wisteria appear before the leaves, and the 12 inch (300 mm) long clusters open from base to tip at the same time. The flowering period is short, but the masses of flowers with their slight fragrance make a wonderful display. Annual pruning in winter to reduce size, as well as regular summer pruning, is necessary to control this vigorous vine. Cold winters may damage flower buds. Grow only grafted or layered plants or cuttings, as seedlings may not bloom for many years.

Wisteria sinensis 'Alba'

Wisteria venusta syn. *W. brachybotrys* 'Alba'
SILKY WISTERIA, ○
JAPANESE WISTERIA

Family: LEGUMINOSAE
Origin: Japan.
Flowering time: Spring.
Climatic zone: 5, 6, 7, 8, 9.
Description: Large, white, long-stalked flowers are carried on 6-inch-long (150 mm) sprays. Such a spectacular display of massed blossoms makes this one of the best of the white wisterias. Silky hairs on the surface of the leaflets give the species its name. The leaves have nine to thirteen broad leaflets. Trained to a tree shape, this plant will bloom profusely, and is a magnificent specimen, especially when it becomes old. It needs constant pruning if it is to develop tree proportions, but looks beautiful, even when bare-branched in the winter.

Wisteria venusta

Achillea ageratifolia

Achillea millefolium

Anaphalis cinnamomea
PEARLY EVERLASTING ◐

Family: COMPOSITAE
Origin: India, Burma.
Flowering time: Late summer.
Climatic zone: 5, 6, 7, 8, 9, 10.
Dimensions: Up to 2½ feet (750 mm) high.
Description: This attractive herbaceous perennial forms a wide clump of downy grey-green leaves and in summer is covered with globular clusters of white flowers. An adaptable plant which can be grown with success in a wide range of soils and conditions, it prefers a semishaded, protected position and good soil drainage. It can be propagated either by seed or by division.

Achillea ageratifolia
YARROW ○

Family: COMPOSITAE
Origin: Greece.
Flowering time: Summer.
Climatic zone: 5, 6, 7, 8, 9, 10.
Dimensions: Up to 6 inches (150 mm) high.
Description: A handsome, low-growing, spreading shrub, it has a covering of grey-green foliage, and masses of small, white, daisy-like flowers with yellow centers. Plant it in an open, sunny position in light, well-drained soil that has been enriched with plenty of organic matter. It is easily propagated either by division during autumn or spring, or by cuttings.

Actaea rubra
RED BANEBERRY, ◐ ●
RED COHOSH (U.S.A.)

Family: RANUNCULACEAE
Origin: North America.
Flowering time: Spring.
Climatic zone: 3, 4, 5, 6, 7, 8.
Dimensions: 18 inches to 2 feet (450–600 mm) high.
Description: The two main features of this plant are its stems of small, white flowers in spring and its clusters of glistening scarlet berries in autumn. The berries are poisonous, hence the name baneberry. Although adaptable and very hardy, it grows best in cool, shaded positions in moist and fertile soils. The clumps of green, coarse, ferny leaves contrast well with other foliage. Propagation is by division, or from seeds which take many months to germinate.
Varieties/cultivars: *A. r.* var. *album*, *A. r.* var. *neglecta*.

Anaphalis cinnamomea

Achillea millefolium
COMMON YARROW, ○
MILFOIL

Family: COMPOSITAE
Origin: Europe, Caucasus, Himalayas, Siberia.
Flowering time: Summer.
Climatic zone: 3, 4, 5, 6, 7, 8, 9, 10.
Dimensions: 2 feet (600 mm) high.
Description: This plant, with its invasive roots, spreads quickly and can be a troublesome weed if it infests a lawn. Each root produces a clump of feathery, dark-green leaves and the strong, wiry stems produce a white flower head. It is strongly resistant to both cold and drought and will grow in all types of soil, particularly sandy soils near the sea. Propagation is easy by division in spring or autumn.
Other colors: Pink, red.
Varieties/cultivars: 'Cerise Queen', 'Red Beauty', 'Fire King'.

Actaea rubra var. *album*

Anaphalis nubigena

Anaphalis nubigena
PEARLY ○
EVERLASTING

Family: COMPOSITAE
Origin: Himalayas.
Flowering time: Summer.

Climatic zone: 4, 5, 6, 7, 8, 9.
Dimensions: 8–12 inches (200–300 mm) high.
Description: This tufted plant has silvery-gray, woolly leaves with inrolled margins. The little starry, daisy-like flowers are on wide branching stems above the foliage. They are excellent for cutting and can be successfully dried. The plant quickly makes a large clump if grown in any good garden soil in an open position, but will droop if the roots are allowed to dry out. It can be propagated from seed but is usually divided in spring.

Androsace lanuginosa

Anaphalis triplinervis

Anaphalis triplinervis
PEARLY EVERLASTING ○ ◑

Family: COMPOSITAE
Origin: Himalayas.
Flowering time: Late summer–autumn.
Climatic zone: 3, 4, 5, 6, 7, 8, 9.
Dimensions: Up to 18 inches (450 mm) high.
Description: This is a tufted plant which forms a clump of silver-gray foliage. This later becomes buried beneath the wide sprays of crisp, white daisies which are excellent for cutting and drying. To dry them, hang the cut flower heads upside down. An ideal plant for the edge of a border, pearly everlasting makes a pleasing combination with pink flowers. It is an easy plant to grow, but will not tolerate drought.
Varieties/cultivars: 'Summer Snow'

Androsace lanuginosa
ROCK JASMINE ○

Family: PRIMULACEAE
Origin: Himalayas.
Flowering time: Summer.
Climatic zone: 4, 5, 6, 7, 8.
Dimensions: Up to 4 inches (100 mm) high.
Description: This low-growing, tussock-forming alpine perennial has trailing stems of silvery foliage in rosettes. The white to pale pink flowers occur in dense terminal clusters. It is an excellent rock garden plant in the right conditions, due to showy flowering and cascading habit. It prefers well-composted, well-drained soils and an open, sunny position. Cuttings can be taken in spring.

Anemone sylvestris
SNOWDROP ANEMONE, SNOWDROP WINDFLOWER ◑ ●

Family: RANUNCULACEAE
Origin: Europe–Siberia.
Flowering time: Late spring–summer.
Climatic zone: 3, 4, 5, 6, 7, 8.
Dimensions: 18 inches (450 mm) high.
Description: In light soil, this anemone spreads freely and quickly but is more restrained in heavier clay soils. The erect to somewhat nodding white flowers are pleasantly fragrant and set

Anemone sylvestris

off by a group of yellow stamens in the center. The blooms are followed by clusters of woolly seed heads. It is best propagated by seed, although the clumps formed in light soil can be easily divided.
Varieties/cultivars: 'Grandiflora'.

Anemone vitifolia 'Robustissima'

Anemone vitifolia 'Robustissima'
JAPANESE ANEMONE ○ ◑

Family: RANUNCULACEAE
Origin: Himalayas–China.
Flowering time: Late summer–autumn.
Climatic zone: 5.
Dimensions: 2–3 feet (approx. 1 meter) high.
Description: The Japanese anemone, a delight in the autumn garden when the summer blooms are fading, has showy flowers borne on longish stem clusters. The plant grows in clumps which are slow to develop in their first year, but then spread rapidly and prefer to remain undisturbed. It prefers rich, well-drained soil, with ample water in dry conditions, especially if it is grown in full sun. It makes an attractive show planted with Michaelmas daisies and old-fashioned autumn climbing roses. Japanese anemone is a good cut flower.

Anemone x *hybrida*
JAPANESE ANEMONE, ◑ ●
JAPANESE WINDFLOWER

Family: RANUNCULACEAE
Origin: U.K.
Flowering time: Late summer–autumn.
Climatic zone: 5, 6, 7, 8, 9.
Dimensions: Up to 4 feet (over 1 meter) high.
Description: This is one of the most elegant and beautiful of the autumn perennials, with its rounded blooms produced on ascending branching stems over a period of many weeks. Once established, the plant can spread quite rapidly, making fine clumps of trifoliate dark-green leaves. Derived from the

Anemone x *hybrida*

species *A. hupehensis*, which is pink-flowered, there are now many shades of color in this garden hybrid, the single white being one of the most popular. This anemone prefers good soil and moist conditions.
Other colors: Deep pink, rosy pink, red.
Varieties/cultivars: 'Honorine Jobert', 'Queen Charlotte', 'Whirlwind', 'Margarete', 'Lorelei'.

Arabis caucasica
ROCK CRESS ○

Family: CRUCIFERAE
Origin: Caucasus.
Flowering time: Late spring–summer.
Climatic zone: 4, 5, 6, 7, 8, 9.
Dimensions: 6–10 inches (150–250 mm) high.
Description: The most widely grown rock cress, this vigorous trailing plant is suited to a spacious walled garden which will allow it plenty of room. It will also grow on a sunny bank and does best in poor soil and an open position. Cut it back after flowering. The cuttings will easily take root in a pot or in the ground, or the plant can also be divided. The leaves are grayish-green and the flowers slightly scented.
Varieties/cultivars: 'Flore Pleno', and a variegated leaf form.

Arabis caucasica

Arabis procurrens
ROCK CRESS ○ ◑

Family: CRUCIFERAE
Origin: Southeastern Europe.
Flowering time: Spring.
Climatic zone: 4, 5, 6, 7, 8, 9.
Dimensions: Up to 12 inches (300 mm) high.
Description: Rock cress is one of the more showy species in this group of low-

Arabis procurrens

growing members of the mustard family. The flowers are quite large for the size of the plant, and are borne on slender heads. The foliage spreads at ground level by a series of short runners. Ideal for rock gardens, the plant thrives in poor soils and dry conditions, but needs a well-drained position. Plant it in either full sun or partial shade.

Argemone glauca

Argemone glauca
PRICKLY POPPY　〇

Family: PAPAVERACEAE
Origin: North America.
Flowering time: Summer.

Climatic zone: 9, 10.
Dimensions: Up to 2 feet (600 mm) high.
Description: These exquisite, soft white poppy flowers have bright yellow stamens that exude a sticky sap. The prickly stems are unpleasant to touch except with gloves. The plant is ideal for borders or mixed beds of annuals and likes full sun and warm weather. The soil should be light and well-drained. The seeds can be sown in summer and the seedlings transplanted in autumn for flowering the following year.

Armeria maritima
THRIFT, COMMON THRIFT 〇
(U.K.), SEA PINK

Family: PLUMBAGINACEAE
Origin: Northern hemisphere (mainly coastal and mountainous areas).
Flowering time: Summer.
Climatic zone: 3, 4, 5, 6, 7, 8.
Dimensions: 6–12 inches (150–300 mm) high.
Description: This is a useful edging or front-of-the-border plant with rich green, grass-like foliage. Erect and rigid stems bear individual flower heads in the shape of a globe, each made up of many small flowers. It prefers a light, open soil and grows particularly well near the sea as indicated by its name, sea pink. Propagation can be by seed or, better still, by division or cuttings taken in early autumn.
Other colors: Pink, red, purple.
Varieties/cultivars: 'Alba', 'Grandiflora', 'Purpurea', 'Rubra', 'Splendens'.

Artemisia lactiflora
CHINESE MUGWORT, 〇 ◑
WHITE MUGWORT,
GHOSTPLANT (U.S.A.)

Family: COMPOSITAE
Origin: China, India.
Flowering time: Late summer–autumn.
Climatic zone: 4, 5, 6, 7, 8.
Dimensions: 4–5 feet (1.5 meters) high.
Description: This strong-growing plant is useful in the background of a garden bed as a foil for more brightly colored subjects. It has jagged, green leaves and conspicuous sheaves of tiny, creamy-white flowers which are long-lasting and suitable for cutting. Because of their color, the flowers tend to look "dirty" when placed near white flowers or silver foliage and are better when grouped with yellow or blue flowers. It prefers a moist and fertile soil.

Artemisia lactiflora

Armeria maritima 'Alba'

Aruncus dioicus

Aruncus dioicus
GOATSBEARD

Family: ROSACEAE
Origin: Northern hemisphere.
Flowering time: Summer.
Climatic zone: 3, 4, 5, 6, 7, 8, 9.
Dimensions: 4–7 feet (1.2–2 meters) high.
Description: Goatsbeard is a handsome plant which forms a massive clump of fernlike foliage from which arise large plumes of minute creamy-white flowers. It can be used successfully as an isolated specimen, but is also good for general use, especially as a companion to shrub roses. It is easy to grow in most soils, but prefers moist conditions. Propagate by division or seed.
Varieties/cultivars: 'Kneiffii'.

Boltonia asteroides
WHITE BOLTONIA, FALSE CHAMOMILE, FALSE STARWORT (U.S.A.)

Family: COMPOSITAE
Origin: North America.
Flowering time: Autumn.
Climatic zone: 4, 5, 6, 7, 8, 9.
Dimensions: 5–6 feet (2 meters) high.
Description: This is an easily grown plant in most types of soil and ideal as a background plant. Massed heads of tiny, daisy-like flowers are produced in such vast quantities that the plants may need staking for support when in bloom. The pale-green leaves are quite small and insignificant. It is propagated by division in winter and is somewhat susceptible to mildew in warm, moist conditions.
Other colors: Pink, purple.
Varieties/cultivars: 'Snowbank'.

Boltonia asteroides

Campanula persicifolia 'Alba'
PEACH-LEAVED BELLFLOWER, PAPER BELLFLOWER (U.K.)

Family: CAMPANULACEAE
Origin: Cultivar.
Flowering time: Summer.
Climatic zone: 4, 5, 6, 7, 8, 9.
Dimensions: 2–3 feet (1 meter) high.
Description: This is a popular perennial which forms wide clumps of dense, narrow leaves and strong but slender stems bearing large, cup-shaped flowers. Being evergreen, it makes a useful groundcover throughout the year. It flowers over a long period and is good for cutting. It can be grown from seed, or propagated by root division in autumn or spring.

Campanula persicifolia 'Alba'

Cerastium tomentosum
SNOW-IN-SUMMER

Family: CARYOPHYLLACEAE
Origin: Italy and Sicily.
Flowering time: Summer.
Climatic zone: 5, 6, 7, 8, 9.
Dimensions: 4–6 inches (100–150 mm) high.
Description: A delightful groundcover plant, snow-in-summer spreads quickly in a sunny or lightly shaded spot. Its silvery-white foliage and white flowers give it its common name. It will grow in most soils, even sand, and is useful for retaining soil on steep banks as it puts down roots from each stem. Because it is invasive, it is not recommended for small gardens or choice spots. It is easily divided at any time except mid-winter.

Cerastium tomentosum

Chrysanthemum frutescens
PARIS DAISY, MARGUERITE DAISY

Family: COMPOSITAE
Origin: Canary Islands.
Flowering time: Spring–autumn and winter.
Climatic zone: 9, 10.
Dimensions: 3 feet (1 meter) high.
Description: This shrub-like evergreen perennial is of great value in the garden as it is covered in a mass of flowers for a long period if the spent blooms are removed. It has neatly divided, light-green foliage and does well in most garden soils, provided it gets plenty of water in summer. It makes a good specimen for planting in large

Chrysanthemum frutescens

containers and can be easily propagated from cuttings taken in spring or autumn.

Other colors: Pink, yellow.
Varieties/cultivars: 'Coronation', 'Mary Wootton'.

Chrysanthemum leucanthemum
OX-EYE DAISY, COMMON DAISY

Family: COMPOSITAE
Origin: Europe, Asia.
Flowering time: Early to late summer.
Climatic zone: 3, 4, 5, 6, 7, 8, 9, 10.

Chrysanthemum leucanthemum

Dimensions: 2 feet (600 mm) high.
Description: This is the common, white field daisy which can be quite attractive when mass-planted, although it often becomes a nuisance in gardens. The flower heads, usually solitary, are on a long, sturdy stalk which rarely needs staking for wind protection. The cut flowers last quite well indoors. This hardy perennial reseeds easily and so spreads rapidly.
Varieties/cultivars: 'Maistern'.

Chrysanthemum x *superbum*

Chrysanthemum x *superbum* syn.
C. maximum
SHASTA DAISY

Family: COMPOSITAE
Origin: Hybrid.
Flowering time: Summer.

Climatic zone: 5, 6, 7, 8, 9.
Dimensions: 3 feet (1 meter) high.
Description: A robust plant, shasta daisy is coarser in all its parts than most other chrysanthemums. The daisy flowers it produces are large, up to 5 or 6 inches (130–150 mm) across, and last well when cut. It is one of the easiest plants to cultivate in almost any position, although it does best in full sun. It is available in single and double forms and there are now several cultivars. Plant it out in autumn, and lift and divide the clumps every two years.
Varieties/cultivars: 'Wirral Supreme', 'Aglaia', 'Fiona Coghill', 'September Snow', 'Mayfield Giant'.

Crambe cordifolia

Crambe cordifolia
HEARTLEAF CRAMBE, SEA KALE

Family: CRUCIFERAE
Origin: Caucasus.
Flowering time: Early summer.
Climatic zone: 5, 6, 7, 8, 9.
Dimensions: 6 feet (2 meters) high.
Description: This is a massive plant with bold basal leaves, gray-green in color and often deeply lobed or cut. The intricately branched flowering stems carry clouds of tiny, white flowers, rather strongly scented. It is a most effective plant for a large garden, given well-drained, slightly alkaline soil and a position preferably in full sunshine. It is sometimes attacked by the caterpillars of the cabbage white butterfly. Propagate it from root cuttings in late winter or early spring.
Varieties/cultivars: 'Grandiflora'.

Dicentra cucullaria

Dicentra cucullaria
DUTCHMAN'S- ◯ ◖
BREECHES, WHITE EARDROPS

Family: FUMARIACEAE
Origin: Eastern United States.
Flowering time: Late spring.
Climatic zone: 4, 5, 6, 7, 8, 9.
Dimensions: 8 inches (200 mm) high.
Description: This is a graceful, stemless plant with numerous feathery basal leaves. The pendant flowers, on their slender, arching stalks, are divided into two spurs, giving the bloom a forked appearance similar to the trousers worn by Dutch peasants, hence the common name. It prefers a rich, well-drained soil and is frost-resistant, but drought-tender. It can be propagated by seed or division.

Dictamnus albus
GAS PLANT, BURNING ◯ ◖
BUSH, DITTANY (U.K.)

Family: RUTACEAE
Origin: Eastern Europe.
Flowering time: Summer.
Climatic zone: 3, 4, 5, 6, 7, 8, 9.
Dimensions: 2–3 feet (up to 1 meter) high.
Description: A bushy perennial with simple upright stems, this plant is not extensively cultivated but is worth growing for the tangy lemon perfume of its leaves and its elegant flowers. It grows best in a fertile soil in a sunny position. The volatile oil from this plant will ignite if a lighted match is held near the developing seed pods on a windless day. The ripe seed pods explode

violently in warm, dry weather and the seeds can take up to a year to germinate.
Other colors: Red, purple.
Varieties/cultivars: 'Purpureus', 'Rubrus'.

Dictamnus albus

Dianthus arenarius
PRUSSIAN PINK, GRASS ◖
PINK (U.K.)

Family: CARYOPHYLLACEAE
Origin: Eastern Europe.
Flowering time: Summer.
Climatic zone: 4, 5, 6, 7, 8, 9.

Dianthus arenarius

Dimensions: 8–12 inches (200–300 mm) high.
Description: A useful mat-forming plant with masses of single, heavily fringed, white flowers with a greenish eye. This species prefers a semishaded position and a slightly gritty soil that has been enriched with a potassium-rich fertilizer. Make sure that plenty of water is supplied, especially during the warm summer months. Prussian pink is easily grown from either seed or cuttings.

Dietes vegeta syn. *Moraea iridioides*
AFRICAN IRIS ◯ ◖

Family: IRIDACEAE
Origin: South Africa.
Flowering time: Summer.

Dietes vegeta

Climatic zone: 9, 10.
Dimensions: Up to 2 feet (600 mm) high.
Description: The glorious lily-like flowers of this species appear in profusion on long, slender stems during the warm weather. Even when the plant is not in flower, the evergreen, sword-like foliage, in large clumps, is most attractive and makes an excellent feature. In its native environment, African iris is found growing in semishade under spreading trees. It can withstand extremely dry conditions, prefers light and well-drained soils, and is often grown as a low hedge. Once established it will readily self-seed.

Dimorphotheca ecklonis syn.
Osteospermum ecklonis
WHITE VELDT DAISY,
SAILOR BOY DAISY ○

Family: COMPOSITAE
Origin: South Africa.
Flowering time: Summer–autumn.
Climatic zone: 9.
Dimensions: Up to 3 feet (1 meter) high.
Description: In a frost-free climate, this plant grows into a vigorous, upright, shrubby bush. It prefers a light, well-drained soil and is able to withstand periods of dryness. The petals of the daisy-like flower, white on top and purple underneath, close at night time. The long, narrow, light-green leaves are lightly toothed around the margin. It is easily propagated from cuttings and can also be grown from seed.
Varieties/cultivars: var. *prostrata*, 'Whirligig', 'Pink whirls'.

Epilobium glabellum

Epilobium glabellum
FIREWEED, WILLOW
HERB ○ ◑

Family: ONAGRACEAE
Origin: New Zealand.
Flowering time: Summer.
Climatic zone: 8, 9, 10.
Dimensions: Up to 15 inches (375 mm) high.
Description: The shining, light-green leaves of this little alpine perennial form attractive clumps which gradually expand, but are never a nuisance. The tumbled masses of funnel-shaped flowers are followed by fluffy seed heads. As it comes from the rocky subalpine and alpine slopes, it needs an open, well-drained soil that is reasonably fertile. It can be propagated by division during spring.
Other colors: Yellow, pink.
Varieties/cultivars: 'Sulphureum'.

Dimorphotheca ecklonis

Epimedium x *youngianum* 'Niveum'
SNOWY BARRENWORT ◑

Family: BERBERIDACEAE
Origin: Hybrid cultivar.
Flowering time: Spring.
Climatic zone: 5, 6, 7, 8, 9.
Dimensions: 6–12 inches (150–300 mm) high.

Epimedium x *youngianum* 'Niveum'

Description: This perennial is valued for its delicate-looking, but leathery-textured, leaves made up of heart-shaped leaflets on wiry stems. They are light green with pink veins in spring, turning to reddish-bronze in autumn. The flowers, borne in pendulous white clusters, composed of eight sepals and four petals, are excellent for cutting. It grows well in cool and temperate areas in light shade and moist soil that is well-nourished. The clumps may be divided in autumn or spring.

Erigeron mucronatus

Erigeron mucronatus syn.
E. karvinskianus
BONYTIP FLEABANE,   ○   ◑
MEXICAN FLEABANE (U.K.),
BABY'S TEARS (Aust.)

Family: COMPOSITAE
Origin: Mexico–Venezuela.
Flowering time: Spring–summer and autumn.
Climatic zone: 8, 9, 10.
Dimensions: 8 inches (200 mm) high.
Description: This attractive little plant self-seeds vigorously and will fill up many a bare space with endless clouds of little white and pink daisies. It is excellent around steps or in gaps in brick or stone paving. It also spreads by means of underground runners. It dies down in winter but will reappear in spring. It seems to do best in light, well-drained, sandy soil of low fertility, especially in areas near the sea.

Eryngium bourgatii
MEDITERRANEAN   ○
ERYNGO (U.S.A.), SEA HOLLY

Family: UMBELLIFERAE
Origin: Pyrenees.
Flowering time: Summer.
Climatic zone: 6, 7, 8, 9, 10.
Dimensions: 2 feet (600 mm) high.
Description: This is an eye-catching plant because of its unusual foliage. The leaves are crisp and curly, gray-green in color with white veins, and form a basal rosette. The blue-green, thistle-like flowers are protected by silvery-white bracts tipped with spines. It thrives in full sun and well-drained, sandy soil

that is moderately fertile. The flower heads are most useful for dried floral arrangements. Seed in spring or root cuttings in late winter are the best means of propagation.

Eryngium bourgatii

Filipendula vulgaris 'Flore Pleno'

Filipendula vulgaris 'Flore Pleno' syn.
F. hexapetala 'Flore Pleno'
DOUBLE-FLOWERED   ○   ◑
DROPWORT, MEADOWSWEET

Family: ROSACEAE
Origin: Eastern Europe, Siberia.
Flowering time: Summer.
Climatic zone: 4, 5, 6, 7, 8, 9.
Dimensions: Up to 2 feet (600 mm) high.
Description: This plant has finely divided foliage like that of the carrot and produces double, creamy-white flowers in a loose raceme. It will tolerate

reasonably dry conditions and will grow well in either full sun or partial shade. It makes an excellent border subject when mixed with other plants of a different texture. It is usually propagated by division in autumn or spring.

Fragaria chiloensis
CHILOE STRAWBERRY,   ○   ◑
BEACH STRAWBERRY

Family: ROSACEAE
Origin: Western North and South America from Alaska to Chile.
Flowering time: Spring.
Climatic zone: 5, 6, 7, 8, 9.
Dimensions: Up to 6 inches (150 mm) high.
Description: This is a low, spreading, groundcover plant which sends out stems, or runners, after it has finished flowering and fruiting. The attractive leaves are green and glossy above and pale bluish-white beneath. The fruit is large, firm and dark-red, this plant being one of the parents of our dessert strawberries. It prefers a position in cool, moist, fertile soil open to sunshine.

Fragaria chiloensis

Gypsophila paniculata

Helleborus corsicus

Gillenia trifoliata
INDIAN-PHYSIC, BOWMAN'S-ROOT (U.S.A.)

Family: ROSACEAE
Origin: Eastern North America.
Flowering time: Summer.
Climatic zone: 4, 5, 6, 7, 8, 9.
Dimensions: 3 feet (1 meter) high.
Description: Indian-physic is a dainty and refined perennial with wiry, reddish stems and leaves divided into three parts. It forms a clump from which it sends up stems of small white flowers in airy clusters. After the petals fall, the red calyces persist and remain decorative until the seeds ripen. It can be grown in full sun except in very hot regions, and any type of soil that is not too dry seems to suit it. Propagate it by division of the clumps in spring.

Gypsophila paniculata
BABY'S-BREATH, CHALK PLANT

Family: CARYOPHYLLACEAE
Origin: Central Europe – central Siberia.
Flowering time: Summer.
Climatic zone: 3, 4, 5, 6, 7, 8, 9.
Dimensions: Up to 3 feet (1 meter) high.

Description: A wide-spreading plant up to 3 feet (1 meter) in diameter, baby's-breath produces dense tufts of intricately branched, erect stems covered in a froth of tiny star-like flowers. It prefers a neutral or slightly alkaline soil and resents disturbance of the roots once established. The plant's cloud-like appearance makes a dramatic contrast with other more striking subjects in the garden. It can be grown from seed.
Other colors: Pink.
Varieties/cultivars: 'Bristol Fairy', 'Flamingo', 'Rosy Veil'.

Gillenia trifoliata

Helleborus corsicus syn. *H. lividus corsicus*, *H. argutifolius*
CORSICAN HELLEBORE

Family: RANUNCULACEAE
Origin: Corsica, Sardinia.
Flowering time: Winter–spring.
Climatic zone: 6, 7, 8, 9.
Dimensions: 2–3 feet (up to 1 meter) high.
Description: This handsome, evergreen perennial produces large, three-part leaves, serrated at the edges, during its first year. From the top of a short leafy stem the flower stalk develops in the second year. The single, upright spike bears a cluster of fifteen to twenty cup-shaped flowers of an unusual pale green, which last for many months. It is ideal for growing under deciduous trees in a moist, fertile soil. Propagate it from seed or by division, but exercise care with division; the roots are brittle.

Helleborus foetidus

Helleborus foetidus
STINKING HELLEBORE, SETTERWORT, BEAR'S FOOT

Family: RANUNCULACEAE
Origin: Western Europe.
Flowering time: Winter–spring.
Climatic zone: 6, 7, 8, 9.
Dimensions: Up to 3 feet (1 meter) high.
Description: This plant has handsome, deeply divided, dark-green leaves which form a compact clump. The flowers are airy clusters at the end of the stems, thimble-shaped and of a pale green color edged with maroon. The plant has tough roots that penetrate the soil for a considerable depth. The shiny foliage makes an excellent foil for silver-leaved plants, and the masses of blooms stay fresh for some time. The plant self-seeds readily.

Helleborus lividus
MAJORCA HELLEBORE

Family: RANUNCULACEAE
Origin: Majorca.
Flowering time: Early spring.
Climatic zone: 9.
Dimensions: 12 inches (300 mm) high.
Description: This perennial has leathery leaves divided into three parts and overlaced with gray-white markings and purple beneath. The clusters of flowers appear on leafy stems in the second year and are yellowish-green flushed purplish-pink and delicately scented. The fragrance is most noted when the plant is grown under cover. Best grown under glass in cold climates.

Helleborus lividus

Helleborus niger

Helleborus niger
CHRISTMAS ROSE, BLACK HELLEBORE

Family: RANUNCULACEAE
Origin: Central Europe – Yugoslavia.
Flowering time: Winter.
Climatic zone: 4, 5, 6, 7, 8, 9.
Dimensions: 8–12 inches (200–300 mm) high.
Description: The leathery leaves are evergreen and the single flowers, up to 3 inches (75 mm) across, are pure white, becoming pinkish as they age. The name black hellebore refers to the color of the roots. It thrives best in heavy, moist soils in either full or partial shade. This plant has been in cultivation since the Middle Ages and is a welcome sight after Christmas in the northern hemisphere.
Other colors: Pink.
Varieties/cultivars: 'Louis Cobbett', 'Altifolius', 'Praecox'.

Iberis sempervirens
PERENNIAL CANDYTUFT

Family: CRUCIFERAE
Origin: Mediterranean region.
Flowering time: Spring.
Climatic zone: 7, 8, 9.
Dimensions: Up to 12 inches (300 mm) high.
Description: This makes a fine edging plant or can be planted among rocks. Usually evergreen, it becomes covered in a mass of flattish white flower clusters. To avoid the formation of a noticeable space in the center of the plant after flowering, the stems should be lightly cut back. It prefers a sunny position but will stop flowering if allowed to dry out. It is easily propagated by division or from seed.
Varieties/cultivars: 'Little Gem', 'Plena'.

Iberis sempervirens

Lamium maculatum
SPOTTED DEAD NETTLE

Family: LABIATAE
Origin: Most of Europe – Russia and Turkey.
Flowering time: Early summer.
Climatic zone: 5, 6, 7, 8, 9.
Dimensions: 6–8 inches (150–200 mm) high.
Description: This useful groundcover plant has white flowers and attractively marked foliage. The mid-green leaves with their silver stripe will form a carpet under trees and in shaded areas. The semi-prostrate stems send out runners which will put down roots and these can be easily cut off and replanted elsewhere. It will thrive in poor soils and

Lamium maculatum 'White Nancy'

is useful for planting under hedges and for covering steep banks.
Other colors: Mauve-pink.
Varieties/cultivars: 'Beacon Silver', 'White Nancy', 'Roseum'.

Leontopodium alpinum
EDELWEISS ○

Family: COMPOSITAE
Origin: Central Europe.
Flowering time: Summer.
Climatic zone: 4, 5, 6, 7, 8.
Dimensions: 6 inches (150 mm) high.
Description: This well-known alpine plant from the European mountains produces small, low tufts of gray, furry leaves. It has clustered heads of small flowers, each surrounded by a collar of grayish-white, felted bracts. It is grown more for its romantic associations than its beauty. It needs well-drained soil in a sunny spot and resents the winter wet, which may cause it to rot. It can be grown readily from seed.

Leontopodium alpinum

Macleaya cordata

Macleaya cordata syn. *Bocconia cordata*
PLUME POPPY ○ ◑

Family: PAPAVERACEAE
Origin: China, Japan.
Flowering time: Summer.
Climatic zone: 4, 5, 6, 7, 8, 9.
Dimensions: 7 feet (2 meters) high.

Description: This tall perennial combines handsome foliage with delightful, small white flowers that appear in masses of feathery plumes. The gray-green leaves, not unlike those of the culinary fig, are gray-white and downy underneath. At its best in reasonably moist soils, it is deciduous, self-supporting in spite of its height, and spreads by suckering roots. In hot areas, some shade is necessary. It should be planted in autumn or spring, divided in spring, or grown from root cuttings in late winter.

Minuartia verna syn. *Arenaria verna* var. *caespitosa*
IRISH MOSS, SPRING ◑ ●
SANDWORT (U.K.)

Family: CARYOPHYLLACEAE
Origin: European and Rocky Mountains.
Flowering time: Late spring.
Climatic zone: 4, 5, 6, 7, 8.
Dimensions: 2 inches (50 mm) high.
Description: This alpine perennial produces dense, mosslike clumps and, in sufficient sunshine, small starry flowers. It grows well in ordinary soil but with the addition of leaf mold it will thrive. It tolerates full shade and partial sun.
Varieties/cultivars: 'Aurea'.

Minuartia verna

Paeonia lactiflora 'Lady Alexander Duff'

Paeonia lactiflora and hybrids
CHINESE PEONY ○ ◐

Family: RANUNCULACEAE
Origin: China, Siberia, Mongolia.
Flowering time: Early summer.
Climatic zone: 3, 4, 5, 6, 7, 8, 9.
Dimensions: 2–3 feet (up to 1 meter) high.
Description: This species, which has large, white, fragrant flowers, is the parent of many garden peony hybrids. These cultivars offer great variety in shape and color and are easy to grow given the right conditions. They need deep, fertile, neutral to slightly alkaline soil, well-drained, but moisture-retentive. A sunny position suits best, with an annual mulch over the crowns to keep them cool and moist during hot weather. They resent disturbance. Propagate by root division in autumn, but only when essential.
Other colors: Pink, crimson, scarlet.
Varieties/cultivars: 'Whitleyi Major', 'The Bride', 'Solange', 'Sarah Bernhardt', 'The Moor', 'Victoria', 'Duchesse de Nemours', 'Bunker Hill', 'Pink Delight', 'Lady Alexander Duff'.

Pachysandra terminalis
JAPANESE SPURGE ◐ ●

Family: BUXACEAE
Origin: China, Japan.
Flowering time: Spring.
Climatic zone: 4, 5, 6, 7, 8, 9.
Dimensions: Up to 12 inches (300 mm) high.
Description: This is a widely grown, evergreen groundcover with handsome, spoon-shaped leaves of a glossy dark green, and spikes of small, scented flowers. It does well in moist, well-drained soil in shaded areas. Too much exposure to the sun tends to turn the foliage yellow. It spreads quickly by underground stems and is vigorous and tough enough for planting in public places. Propagate by division in spring.
Varieties/cultivars: 'Variegata'.

Pachysandra terminalis

Phlox paniculata

Phlox paniculata and cultivars
PERENNIAL PHLOX, ○
GARDEN PHLOX, BORDER
PHLOX (U.K.)

Family: POLEMONIACEAE
Origin: Eastern North America.
Flowering time: Late summer.
Climatic zone: 4, 5, 6, 7, 8, 9.
Dimensions: 2–3 feet (up to 1 meter) high.
Description: The many cultivars of this species are easy to grow and provide masses of long-lasting color in border gardens. A sunny position is best, in a fairly rich soil with applications of liquid fertilizer during the growing period. The dense flower heads are fragrant and useful for cutting. The plants are prone to the fungal disease powdery mildew and to spider mites. Propagate it from root cuttings in winter or by division in spring.
Other colors: Pink, red, pale-blue, violet, salmon.
Varieties/cultivars: 'Mars', 'Purple King', 'Leo Schlageter', 'Mount Fuji', 'September Schnee', and others.

Physostegia virginiana 'Summer Snow'

Physostegia virginiana 'Summer Snow'
FALSE ○ ◐
DRAGONHEAD, OBEDIENT
PLANT

Family: LABIATAE
Origin: Cultivar.
Flowering time: Late summer–early autumn.
Climatic zone: 4, 5, 6, 7, 8, 9.
Dimensions: Up to 4 feet (over 1 meter) high.
Description: This is an easy-to-grow, herbaceous perennial with leafy, upright stems, and spikes of tubular white flowers. The individual flowers have hinged stalks and will remain in any position they are moved to, hence the name obedient plant. The leaves are long and tapered, and toothed around the margins. It thrives in any fertile soil, but the soil must not be allowed to dry out. Propagation is best by the division of established plants in spring.

Polygonatum x *hybridum*

Polygonatum x *hybridum*
SOLOMON'S-SEAL, DAVID'S HARP

Family: LILIACEAE
Origin: Hybrid.
Flowering time: Late spring.
Climatic zone: 5, 6, 7, 8, 9.
Dimensions: 2 feet (600 mm) high.
Description: This plant likes being left undisturbed to allow the rhizomes to spread. A woodland plant, it looks particularly attractive when associated with ferns and hostas. The broad, green leaves are attractive and the dainty tubular flowers, carried one or two at a time, are fragrant. The leaves turn a buttery yellow in autumn. Any good garden soil will suit, provided it contains organic matter and is cool and moisture-retentive.
Varieties/cultivars: 'Flore Pleno'.

Potentilla tridentata
CINQUEFOIL, THREE-TOOTHED CINQUEFOIL

Family: ROSACEAE
Origin: North America.
Flowering time: Summer.
Climatic zone: 5, 6, 7, 8.
Dimensions: 6–10 inches (150–200 mm) high.
Description: This plant has trifoliate, evergreen, leathery leaflets, quite shiny on the upper surface. It is easy to grow in most types of soils provided they are well-drained, but it will not tolerate extra-dry conditions. Although not a particularly showy plant, it flowers for a prolonged period. It looks its best at the front of a border or in a rockery, and the stems can be cut back after flowering. Propagate it by seed or division in spring.

Potentilla tridentata

Rheum alexandrae
RHUBARB (not culinary)

Family: POLYGONACEAE
Origin: Himalayas.
Flowering time: Summer.
Climatic zone: 5, 6, 7, 8, 9.
Dimensions: 3 feet (1 meter) high.
Description: This is a curious species that scarcely resembles a rhubarb as growing all the way down the stems are straw-colored bracts which sheath the flowers and look like tiles on a house. The bracts protect the flowers and ripening seeds. The leaves are oval, dark shining green, and prominently ribbed. A fine plant, it is difficult to cultivate unless the climate is moist and cool. Propagation is by division, or by sowing seeds in spring.

Rheum alexandrae

Rodgersia podophylla

Rodgersia podophylla
BRONZE LEAF, RODGERS' FLOWER

Family: SAXIFRAGACEAE
Origin: China, Japan.
Flowering time: Summer.
Climatic zone: 5, 6, 7, 8, 9.
Dimensions: 3–4 feet (approx. 1 meter) high.
Description: This plant, with its superb ornamental foliage, is very suitable for moist garden situations or beside water. The large, divided leaves are bronze when young, then turn green, and finally take on dark coppery tones as they mature in summer. The fluffy flowers are carried on arching stems well above the foliage. Strong winds can damage the foliage, so the plant should be given a sheltered position where it will form large colonies in time.

Romneya coulteri

Saxifraga stolonifera

Romneya coulteri
CALIFORNIA TREE POPPY, ○
MATILIJA POPPY

Family: PAPAVERACEAE
Origin: California.
Flowering time: Summer–autumn.
Climatic zone: 8, 9, 10.
Dimensions: Up to 8 feet (over 2 meters) high.
Description: Although a somewhat difficult plant to establish as it resents any root disturbance, the flowers make it well worth the effort. These are silky and crinkled, up to 6 inches (150 mm) wide, and sweetly fragrant. They contrast well with the green-gray, deeply divided foliage. The plant prefers a warm and well-drained position in normal garden soil, even slightly alkaline. It can be propagated by root cuttings, but disturbing the roots in this way can unfortunately result in the death of the parent plant.

Saxifraga stolonifera syn. *S. sarmentosa*
STRAWBERRY ◑ ●
GERANIUM (U.K.), MOTHER OF
THOUSANDS, CREEPING
SAILOR

Family: SAXIFRAGACEAE
Origin: Eastern Asia.
Flowering time: Summer.
Climatic zone: 8, 9, 10.
Dimensions: Up to 18 inches (450 mm) high.
Description: This plant has long, prostrate stems which send out roots and then develop rosettes of round and toothed, glossy leaves. These are veined,

marbled, and colored a strawberry pink underneath. Delicate, small, white flowers are borne on loose panicles, standing above the foliage. It makes a useful and most decorative basket or pot plant, as well as a good groundcover provided it is given room to spread in a warm, sheltered spot. It can be propagated from seed in spring or by division in summer.
Varieties/cultivars: 'Tricolor'.

Shortia galacifolia
OCONEE-BELLS ◑ ●

Family: DIAPENSIACEAE
Origin: Eastern North America.
Flowering time: Summer.

Climatic zone: 4, 5, 6, 7, 8, 9.
Dimensions: Up to 6 inches (150 mm) high.
Description: The small, delicate, white blooms of oconee-bells resemble frilled bells. They emerge from their low foliage on slender, leafless stalks and have a nodding habit. The plant is not an easy one to grow, and once established should not be moved. It is an excellent choice for a rock garden. Grow it in cool, moist, well-drained, acid soil enriched with humus. Use peat moss as humus in clay-loam soils to make them acid. Propagate by division in early spring.

Smilacina racemosa
FALSE SPIKENARD, ◑ ●
FALSE SOLOMON'S SEAL

Family: LILIACEAE
Origin: North America.
Flowering time: Late spring.
Climatic zone: 3, 4, 5, 6, 7, 8, 9.

Smilacina racemosa

Shortia galacifolia

Dimensions: Up to 3 feet (1 meter) high.
Description: This plant has erect to ascending stems of fresh green leaves and spikes of fluffy, creamy-white flowers, deliciously lemon-scented. As the flowers age they become tinged with pink and can be followed by red berries. The plant makes a good combination with ferns and primulas. It prefers shaded conditions in a lime-free soil and, with consistent moisture, is not difficult to grow. Propagate it by division in spring.

Trillium grandiflorum

Verbascum chaixii 'Album'

Symphytum grandiflorum

Symphytum grandiflorum
GROUND-COVER COMFREY, CREEPING COMFREY (U.K.)
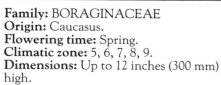

Family: BORAGINACEAE
Origin: Caucasus.
Flowering time: Spring.
Climatic zone: 5, 6, 7, 8, 9.
Dimensions: Up to 12 inches (300 mm) high.
Description: This perennial herb makes an excellent groundcover, spreading by means of underground stems. The dark-green leaves are broad and hairy, and make a close carpet on the soil. The buds arise on hooked stems and open to tubular, cream flowers. The plant prefers moist, but not boggy, soil, and is easy to grow. Propagation is usually by division in spring or autumn.
Varieties/cultivars: 'Variegatum'.

Trillium grandiflorum
WAKE ROBIN, SNOW TRILLIUM, TRINITY FLOWER

Other common names: WOOD LILY (U.K.)
Family: LILIACEAE
Origin: Eastern North America.
Flowering time: Spring–early summer.
Climatic zone: 5, 6, 7, 8, 9.
Dimensions: 12–18 inches (300–450 mm) high.
Description: This woodland plant has undeniable appeal, but is often difficult to grow among other plants in a border. Each erect stem bears three leaves, three calyx lobes, and three petals — hence the names "trillium" and "trinity". The foliage dies down in summer and the plant can be lifted and divided then. It likes moist but well-drained soil, enriched with plenty of leaf mold, which must never be allowed to dry out.
Other colors: Pink.
Varieties/cultivars: 'Roseum'.

Verbascum chaixii 'Album'
CHAIX'S MULLEIN, NETTLE-LEAVED MULLEIN

Family: SCROPHULARIACEAE
Origin: Southern and central Europe.
Flowering time: Summer.
Climatic zone: 5, 6, 7, 8, 9.
Dimensions: 3 feet (1 meter) high.
Description: This variety has delightful, pure white flowers with rose-colored stamens, borne on showy spikes which rise from large basal leaves which are gray and hairy and often up to 12 inches (300 mm) long. An easy plant to grow, it likes a light, sandy, well-drained soil. It looks well combined with other plants in a border or wild garden, and is attractive with campanulas and as a contrast to rounded gray shrubs. It can be propagated by seed in spring.

Yucca filamentosa

Yucca filamentosa
ADAM'S-NEEDLE

Family: AGAVACEAE
Origin: Southeastern United States.
Flowering time: Late summer.
Climatic zone: 5, 6, 7, 8, 9.
Dimensions: 5 feet (over 1 meter) high.
Description: The grayish-green leaves of this semidesert plant are almost bayonet-like and have thread-like hairs along their margin — representing the needle and thread. The tall, beautiful flower spikes rising from these basal leaves are deliciously fragrant in the evening. The sharp outlines of this plant make it a useful specimen when landscaping. It does best in well-drained, sandy loam and càn be propagated by seeds or offsets.
Varieties/cultivars: 'Variegata', 'Golden Sword'.

Abeliophyllum distichum

Abeliophyllum distichum
KOREAN ABELIALEAF, WHITE FORSYTHIA ○

Family: OLEACEAE
Origin: Korea.
Flowering time: Spring.
Climatic zone: 5, 6, 7, 8, 9.
Dimensions: 3–5 feet (approx. 1–2 meters) high.
Description: Korean abelialeaf is a very pretty, slow-growing, deciduous shrub with arching stems. The white, bell-like flowers appear in early spring, covering leafless stems. Plant it in a shrub border or use it at the back of a perennial garden. It is easy to grow in most garden soils. Pruning should be carried out as soon as the flowers have finished, as flowers appear on wood from the previous year. New growth can be stimulated by removing old wood to the ground.

Adenandra uniflora
ADENANDRA, ENAMEL FLOWER ○ ◑

Family: RUTACEAE
Origin: South Africa.
Flowering time: Spring–summer.
Climatic zone: 8, 9, 10.
Dimensions: 3 feet (1 meter) high.
Description: This is a bushy, evergreen shrub with small, tapering leaves and numerous white flowers which have a rose-pink rib down the center of each petal and purplish-brown anthers. Adenandra looks pretty when grown in the front of a shrub border. It is a hardy shrub which, because of its naturally

Adenandra uniflora

compact shape, does not require pruning. It will tolerate most garden soils. In spring apply a handful of complete plant food around the base of the plant.

Aesculus parviflora
DWARF HORSE CHESTNUT (U.S.A.), BOTTLEBRUSH BUCKEYE (U.K.) ○ ◑

Family: HIPPOCASTANACEAE
Origin: Southeastern United States.
Flowering time: Summer.
Climatic zone: 4, 5, 6, 7, 8, 9.
Dimensions: 8–12 feet (2–4 meters) high.

Arctostaphylos uva-ursi

Description: Bottlebrush buckeye is a spreading, suckering, free-flowering, deciduous shrub. The white flowers have very showy, dark-pink anthers and the leaves color attractively during autumn. Plant it as a specimen plant or in a shrub border, giving it plenty of room so that its spreading shape can be appreciated. It is not suitable for a small garden as suckers can spread widely creating thickets up to 20 feet (6 meters) across. It will thrive in almost any garden soil. A mulch of manure or compost around the roots in spring will provide food and keep the roots moist.

Arctostaphylos uva-ursi
BEARBERRY, RED BEARBERRY, KINNIKINNICK (U.S.A.) ○

Family: ERICACEAE
Origin: North America, Europe, Asia, circumpolar.
Flowering time: Spring.
Climatic zone: 2, 3, 4, 5, 6, 7, 8, 9.
Dimensions: Up to 6 inches (150 mm) high.
Description: Bearberry is an interesting, creeping, mountain or cold climate shrub. Its white, bell-shaped flowers are tinged with pink, and are followed by red berries. The prostrate stems are often up to 7 feet (2 meters) long. Because of its dense foliage it makes a good groundcover for large banks. Bearberry needs a well-drained, acid soil and, because it is salt-tolerant, will grow in sandy soils near the sea.

Aesculus parviflora

Ardisia crispa

Ardisia crispa syn. *A. crenulata,*
A. crenata
CORALBERRY,
SPICEBERRY, CORAL ARDISIA

Family: MYRSINIACEAE
Origin: Southeastern Asia.
Flowering time: Summer.
Climatic zone: 9, 10.
Dimensions: 3 feet (1 meter) high.
Description: This is a popular small
shrub for shady situations and for use as
an indoor plant. The fragrant, star-
shaped, white flowers appear in terminal
clusters and are followed by a heavy
crop of scarlet berries, which remain on
the plant throughout autumn and
winter. The glossy, dark-green leaves
have wavy margins. Coralberry requires
a hot climate and a well-drained soil. In
colder climates, it thrives as an indoor
pot plant.

Aronia arbutifolia
RED CHOKEBERRY

Family: ROSACEAE
Origin: Eastern North America.
Flowering time: Spring–summer.
Climatic zone: 5, 6, 7, 8.
Dimensions: 6–8 feet (2–3 meters) high.
Description: This deciduous shrub has
white flowers, tinted with pink, which
are followed in autumn by masses of
small, round berries that remain on the
plant for a long period. The long, glossy
green leaves with their gray undersides
turn red in autumn. The plant will
thrive in normal to acid soil. It increases
freely by suckers which can easily be
divided.
Varieties/cultivars: 'Erecta'.

Aronia arbutifolia

Aronia melanocarpa
BLACK CHOKEBERRY

Family: ROSACEAE
Origin: Eastern North America.
Flowering time: Spring.
Climatic zone: 5, 6, 7, 8, 9.
Dimensions: 2–3 feet (up to 1 meter)
high.

Description: Black chokeberry is a low-
growing shrub which is covered in white
flowers during spring. These are
followed by lustrous, deep purple-black
berries. It looks most striking at the
back of a herbaceous border or planted
with low-growing asters. Black
chokeberry requires a free-draining soil.

Aronia melanocarpa

199

Azalea indica 'Alba Magna'

Azalea indica 'Alba Magna'
INDIAN AZALEA, EVERGREEN AZALEA ○ ◑

Family: ERICACEAE
Origin: Cultivar.
Flowering time: Spring.
Climatic zone: 6, 7, 8, 9.
Dimensions: 6 feet (2 meters) high.
Description: A beautiful evergreen shrub, Indian azalea is covered in a profusion of large, white flowers during spring. It requires a well-drained, acid soil which should be enriched with leaf mold, compost, or peat before planting. Azaleas have a very shallow root system, which should not be allowed to dry out during summer. Drying out can be prevented by mulching the root area.

Bouvardia longiflora
WHITE BOUVARDIA ○

Family: RUBIACEAE
Origin: Mexico.
Flowering time: Summer–autumn.

Bouvardia longiflora

Climatic zone: 9, 10.
Dimensions: 3–5 feet (approx. 1–2 meters) high.
Description: This pretty shrub has terminal heads of long, fragrant, white, jasmine-like flowers, and glossy green leaves. Plant white bouvardia near a doorway, window, or garden seat where the perfume can be appreciated. It will grow in any well-drained soil and should be pruned lightly after flowering has finished. Apply a handful of complete plant food in early spring.
Varieties/cultivars: There are numerous varieties throughout the world.

Buddleia davidii 'White Bouquet'
BUTTERFLY BUSH ○ ◐

Family: LOGANIACEAE
Origin: Cultivar.
Flowering time: Summer–autumn.
Climatic zone: 5, 6, 7, 8, 9.
Dimensions: 6–10 feet (2–3 meters) high.
Description: The fragrant, white flowers of this shrub have yellow eyes and are borne in large clusters which attract butterflies, hence the common name. Butterfly bush is a strong shrub with long, slender, dark-green leaves which are felted underneath. It grows well near the sea. A rapid grower, especially in sheltered sites, it likes good drainage. A yearly prune during winter produces a nicely shaped bush.

Buddleia davidii 'White Bouquet'

Calliandra portoricensis
WHITE TASSEL FLOWER, SNOWFLAKE ACACIA, WHITE POWDER PUFF ○

Family: LEGUMINOSAE
Origin: Southern Mexico–Panama, West Indes.
Flowering time: Spring–autumn.
Climatic zone: 9, 10.
Dimensions: 8–12 feet (approx. 2–4 meters) high.
Description: Admired for its fern-like foliage and long flowering period, this handsome shrub produces fragrant, fluffy white flowers that resemble flakes of snow. Unless grown where there are

Calliandra portoricensis

hot, dry summers, it tends to produce an abundance of foliage and odd-shaped flowers. Plant it in well-drained soil that has been enriched with leaf mold or compost. An occasional spring pruning will keep the shrub in good shape.

Calocephalus brownii

Calocephalus brownii
CUSHION BUSH, SKELETON PLANT ○

Family: COMPOSITAE
Origin: Australia.
Flowering time: Summer.
Climatic zone: 9, 10.
Dimensions: Up to 3 feet (1 meter) high.
Description: Cushion bush is a round, silvery, mound-like shrub with silvery-white, multi-branched stems and minute leaves which clasp the stem. The small, greenish-yellow flowers are insignificant compared with the foliage. Cushion bush grows in any soil and suits rockeries where its silvery appearance contrasts with other green shrubs. Alternatively, it is an ideal plant for a gray or white garden scheme. It is often found growing naturally on sandy and rocky seashores. Prune it after flowering has finished to maintain its bushy habit.

Carissa grandiflora
NATAL PLUM, AMATUNGULA (U.S.A.) ○

Family: APOCYNACEAE
Origin: South Africa.
Flowering time: Throughout the year.
Climatic zone: 9, 10.
Dimensions: Up to 15 feet (5 meters) high.
Description: A bushy shrub covered in long spines, natal plum is often used for

Carissa grandiflora

hedging. It has oval leaves and pretty, fragrant, white flowers which are 2 inches (50 mm) wide. The flowers are followed by egg-shaped berries, tasting similar to cranberries, which can be eaten fresh or made into a sauce. Natal plum is easy to grow and will thrive if given ample amounts of summer water. Mulching around its roots will help to keep the soil moist.

Carpenteria californica
CALIFORNIAN MOCK ORANGE ○

Family: PHILADELPHACEAE
Origin: California.
Flowering time: Summer.
Climatic zone: 8, 9, 10.
Dimensions: 6–8 feet (2–3 meters) high.
Description: A beautiful, bushy

Carpenteria californica

evergreen, this shrub has long, smooth, narrow leaves which are bright green above and rather downy underneath. The fragrant flowers with their creamy-white central stamens are about 2½ inches (62 mm) across and borne in terminal clusters. Californian mock orange requires a moist but well-drained soil, otherwise the foliage will burn during summer. Add plenty of compost or manure to the soil and keep it mulched with this.
Varieties/cultivars: 'Ladham's Variety'.

Chaenomeles speciosa 'Nivalis'

Chaenomeles speciosa 'Nivalis'
FLOWERING QUINCE, ○ ◑ JAPONICA, JAPANESE QUINCE (U.K.)

Family: ROSACEAE
Origin: China.
Flowering time: Spring.
Climatic zone: 5, 6, 7, 8, 9.
Dimensions: 6–10 feet (2–3 meters) high.
Description: This deciduous shrub has spiny, smooth branches and oval leaves which may turn shades of red, orange, or yellow during autumn. 'Nivalis' is valued for its large, pure-white flowers which appear before the leaves in early spring. It makes a delightful feature plant or can be used with evergreen shrubs in a border. Flowering quince is easy to grow in any garden soil. Apply a handful of complete plant food in late winter to ensure a good flower display.

SHRUBS

Chamelaucium uncinatum

GERALDTON WAXFLOWER ○

Family: MYRTACEAE
Origin: Western Australia.
Flowering time: Late spring–summer.
Climatic zone: 9, 10.
Dimensions: 9 feet (3 meters) high.
Description: Geraldton waxflower is a spreading, open shrub with fine foliage. The terminal sprays of dainty, waxy-textured flowers are white but can vary in color to pink or purple. The flowers are ideal for indoor decoration as they will last for a long time when picked. The shrub requires a sandy soil that contains some lime. It resents root disturbance so care should be taken not to cultivate in close proximity to it.
Other colors: Dark plum.
Varieties/cultivars: 'University'.

Chamelaucium uncinatum

Choisya ternata

MEXICAN ORANGE BLOSSOM ○ ◑

Family: RUTACEAE
Origin: Mexico.
Flowering time: Spring.
Climatic zone: 7, 8, 9, 10.
Dimensions: 6–8 feet (2–3 meters) high.
Description: A compact, evergreen shrub, the dark-green, glossy leaves of Mexican orange blossom make a striking contrast with the abundant clusters of crisp, white, fragrant flowers. The leaves have an interesting aroma when crushed. Plant it near a door or window so that the delightful perfume can be appreciated. It is an adaptable shrub, growing just as well in full sun as in partial shade. It likes a well-drained, humus-rich soil, but can be damaged by prolonged frosty winters.

Choisya ternata

Cistus ladanifer

CRIMSON SPOT ROCK ROSE, GUM CISTUS, CRIMSON SPOT SUNROSE (U.K.) ○

Other common names: GUM SUNROSE (U.K.)
Family: CISTACEAE
Origin: Southwestern Europe.
Flowering time: Summer.
Climatic zone: 7, 8, 9.
Dimensions: Up to 6 feet (2 meters) high.
Description: This erect species has lance-shaped leaves, and interesting, fragrant, white flowers with a yellow center and a purple blotch on each petal. The flowers are at least 3½ inches (85 mm) across. Crimson spot rock rose is a very hardy plant that will withstand

salt winds and drought, although it may be killed by severe winters. It will thrive if given a well-drained, shady soil and a very hot, sunny position in the garden. Plant it alone, as a feature plant, or in a herbaceous garden.
Other colors: Pure white.
Varieties/cultivars: 'Albiflorus', 'Maculatus'.

Cistus salviifolius

ROCK ROSE, SAGE-LEAVED SUNROSE (U.K.) ○

Family: CISTACEAE
Origin: Southern Europe.
Flowering time: Summer.
Climatic zone: 7, 8, 9.
Dimensions: 3 feet (1 meter) high.
Description: This pretty, low-growing shrub, with its sage-like, grayish-green leaves, has white flowers with a yellow center. Plant it in a large rockery or at the front of a shrub border. It looks

Cistus salviifolius

Cistus ladanifer

202

interesting when planted either with dark-green shrubs or as part of a white and gray garden theme. Rock rose will thrive if given a well-drained, sandy soil and full sun in the hottest part of the garden. It can be killed by severe winters.

Varieties/cultivars: 'Prostratus'.

Clerodendrum trichotomum

Clerodendrum trichotomum
HARLEQUIN GLORY BOWER

Family: VERBENACEAE
Origin: China, Japan.
Flowering time: Summer–autumn.
Climatic zone: 5, 6, 7, 8, 9.
Dimensions: 8–12 feet (3–4 meters) high.
Description: Throughout summer, this attractive shrub is covered in fragrant, white flowers which are enclosed in maroon calyces. The flowers are followed by bright-blue berries still surrounded by the colorful calyces, hanging among the large leaves in their autumn tonings. It makes an interesting feature shrub, looking as wonderful when in flower as when covered with berries. Plant it in well-drained soil that has been previously enriched with manure or compost.

Clethra alnifolia
SWEET PEPPERBUSH, SUMMER SWEET CLETHRA, SPIKED ALDER (U.S.A.)

Family: CLETHRACEAE
Origin: Eastern United States.
Flowering time: Summer.
Climatic zone: 4, 5, 6, 7, 8, 9.
Dimensions: 6–9 feet (2–3 meters) high.
Description: This hardy, deciduous shrub has long leaves and is covered in a profusion of very fragrant, terminal spikes of white flowers in summer. It

Clethra alnifolia

should be planted close to a door or window so that the delicious perfume can be appreciated. It is very easy to grow and will thrive in a moist, neutral to acid soil. Keep the soil around the base of the plant mulched with manure or compost. This will not only feed the shrub, but keep the soil moist.
Other colors: Pink.
Varieties/cultivars: 'Pink Spires', 'Rosea', 'Paniculata'.

Cleyera japonica

Cleyera japonica
SASAKI

Family: THEACEAE
Origin: Japan, China, Korea, Taiwan.
Flowering time: Spring.
Climatic zone: 8, 9.
Dimensions: 6–10 feet (2–3 meters) high.
Description: This slow-growing shrub has a distinctive growth habit. The branches spread rigidly and are very densely covered in dark-green, shining leaves. In spring, it can be covered in a profusion of small, white flowers.

Some of the leaves may turn red in winter, even though it is an evergreen. It likes sandy loam and responds to regular fertilizing in spring.

Convolvulus cneorum
SILVERBUSH

Family: CONVOLVULACEAE
Origin: Southeastern Europe.
Flowering time: Spring–summer.
Climatic zone: 7, 8, 9, 10.
Dimensions: Up to 3 feet (1 meter) high.
Description: The white flowers of this compact, little evergreen shrub look at first like partly opened umbrellas, but when fully open are about 2 inches (50 mm) across. The slender, silvery-gray foliage is covered in silky hairs. Silverbush makes a good non-invasive shrub in large rock gardens or can be included in a herbaceous border. It will thrive in a sunny position in sandy, well-drained soil, but may be killed by severe winters. Fertilize it with a handful of complete plant food in early spring.

Convolvulus cneorum

Cornus alba

Cornus sanguinea

Cornus alba
RED-BARKED DOGWOOD, TARTARIAN DOGWOOD
○ ◑

Family: CORNACEAE
Origin: Eastern Asia.
Flowering time: Early summer.
Climatic zone: 3, 4, 5, 6, 7, 8, 9.
Dimensions: 6–10 feet (2–3 meters) high.
Description: The white flowers of tartarian dogwood appear in profusion during early summer. An added feature is the deep-red, twiggy branches which add some color to the garden during the winter months. The oval leaves may color well in autumn. There are many different varieties of this plant, the majority of them having variegated leaves. Tartarian dogwood will grow well in either wet or dry soil.
Varieties/cultivars: There are numerous cultivars throughout the world. Flower color is generally white, but the color of the branches ranges from black-purple to bronze.

Cornus sanguinea
COMMON DOGWOOD, BLOOD-TWIG DOGWOOD
○ ◑

Family: CORNACEAE
Origin: Europe, southwestern Asia.
Flowering time: Summer.
Climatic zone: 4, 5, 6, 7, 8, 9.
Dimensions: 4–6 feet (1–2 meters) high.
Description: Grown throughout England as a hedgerow plant, this attractive, hardy shrub has dark-reddish stems and oval leaves that turn a rich purple in autumn. The off-white, scented flowers are followed in autumn

by large clusters of black fruits. Plant it in a shrub border or with evergreen plants in an informal hedge. Prune it every second spring to encourage new shoots.

Cornus stolonifera syn. *C. sericea*
RED OSIER, DOGWOOD
○ ◑

Family: CORNACEAE
Origin: North America.
Flowering time: Spring.
Climatic zone: 3, 4, 5, 6, 7, 8, 9.
Dimensions: 6 feet (2 meters) high.
Description: This is a rampant, suckering, hardy shrub which forms a dense thicket of purplish-red, upright

Cornus stolonifera

branches. The off-white flowers are followed by white berries. It thrives in wet soil and is often used for hedges, especially on large estates. It can be pruned heavily in late winter if required. Mulch around the base of the plant with manure, compost, or grass clippings to keep the soil moist.
Varieties/cultivars: 'Flaviramea'.

Cornus stolonifera 'Flaviramea'

Cornus stolonifera 'Flaviramea' syn. *C. sericea* 'Flaviramea'
YELLOWTWIG, DOGWOOD
○ ◑

Family: CORNACEAE
Origin: Cultivar.
Flowering time: Spring.
Climatic zone: 3, 4, 5, 6, 7, 8, 9.
Dimensions: 4–6 feet (1–2 meters) high.
Description: The white flowers of this low, spreading, deciduous shrub are produced in clusters and are followed by small, round, black berries. It has shining, bright greenish-yellow bark and looks particularly attractive when planted with the red-stemmed species, *C. sanguinea*. This hardy shrub will thrive in moist or wet conditions. If planted in ordinary garden soil, make sure the area around the base of the plant is continually mulched to keep the moisture in the soil, and supply ample water in the summer.

Correa alba
WHITE CORREA, AUSTRALIAN FUCHSIA
○ ◑

Family: RUTACEAE
Origin: Eastern Australia, Tasmania.
Flowering time: Winter.

Correa alba

Cyrilla racemiflora

Climatic zone: 9, 10.
Dimensions: 5 feet (approx. 2 meters) high.
Description: This rounded shrub has circular leaves with a waxy bloom. The white flowers are valued for providing winter color when, in most places, other flowers are scarce. Although this is the main flowering period there are usually some flowers on the plant throughout the year. They attract nectar-feeding birds. It is very salt-resistant and therefore suitable for seaside planting. The soil should be well drained and fed with an organic fertilizer in early spring.

Cyrilla racemiflora
LEATHERWOOD, SWAMP CYRILLA ○

Family: CYRILLACEAE
Origin: Southeastern United States, West Indies, eastern South America.
Flowering time: Summer.
Climatic zone: 6, 7, 8, 9, 10.
Dimensions: 10–15 feet (3–5 meters) high.
Description: The white flowers of this pretty shrub are borne in whorls of slender racemes at the base of the current year's shoots. The lance-shaped leaves may turn crimson in autumn. The shrub looks most attractive in a woodland garden. It requires an acid soil. Mulching around the base with oak leaves or peat will keep the soil acidic. It is easily propagated from cuttings taken in summer, or by seed.

Cytisus x *kewensis*
KEW BROOM ○

Family: LEGUMINOSAE
Origin: Hybrid.
Flowering time: Early summer.
Climatic zone: 6, 7, 8, 9.
Dimensions: 12 inches (300 mm) high.
Description: This is a deciduous, semiprostrate, mat-forming hybrid which was raised at Kew Gardens in England. The small trifoliate leaves are slightly hairy on the edges and underneath. The creamy-white flowers are produced in abundance, making a most magnificent display. Plant it in large rockeries, on banks, or at the front of shrub borders. Kew broom likes a free-draining soil.

Cytisus x *kewensis*

Cytisus 'Snow Queen'

Cytisus x *praecox*

Cytisus 'Snow Queen'
BROOM, WHITE BROOM ○

Family: LEGUMINOSAE
Origin: Cultivar.
Flowering time: Spring.
Climatic zone: 6, 7, 8, 9.
Dimensions: 3–4 feet (approx. 1 meter) high.
Description: White broom looks magnificent when covered in its masses of white flowers in spring. These look impressive especially if near plants with dark-green foliage. Plant it at the front of a shrub border, or at the back of a herbaceous border. The main requirement of white broom is well-drained soil.

Cytisus x *praecox*
WARMINSTER BROOM ○

Family: LEGUMINOSAE
Origin: Hybrid.
Flowering time: Early summer.
Climatic zone: 6, 7, 8, 9.
Dimensions: 3–4 feet (approx. 1 meter) high.
Description: This extremely pretty plant has a dainty, loose habit. When in bloom it becomes a tumbling mass of creamy white as the long, thin stems hang down with the sheer weight of the flowers. It makes a delightful feature plant and fits in well with herbaceous plants in a border. Plant it in well-drained soil and fertilize it in spring with a handful of complete plant food.
Other colors: Golden yellow.
Varieties/cultivars: 'Alba', 'Allgold', 'Gold Spear', 'Hollandia'.

Daphne odora 'Alba'
FRAGRANT DAPHNE, ○ ◑
WINTER DAPHNE

Family: THYMELAEACEAE
Origin: Cultivar.
Flowering time: Winter–spring.
Climatic zone: 7, 8, 9.
Dimensions: 3 feet (1 meter) high.
Description: An attractive shrub, fragrant daphne has a spreading habit and smooth, showy, deep-green leaves. The extremely fragrant flowers are in tight clusters, each composed of thirty to forty flowers. The shrub requires a cool soil which must be crumbly and well-drained. Before planting, dig in leaf mold or peat. Do not use chemical fertilizers. A mulch of leaf mold annually will suffice to feed the plant and will not harm it.

Daphne x *burkwoodii* 'Albert Burkwood'
BURKWOOD DAPHNE ○ ◑

Family: THYMELAEACEAE
Origin: Hybrid.
Flowering time: Summer.
Climatic zone: 5, 6, 7, 8, 9.
Dimensions: Up to 3 feet (1 meter) high.
Description: This is a useful, low-growing, semi-evergreen shrub for the front border. In summer the stem tips are crowned with clusters of fragrant white flowers which age to pink. Burkwood daphne thrives in a neutral to limy soil. Do not use chemical fertilizer as, like other daphnes, it is easily killed with such kindness. A mulch of leaf mold or manure applied around the plant in spring is all that is required.

Daphne odora 'Alba'

Daphne x *burkwoodii* 'Albert Burkwood'

Datura suaveolens

Datura suaveolens syn. *Brugmansia suaveolens*
ANGEL'S-TRUMPET ○ ◑

Family: SOLANACEAE
Origin: Mexico.
Flowering time: Summer.
Climatic zone: 9, 10.
Dimensions: 6–10 feet (2–3 meters) high.
Description: This large shrub has flannel-like leaves and bears large, hanging, trumpet-shaped, fragrant flowers during summer. It makes an eye-catching specimen shrub. Quick-growing, it flourishes in warm temperate to tropical climates, but withstands cold if it is cut back to near ground level during winter. In spring, new shoots will burst forth and flower during the first season. Angel's-trumpet is often grown in conservatories in cold climates.

Deutzia gracilis

Deutzia gracilis
SLENDER DEUTZIA ○

Family: PHILADELPHACEAE
Origin: Japan.
Flowering time: Early summer.
Climatic zone: 4, 5, 6, 7, 8, 9.
Dimensions: Up to 4 feet (approx. 1 meter) high.
Description: This elegant, deciduous shrub maintains a bushy form and has yellow-gray bark on its hollow stems. It is excellent in cool-climate gardens, where its many-flowered heads of pure-white flowers are a delight in the summer. Prune it immediately after it has finished flowering.

Deutzia scabra

Deutzia scabra
FUZZY DEUTZIA ○

Family: PHILADELPHACEAE
Origin: Japan, China.
Flowering time: Early summer.
Climatic zone: 5, 6, 7, 8, 9.
Dimensions: Up to 8 feet (approx. 3 meters) high.
Description: This widely cultivated deciduous shrub has produced some well-known cultivars including those with double flowers. The species produces abundant spikes, up to 5 inches (125 mm) long, of star-shaped flowers, which may show a faint flush of pink on the outside of the petals. Arising from the base, the branches are erect, arching canes, with the upper twigs coppery-green and furry and the older wood peeling in small shreds. The shrub should be pruned immediately after flowering by removing the oldest canes at the base.
Varieties/cultivars: 'Candidissima', 'Pride of Rochester'.

Deutzia x *lemoinei*
LEMOINE DEUTZIA ○

Family: PHILADELPHACEAE
Origin: Hybrid.
Flowering time: Early summer.
Climatic zone: 4, 5, 6, 7, 8, 9.
Dimensions: Up to 7 feet (2 meters) high.
Description: This hybrid from *D. gracilis* and *D. parviflora* was produced by Victor Lemoine of Nancy in France. A many-branched, deciduous shrub, it grows erect and has narrow leaves, up to 4 inches (100 mm) long, which are sharply toothed. The pure-white flowers are very numerous and, though individually only ¾ inch (18 mm) wide, they appear in spikes up to 4 inches (100 mm) long. Annual pruning after flowering is advisable to encourage strong growth.

Deutzia x *lemoinei*

Erica carnea 'Springwood White'

Escallonia bifida

Erica carnea 'Springwood White'
WINTER HEATH ○

Family: ERICACEAE
Origin: Cultivar.
Flowering time: Midwinter–early spring.
Climatic zone: 5, 6, 7.
Dimensions: Up to 1 foot (300 mm) high.
Description: Considered the finest white cultivar of Erica, this is a low, spreading shrub with masses of showy, urn-shaped flowers. Hardy and easy to cultivate, plant it in an open, sunny position in moderately rich, well-drained soil that is slightly acidic. It is ideal for grouping with dwarf rhododendrons and conifers which like the same growing conditions. Prune back immediately after flowering to maintain a neat shape.

Escallonia bifida syn. *E. montevidensis*
ESCALLONIA ○

Family: ESCALLONIACEAE
Origin: Uruguay, southern Brazil.
Flowering time: Summer–mid-autumn.
Climatic zone: 8, 9.
Dimensions: 13 feet (4 meters) high.
Description: The most beautiful of the white-flowered escallonias is this handsome evergreen shrub with a loose, open habit. It sometimes attains a tree-like form. The sweetly honey-scented flowers are star-shaped, ½ inch (12 mm) wide, and attached to the stem by a bell-shaped receptacle. Its shoots are hairless but sometimes slightly sticky, and its elliptic or spatula-shaped leaves, up to 3 inches (75 mm) long, are sprinkled on their undersides with small resinous

dots. Easy to cultivate, this shrub flowers generously over a long period and is suitable for seaside conditions. In colder climates, the protection of a wall is necessary as the shrub may be killed by severe winters.

Exochorda racemosa
PEARLBUSH ○

Family: ROSACEAE
Origin: China.
Flowering time: Spring.
Climatic zone: 5, 6, 7, 8, 9.
Dimensions: Up to 15 feet (5 meters) high.
Description: This is a deciduous shrub of considerable beauty, much prized for its showy display of paper-white flowers, which coincides with lilac flowering

Exochorda racemosa

time. Its buds in racemes are said to look like a string of pearls. The five petals of the open flowers spread to 1½ inches (35 mm) wide with many stamens arranged around the rim of the green center. Grown in slightly acid soil, the shrub needs to have the oldest branches pruned back to the base in late winter.

Fothergilla gardenii

Fothergilla gardenii
DWARF FOTHERGILLA ○

Family: HAMAMELIDACEAE
Origin: Southeastern United States.
Flowering time: Spring.
Climatic zone: 5, 6, 7, 8, 9.
Dimensions: 3 feet (1 meter) high.
Description: An attractive and unusual spring-bloomer, this small, deciduous shrub deserves greater popularity. The masses of flower spikes are without petals and appear as erect dish-mop heads of fragrant, white stamens measuring 1 inch (25 mm) long. These

bloom before the leaves unfold. In autumn, the leaves are a brilliant display of orange-crimson color. Plant the bush among other favorites in the shrub garden, preferably with an evergreen as a background so that the fluffy flower heads can be seen at their best.

Fothergilla major

Fothergilla major syn. *F. monticola*
WITCH ELDER,
FOTHERGILLA, MOUNTAIN
SNOW

Family: HAMAMELIDACEAE
Origin: Southeastern United States.
Flowering time: Spring.
Climatic zone: 5, 6, 7, 8, 9.
Dimensions: 6 feet (2 meters) high.
Description: The genus name honors John Fothergill, an eighteenth-century English physician and friend of Benjamin Franklin, who introduced many American plants into cultivation in England. Witch elder is a shrub with either an open, spreading habit or a rounded habit. Its roundish or heart-shaped leaves, becoming brilliant scarlet or crimson in autumn, make it one of the finest of the autumn coloring plants. In spring, it also offers a conspicuous show of terminal heads, up to 2 inches (50 mm) long, the petalless flowers relying on the spikes of stamens for their display. A lime-free soil will ensure continuous good growth.

Gardenia jasminoides 'Florida'
FLORIST'S GARDENIA

Family: RUBIACEAE
Origin: Cultivar.
Flowering time: Spring–summer.
Climatic zone: 9, 10.
Dimensions: Up to 5 feet (approx. 2 meters) high.
Description: Growing in warm

Gardenia jasminoides 'Florida'

climates, gardenias are cherished for their perfume, their white perfection, and their long flowering period. The glossy green leaves, up to 4 inches (100 mm) long, are also attractive all year. The solitary flowers stand clear of the top-most leaves and open from bright green buds in a spiral of overlapping petals to a width of 2½ inches (60 mm). The plants thrive in a slightly acid soil and should be planted near a doorway, window, or outdoor sitting area, where their perfume can be appreciated. Florists use the flowers because of their perfume and longevity.

Gardenia jasminoides 'Magnifica'
LARGE FLOWERED
GARDENIA, FLORIST'S
GARDENIA

Family: RUBIACEAE
Origin: Cultivar.
Flowering time: Spring–summer.
Climatic zone: 9, 10.
Dimensions: Up to 8 feet (approx. 2 meters) high.
Description: This cultivar is a larger shrub than G. *jasminoides* 'Florida', being both taller and wider. Its leaves are also larger, 4½ inches (112 mm) long, more lustrous, and a brighter green. Most of the twenty large, unfurling petals of the flowers spread out to measure 4½ inches (112 mm) wide, but some remain unopened and stand erect in the center. Their perfume is heady. Among the choicest of evergreen flowering shrubs, this gardenia adds distinction to shrub beds and borders. A hot-climate plant, plenty of water and an acid fertilizer are essential.

Gardenia jasminoides 'Magnifica'

Gardenia jasminoides 'Prostrata'

Gardenia jasminoides 'Prostrata' syn. 'Radicans'
DWARF GARDENIA,
FLORIST'S GARDENIA

Family: RUBIACEAE
Origin: Cultivar.
Flowering time: Spring–summer.
Climatic zone: 9, 10.
Dimensions: 12 inches (300 mm) high.
Description: This low, broad-spreading cultivar is an excellent small-scale groundcover. The lower branches often self-layer. The leaves are narrow and small, about 1½ inches (35 mm) long, and a bright, glossy green. The fragrant flowers are semidouble, about 1½ inches (35 mm) wide, with somewhat twisted petals. The miniature flower makes a perfect buttonhole. As well as being an excellent border shrub, this evergreen makes a very effective, low, informal hedge if enough shrubs are planted close together. A hot, humid summer is its main requirement, but plenty of water and regular feeding with an acid plant food is necessary for good flowering. It is also a good container plant, so a greenhouse environment will enable it to cope with cold climates.

Gaultheria procumbens

Gaultheria procumbens
WINTERGREEN, CHECKERBERRY

Family: ERICACEAE
Origin: Eastern United States.
Flowering time: Spring.
Climatic zone: 3, 4, 5, 6, 7, 8, 9.
Dimensions: 6 inches (150 mm) high.
Description: Wintergreen is found growing naturally in acid soils in dry and moist woodlands over areas that are vastly different climatically. Spreading by means of rhizomes, the stems of this prostrate, creeping shrub stand erect with the foliage crowded near the top. The evergreen leaves are up to 2 inches (50 mm) long. About 1/3 inch (8 mm) long, the waxy, white, bell-shaped flowers are solitary and hang from the leaf axils. The highly decorative, bright scarlet fruits are spicy and aromatic and much sought after as winter food by deer, grouse, and partridges.

Gaultheria shallon
SALAL, SHALLON

Family: ERICACEAE
Origin: Western United States.
Flowering time: Early summer.
Climatic zone: 6, 7, 8, 9.
Dimensions: Up to 5 feet (approx. 2 meters) high.
Description: This plant forms a pleasing ornamental, open shrub. It has many hairy stems with broad, ovate leaves which measure up to 5 inches (125 mm) long and are hairless when mature. The felted blooms, which can be tinged with pink, are about 1/2 inch (12 mm) long and are suspended like bells in terminal clusters of slender racemes. They are followed by edible,

purple fruits which turn black when mature. Esteemed for its attractive leaves, flowers, and fruit, this shrub is a good choice in a lightly shaded shrub border or woodland garden, although it can be very invasive when grown in moist, acid soil.

Genista monosperma
WHITE BROOM, WHITE WEEPING BROOM, BRIDAL VEIL BROOM

Family: LEGUMINOSAE
Origin: Spain, Portugal, North Africa.
Flowering time: Spring.
Climatic zone: 9, 10.
Dimensions: Up to 10 feet (3 meters) high.
Description: Somewhat straggly, this

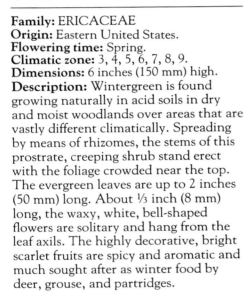

Genista monosperma

Gaultheria shallon

deciduous shrub has rush-like, wide-spreading, pendant branches that are silky-haired when young. When they appear, the leaves are sparse, up to 3/4 inch (18 mm) long, narrow, and also covered with silky hairs. The very fragrant flowers, each about 1/2 inch (12 mm) wide, are scattered abundantly along the branches in short racemes. They, too, have a silky-haired covering. Dry, well-drained, alkaline soils with poor fertility best simulate the conditions of their native habitat. Annual pruning and thinning out of the oldest branches is recommended.

Grevillea banksii 'Alba'
BANKS' WHITE GREVILLEA

Family: PROTEACEAE
Origin: Cultivar.
Flowering time: Spring–early summer.
Climatic zone: 9, 10.
Dimensions: Up to 13 feet (4 meters) high.
Description: This upright, many-branched shrub has leaves of dark green with silky hairs giving a white appearance to their undersides. The leaves can measure up to 12 inches (300 mm) long. The flowers are produced in profusion, with forty to eighty crowded on an erect, terminal, cylindrical head up to 4 inches (100 mm) long. This white form of the red-flowering species has the same

Grevillea banksii 'Alba'

reputation as the red for blooming intermittently after the main flowering period is over. Thriving in a sunny position, it is a very hardy and rewarding plant. It attracts birds.

Hakea acicularis

Hakea acicularis syn. *H. sericea*
BUSHY NEEDLEWOOD, SILKY HAKEA ○

Family: PROTEACEAE
Origin: Southeastern Australia.
Flowering time: Winter–spring.
Climatic zone: 9, 10.
Dimensions: 9 feet (3 meters) high.
Description: Care should be taken when positioning this shrub in the garden as its stiff, needle-like leaves, which spread in all directions, have sharp points which can prick the unwary. However, planted as an impenetrable hedge, this species would have few equals. The perfumed flowers, which sometimes show a tinge of pink, appear mostly as small clusters in the upper leaf axils and are a dainty foil to

the leaves. The prominent, woody fruits, measuring up to 1½ inches (35 mm) long, persist on the plant, unopened, for several years unless disturbed by fire or injury. It is easy to grow in well-drained soil.

Hebe albicans

Hebe albicans
NEW ZEALAND LILAC, SHRUBBY VERONICA (U.K.) ○

Family: SCROPHULARIACEAE
Origin: New Zealand.
Flowering time: Summer–autumn.
Climatic zone: 7, 8, 9.
Dimensions: Up to 3 feet (1 meter) high.
Description: This is a splendid dwarf, evergreen shrub with a dense, rounded shape. The gray-green leaves arranged opposite one another on the stem give way at the top to the flower heads. Here, numerous 1 inch (25 mm) long spikes of flowers cover the plant throughout its long flowering period. Hardy in most soils which are well drained, this is another species that can tolerate difficult locations near the sea. Pruning is not needed.

Hebe diosmifolia

Hebe diosmifolia
VERONICA ○ ◑

Family: SCROPHULARIACEAE
Origin: New Zealand.
Flowering time: Summer.
Climatic zone: 6, 7, 8, 9.
Dimensions: Up to 3 feet (1 meter) high.
Description: A small, neat shrub, this species has glossy green foliage and flat clusters of small white flowers, tinged with palest lilac. Like most veronicas it thrives in rich, well-drained soil if planted in an open, sunny position. It can withstand both frosts and drought conditions and can be easily propagated by cuttings taken at any time of the year.

Hebe odora

Hebe odora syn. *H. buxifolia*
WHITE SPEEDWELL, SHRUBBY VERONICA ○

Family: SCROPHULARIACEAE
Origin: New Zealand mountains.
Flowering time: Spring–summer.
Climatic zone: 8, 9.
Dimensions: Up to 6 feet (2 meters) high.
Description: Of the one hundred species of *Hebe*, all but a few are natives of New Zealand. This plant is a small, erect, evergreen shrub with polished green leaves less than 1 inch (25 mm) long. The flowers grow on 1–2-inch (25–50 mm) terminal spikes. When *H. odora* is in full bloom, the profusion of flowers almost hides the leaves. Very ornamental, this species is also invaluable for seaside and industrial estate planting.

Hebe salicifolia

Hebe salicifolia
KOROMIKO, SHRUBBY VERONICA

Family: SCROPHULARIACEAE
Origin: New Zealand, southern Chile.
Flowering time: Summer.
Climatic zone: 7, 8, 9.
Dimensions: Up to 15 feet (5 meters) high.
Description: With the specific name meaning "leaves like a *Salix* (or willow)" it is no surprise to find this evergreen species has narrow leaves up to 6 inches (150 mm) long, tapering to a point at the tips. They usually have toothed margins. The flower spikes are slender and cylindrical and are sometimes more than 6 inches (150 mm) long. The small, white, individual blooms can be tinged with pale to darker lilac. This is a shrub which is ideally suited to seaside areas and, as with the other *Hebe* species, is one of the easiest plants to maintain in the garden. It is a parent of many hardy hybrids. It does not, however, tolerate prolonged winter cold.

Hibiscus mutabilis
COTTON ROSE, CONFEDERATE ROSE, ROSE COTTON

Other common names: ROSE OF SHARON
Family: MALVACEAE
Origin: Southeastern China.
Flowering time: Autumn.
Climatic zone: 9, 10.
Dimensions: Up to 13 feet (4 meters) high.
Description: *Mutabilis*, meaning "to change", indicates the change in flower color, from white when they emerge to deep-red as they age. This transition means that the shrub is liberally clothed in flowers of white and red, as well as all the intervening shades of pink. The long-stalked leaves are also distinctive. They are wider than they are long, about 7 inches (175 mm) across, with three to seven coarsely toothed, shallow triangular lobes, and both they and the young stems are thickly covered with yellowish hairs. It needs protection from frost and wind, and enjoys full sun and a well-drained soil.

Hibiscus mutabilis

Hydrangea arborescens 'Grandiflora'

Hydrangea arborescens
TREE HYDRANGEA, SMOOTH HYDRANGEA

Family: HYDRANGEACEAE
Origin: Southeastern United States.
Flowering time: Summer.
Climatic zone: 4, 5, 6, 7, 8, 9.
Dimensions: Up to 5 feet (approx. 2 meters) high.
Description: This ornamental, deciduous shrub has a somewhat loose and straggling growth. Its leaves are large and egg-shaped. Its flattish flower clusters are up to 6 inches (150 mm) across, consisting of masses of small, fertile flowers and a dappling of a few large, showy, sterile ones on the outer edges. *H. arborescens* 'Grandiflora', known as Hills of Snow, is very popular and the more commonly cultivated form. An annual prune after flowering will keep this shrub compact. The cut blooms are very decorative in vases.
Varieties/cultivars: 'Grandiflora'.

Hydrangea quercifolia

Hydrangea quercifolia
OAK-LEAVED HYDRANGEA

Family: HYDRANGEACEAE
Origin: Southeastern United States.
Flowering time: Summer.
Climatic zone: 5, 6, 7, 8, 9.
Dimensions: Up to 6 feet (2 meters) high.
Description: This beautiful deciduous shrub is an elegant inclusion in an open woodland garden or positioned in light shade. Many cultivate it for its bold, handsome foliage. The leaves are 8 inches (200 mm) long, with three to five deep lobes, whitish on their undersides when newly opened, and changing in autumn to produce a spectacular display of bronzy-purple. The flower clusters are in 12-inch-long (300 mm) pyramids of long-stalked, showy, sterile blooms, as well as smaller, fertile ones. They age to a rosy-purple. It requires a humus-rich soil and may be damaged by severe winters.

Itea virginica

Itea virginica
VIRGINIA WILLOW, ◯ ◖
SWEETSPIRE

Family: ITEACEAE
Origin: Southeastern United States.
Flowering time: Summer.
Climatic zone: 5, 6, 7, 8, 9.
Dimensions: Up to 10 feet (3 meters)
high.
Description: A native of wet woods
and swamps of the coastal region, this
deciduous shrub branches into many
slender stems which support its
handsome leaves. Up to 4 inches
(100 mm) long, with finely toothed
margins, they turn beautiful shades of
red in autumn. The small, fluffy,
creamy-white flowers, which are tinged
with green, are sweetly fragrant and
produced in great profusion in semi-
erect racemes measuring up to 6 inches
(150 mm) long. Humus-rich soil is
preferred and the protection of a wall or
sheltered corner is desirable.

Leucothoe axillaris syn. *L. catesbaei*
COAST LEUCOTHOE ◖

Family: ERICACEAE
Origin: Southeastern United States.
Flowering time: Summer.
Climatic zone: 5, 6, 7, 8, 9.
Dimensions: Up to 6 feet (2 meters) high.
Description: Named after Leucothoë, a
legendary princess of Babylon who was
believed to have been changed into a

Leucothoe axillaris

shrub by the god Apollo, this excellent
evergreen shrub is generally similar to
L. fontanesiana. It is, however, a native
of moist woodlands of the coastal plain.
The flower heads, which are about
3 inches (75 mm) long, are crowded with
broad, urn-shaped flowers. The leaves
are bluntly pointed and only sparsely
toothed. This shrub likes moist, acid
soil.

Leucothoe fontanesiana
DROOPING ◯ ◖
LEUCOTHOE

Family: ERICACEAE
Origin: Eastern United States.
Flowering time: Early summer.
Climatic zone: 5, 6, 7, 8, 9.
Dimensions: Up to 6 feet (2 meters) high.
Description: This is an attractive and
useful evergreen shrub for lightly shaded
garden areas, and open woodlands
where naturalistic effects are sought. Its
native habitat is along banks of
mountain streams. The flowers, which
are small, urn-shaped, and drooping,
appear in clusters up to 4 inches
(100 mm) long, all along the graceful,
arching stems. The stems, reddish when
young, support lance-like, leathery
leaves which, in the cold months and

Leucothoe fontanesiana

especially in exposed positions, become
tinged with deep reds and bronzy-
purples. An acid, peaty soil is necessary
which is moist but well-drained.

Ligustrum japonicum 'Rotundifolium'

Ligustrum japonicum
JAPANESE PRIVET, JAPANESE TREE PRIVET ○

Family: OLEACEAE
Origin: Japan, Korea.
Flowering time: Late summer–autumn.
Climatic zone: 7, 8, 9.
Dimensions: Up to 10 feet (3 meters) high.
Description: Sometimes assuming a tree-like form, this dense, evergreen shrub has shiny olive-green leaves over 4 inches (100 mm) long. The flowers are small and are borne in large clusters up to 6 inches (150 mm) long, on the terminal shoots. Many people find their scent unpleasant. These plants make an effective hedge, screen, or background. They can be clipped into formal shapes or left as a natural wall of greenery, and thrive even when neglected or grown in poor soils.
Varieties/cultivars: 'Rotundifolium'.

Ligustrum lucidum
CHINESE PRIVET ○

Family: OLEACEAE
Origin: Japan, Korea, China.
Flowering time: Late summer–autumn.
Climatic zone: 7, 8, 9.
Dimensions: Up to 30 feet (9 meters) high.
Description: Occasionally seen as a beautiful, symmetrical tree with an attractive, fluted trunk, this evergreen can also be clipped as a hedge. It has large, glossy green, pointed leaves, up to 6 inches (150 mm) in length, and large, handsome clusters of flowers with petals as long as the corolla tubes that support

them. All privets have some unwelcome characteristics. The scent of the flowers is offensive to some people, and the roots are "hungry" and impoverish nearby soil.
Varieties/cultivars: 'Excelsum Superbum', 'Tricolor'.

Ligustrum lucidum

Ligustrum ovalifolium

Ligustrum ovalifolium
CALIFORNIA PRIVET (U.S.A.), ○ OVAL LEAF PRIVET (U.K.), HEDGING PRIVET (U.K.)

Family: OLEACEAE
Origin: Japan.
Flowering time: Summer.
Climatic zone: 5, 6, 7, 8, 9.
Dimensions: Up to 13 feet (4 meters) high.
Description: This favorite hedge plant grows erect and stiff, but possesses the fine twiggy growth so essential for the formation of a good, dense hedge. It can

be grown successfully in poor soils and remains semi-evergreen, except in very severe winters when it becomes deciduous. The short-stalked flowers appear in profuse clusters, up to 4 inches (100 mm) long. Many people dislike their smell. The leaves, which are glossy green and pointed, are up to 2½ inches (62 mm) long.
Varieties/cultivars: 'Aureum', 'Argenteum'.

Lonicera nitida 'Aurea'

Lonicera nitida
BOX-LEAF HONEYSUCKLE

Family: CAPRIFOLIACEAE
Origin: Western China.
Flowering time: Spring.
Climatic zone: 7, 8, 9.
Dimensions: Up to 6 feet (2 meters) high.
Description: This twiggy, evergreen shrub is a vigorous grower, stands clipping well, and makes a dense, compact hedge. The tiny, sweetly fragrant flowers appear in pairs from the leaf axils, and are followed by bluish-purple berries, ¼ inch (6 mm) wide. The leaves are small, thick, glossy, oval to rounded in shape, and up to ½ inch (12 mm) long. When training it as a hedge, establish a good basic framework when the plant is young by regular pruning. Grow in well-drained but moist soil.
Varieties/cultivars: Several cultivars are available.

Loropetalum chinense
FRINGE FLOWER, LOROPETALUM ○

Family: HAMAMELIDACEAE
Origin: China.
Flowering time: Spring.
Climatic zone: 8, 9, 10.

Loropetalum chinense

Dimensions: Up to 12 feet (4 meters) high.
Description: This neat-foliaged, evergreen shrub grows well among azaleas and other shrubs which have the same well-drained, acid soil requirements. The showy flowers consist of four soft, strap-shaped petals about 1 inch (25 mm) long, freely produced in clusters of six to nine to give a fringed appearance to the shrub. The leaves are rough to the touch, egg-shaped, and up to 2 inches (50 mm) long. A warm, sheltered position is necessary for this shrub. It does not tolerate severe winter weather. It appreciates an application of lime-free compost.

Magnolia stellata
STAR MAGNOLIA ○ ◑

Family: MAGNOLIACEAE
Origin: Japan.
Flowering time: Spring.
Climatic zone: 5, 6, 7, 8, 9.
Dimensions: Up to 15 feet (5 meters) high.
Description: Slow-growing and deciduous, this shrub is distinctive and charming. With its many spreading branches, it grows wider than it does high and is prized for its brilliant spring floral display. The fragrant, star-like flowers burst open on bare branches. They comprise up to twenty-one petals and sepals, which look alike and are narrow, strap-shaped, 1½ inches (35 mm) long, and bend backwards with age. The leaves are broadly oval to

Magnolia stellata

oblong and up to 5 inches (125 mm) long. Plant in fertile, well-drained soil with plenty of humus.
Other colors: Pink, purplish-pink.
Varieties/cultivars: 'Rosea', 'Rubra'.

Melaleuca armillaris
HONEY MYRTLE, ○
BRACELET HONEY MYRTLE

Family: MYRTACEAE
Origin: Eastern Australia.
Flowering time: Spring–summer.
Climatic zone: 9, 10.
Dimensions: Up to 17 feet (approx. 5 meters) high.
Description: This is a hardy, fast-growing, evergreen, bushy shrub, or

Melaleuca armillaris

small tree, which often grows wider than it does tall. Narrow, 1-inch-long (25 mm) leaves, thickly covering the many fine stems, form a dense, impenetrable barrier, making this an excellent choice for a windbreak or screen. The flowers are arranged in a spike up to 2½ inches (60 mm) long. Their conspicuous stamens give the whole flower the appearance of a "bottlebrush". The woody, capsular fruit with their seeds remain on the plant for several years. It grows well in most soils and will tolerate lime.

Melaleuca incana

Melaleuca incana
GRAY HONEY MYRTLE ○

Family: MYRTACEAE
Origin: Western Australia.
Flowering time: Late spring–early summer.
Climatic zone: 9, 10.
Dimensions: Up to 10 feet (3 meters) high.
Description: The Latin word *incana* meaning "quite gray", refers to the color of the foliage of this attractive and useful evergreen shrub. The twenty to forty tiny flowers are densely crowded onto spikes up to 1 inch (25 mm) long. The leaves are small, up to ½ inch (12 mm) long, and their soft, white, hairy covering extends also to the twigs supporting them. These leaves assume a grayish-purple tinge in winter. This species requires an extremely well-drained situation in open, light soil.

Melaleuca linariifolia 'Snowstorm'

Melaleuca linariifolia 'Snowstorm'
SNOW-IN-SUMMER ○

Family: MYRTACEAE
Origin: Cultivar.
Flowering time: Late spring–summer.
Climatic zone: 9, 10.
Dimensions: Up to 5 feet (approx. 2 meters) high.
Description: This is a registered dwarf form of the well-known evergreen tree species. As its cultivated name indicates, at flowering time the display of flowers covers the plant so profusely that the fine, narrow leaves are not visible. The flower head is a slender spike containing thirty to forty-five flowers massed along its 2½-inch (60-mm) length. The light perfume is reminiscent of honey. The bark is thick, spongy, white, and papery, and the 1 inch (25 mm) long, leaves contain sweet-smelling oil glands. This shrub will thrive even in exposed positions in seaside gardens.

Murraya paniculata syn. *M. exotica*
MOCK ORANGE, ○ ◑
ORANGE JESSAMINE

Family: RUTACEAE
Origin: South East Asia.
Flowering time: Spring and intermittently.
Climatic zone: 9, 10.
Dimensions: Up to 10 feet (3 meters) high.
Description: This evergreen, ornamental shrub is highly esteemed in gardens or containers in the tropics and subtropics. The blooms, deliciously scented, open to a trumpet shape, about 1 inch (25 mm) across, in clusters of ten to twenty. The decorative oval fruit ripens to a bright red. The plant often

flowers several times a year. The leaves are a bright, shining green, with three to nine leaflets, each up to 2 inches (50 mm) long, and, because this species belongs to the same family as *Citrus*, they emit a sweet smell when handled. This shrub requires lots of water and a humus-rich soil.

Murraya paniculata

Myoporum parvifolium

Myoporum parvifolium
CREEPING MYOPORUM ○

Family: MYOPORACEAE
Origin: Eastern Australia.
Flowering time: Spring.
Climatic zone: 9, 10.
Dimensions: Up to 10 inches (250 mm) high.
Description: This prostrate, evergreen shrub makes an excellent mat-forming plant, spreading readily to 3 feet (1 meter) and sending down roots as its trailing stems proceed. Tiny, white, star-

like flowers are borne all along the stems. The rich green of the foliage of this hardy plant is also a feature. The leaves are narrow, fleshy, and thickly produced. Fine-, medium-, and broad-leaved as well as purple-stemmed forms are available. Well-drained soil in a sunny position gives the best results.

Myrtus communis

Myrtus communis
COMMON MYRTLE ○

Family: MYRTACEAE
Origin: Western Asia.
Flowering time: Summer.
Climatic zone: 8, 9, 10.
Dimensions: Up to 15 feet (5 meters) high.
Description: Esteemed since classical times as a symbol of love and peace, myrtle is often traditionally included in the bride's bouquet, from which cuttings are grown, to be kept as carefully tended plants throughout life. This dense, leafy, evergreen shrub has leaves that are glossy, spicily aromatic, elliptic to lance-shaped, and nearly 2 inches (50 mm) long. The four petals of the solitary flowers spread wide to ¾ inch (18 mm) across, to display a profusion of long stamens. The fruit is ½ inch (12 mm) long and ripens to bluish-black. Although fairly hardy, it grows best against a sunny, sheltered wall. In cooler climates, myrtle should be kept in a greenhouse in winter.
Varieties/cultivars: 'Flore Pleno', 'Microphylla', 'Tarentina', 'Variegata'.

Nandina domestica

Olearia x *haastii*

Nandina domestica
SACRED BAMBOO, HEAVENLY BAMBOO

○ ◑ ●

Family: BERBERIDACEAE
Origin: India–eastern Asia.
Flowering time: Spring.
Climatic zone: 7, 8, 9.
Dimensions: Up to 8 feet (approx. 2 meters) high.
Description: Somewhat like a bamboo in appearance, this evergreen shrub is grown in gardens and tubs for its ornamental qualities. Much of its beauty lies in the delicate tracery of the fine leaflets on leaves which can be up to 1½ feet (450 mm) long and which may assume brilliant shades of red to purple in autumn. The flowers, while not showy, are produced in terminal, pyramidal clusters, 12 inches (300 mm) long. The fruits, considered by some to be the most attractive feature of the plant, ripen to a handsome, rich red. It prefers a sheltered position away from cold winds and may be damaged by severe winters. Plant in humus-rich, neutral to acid soil.
Varieties/cultivars: 'Nana Compacta'.

Olearia x *haastii*
NEW ZEALAND DAISYBUSH

○

Family: COMPOSITAE
Origin: Hybrid.
Flowering time: Late summer.
Climatic zone: 7, 8, 9.
Dimensions: Up to 10 feet (3 meters) high.
Description: A wild hybrid between two New Zealand species, this shrub is one of the hardiest and, at the same time, the most floriferous and popular of the daisybushes. It is a many-branching, rounded shrub with small, crowded, oblong to egg-shaped leaves which are glossy green with white-felted undersides. The individual flower heads, about ⅓ inch (8 mm) across with yellow centers, are in flattish, long-stalked clusters up to 3½ inches (85 mm) in diameter. Ideally suited for hedges and thriving in seaside gardens, this shrub will withstand some frost. Well-drained but moist soil in a reasonably sunny position is required.

Osmanthus delavayi
DELAVAY OSMANTHUS

○ ◑

Family: OLEACEAE
Origin: Western China.
Flowering time: Spring.
Climatic zone: 7, 8, 9.
Dimensions: Up to 8 feet (approx. 2 meters) high.
Description: Introduced into Europe

Osmanthus delavayi

by Abbé Delavay as recently as 1890, this shrub is one of China's gems. It is a beautiful, fairly slow-growing, evergreen shrub densely covered with small, lustrous green, ovate leaves about 1 inch (25 mm) long. The freely produced tubular flowers are fragrant and jasmine-like, arising in small clusters from the leaf axils. The berry-like fruits, about ½ inch (12 mm) long, ripen in summer to a bluish-black. Although reasonably hardy, the shrub likes protection from the fiercest sun, and does not survive severe winters. Humus-rich, well-drained soil in a sheltered site is preferred.

Osmanthus fragrans

Osmanthus fragrans
SWEET OSMANTHUS, FRAGRANT TEA OLIVE, SWEET OLIVE

◑

Family: OLEACEAE
Origin: Himalayas–China.
Flowering time: Summer.
Climatic zone: 8, 9.
Dimensions: Up to 25 feet (8 meters) high.
Description: This evergreen shrub is grown for the beautiful, rich fragrance of its bell-shaped flowers. In its native lands, it has been cultivated for many centuries as an ornamental. Its dried flowers make a scented tea and, it is said, are used to keep clothes insect-free. It can be found in the garden in mild climates and in greenhouses in colder regions. The leaves are oval or oblong, up to 4 inches (100 mm) long, and finely toothed on the margins. A dense shrub, it can be trained as an espalier or small tree, or clipped as a hedge. Semishade and rich, acid soil suit it best.

Philadelphus coronarius

Philadelphus coronarius
COMMON MOCK ORANGE, SWEET MOCK ORANGE ○

Family: SAXIFRAGACEAE
Origin: Europe, southwestern Asia.
Flowering time: Early summer.
Climatic zone: 4, 5, 6, 7, 8, 9.
Dimensions: Up to 10 feet (3 meters) high.
Description: A deciduous shrub, sweet mock orange gives a splendid display of spring blossom. These very fragrant flowers, each about 1½ inches (35 mm) across, open wide to display four distinct, rounded petals and appear in five-to-seven-flowered heads at the ends of the many erect stems. The narrow leaves measure up to 3 inches (75 mm) long, have toothed margins, and change from a dark green to dull yellow in autumn. This very commonly cultivated species is particularly suited to dry soils.
Varieties/cultivars: 'Aureus', 'Variegatus'.

Philadelphus mexicanus
MEXICAN MOCK ORANGE ○

Family: SAXIFRAGACEAE
Origin: Southern Mexico, Guatemala.
Flowering time: Late spring.
Climatic zone: 9, 10.
Dimensions: Up to 6 feet (2 meters) high.
Description: Mexican mock orange is an evergreen shrub whose numerous slender branches arise from the base and arch outwards to form a loose, rounded shape. It is included in gardens for its

spring floral display. The sweetly perfumed flowers measure about 1½ inches (35 mm) across and occur singly or in clusters of three on small shoots from the upper branches. The softly textured leaves are up to 2½ inches (60 mm) across and somewhat furry, as are the new stems. Requiring little in the way of cultivation, these shrubs respond to pruning immediately after flowering.

Philadelphus mexicanus

Philadelphus x *lemoinei*

Philadelphus x *lemoinei*
LEMOINE MOCK ORANGE ○

Family: SAXIFRAGACEAE
Origin: Hybrid.
Flowering time: Late spring.
Climatic zone: 5, 6, 7, 8, 9.
Dimensions: Up to 6 feet (2 meters) high.
Description: This is one of an array of hybrids bred during the nineteenth century by Victor Lemoine in France. Its parents are *P. coronarius* and *P. microphyllus*. The profusion of 1-inch-

wide (25 mm) flowers, with their many golden-yellow anthers standing out against the white of the petals, and with their sweet fragrance, are this deciduous shrub's main attraction. They are produced on short stalks in terminal clusters of from three to five flowers. The leaves are up to 3 inches (75 mm) long. Any well-drained garden soil in a sunny position will ensure a rewarding display of flowers.
Varieties/cultivars: 'Avalanche', 'Boule d'Argent', 'Innocence', 'Manteau d'Hermine'.

Philadelphus x *virginalis*

Philadelphus x *virginalis*
VIRGINAL MOCK ORANGE ○

Family: SAXIFRAGACEAE
Origin: Hybrid.
Flowering time: Spring.
Climatic zone: 5, 6, 7, 8, 9.
Dimensions: Up to 10 feet (3 meters) high.
Description: This deciduous hybrid shrub is understandably popular, producing displays of double or semidouble blooms of superb quality. The flowers are generally large, up to 2 inches (50 mm) in diameter, and occur in abundance in clusters of five to seven on the many erect shoots. The rich fragrance of the flowers, which is likened to orange blossom, makes them an excellent inclusion in bridal bouquets. The leaves are up to 3 inches (75 mm) long with a coarsely toothed margin. Well-drained soil and a sunny position are preferred.
Varieties/cultivars: 'Virginal'.

Physocarpus opulifolius

Pieris formosa

Physocarpus opulifolius
COMMON NINEBARK ○ ◑

Family: ROSACEAE
Origin: Eastern North America.
Flowering time: Spring.
Climatic zone: 3, 4, 5, 6, 7, 8, 9.
Dimensions: Up to 10 feet (3 meters) high.
Description: The name common ninebark refers to the shedding and peeling bark seen on all species of *Physocarpus*. These deciduous shrubs are closely related to spiraeas although they are less showy in bloom. They thrive in almost any open position, are hardy, vigorous, and remarkably free from pests and diseases. The small flowers, which are sometimes tinged with pink, form profuse clusters, nearly 2 inches (50 mm) wide, along the many arching stems. The leaves are three-lobed and about 3 inches (75 mm) long. Moderately fertile, well-drained soil in a sunny or partially shaded position will ensure best results.
Varieties/cultivars: 'Intermedius', 'Luteus'.

Pieris formosa
HIMALAYAN ◑ ● ANDROMEDA, LILY-OF-THE-VALLEY SHRUB

Family: ERICACEAE
Origin: Himalayas.
Flowering time: Spring–early summer.
Climatic zone: 7, 8, 9.
Dimensions: Up to 10 feet (3 meters) high.
Description: Attractive throughout the year, this is a magnificent evergreen shrub whose large leaves are leathery and a lustrous green, with a fine-toothed margin. When new they are attractively copper-tinted. The flowers, resembling lily-of-the-valley flowers, are clustered together into large panicles which hang from the terminal shoots. The presentation of attractive flowers and foliage in a compact form makes this a highly decorative shrub. However, some consider it is surpassed by the cultivar 'Forrestii', whose young growth is brilliant red. A rich, lime-free soil and a cool, moist, sheltered position are essential for best results. This shrub may be damaged by prolonged, frosty winters.
Varieties/cultivars: 'Forrestii'.

Pieris japonica
JAPANESE PIERIS, ◑ ● JAPANESE PEARL FLOWER, JAPANESE ANDROMEDA

Family: ERICACEAE
Origin: Japan.
Flowering time: Spring.
Climatic zone: 5, 6, 7, 8, 9.
Dimensions: Up to 10 feet (3 meters) high.

Pieris japonica 'Bert Chandler'

Description: Somewhat hardier than *P. formosa*, this is another very attractive evergreen shrub which, under favorable conditions, can reach a height of 30 feet (9 meters) but mostly does not exceed shrub dimensions. Its narrow leaves, up to 4 inches (100 mm) long, with a coppery tinge when young, mature to a dark, lustrous green. The pitcher-shaped flowers, individually up to ¼ inch (6 mm) long, are displayed in spreading clusters of eight or ten drooping racemes which measure about 6 inches (150 mm) long. The buds for these sprays appear in autumn. Plant in neutral to acid, peaty soil and provide shelter from cold winds.
Other colors: Pink.
Varieties/cultivars: 'Bert Chandler', 'Pygmaea', 'Variegata', Daisen', 'Christmas Cheer'.

Prunus glandulosa 'Alba Plena'

Prunus glandulosa 'Alba Plena'
DOUBLE WHITE DWARF ○ FLOWERING ALMOND, CHINESE BUSH CHERRY

Family: ROSACEAE
Origin: Cultivar.
Flowering time: Spring.
Climatic zone: 4, 5, 6, 7, 8, 9.
Dimensions: Up to 4 feet (over 1 meter) tall.
Description: Double white dwarf flowering almond, with its many slender, erect shoots, forms a neat, bushy shrub. It is grown for its spring display of large double flowers which are produced in such profusion that they bend the stems with their weight. Sprays of blossom are often cut for house decoration. The leaves, opening after the flowers, are up to 4 inches (100 mm) long and provide good autumn color. This shrub requires a warm sheltered position and can be pruned hard after flowering.

Plumbago auriculata 'Alba'

Pyracantha coccinea

Plumbago auriculata 'Alba' syn.
P. capensis 'Alba'
PLUMBAGO, CAPE
PLUMBAGO LEADWORT

Family: PLUMBAGINACEAE
Origin: Cultivar.
Flowering time: Summer, autumn.
Climatic zone: 9, 10.
Dimensions: Up to 10 feet (3 meters) tall.
Description: This is the white-flowering cultivar of the blue-flowering species. It is an upright, straggling, and partly climbing, evergreen shrub which responds well to pruning and is most effective against a wall or as a hedge. The flowers appear almost continually in warm, sunny conditions. They are in rounded clusters with five spreading petals at the top of a slender tube. Viscous glands at the base of the flowers make them very sticky to the touch. The 4-inch-long (100 mm) leaves are dull green. Well-drained soil and a partially shady or sunny site suit this warm-climate plant. It spreads rapidly from suckers.

Pyracantha coccinea
SCARLET FIRETHORN,
COMMON FIRETHORN (U.K.)

Family: ROSACEAE
Origin: Southern Europe–western Himalayas.
Flowering time: Spring–early summer.
Climatic zone: 6, 7, 8, 9.
Dimensions: Up to 15 feet (5 meters) high.
Description: The rich red fruits, formed in dense clusters in autumn and winter, and the thorny branches, have given

the name "scarlet firethorn" to this shrub. The creamy-white flowers, looking like those of a hawthorn but smaller, appear in profusion, and are followed by the fruits, each about 1/3 inch (8 mm) wide. The evergreen leaves, which are about 1 1/2 inches (37 mm) long, are narrow and oval with finely-toothed margins. This is an excellent shrub to grow in fertile, moist, well-drained soil.
Varieties/cultivars: 'Lalandei'.

Sambucus nigra

Sambucus nigra
ELDER, EUROPEAN
ELDER

Family: CAPRIFOLIACEAE
Origin: Europe, western Asia, North Africa.
Flowering time: Summer.
Climatic zone: 5, 6, 7, 8, 9.
Dimensions: 10–30 feet (3–9 meters) high.

Description: European elder has been cultivated over a long period in history. It is a familiar large, deciduous shrub and is sometimes seen as a smallish tree with a rugged, fissured bark. It has attractive leaves with from five to seven leaflets, each up to 4 inches (100 mm) long. In autumn the leaves may change from their summer mid-green to bright yellow or dull purple. The flowers appear as flattened heads, up to 7 inches (175 mm) across, of masses of sweetly fragrant blooms. The fruits are glossy black and, with the flowers, are used in country wine-making. Moisture-retentive but well-drained soil creates ideal growing conditions.
Varieties/cultivars: 'Albovariegata', 'Aurea', 'Lanciniata', 'Purpurea'.

Serissa foetida
SERISSA

Family: RUBIACEAE
Origin: South East Asia.
Flowering time: Autumn.
Climatic zone: 9, 10.
Dimensions: Up to 3 feet (1 meter) high.
Description: Outdoors, in frost-free regions, this useful shrub is seen in shrubberies, rock gardens, and borders, commonly growing broader than it does tall. The attractive, small flowers, pink in bud, solitary or in small clusters, open to 1/2 inch (12 mm) across with petals that are hairy on the insides. In warm situations, serissa flowers for most of the year. The leaves are elliptic, up to 1 inch (25 mm) long, and dark green, with an unpleasant odor when crushed. In cooler climates they make good container plants in greenhouses where they grow well with minimum care.
Varieties/cultivars: 'Variegata'.

Serissa foetida

Skimmia japonica 'Fragrans'

Skimmia reevesiana

Skimmia japonica
JAPANESE SKIMMIA ○ ◐

Family: RUTACEAE
Origin: Japan.
Flowering time: Spring.
Climatic zone: 7, 8, 9.
Dimensions: Up to 5 feet (approx. 2 meters) high.
Description: Among the most satisfactory broadleaf evergreens for shady areas, this shrub is also excellent for industrial or city areas and seaside gardens. Skimmias are slow-growing and compact, spreading wider than they are tall. The four-petaled, fragrant, white flowers appear in large panicles above the foliage. They are also grown for their decorative red fruits, about ¼ inch (6 mm) in diameter, which follow the flowers and last on the plants throughout winter. There are male and female flowers on different plants. Fruits are only produced if both sexes are planted together, one male to three females. Humus-rich soil is preferred.
Varieties/cultivars: 'Foremanii', 'Fragrans', 'Rubella', 'Rogersii'.

Skimmia reevesiana
SKIMMIA ●

Family: RUTACEAE
Origin: China, Taiwan, Philippines.
Flowering time: Late spring.
Climatic zone: 7, 8, 9.
Dimensions: Up to 2 feet (600 mm) high.
Description: This dwarf shrub forms a low, compact mound. It is slow-growing and because it withstands polluted air better than most evergreens, it is excellent for city gardens. It is also good

planted beneath trees as it thrives in shade. The leaves are elliptic, up to 4 inches (100 mm) long, and dark green. The fragrant flowers are bisexual (unlike those of Japanese skimmia), small, about ½ inch (12 mm) wide, and are borne in a dense head up to 3 inches (75 mm) long. They are followed by oval, matte, crimson-red fruits which remain on the plant all winter.
Varieties/cultivars: 'Variegata'.

Spiraea cantoniensis 'Flore Pleno'
MAY, REEVES SPIRAEA ○

Family: ROSACEAE
Origin: Southeastern China.
Flowering time: Spring.
Climatic zone: 7, 8, 9.
Dimensions: Up to 5 feet (approx. 2 meters) high.
Description: The generic name comes from the Greek *speira* meaning a wreath, which appropriately describes

Spiraea cantoniensis 'Flore Pleno'

this shrub when it is in full flower with its branches garlanded with clusters of blooms. These clusters, up to 2 inches (50 mm) wide, are rounded and contain twenty to twenty-five diminutive flowers. They grow in such profusion along the length of the arching stems that the stems can be bent to the ground. The narrow leaves, up to 2½ inches (60 mm) long, are dark green with irregularly toothed margins. Pruning, immediately after flowering, is essential.
Varieties/cultivars: 'Lanceata'.

Spiraea prunifolia

Spiraea prunifolia syn. *S. p.* 'Plena'
BRIDAL-WREATH ○

Family: ROSACEAE
Origin: Japan.
Flowering time: Spring.
Climatic zone: 4, 5, 6, 7, 8, 9.
Dimensions: Up to 6 feet (2 meters) high.
Description: This popular plant is only known in cultivation and was first introduced into Europe from Japan in about 1845. It is a dense shrub with many slender, arching branches and grows almost as broad as it does high. The flowers are double and almost ½ inch (12 mm) across. They are borne in tight, button-like, stalkless clusters along the branches. The young shoots are slightly hairy, and the elliptic leaves, which open after the flowers, are up to 2 inches (50 mm) long. Autumn interest is provided by the orange and red foliage. Prune after flowering.

Spiraea thunbergii

Spiraea thunbergii
THUNBERG SPIRAEA ○

Family: ROSACEAE
Origin: China.
Flowering time: Spring–summer.
Climatic zone: 5, 6, 7, 8, 9.
Dimensions: Up to 6 feet (2 meters) high.
Description: Generally the earliest of the spiraeas to bloom, its pure white flowers often smother the arching branches of this graceful, deciduous shrub. It has a dense twiggy habit, often broader than it is tall, with slender downy stems. The leaves, which are narrow and shiny, about 1 inch (25 mm) long with a toothed margin, turn in autumn to shades of orange and scarlet. The flowers occur in numerous, but small, stalkless clusters of two to five flowers. Late frosts are a hazard to the early flowers of this popular shrub. Remove dead flower heads and stems if unsightly.

Spiraea x *arguta*
BRIDAL WREATH (U.K.), ○
GARLAND SPIRAEA

Family: ROSACEAE
Origin: Hybrid.
Flowering time: Late spring.
Climatic zone: 4, 5, 6, 7, 8, 9.
Dimensions: Up to 6 feet (2 meters) high.
Description: One of the most effective and free-flowering of the spiraeas, bridal wreath is a hybrid of *S. thunbergii* and *S. multiflora*. It is a dense-growing, deciduous shrub with graceful, slender branches and, in habit, resembles *S. thunbergii*. However, its leaves are broader and it blooms later in spring so that its flowers are not so subject to damage by late frosts. To maintain a

Spiraea x *arguta*

tidy appearance, prune this shrub hard immediately after flowering. Alternatively, if large flowers are desired, remove dead flower heads and stems only if unsightly. Otherwise, it is very easy and rewarding to grow.

Spiraea x *vanhouttei*
VANHOUTTE SPIRAEA ○

Family: ROSACEAE
Origin: Hybrid.
Flowering time: Summer.
Climatic zone: 4, 5, 6, 7, 8, 9.
Dimensions: Up to 8 feet (approx. 2 meters) high.
Description: A hybrid from *S. cantoniensis* and *S. trilobata*, this deciduous shrub, slender and vigorous with beautifully arching branches, is one of the most commonly cultivated spiraeas. The leaves are coarsely toothed, up to 1½ inches (35 mm) long, sometimes with three to five lobes, and blue-green in color. They show off the great numbers of many-flowered clusters

Spiraea x *vanhouttei*

of blooms which smother the stems. This showy shrub may also produce good autumn color in the leaves and makes an excellent hedge. Prune after flowering by removing dead stems and flower heads.

Styrax americanus

Styrax americanus
SNOWBELL ○

Family: STYRACACEAE
Origin: Southeastern United States.
Flowering time: Early summer.
Climatic zone: 6, 7, 8, 9.
Dimensions: Up to 9 feet (3 meters) high.
Description: Not the easiest of plants to grow, this deciduous shrub, with its refined and graceful habit, combines well with other trees and shrubs in a mixed border. The leaves on the ascending branches are narrow, bright green, minutely toothed, and up to 3½ inches (85 mm) long. Its flowers are bell-shaped, up to ½ inch (12 mm) long, and hang by hairy stalks, either solitary or in clusters of up to four. Egg-shaped fruits about ⅓ inch (8 mm) long follow. A sandy, porous soil enriched with compost will ensure the best results. Protect from strong, cold winds. This shrub may be damaged by severe winters.

Symphoricarpos albus 'Laevigatus'
SNOWBERRY, ○ ◑ ●
WAXBERRY

Family: CAPRIFOLIACEAE
Origin: Cultivar.
Flowering time: Summer–autumn.

Symphoricarpos albus 'Laevigatus'

Climatic zone: 3, 4, 5, 6, 7, 8, 9.
Dimensions: Up to 4 feet (approx. 1 meter) high.
Description: Having clusters of small, bell-shaped flowers, this deciduous shrub is mainly grown for its abundant display of fruits which appear in late summer and autumn and are retained for a long period. The fruits are round, white berries about ½ inch (12 mm) in diameter and are prized by floral arrangers for winter decoration. The shrubs, with slender, erect, downy shoots, form dense thickets of upright stems. The leaves are about 1 inch (25 mm) long. Snowberries will grow in shade, and in city and seaside environments.

Syringa vulgaris 'Madame Lemoine'
LILAC ○ ◑

Family: OLEACEAE
Origin: Cultivar.
Flowering time: Early summer.
Climatic zone: 4, 5, 6, 7, 8, 9.
Dimensions: Up to 15 feet (5 meters) high.
Description: This horticultural cultivar of the common lilac is grown, as are all lilacs, for its deliciously perfumed flowers. These cover the plant in great panicles, up to 8 inches (200 mm) long, of multiple blooms. The flowers are creamy-yellow in bud, opening to pure white. The leaves are heart-shaped and up to 5 inches (125 mm) long. Grow in fertile, moist soil.

Syringa vulgaris 'Madame Lemoine'

Teucrium chamaedrys
WALL GERMANDER ○

Family: LABIATAE
Origin: Central and southern Europe–southwestern Asia.
Flowering time: Late summer.
Climatic zone: 6, 7, 8, 9.
Dimensions: Up to 12 inches (300 mm) high.
Description: A small, erect shrub, well suited to a sunny border, *T. chamaedrys* has toothed, glossy, deep-green leaves and tiny, tubular flowers which are pale to deep rosy-purple and appear in terminal whorls. Plant in well-drained soil in a sunny position.

Vaccinium corymbosum
SWAMP BLUEBERRY, HIGHBUSH BLUEBERRY ○

Family: ERICACEAE
Origin: Eastern North America.
Flowering time: Early summer–mid summer.
Climatic zone: 3, 4, 5, 6, 7, 8, 9.
Dimensions: Up to 12 feet (4 meters) high.
Description: While showy autumn leaves and attractive berries are notable features of this deciduous shrub, the flowers, in clusters of small, urn-shaped blooms, are also attractive. When they open, the leaves are half-grown. The leaves are bright green and when mature are about 3 inches (75 mm) long. With autumn, they turn brilliant shades of bronze and scarlet. The comparatively large berries, about ⅓ inch (8 mm) in diameter, are black with a "blue" bloom and are sweet and edible. Larger fruits are produced on commercial cultivars. For best results, plant in a moist, acid, peaty soil.
Varieties/cultivars: 'Early Blue', 'Grover', 'Jersey', 'Pemberton'.

Vaccinium corymbosum

Teucrium chamaedrys

Viburnum carlesii

Viburnum carlesii
KOREAN VIBURNUM

Family: CAPRIFOLIACEAE
Origin: Korea.
Flowering time: Spring.
Climatic zone: 4, 5, 6, 7, 8, 9.
Dimensions: Up to 5 feet (approx.
2 meters) high.
Description: Since W. R. Charles, a
British diplomat, discovered this
deciduous plant in Korea, it has become
one of the most popular of shrubs. It is
a rounded bush whose leaves, downy on
both sides, look dull until autumn
comes, when they turn shades of yellow
and red. The buds are pink and the
flowers exquisitely fragrant. Supported
by a rose-pink tube, the petals are pure
white on the inside. The flower heads,
produced in profusion, are
hemispherical, about 3 inches (75 mm)
across, and appear with the new leaves.
A hardy plant, it prefers fertile, well-
drained soil.

Viburnum dentatum
ARROWWOOD

Family: CAPRIFOLIACEAE
Origin: Eastern United States.
Flowering time: Late spring.
Climatic zone: 2, 3, 4, 5, 6, 7, 8, 9.
Dimensions: Up to 15 feet (5 meters)
high.
Description: The common name of this
deciduous shrub refers to the strong,
straight basal shoots which the
American Indians are said to have used
for making arrows. The leaves are oval,
up to 3 inches (75 mm) long, and
coarsely toothed, with hairs on both

Viburnum dentatum

surfaces. In autumn they may become
shining red. Produced in long-stemmed
clusters measuring about 3 inches
(75 mm) in diameter, the flowers are
small with long, protruding stamens.
The egg-shaped fruits are blue-black. A
sunny position and well-drained soil are
preferred.

Viburnum farreri syn. *V. fragrans*
FRAGRANT VIBURNUM

Family: CAPRIFOLIACEAE
Origin: Northern China.
Flowering time: Winter.
Climatic zone: 6, 7, 8.
Dimensions: Up to 10 feet (3 meters)
high.
Description: With its very fragrant
flowers opening well in advance of its
foliage, this shrub is a most valuable,
deciduous, winter-flowering plant. The
leaves are up to 4 inches (100 mm) long,
elliptic, and toothed, with conspicuous,

Viburnum farreri 'Candidissimum'

parallel veins. The flowers are produced
in somewhat rounded clusters up to
2 inches (50 mm) wide, and retain a
blush of pink after opening from pink
buds. Hardy, this plant prefers a fertile,
well-drained, sunny position.
Varieties/cultivars: 'Candidissimum',
'Nanum'.

Viburnum japonicum

Viburnum japonicum
JAPANESE VIBURNUM

Family: CAPRIFOLIACEAE
Origin: Japan.
Flowering time: Spring.
Climatic zone: 8, 9.
Dimensions: Up to 25 feet (8 meters)
high.
Description: Sometimes seen as a small
tree, this handsome evergreen shrub has
glossy, leathery, dark-green leaves up to
6 inches (150 mm) long. The paler
undersides are spotted and the leaf
margins near the tips may be toothed.
On mature plants, the small, fragrant
flowers are borne in dense, rounded
clusters. Small numbers of red fruits are
produced and are particularly sparse on
young specimens. Japanese viburnum
has conspicuous, warty young shoots
and relatively flat flower clusters. Plant
in a sunny position in well-drained soil.
It may be killed or damaged by severe
winters and needs a sheltered site.

Viburnum macrocephalum 'Sterile'
CHINESE SNOWBALL

Family: CAPRIFOLIACEAE
Origin: Cultivar.
Flowering time: Late spring.
Climatic zone: 6, 7, 8, 9.

Viburnum macrocephalum 'Sterile'

Dimensions: Up to 12 feet (4 meters) high.

Description: Chinese snowball is a semi-evergreen shrub which will lose all its leaves in a severe winter. Its leaves are finely toothed, up to 4 inches (100 mm) long, and furry on both surfaces. The flowers give a spectacular display of open-faced, sterile blooms in large, globular heads up to 6 inches (150 mm) across, reminiscent of the sterile forms of *Hydrangea macrophylla*. There is some doubt as to whether the wild form, with fertile flowers, is still in cultivation. This cultivar thrives in a sunny, well-drained location.

Viburnum odoratissimum
SWEET VIBURNUM ○

Family: CAPRIFOLOACEAE
Origin: China.
Flowering time: Summer.
Climatic zone: 6, 7, 8, 9, 10.
Dimensions: Up to 13 feet (4 meters) high.
Description: This viburnum is a delightful, fragrant, deciduous tree which appears quite ordinary until in flower when it is covered with dense, terminal clusters of small, white flowers. Plant in an open, sunny position in medium to light, well-drained soil, and mulch around the base well with

organic matter to keep the ground cool in summer. This viburnum cannot withstand very dry summers or extremely cold winters, and should be positioned with some thought to protection from strong winds.

Viburnum odoratissimum

Viburnum plicatum

Viburnum plicatum syn. *V. tomentosum* 'Plicatum'
JAPANESE SNOWBALL ○ ◑

Family: CAPRIFOLIACEAE
Origin: China, Japan.
Flowering time: Late spring.
Climatic zone: 4, 5, 6, 7, 8, 9.
Dimensions: Up to 10 feet (3 meters) high.

Description: This is the finest of the snowball bushes and rates very highly among the hardy ornamental shrubs. It is deciduous, with wide-spreading, arching branches. Its leaves, egg-shaped and toothed on the margins, are up to 4 inches (100 mm) long and hairy on their undersides. They color in the autumn. The conspicuous, sterile flowers are arranged in globular heads measuring up to 3 inches (75 mm) across. They are produced in a double row along the length of each stem of the previous year's growth and persist for several weeks. Make this a feature plant as it is hardy and prefers a reasonably sunny, well-drained site.
Varieties/cultivars: *V. p.* var. *tomentosum*, *V. p. t.* 'Lanarth', *V. p. t.* 'Mariesii', *V. p. t.* 'Pink Beauty', *V. p. t.* 'Rowallane'.

Viburnum plicatum var. *tomentosum* 'Mariesii'

Viburnum plicatum var. *tomentosum* 'Mariesii'
DOUBLEFILE VIBURNUM ○ ◑

Family: CAPRIFOLIACEAE
Origin: Cultivar.
Flowering time: Summer.
Climatic zone: 4, 5, 6, 7, 8, 9.
Dimensions: Up to 8 feet (approx. 2 meters) high.
Description: A cultivar of *V. plicatum* var. *tomentosum*, the original wild species of *Viburnum*, 'Mariesii' has a much stronger tiered habit than its parent and is very free-flowering, making it a most desirable addition to the garden. Plant 'Mariesii' in a well-drained, reasonably sunny position.

Viburnum rhytidophyllum

Viburnum rhytidophyllum
LEATHERLEAF VIBURNUM

Family: CAPRIFOLIACEAE
Origin: China.
Flowering time: Late spring–early summer.
Climatic zone: 5, 6, 7, 8, 9.
Dimensions: Up to 15 feet (approx. 5 meters) high.
Description: The hardiest of the evergreen viburnums, this shrub, which becomes as broad as it is tall, is thickly covered with narrow leaves up to 7 inches (175 mm) long. These are distinctive because of their much-wrinkled upper surfaces and the dense felting of yellowish hairs on the undersurfaces. The flowers, which individually measure ¼ inch (6 mm) across, are yellowish-white and are gathered into large, flat clusters up to 8 inches (200 mm) wide. The red, oval fruits become black when mature. Plant in well-drained soil.

Viburnum sieboldii
SIEBOLD VIBURNUM

Family: CAPRIFOLIACEAE
Origin: Japan.
Flowering time: Early spring.
Climatic zone: 7, 8, 9.
Dimensions: Up to 30 feet (9 meters) high.
Description: One of the most handsome viburnums, this deciduous shrub has a shapely, rounded form. The elliptic leaves are coarsely toothed, up to 6 inches (150 mm) long, with conspicuous veins, and while the upper surfaces are glossy, the undersides are hairy. Numerous small, creamy-white flowers are produced in rounded, open clusters up to 4 inches (100 mm) long. The distinctive oval fruits are pink, maturing to blue-black. The new leaves of spring and fallen leaves of autumn emit an objectionable smell when crushed. Plant in well-drained soil. Propagate from seed when ripe, or by layering in late winter.

Viburnum tinus

Viburnum tinus
LAURUSTINUS

Family: CAPRIFOLIACEAE
Origin: Southeastern Europe.
Flowering time: Late autumn–early spring.
Climatic zone: 7, 8, 9.
Dimensions: Up to 10 feet (3 meters) high.
Description: This shrub is a most popular evergreen. Its dense, bushy habit, with foliage growing from ground level, makes it an excellent informal hedge. Its glossy, oval, dark-green leaves, up to 4 inches (100 mm) long, thickly cover the stems. This valuable winter-flowering shrub can have its long flowering period extended if there are spells of mild weather. The flowers, each ¼ inch (6 mm) wide, emerge from pink buds in flat clusters about 4 inches (100 mm) across. The plant tolerates light shade and grows well in seaside locations. It may be damaged or killed by severe winters.
Varieties/cultivars: 'Eve Price', 'Variegatum', *V. t.* var. *hirtulum*, *V. t.* var. *lucidum*.

Viburnum x *burkwoodii*
BURKWOOD VIBURNUM

Family: CAPRIFOLIACEAE
Origin: Hybrid.
Flowering time: Spring.
Climatic zone: 5, 6, 7, 8, 9.
Dimensions: Up to 6 feet (2 meters) high.
Description: This upright shrub is semi-evergreen to evergreen. It is a more vigorous grower than its parent,

Viburnum sieboldii

V. carlesii, from which it inherits its fragrant, pink-budded, white flowers. Rounded, and measuring up to 3 inches (75 mm) across, the beautiful flower heads open after the new leaves. The egg-shaped leaves are slightly toothed, up to 4 inches (100 mm) long, and a shiny, rich green on the upper surface, with grayish-brown felting on the underside. The fruits are red, maturing to black. Hardy, it prefers a well-drained but not dry soil. It is well-suited to training up a wall, where it may grow up to 10 feet (3 meters) high.
Varieties/cultivars: 'Chenaultii', 'Park Farm Hybrid'.

Viburnum x *burkwoodii*

Viburnum x *carlcephalum*

Viburnum x *carlcephalum*
FRAGRANT SNOWBALL

Family: CAPRIFOLIACEAE
Origin: Hybrid.
Flowering time: Spring.
Climatic zone: 5, 6, 7, 8, 9.
Dimensions: Up to 10 feet (3 meters) high.
Description: Fragrant snowball is a splendid, compact, deciduous shrub producing large, rounded flower heads up to 5 inches (125 mm) across. The flowers are very fragrant and open from pink buds. The broad leaves are up to 4 inches (100 mm) long, shiny green on the upper surface and covered with fine hairs on the undersides. After hot summers they color to rich shades of orange and crimson in autumn. A robust grower, plant from autumn to spring in well-drained soil.

Vitex agnus-castus 'Alba'

Vitex agnus-castus 'Alba'
CHASTE TREE

Family: VERBENACEAE
Origin: Cultivar.
Flowering time: Summer.
Climatic zone: 8, 9, 10.
Dimensions: Up to 20 feet (6 meters) high.
Description: Chaste tree is an ornamental, deciduous shrub which can withstand sea winds in warmer regions. The fragrant flowers are small and tubular and grow in spikes up to 7 inches (175 mm) long, clustered at the ends of the erect stems. The shrub's velvety appearance is due to the short gray hairs on the undersurface of the dark-green leaves. The new shoots are

also hairy, and they and the leaves are strongly aromatic when bruised. The leaves consist of five or seven narrow leaflets up to 4 inches (100 mm) in length. Plant in autumn or spring against a wall in a sunny position. Fertile, well-drained soil is preferred.

Zenobia pulverulenta

Zenobia pulverulenta syn. *Z. speciosa*
ZENOBIA, ANDROMEDA

Family: ERICACEAE
Origin: Southeastern United States.
Flowering time: Early summer.
Climatic zone: 5, 6, 7, 8, 9.
Dimensions: To 6 feet (2 meters) high.
Description: Named after Zenobia, a queen of ancient Syria, this single species of *Zenobia* is a beautiful deciduous or semi-evergreen, small shrub. The narrow leaves, up to 3 inches (75 mm) long, are covered by a conspicuous gray bloom which is more noticeable when they are young. The flowers are fragrant and bell-shaped, resembling a large lily-of-the-valley. About ½ inch (12 mm) long, they appear on whitish stems in drooping clusters. Zenobia requires a lime-free, moist soil and is an excellent companion plant for *Pieris*, *Leucothoe* and *Rhododendron*.
Varieties/cultivars: *Z. p.* var. *nuda*.

Aesculus hippocastanum
COMMON HORSE CHESTNUT ○

Family: HIPPOCASTANACEAE
Origin: Northern Greece, Albania, Bulgaria.
Flowering time: Late spring–early summer.
Climatic zone: 3, 4, 5, 6, 7, 8, 9.
Dimensions: 60–120 feet (20–36 meters) high.
Description: Horse chestnut is one of the finest of all the deciduous broadleaf trees, with its handsome canopy of huge, radiating leaves, bright green in spring and turning yellow in autumn. Its wonderful spikes of white flowers flecked with red, sit up like candles in spring. In autumn children use the seeds to play the game of "conkers". The leaves create such a dense shade that nothing much will grow beneath the tree. Slow-growing, it is not fussy regarding soil type.
Other colors: Crimson.
Varieties/cultivars: 'Baumannii', A. x carnea 'Briotii'.

Aesculus hippocastanum

Amelanchier arborea
SHADBLOW (U.S.A.), SERVICEBERRY, JUNE-BERRY (U.K.) ○ ◑

Family: ROSACEAE
Origin: Eastern North America.
Flowering time: Spring, northern hemisphere.
Climatic zone: 4, 5, 6, 7, 8, 9.
Dimensions: 30–50 feet (10–17 meters) high.
Description: The most vigorous and

Amelanchier arborea

tallest-growing of the amelanchiers, A. arborea is similar to the much smaller A. canadensis, but its pure white, star-shaped flowers are larger and hang more loosely. Deciduous, toothed leaves appear in spring from pointed buds. In summer, bunches of edible black berries hang among the foliage. Autumn changes the color of the foliage to subtle reds, oranges, and browns. This tree requires lime-free soil, with plenty of water in dry spells. It is susceptible to rust and fire-blight disease in some areas.

Amelanchier laevis
ALLEGHENY SERVICEBERRY (U.S.A.), SHADBLOW (U.S.A.), SHADBUSH (U.K.) ○ ◑

Family: ROSACEAE
Origin: Eastern North America.
Flowering time: Spring, northern hemisphere.

Amelanchier laevis

Climatic zone: 4, 5, 6, 7, 8, 9.
Dimensions: 20–35 feet (6–11 meters) high.
Description: Masses of pure white, star-shaped, fragrant flowers hanging in slender, nodding clusters bedeck this pretty tree in spring. Tender young leaves emerging as a delicate pink turn to a rich red color in autumn. In summer, birds love the clusters of sweet edible berries, which start as purplish black and later turn to red. A. laevis forms a more tree-like shape than most amelanchiers and pruning is rarely necessary. Give it extra water during dry spells. Plant it in a lime-free soil in a moist situation.

Amelanchier x lamarkii

Amelanchier x lamarkii
SHADBUSH ○ ◑

Family: ROSACEAE
Origin: Northern Europe.
Flowering time: Spring.
Climatic zone: 4, 5, 6, 7, 8, 9.
Dimensions: Up to 25 feet (8 meters).
Description: A most attractive deciduous tree, often confused with A. canadensis, however distinguished by the new foliage growth which is coppery-red and covered with silken hairs. The small white flowers appear in profusion, making a dramatic, if short-lived, display. It prefers a well drained, slightly acid soil and a sheltered position. Although frost resistant, it cannot withstand long periods without water.

Arbutus menziesii

Arbutus menziesii
MADRONE (U.K.), ○ ◑
MADRONA, OREGON LAUREL

Family: ERICACEAE
Origin: British Columbia–California.
Flowering time: Spring, northern hemisphere; late winter and spring, southern hemisphere.
Climatic zone: 7, 8, 9.
Dimensions: 25–100 feet (7–30 meters) high.
Description: Often called the Californian version of the strawberry tree, this magnificent tree adds drama and beauty to gardens in many climates. In its native habitat it grows to large proportions, but in gardens it rarely exceeds 30 feet (10 meters). It bears clusters of small, white flowers similar to those of heather, which belongs to the same family. In autumn, handsome, round fruits change color from yellow to orange to red amid rich green leaves. This species can tolerate some lime though it prefers neutral to acid conditions and should be planted in any moderately rich, well-drained soil. Excellent in that it can tolerate hot, dry conditions.

Arbutus unedo
STRAWBERRY TREE ○

Family: ERICACEAE
Origin: Mediterranean region and southwestern Eire.
Flowering time: Autumn to early winter, southern hemisphere; late autumn, northern hemisphere.
Climatic zone: 7, 8, 9.
Dimensions: 20–25 feet (6–8 meters) high.

Description: Every part of this tree is attractive — its almost translucent-petaled flowers which look like lily-of-the-valley, the red, round fruits that follow, and the rich red stringy bark of the trunk and branches. All three delights can be enjoyed in autumn when the tree is covered in fragrant, white flowers, blooming amid the previous year's fruit. Easily grown, this evergreen is perfect for small gardens. Enrich soil with some well-rotted compost or cow manure prior to planting, and ensure that drainage is adequate. It can be damaged by severe winters.
Other colors: Pink.

Arbutus unedo

Callistemon salignus
WHITE BOTTLEBRUSH, ○
WILLOW BOTTLEBRUSH

Family: MYRTACEAE
Origin: Australia (southern Queensland–Tasmania).
Flowering time: Mid-spring–summer.

Callistemon salignus

Climatic zone: 8, 9.
Dimensions: 27–40 feet (8–12 meters) high.
Description: This is one of the hardiest of the bottlebrushes and will grow in both hemispheres. The leaves, soft, downy, and pink when new, turn green at maturity and are aromatic when crushed. The flowers are actually a pale creamy-yellow and bloom in abundance. New shoots emerge from the flowering tips, which may be pruned to encourage bushier growth and longer life. These evergreen bottlebrushes grow in most soils, dry or wet.
Other colors: Pink.

Catalpa bignonioides

Catalpa bignonioides
SOUTHERN CATALPA ○
(U.S.A.), INDIAN BEAN TREE
(U.K.)

Family: BIGNONIACEAE
Origin: Southeastern United States.
Flowering time: Spring.
Climatic zone: 5, 6, 7, 8, 9.
Dimensions: 30–40 feet (9–12 meters) high.

Description: Big, bold, and beautiful, southern catalpa is unfortunately not very long-lived. This exotic-looking, rounded tree on a sturdy trunk is much admired for its wonderful clusters of fragrant, white flowers spotted with yellow, and its huge, heart-shaped leaves. Its rapid growth makes it a most desirable tree for new gardens. Because it needs a lot of space, it is best planted in large gardens. It will tolerate wet and dry conditions and withstand frost. Its leaves, though attractive, have an unpleasant smell.
Varieties/cultivars: 'Aurea' (yellow-tinted foliage).

Cedrela sinensis

Cedrela sinensis syn. *Toona sinensis*
CHINESE CEDAR, CHINESE TOON ○

Family: MELIACEAE
Origin: Northern and western China.
Flowering time: Summer, northern hemisphere.
Climatic zone: 6, 7, 8, 9.
Dimensions: 20–70 feet (6–21 meters) high.
Description: Given the right conditions, this deciduous tree is perfect for the larger garden. A fast-grower, it will, if carefully pruned, develop a single trunk and rounded canopy. Its huge leaves, made up of numerous leaflets, are pinkish, onion-flavored, and edible when young, turning to green in summer and yellow in autumn. Flowers hang in 12-inch (300-mm) long clusters. It needs hot summers, complete protection from winds, and excellent drainage, and is found in such diverse places as wilderness areas in Victoria, Australia, and the streets of Paris.

Chionanthus retusus
CHINESE FRINGE TREE ○

Family: OLEACEAE
Origin: China.
Flowering time: Summer.
Climatic zone: 6, 7, 8, 9.
Dimensions: 10–20 feet (3–6 meters) high.
Description: This superb deciduous tree, often shrub-like, is covered with white, fine-petaled flowers during summer. It is an ideal choice for the cool, temperate garden because of its size and its tolerance of a wide range of soils. Chinese fringe tree prefers a sunny aspect with protection from the wind.

Chionanthus virginicus
OLD-MAN'S-BEARD, FRINGE TREE (U.K.) ○

Family: OLEACEAE
Origin: Gulf and lower Atlantic states of United States.
Flowering time: Late spring.
Climatic zone: 5, 6, 7, 8, 9.
Dimensions: 10–30 feet (3–9 meters) high.
Description: *Chionanthus* is derived from Greek words meaning snowflower. Pure white, fragrant flowers in loosely branched clusters grow at the end of branches produced from the previous year's growth. Later, dark-blue fruits ripen on the female trees. The fringe tree, with its single trunk and spreading canopy, makes an ideal shade tree. In autumn, the leaves turn yellow and often remain on the tree, especially in milder areas. Rather slow-growing — 8 feet or so (about 2 meters) in 20 years — it likes rich, moist soils on a wind-sheltered site, in a cool, humid climate.

Chionanthus retusus

Chionanthus virginicus

Citharexylum spinosum
FIDDLEWOOD ○

Family: VERBENACEAE
Origin: West Indies, Central America.
Flowering time: Mid-summer–mid-winter.
Climatic zone: 9, 10.
Dimensions: 16–40 feet (5–12 meters) high.
Description: *C. spinosum* is conspicuous

Citharexylum spinosum

among green trees in late winter when its own leaves turn a beautiful shade of apricot before some of them drop. Creamy-colored spikes of deliciously perfumed flowers appear in warm weather. New leaves are a glossy, bright green. Happy in most soils, it needs plenty of mulch and water in hot, dry weather. A fast-grower, it responds well to fertilizer and to pruning, which makes it an ideal plant for hedging. Plant it near the house in large containers so that the perfume, especially at night, can be enjoyed.

Clethra arborea

Clethra arborea
LILY-OF-THE-VALLEY TREE ○

Family: CLETHRACEAE
Origin: Madeira.
Flowering time: Late spring, southern hemisphere; late summer, northern hemisphere.
Climatic zone: 9, 10.
Dimensions: 10–20 feet (3–6 meters) high.
Description: Would that this delightful, small, evergreen tree could be grown in a wider range of climates. The nodding clusters of flowers resemble those of lily-of-the-valley, hence its name. Its glossy, elliptic leaves, 2–5 inches (50–130 mm) long, are similar to those of the rhododendron but serrated. It enjoys a mild, coastal climate and humus-rich, lime-free soils. If it is growing where autumns are always hot, dry, and long, giving time for the tender wood to harden, it may survive brief, light frosts. It develops into a multi-stemmed tree, unlike other *Clethra* which are shrub-like.
Varieties/cultivars: 'Flore-pleno' (double-flowered form).

Cornus capitata
STRAWBERRY TREE, ○
EVERGREEN DOGWOOD,
BENTHAM'S CORNEL

Family: CORNACEAE
Origin: Himalayas, western China.
Flowering time: Summer.
Climatic zone: 8, 9.
Dimensions: 20–30 feet (6–10 meters) high.
Description: One of the many beautiful dogwoods, this small, slow-growing, evergreen species is happiest in the mildest of climates. The actual flowers are quite small, but are surrounded by four to six cream-colored bracts which are what really attract the eye. These splendid "flowers" are followed by strawberry-shaped fruits, 1–1½ inches (25–40 mm) wide, which turn from yellow to crimson. The young shoots harden into sprays of dull green, leathery leaves.

Cornus capitata

Cornus florida

Cornus florida
FLOWERING DOGWOOD ○
(U.K.), EASTERN DOGWOOD

Family: CORNACEAE
Origin: Eastern United States (south of Massachusetts).
Flowering time: Late spring–early summer, northern hemisphere; late spring, southern hemisphere.
Climatic zone: 5, 6, 7, 8, 9.
Dimensions: 13–30 feet (4–9 meters) high.
Description: *C. florida* is a spectacular sight when in full flower. Petal-like bracts surround the tiny, greenish flowers, which are carried on upturned twigs along horizontal branches. Very often the canopy spreads wider than the height of the tree, the main trunk dividing at an early stage of growth. The flowers are followed in autumn by scarlet fruits and red to purplish leaves. It needs excellent drainage, but will not tolerate drought conditions.
Other colors: Red, pink.
Varieties/cultivars: 'Pleniflora', *C. f.* var. *rubra*.

Cornus kousa

Cornus kousa
JAPANESE DOGWOOD, ○ ◑
KOREAN DOGWOOD

Family: CORNACEAE
Origin: Japan, Korea, China.
Flowering time: Early summer.
Climatic zone: 5, 6, 7, 8, 9.
Dimensions: 16–20 feet (5–6 meters) high.
Description: This small, deciduous tree is mostly grown for its summer display of white, showy bracts. It has a preference for acid soils and summer moisture. Its distinctive strawberry-like fruit in late summer and its bright autumn foliage are added features. Its size makes it suitable for small gardens.
Other colors: Pink.
Varieties/cultivars: 'Chinensis', 'Rubra'.

Crataegus crus-galli
COCKSPUR THORN, ○
COCKSPUR HAWTHORN

Family: ROSACEAE
Origin: Northeastern United States and adjacent Canada.
Flowering time: Spring.
Climatic zone: 5, 6, 7, 8, 9.
Dimensions: 13–30 feet (4–9 meters) high.
Description: Cockspur thorn lights up each spring as small clusters of tiny rose-like flowers decorate this attractive, deciduous tree. The orange to scarlet foliage provides a foil for the crimson berries in autumn. It develops a small trunk which branches low down. Formidable, sharp thorns (up to 4 inches (100 mm) in length) cover the

Crataegus crus-galli

branches, making it an ideal barrier plant, although it will not stand much clipping. It grows best in cool climates in limy soils, and tolerates drought and pollution. In disease-prone areas, check for fireblight regularly.

Crataegus phaenopyrum
WASHINGTON THORN ○

Family: ROSACEAE
Origin: Southeastern United States.
Flowering time: Spring, northern hemisphere; late spring–early summer, southern hemisphere.
Climatic zone: 5, 6, 7, 8, 9.
Dimensions: 20–30 feet (6–9 meters) high.
Description: Often described as the best of the hawthorns, C. phaenopyrum is deciduous and easy to grow. Profuse, pear-like blossom sits well clear of the

foliage in spring, and is followed by numerous clusters of bright red "berries" in autumn. Orangy-red foliage at this time produces what looks like a tree on fire! Its single, short trunk and shapely canopy make it an excellent small shade tree, and its very sharp, slender thorns 2–2½ inches (50–65 mm) long make it a good barrier plant. It prefers cool climates and deep, rich soils.

Crataegus phaenopyrum

Crataegus x lavallei
LAVALLE THORN ○

Family: ROSACEAE
Origin: Hybrid.
Flowering time: Mid-spring, northern hemisphere; late spring, southern hemisphere.
Climatic zone: 5, 6, 7, 8, 9.
Dimensions: 16–25 feet (5–7 meters) high.
Description: The hardy hawthorns are all reliable for their show of spring flowers and autumn color. C. lavallei is no exception. Pretty, white flowers,

Crataegus x lavallei

marked with a red disk, produce brick-red fruits in autumn which hang on into winter. Autumn leaf coloration varies from reddish-brown to purplish-red. Sparse, stout, dark-red thorns 2 inches (50 mm) in length on the branches make it a suitable small barrier tree, or it can be grown as a small shade tree if the lower branches are cut away from the trunk to form a partial standard. Deciduous, though in mild climatic conditions only a percentage of the foliage falls in winter.

Davidia involucrata

Dombeya tiliacea

Davidia involucrata
HANDKERCHIEF TREE, ○ ◑ DOVE TREE

Family: DAVIDIACEAE
Origin: Southwestern China.
Flowering time: Late spring–early summer.
Climatic zone: 6, 7, 8, 9.
Dimensions: 40–50 feet (12–15 meters) high.
Description: This deciduous tree is named after the nineteenth-century plant collector and missionary, Abbé Armand David. The common name refers to the conspicuous white bracts which flutter in the breeze like handkerchiefs waving. The floral display, which begins just as the tree's foliage opens, lasts for several weeks. The tree is welcome in the garden because it tolerates a wide range of climates.

Dombeya tiliacea
NATAL CHERRY, ○ WEDDING FLOWER

Family: BYTTNERIACEAE
Origin: South Africa (frost-free areas of Eastern Cape, Natal, Transvaal).
Flowering time: Autumn–winter,

northern hemisphere; autumn–spring, southern hemisphere.
Climatic zone: 9, 10.
Dimensions: 13–25 feet (4–7 meters) high.
Description: Like all dombeyas, this is a small tree for tropical to subtropical areas only. In autumn it becomes weighed down by what look like huge clusters of cherry blossom. These perfumed flowers later fade to a pale brown, becoming papery and persistent. Although the tree is evergreen, some of the dark-green leaves turn yellow or red in autumn. The mature tree is slim, with a rounded crown. Grow it in fertile, well-drained soils, in a warm, wind-sheltered position.
Other colors: Rose-pink.
Varieties/cultivars: 'Dregiana'.

Eucalyptus citriodora
LEMON-SCENTED GUM ○

Family: MYRTACEAE
Origin: Australia (tropical Queensland).
Flowering time: Winter, southern hemisphere.
Climatic zone: 9, 10.
Dimensions: 30–65 feet (10–20 meters) high.
Description: Tall, slender, and graceful describes this popular, ornamental, evergreen eucalypt. Its elevated canopy makes this tree a marvellous feature in parks and gardens when planted in small groups. Its smooth, pale gray-pink

Eucalyptus citriodora

to white bark is then really appreciated. The flowers are pretty, and its rough leaves give off a strong lemon scent when the breeze blows or when they are crushed. Grow it in well-drained sites, but give it water in dry spells. Do not spoil its shape by lopping. In cold climates it is often grown as a greenhouse pot plant for its scented foliage.

Eucalyptus scoparia

Eucalyptus scoparia
WALLANGARRA WHITE GUM, WILLOW GUM   ○

Family: MYRTACEAE
Origin: Australia (N.S.W. and Queensland border).
Flowering time: Late spring–summer, southern hemisphere.
Climatic zone: 9, 10.
Dimensions: 30–40 feet (10–12 meters) high.
Description: One of the loveliest eucalypts, willow gum is grown widely in hot climates as an evergreen, ornamental, shade, or screen tree. Graceful, willowy leaves cover the slender canopy. It has attractive white flowers, and the smooth bark is a wonderful, subtle medley of white and creamy-yellow, often daubed with areas of blue and pink which intensify in color when wet. Plant it in coarse, well-drained soils, giving plenty of water in dry weather.

Eucryphia lucida
LEATHERWOOD   ○ ◑

Family: EUCRYPHIACEAE
Origin: Australia (Tasmania).
Flowering time: Summer, northern hemisphere; late summer–early autumn, southern hemisphere.
Climatic zone: 8, 9.
Dimensions: 10–30 feet (3–9 meters) high.
Description: Native to rainforest areas of Tasmania, this slender evergreen tree is popular with bees. Leatherwood honey has a very distinctive, strong, and pungent flavor. The beautiful, delicate-looking, fragrant flowers with numerous stamens have been likened to small, single camellias, and cover the

crown in abundance. Not easy to cultivate unless conditions are just right, it enjoys cool, moist conditions. It will not endure harsh, drying winds or frosty winters. *Lucida*, Latin for bright and shiny, refers to the glossy leaves.

Eucryphia lucida

Eugenia smithii syn. *Acmena smithii*
LILLY PILLY   ○ ◑

Family: MYRTACEAE
Origin: East coast of Australia (Cape Howe to Cape York).
Flowering time: Late spring–summer, southern hemisphere.
Climatic zone: 9, 10.
Dimensions: 25–30 feet (7–10 meters) high.
Description: If you live in a warm climate, this evergreen tree will certainly enhance your garden. Everything comes in abundance; indeed, the Greek word *acmena* means buxom. Glossy green leaves, numerous fluffy flowers, followed by clusters of white to purplish, edible fruits keep this plant looking good all year. Prune it to form a hedge or screening plant, or allow it to grow as a tree, pruning to a single trunk. It likes well-drained soils, and plenty of water in hot, dry weather.

Eugenia smithii

Franklinia alatamaha

Franklinia alatamaha
FRANKLIN TREE   ○

Family: THEACEAE
Origin: Georgia, United States.
Flowering time: Late summer–autumn.
Climatic zone: 6, 7, 8, 9, 10.
Dimensions: Up to 30 feet (9 meters) high.
Description: This tree, discovered close to the mouth of the Alatamaha River in 1765, was named in honor of Benjamin Franklin. It has not been seen in the wild since 1803, so all known specimens are the result of the original collection of seeds. This history makes it an interesting tree, but it is also highly ornamental. Given a hot continental summer, the 3-inch (75-mm) wide, open, cup-shaped flowers with their conspicuous yellow stamens are produced in profusion. In autumn, the large, lustrous, green leaves, 6 inches (150 mm) long, turn crimson before they fall. It requires an acid soil and cannot tolerate cold winters.

Fraxinus ornus
MANNA ASH (U.K.), FLOWERING ASH   ○

Family: OLEACEAE
Origin: Southern Europe–Turkey.
Flowering time: Late spring–early summer.

Fraxinus ornus

Climatic zone: 5, 6, 7.
Dimensions: 20–65 feet (6–20 meters) high.
Description: Manna ash is grown in southern Italy and Sicily for its sap which hardens to a sugary substance called manna and is used medicinally. The tree is readily distinguished from other ashes by the showy clusters of fragrant flowers opening in late spring just after the new leaves have appeared. In its native habitat it is found growing in mixed woods, thickets, and rocky places, so the ideal place for this deciduous tree is in similar positions in large gardens for a natural effect.

Gordonia axillaris
GORDONIA, FALSE CAMELLIA ○ ◖

Family: THEACEAE
Origin: Taiwan, southern China, Vietnam.
Flowering time: Late autumn–early winter.
Climatic zone: 8, 9, 10.
Dimensions: 30 feet (10 meters) high.
Description: Gordonia, a close relative of the camellia, is an evergreen tree which is slow to establish. It is noted for its showy, solitary, white flowers, with their prominent stamens. The flowering cycle can last from two to three months, the fallen blooms producing a showy carpet beneath the tree. Gordonias respond equally well to full sun or dappled shade, but tolerate nothing more than light frosts — severe winters can kill them. Its soil requirements are similar to those of camellias — a light, well-drained, acid soil enriched with well-rotted compost to encourage rapid growth. The two can be grown successfully together.

Hakea laurina
PINCUSHION HAKEA, SEA URCHIN ○

Family: PROTEACEAE
Origin: Western Australia.
Flowering time: Autumn–winter, southern hemisphere.
Climatic zone: 9, 10.
Dimensions: 10–20 feet (3–6 meters) high.
Description: Its curious and beautiful flowers are the main attraction of this pretty hakea. The globular flower clusters, with their protruding, creamy-colored styles, look like round pincushions when fully opened. Sprays, attached to branches, make good cut flowers in autumn and winter. Give this evergreen tree a sunny, well-drained position in a dry atmosphere similar to that of its native home in Western Australia and its adopted home in California. It grows fairly quickly into a small, low-branching tree. Prune it lightly after flowering.

Hakea laurina

Hakea salicifolia syn. *H. saligna*
WILLOW-LEAVED HAKEA ○

Family: PROTEACEAE
Origin: Australia (coastal N.S.W. and Queensland).
Flowering time: Spring–early summer, southern hemisphere.
Climatic zone: 9, 10.
Dimensions: 10–20 feet (3–6 meters) high.
Description: Unlike most hakeas, which need well-drained soils, the willow-leaved hakea will grow in wetter conditions, often being found in good soils near permanent, running streams in its native habitat. It will tolerate some frost and is most useful in the home garden as a quick-growing, evergreen, screen plant. It has attractive, white flowers borne in showy, dense clusters. Tip-prune it regularly to keep the screen or hedge dense, but do wait until the flowers have finished. Hakeas form decorative, woody fruits after flowering, so you have to decide whether to keep these or prune the plant.
Varieties/cultivars: 'Fine Leaf'.

Gordonia axillaris

Hakea salicifolia

Liriodendron tulipifera
TULIP TREE, WHITEWOOD, ○ YELLOW POPLAR

Family: MAGNOLIACEAE
Origin: Southeastern United States.
Flowering time: Early summer.
Climatic zone: 4, 5, 6, 7, 8, 9.
Dimensions: 50–200 feet (15–60 meters) high.
Description: This magnificent tree,

Halesia carolina

Halesia carolina syn. *H. tetraptera*
SILVER-BELL TREE, ○ ◑
SNOWDROP TREE (U.K.),
CAROLINA SILVERBELL

Family: STYRACACEAE
Origin: Southeastern United States.
Flowering time: Spring.
Climatic zone: 5, 6, 7, 8, 9.
Dimensions: 10–30 feet (3–9 meters) high.
Description: Halesias enjoy similar conditions to rhododendrons and azaleas — moist, rich, well-drained, lime-free soil. Requiring filtered sun and protection from strong winds, these plants would revel in a light, woodland setting. Easily grown, they are hardy in cold winter areas. Train them to a single stem whilst young or the plants will become too bushy. You have plenty of time for they grow slowly — about 12 feet (4.5 meters) in 15 years. In late spring, an excellent display of pendulous clusters of white, bell-shaped flowers appear just before the new leaves begin to open. The leaves turn yellow in autumn.

Hoheria glabrata
HOUHERIA ○ ◑ ●

Family: MALVACEAE
Origin: New Zealand (North Island).
Flowering time: Summer (northern hemisphere); late summer (southern hemisphere).
Climatic zone: 8, 9.
Dimensions: Up to 30 feet (9 meters) high.

Description: Native to the North Island of New Zealand, the Latin name *Hoheria* is derived from the Maori name "houhere". *H. glabrata* has pale green, oval leaves with serrated margins, and fragrant white trumpet-shaped flowers occurring in terminal clusters. Grows best in organically rich, well-drained soil and is frost resistant, but drought tender. Useful as a screen or background plant, it can be propagated either by seed or from cuttings.

Liriodendron tulipifera

Hoheria glabrata

which grows huge and fast on a straight trunk, can be grown in the very large garden. The handsome leaves differ markedly from any other broadleaf, looking rather like a maple leaf with the middle lobe cut off. One cultivar develops leaves that are almost rectangular. The flowers resemble tulips. Carried on the branchlet tips, these are greenish-yellow with a band of orange, and often only appear when the tree is twenty to twenty-five years old. Tulip tree prefers deep, crumbly soils and a cool, wet spring season. Deciduous, with yellow leaves in autumn, it withstands pollution.
Varieties/cultivars: 'Fastigiatum' (narrow tree, for limited space), 'Aureo-marginatum' (variegated foliage).

Magnolia grandiflora
BULL BAY MAGNOLIA (U.K.), SOUTHERN MAGNOLIA (U.S.A.) ○

Family: MAGNOLIACEAE
Origin: Florida–Texas, North Carolina, United States.
Flowering time: Mid-summer.
Climatic zone: 7, 8, 9, 10.
Dimensions: 80 feet (25 meters) high.
Description: This is a slow-growing, broad-domed, evergreen tree, with dark, glossy green leaves and spectacular, solitary, bowl-shaped white flowers. Its size, longevity, and grandeur make it very suitable for use in large-scale landscapes, such as parklands, avenues, and malls. It prefers a well-drained, sandy loam which is slightly acid. Summer moisture is essential, and frost protection is necessary when the tree is young. Prune to shape the tree and raise the crown in its early years.
Varieties/cultivars: Several cultivars are available.

Magnolia grandiflora

Malus baccata 'Jackii'

Malus baccata hybrids and cultivars
SIBERIAN CRAB APPLE ○

Family: ROSACEAE
Origin: Eastern Asia.
Flowering time: Mid–late spring.
Climatic zone: 2, 3, 4, 5, 6, 7, 8, 9.
Dimensions: 15–40 feet (5–12 meters) high.
Description: Any plant that can grow in Siberia is tough. Siberian crab apple is a beautiful tree, smothered in fragrant, white blossom in spring, and later by yellow to red fruits which remain after the leaves have dropped. It has been used by breeders since the end of the eighteenth century to yield a fair number of hybrids and cultivars. A most successful cultivar, 'Manchuria', is the first of all the crab apples to flower. The species plant is resistant to apple scab and is long-lived. It does best in cool, moist climates, and is deciduous.
Varieties/cultivars: There are many cultivars available.

Malus 'Golden Hornet'
ORNAMENTAL CRAB APPLE ○

Family: ROSACEAE
Origin: Cultivar.
Flowering time: Mid-spring.
Climatic zone: 4, 5, 6, 7, 8, 9.
Dimensions: 13–25 feet (4–7 meters) high.
Description: Ornamental crab apple has white to palest pink flowers in spring, followed by delightful yellow fruits (¾ inch (20 mm) across) which hang on the tree into winter. Heavy crops weigh down its slender branches, creating a graceful, weeping appearance. Delicious jelly can be made from the apples. Like all other crabs, they are best pruned only when young, in this

Malus 'Golden Hornet'

case to a single trunk. Thereafter flowering and fruiting are better if the tree is left undisturbed. This deciduous tree does best in cool, moist climates and good soils.

Malus 'John Downie'
ORNAMENTAL CRAB APPLE ○

Family: ROSACEAE
Origin: Cultivar.
Flowering time: Spring.
Climatic zone: 4, 5, 6, 7, 8, 9.
Dimensions: 13–20 feet (4–6 meters) high.
Description: This crab apple is grown for its luscious fruit, which are good for eating straight off the tree or for making jam. The white flowers in spring are followed by a generous crop of bright orange and red fruits in autumn, which, if not picked, remain through the winter. Do not crowd this pretty deciduous tree among other trees. It prefers a cool, moist climate and good soils.

Malus 'John Downie'

Melaleuca linariifolia

Melaleuca linariifolia
FLAXLEAF PAPERBARK, SNOW IN SUMMER ○

Family: MYRTACEAE
Origin: Australia (Queensland and N.S.W.).
Flowering time: Late spring, northern hemisphere; late spring–summer, southern hemisphere.
Climatic zone: 9, 10.
Dimensions: 16–30 feet (5–9 meters) high.
Description: A hot climate tree, snow in summer certainly lives up to its name when a cloudburst of white flowers envelops it all at once. The flowers, though otherwise similar to the bottlebrush, differ in that the stamens are joined together in groups. Birds find the honey attractive. Often developing several trunks, it is a good foil tree, and its flaky bark makes it team well with shrubby plants. It will grow in any soil, and has needle-like, evergreen leaves.

Melaleuca quinquenervia
BROAD-LEAVED PAPERBARK, PAPERBARK (U.K.), CAJEPUT TREE, SWAMP TEA TREE ○

Family: MYRTACEAE
Origin: Australia (east coast from Cape York to Shoalhaven).
Flowering time: Spring–late summer and intermittently.

Melaleuca quinquenervia

Climatic zone: 9, 10.
Dimensions: 27–75 feet (8–23 meters) high.
Description: So good is this tree at adaptation, it is planted worldwide for many purposes. It will grow in dry or wet ground, and in some countries it is used to stabilize swampy ground. Unfortunately, it has become too successful in Florida, where it threatens to overtake the Everglades. Its fluffy, cream flowers are similar to those of the bottlebrush, except that the stamens of *Melaleuca* are united in bundles. White, flaky bark contrasts with the dark-green leaves, with their five parallel veins. An

evergreen, it is best grown from seed or semihardwood cuttings in large home gardens as a background plant.
Varieties/cultivars: 'McMahon's Golden'.

Michelia doltsopa
MICHELIA, WONG-LAN ○ ◑

Family: MAGNOLIACEAE
Origin: Eastern Himalayas–western China.
Flowering time: Winter–spring.
Climatic zone: 8, 9, 10.
Dimensions: 20–40 feet (6–12 meters) high.
Description: This neat, pyramid-shaped tree, with its rich green leaves is popular in many home gardens. The large, showy white flowers are fragrant and measure 4 inches (100 mm) across, with 12–16 narrow petals. Plant it as an individual in a lawn or use it as a

Michelia doltsopa

background tree. Do not plant it too near the house, because perfume from the flowers, although pleasant at first, can become rather overpowering. Fast-growing and easy to grow in mild climates, it likes a rich, well-drained soil. Sow this evergreen from seed in spring.

Oxydendrum arboreum
SOURWOOD, SORREL TREE (U.K.) ○ ◑

Family: ERICACEAE
Origin: Southeastern United States.
Flowering time: Mid-summer–late summer.

Oxydendrum arboreum

Climatic zone: 5, 6, 7, 8, 9.
Dimensions: 20–50 feet (6–15 meters) high.
Description: Sourwood is worth growing for its brilliant coloring in autumn, when its leaves turn a fiery red before they fall. Slender heads of fragrant flowers droop from the tips of shoots in summer, attracting birds and bees to their honeyed nectar. Belonging to the same family as rhododendrons, it enjoys similar conditions — moist, acid soil with other trees nearby, in a light glade, for example. It can be grown from seed, cuttings, or layers, but is slow-growing and dislikes polluted air.

Photinia x *fraseri* 'Robusta'
RED-LEAF PHOTINIA ○

Family: ROSACEAE
Origin: Hybrid.
Flowering time: Spring–early summer, southern hemisphere; late spring–summer, northern hemisphere.

Photinia x *fraseri* 'Robusta'

Climatic zone: 4, 5, 6, 7, 8.
Dimensions: 13–16 feet (4–5 meters) high.
Description: This handsome, evergreen shrub has white, bitter-smelling flowers which fade to brown. Carried in clusters 5–6 inches (120–150 mm) across, they appear above the upper leaves. Fleshy, green fruits follow, ripening to red in autumn. It has showy foliage — the new leaves are a shiny, coppery-red which then mature to a deep green; older leaves turn crimson in autumn before they fall. Tolerant of regular clipping which induces plenty of new growth, photinias are often used as hedging plants, or as a background foil.
Varieties/cultivars: 'Red Robin', 'Americanum'.

Plumeria rubra

Plumeria rubra syn. *P. acutifolia*
FRANGIPANI, ○
GRAVEYARD TREE (Asia)

Family: APOCYNACEAE
Origin: Central America, Mexico, Venezuela.
Flowering time: Summer–autumn, northern and southern hemispheres; most of year in tropical areas.
Climatic zone: 9, 10.
Dimensions: 10–27 feet (3–8 meters) high.
Description: You can often smell this wonderful tree before you see it, so pervasive is its perfume. Glorious flowers, carried on stubby branches, cover the tree in bloom. It can be grown successfully only in warmer gardens in full sun, protected from the wind.

Cuttings taken from hardened stem tips about 4–6 inches (100–150 mm) long are planted in early spring. The stems contain a milky sap. Deciduous, it is often planted as a street tree in tropical countries.

Prunus cerasifera and cultivars
CHERRY PLUM, ○
MYROBALAN CHERRY

Family: ROSACEAE
Origin: Southeastern Europe–central Asia.
Flowering time: Late winter–early spring.
Climatic zone: 4, 5, 6, 7, 8, 9.
Dimensions: 15–30 feet (5–9 meters) high.
Description: Flowering cherry plums really are a study in themselves, with so many beautiful varieties and cultivars bred from the species. One of the more notable ones is 'Pissardii', first noticed in the Shah of Persia's garden by the French gardener Pissardt. Its flowers are

Prunus cerasifera

white to blush-pink and the foliage is purple. A further development from America produced 'Pissardii Thundercloud', with pink flowers and deep, smoky, purplish-red foliage. Others are listed below. All are deciduous, easy to grow, and do best in full sun. Their dark-colored foliage can be used, sparingly, for contrast in the garden.
Varieties/cultivars: 'Festeri' and 'Nigra' (single pale pink), 'Vesuvius' (white to blush-pink), 'Elvins', 'Rosea' (salmon-pink flowers, bronze-green foliage).

Prunus cerasifera 'Elvins'
CHERRY PLUM ○

Family: ROSACEAE
Origin: Cultivar.
Flowering time: Spring.
Climatic zone: 4, 5, 6, 7, 8, 9.
Dimensions: 10–13 feet (3–4 meters) high.
Description: 'Elvins', developed in Victoria in about 1940, is a small tree that can enhance many small gardens in cool to temperate climates. Each spring it appears as a froth of pure white flowers which, though enchanting, have a very brief life. This deciduous tree has a mass of slender shoots spreading out from a short trunk. Plant it with other blossom trees for an outstanding spring show.

Prunus cerasifera 'Elvins'

Prunus dulcis syn. *P. amygdalus*
ALMOND, COMMON ○
ALMOND

Family: ROSACEAE
Origin: Western Asia.
Flowering time: Late winter–early spring.
Climatic zone: 7, 8, 9.
Dimensions: 20–30 feet (6–9 meters) high.
Description: Almonds, which are among the very first trees to blossom, are followed soon after by the peach trees. Plant them together for an extended blooming period. The species almond is a spreading, deciduous tree, extensively grown in Sicily for commercial purposes. It grows well in a dryish climate in well-drained soils. It has been crossed with *P. persica* to produce the cultivar 'Pollardii'. Often flowering in late winter, it needs protection from inclement weather. The almond looks wonderful against a

Prunus dulcis

backdrop of large evergreens which also provide protection.
Varieties/cultivars: *P. d.* var. *praecox*, 'Macrocarpa' (large, very pale pink to white flowers), 'Roseoplena' (double pale pink flowers).

Prunus lusitanica
PORTUGAL LAUREL ○ ◑

Family: ROSACEAE
Origin: Spain, Portugal.
Flowering time: Early summer.
Climatic zone: 7, 8, 9.
Dimensions: 13–40 feet (4–12 meters) high.
Description: Suitable for clipping, Portugal laurel makes an elegant round-

Prunus lusitanica

topped tree, or a formal or informal hedge or screen. Evergreen and elegant all year with glossy green foliage, there comes a bonus in spring as slender, long heads of cream, fragrant flowers appear, followed in summer by red berries that turn purplish-black. It withstands poor, chalky soils, and looks most effective in large gardens lining a driveway or screening off unattractive areas.
Varieties/cultivars: 'Variegata', 'Myrtifolia'.

Prunus mume 'Alba Plena'
JAPANESE APRICOT (U.K.) ○

Family: ROSACEAE
Origin: Cultivar.
Flowering time: Early spring.
Climatic zone: 7, 8, 9, 10.
Dimensions: 10–27 feet (3–8 meters) high.
Description: Japanese apricot flowers at

Prunus mume 'Alba Plena'

the same time as many of the almonds, but needs more protection from the elements. If planted in a cold-climate garden, place it against the warmest-facing wall. The pure white, semidouble flowers decorating this deciduous tree each winter are at their best after a summer of good sunshine. Cool, moist soil conditions are preferred, however a rich and well-drained soil that is watered consistently should produce good flowering results.

Prunus serrulata hybrids and cultivars
JAPANESE FLOWERING CHERRY ○

Family: ROSACEAE
Origin: Japan, China, Korea.
Flowering time: Mid–late spring.
Climatic zone: 6, 7, 8, 9.
Dimensions: 13–27 feet (4–8 meters) high.
Description: The many cultivars bred from this species are mostly wide, flat-topped, small trees. Most of them flower in mid-spring, producing extremely beautiful clusters of flowers hanging from long stalks. The shiny trunks are often marked by horizontal scars and the leaves color yellow through red in autumn. Give these wide-spreading, deciduous cultivars plenty of space for best effect. They need a moist, elevated site.
Varieties/cultivars: 'Shirotae' (Mt. Fuji), 'Snow Goose' (masses of pure white flowers), 'Shimidsu Sakura' (large, double

Prunus serrulata 'Mt. Fuji'

white flowers pink-tinged in bud), 'Shirofugen', 'Purpurea' (white flowers, rich purple foliage), 'Kiku-shidare Sakura' (double, clear, deep-pink flowers), 'Tai Haku', 'Fugenzo', 'Autumn Glory' (pale blush flowers), 'Ojochin', 'Ichiyo'.

Prunus subhirtella 'Alba'
WHITE SPRING, WEEPING SPRING CHERRY ○

Family: ROSACEAE
Origin: Cultivar.
Flowering time: Spring.
Climatic zone: 6, 7, 8, 9.

Prunus subhirtella 'Alba'

Dimensions: 3–10 feet (1–3 meters) high.
Description: Graceful at any time, this little tree is a most glorious sight in spring when it is smothered in cascades of hanging flowers. The pink buds open to a single white flower. Plant white spring in a lawn or at a focal point in the garden where it is shown at its best. Deciduous, its leaves color attractively in autumn. It likes a cool climate.

Prunus 'Ukon'

Prunus 'Ukon' syn. *P. serrulata luteovirens*
JAPANESE FLOWERING CHERRY (U.K.), GREEN JAPANESE FLOWERING CHERRY ○

Family: ROSACEAE
Origin: Japan.
Flowering time: Mid-spring.
Climatic zone: 6, 7, 8, 9.
Dimensions: 15–30 feet (5–9 meters) high.
Description: The most unusual coloring of the flowers sets this Japanese flowering cherry apart from the others. In mid-spring the flower buds appear lime-green in color, opening to reveal pale greenish-yellow to white petals, with a hint of rose along the central rib. When leaves appear, they are a pale bronze-green which soon turns to green. Later in autumn they become a rusty-purple color. Like all cherries, this tree is deciduous, needing a moist, elevated, cool site.

Pyrus calleryana

Pyrus calleryana
CALLERY PEAR, CHINESE ○ WILD PEAR, BRADFORD PEAR (U.K.)

Family: ROSACEAE
Origin: Central and southeastern China.
Flowering time: Spring.
Climatic zone: 6, 7, 8, 9.
Dimensions: 25–30 feet (7–9 meters) high.
Description: Trouble-free and unfussy, this species grows in the wilds of China as a medium-sized, deciduous tree. Pyramidal in outline, it forms a dense, much-branched canopy and lives to a great age. Frothy sprays of attractive white flowers appear each spring, followed by small, brown fruits on slender stalks. The leaves are glossy green, turning to red in autumn. Callery pear needs full sun and occasional pruning to thin out dense, thorny branches. It tolerates lime soils and thrives even when neglected.
Varieties/cultivars: 'Bradford', 'Chanticleer'.

Pyrus salicifolia 'Pendula'
WILLOW-LEAVED PEAR ○ (U.K.), WEEPING SILVER PEAR

Family: ROSACEAE
Origin: Cultivar.
Flowering time: Early spring.
Climatic zone: 5, 6, 7, 8, 9.
Dimensions: 15–20 feet (5–6 meters) high.
Description: Many pears grow rather too large and unruly for the average garden, but this little deciduous tree is

Pyrus salicifolia 'Pendula'

perfect for many landscape situations. Tightly packed, small flowers in flat heads appearing in spring are followed by small, brown, inedible fruits. Long, grayish leaves, covered in a silvery down, hanging from slender, drooping branches, make this tree a perfect foil for more somber-colored plants. Planted in a white garden among flowering perennials, it adds a graceful harmony. It revels in full sun in cool-climate gardens, and is not fussy as to soil conditions.

Pyrus ussuriensis
USSURIAN PEAR, ○ CHINESE PEAR, MANCHURIAN PEAR

Family: ROSACEAE
Origin: Northeastern China–eastern U.S.S.R., Korea, northern Japan.
Flowering time: Spring.
Climatic zone: 5, 6, 7, 8, 9.

Pyrus ussuriensis

Dimensions: 40–50 feet (12–15 meters) high.

Description: Eventually growing to about 50 feet (15 meters) in height, Ussurian pear develops a broad crown on a straight trunk. It is a perfect deciduous tree for a large country garden where informality is the keynote. Flat heads of pretty, white flowers, often tinged pink in the bud, appear in spring and are followed by yellowish, round fruits. These can become a nuisance if they fall on a public footpath. The broad, shiny, green leaves turn reddish in autumn. Like all pears it needs full sun. This species is resistant to fireblight disease.

Robinia pseudoacacia
BLACK LOCUST (U.K.), FALSE ACACIA, COMMON ACACIA ○

Family: LEGUMINOSAE
Origin: Eastern and central United States.
Flowering time: Early summer, northern hemisphere; mid–late spring, southern hemisphere.
Climatic zone: 3, 4, 5, 6, 7, 8, 9.
Dimensions: 40–65 feet (12–20 meters) high.
Description: Now at home in many countries of both hemispheres, this tree thrives in dry soils, but casts only a light shade from its open canopy. Zig-zag branches carry bright green leaves — and thorns! Its delightful, fragrant, pea-like flowers are borne in clusters, partially hidden by foliage. Fast-growing, it is valued for its durable timber. The leaves arrive late and fall early, providing sun and shade when most needed.
Varieties/cultivars: 'Frisia', 'Inermis'.

Rothmannia globosa syn. *Gardenia globosa*
TREE GARDENIA ◑

Family: RUBIACEAE
Origin: South Africa.
Flowering time: Spring.
Climatic zone: 9, 10.
Dimensions: 9–12 feet (3–4 meters) high.
Description: A close relative of the gardenia, this evergreen tree with its upright stems forms a small multi-branched dome. It is covered with small, bell-shaped, cream flowers in spring, followed by black, round, woody seed capsules which remain on the tree. Rothmannias like only mild climates and survive best in acid soils with summer moisture. They are usually grown for their sweet fragrance.

Salix caprea

Salix caprea
GOAT WILLOW, SALLOW, PUSSY WILLOW ○

Family: SALICACEAE
Origin: Europe–southwestern Asia.
Flowering time: Late winter–mid-spring.
Climatic zone: 5, 6, 7, 8, 9.
Dimensions: 27–33 feet (8–10 meters) high.
Description: Like all willows, goat willow likes water. It is a small, shrubby, deciduous tree, loved for its pretty, furry catkins. Male and female catkins grow on separate trees. Female catkins are silky and silvery. Male catkins are larger, and silky-white, turning to yellow. More graceful and needing less space is the cultivar 'Pendula'. The male tree produces ornamental yellow catkins. 'Pendula' is usually grafted onto the species as a standard trunk about 6½ feet (2 meters) tall. Plant it near water or in boggy ground.
Varieties/cultivars: See description.

Robinia pseudoacacia

Rothmannia globosa

Sophora japonica

Sophora japonica
JAPANESE PAGODA TREE, ○
CHINESE SCHOLAR TREE

Family: LEGUMINOSAE
Origin: China, Korea, Japan.
Flowering time: Late summer.
Climatic zone: 5, 6, 7, 8, 9.
Dimensions: 40–70 feet (12–21 meters) high.
Description: Admired for its beautiful foliage, the Japanese pagoda tree has bright leaves and clusters of flowers which later form pods. The leaves of this shapely tree stay fresh-looking into winter. Grow it from seed in well-drained soil and protect the young plants from frost. The cultivar, 'Pendula', is grafted onto a standard *Sophora japonica* and develops drooping, contorted branches. It tolerates pollution.
Varieties/cultivars: See description.

Sorbus alnifolia
KOREAN MOUNTAIN ASH, ○
WHITEBEAM (U.K.)

Family: ROSACEAE
Origin: Eastern Asia.
Flowering time: Late spring.
Climatic zone: 6, 7, 8, 9.
Dimensions: 30–50 feet (9–15 meters) high.
Description: All year round there is something to enjoy on this comely tree. In spring, the abundant, flat-topped heads of white flowers become delightful, tiny, pinkish-orange berries which remain hanging on the tree. In autumn, the broad leaves turn to a beautiful orange-brown, and in winter, the beautiful gray bark is the tree's eye-catching feature. Plant it with other deciduous trees for glorious autumn color, or against dark-green evergreens for dramatic effect. Easily grown from seed, it performs best in cool, elevated sites, and must be given extra water during hot, dry spells.

Sorbus alnifolia

Sorbus aria

Sorbus aria
WHITEBEAM (U.K.) ○

Family: ROSACEAE
Origin: Southern and central Europe, U.K.
Flowering time: Spring.
Climatic zone: 6, 7, 8, 9.
Dimensions: 25–45 feet (8–14 meters) high.
Description: If you first see this tree in spring, you can be forgiven for thinking that it is in flower, for as the leaves open, in an upright position, they show only the silvery-white, hairy undersides. The flowers follow, in heavily scented clusters. Bunches of abundant red fruits and russet-colored foliage glow in autumn. It prefers well-drained, lime soils and with its silvery foliage will brighten a dull corner in the garden. It makes a good coastal tree and can withstand pollution. In some areas it is attacked by leaf skeletonizers.
Varieties/cultivars: 'Chrysophylla' (yellow leaves), 'Decaisneana' (large leaves), 'Lutescens', (hairy, gray-green leaves), 'Pendula' (small, weeping tree; leaves small and narrow).

Sorbus aucuparia

Sorbus aucuparia
COMMON MOUNTAIN ○
ASH (U.K.), ROWAN TREE,
EUROPEAN MOUNTAIN ASH

Family: ROSACEAE
Origin: Europe, western Asia, North Africa.
Flowering time: Summer.
Climatic zone: 3, 4, 5, 6, 7, 8, 9.
Dimensions: 20–50 feet (6–15 meters) high.
Description: The common mountain ash has ash-like leaves, made up of small leaflets and contrasting with the dramatic display of bright red berries which appear after the large clusters of cream flowers. Thriving on acid soils, but short-lived on chalky soils, it prefers a well-drained site, with plenty of mulch and water in warm, dry spells. It can be susceptible to borer in the U.S.A. In autumn the leaves produce a range of color from yellow through to red, before they fall.
Varieties/cultivars: 'Cardinal Royal', 'Asplenifolia', 'Beissneri', 'Edulis', 'Fastigiata','Sheerwater Seedling', 'Xanthocarpa'.

Sorbus domestica

Stewartia pseudocamellia

Sorbus domestica
SERVICE TREE, TRUE SERVICE TREE ○

Family: ROSACEAE
Origin: Southern and central Europe, North Africa, western Asia.
Flowering time: Late spring.
Climatic zone: 5, 6.
Dimensions: 33–60 feet (10–18 meters) high.
Description: This deciduous tree is distinguished from the rowans by its scaly bark, often used in tanning, and by its more open and wider-spreading branches. The pretty, feathery foliage colors later than that of other service trees and the attractive, rounded or pear-shaped berries turn from green to brown in autumn. Larger than those of the common rowan, they are edible only after a frost and are used in alcoholic beverages. The winter buds of this tree are shiny and sticky. Demanding no special conditions, it is an easy tree to grow.

Stewartia pseudocamellia
STEWARTIA ◑

Family: THEACEAE
Origin: Japan.
Flowering time: Summer.
Climatic zone: 7, 8, 9.
Dimensions: Up to 35 feet (12 meters) high.
Description: A spreading deciduous tree that is valued for its foliage, flowers, and attractive flaking bark. The large but delicate, single white flowers resemble camellias and require similar conditions that is, a well-drained, acid soil with plenty of mulch to keep the roots cool, and extra water in warm, dry spells. Planted in semishade with azaleas and camellias it will give a fine show of summer flowers for some weeks, long after the azaleas and camellias have finished. Autumn brings more interest as the foliage turns brilliant shades of red and orange.

Styrax japonica
JAPANESE SNOWDROP ○ ◑ TREE, JAPANESE SNOW-BELL TREE (U.K.)

Family: STYRACACEAE
Origin: Japan, Korea, China, Taiwan, Philippines.
Flowering time: Late spring–summer.
Climatic zone: 5, 6, 7, 8, 9.
Dimensions: 10–25 feet (3–8 meters) high.
Description: This graceful little tree,

Styrax japonica 'Fargesii'

when in bloom, is profusely covered with snowdrop-like, waxy, fragrant flowers. Plant it on a bank or terrace where you can look up at the flowers. Another delight is the pinkish-orange fissuring appearing between ridges in the trunk. The wide-spreading, horizontal branches carry bright, glossy green leaves through the summer, which turn yellow and red in autumn. A slow-grower, this deciduous tree likes cool gardens and well-drained but moist, lime-free soils.
Varieties/cultivars: 'Fargesii'.

Syzygium jambos

Syzygium jambos
ROSE APPLE, JAMBU, ○ MALABAR PLUM

Family: MYRTACEAE
Origin: Tropical South East Asia, Indonesia, naturalized in West Indies.
Flowering time: Spring–autumn.
Climatic zone: 9, 10.
Dimensions: 30–40 feet (9–12 meters) high.
Description: The glossy green leaves of this evergreen are bright crimson when young, and its showy, fluffy flowers, which bloom for months, are followed by pretty, fragrant, creamy-yellow fruits, tinged with rosy-pink. Insects are attracted to the nectar-bearing flowers, and flavorsome jams and jellies can be made from the fruits. When mature, jambu forms a broad dome on a short trunk, casting a welcome, dense shade. It needs no special attention.

YELLOW FLOWERS

Calceolaria x *herbeohybrida*
SLIPPERWORT ○

Family: SCROPHULARIACEAE
Origin: Hybrid.
Flowering time: Late spring–midsummer.
Climatic zone: 7, 8, 9.
Dimensions: Up to 18 inches (450 mm) high.
Description: A dramatic, giant-flowering hybrid available in various shades of yellow, orange, and red, spotted and blotched in many combinations. The flowers are borne in terminal trusses, are pouch-shaped, and can reach 2 inches (50 mm) across. In the right conditions this hybrid can be treated as a biennial. Plant in moderately rich, acid soil and ensure that drainage is good. Care must be taken not to overwater as it resents waterlogged root conditions. The best display is achieved by group planting which also suits its preference for slightly crowded root conditions.

Calceolaria x *herbeohybrida*

Calendula officinalis
POT MARIGOLD ○

Family: COMPOSITAE
Origin: Southern Europe.
Flowering time: Summer–autumn.
Climatic zone: 4, 5, 6, 7, 8, 9.
Dimensions: 1–2 feet (300–600 mm) high.
Description: This hardy and fast-growing annual blooms over many months, bringing a real splash of color to the garden, with its bright and showy, yellow-orange flowers. Sow seeds in early spring, when frosts have finished, in an open position, in moderately rich and well-drained soil.

Keep the seedlings well-watered during the growing period (10 weeks) and, once they are established, mulch with well-rotted manure to keep weeds down and encourage good flower production. If the seeds are allowed to ripen on the flower and fall, they will germinate the following season.

Calendula officinalis

Coreopsis tinctoria
GOLDEN COREOPSIS, ○
CALLIOPSIS

Family: COMPOSITAE
Origin: North America.
Flowering time: Summer.
Climatic zone: 6, 7, 8, 9, 10.
Dimensions: Up to 2 feet (600 mm) high.
Description: This self-seeding, very hardy annual has flat, daisy-like flowers which appear at the tops of the stems. The flowers are up to 2 inches (50 mm) wide, yellow-petaled with a red-brown center, and the foliage is fern-like. Because they are so brightly colored and their stems are so long (up to 18 inches (450 mm)), coreopsis are popular with both florists and home decorators. Easily grown in most soils and conditions, it may require some support when flowering.
Varieties/cultivars: 'Nana' (dwarf), also double-flowered form.

Helianthus annuus
ANNUAL SUNFLOWER, ○
EVERLASTING, COMMON
SUNFLOWER

Family: COMPOSITAE
Origin: North America, Mexico.
Flowering time: Summer–autumn.
Climatic zone: 6, 7, 8, 9, 10.
Dimensions: Up to 10 feet (3 meters) high.
Description: One of the tallest of the annuals, sunflowers need to be grown in special open, sunny situations to be seen at their best. The bright yellow flowers, which may be 12 inches (300 mm) across, are borne on long, hairy stems, and face the sun. Because of their size, they are seldom used in the home, but are very suitable for large-scale

Coreopsis tinctoria

arrangements in foyers and other large spaces in buildings. Both humans and birds love the mature seeds, which are not only nutritious, but also produce a valuable oil. Sunflowers will grow in any soil, but really thrive in ground that has been enriched with plenty of organic matter. Full sun and some protection from strong wind is important.
Other colors: Wine-red.
Varieties/cultivars: 'Purpureus'. Also dwarf forms to 3 feet (1 meter) high.

Helichrysum bracteatum

Helianthus annuus

Helichrysum bracteatum
STRAWFLOWER, EVERLASTING

Family: COMPOSITAE
Origin: Australia.
Flowering time: Summer–autumn.
Climatic zone: 5, 6, 7, 8, 9, 10.
Dimensions: Up to 3 feet (1 meter) high.
Description: This very hardy plant is a short-lived perennial, but is usually grown as an annual. Its long stems, up to 18 inches (450 mm) high, are topped with brightly colored, paper-textured flowers that last many weeks on the plant. They are very useful for floral work, particularly as a dried specimen, when they are truly everlasting. Choose a warm, sunny, and sheltered position, and water regularly for a good flower display.
Varieties/cultivars: 'Monstrosum' (large size flowers).

Hunnemania fumariifolia
MEXICAN TULIP POPPY, GOLDEN CUP

Family: PAPAVERACEAE
Origin: Mexico.
Flowering time: Summer–autumn.
Climatic zone: 4, 5, 6, 7, 8, 9, 10.
Dimensions: Up to 2 feet (600 mm) high.
Description: The foliage of this sun-loving plant is slightly gray and feathery, making a soft background for the bright yellow, cup-shaped flowers. Up to 3 inches (75 mm) wide, these are borne on upright stems about 12 inches (300 mm) long. The petals curve inwards slightly towards the center of the flower. The soil should be moderately rich, but well-drained. It can withstand very dry summers.

Hunnemania fumariifolia

Layia platyglossa syn. *L. elegans*
TIDY TIPS

Family: COMPOSITAE
Origin: California.
Flowering time: Summer–autumn.
Climatic zone: 4, 5, 6, 7, 8, 9.
Dimensions: Up to 2 feet (600 mm) high.
Description: This is an attractive garden flower for sunny situations and, although it thrives in dry climates, it does not respond in temperatures continuously over 95°F (35°C). It prefers much cooler weather. The flower stems are up to 12 inches (300 mm) long, and the individual, daisy-like flowers have a clear yellow center, a ring of yellow florets with white tips. Flowers may be up to 2 inches (50 mm) wide. Moist, rich soil and full sun will yield good results.

Layia platyglossa

Limnanthes douglasii

Limnanthes douglasii
MEADOW FOAM, POACHED EGG PLANT

Family: LIMNANTHACEAE
Origin: North America.
Flowering time: Late spring–summer; summer–autumn.
Climatic zone: 4, 5, 6, 7, 8, 9.
Dimensions: Up to 12 inches (300 mm) high.
Description: This low-growing plant may be used in rock gardens, or at the front of borders, preferably in moist conditions. It will not tolerate dry heat in summer. The flowers are up to 1 inch (25 mm) wide, have broadly notched petals which are yellow with a broad white tip. These show above a bed of dense fern-like foliage. Rather sensitive to cultivate, meadow foam likes open sun, but cool, moist soil. Sow in autumn or in spring.
Varieties/cultivars: 'Sulphurae'.

Mentzelia lindleyi
BLAZING STAR, BARTONIA (U.K.)

Family: LOASACEAE
Origin: California.
Flowering time: Summer–autumn.
Climatic zone: 5, 6, 7, 8, 9.

Dimensions: Up to 2 feet (600 mm) high.
Description: This annual has broadly-cut, toothed leaves. The flowers open flat and are the clearest shiny yellow, with slightly darker stamens. The fragrant, single-stemmed flowers are up to 2½ inches (60 mm) wide. A most versatile plant, it thrives in most soils, preferring full sun in cooler climates and good drainage.

Mentzelia lindleyi

Nemesia strumosa
NEMESIA

Family: SCROPHULARIACEAE
Origin: South Africa.
Flowering time: Spring.
Climatic zone: 4, 5, 6, 7, 8, 9.
Dimensions: Up to 12 inches (300 mm) high.
Description: While the individual flowers of nemesia are small (1 inch (25 mm) wide), they are produced in great quantity to give a vivid display of color. They appear on top of leafy stems. Grown closely together, the

Nemesia strumosa cultivar

plants form a wonderful flowering border. The flowers mature quickly, but do not persist in hot climates (i.e. in temperatures over 85°F (30°C)). They are short-lived when picked and cannot be used in floral decoration. For beautiful blooms add lots of manure or fertilizer to the soil before planting. Choose a sunny position and ensure that drainage is good.

Other colors: Pale blue.
Varieties/cultivars: 'Compacta', 'Carnival', 'Blue Gem'.

Sanvitalia procumbens
CREEPING ZINNIA ○

Family: COMPOSITAE
Origin: Mexico, Guatemala.
Flowering time: Summer.
Climatic zone: 5, 6, 7, 8, 9, 10.
Dimensions: Up to 6 inches (150 mm) high.
Description: This is a sprawling groundcover or trailing plant which produces clusters of bright, daisy-like flowers in midsummer. Even though the flowers are only 1 inch (25 mm) in diameter, the spreading capacity of the plant and the masses of flowers produced makes it highly suitable for use in hanging baskets in a warm situation. Seeds should be sown directly where the plant is to grow, as creeping zinnia does not transplant well. The soil should be moderately rich with good drainage.

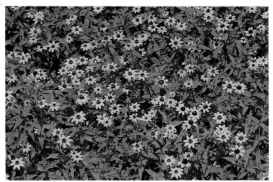

Sanvitalia procumbens

Tagetes erecta
AFRICAN MARIGOLD, AZTEC MARIGOLD, AMERICAN MARIGOLD ○

Family: COMPOSITAE
Origin: Mexico.
Flowering time: Summer–autumn.
Climatic zone: 4, 5, 6, 7, 8, 9, 10.

Tagetes erecta cultivar

Dimensions: Up to 3 feet (1 meter) high.
Description: These tall, attractive, summer-flowering plants are among the most popular in the yellow color range. They are easily grown in average warm conditions. Each plant produces abundant, pompom-like flowers for up to two months. The stems are up to 18 inches (450 mm) long and bear large, densely petaled double flowers up to 6 inches (150 mm) wide. Not very demanding, it grows in any fertile garden soil. Water well during the growing period.
Other colors: Cream, orange, orange-red.
Varieties/cultivars: Many cultivars including 'Jubilee', 'Golden Girl', 'African Queen'.

Tagetes patula
FRENCH MARIGOLD ○

Family: COMPOSITAE
Origin: Mexico, Guatemala.
Flowering time: Late summer–autumn.
Climatic zone: 4, 5, 6, 7, 8, 9, 10.
Dimensions: Up to 2 feet (600 mm) high.
Description: While the French marigold likes the sun, it prefers cooler conditions than its so-called African namesake. The plant is bushy and produces many flowers of a smaller size (up to 3 inches (75 mm) wide), which are useful for floral work and home decoration. They are usually yellow to orange with darker reddish marks towards the center, and are borne singly on short stems. Plant in an open, sunny location. Water and feed it regularly in the growing period.
Other colors: Clear orange, clear red.
Varieties/cultivars: 'Honeycomb', 'Gypsy', 'Petite Yellow', 'Petite Orange', 'Queen Sophia', 'Freckle Face', 'Cinnabar', 'Tiger Eyes'.

Tagetes patula cultivar

Tropaeolum majus cultivar

Tropaeolum majus
NASTURTIUM, INDIAN CRESS ◑

Family: TROPAEOLACEAE
Origin: South America (cool mountain areas).
Flowering time: Summer.
Climatic zone: 4, 5, 6, 7, 8, 9.
Dimensions: Trailing or climbing, to 10 feet (3 meters) long. Dwarf types to 12 inches (300 mm) high.
Description: Nasturtium is a climbing or trailing plant with long stems, which may be supported on a trellis or wire fence or allowed to hang from baskets. It has unusually shaped flowers, 2½ inches (60 mm) wide with five petals opening out and curving slightly backwards. The largest petal lengthens to a spur which bears nectar. The leaves are large, flat, and are edible with a pleasant, sharp flavor. The plant prefers a sheltered position where it may persist for years. It seeds prolifically and the seeds too are edible when soft and green. They are used as a substitute for capers. Moderate to poor soils are preferable — too much fertilizer encourages foliage growth at the expense of the flowers.
Other colors: Orange to ruby-red.
Varieties/cultivars: Dwarf cultivars are 'Jewel', 'Cherry Rose', 'Whirly Bird', 'Alaska', which are all compact and non-trailing. 'Gleam' types are semitrailing and used as groundcover.

Calochortus venustus

Calochortus venustus
MARIPOSA LILY ◯

Family: LILIACEAE
Origin: North America and Mexico.
Flowering time: Early summer, northern hemisphere; summer, southern hemisphere.
Climatic zone: 7, 8, 9.
Dimensions: Up to 18 inches (450 mm) high.
Description: Mariposa lily is an American wildflower with one to three bowl-shaped flowers per stem, with patches of deep red on the stem. The flower color is very variable. The leaves are sparse and grass-like, hence the name *Calochortus*, which is Greek for "beautiful grass". Plant it in rock or native gardens and among pebble paths. It is a good choice for a newly established garden, where the soil is not too rich, but it does not like manure, frosty conditions, or very wet areas. It can be grown in pots on a sunny deck.
Other colors: White, cream, pinkish-purple, red.

Crocus chrysanthus and cultivars
WINTER CROCUS ◯ ◑

Family: IRIDACEAE
Origin: Yugoslavia to Turkey.
Flowering time: Late winter to spring.
Climatic zone: 5, 6, 7, 8, 9.

Dimensions: Up to 4 inches (100 mm) high.
Description: The native form is yellow. This variable plant has produced many cultivars and is a favorite with alpine and cold climate gardeners. It provides a spectacular display in rock gardens, outdoor pots and indoor pans. Crocus forms clumps and needs little attention. Pre-cooled bulbs should be planted in semishaded areas. In their native element they thrive in enriched soils and sunny or lightly shaded positions. If plenty of water is provided a few bulbs will quickly spread and become a colorful colony in the garden.
Other colors: Blue, gold, cream, white.
Varieties/cultivars: 'Blue Pearl', 'E. A. Bowles', 'Cream Beauty', 'Warley', 'Zwanenburg Bronze'.

Crocus chrysanthus and cultivars

Eucomis comosa

When planted the tops of the bulbs should be well below the soil surface to give frost protection in winter. Water well in summer.
Other colors: Purple, cream.

Eranthis hyemalis

Fritillaria imperialis 'Lutea Maxima'

Eranthis hyemalis
WINTER ACONITE

Family: RANUNCULACEAE
Origin: France–Bulgaria.
Flowering time: Spring.
Climatic zone: 3, 4, 5, 6, 7, 8.
Dimensions: 4 inches (100 mm) high.
Description: Related to the buttercup, these hardy plants are best naturalized. Nestling at the base of large trees or around shrubs, they will produce flowers for up to four weeks. Propagation is by offsets from the tubers or by seed. Both seeds and tubers need to be soaked overnight in warm water. Plant them in generous clusters in compost for a good spring display. Mice may be a problem in some areas.
Varieties/cultivars: *E.* x *tubergenii.*

Eucomis comosa syn. *E. punctata*
PINEAPPLE LILY

Family: LILIACEAE
Origin: South Africa.
Flowering time: Late summer–autumn.
Climatic zone: 7, 8, 9, 10.
Dimensions: Up to 2½ feet (750 mm) high.
Description: Dozens of flowers mass on the thick stem to form a spike, capped by a pineapple-like tuft of leaves. The name *Eucomis* comes from the Greek for "beautiful topknot". The flowers turn green with age and will bloom for several months. These sun-lovers make beautiful plants for a sheltered border. They also do well in cool greenhouses. Plant in rich, composed soil near a sunny wall protected from the wind.

Fritillaria imperialis
CROWN IMPERIAL

Family: LILIACEAE
Origin: Iran–Kashmir.
Flowering time: Early spring.
Climatic zone: 5, 6, 7, 8, 9.
Dimensions: Up to 3 feet (1 meter) high.
Description: This bulb is noted for its eye-catching flower-head. At the top of an erect stem is a crown of bell-shaped flowers surrounded by a rosette of shiny leaves. *Fritillaria* has a regal form and is happy in full sun or partial shade. It requires rich, well-drained soil. Leave the bulbs undisturbed in the ground.
Varieties/cultivars: 'Lutea Maxima'.

Fritillaria pudica

Fritillaria pudica
YELLOW FRITILLARY, YELLOW BELL ◯ ◑

Family: LILIACEAE
Origin: Western North America.
Flowering time: Spring.
Climatic zone: 6, 7, 8, 9.
Dimensions: Up to 9 inches (225 mm) high.
Description: Yellow fritillary is not unlike golden snowdrop. Plant it in open woodland, in rock garden pockets, and along paths and driveways. Providing it has good sunlight, perfect drainage, and very little humus, it will produce abundant offset bulbs, which should be dug up, divided, and replanted every second or third year. The bulbs should be replanted as soon as they are dug up as they can dry out very rapidly. Bunches of these yellow bells make very pretty spring floral arrangements indoors.

Gladiolus hybrids
GLADIOLI ◯

Family: IRIDACEAE
Origin: Hybrid.
Flowering time: Summer.
Climatic zone: 7, 8, 9, 10.
Dimensions: Up to 3 feet (1 meter) high.
Description: There are over 200 species of gladioli which take their name from their sword-like leaves, the Latin *gladius* meaning sword. Miniature to giant varieties are available, with an almost endless range of forms and colors. They require some attention because of their susceptibility to virus and fungal disease

Gladiolus 'Georgette'

which can spread and ruin the corms. They are best planted en masse in garden beds in good sun, protected from wind, and the smaller varieties make splendid pot plants. Gladioli are widely cultivated commercially for the cut flower trade.
Other colors: Red, white, purple, pink, lilac.
Varieties/cultivars: There are many varieties and cultivars available.

Hypoxis longifolia
STAR GRASS ◯

Family: AMARYLLIDACEAE
Origin: South Africa.
Flowering time: Autumn.
Climatic zone: 9, 10.
Dimensions: Up to 12 inches (300 mm) high.
Description: A low-growing, spreading groundcover, *H. longifolia* is distinguished by its long, slender, glossy leaves and brilliant yellow, star-like flowers. The underside of the yellow petals is green. Grown from large tubers, it is a warm climate plant preferring a warm, sunny position in moderately rich, slightly acid soil that

Hypoxis longifolia

has good drainage. Protect from wet winter weather and frosts. Every four years the plants should be lifted and separated.

Iris danfordiae
WINTER IRIS ◯

Family: IRIDACEAE
Origin: Turkey.
Flowering time: Winter–spring.
Climatic zone: 6, 7, 8, 9.
Dimensions: Up to 4 inches (100 mm) high.
Description: The short stems of this iris make it ideal for rock gardens, where the honey-scented, bright yellow blooms will flower for many weeks. Plant the bulbs 4 inches (100 mm) deep in well-drained soil enriched with compost. Although hardy, they need a sunny, protected position and regular fertilizing.

Iris danfordiae

Ixia maculata

Ixia maculata
AFRICAN CORN LILY ○

Family: IRIDACEAE
Origin: South Africa.
Flowering time: Spring–summer.
Climatic zone: 8, 9.
Dimensions: Up to 18 inches (450 mm) high.
Description: A tender corm, *Ixia maculata* produces brilliant and graceful corn-colored flowers. Each long stem carries numerous blooms opening successively from the base up. The corm multiplies quickly in warmer climates and is a good choice for sunny edges and borders, where light to medium, well-drained soil is available. In colder climates, it can be successfully cultivated in a greenhouse. If pot-planting outdoors, put six to twelve corms in a large pot. *Ixia* is a very pretty plant, producing good cut flowers.

Narcissus bulbocodium
HOOP-PETTICOAT ○ ◖
DAFFODIL

Family: LILIACEAE
Origin: Spain, Portugal, France, Northwestern Africa .
Flowering time: Spring.
Climatic zone: 5, 6, 7, 8.
Dimensions: Up to 6 inches (150 mm) high.
Description: Hoop-petticoat daffodil has almost cylindrical leaves which are longer than the flower stems. The flowers are shades of bright yellow, with very large trumpets and six very small, narrow petals. Plant the bulbs in naturalized settings where they can be left undisturbed. The informal nature of the flower and its brilliant color make it an interesting inclusion in the spring garden.

Narcissus bulbocodium

Narcissus (daffodil)

Narcissus (daffodil)
DAFFODIL, NARCISSUS ○ ◐

Family: AMARYLLIDACEAE
Origin: Southern Europe–Asia.
Flowering time: Spring.
Climatic zone: 5, 6, 7, 8, 9.
Dimensions: Up to 18 inches (450 mm) high.
Description: This is one of the biggest and most popular genera for gardeners. *Narcissus* was named after the celebrated youth who fell in love with his own image. The daffodil, with its trumpet-shaped corona surrounded by six tepals, may be naturalized, planted in clumps between shrubs, or grown in pots. Praised by poets and gardeners alike, it is beautiful indoors and out.
Other colors: White, pink.
Varieties/cultivars: The many cultivars include 'King Alfred', 'Mount Hood', 'Romance', 'Mrs. R. O. Backhouse'.

Narcissus (Tazetta hybrids)
JONQUIL ○ ◐

Family: AMARYLLIDACEAE
Origin: Southern Europe, Algeria.
Flowering time: Late spring.
Climatic zone: 6, 7, 8.
Dimensions: 18 inches (450 mm) high.

Description: Jonquil is like a bunch-flowered narcissus, but with rush-like, dark green leaves. Strongly fragrant, they tend to flower earlier than daffodils. They are seen at their best in drifts under deciduous trees or naturalized in lawn areas. Jonquils are an old, familiar, hardy favorite in all gardens. Cool, moist, and well-drained soil conditions are essential for healthy growth. In warmer districts, wait until the ground has cooled in autumn before planting. Incorporate plenty of well-rotted compost.

Narcissus (Tazetta hybrids)

Ranunculus asiaticus
RANUNCULUS, TURBAN FLOWER ○

Family: RANUNCULACEAE
Origin: Southwestern Asia and Crete.
Flowering time: Late spring, early summer.

Climatic zone: 6, 7, 8, 9.
Dimensions: Up to 18 inches (450 mm) high.
Description: The small claw-like tubers of ranunculus are planted and then lifted in order to promote optimum flowering. Ranunculus display solitary, open, single or double flowers on erect stems. The flowers are surrounded by a mass of segmented foliage. They are most suited to being mass-planted in full sun or used in a perennial border. They are also very attractive as cut flowers. Cool, moist soil conditions are important, and bulbs will rot if planted during warm weather. The soil should be well-drained and rich in organic matter.
Other colors: White, pink, red, copper, bronze.

Sternbergia lutea
YELLOW AUTUMN ○ CROCUS (U.K.), WINTER DAFFODIL, LILIES-OF-THE-FIELD

Family: AMARYLLIDACEAE
Origin: Mediterranean Europe–Turkey, Iran, and adjacent U.S.S.R.
Flowering time: Autumn.
Climatic zone: 6, 7, 8, 9.
Dimensions: Up to 6 inches (150 mm) high.
Description: These golden-yellow flowers, which resemble crocuses and are believed by some to be the biblical "lilies-of-the-field", flourish in rocky mountain areas. They are ideal grown indoors in pots, or outdoors in rock garden pockets, or naturalized in lawns.

Ranunculus asiaticus

Sternbergia lutea

Provided they have good sun and regular watering, they need little attention. The bulbs should be planted in sandy, well-drained soil which has had an application of compost. Lift and divide them in summer to propagate.

Tigridia pavonia

Tigridia pavonia
JOCKEY'S CAP LILY, MEXICAN TIGER FLOWER, PEACOCK TIGER FLOWER (U.K.) ○

Family: IRIDACEAE
Origin: Mexico, Guatemala.
Flowering time: Summer.
Climatic zone: 8, 9, 10.
Dimensions: Up to 18 inches (450 mm) high.
Description: These spectacular flowers look like large butterflies and can measure up to 6 inches (150 mm) across.

Resting on tall, gladiolus-like stems, they are most effective planted en masse in drifts or clumps. In warmer areas, the clumps should not be disturbed for three to four years after planting. In colder climates they should be lifted annually in autumn and replanted in spring. Plant in moist, fertile soil in a sunny position protected from the wind. Water regularly.
Other colors: Red.

Triteleia ixioides syn. *Brodiaea ixioides, B. lutea*
TRITELEIA ○

Family: LILIACEAE
Origin: California, Oregon.
Flowering time: Summer.
Climatic zone: 7, 8, 9.
Dimensions: 12–18 inches (300–450 mm) high.
Description: This plant produces clusters of starry, yellow flowers boldly veined with purplish-brown and having six, widely expanding petal lobes. It likes a sunny, open position with light to medium, well-drained soil. It will grow in sandy or gritty soils and is useful for newly established gardens where soils are still being built up. Frosts do not bother it, but it dislikes drought, so plenty of water is needed. It does well in borders and pots.

Triteleia ixioides

257

Allamanda cathartica

Allamanda cathartica
ALLAMANDA, GOLDEN ALLAMANDA ○

Family: APOCYNACEAE
Origin: Guyana.
Flowering time: Summer, autumn.
Climatic zone: 9, 10.
Description: A warmth-loving, tropical vine with clear, bright yellow flowers and strong, vigorous shoots, the allamanda will decorate posts, pillars, and fences with its glossy green foliage. Rich soil, good drainage, and ample water will ensure a handsome appearance. This lovely evergreen vine is only suitable for warm tropical conditions, but makes a good addition to a warm greenhouse.
Varieties/cultivars: 'Hendersonii' (orange-yellow), 'Nobilis' (clear yellow), 'Schottii' (yellow, striped with brown).

Bignonia capreolata
TRUMPET FLOWER, CROSS VINE ○

Family: BIGNONIACEAE
Origin: Southeastern United States.
Flowering time: Spring.

Bignonia capreolata

Climatic zone: 8, 9, 10.
Description: This evergreen climber will grow as high as 45–50 feet (12 meters). The tendrils at the end of the branchlets cling by tiny hooks and disks, and the funnel-shaped flowers, 2 inches (50 mm) wide, are orangey-yellow, and hang in clusters. With rich, moist soil, and good drainage, this vigorous vine will quickly spread to become large and shrubby, unless trained and tied to achieve a climbing habit. It cannot withstand heavy frosts.
Other colors: Red.
Varieties/cultivars: 'Atrosanguinea'.

Billardiera longiflora

Billardiera longiflora
PURPLE APPLEBERRY ○
(Aust.)

Family: PITTOSPORACEAE
Origin: Southeastern Australia.
Flowering time: Summer–autumn.
Climatic zone: 8, 9, 10.
Description: An evergreen climber suited to moist forest conditions, the purple appleberry is a slight vine with narrow, dark-green leaves. The flowers are pale greenish-yellow with purple shading and are followed by shiny purple-blue berries which remain hanging from the slender branches for a long period. Support is needed to control its wandering habit, and it can be grown in a container up a wire or trellis. It needs well-drained soil and protection from the wind.

Clematis tangutica
GOLDEN CLEMATIS ○

Family: RANUNCULACEAE
Origin: Central Asia.
Flowering time: Summer–autumn.
Climatic zone: 5, 6, 7, 8, 9.
Description: An unusual clematis, this deciduous climber with finely divided foliage becomes a graceful, elegant vine of up to 20 feet (7 meters) high. The flowers are bell-shaped with golden-yellow petal-like sepals, 2 inches (50 mm) long and stalks 3–4 inches (75–100 mm) long. It is a vigorous vine, very hardy and free-flowering. Golden clematis needs a sunny position, but its roots must be kept cool.
Varieties/cultivars: 'Gravetye'.

Clematis tangutica

Gelsemium sempervirens
CAROLINA JASMINE, ○ ◐ CAROLINA JESSAMINE

Family: LOGANIACEAE
Origin: Southeastern United States, Mexico–Guatemala.
Flowering time: Late winter–spring.

Gelsemium sempervirens

Climatic zone: 9, 10.
Description: The strong, slender branches of this dainty little evergreen vine bear small, funnel-shaped flowers about 1 inch (30 mm) across. They are bright yellow and slightly fragrant among narrow leaves. The vine looks attractive climbing up a trellis, lattice, or archway. It also makes a useful groundcover but should be kept away from children as the plant is poisonous. A hot climate plant, a greenhouse environment is essential in cooler areas.

Hibbertia scandens
SNAKE VINE, GOLDEN   ○ ◑
GUINEA VINE

Family: DILLENIACEAE
Origin: Australia (Queensland, N.S.W.).
Flowering time: Spring, summer, autumn.
Climatic zone: 9, 10.
Description: The shiny leaves are attractive all year on this fast-growing, but non-invasive climber. It is a versatile plant which can be grown as a groundcover, as a container plant, as a trailer over a wall or low fence, or as a climber. Clear, rich yellow flowers 2 inches (50 mm) across are scattered over the vine from spring to summer. It tolerates some shade but prefers a sunny position. Very well-drained, sandy soil is essential. This is a warm climate plant which requires a greenhouse in cool areas.

Lonicera caprifolium

Lonicera caprifolium
SWEET   ○ ◑
HONEYSUCKLE

Family: CAPRIFOLIACEAE
Origin: Europe, western Asia.
Flowering time: Late spring–early summer.
Climatic zone: 5, 6, 7, 8, 9.
Description: Sweet honeysuckle is a vigorous and hardy deciduous climber with attractive foliage and masses of showy flowers that are white to deep

creamy yellow, sometimes tinged with pink. The flowers are followed by orange berries. Plant in rich, well-drained soil that retains moisture well, and choose either a sunny or semishaded position offering some support to the young shoots to encourage climbing.
Other colors: Reddish-purple.
Varieties/cultivars: 'Pauciflora'.

Lonicera hildebrandiana

Lonicera hildebrandiana
GIANT BURMESE   ○ ◑
HONEYSUCKLE

Family: CAPRIFOLIACEAE
Origin: Burma, Cambodia, southern China.
Flowering time: Summer.
Climatic zone: 9, 10.
Description: Everything about this honeysuckle is big. Huge, highly-perfumed flowers 6–7 inches (150–175 mm) long changing from cream to orange-yellow hang from strong, sturdy stems. The leaves are large and glossy, up to 6 inches (150 mm) long. It grows best in good soil with plenty of water. A very vigorous climber, it needs plenty of space to grow, or regular pruning and thinning out of older branches to control its size. The stems become thick and woody when mature.

Hibbertia scandens

Lonicera periclymenum
WOODBINE, HONEYSUCKLE (U.K.) ○

Family: CAPRIFOLIACEAE
Origin: Europe, western Asia, North Africa.
Flowering time: Summer.
Climatic zone: 4, 5, 6, 7, 8, 9.
Description: A handsome climber, honeysuckle has showy clusters of fragrant, creamy flowers with pink or crimson buds. It likes temperate conditions, a moderately rich soil with good drainge, and an open, sunny position. Provide plenty of support to display this climber to best advantage. It is an excellent choice for covering a wall or trellis.
Varieties/cultivars: 'Belgica', 'Serotina'.

Lonicera periclymenum

Macfadyena unguis-cati syn. *Bignonia* and *Doxantha unguis-cati*
CAT'S-CLAW CREEPER ○

Family: BIGNONIACEAE
Origin: Argentina–Mexico.
Flowering time: Spring.
Climatic zone: 9, 10.

Macfadyena unguis-cati

Description: This is the vine to choose when there is no support or frame available. A vigorous climber, it will cling to any surface with its dainty, claw-like tendrils. It does no damage to the surface, and can be peeled off if necessary, and grown again. Trumpet-shaped flowers, 3 inches (75 mm) wide, stand out from the evergreen foliage to form a brilliant yellow curtain in spring. Warm zones will produce rampant growth which is difficult to control. It is better grown in cooler climates. It needs a lot of sun to flower freely.

Rosa banksiae
BANKS' ROSE, LADY BANKS' ROSE, BANKSIA ROSE (Aust.) ○

Family: ROSACEAE
Origin: Southern China.
Flowering time: Spring, summer.
Climatic zone: 7, 8, 9.
Description: Many thornless stems, up to 20 feet (6 meters) long, make a wide base on this shrubby climber. Tiny, double, buff-yellow blooms which are delicately fragrant appear in spring or summer. A strong pergola or other support is required, or its overall size can be reduced by regular pruning and thinning. Although evergreen in warm and moderate climates, it is deciduous where the winters are cold. Because its stems are thornless, it is an excellent choice for growing over arbors or planting near paths.
Varieties/cultivars: 'Lutea' (golden yellow), 'Lutescens' (creamy yellow), 'Alba Plena' (double white).

Rosa 'Mermaid'
MERMAID ROSE ○

Family: ROSACEAE
Origin: Hybrid.
Flowering time: Early–late summer.
Climatic zone: 7, 8, 9.
Description: This is a popular climbing rose with large, single, open flowers, and a dense ring of yellow stamens. The flowers appear on the previous year's wood, so pruning should be selective, some old and some new wood should be retained each year. A strong-growing evergreen it will climb up into trees and hang in great festoons from the branches, or it can be tied to fences or pergolas where the lovely blooms can be seen more easily. It does not tolerate severe cold.

Rosa 'Mermaid'

Rosa banksiae

Senecio macroglossus

Senecio macroglossus
KENYA IVY, CAPE IVY (U.K.), WAX VINE (U.K.) ○ ◑

Family: COMPOSITAE
Origin: South Africa (East Cape Province).
Flowering time: Winter.
Climatic zone: 8, 9, 10.
Description: As the name implies, the thick, waxy, young leaves are shaped like ivy, but, unexpectedly, the flowers are long-stalked, daisy-like, 2 inches (50 mm) wide, and in considerable numbers so they are quite showy. It is a handsome climber when growing over a low wall, or trained up a pillar. A warm and rather dry position suits it best. Protect from frost when it is young, but it becomes a little more tolerant of cold when mature. Try it in a hanging basket where the glossy leaves will look interesting all year, with the bonus of flowers in winter. In cold areas, it makes a perfect house or greenhouse plant.
Varieties/cultivars: 'Variegatum'.

Solandra maxima syn. *S. guttata*, *S. grandiflora*
GOLDEN CUP VINE, CUP OF GOLD ○ ◑

Family: SOLANACEAE
Origin: Mexico.
Flowering time: Late winter and spring.
Climatic zone: 9, 10.
Description: This rampant, evergreen vine will grow 40 feet (12 meters) high or more and grows superbly even in quite poor soils. It is tolerant of salt spray and windy positions. With good soil and adequate water it needs plenty of space.

Solandra maxima

The huge, golden flowers up to 8 inches (200 mm) across are produced sporadically in winter and spring. It needs a very strong support and can cover a fence very quickly. Too heavy and thick-stemmed to be controlled by pruning, it is not suitable for a small garden. As this is a hot climate plant, a greenhouse is essential in cold areas.

Stigmaphyllon ciliatum
BRAZILIAN GLORY VINE, GOLDEN VINE, GOLDEN CREEPER (U.K.) ○

Other common names: BUTTERFLY VINE (U.K.)
Family: MALPIGHIACEAE

Stigmaphyllon ciliatum

Origin: Tropical America.
Flowering time: Summer, autumn.
Climatic zone: 9, 10.
Description: The unusual flowers on this delightful climber hang in small clusters. The petals are fringed and appear to be on little stems, giving the golden-yellow blooms a lacy appearance. Its fast-growing, twining habit makes it useful for covering fences, lattices, or frames, or it can be used as a groundcover. The heart-shaped leaves are glossy and attractive all year. If grown in the cooler zones, this plant needs a greenhouse, but it prefers a warm, humid climate.

Tropaeolum peregrinum

Tropaeolum peregrinum
CANARY-BIRD FLOWER, CANARY CREEPER ◑

Family: TROPAEOLACEAE
Origin: Peru.
Flowering time: Late summer and autumn.
Climatic zone: 5, 6, 7, 8, 9, 10.
Description: The canary creeper is a smooth-stemmed, much-branched climber, which will reach a height of 10–15 feet (3–4 meters). The flowers are bright yellow, frilled and fringed, and have a green spur holding the nectar. Ample water is needed and a frame or support to hold this graceful plant with its somewhat succulent growth. It is happy in partial shade, and should be given space to grow by itself. It does not seem to be at its best with competition from other climbers. In frost-free areas it grows as a short-lived perennial, otherwise it is treated as an annual.

Achillea filipendulina
FERN LEAF YARROW ○

Family: COMPOSITAE
Origin: Caucasus, Iran, Afghanistan.
Flowering time: Summer.
Climatic zone: 4, 5, 6, 7, 8, 9.
Dimensions: 3 feet (1 meter) high.
Description: This is a most distinctive plant whose stout, leafy, erect stems bear feathery, finely divided, green leaves. The flower heads, like a yellow plate, are up to 5 inches (125 mm) across, and the foliage has a strong, spicy odor. It is a very useful perennial in borders, the flowers lasting for a long time. They can also be successfully dried. The plant needs good drainage, but the soil should be reasonably moisture-retentive. Propagate it by division in spring.
Varieties/cultivars: 'Gold Plate', 'Canary Bird', 'Sungold', 'Parker's Variety'.

Achillea filipendulina

Achillea tomentosa
YARROW ○

Family: COMPOSITAE
Origin: Central Europe–western Asia.
Flowering time: Summer–early autumn.
Climatic zone: 4, 5, 6, 7, 8, 9.
Dimensions: 4–6 inches (100–150 mm) high.
Description: Found on dry, sunny slopes in sandy or stony soils, this mat-forming plant is very easy to grow. It is well-suited to a rock garden or herbaceous border. The leaves are silver-gray and hairy and, if bruised, emit an aromatic fragrance. The flower heads appear in flattened clusters on

Achillea tomentosa

long stalks and can be used for dried floral arrangements. They should be picked, tied in bunches, and hung downwards in a sheltered place. In this way they will keep their form and color. Propagate woolly yarrow by division.
Varieties/cultivars: 'Maynard Gold'.

Adonis amurensis
AMUR ADONIS, ○ ◑
PHEASANT'S EYE

Family: RANUNCULACEAE
Origin: Japan, Manchuria.
Flowering time: Early spring.
Climatic zone: 4, 5, 6, 7, 8, 9.
Dimensions: 8–12 inches (200–300 mm) high.
Description: This is a pretty plant for the front of the border, with anemone-like flowers and much-divided, ferny leaves. A well-drained, fertile soil suits it best, but it should be kept consistently moist. Plant it in autumn and propagate

Adonis amurensis 'Yatsubusa'

it by division, or seed sown immediately after gathering. Germination is slow. Grow amur adonis in clumps a little distance from other plants with hungry roots.
Varieties/cultivars: 'Fukujukai', 'Nadeshiku', 'Pleniflora', 'Yatsubusa'.

Alchemilla mollis
LADY'S-MANTLE ○ ◑

Family: ROSACEAE
Origin: Eastern Europe–Turkey.
Flowering time: Early summer.
Climatic zone: 4, 5, 6, 7, 8, 9.
Dimensions: 18 inches (450 mm) high.
Description: Both the leaves and the flowers of this perennial have a special beauty, making it popular with many gardeners. The soft-green leaves are rounded and downy, with radiating veins prolonged into gentle, toothed scallops. They hold drops of water like pearls. The flowers are a froth of tiny lime-green stars produced in feathery sprays which last for weeks. Lady's-mantle is the ideal foil for white or blue flowers. It can be propagated by division or seed and often self-sows if the soil remains moist.

Alchemilla mollis

Alyssum saxatile syn. *Aurinia saxatile*
BASKET-OF-GOLD, GOLD ○
DUST ALYSSUM

Family: CRUCIFERAE
Origin: Central and southeastern Europe.
Flowering time: Spring.
Climatic zone: 4, 5, 6, 7, 8, 9, 10.
Dimensions: 8–12 inches (200–300 mm) high.
Description: This bushy rock-garden plant flourishes in almost any soil, provided it is well-drained and not too

Alyssum saxatile

moist. Above the gray-green leaves the branched clusters of flowers are produced in profusion and, if allowed to cascade over a wall, can be most eye-catching. Water it only during dry periods and cut back quite hard after flowering to prevent it becoming woody and straggly. It is easily propagated by seed in spring or cuttings in late summer.
Varieties/cultivars: 'Citrinum'.

Angelica archangelica

Angelica archangelica
ANGELICA,
ARCHANGEL, WILD PARSNIP

Family: UMBELLIFERAE
Origin: Syria.
Flowering time: Summer.
Climatic zone: 5, 6, 7, 8, 9.
Dimensions: 6½ feet (2 meters) high.
Description: Angelica is a biennial herb with yellow flowers and soft green leaves. It was said to have been given to mankind by the Archangel Michael as protection against the plague. The stems can be cooked with sugar and eaten as

candied fruit. The leaves may be dried to make a tea. It may be placed among shrubs or in the herb garden. Plant it in fertile, moist, well-dug soil and protect it from the wind.

Anthemis sancti-johannis
SAINT JOHN'S
CHAMOMILE

Family: COMPOSITAE
Origin: Bulgaria.
Flowering time: Summer.
Climatic zone: 5, 6, 7, 8, 9.
Dimensions: 1–3 feet (up to 1 meter) high.
Description: These large and beautiful daisy-like flowers, up to 2 inches (50 mm) wide, make a great splash in the garden against the elegantly lobed foliage. Nowadays the true species is rarely seen because it has cross-pollinated so prolifically with the species *A. tinctoria*. Clump-forming, it grows best in a sunny position in a well-drained soil and should be divided and replanted each spring to keep it growing vigorously. It can be grown from seed or cuttings.

Anthemis sancti-johannis

Anthemis tinctoria
GOLDEN MARGUERITE,
OX-EYE CHAMOMILE

Family: COMPOSITAE
Origin: Europe.
Flowering time: Late summer.
Climatic zone: 4, 5, 6, 7, 8, 9.
Dimensions: Up to 3 feet (1 meter) high.
Description: This showy garden plant produces a basal clump of leaves like parsley, above which masses of daisy flowers are produced for many weeks. They were once used by the French to make a fine yellow dye. For garden purposes, the original species has been much surpassed by a vast number of improved hybrids. It does not require a

Anthemis tinctoria

very rich soil, but needs a fairly open position. Propagate it by division in spring or autumn.
Varieties/cultivars: 'Moonlight', 'Golden Dawn', 'Perry's Variety'.

Arctotis x *hybrida* syn. *Venidio-arctotis*
AFRICAN DAISY (U.K.),
AURORA DAISY

Family: COMPOSITAE
Origin: Hybrid.
Flowering time: Summer.
Climatic zone: 8, 9, 10.
Dimensions: 1–2 feet (300–600 mm) high.
Description: The numerous hybrids of this daisy vary in height, leaf shape, and color. The beautifully colored daisy flowers open only in full sunlight and the plants do best in an open, sunny position in rich, damp soil. They respond well to organic feeding and regular watering and dislike very cold weather and wet conditions. In cold climates, a greenhouse is desirable. They can be lifted and grown indoors as pot plants in winter. Keep them bushy by pinching out the growing points. They can be grown from seed.
Other colors: White, pink, red, bronze, purple.
Varieties/cultivars: Many cultivars are available.

Arctotis x *hybrida*

Artemisia stellerana

Artemisia stellerana
BEACH WORMWOOD (U.K.), DUSTY MILLER, OLD WOMAN ○

Family: COMPOSITAE
Origin: Northeastern Asia.
Flowering time: Summer.
Climatic zone: 5, 6, 7, 8, 9.
Dimensions: Up to 2 feet (600 mm) high.
Description: Beach wormwood has dense heads of yellow flowers and chrysanthemum-like silvery-gray foliage which makes it an attractive perennial planted among beds of summer flowers. Unlike other *Artemisia*, it can withstand humid conditions. In general, poor, sandy soils suit it better than rich ones, but they must be well-drained and in a sunny position. Many of the *Artemisia* group are used medicinally or, like the herb tarragon, in cooking.

Buphthalmum salicifolium
YELLOW OX-EYE DAISY ○ ◑

Family: COMPOSITAE
Origin: Central Europe.
Flowering time: Summer.
Climatic zone: 4, 5, 6, 7, 8, 9.
Dimensions: Up to 2 feet (600 mm) high.

Buphthalmum salicifolium

Description: This perennial prefers limy soils which are not too fertile. When in flower it is often staked but looks better when allowed to flop and make a large mass of narrow, dark-green leaves under the stems of the brightly colored daisy flowers. It is both drought- and frost-resistant and forms a clump about 2 feet (600 mm) wide. It can be increased by seed but is usually propagated by division in autumn or spring.

Caltha palustris

Caltha palustris
MARSH MARIGOLD, ○ ◑ KING CUP, COWSLIP (U.S.A.)

Family: RANUNCULACEAE
Origin: Northern temperate zone.
Flowering time: Spring.
Climatic zone: 3, 4, 5, 6, 7, 8, 9.
Dimensions: Up to 18 inches (450 mm) high.
Description: This moisture-loving plant is found in nature in marshy meadows and beside streams. In cultivation, it will grow in any wet soil, but prefers a sunny site. It makes a clump of shining, rounded leaves with brownish yellow branching stems covered with single flowers filled with rich yellow stamens. This perennial looks best when planted beside water, such as an ornamental pond. Propagate it by division or by seed.
Varieties/cultivars: 'Flore Pleno' (double).

Canna x generalis
INDIAN SHOT (U.K.), ○ CANNA LILY

Family: CANNACEAE
Origin: Hybrid.
Flowering time: Summer–autumn.

Canna x generalis

Climatic zone: 5, 6, 7, 8, 9, 10.
Dimensions: Up to 5 feet (approx. 2 meters) high.
Description: These cultivated varieties are all hybrids obtained by crossing three distinct canna species. They are most decorative plants, both for flowers and foliage, and suit both summer bedding and pot planting. The three-petaled tubular flowers appear on terminal racemes and are most striking. The leaves vary from pale- to dark-green to bronze and claret shades. They require enriched soil, a sunny site, and copious water during dry weather. Dead blooms should be continuously removed to ensure a long flowering period. They should be cut down to ground level in winter and the rhizomes can then be divided. Protect against frost. In cold areas, they should be lifted in autumn and replanted in spring.
Other colors: Pink, white, red, orange, speckled.
Varieties/cultivars: Many cultivars are available including 'Eureka', 'The President', 'King Humbert', 'Wyoming', 'Copper Giant', 'Bonfire', 'Brilliant', 'Coq d'Or', 'America', 'Striped Beauty'.

Centaurea macrocephala
YELLOW HARDHEAD, ○ GLOBE CENTAUREA, YELLOW KNAPWEED (U.K.)

Family: COMPOSITAE
Origin: Caucasus.
Flowering time: Summer.
Climatic zone: 3, 4, 5, 6, 7, 8, 9.
Dimensions: 3 feet (1 meter) high.
Description: A well-grown plant of this species may produce between twenty

Centaurea macrocephala

and thirty stems topped with golden flowers enclosed in brown calyxes which look like a fur coating. The rough, oblong leaves are stemless, giving the plant a very dense appearance. The flowers make excellent specimens for drying. Fertile, moist but well-drained soils seem to suit them best, although they are easy to grow in most garden soils.

Cephalaria gigantea

GIANT SCABIOUS

Family: DIPSACACEAE
Origin: Siberia.
Flowering time: Summer.
Climatic zone: 5, 6, 7, 8, 9.
Dimensions: Up to 6 feet (2 meters) high.
Description: This quite large perennial is best used as a background plant as it tends to be rather ungainly. It has dark-green, divided leaves and wiry stems ending in the large scabious-like flowers. The blooms are excellent for cutting purposes. It is a hardy plant needing only a normal, fertile soil to give good results. Propagate it from seed or by division in spring.

Cephalaria gigantea

Cheiranthus cheiri

Cheiranthus cheiri

WALLFLOWER ○

Family: CRUCIFERAE
Origin: Southern Europe.
Flowering time: Early spring–early summer, northern hemisphere; summer, southern hemisphere.
Climatic zone: 7, 8, 9.
Dimensions: Up to 16 inches (400 mm) high.
Description: In ancient times, maidens carried these flowers during festivals and the Elizabethans called them gilloflowers, or "yellow flowers". These popular perennials, grown as annuals or biennials, look pretty against a sunny wall in a cottage garden. Although the old-fashioned yellow and brown wallflowers are still the favorites, there are now many different colors to choose from. Flowering for several weeks, the plants are suited to beds and borders in a sunny position, protected from the wind.
Other colors: Many varied colors including red.
Varieties/cultivars: 'Harpur Crewe', 'Rufus'.

Chelidonium majus

GREATER CELANDINE, ○
SWALLOW-WORT

Family: PAPAVERACEAE
Origin: Europe, Asia.
Flowering time: Late spring–late summer.
Climatic zone: 5, 6, 7, 8, 9.
Dimensions: 2 feet (600 mm) high.
Description: This rather weedy plant is best suited to a wild garden. It forms a basal rosette of quite attractive, coarsely-toothed and lobed foliage. In its second year, erect branching stems of small flowers rise from the rosette. These stems, when broken, emit a

Chelidonium majus

bright yellow, somewhat caustic juice. It self-sows readily but dislikes boggy locations and over-wet conditions. There is a semi-double-flowered form which also self-sows readily.
Varieties/cultivars: 'Flore Pleno'.

Coreopsis lanceolata

TICKSEED, LANCE ○ ◐
COREOPSIS

Family: COMPOSITAE
Origin: Eastern United States.
Flowering time: Summer.
Climatic zone: 5, 6, 7, 8, 9.
Dimensions: 2–3 feet (up to 1 meter) high.
Description: This is a short-lived perennial which thrives in any well-drained soil. If the soil is too fertile, it tends to produce more foliage than flowers. Dead flowers should be removed to keep the plant flowering constantly. Any position in the garden usually suits it, but it does not like to be disturbed and needs regular but restrained watering. It can be propagated by division in spring or autumn.
Varieties/cultivars: 'Sunray', 'Baby Sun'.

Coreopsis lanceolata

Coreopsis verticillata

Coreopsis verticillata
THREADLEAF COREOPSIS, TICKSEED

Family: COMPOSITAE
Origin: Southeastern United States.
Flowering time: Summer–autumn.
Climatic zone: 4, 5, 6, 7, 8, 9.
Dimensions: 2 feet (600 mm) high.
Description: This species is distinctive because of its foliage which is finely divided into thread-like segments. The daisy-like flowers, 1–2 inches (30–40 mm) wide, are produced in great profusion over a number of months, and are useful for cutting. It is easy to grow and will withstand dry conditions for a long period. Once established, it increases quite readily to form wide clumps. The usual method of propagation is by division.
Varieties/cultivars: 'Golden Shower', 'Moonbeam', 'Zagreb'.

Dietes bicolor
FORTNIGHT LILY

Family: IRIDACEAE
Origin: South Africa.
Flowering time: Summer.
Climatic zone: 9, 10.
Dimensions: Up to 12 inches (300 mm).
Description: Fortnight lily forms a spectacular clump of arching, slender, green leaves and showy, yellow flowers with brown blotches on three of the six petals. The flower, resembling iris in shape, is borne on graceful stems. Drought-resistant, it prefers a rich and well-drained soil and a semishaded position. It can be planted as a low-growing hedge which, when established, will annually self-seed to create a thick, lush clump.

Dietes bicolor

Digitalis grandiflora

Digitalis grandiflora
YELLOW FOXGLOVE

Family: SCROPHULARIACEAE
Origin: Southern and central Europe–western Turkey.
Flowering time: Summer.
Climatic zone: 4, 5, 6, 7, 8, 9.
Dimensions: 2–3 feet (up to 1 meter) high.
Description: This clump-forming perennial has broad, slightly hairy leaves and produces tall flower spikes of showy blooms arranged on only one side of the spike. It prefers moist but well-drained soils, rich in organic matter. All species of the *Digitalis* genus are poisonous, but they are worthy garden subjects. Yellow foxglove can be easily propagated by seed.

Doronicum cordatum syn. *D. columnae*
LEOPARD'S-BANE

Family: COMPOSITAE
Origin: Eastern Europe.
Flowering time: Late spring.

Doronicum cordatum

Climatic zone: 4, 5, 6, 7, 8, 9.
Dimensions: 1–2 feet (300–600 mm) high.
Description: An easy-to-grow perennial
with heart-shaped, serrated leaves and
short stems of daisy-like flowers,
leopard's-bane flowers in spring with the
daffodils. Partial shade is needed in hot
climates, where it may become dormant.
It does best in a moist soil even during
its dormant period. Slugs and snails are
particularly partial to the new shoots.
The flowers are excellent for cutting and
often a second crop is produced in
autumn. Dividing the roots in spring
will produce new plants.
Varieties/cultivars: 'Miss Mason',
'Madame Mason', 'Spring Beauty',
'Magnificum'.

Doronicum plantagineum
LEOPARD'S-BANE   ○ ◐

Family: COMPOSITAE
Origin: Western Europe.
Flowering time: Spring.
Climatic zone: 4, 5, 6, 7, 8, 9.
Dimensions: 2 feet (600 mm) high.
Description: The hairy, kidney-shaped
leaves of this perennial are slightly
toothed and the upper ones clasp the
stem. It makes a lovely contrast in the
garden when planted with euphorbias
and honesty (*Lunaria*). Easy to grow, it
likes moist and fertile soil and the flower
stems are excellent for picking. A
number of hybrids have now been
produced, and this species is largely
passed over by gardeners in favor of the
new cultivars. It can be propagated by
division.
Varieties/cultivars: 'Harpur Crewe',
'Excelsum'.

Epimedium perralderianum
ALGERIAN BARRENWORT   ○ ◐ ●

Family: BERBERIDACEAE
Origin: Algeria.
Flowering time: Spring.
Climatic zone: 5, 6, 7, 8, 9.
Dimensions: 12 inches (300 mm) high.
Description: This spreading perennial
has very attractive foliage, the shiny,
rich-green leaves being bronze-tinted

Epimedium perralderianum

when young. It forms wide clumps, with
the little brown-spurred flowers
appearing on wiry stems just above the
leaves. Like all epimediums it can be
used in the front of a border or as a
groundcover under trees. It retains its
leaves throughout the year. It is best
propagated by division after flowering.
Varieties/cultivars: 'Fronleiten'.

Euphorbia characias var. *wulfenii*

Euphorbia characias var. *wulfenii*
POISON SPURGE (U.S.A.)   ○

Family: EUPHORBIACEAE
Origin: Eastern Mediterranean region.
Flowering time: Late winter–late spring.
Climatic zone: 8, 9.
Dimensions: 4 feet (over 1 meter) high.
Description: This is a handsome and
eye-catching plant in the garden because
of its unusual color. The tall, imposing
flower stems are clothed in gray-green
leaves and topped with yellowish-green
flowers. These decorative parts are
really bracts, the flowers themselves
being small and insignificant. When cut,
the stems exude a milky sap which is
poisonous and may irritate the skin. It
prefers a relatively dry position and
makes an effective color contrast with
bronze foliage. Propagate it by seed in
early spring or soft cuttings in summer.

Doronicum plantagineum

Gaillardia aristata

Gaillardia aristata
BLANKET FLOWER   ○

Family: COMPOSITAE
Origin: Central–northwestern United States.
Flowering time: Summer.
Climatic zone: 4, 5, 6, 7, 8, 9.
Dimensions: 2–3 feet (up to 1 meter) high.
Description: Blanket flower is a very showy perennial, although it is often not long-lived, especially if the soil becomes overly wet. It blooms in the first year from seed and is a parent of most of the garden forms grown today. The plant tends to be sticky and aromatic and the large, daisy-shaped flowers are excellent for cutting. It is easily raised from seed, but the many named hybrids are propagated from root cuttings. Over-fertilizing may cause the plant to collapse.
Other colors: Red, orange.
Varieties/cultivars: 'Croftway Yellow', 'Wirral Flame', 'The King', 'Ipswich Beauty', 'Mandarin', 'Dazzler'.

Gerbera jamesonii
BARBERTON DAISY,   ○ ◑
AFRICAN DAISY, TRANSVAAL
DAISY

Family: COMPOSITAE
Origin: South Africa.
Flowering time: Spring–summer.
Climatic zone: 9, 10.

Dimensions: 18 inches (450 mm) high.
Description: From clumps of dark-green, lobed, and rather coarse leaves arise single, strong flower stems. The perfect shape of the bloom makes it look almost artificial. As a cut flower, it lasts a long time in water. Not particularly easy to grow, Barberton daisy prefers neutral to slightly alkaline soil that is well-drained. It can be propagated by division in autumn if the young plants are protected from frost. If grown from seed, the seed must be very fresh.
Other colors: White, red, orange, pink.
Varieties/cultivars: Many semidouble and double varieties.

Gerbera jamesonii

Hedychium gardnerianum
FALSE GINGER LILY,   ○ ◑
KAHILI GINGER

Family: ZINGIBERACEAE
Origin: India.
Flowering time: Late summer–autumn.

Hedychium gardnerianum

Climatic zone: 9, 10.
Dimensions: Up to 4 feet (approx. 1 meter) high.
Description: Growing from a large rhizome, the tall stems have paddle-shaped leaves for most of their length and are topped with an exotic flower head composed of many orchid-like flowers. The perfume is very pronounced and spicy. It is rather like a canna lily and responds to similar treatment of cutting the flowering stems back to ground level in winter. It requires a moist soil enriched with organic matter. The rhizomes can be divided in winter.

Helianthus angustifolius

Helianthus angustifolius
SUNFLOWER, SWAMP   ○
SUNFLOWER

Family: COMPOSITAE
Origin: Southeastern United States.
Flowering time: Late summer–autumn.
Climatic zone: 6, 7, 8, 9.
Dimensions: 5 feet (approx. 2 meters) high.
Description: This is an easily grown perennial with coarse, hairy leaves and stiff, upright flower stems. It prefers a moist, fairly fertile soil, but even when it is planted at the back of a border, the roots can be invasive. For this reason it should be divided at least every three years. It is closely related to the Jerusalem artichoke. It can be used as a cut flower and is propagated by division in autumn.

Helenium autumnale

Helenium autumnale
SNEEZEWEED, FALSE SUNFLOWER ○

Family: COMPOSITAE
Origin: Eastern and central northern North America.
Flowering time: Late summer–autumn.
Climatic zone: 3, 4, 5, 6, 7, 8, 9.
Dimensions: 5 feet (approx. 2 meters) high.
Description: This plant is usually so covered with flowers that it requires staking. It is very useful as a background plant, but the strong colors need to be softened by grouping it with good greenery and some creamy-white flowers. It is the parent plant to several horticultural varieties. It grows in almost any soil, provided it is well-drained. Propagation is by division in autumn or spring.
Other colors: Red, orange, bronze.
Varieties/cultivars: 'Riverton Beauty', 'Riverton Gem', 'Bruno', 'Crimson Beauty', 'Wyndley', 'Coppelia'.

Helianthus x *multiflorus*
PERENNIAL SUNFLOWER ○ ◑

Family: COMPOSITAE
Origin: Hybrid.
Flowering time: Late summer.
Climatic zone: 4, 5, 6, 7, 8, 9.
Dimensions: 3–6 feet (1–2 meters) high.
Description: This robust and very showy perennial performs best in moist, well-drained soils. It is a thin-leafed plant producing tall, branched flowering stems which should be cut back after flowering to the basal clump. The wide daisy-like flowers are yellow with a large central disk. It is a plant that spreads quickly and requires regular division. It is best planted at the back of the border and will need staking. There are now many cultivars and they are propagated easily by division.
Varieties/cultivars: 'Loddon Gold', 'Soleil d'Or', 'Miss Mellish', 'Triomphe de Gard'.

Heliopsis helianthoides var. *scabra*

Heliopsis helianthoides var. *scabra*
ORANGE SUNFLOWER, ROUGH HELIOPSIS, OX-EYE ○

Family: COMPOSITAE
Origin: Eastern North America.
Flowering time: Late summer.
Climatic zone: 4, 5, 6, 7, 8, 9.
Dimensions: Up to 4 feet (over 1 meter) high.
Description: Like most of the sunflower-type plants, this is a long-lasting perennial giving strong color to border plantings. The flowers range from single to fully double and are produced quite prolifically. It is a reasonably compact plant with very rough stems and leaves and is easily grown in most types of soil. Several garden varieties have been bred from the species. It is propagated by division in spring.
Other colors: Orange.
Varieties/cultivars: 'Light of Loddon', 'Orange King', 'Patula', 'Summer Sun', 'Gold Greenheart'.

Helianthus x *multiflorus*

Hemerocallis x *hybrida*

Hemerocallis x *hybrida*
DAYLILY

Family: LILIACEAE
Origin: Hybrids.
Flowering time: Spring–summer.
Climatic zone: 4, 5, 6, 7, 8, 9.
Dimensions: Up to 3 feet (1 meter) high.
Description: The elegance and charm of these plants and the range of flower colors make them an asset in any garden. Easy to grow and tolerant, they thrive in any good soil, preferably a moist one, and although each flower only lasts a day or two, the blooms open successively over a long period. The clumps of arching leaves are attractive and many turn bright yellow in autumn. The plant can be divided at any time, although spring is best, as the new growth appears.
Other colors: White, red, pink, bronze, violet, orange.
Varieties/cultivars: 'Black Cherry', 'Diva', 'Bride Elect', 'Green Magic', 'Pink Damask', 'Royal Crown'.

Iris pseudacorus
YELLOW FLAG, YELLOW IRIS

Family: IRIDACEAE
Origin: Europe, western Asia.
Flowering time: Summer.
Climatic zone: 4, 5, 6, 7, 8, 9.
Dimensions: 4 feet (over 1 meter) high.
Description: This is an aquatic iris that thrives in water or in boggy ground beside streams and ponds. It colonizes quite rapidly and large clumps can make a stunning picture, especially when associated with blue flowers. The graceful, slender foliage is attractive, and there is a variegated form with yellow-striped leaves turning green in summer. This flower is the Fleur de Lys of heraldry. It is propagated by division.
Varieties/cultivars: 'Golden Fleece', 'Variegata'.

Iris pseudacorus

Ligularia stenocephala
ROCKET LIGULARIA

Family: COMPOSITAE
Origin: Northern China.
Flowering time: Summer.
Climatic zone: 4, 5, 6, 7, 8, 9.
Dimensions: 4–6 feet (up to 2 meters) high.
Description: In its natural habitat, this perennial is found in damp mountain meadows and forests and therefore needs a deep, fertile, and moist soil. The dark-green leaves are elegant, decorative, and deeply lobed and extend up the almost black-colored stems. The spikes of daisy-like flowers look quite imposing, especially when planted near water. Hot sun can wilt the large leaves and slugs and snails are fond of them. Propagation is by division in spring.
Varieties/cultivars: 'The Rocket'.

Linum flavum
GOLDEN FLAX, YELLOW FLAX (U.K.) ○

Family: LINACEAE
Origin: Central and southeastern Europe.
Flowering time: Summer.
Climatic zone: 5, 6, 7, 8, 9.
Dimensions: 1–2 feet (300–600 mm) high.
Description: This woody-based species forms mounds of spoon-shaped leaves in rosettes, above which rise the wiry stems of satiny-textured flowers. Flowering will be prolonged if the faded blooms are regularly removed. It requires a well-drained soil in an open position and makes a very satisfactory rock garden plant. The usual method of propagation is by seed in spring or by cuttings in summer.
Varieties/cultivars: 'Compactum'.

Ligularia stenocephala 'The Rocket'

Linum flavum

Lysimachia punctata
YELLOW ○ ◑
LOOSESTRIFE, CIRCLE FLOWER

Family: PRIMULACEAE
Origin: Southeastern Europe.
Flowering time: Summer.
Climatic zone: 4, 5, 6, 7, 8, 9.
Dimensions: 3 feet (1 meter) high.
Description: This plant is best grown in a wild garden as it spreads readily and the underground rhizomes can be very invasive. It prefers moist or wet soils and usually looks good when planted near water. The spikes of brightly colored flowers, in whorls around the leaf axils, last for a considerable period without any maintenance. The clumps need to be reduced regularly, and it is propagated by division.

Lysimachia punctata

Meconopsis cambrica

Meconopsis cambrica
WELSH POPPY ○ ◑

Family: PAPAVERACEAE
Origin: Western Europe.
Flowering time: Late spring.
Climatic zone: 6, 7, 8, 9.
Dimensions: 18 inches (450 mm) high.
Description: This delightful little plant forms clumps of ferny leaves, the papery flowers swaying above them on fine stems. It blooms for a long period and seeds readily so that the plant soon naturalizes itself. Although it seems to flourish in most conditions, it prefers a well-drained soil, rich in humus. There is a double-flowered form which does not self-seed as readily. Welsh poppy is one of the easiest of the *Meconopsis* genus to grow.
Other colors: Orange.
Varieties/cultivars: M. c. var. *aurantiaca*, 'Flore Pleno'.

Mimulus guttatus
COMMON MONKEY ◑
FLOWER

Family: SCROPHULARIACEAE
Origin: Western North America.
Flowering time: Summer–autumn.

Climatic zone: 5, 6, 7, 8, 9.
Dimensions: Up to 2 feet (600 mm) high.
Description: Cool conditions are essential for this plant, although it is widely grown throughout America. The 2 inches (50 mm) long flowers are tubular, expanding to five rounded petal lobes at the mouth. Basically yellow, each flower has a red-spotted throat. Several flowers are borne on a single stem which makes the plant useful for pot culture, especially as it will flourish indoors. The soft leaves may be eaten in salads. Ideal for damp, partially shady corners.

Mimulus guttatus

Oenothera fruticosa

Papaver alpinum

Oenothera fruticosa
COMMON SUNDROPS, EVENING PRIMROSE ○

Family: ONAGRACEAE
Origin: Eastern United States.
Flowering time: Summer.
Climatic zone: 5, 6, 7, 8, 9.
Dimensions: 18 inches (450 mm) high.
Description: The foliage is small, narrow, and pointed and forms dark clumps, over which the stiff stems of the flowers appear. The flowers are reddish in bud before they open out into silky, cup-shaped, yellow blooms. Unlike some of the evening primroses, which belong to the same genus, these flowers remain open all day. It is a suitable plant for edging purposes or for rock garden pockets. Propagate it by seed, division, or by cuttings. It is sometimes confused with *O. tetragona*, a very closely related species.
Varieties/cultivars: 'Yellow River', 'William Cuthbertson'.

Papaver alpinum
ALPINE POPPY ○ ◑

Family: PAPAVERACEAE
Origin: European alps.
Flowering time: Summer.
Climatic zone: 5, 6, 7, 8, 9.
Dimensions: 6 inches (150 mm) high.
Description: The rock garden is the place for this tiny, tufted perennial with pretty four-petaled, bowl-shaped flowers. If conditions are ideal, it will often seed itself and grow in unlikely spots, especially gravel paths. It forms a close-growing, compact plant with much-segmented leaves. It needs open, well-drained soil. With a little attention, it makes an excellent pot plant. Propagate it from seed which should be fresh.
Other colors: White, red.

Phlomis russeliana
BORDER JERUSALEM SAGE ○ ◑

Family: LABIATAE
Origin: Turkey.
Flowering time: Summer.
Climatic zone: 5, 6, 7, 8, 9.
Dimensions: 3 feet (1 meter) high.
Description: This is a plant for a warm, well-drained position in the garden. The finely wrinkled, sage-like leaves are

Phlomis russeliana

evergreen, and the hooded flowers are formed in whorls around the stem. It is excellent in gardens by the seaside or in a border of gray-leaved plants. It will tolerate even strongly alkaline soils, but needs protection in cold winters. It can be propagated by seed or by division.

Potentilla eriocarpa
CINQUEFOIL ○

Family: ROSACEAE
Origin: Himalayas.
Flowering time: Spring–autumn.
Climatic zone: 4, 5, 6, 7, 8, 9.
Dimensions: Up to 2 inches (50 mm) high.
Description: This matt-forming groundcover spreads to 12 inches (300 mm) in width, with a dense covering of hairy, gray-green foliage and a dramatic display of showy, bright yellow flowers over many weeks. Position in an open, sunny location in well-drained, moderately rich soil. It grows extremely well in rocky soil, making a delightful addition to the rock garden.

Potentilla eriocarpa

Primula veris
COWSLIP, COWSLIP PRIMROSE (U.S.A.) ◑ ●

Family: PRIMULACEAE
Origin: Europe–western Asia.
Flowering time: Spring.
Climatic zone: 5, 6, 7, 8, 9.
Dimensions: 8–12 inches (200–300 mm) high.
Description: As this species grows wild

Primula veris

in cool, fresh meadows and open woodlands, it prefers a moist, well-drained soil, but will not tolerate dryness. The broad and wrinkled leaves form a basal rosette, and the erect stems bear drooping, bell-shaped flowers with a pleasant fragrance. It can be propagated by division in autumn or spring or from chilled, fresh seed. In ancient times an infusion of the roots and flowers was believed to have a sedative effect.
Other colors: White, pink, red, purple.
Varieties/cultivars: 'Alba', 'Aurea', 'Caerulea'.

Primula vulgaris
COMMON PRIMROSE, ENGLISH PRIMROSE (U.S.A.) ◑ ●

Family: PRIMULACEAE
Origin: Europe–western Asia.
Flowering time: Spring.
Climatic zone: 5, 6, 7, 8, 9.
Dimensions: 6 inches (150 mm) high.
Description: Common primrose is one of the best-known wildflowers in Europe, where it sometimes forms carpets of yellow in sheltered and shaded areas. It prefers moist, humus-rich soil, as found in woodland

surroundings. The rough and wrinkled green leaves form a rosette from which the flower stems arise. This species has given rise to a number of garden varieties. It is very useful in planters or rockeries, and the clumps can be divided in autumn.
Other colors: White, red, purple, pink.
Varieties/cultivars: *P. v.* var. *sibthorpii*, 'Alba Plena'.

Primula x *polyantha* 'Barrowby Gem'

Primula x *polyantha* syn. *P.* x *tommasin*, *P.* x *variabilis*
POLYANTHUS ◑ ●

Family: PRIMULACEAE
Origin: Hybrids.
Flowering time: Late winter–spring.
Climatic zone: 5, 6, 7, 8, 9.
Dimensions: Up to 9 inches (225 mm) high.
Description: These popular plants are chiefly derived from *P. veris* and *P. vulgaris*. They have coarse green leaves and bunched flower heads in a variety of colors. They will grow in practically any soil, but grow best when the soil is kept moist and decayed animal manure is dug in. After flowering, they should not be left in a hot, dry place, but dug up and replanted in cool shade. Protect them from attack by slugs and snails. They can be divided after flowering.
Other colors: White, cream, pink, red, blue.
Varieties/cultivars: 'Garryarde Guinevere', 'Pacific Giants', 'Barrowby Gem'.

Primula vulgaris

Ranunculus acris 'Flore Pleno'

Ranunculus acris 'Flore Pleno'
DOUBLE MEADOW ○ ◑
BUTTERCUP, BACHELOR'S
BUTTONS

Family: RANUNCULACEAE
Origin: Cultivar.
Flowering time: Late spring.
Climatic zone: 5, 6, 7, 8, 9.
Dimensions: 3 feet (1 meter) high.
Description: Derived from the common
European meadow buttercup, this
attractive plant forms wiry, branching
stems with neat, shining, and fully
double flowers. It often flowers twice in
a season and is a non-invasive, clump-
forming perennial. Propagation is by
division in autumn or spring. This plant
is poisonous.

Rudbeckia fulgida
CONEFLOWER, ○ ◑
BLACK-EYED SUSAN

Family: COMPOSITAE
Origin: Eastern United States.
Flowering time: Summer–autumn.
Climatic zone: 3, 4, 5, 6, 7, 8, 9.
Dimensions: 2 feet (600 mm) high.
Description: A sturdy and hardy plant
with rough, narrow leaves and tall stems
of flowers, it looks best in bold groups.
The flowers last for a long time and are

Rudbeckia fulgida var. *deamii* ,

suitable for cutting. It will tolerate light
frosts and most garden conditions, and
does exceptionally well on heavy soils but
needs plenty of water during summer.
Propagation is mainly by division in
spring or by sowing seed.
Varieties/cultivars: *R. f.* var. *speciosa*,
R. f. var. *sullivantii* 'Goldsturm',
R.f. var.*deamii* .

Rudbeckia hirta
BLACK-EYED SUSAN, ○
CONEFLOWER, GLORIOSA
DAISY

Family: COMPOSITAE
Origin: Eastern North America.
Flowering time: Summer.
Climatic zone: 5, 6, 7, 8, 9, 10.
Dimensions: Up to 3 feet (1 meter) high.
Description: Originally a short-lived
perennial, black-eyed Susan is now
mostly grown as a hardy annual. It is
grown widely for its continuous
flowering and ability to stand up to
hard conditions. The flowers may be
4–6 inches (100–150 mm) in diameter

Rudbeckia hirta

and mostly in shades of deep yellow to orange, but always with a contrasting black center. Given its height, the plant is best situated towards the rear of a border, in association with others of complementary tones. It looks spectacular mass-planted in parks and other large areas. Indoors it is also very useful for floral work. It is easily grown from seed and thrives in warm, sunny situations. Grows well in most soils and conditions, providing drainage is good.
Other colors: See Description.
Varieties/cultivars: 'Gloriosa', 'Marmalade', 'Gold Flame'.

Rudbeckia nitida
BLACK-EYED SUSAN, CONEFLOWER   ○ ◑

Family: COMPOSITAE
Origin: Southeastern United States.
Flowering time: Late summer.
Climatic zone: 5, 6, 7, 8, 9.
Dimensions: 4 feet (over 1 meter) high.
Description: The single daisy flowers with their green central cone have a certain freshness in their appearance even on a hot summer's day. This plant is good in a large garden, but can be blown about by wind so some support is necessary. The rounded, lance-shaped leaves are attractive and the flowers are

excellent for cutting. If grown on light soils, it needs plenty of organic matter added. Propagate it by division or cuttings in spring.
Varieties/cultivars: 'Herbstsonne', 'Goldquelle'.

Santolina chamaecyparissus
LAVENDER COTTON   ○ ◑

Family: COMPOSITAE
Origin: Mediterranean region.
Flowering time: Spring–summer.
Climatic zone: 6, 7, 8, 9, 10.
Dimensions: 1–2 feet (300–600 mm) high.

Santolina chamaecyparissus

Description: The finely dissected and heavily felted foliage forms attractive mounds of silvery white, making this a most useful plant in garden borders. The leaves have a strong, aromatic odor when bruised, and the button flowers, on almost leafless stems, are useful for picking and drying. It does best in an open situation in well-drained soil. This plant is evergreen but should be cut back hard, almost to ground level in spring, to prevent it from becoming straggly. It can be propagated by stem cuttings in the summer.
Varieties/cultivars: 'Weston'.

Senecio cineraria syn. *Cineraria maritima, Senecio maritimus*
DUSTY-MILLER (U.K.), SEA RAGWORT, SILVER CINERARIA   ○

Family: COMPOSITAE
Origin: Mediterranean region.
Flowering time: Summer.
Climatic zone: 7, 8, 9.
Dimensions: 2 feet (600 mm) high.
Description: The jagged, lobed leaves of this plant are felted in a silvery gray color making it a useful foil for other colors in a garden border. Like so many gray-leaved plants it grows exceptionally well near the seaside and can survive dry conditions, but not frost. Weak and exhausted growth should be removed after flowering and the plant regularly trimmed. The small, rayed flower heads appear in compound corymbs. Propagation is by cuttings or clump division in autumn, and also by seed.
Varieties/cultivars: 'White Diamond', 'Hoar Frost', 'Dwarf Silver'.

Rudbeckia nitida

Senecio cineraria syn. *Cineraria maritima*

Sisyrinchium striatum

Sisyrinchium striatum
SATIN FLOWER   ○ ◐

Family: IRIDACEAE
Origin: Southern Chile.
Flowering time: Summer.
Climatic zone: 7, 8, 9, 10.
Dimensions: 2 feet (600 mm) high.
Description: The gray-green, sword-like leaves of satin flower grow in clumps similar to bearded iris and from them arise the slender spikes of flowers. The flowers fade in the afternoon. When grown in an open, well-drained location, it will freely set seed. It is usually propagated from seed.
Varieties/cultivars: 'Aunt May'.

Solidago canadensis
GOLDEN ROD   ○

Family: COMPOSITAE
Origin: North America.
Flowering time: Summer.
Climatic zone: 4, 5, 6, 7, 8, 9.
Dimensions: Up to 5 feet (approx. 2 meters) high.
Description: This species is one of the parents of the many hybrid forms of golden rod available today. It forms wide clumps and has narrow, downy leaves and broad, pyramidal clusters of flowers. A very easily grown plant, it is useful at the back of the border, but it

can be quite invasive and spreads seed prolifically. The garden cultivars are less weedy and more acceptable. It grows in any good garden soil, and was once used medicinally as a poultice and a tonic. Propagate it by division.
Varieties/cultivars: 'Golden Wings', 'Goldenmosa', 'Lesdale', 'Cloth of Gold', 'Lemore', 'Golden Thumb'.

Solidago canadensis

Thalictrum speciosissimum syn. *T. flavum glaucum*
YELLOW MEADOW RUE   ○ ◐

Family: RANUNCULACEAE
Origin: Europe, temperate Asia.
Flowering time: Summer.
Climatic zone: 5, 6, 7, 8, 9.
Dimensions: Up to 5 feet (approx. 2 meters) high.
Description: The handsome foliage is blue-green in color and delicately lobed and divided. The tiny flowers are formed in dense panicles on tall stems. This is a most useful plant in the garden especially in blue-and-yellow color schemes. It will grow in most types of soil, but requires good watering during dry weather and may need support to hold the flower heads high. It becomes dormant in winter and can be divided or else propagated from seed.
Varieties/cultivars: 'Illuminator'.

Thalictrum speciosissimum

Trollius europaeus
GLOBEFLOWER   ◐

Family: RANUNCULACEAE
Origin: Europe–Caucasus, Canada.
Flowering time: Late spring–summer.
Climatic zone: 3, 4, 5, 6, 7, 8, 9.
Dimensions: 2 feet (600 mm) high.
Description: This is a plant for moist, boggy soils, good for growing in a

Trollius europaeus

Climatic zone: 4, 5, 6, 7, 8, 9.
Dimensions: Up to 2 feet (600 mm) high.
Description: This dainty woodland plant, closely related to Solomon's seal, has a thick, creeping rootstock. The narrowly oval to oblong leaves on arching stems are half unrolled as the pretty bell-shaped flowers hang from the stem. When they have faded, the leaves straighten out and remain fresh throughout summer. It needs a moist, slightly acid soil, with protection from the wind. It is easily propagated by division of the rhizomes in autumn.
Varieties/cultivars: 'Pallida'.

Verbascum phoeniceum

sunken garden or beside an ornamental pond. The leaves form a basal clump which gradually increases with age. In high altitudes it can take full sun, but it usually requires some protection. The flowers, which are single and solitary, are mildly fragrant. There are now a number of hybrid cultivars available. It is propagated by division in autumn or spring.
Varieties/cultivars: 'Superbus', 'Canary Bird', 'Orange Princess', 'Empire Day', 'Lemon Queen', 'Fire Globe'.

Trollius x *cultorum* 'Golden Queen'
GLOBEFLOWER   ◐ ◑

Family: RANUNCULACEAE
Origin: Hybrid
Flowering time: Summer.

Climatic zone: 4, 5, 6, 7, 8, 9.
Dimensions: 2–3 feet (up to 1 meter) high.
Description: This garden form is distinct from the true species which is now claimed not to be in cultivation. The formation of the flower is a little different from other globeflowers as the inside is filled with slender, petal-like orange stamens. It requires moist, well-drained soil that is well nourished, and looks splendid beside a green lawn or a stretch of water. Propagate it by division in autumn.

Verbascum phoeniceum hybrids
MULLEIN   ◯ ◑

Family: SCROPHULARIACEAE
Origin: Hybrids.
Flowering time: Summer.
Climatic zone: 6, 7, 8, 9.
Dimensions: 3–6 feet (1–2 meters) high.
Description: These lovely perennial hybrids are useful garden plants with a wide range of colors. From a rosette of large, gray-felted leaves, a tall flower spike arises bearing masses of small flowers. Mullein look best when grown in large numbers and at the back of a border with delphiniums and lupins. They thrive in well-drained, even poor, dry soil. Some plants may need staking if exposed to the wind. Cut them back after flowering and divide in autumn or spring.
Other colors: White, pink, mauve, bronze.
Varieties/cultivars: 'Bridal Bouquet', 'Miss Willmott', 'C. L. Adams', 'Cotswold Queen', 'Gainsborough'.

Uvularia grandiflora

Uvularia grandiflora
MERRYBELLS, MOUNTAIN   ◑
MERRYBELLS, BELLWORT

Family: LILIACEAE
Origin: Eastern North America.
Flowering time: Late spring.

Trollius x *cultorum* 'Golden Queen'

Abutilon megapotamicum

Abutilon megapotamicum
BRAZIL FLOWERING MAPLE, BRAZILIAN LANTERN FLOWER ◑

Family: MALVACEAE
Origin: Brazil.
Flowering time: Summer and autumn.
Climatic zone: 9, 10.

Dimensions: Up to 6 feet (2 meters) tall.
Description: This evergreen plant with its drooping stems and pendulous flowers looks attractive in a hanging basket or spilling over the edge of a large container or retaining wall. The leaves are arrow-shaped, slender, and up to 4 inches (100 mm) long. Each flower, with its yellow petals and purple anthers, is suspended by a slender stem holding a bell-shaped red calyx from which the petals unfurl to a diameter of 1 inch (25 mm). It dislikes cold climates, where a greenhouse is essential.
Varieties/cultivars: 'Variegatum'.

Abutilon x *hybridum* 'Golden Fleece'
FLOWERING MAPLE ○

Family: MALVACEAE
Origin: Hybrid.
Flowering time: Summer–autumn.
Climatic zone: 9, 10.

Dimensions: Up to 7 feet (approx. 2 meters) high.
Description: This charming, warm-climate shrub is generally grown for its pendulous, bell-shaped, golden yellow flowers and handsome, long-stalked, maple-like leaves. The best position is against a warm, sunny, and sheltered wall where well-drained, moderately rich soil will help produce an abundance of flowers in summer. Water well in summer and pinch back to encourage branching and increased flower display. *Abutilon* can also be trained around a column if the conditions are warm and sheltered.
Other colors: Orange, crimson, orange-yellow, creamy yellow, yellow with purple veins.
Varieties/cultivars: 'Ashford Red', 'Boule de Neige', 'Canary Bird', 'Fireball', 'Nabob', 'Orange Glow', 'Souvenir de Bob', 'Emperor', 'Vesuvius', 'Tunisia'.

Abutilon x *hybridum* 'Golden Fleece'

278

Banksia robur

SWAMP BANKSIA, BROAD-LEAVED BANKSIA

Family: PROTEACEAE
Origin: Australia (Queensland, N.S.W.).
Flowering time: Winter–spring.
Climatic zone: 9, 10.
Dimensions: Up to 7 feet (2 meters) tall.
Description: In its swampy native habitat, this unusual shrub, with its coarse, wide-spreading branches, grows broader (9 feet (3 meters)) than it does tall. The flowers are in dense, erect spikes, or "brushes", 6 inches (150 mm) long, yellowish-green at first, deepening to bronze-green with black stigmas. The large, elliptic leaves, 10 inches (250 mm) long, with sharp, irregular teeth on the margins, are smooth and dark green on the upper surface and rusty-red and furry on the undersurface. Prefers well-drained, heavy soil that is slightly acid.

Berberis darwinii

BARBERRY (U.K.), DARWIN BARBERRY

Family: BERBERIDACEAE
Origin: Chile.
Flowering time: Early spring.
Climatic zone: 7, 8, 9.

Berberis darwinii

Dimensions: Up to 10 feet (3 meters) high.
Description: First discovered in Chile in 1835 by Charles Darwin on the voyage of the *Beagle*, this early-flowering species is one of the finest of all flowering shrubs. The orange-yellow flowers numbering from ten to thirty, are arranged in drooping flower heads up to 4 inches (100 mm) long. It is a densely-branched shrub with the new growth arching outwards. The leaves are holly-like, three-pointed and spiny-toothed up to ¾ inch (18 mm) long, and a rich glossy green. Dark-blue-purple waxy berries make a fine autumn and winter display. A sheltered position is preferred together with well-drained soil to ensure good results.

Berberis thunbergii 'Crimson Pygmy'

Berberis thunbergii 'Crimson Pygmy'

BARBERRY, JAPANESE BARBERRY

Family: BERBERIDACEAE
Origin: Japan.
Flowering time: Spring.
Climatic zone: 4, 5, 6, 7, 8, 9.
Dimensions: Up to 2 feet (600 mm) high.
Description: Also known as 'Atropurpurea Nana' and 'Little Favorite', this dwarf cultivar was raised in Holland in 1942. The pale yellow flowers form in small clusters and are followed by bright red berries which persist all winter. The rich reddish-purple color of the foliage intensifies as winter approaches. This charming compact shrub is excellent in rock gardens and, with its thorns, makes an impenetrable low hedge. Hardy, it needs a well-drained soil.

Berberis darwinii

Buddleia globosa

Buddleia globosa
GOLDEN HONEY BALLS,
GLOBE BUDDLEIA (U.K.),
ORANGE BALL TREE

Family: LOGANIACEAE
Origin: Chile, Peru.
Flowering time: Summer.
Climatic zone: 7, 8, 9.
Dimensions: Up to 15 feet (5 meters) high.
Description: This is a striking, wide-spreading, semi-evergreen shrub which is deciduous if the winter is severe. The common names describe the tight ball-like clusters of flowers which are arranged in loose clusters at the tips of the stems. They have a pronounced honey fragrance and flower for several weeks. The handsome, lance-shaped leaves, up to 8 inches (200 mm) long, are dark-green and wrinkled above, with felted, tawny hairs on their undersides. Plant in well-drained soil in a sunny position.
Varieties/cultivars: 'Lemon Ball'.

Caesalpinia gilliesii
BIRD-OF-PARADISE BUSH

Family: CAESALPINACEAE
Origin: Argentina.
Flowering time: Summer.
Climatic zone: 9, 10.
Dimensions: Up to 10 feet (3 meters) high.
Description: This is a non-prickly, straggly, evergreen shrub or small tree. The flowers, crowded thirty or forty together in racemes up to 5 inches (125 mm) long, consist of rich yellow petals from which bright red, showy stamens protrude. The cluster of stamens can be as long as 3 inches

Caesalpinia gilliesii

(75 mm). The new shoots are sticky and hairy and the numerous small, dainty leaflets make the foliage appear very feathery and graceful. An open, sunny position with well-drained soil fertilized with a complete plant food will ensure good results for this warm climate plant.

Cassia artemisioides
SILVER CASSIA

Family: CAESALPINACEAE
Origin: Australia.
Flowering time: Early spring–summer.
Climatic zone: 9, 10.
Dimensions: Up to 4 feet (over 1 meter) high.
Description: Compact and bushy, this attractive, evergreen shrub has beautiful silvery gray shoots and feathery foliage. The leaves are finely divided into six or eight narrow leaflets. The abundant bright yellow flowers, each about ½ inch (12 mm) in diameter, form flower heads 6 inches (150 mm) long, arising in the leaf axils. The seed pods are flat and about 3 inches (75 mm) long. Excellently adapted to hot dry conditions, this plant requires full sun and exceptionally well-drained, open, sandy soil.

Cassia artemisioides

Chimonanthus praecox syn. *C. fragrans*
WINTERSWEET

Family: CALYCANTHACEAE
Origin: China.
Flowering time: Winter.
Climatic zone: 7, 8, 9.
Dimensions: Up to 8 feet (2.4 meters) high.
Description: This deciduous shrub spreads as wide as it grows tall. The bare stems of the previous year produce

Chimonanthus praecox

exceedingly fragrant flowers during the winter months. They open to 1 inch (25 mm) across, the outer petals being a translucent greenish-yellow and the inner ones stained a purplish-brown. Cutting the flowered stems to bring the perfume indoors, is also an effective method of pruning. The short-stalked, ovalish, dark-green leaves are up to 6 inches (150 mm) long. A good wall shrub, it prefers a sheltered, sunny position in well-drained, humus-rich soil.
Varieties/cultivars: 'Grandiflorus', 'Luteus'.

Colutea arborescens
BLADDER SENNA

Family: LEGUMINOSAE
Origin: Southeastern Europe.
Flowering time: Early summer.
Climatic zone: 6, 7, 8, 9.
Dimensions: Up to 12 feet (4 meters) high.
Description: This deciduous shrub sometimes naturalizes too readily to be included with selected plantings, but it will succeed in many inhospitable situations as long as the soil is not too wet and the position is not too shaded. The leaves, which are up to 6 inches (150 mm) long, consist of seven to thirteen leaflets each 1 inch (25 mm) long. The bright yellow flowers are about ¾ inch (18 mm) long and are arranged in racemes of three to eight flowers. The papery and inflated bladder-like pods are about 3 inches (75 mm) long and are sometimes flushed with red. Grow it in well-drained soil.

Colutea arborescens

Corylopsis veitchiana

Corylopsis veitchiana
WINTERHAZEL

Family: HAMAMELIDACEAE
Origin: China.
Flowering time: Spring.
Climatic zone: 7, 8, 9, 10.
Dimensions: Up to 6½ feet (2 meters) high.
Description: A bushy, rounded, deciduous shrub, this species has slender, pointed leaves and showy catkin-like racemes of fragrant primrose-yellow flowers which create a dense display. For good results this shrub requires humus-rich, slightly acid soil and should be positioned in a semishaded, protected site. It can be propagated either from ripe seed cuttings, or by layering in spring.

Corylopsis spicata

Cytisus scoparius

Corylopsis spicata
SPIKE WINTER HAZEL ○

Family: HAMAMELIDACEAE
Origin: Japan.
Flowering time: Spring.
Climatic zone: 5, 6, 7, 8, 9.
Dimensions: Up to 8 feet (2.4 meters) high.
Description: Spike winter hazel is a wide-spreading shrub with a subtle display of bright yellow blooms, sometimes appearing in late winter. The open, cup-shaped flowers are produced in pendant spikes up to 2 inches (50 mm) long of six to twelve flowers with hairy calyxes. The stamens are much the same length as the petals and the anthers are purple. The rounded leaves are about 4 inches (100 mm) long with grayish-green, hairy undersides supported by 1 inch (25 mm) long densely hairy stalks. Humus-rich, acid to neutral soil is preferred.

Cytisus scoparius syn. *Sarothamnus scoparius*
COMMON BROOM, ○
SCOTCH BROOM

Family: LEGUMINOSAE
Origin: Western and central Europe.
Flowering time: Late spring–early summer.
Climatic zone: 6, 7, 8, 9.
Dimensions: Up to 10 feet (3 meters) high.
Description: Freely naturalizing, this shrub grows in great numbers in many areas, where its glowing flowers can turn a whole hillside golden. It is a deciduous, erect shrub with many evergreen branches. The leaf usually consists of three leaflets about ½ inch (12 mm) long. The profuse flowers are produced singly or in pairs, and measure about 1 inch (25 mm) long. Many cultivars are available, with flower colors ranging from cream to shades of yellow with splashes of reds and browns. Although hardy, it prefers a well-drained, sunny site.
Varieties/cultivars: 'Andreanus', 'Cornish Cream', 'Golden Sunlight', 'Sulphureus', 'Firefly'.

Cytisus x *spachianus*
YELLOW BROOM, ○ ◑
CANARY ISLAND BROOM (U.K.)

Family: LEGUMINOSAE
Origin: Hybrid.
Flowering time: Winter–spring.
Climatic zone: 9, 10.
Dimensions: Up to 6 feet (2 meters) high.
Description: This tender, evergreen shrub has deep-green foliage with silky down beneath and rich yellow, fragrant, pea-shaped flowers in slender racemes. Often grown as a pot plant under the name *Genista fragrans*, this species prefers a light, well-drained, slightly acid soil and plenty of water during spring and summer. Intolerant of severe winters.
Other colors: Brown, crimson, orange, scarlet, deep yellow, pale cream.
Varieties/cultivars: 'Andreanus', 'Cornish Cream', 'Dorothy Walpole', 'Firefly', 'Lady Moore', 'Lord Lambourne'.

Cytisus x *spachianus*

Enkianthus campanulatus
ENKIANTHUS, RED- ○ ◑
VEIN BELL FLOWER, REDVEIN
ENKIANTHUS

Family: ERICACEAE
Origin: Japan.
Flowering time: Early summer.

Enkianthus campanulatus

Climatic zone: 4, 5, 6, 7, 8, 9.
Dimensions: Up to 12 feet (4 meters) high.
Description: This erect, deciduous shrub is an excellent companion for rhododendron, because they both require lime-free soil. The bell-shaped flowers, up to ½ inch (12 mm) long, are yellow to yellow-orange and streaked with red. Five to fifteen flowers form flower heads, which appear in great profusion and last on the shrub for about three weeks. The elliptic leaves, which are about 3 inches (75 mm) long with bristly, toothed margins, appear before the flowers open, and turn gold and red in autumn. The cut flowers are useful for floral decoration. Lime-free loamy soil which is well-drained is preferred.

Euryops pectinatus
GRAY EURYOPS ○

Family: COMPOSITAE
Origin: South Africa.
Flowering time: Spring–summer.
Climatic zone: 8, 9, 10.
Dimensions: Up to 5 feet (approx. 2 meters) high.
Description: In a warm, sunny position and well-drained soil, this half-hardy evergreen shrub will flower for months and provide constant color in the garden. The daisy-like flowers, 2 inches (50 mm) across and borne in great numbers on erect, 6-inch-long (150 mm) stems, are clustered towards the end of the branches. The leaves are up to 3 inches (75 mm) long and deeply lobed, and both leaves and stems are densely felted with gray or white hairs. Cutting the flower heads for indoor decoration

provides sufficient pruning for this plant. In cooler climates, this plant makes an attractive pot plant for a greenhouse or patio.

Euryops pectinatus

Forsythia viridissima
GOLDEN-BELLS, SPRING ○
BELLS (U.K.), FORSYTHIA

Family: OLEACEAE
Origin: Eastern China.
Flowering time: Spring.
Climatic zone: 5, 6, 7, 8, 9.
Dimensions: Up to 10 feet (3 meters) high.
Description: Golden-bells is normally the last forsythia to flower. The flowers, which consist of four strap-shaped petals, cover the length of the erect,

Forsythia viridissima 'Bronxensis'

square stems in clusters of up to six. Each bright yellow flower is 1¼ inches (30 mm) wide. The leaves are lance-like, up to 6 inches (150 mm) long, and turn purple-red before they fall. Easy to grow, forsythia is effective planted in large masses with an evergreen background. Well-drained soil in a sunny position is necessary for good flower production.
Varieties/cultivars: 'Bronxensis', 'Koreana'.

Forsythia x *intermedia*

Forsythia x *intermedia*
GOLDEN-BELLS, SPRING ○
BELLS (U.K.), FORSYTHIA

Family: OLEACEAE
Origin: Hybrid.
Flowering time: Spring.
Climatic zone: 5, 6, 7, 8, 9.
Dimensions: Up to 10 feet (3 meters) high.
Description: This hybrid (derived from *F. suspensa* and *F. viridissima*) and its cultivated varieties are regarded as being among the most beautiful of the forsythias. So many clusters of flowers appear along the length of each stem that it seems to be a solid block of color. The flower, with its four strap-shaped petals, is about 1 inch (25 mm) wide. The branches are arching or spreading and the oblong or oval leaves, up to 5 inches (125 mm) long, are toothed or sometimes divided into three. Plant in any well-drained garden soil. Pruning every few years encourages a neater, more compact shape.
Varieties/cultivars: 'Primulina', 'Spectabilis', 'Vitellina'.

Fremontodendron californicum

Genista hispanica

Fremontodendron californicum syn.
Fremontia californicum
FLANNEL BUSH,
FREMONTIA (U.K.)

Family: STERCULIACEAE
Origin: California, Arizona.
Flowering time: Spring–summer.
Climatic zone: 8, 9.
Dimensions: Up to 20 feet (6 meters) high.
Description: Previously named *Fremontia*, this evergreen shrub is excellent as a single specimen, in groups, or espaliered. The flowers, which open flat, are up to 2¼ inches (56 mm) across and although they are produced singly from the leaf axils, they are numerous. The thick, dull green leaves are covered on their undersides with irritant hairs which easily rub off and can be painful if they get into eyes. Each leaf is up to 3 inches (75 mm) long and more or less three-lobed, with three veins radiating from the heart-shaped base. This shrub thrives in dry conditions.

Genista hispanica
SPANISH GORSE

Family: LEGUMINOSAE
Origin: Southwestern Europe.
Flowering time: Early summer.

Climatic zone: 7, 8, 9.
Dimensions: Up to 2 feet (600 mm) high.
Description: Closely allied to *Cytisus*, this small, deciduous shrub grows as a rounded, prickly mound with intertwining, prominently spined branches and hairy shoots. The stalkless leaves are less than ½ inch (12 mm) long and densely covered with silky hairs on the undersides. The flowers, about ⅓ inch (8 mm) long, are in crowded clusters of up to twelve and are produced so abundantly that they completely cover the shrub for up to two months. This plant is easy to grow in soils that are dry and infertile, although it can be damaged or killed by severe winters.

Genista tinctoria
DYER'S GREENWEED

Family: LEGUMINOSAE
Origin: Mediterranean Europe, Caucasus, Turkey.
Flowering time: Summer–early autumn.
Climatic zone: 3, 4, 5, 6, 7, 8, 9.
Dimensions: Up to 2 feet (600 mm) high.
Description: This shrub is hardy and has naturalized in many areas on poor, gravelly soils. Typically, it has many upright branches which are spineless. The pea-shaped flowers are produced in great profusion in long, terminal

racemes over a long period. The narrow, oblong pods are often slightly hairy like the leaves, which are nearly ½ inch (12 mm) long. This is the best known and hardiest of the genistas, but some of its cultivars are more attractive for planting in gardens.
Varieties/cultivars: G. t. var. *prostrata*, 'Plena', 'Royal Gold'.

Genista tinctoria var. *prostrata*

Hamamelis mollis
CHINESE WITCH
HAZEL

Family: HAMAMELIDACEAE
Origin: Western China.
Flowering time: Winter.
Climatic zone: 5, 6, 7, 8, 9.
Dimensions: 10–20 feet (3–6 meters) high.
Description: This slow-growing, deciduous shrub or tree is perhaps the

Hamamelis mollis

(18 mm) long, and arranged in clusters. The leaves are oval, 6 inches (150 mm) long, coarsely toothed, and turn golden yellow before they fall. This large shrub, which is the source of commercial witch hazel, is occasionally seen as a small, broad-domed tree.

Hypericum calycinum
SHRUBBY ST. JOHNS ◯ ◑ WORT, AARON'S BEARD, ROSE OF SHARON

Family: HYPERICACEAE
Origin: Southeastern Bulgaria, Turkey.
Flowering time: Summer–autumn.
Climatic zone: 6, 7, 8, 9.
Dimensions: 1–2 feet (300–600 mm) high.
Description: This semi-evergreen, dwarf shrub is one of the finest of the hypericums. Spreading by stems that can take root where they touch the ground, it forms a dense mat which makes it an excellent groundcover, but it can become a nuisance if allowed to spread unchecked. The flowers, which appear over the whole of a long summer season, are up to 4 inches (100 mm) wide, occur singly or in pairs, and have numerous stamens. The leaves are oblong and up to 4 inches (100 mm) long. The plant thrives in either sun or partial shade, and in dry soils.

finest witch hazel in bloom and certainly the most popular. It is distinguished from the other species by the soft hair on its young shoots and the undersides of its leaves. It has large, rounded leaves to 6 inches (150 mm) long. The fragrant flowers consist of four narrow, strap-shaped petals which emerge crumpled from the buds. When fully open, they are ¾ inch (18 mm) long, reddish at the base, and a welcome sight in the cold months.
Varieties/cultivars: 'Pallida'.

Climatic zone: 4, 5, 6, 7, 8, 9.
Dimensions: Up to 20 feet (6 meters) high.
Description: This deciduous shrub flowers as the leaves drop in autumn. The fragrant flowers have four strap-shaped petals which are up to ¾ inch

Hamamelis virginiana

Hamamelis virginiana
WITCH HAZEL ◯ ◑

Family: HAMAMELIDACEAE
Origin: Eastern North America.
Flowering time: Autumn.

Hypericum calycinum

SHRUBS

Hypericum kalmianum

Hypericum kalmianum
KALM ST. JOHNS WORT, ◯
SHRUBBY ST. JOHNS WORT

Family: HYPERICACEAE
Origin: Northeastern North America.
Flowering time: Summer.
Climatic zone: 4, 5, 6, 7, 8, 9.
Dimensions: Up to 3 feet (1 meter) high.
Description: This dense, compact, evergreen shrub exists as a native over large areas of the eastern United States and is a popular garden inclusion. The stems are pale green when young, and when mature are often gnarled with pale brown, flaky bark. Its leaves, up to 2½ inches (60 mm) long, are narrowly oblong. The flowers, almost stalkless, open wide to 2 inches (50 mm) across to display five rounded petals and a show of stamens. They appear in the axils of the leaves as solitary flowers or in groups of two or three. Plant in a sunny position, in well-drained soil.

Hypericum x *moseranum* 'Tricolor'

Hypericum x *moseranum*
GOLD FLOWER, SHRUBBY ◯
ST. JOHNS WORT

Family: HYPERICACEAE
Origin: Hybrid.
Flowering time: Summer.

Climatic zone: 7, 8, 9.
Dimensions: Up to 2 feet (600 mm) high.
Description: Raised in France in 1887 from *H. calycinum* and *H. patulum*, this low-growing shrub does not, however, spread by rooting stems like *H. calycinum*. With its numerous arching, reddish branches it is an excellent dwarf shrub for rock gardens. The flowers, solitary or in clusters of up to five in number, are 2½ inches (60 mm) across, with conspicuous reddish anthers, and are borne over a long summer. The egg-shaped leaves, up to 2¼ inches (54 mm) long, are grayish on their undersides. Cut back to ground level if winters are harsh. A sunny, well-drained site is preferred.
Varieties/cultivars: 'Tricolor'.

Illicium anisatum

Illicium anisatum syn. *I. religiosum,*
I. japonicum
JAPANESE STAR
ANISE

Family: ILLICIACEAE
Origin: China, Japan, Taiwan.
Flowering time: Spring.
Climatic zone: 8, 9.
Dimensions: Up to 25 feet (8 meters) high.
Description: Related to the magnolia, this outstanding evergreen shrub thrives in conditions congenial to Rhododendron. It is slow-growing and aromatic and is often found in Buddhist cemeteries or near temples, where its wood is used in incense. Its lustrous, oval leaves, which are also aromatic, are thick, fleshy, deep-green, and up to 4 inches (100 mm) long. The many-petaled flowers are pale yellow, about 1 inch (25 mm) across, and appear even on young plants. This species is poisonous, and needs a sheltered site in cooler climates.
Varieties/cultivars: 'Variegatum'.

286

Itea ilicifolia

Itea ilicifolia
HOLLY-LEAF
SWEETSPIRE

Family: SAXIFRAGACEAE
Origin: Western China.
Flowering time: Late summer.
Climatic zone: 7, 8, 9.
Dimensions: Up to 9 feet (3 meters) high.
Description: This handsome evergreen shrub has holly-like, spiny-toothed, broad leaves up to 4 inches (100 mm) long, which are a rich, glossy green on the upper surface and paler beneath. The pale greenish-yellow flowers, which are produced in arching, trailing, slender, catkin-like racemes up to 12 inches (300 mm) long, cover the plant in late summer. These shrubs can be used in much the same manner as hollies — in groups, as single specimens, as hedges, or combined with other plants in the shrub garden. Plant in well-drained, humus-rich soil in sun or partial shade. A sheltered position is preferred, especially in cooler climates.

Jasminum humile 'Revolutum'
YELLOW JASMINE,
SHRUBBY YELLOW JASMINE,
ITALIAN JASMINE

Family: OLEACEAE
Origin: Cultivar.
Flowering time: Summer–autumn.
Climatic zone: 7, 8, 9.
Dimensions: Up to 10 feet (3 meters) high.
Description: Although rather sprawling in habit, this beautiful evergreen shrub forms a more or less

rounded shape. Its deep-green leaves with three to seven leaflets, the terminal one being the longest and measuring up to 2½ inches (60 mm) long, form a splendid background for the deep-yellow, sometimes fragrant flowers. On a long tube, the spreading petals, measuring ¾ inch (18 mm) across, are arranged in clusters of six to twelve or more. This shrub is an ideal plant for a sunny, protected situation such as against a wall. It does not tolerate severe winters. Well-drained but moist soil is preferred.

Jasminum humile 'Revolutum'

Jasminum mesnyi

Jasminum mesnyi syn. *J. primulinum*
PRIMROSE JASMINE

Family: OLEACEAE
Origin: Western China.
Flowering time: Spring.
Climatic zone: 8, 9, 10.
Dimensions: Up to 3 feet (1 meter) high.
Description: Sometimes included among the climbing plants, this very attractive evergreen shrub has weak stems which emerge from the base and,

arching outwards, scramble over any support. The flowers of deep-yellow open to 1½ inches (35 mm) across on a slender tube ½ inch (12 mm) long. They are often semidouble and are produced in succession over a long spring season on the 1- and 2-year-old outer stems for a length of 3 feet (1 meter) or more. The leaves, which grow opposite one another on the stems, consist of three leaflets and are up to 4 inches (100 mm) long. Well-drained, moist soil is preferred. This plant may be killed by severe winters.

Kerria japonica 'Pleniflora'

Kerria japonica 'Pleniflora' syn. 'Flore Pleno'
KERRIA, JEW'S
MALLOW, BACHELORS
BUTTONS (U.K.)

Family: ROSACEAE
Origin: Cultivar.
Flowering time: Spring.
Climatic zone: 5, 6, 7, 8, 9.
Dimensions: Up to 6 feet (2 meters) high.
Description: A cultivar of the only species of *Kerria*, this deciduous, suckering shrub has been a favorite in gardens since its introduction into Europe in 1834. Long, slender, cane-like stems from the previous year support the flowers, which are clear golden-yellow, up to 1¾ inches (42 mm) across, and which open to show their petals and numerous stamens. The egg-shaped leaves, which are about 4 inches (100 mm) long with double-toothed margins, are bright green, smooth on the upper surface, and hairy on the underside. They turn yellow in autumn. Grow in any well-drained soil. It tolerates both sun and partial shade.

Lantana camara 'Drap d'Or'
COMMON LANTANA, ○
YELLOW SAGE (U.K.)

Family: VERBENACEAE
Origin: Cultivar.
Flowering time: Year round.
Climatic zone: 9, 10.
Dimensions: Up to 6 feet (2 meters) high.
Description: Deep golden-yellow flowers and a more compact growth habit distinguish this cultivated variety from other *Lantana* species. Otherwise it has similar characteristics — the crushed leaves give off the familiar pungent smell, the stems are prickly, and the foliage is covered in short hairs. The leaves are oval, wrinkled, up to 5 inches (125 mm) in length, with toothed margins. The small flowers are arranged in flattish clusters of twenty to thirty, measuring up to 2 inches (50 mm) across. The black fruits which follow are mostly sterile (and do not present the same problem as the non-cultivated lantanas whose readily germinating seeds are widely dispersed by birds).

Lantana camara 'Drap d'Or'

Laurus nobilis
SWEET BAY, BAY ○ ◐
LAUREL

Family: LAURACEAE
Origin: Mediterranean region.
Flowering time: Late spring.
Climatic zone: 7, 8, 9.
Dimensions: Up to 20 feet (6 meters) high.
Description: In cultivation since 1562, this is the true laurel that the ancients made into wreaths for poets and crowns for triumphant heroes. Because it stands

Laurus nobilis

clipping well it is today often grown beside doorways and trimmed to shape. Although in the wild it can reach a height of 40 feet (12 meters), in a cultivated garden it is well suited to large containers. The evergreen leaves are narrow, up to 5 inches (125 mm) long, a rich dark-green, and are the bay leaves much esteemed by cooks the world over. Small clusters of fragrant, yellowish flowers are followed by small berries which ripen to purplish-black. Plant in spring in moderate soil in a sunny or partially shady position. It is tolerant of some frost but may be damaged by severe winters.
Varieties/cultivars: 'Angustifolia'.

Lindera benzoin
SPICE BUSH ○ ◐

Family: LAURACEAE
Origin: Eastern North America.
Flowering time: Spring.
Climatic zone: 6, 7, 8, 9.

Lindera benzoin

Dimensions: Up to 15 feet (5 meters) high.
Description: Of compact habit, this is a magnificent deciduous, tall shrub. Its long leaves are aromatic when bruised. Bright green in summer, the leaves in autumn may turn a glorious butter-yellow with rich pink tints. The small flowers are petalless, their calyces being yellow-green. The berry-like fruits are red. Plant in partial shade or full sun in moist soil.

Mahonia aquifolium

Mahonia aquifolium
OREGON GRAPE, ○ ◐
HOLLY MAHONIA

Family: BERBERIDACEAE
Origin: Northwestern North America.
Flowering time: Spring.
Climatic zone: 6, 7, 8, 9.
Dimensions: Up to 4 feet (approx. 1 meter) high.
Description: This very beautiful evergreen shrub looks attractive planted under deciduous trees. The showy flowers are produced in dense, golden-yellow clusters of racemes up to 3 inches (75 mm) long. Masses of attractive blue-black berries follow with their covering of purple bloom. The handsome leaves, up to 10 inches (250 mm) long, consist of five to nine oblong leaflets each up to 3 inches (75 mm) long with shallow-toothed margins. In autumn bronze and purple tints are added to their rich, glossy green. Grow in humus-rich, well-drained soil.
Varieties/cultivars: 'Atropurpureum', 'Moseri'.

Mahonia bealei

Description: Often known as *O. multiflora*, this evergreen shrub has leathery, elliptic leaves which are up to 2 inches (50 mm) long and have sharply toothed margins and prominent midribs. The bronze-colored spring foliage is followed by the fragrant flowers, resembling yellow buttercups, about ¾ inch (18 mm) wide, which are freely produced at the ends of the many lateral shoots. The fruits which quickly follow are kidney-shaped and bright green at first, maturing to a glossy black. Their curious appearance is heightened by the enlarged, bright crimson, waxy receptacles to which they are attached. Hardy, it is easy to propagate as seedlings are freely produced.

Phlomis fruticosa
JERUSALEM SAGE   ○

Family: LABIATAE
Origin: Southwestern Europe.
Flowering time: Summer.
Climatic zone: 7, 8, 9.
Dimensions: Up to 4 feet (approx. 1 meter) high.
Description: Jerusalem sage is a small, broad, evergreen shrub excellent for a sunny position in well-drained soil. Its many branches are densely hairy, as are the ovalish, wrinkled leaves, which are up to 4 inches (100 mm) long. The hairs on their upper surface are green, while those on the undersides are more dense and white or yellowish. The flowers, which are dusky yellow and more than 1 inch (25 mm) long, form rounded clusters at the tops of the stems. Pruning the spent flower heads will increase flowering and maintain the bush's compact shape.

Mahonia bealei
LEATHERLEAF MAHONIA   ○ ◑

Family: BERBERIDACEAE
Origin: China.
Flowering time: Late winter–late spring.
Climatic zone: 6, 7, 8, 9.
Dimensions: Up to 8 feet (approx. 2 meters) high.
Description: The hardiest of the Asian mahonias and, with M. *aquifolium* and M. *repens*, the most cold-resistant, this popular evergreen shrub has stout, upright stems. The fragrant, lemon-yellow flowers are clustered into erect racemes up to 6 inches (150 mm) long. The fruits are a waxy bluish-black. The leaves are stiff, leathery, semi-glossy, deep green and up to 1½ feet (450 mm) long, with nine to fifteen round to oval leaflets each up to 4 inches (100 mm) in length. There are a few large, spiny teeth on the margins. It is adaptable to both sun and partial shade as long as a humus-rich soil is provided.

Ochna serrulata

Ochna serrulata syn. *O. atropurpurea*
BIRD'S EYE BUSH, MICKEY-MOUSE PLANT, CARNIVAL BUSH   ○

Family: OCHNACEAE
Origin: South Africa.
Flowering time: Summer.
Climatic zone: 9.
Dimensions: Up to 10 feet (3 meters) high.

Phlomis fruticosa

Potentilla fruticosa

Reinwardtia, yellow flax is a splendid small, evergreen shrub for warm, sunny, and preferably humid locations and, in warm greenhouses, makes an attractive pot plant. The bright golden-yellow, nearly circular flowers are about 2 inches (50 mm) in diameter and open wide above a slender tube. They fall quickly, but are produced in abundance over a long period. The soft, thin, narrow leaves, about 3 inches (75 mm) long, are bright green. The plant should be pruned to shape in early spring.

Ribes odoratum
YELLOW FLOWERING CURRANT, BUFFALO CURRANT (U.K.)

Family: SAXIFRAGACEAE
Origin: Central United States.
Flowering time: Late spring.
Climatic zone: 5, 6, 7, 8, 9.
Dimensions: Up to 12 feet (4 meters) high.
Description: Closely related to the fruiting currants and gooseberries, this ornamental, deciduous shrub is charming in bloom, when its numerous clove-scented, bright yellow, tubular flowers emerge in drooping, hairy racemes of up to ten. The racemes are 2 inches (50 mm) long. Small, smooth, black, edible fruits follow. The leaves are three- or five-lobed, smooth, though at first hairy, and measure up to 3 inches (75 mm) in length and width. They color to scarlet in autumn. Pruning after flowering produces a compact shape. A well-drained but moist soil and a sunny or partially shaded position are preferred.

Potentilla fruticosa
SHRUBBY CINQUEFOIL

Family: ROSACEAE
Origin: Northern temperate zone, mountains further south.
Flowering time: Summer.
Climatic zone: 2, 3, 4, 5, 6, 7, 8, 9.
Dimensions: Up to 3 feet (1 meter) high.
Description: Usually a rounded bush growing as wide as it does tall, this deciduous shrub is hardy, thrives in any soil, and has flowers like small, single roses which are displayed over a long summer season. Its erect stems bear hairy green to grey leaves divided into five to seven leaflets up to 1 inch (25 mm) long. The open-faced, bright yellow flowers, up to 2 inches (50 mm) in diameter, are numerous and showy. This shrub is the parent of several hybrids as well as producing many cultivated varieties.
Other colors: White, red, orange, cream.
Varieties/cultivars: Many cultivars are available, including 'Grandiflora', 'Katherine Dykes', 'Vilmoriniana', 'Berlin Beauty', 'Klondyke', 'Longacre'.

Reinwardtia indica syn. *R. trigyna*, *Linum trigynum*
YELLOW FLAX

Family: LINACEAE
Origin: Northern India.
Flowering time: Winter–spring.
Climatic zone: 9, 10.
Dimensions: Up to 3 feet (1 meter) high.
Description: The most commonly cultivated of the few species of

Reinwardtia indica

Ribes odoratum

Senecio greyi

Senecio greyi
GROUNDSEL, SHRUBBY GROUNDSEL ○

Family: COMPOSITAE
Origin: New Zealand.
Flowering time: Summer.
Climatic zone: 7, 8, 9.
Dimensions: Up to 6 feet (2 meters) high.
Description: Considered by some the loveliest of the New Zealand *Senecio* species, this very popular wide-spreading, evergreen shrub brings soft shades of white-gray to the garden, with the young shoots, undersides of the leaves, and leaf stalks all densely covered in a felt of white hairs. The bright yellow, daisy flower heads, up to 1 inch (25 mm) wide, are arranged in broad clusters up to 6 inches (150 mm) long. The oblong leaves are up to 4 inches (100 mm) long. This shrub is ideal for seaside planting, but cannot tolerate severe winters.

Spartium junceum
SPANISH BROOM, WEAVER'S BROOM ○

Family: LEGUMINOSAE
Origin: Southwestern Europe.
Flowering time: Summer–autumn.
Climatic zone: 8, 9.
Dimensions: Up to 8 feet (approx. 2 meters) high.
Description: Closely related to *Cytisus* and *Genista*, this single species of *Spartium* is a wonderful seaside shrub

Spartium junceum

thriving in well-drained soils in a sunny situation. The fragrant flowers measure 1 inch (25 mm) long and wide, and look like small, golden-yellow sweet peas arranged in showy, loose, terminal racemes up to 1½ feet (450 mm) long. Because its leaves are small and inconspicuous on the erect, rush-like, green stems, the shrub seems almost leafless. Prune in early spring to keep it shapely. The shrub is tolerant of moderate frost but not severe winters.

Ulex europaeus
COMMON GORSE, FURZE, WHIN ○

Family: LEGUMINOSAE
Origin: Western Europe–southern Scandinavia.
Flowering time: Late winter–late spring.
Climatic zone: 6, 7, 8, 9.
Dimensions: Up to 6 feet (2 meters) high.
Description: Closely resembling the related *Cytisus*, this fiercely spiny, evergreen shrub has been known to produce flowers over the whole year, but only in dry, sandy soil in full sun and in a mild climate. The brilliant yellow pea flowers are up to ¾ inch (18 mm) long, almond-scented, and form loose to dense clusters at the ends of the branches. Young plants have three leaflets, but on older specimens the leaves are scale-like or represented by spines. Naturalized in many areas, sometimes to the point of being a pest, gorse grows well in association with heather. It is suitable for clipping as a hedge.
Varieties/cultivars: 'Plenus'.

Ulex europaeus

Acacia baileyana

Acacia baileyana
COOTAMUNDRA WATTLE, BAILEY WATTLE, BAILEY ACACIA ○

Family: LEGUMINOSAE
Origin: Australia, N.S.W.
Flowering time: Winter–spring.
Climatic zone: 9, 10.
Dimensions: 20–40 feet (6–12 meters) high.
Description: One of the most popular and widely grown of the acacias, Cootamundra wattle is smothered in golden balls of small, fluffy, fragrant flowers in winter. Its bluish or silvery-gray leaves consist of many, divided leaflets, producing a soft, feathery appearance. It can be grown successfully in most soils and conditions, providing drainage is excellent. Like all wattles it is fast-growing which makes it a valuable plant for new gardens for use as a screen or a shade tree. Another asset in landscaping is its role as a "nurse" plant — it fills in space and protects much slower-growing plants. In cold areas, it needs to be grown under glass. Tip-prune it after flowering, to prolong its life.
Varieties/cultivars: 'Purpurea'.

Acacia dealbata
SILVER WATTLE, MIMOSA ○

Family: LEGUMINOSAE
Origin: Eastern Australia.
Flowering time: Spring.
Climatic zone: 8, 9, 10.
Dimensions: 33–66 feet (10–20 meters) high.

Description: In the wild, silver wattle grows by permanent creeks. With its profuse flower heads of highly fragrant flowers it is a favorite in France for the perfume industry. After blooming, the tree takes on a hazy pink hue, as masses of pods hang among the silvery, feathery foliage. Fast-growing and evergreen, it is best grown in a very large, natural garden, near a running creek. It is easily grown from seed in spring, but the seed must be soaked in freshly boiled water which is allowed to cool slowly for 24 hours before sowing.

Acacia dealbata

Acacia longifolia
SYDNEY GOLDEN WATTLE, SALLOW WATTLE ○

Family: LEGUMINOSAE
Origin: Eastern and southern Australia.
Flowering time: Spring.
Climatic zone: 9, 10.
Dimensions: 10–20 feet (3-6 meters) high.
Description: At home in many warm, temperate climates, this evergreen tree is used extensively in California as a street tree, while in South Africa it has reached almost weed proportions. Profuse, fragrant fingers of fluffy flowers appear each spring. Beautiful, fast-growing, and resistant to salt spray, it will bind soil when planted on a bank, or very quickly create a screen for a new garden. *Acacia longifolia* var. *sophorae* is a much smaller, spreading form which will bind sand in beach gardens. Grow new plants from seed in spring, soaking them in warm water for 12 hours before planting.
Varieties/cultivars: *A. l.* var. *sophorae*.

Acer platanoides
NORWAY MAPLE ○

Family: ACERACEAE
Origin: Scandinavia, western Europe, western Asia.
Flowering time: Early spring.
Climatic zone: 3, 4, 5, 6, 7, 8, 9.
Dimensions: 50–100 feet (15–30 meters) high.
Description: Found over large areas in its natural habitat, this tree is also extensively cultivated. Attractive clusters of yellow flowers appear just before the fine, green leaves, which turn yellow briefly in autumn before falling. One of the fastest-growing of the maples, it prefers cool, moist gardens in areas high above sea level, but will withstand pollution. Because it produces a dense canopy, not much will grow beneath this tree. Plant it where shade is required, perhaps in a paved area with garden seats.
Varieties/cultivars: 'Crimson King', 'Drummondii', 'Dissectum', 'Erectum', 'Faasen's Black', 'Reitenbachii', 'Schwedleri', 'Goldsworth Purple', 'Laciniatum', 'Lorbergii'.

Acacia longifolia

Acer platanoides

Azara lanceolata

Azara lanceolata
AZARA

Family: FLACOURTIACEAE
Origin: Chile.
Flowering time: Midsummer.
Climatic zone: 8, 9.
Dimensions: Up to 20 feet (6 meters) high.
Description: This is a neat and pretty evergreen tree covered in slender, dark green, glossy foliage. The strongly fragrant flowers are mustard-yellow, and followed by pretty, pale mauve berries. To achieve good results position in a warm, sheltered site in rich, moist soil that is slightly acid. Mulch well around the base, and ensure there is a good supply of water during summer. Avoid planting close to other species, as the roots produce a growth inhibitor.

Banksia serrata
RED HONEYSUCKLE,
SAW BANKSIA

Family: PROTEACEAE
Origin: Eastern Australia.
Flowering time: Summer.
Climatic zone: 9, 10.
Dimensions: Up to 30 feet (9 meters) high.
Description: Banksias are a useful shrub in poor, sandy, coastal soil and are salt-resistant. The spikes of golden flowers, which look like erect cylinders, are about 6 inches (150 mm) long. The fruits are woody seed cells. The shiny

Banksia serrata

leaves are leathery, narrow, and up to 6 inches (150 mm) long, with closely toothed margins. Plant in acid, well-drained, sandy to loamy soil.

Caesalpinia ferrea syn. *Poinciana ferrea*
BRAZILIAN IRONWOOD,
LEOPARD TREE

Family: CAESALPINACEAE
Origin: Eastern Brazil.
Flowering time: Spring.
Climatic zone: 9, 10.
Dimensions: 33–50 feet (10–15 meters) high.
Description: The beautiful mottling of the trunk, caused by peeling bark, gives this tree the name leopard. In spring,

Caesalpinia ferrea

the top of the tree is lit up with vivid yellow blossoms, and its soft, feathery foliage, reddish at first but bright green when mature, adds a touch of elegance. Ideal in the subtropical garden, it is a fairly fast grower, making a good shade tree, but needing plenty of room. It grows well in coastal areas, but not the dry inland. Grow it from seed that has been soaked for several hours in warm water.

Caragana arborescens

Caragana arborescens
SIBERIAN PEA TREE, PEA
SHRUB

Family: FABACEAE
Origin: Siberia, Mongolia.
Flowering time: Late spring, northern hemisphere.
Climatic zone: 3, 4, 5, 6, 7, 8, 9.
Dimensions: 15–20 feet (5–6 meters) high.
Description: The deciduous Siberian pea tree was first introduced into England in the mid-eighteenth century and has since been used as a hedge or windbreak in dry, exposed areas. The attractive yellow flowers appear in clusters from buds of the previous year. This tree is best planted in either autumn or winter, and will grow well in most soils and conditions providing drainage is adequate. Being such an adaptable plant it is often used for grafting other desirable varieties.
Varieties/cultivars: 'Lorbergii', 'Nana', 'Pendula'.

Cassia fistula

Cassia fistula
GOLDEN-SHOWER (U.K.), ○ INDIAN LABURNUM, PUDDING-PIPE TREE

Family: CAESALPINACEAE
Origin: Tropical India, Burma, Sri Lanka.
Flowering time: Late summer–early autumn.
Climatic zone: 9, 10.
Dimensions: 20–33 feet (6–10 meters) high.
Description: Showy, large, drooping clusters of clear yellow, fragrant flowers adorn this lovely tree for weeks on end, enhanced by the pretty, fresh-green leaves. The name "pudding-pipe" refers to the long, brown, rather ugly seed pods that hang from the branches. The seeds may be sown in spring after soaking them in warm water for 24 hours to soften their outer coating. Easy to grow in warmer gardens, pudding-pipe tree needs to be protected from frost and cold winds in borderline climates. It thrives in well-drained soils in warm, coastal environments with good rainfall. It sheds its leaves for short periods.

Cornus mas
CORNELIAN CHERRY ○

Family: CORNACEAE
Origin: Central and southern Europe.
Flowering time: Late winter–spring.
Climatic zone: 4, 5, 6, 7, 8, 9.

Dimensions: 17–27 feet (5–8 meters) high.
Description: Cornelian cherry bears profuse clusters of tiny, yellow flowers on naked branches at the end of winter, and produces pretty, bright-red, edible fruits in summer. In autumn, the leaves may turn reddish-purple before falling. Not many other trees will tolerate the conditions this tree does — dry, chalky soils, pollution, exposed situations — and also resist pests and diseases. Often shrubby in habit, cornelian cherry should be pruned to train it as a single trunk. Grow this tree from semihardwood cuttings in late summer.
Varieties/cultivars: 'Aurea', 'Elegantissima', 'Variegata'.

Cornus mas

Genista aetnensis
MOUNT ETNA BROOM ○

Family: LEGUMINOSAE
Origin: Sicily, Sardinia.
Flowering time: Summer, northern hemisphere; late spring–mid-summer, southern hemisphere.
Climatic zone: 8, 9.
Dimensions: 17–20 feet (5–6 meters) high.
Description: Imagine a landscape of black and yellow. That is Mount Etna in summer, when the broom is in full flower on the lava-blackened slopes. Loose clusters of fragrant, clear yellow, pea-shaped flowers weigh down the slender branches of this graceful, little deciduous tree. The silky, downy, sparse leaves appear somewhat silvery. This

Genista aetnensis

broom prefers a well-drained position and tolerates chalky soil; in some areas it is subject to fungal die-back. Grow it in spring from seed that has been soaked for 24 hours in warm water. It requires no pruning.

Grevillea robusta
SILK OAK (U.S.A.), SILKY ○ OAK

Family: PROTEACEAE
Origin: Australia (coastal N.S.W. and Queensland).
Flowering time: Spring, northern hemisphere; late spring–early summer, southern hemisphere.
Climatic zone: 9, 10.

Grevillea robusta

Dimensions: 40–145 feet (12-44 meters) high.
Description: Silky oak is widely grown — as a garden tree, a street tree, a pot plant, indoors and outdoors, and as a rootstock for grafting other grevilleas. Largest of all the grevilleas, it can grow rapidly to 65 feet or more (over 20 meters) in southern hemisphere gardens, and even higher in parts of the northern hemisphere. It has yellowy-orange, toothbrush-shaped clusters of spider-like flowers and deeply-lobed, feathery leaves, somewhat silvery underneath. The tree prefers warm, moist soils. Normally evergreen, it tends to become deciduous if affected by cold and drought. Protect it from frost when young. It can be grown from seed.

Harpephyllum caffrum

Harpephyllum caffrum
KAFFIR PLUM

Family: ANACARDIACEAE
Origin: Southeastern Africa.
Flowering time: Mid–late summer.
Climatic zone: 8, 9, 10.
Dimensions: 33–40 feet (10–12 meters) high.
Description: Give this handsome, evergreen tree plenty of space to develop its wide canopy. The young leaves appear reddish and shiny and can be mistaken for flowers from a distance. They later become dark-green and lustrous giving the tree a rather somber appearance. Delicious jams and jellies are made from the bright, red fruits, which develop from the rather pale, greenish-yellow flowers. Plant it as a shade tree in large coastal gardens where the rainfall is high. It grows easily from large stem cuttings, 12–24 inches (300–600 mm) long in late spring.

Hymenosporum flavum

Hymenosporum flavum
NATIVE FRANGIPANI, AUSTRALIAN FRANGIPANI, SWEET-SHADE (U.K.)

Family: PITTOSPORACEAE
Origin: Australia (northern N.S.W. and Queensland).
Flowering time: Late spring–early summer.
Climatic zone: 9, 10.
Dimensions: 20–66 feet (6–20 meters) high.
Description: In a sunny, open space in the garden, this delightful, evergreen tree grows only a fraction of the height it attains in its natural habitat, where it has to fight for light. The sprays of scented yellow flowers are tubular, with five open lobes. The tree needs to be carefully positioned, because both flowers and leaves are borne towards the end of the thinnish, brittle branches. Because its branching is open and irregular, it throws little shade. Protect it from the wind by planting it either against a fence or wall, or behind a shrubbery. It enjoys warm, coastal areas and free-draining soil.

Koelreuteria paniculata
VARNISH TREE (U.S.A.), GOLDEN RAIN TREE (U.K.), PRIDE OF CHINA TREE

Other common names: WILLOW PATTERN PLATE TREE
Family: SAPINDACEAE
Origin: Northern China, Korea.
Flowering time: Early summer.
Climatic zone: 5, 6, 7, 8.
Dimensions: 20–50 feet (6–15 meters) high.
Description: Golden rain tree grows in a wide range of climates and soils, tolerating drought, but disliking the coastal garden with its salt-laden winds. Its large, drooping clusters of yellow

Koelreuteria paniculata

flowers are followed by long, reddish, papery pods which hang on the tree into winter, and its large, feathery leaves color well in the autumn. Developing a wide canopy when mature, it grows rapidly in warmer climates, but in cooler regions takes about 20 years to attain a height of 18 feet (5 meters). Propagate it from seed or root cuttings.
Varieties/cultivars: 'Fastigiata', 'September' (flowers in late summer).

Laburnum anagyroides

Laburnum anagyroides
COMMON LABURNUM

Family: LEGUMINOSAE
Origin: Central and southern Europe.
Flowering time: Early summer.
Climatic zone: 6, 7, 8, 9.
Dimensions: Up to 20 feet (6 meters).
Description: This charming, small, deciduous tree has a spreading shape and large, drooping clusters of bright yellow, pea-like flowers. It likes cool-climate gardens, and although it can be grown successfully in most soil types, one that is deep and moist will bring the best results. In country gardens do not position it where stock can eat it, as all parts of the plant are poisonous.

Laburnum x watereri 'Vossii'

Laburnum x watereri 'Vossii'
LABURNUM, GOLDEN CHAIN TREE, WATERER'S LABURNUM ○

Family: LEGUMINOSAE
Origin: Hybrid.
Flowering time: Late spring–early summer.
Climatic zone: 6, 7, 8, 9.
Dimensions: 20–30 feet (6–9 meters) high.
Description: This beautiful tree bears long, drooping sprays of yellow, pea-shaped flowers, and has attractive, soft foliage which consists of three leaflets on a common stalk. An avenue of laburnum, flowering vividly yellow in the spring, is an enchanting spectacle. Laburnum is deciduous and grows in almost any position in regions where the winters are cold and the atmosphere moist. All parts of the plant are poisonous so fence off from stock.

Parkinsonia aculeata
MEXICAN PALO VERDE (U.S.A.), JERUSALEM THORN (U.K.) ○

Family: LEGUMINOSAE
Origin: Tropical America.
Flowering time: Spring.
Climatic zone: 9, 10.
Dimensions: 20–27 feet (6–8 meters) high.
Description: Growing rapidly in its early years, this elegant little tree is for

Parkinsonia aculeata

the tropical garden only. Its large clusters of yellow flowers, slightly scented, are followed by seed pods which look like a short string of beads. The soft, green, gracefully drooping branches, with their sparse foliage, cast a delicate tracery of shadow, but carry sharp thorns about 1 inch (25 mm) long. Jerusalem thorn grows well in coastal gardens or in frost-free inland gardens and tolerates alkaline soil and drought. Propagate it from seed.

Tamarindus indica
TAMARIND ○

Family: CAESALPINACEAE
Origin: Tropical Africa, Abyssinia, India.
Flowering time: Summer, then intermittently.
Climatic zone: 10.
Dimensions: 50–80 feet (15–25 meters) high.
Description: In India, it is believed that bad spirits take possession of anyone who sleeps beneath the dense canopy of the tamarind, so dense that nothing grows below it. Abundant, orchid-like flowers, with a delicate scent, fall to create carpets of pale yellow. A hot-

climate, adaptable tree, it grows slowly, tolerating semi-arid conditions, but preferring deep, moist soils. Grow it from seed or buy a grafted specimen for quicker flowering. It is best suited to large, coastal or country gardens. The pulp from the large seed pods is used in curries and drinks.

Tamarindus indica

Description: Growing up to 100 feet (30 meters) in the wild, the tipu is much more manageable as a garden tree. Crinkled, apricot-yellow flowers appear in late spring at the tips of the branches. Pretty, light-green leaflets growing on wide-spreading limbs form the flattened canopy which, sometimes wider than it is high, makes tipu a perfect shade tree. In the subtropics it loses its leaves for a short time only. Grow it from seed.

Thevetia peruviana

Tristaniopsis laurina

Thevetia peruviana
LUCKY NUT, YELLOW OLEANDER, BE STILL TREE ○

Family: APOCYNACEAE
Origin: Tropical America.
Flowering time: Throughout hottest months.
Climatic zone: 9, 10.
Dimensions: 10–30 feet (3–9 meters) high.
Description: With its glossy green leaves and trumpet-shaped, sunshine-yellow flowers, that bloom for much of the year but never fully open, this little tree is a welcome addition to any hot climate garden. Demanding only a sunny spot and a free-draining soil, it forms a neat dome with little or no pruning. Plant it on its own or among lush vegetation. Beware of all parts of this innocent-looking tree — they are poisonous! The hard, triangular seeds are often worn as lucky charms — hence the name, lucky nut. Grow it in the warm months from seed or cuttings.
Other colors: Salmon-orange, white.
Varieties/cultivars: 'Aurantiaca', 'Alba'.

Tipuana tipu

Tipuana tipu
PRIDE-OF-BOLIVIA (U.K.), TIPU TREE, ROSEWOOD ○

Family: LEGUMINOSAE
Origin: Mountains of Bolivia, southern Brazil.
Flowering time: Late spring.
Climatic zone: 9, 10.
Dimensions: 27–40 feet (8–12 meters) high.

Tristaniopsis laurina syn. *Tristania laurina*
KANOOKA, WATER BOX (U.K.), AUSTRALIAN WATER GUM ○

Family: MYRTACEAE
Origin: Australia (coastal Victoria to Queensland).
Flowering time: Summer.
Climatic zone: 9.
Dimensions: 15–50 feet (5–15 meters) high.
Description: A most accommodating tree, Australian water gum, which grows quite large in the wild, can nevertheless be easily grown as a tub plant. Although it is found naturally by river banks, it will adapt to average rainfall conditions, but not to heavy soils. Handsome, glossy green leaves are enhanced in summer by the scented, bee-attracting flowers clustered at the leaf bases. Newly exposed bark appears in shades of pale yellow, gray, and red. Slow-growing, it makes a good shade or background tree. Grow it from seed in spring.

GLOSSARY

ACID SOIL: has a pH of less than 6, turning litmus paper red.

ALKALINE SOIL: has a pH of more than 8, turning litmus paper blue.

ANNUAL: a plant grown from seed that flowers, fruits, then dies within one year or season.

AXIL: the angle or point between a leaf and stem or branch.

BIENNIAL: a plant completing its life cycle in two years.

BRACT: a modified leaf, often at the base of a flower.

BUD: a more or less immature shoot arising from the leaf axil.

CALYX: the outer ring of the flower, consisting of sepals.

CANE: a slender woody stem that is often hollow. Bamboo and most berry fruits produce canes.

CONIFER: a plant that bears its primitive flowers and seeds in cones.

COROLLA: a collective term for sepals and petals.

CORYMB: similar to a raceme, but with the stalks of the lower florets longer than the upper ones, creating a flattened or convex head.

CULTIVAR: a selected plant form introduced into cultivation, which has some horticultural value.

DECIDUOUS: a plant which loses its leaves every year, generally referring to shrubs or trees.

DIVISION: a propagating method where perennials are separated by digging up and dividing the roots and top growth into clumps that can be replanted.

DOUBLE FLOWER: a flower with more than twice the usual number of petals, usually formed from stamens.

ELLIPTIC: describing the shape of a leaf, being in outline the shape of an ellipse.

ESPALIER: a plant which has been trained to lie flat against a wall or trellis featuring a central trunk with opposite pairs of horizontal stems.

EPIPHYTE: a plant which grows on another, using it for support without actually being a parasite, e.g., many orchids.

FAMILY: a natural grouping of plant genera with certain essential characteristics in common.

FLORET: an individual small flower that forms part of a large cluster of flowers, e.g., daisy.

GENUS: a group of species which have common features and characteristics.

GRAFTING: A propagating method where a section of one plant is inserted into the rootstock of another.

GREENHOUSE: a structure surfaced with glass or plastic sheeting which provides a sheltered environment for growing plants.

HARDENING OFF: a method of gradually acclimatising plants into a new temperature situation, usually after being reared in a greenhouse before transplanting into the garden.

HARDY: being able to withstand extremes of cold and frost, or harsh, dry conditions. Varies from zone to zone.

HUMUS: dark brown material produced after composting vegetable and animal matter.

HYBRID: the progeny of a cross between two different species.

INFLORESCENCE: the arrangement of flowers of a plant.

LANCEOLATE: describing the shape of a leaf, being like the head of a lance, tapering at each end.

LATERAL: a stem or shoot arising from a leaf axil of a larger stem.

LEADER: a shoot at the end of a main stem.

LINEAR: very narrow.

LOAM: a moderately fertile soil composed of clay, sand, and humus with a texture that is neither too sandy nor too heavy. Good loam will retain moisture and be rich in humus.

MULCH: a layer of organic material laid at ground level to help reduce weed growth and conserve soil moisture.

NATURALIZED: plants growing in areas or countries where they do not naturally occur, often escapees from gardens.

ORGANIC: material derived from living organisms. In horticulture referring to soil additives of natural orgin, i.e. animal manure, compost from decayed plant remains.

OVATE: describing the shape of a leaf, being oval or egg-shaped in outline.

PANICLE: a many-branched inflorescence.

PERENNIAL: a plant living for more than two years.

PINNATE: a compound leaf with leaflets arranged along either side of a common stalk.

PISTIL: the female section of the flower.

RACEME: a group of flowers arranged along an unbranched stem, each floret having a distinct stalk.

RHIZOME: an underground creeping root system

from which shoots and roots develop.

ROOTSTOCK: the root and base of a plant onto which sections of another plant can be grated.

ROSETTE: a group of leaves arranged in an overlapping, circular fashion.

RUNNER: aerial stems from which roots grow, forming a new plant.

SEPAL: a unit of the calyx protecting the petals.

SESSILE: used of flowers and leaves without individual stalks.

SINGLE FLOWER: a simple flower form with one ring of petals.

SPADIX: a spiked inflorescence in which the axis is fleshy.

SPATHE: a large bract, sometimes pair of bracts, enclosing the spadix.

SPECIES: a collection of individual plants essentially alike when grown in the same conditions. In horticulture and botany it is used as a form of classification.

SPIKE: similar to a raceme but having stalkless florets.

SPORE: a specialized reproductive cell usually formed asexually; the reproductive unit of ferns and fungi.

STAMEN: the male part of the plant, consisting of filament, anther, and pollen.

SUCKER: a shoot arising from the root system or base of a plant.

SYN: a plant name that has been set aside in favor of a new name.

TENDRIL: a spiraling slender shoot by which some climbing plants cling for support.

TERMINAL: at the apex or tip.

TRIFOLIATE: a leaf divided into three leaflets.

TUBER: a fleshy root or stem that stores nutrients for later use.

UMBEL: a rounded, often flattened head of flowers, the stalks of which all arise together from the tip of a stem.

UNISEXUAL: a flower of only one sex.

VAR: a variant species.

WEEPING: a shrub or tree whose branches hang in a pendulous, drooping fashion.

WHORL: a group of three or more structures encircling an axis.

X: denoting a hybrid species.

BIBLIOGRAPHY

Beckett, Kenneth A. 1983. *The Concise Encyclopedia of Garden Plants*. London: Orbis.

Clausen, Ruth Rogers and Nicolas H. Ekstrom. 1989. *Perennials for American Gardens*. New York: Random House.

Hortus Third: A Concise Dictionary of Plants Cultivated in the United States and Canada. 1976. New York: Macmillan.

Johnson, Hugh. 1973. *The International Book of Trees*. London: Mitchell Beazley.

Macoboy, Stirling. 1986. *What Flower is That?* Sydney: Lansdowne.

Moggi, Guido and Luciano Giugnolini. 1983. *Simon and Schuster's Guide to Garden Flowers*. New York: Simon and Schuster.

Readers Digest. 1984. *Guide to Creative Gardening*. London: Readers Digest.

Readers Digest. 1987. *Illustrated Guide to Gardening*. Sydney: Readers Digest

Taylor's Guides to Gardening. 1986. Boston: Houghton Mifflin.

INDEX OF COMMON NAMES

INDEX OF
BOTANICAL NAMES

The Margarets

The Margarets

Sheri S. Tepper

GOLLANCZ

LONDON

The Margarets © Sheri S. Tepper 2007
All rights reserved

The right of Sheri S. Tepper to be identified as the author
of this work has been asserted by her in accordance with the
Copyright, Designs and Patents Act 1988.

First published in Great Britain in 2008 by Gollancz
An imprint of the Orion Publishing Group
Orion House, 5 Upper St Martin's Lane,
London WC2H 9EA
An Hachette Livre UK Company

A CIP catalogue record for this book
is available from the British Library

ISBN 978 0 57508 0 478 (Cased)
ISBN 978 0 57508 0 461 (Trade Paperback)

1 3 5 7 9 10 8 6 4 2

Printed in Great Britain at Mackays of Chatham plc,
Chatham, Kent

The Orion Publishing Group's policy is to use papers that
are natural, renewable and recyclable products and made
from wood grown in sustainable forests. The logging and
manufacturing processes are expected to conform to the
environmental regulations of the country of origin.

www.orionbooks.co.uk

In fond memory of
my friend of sixty-three years,
LAMBERT J. LARSON,
without whose encouragement
I would never have written a word

PLANETS	LOCATIONS	INHABITANTS OF

MARS

Human bases on Phobos and in Valles Marineris
> Margaret Bain
> Louise and Harry Bain, her parents
> Chili Mech, a technician

EARTH

The worldwide Urb, occupying the entire planet's surface
> Dr. David Mackey, Margaret's husband

CHOTTEM (Human colony planet, partly occupied by the Gibbekot)
Perepume, a continent occupied by the Gibbekot
Manland, a continent partially settled by humans
Within Manland: The city of Bray, a sea city
> Stentor d'Lorn, Founder and Tycoon
> Mariah d'Lornschilde, his daughter
> Von Goldereau d'Lornschilde, a cousin

The village of Swylet
> The Gardener, a longtime resident
> Gretamara, [a Margaret] foster daughter of the Gardener
> Benjamin Finesilver, artist and dreamer, husband of Mariah
> Sophia, his daughter
> Grandma Bergamot, Grandfather Vinegar, and other herbal persons

CANTARDENE (Mercan planet, occupied by the K'Famir)
Om-Bak-Zandig-Shadup (Crossroads of the Worlds) freeport
Bak-Zandig-g'Shadup (Street of Many Worlds) pleasure district
> Ongamar, [a Margaret] bondslave, seamstress
> Adille, a K'Famira, a pleasure-female, Ongamar's owner

Bargom, Adille's patron
Lady Ephedra, K'Famira, owner of House Mousselline
Progzo, Adille's father
Draug B'lango, Adille's clan leader
The Hill of Beelshi (site of unspeakable rites)

THAIRY (Human colony planet, also occupied by the Gibbekot)
Town of Bright
Naumi, [a Margaret] foster son of Rastarong
Mr. Wyncamp, school manager
Mr. Weathereye, elderly, odd personage with one eye
various citizens and louts
Fort Point Zibit (site of the academy)
Captain Orley, commandant
Sergeant Orson, in charge of first-year cadets
Grangel, cadet and lout
Jaker, Flek, Poul, Caspor and Ferni, cadets and Naumi's friends

TERCIS (Human colony planet, divided into "Walled-Offs")
Hostility (a Walled-Off)
Rueful (a Walled-Off)
Contrition City
Repentance (a large town)
Remorseful (a small town, site of the school, also a river)
Deep Shameful (a hamlet)
Crossroads (a village in The Valley)
Grandma Mackey [a Margaret]
Dr. Bryan Mackey, her husband
Maybelle and Mayleen, Margaret's daughters
James Joseph Judson (Jimmy Joe), Maybelle's husband
Til and Jeff, their twin sons
Gloriana, their daughter
Falija, Glory's fosterling
Billy Ray Judson, Mayleen's husband
Joe Bob and Billy Wayne (twin sons)
Ella May and Janine Ruth (twin daughters)
Benny Paul, son, twin died at birth
Trish, daughter, twin died at birth
Sue Elaine and Lou Ellen, twin daughters
Orvie John, son, twin died at birth
Little Emmaline, daughter, twin died at birth
[At time of story, Billy Wayne has gone off to the army,
Ella May has joined the Siblinghood of Silence, and Janine
Ruth has moved to Contrition City.]

Pastor Grievy
Abe Johnson
Bamber Joy, Abe's foster son
Others mentioned in passing

FAJNARD (formerly Gentheran planet taken over by the Frossians)
The Fastness—where Gentherans still live
The Grasslands—occupied by
The umox farm
Medicines sans Limites. Volunteer doctors, human
Frossians
Mar-agern, [a Margaret] bondslave, herdswoman
Umoxen, wool-bearing animals, or perhaps not
Ghoss, humans, somewhat modified
Deen-agern, a Ghoss
Rei-agern, a Ghoss
Various Frossian slave drivers and overlords
Howkel and Mrs. Howkel, hayraiders
Mirabel and Maniacal, two of their children
Gizzardiles: inimical creatures

HELL (distant, little-known planet with a tragic history)
One buried Gentheran ship
Wilvia [a Margaret]

CRANESROOST (Human colony planet)

EDEN (Human colony planet)

B'YURNGRAD (Human colony planet)
The prairies, temperate zone
The Siblinghood
The Tribes, former bondslaves of violent disposition
Dark Runner, a tribal boy and man
Wolf Mother, a shamaness
M'urgi, [a Margaret] her apprentice
Fernwold, M'urgi's lover, a member of the Siblinghood
The icelands, an area of severe winters
B'Oag, an oasthouse keeper
Ojlin, his son
G'lil, a young woman rescued at the last moment
Ogric, a worker

AMBIGUOUS INDIVIDUALS OR THINGS OF VARIOUS OR UNCERTAIN LOCATION

Ghyrm, a deadly parasite

Mr. Weathereye

Lady Badness

The Gardener

Dweller in Pain

Flayed One-Drinker of Blood

Whirling Cloud of Darkness-Eater of the Dead

Sysarou, Gentheran Goddess of Abundance and Joy

Ohanja, Gentheran God of Honor, Duty, and Kindness

NONHUMAN RACES

Baswoidin: ancient, secretive, superior

Elos: Omniont race, graceful, sneery, arrogant

Frossian: Mercan race, boneheaded, vaguely humanoid, malign

Garrick: related to the Gentherans

Gentherans: mysterious, beneficent

Gibbekot: humanoid, furry, small

Hrass: Omniont race, tapirlike, unassuming, dirty, cringing

K'Famir: Mercan race, four-legged, four-armed, vicious

K'Vasti: Mercan race, distantly related to K'Famir, less vicious

Pthas: ancient, very wise, now presumed extinct or departed

Quaatar: Mercan race, ancient, prideful, arrogant, vengeful

Thongal: Mercans, hireling spies and killers

Trajians: a very ancient itinerant race, famous as entertainers

ORGANIZATIONS

Siblinghood of Silence: a secret organization including humans and
  Gentherans

ISTO: Interstellar Trade Organization. A regulatory organization of all races
  engaging in interstellar trade

IGC: Intergalactic Court. The final arbiter in conflicts among races

Mercan Combine: Confederation of vile races united by proximity, race,
  language, commerce

Omniont Federation: Similar to the Mercan Combine, but less cutthroat
  and more concerned with ethics

Dominion Central Authority: Oversight body set up by the Gentherans to
  represent off-Earth humans

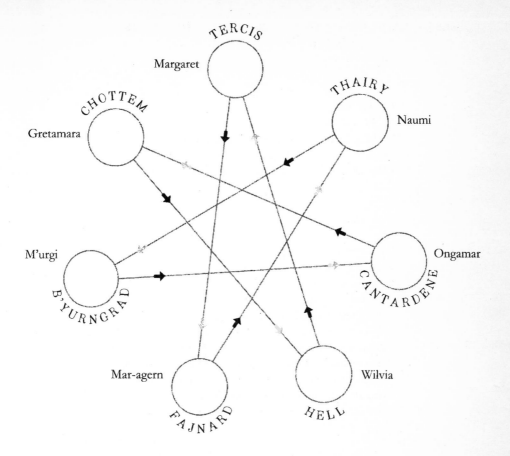

TERCIS

Margaret

THAIRY

Naumi

CHOTTEM

Gretamara

Ongamar

CANTARDENE

M'urgi

B'YURNGRAD

Mar-agern

Wilvia

FAJNARD

HELL

The
Margarets

What the Gardener Told Me Might Have Happened

Once a very long time ago, between fifty and a hundred thousand years, a small group of humans fleeing from predators took refuge in a cave. Clinging to one another during the night, they heard a great roaring, louder and more fierce than the roars of the beasts they knew, and when they peeked out at dawn, they saw that a moon had fallen out of the sky. The sun was just rising, the changeable baby moon they were used to was with Mother Sun, so the fallen moon belonged to someone else.

The someone elses were walking here and there, clanking and creaking. Ahn, the leader of the people, noticed holes around the bottom of the moon, open holes as large as caves. The clanking things were frightening, but not so scary as the animals howling among the nearest trees. Ahn, the leader, had no memory of such things; neither did any of the other of his people. No clanking things. No falling moons.

Ahn nodded, thoughtfully. It was harder when it was a new thing. If they had a memory of the thing, it was easier to figure out what to do. Otherwise, they had to decide, then see what would happen. It did seem to Ahn, however, that hiding inside the moon was a good idea. When the moon went back up into the sky, the beasts couldn't follow. The holes smelled strange, so Ahn went first in case there were bad things inside.

Just as there had been no memory of fallen moons, there had been
no memory of those who owned the moon: the Quaatar, who disliked being fooled with, bothered by, or trespassed upon by anything.
Even if Ahn had had such a memory, the immediacy of his people's
situation might have made him risk it. Since he did not know it, he
had no qualms about leading his people up the vent tubes and thence
into a hydroponic oasis.

The ship's robots found nothing worth ravening upon the world;
the ship departed. Inside, the stowaways lived rather pleasantly on
the juicy bodies of small furry vermin that infested the ship and the
garden produce that fed the noncarnivorous creatures aboard. When
the ship finally landed, the people went out to find themselves not in
the sky, as they had expected, but rather upon some other world,
where their eager senses informed them there were no predators at
all. The world was a paradise, and they fled into it.

Ahn's people never knew how they got there; the Quaatar were
and are a little-known people. The females are said to be solitary,
aquatic, and planet-bound. The males return to the water only to
breed. It is said if one imagines a huge, multilegged lizard, hundreds
of years old, who is able to talk and count from one to six, one has
imagined a Quaatar. The race became starfaring only by accident.
Early in their evolutionary history, they were approached by an advanced people who offered to trade for mining rights on the several
lifeless, metal-rich planets of the system. Galactic Law required that
they need deal only with the most numerous indigenous group. The
Quaatar demanded first that three lesser tribes, the Thongal,
Frossians, and K'Famir, who had long ago branched treacherously
from the Quaatar genetic line, be wiped out. Since Galactic Law did
not permit such a thing, the mining concessionaires offered many
other inducements, finally agreeing, among other things, to move the
other tribes or races far away. The Thongal, Frossians, and K'Famir,
all of whom were more agile and far cleverer than the Quaatar, had
no objection at all to being removed from the dismal swamps of
Quaatar and given drier planets of their own. They were accordingly
transported, leaving the Quaatar alone and unchallenged in their in-
sistence that themselves, their world, and their language were sacred
and inviolable.

For generations the Quaatar traded mining rights for fancy uniforms, medals, starships, and spare parts plus an endless supply of non-Quaatar mechs, techs, and astrogators to keep the ships flying. Though Quaatar owned the ships and appropriated all the fancy titles (captain, chief science officer, and so on), they never learned how to go from point A to point B without relying on non-Quaatar crew members who could count much higher than six to take them there.

The Quaatar had not known they had stowaways until they saw Ahn's people leaving the ship and disappearing into the underbrush. The sight infuriated them. It should be mentioned that an infuriated Quaatar is something no reasonable individual wants to deal with. An aroused Quaatar is somewhat comparable to a tsunami engendered by an earthquake measuring eight or nine on the Richter scale while several supervolcanoes erupt simultaneously during a category five hurricane. The Quaatar ordered the ship to destroy the planet and were dissuaded only when the automatic system governor harshly reminded them the Galactic Court would not allow destruction of living planets.

Quaatar annoyance, once aroused, however, had to be slaked, not least because their vessel, sacred to the holy Quaatar race, had been defiled and would have to be resanctified. All non-Quaatar personnel were sequestered, for their own safety, while every deck was washed down with the blood of sacrificial victims (a supply of whom were always carried on Quaatar ships), who were first flayed to yield skins with which the entire exterior hull had to be scrubbed. Finally, skin, bones, and remaining tissue were ritually burned. This was time-consuming, yielding only mild amusement during the flaying part, and it was all the fault of the stowaways.

When the ritual was completed, the Quaatar turned their attention back to vengeance. Honor demanded that revenge be exacted upon those who had committed the trespass. Since the Quaatar could not find the beings who had fled the ship, they decided to maim them from a distance by using a recently and illicitly obtained brain block ray, which could be set to atrophy parts of the brain of any animal that had one. Since they had no sample stowaway to set the machine with (and would have been unlikely to do it correctly had they had one), they entered an arbitrary and random setting, trusting that their

god, Dweller in Pain, who had been properly propitiated, would see
to the seemliness of the punishment.

Accordingly, the stowaways' brains were fried. This left untouched
the race from which they had come, which was equally guilty since it
had produced the offenders. The Quaatar "captain" ordered the ship
to be returned to the penultimate planet, where the brain block ray,
still on the same setting, was set to cover the entire surface of the
world during one complete revolution.

When the Quaatar departed, they left monitors behind to send
images they later watched with great gratification as several generations of the creatures struggled to compensate for their new handicap. The ray had not made them completely mindless. It had merely
wiped out the memory of certain things. This loss was a considerable
handicap, however, and by the time several generations had passed,
there were only fifteen or twenty thousand of them left.

"Can they ever get it back?" a junior Quaatar asked its elder. Very
young Quaatar sometimes had ideas, before their brains solidified.

The senior drew itself up pompously. "There is no it! The it no
longer exists!"

"Legend says everything exists, you know, where Keeper keeps
everything."

"Tah. Is dirty K'Famir legend! If kept, is in a place these filth
could never find, never!"

"Somebody says Pthas did."

"Tss," the senior sneered. "Dirty K'Famir legend says Pthas went
many places nobody wanted them. K'Famir say Keeper much annoyed by visit of Pthas. K'Famir say Keeper changed rules, told Pthas
only person walking seven roads at once can ever see Keeper. That is
like saying nobody, never. That is good thing. Seven is unlucky for
Quaatar. Six is enough number."

"If something had seven all-same-time universes, it could . . ."

"Enough!" roared the senior. "You are bad-lucking us with utterance? You want go in hold with sacrifices? You want skinning?"

The junior member tardily, wisely, kept silent.

Before continuing their journey, the Quaatar celebrated by torturing several of the non-Quaatar crew members, whose families later
received the generous life insurance payments that had been guaran-

teed by the mining interests before the crew members could have been ordered onto the Quaatar vessel. Thereafter the Quaatar often talked about their vengeance with others of their kind, though always without mentioning the return to the planet of origin or the use to which certain crew members had been put. The return had not been approved by the chiefs of Quaatar, and both the torture of crew members and the use of the brain block was specifically forbidden by the Galactic Court, a body greatly feared though not at all respected by the Quaatar.

In time the Quaatar crew died, those with whom they had spoken died, and nothing about the happening was remembered except the prejudice that had been engendered against a race of bipedal, naked, rather ugly creatures, forever anathema to the Quaatar. The bipeds were Crnk-cha zibitzi, that is half-brained defilers, which was the worst thing they could have been. When humans finally made it off their home planet, the Quaatar greeted their appearance with revulsion, knowing immediately they were not fit for anything but killing, which was generally true of all other races except the Thongal, K'Famir, and Frossians, who were considered merely dirty and occasionally useful.

On the planet where the stowaways had left the ship, however, the people did go on living. They all knew that something was wrong, but they didn't know what it was. Something was missing, something they'd had before and didn't have anymore. Still, the growths were good to eat, with juicy roots, fruits, nuts, succulent leaves. The women had babies that grew very fast, for there was no hunger on this world. No hunger, no danger, no threats. A good place, this world, even though it had no moon at all. Very soon the word for moon was forgotten.

"Wake up little one," said Ahn's woman to the new baby. "Wake up, take milk, grow up fast." The older children played follow the leader, yelling to one another. "Up the tree, over the stump, down the bank, into the water, back again," they cried. "Right, left, right, left, right, left!"

"The fruit is ripe," the women called. "We should all pick it now, it's so juicy and good. We can dry what's left over." Lots of women were having babies.

Seasons were long in this new world, but eventually the winter came, not a cruel winter, just chilly and unpleasant. The people took mud from the riverbank and piled it into walls. They learned to make thick walls, let them dry, then tunnel through them to get from one room to another. When the rooms were nice and dry, they could build new rooms on top. They made baskets from tree roots and limber branches. "We're going out to get fruit," they cried. "We'll bring a basketful."

They cleared everything from around the mud houses, making a smooth, packed-down place where the women could sit making baskets and the children could play. If the children were too noisy, the men would cry, "Cross the ground! Go into the woods!" The woods were safe; there were no beasts. The words for beasts were forgotten.

Rooms piled on rooms until their dwelling was as high as they could build it. "We have to make room for more," they said. Some of them went a day's journey away and started another tower to house some of the children the women were having. Soon each tower had daughter towers out in the woods, many cleaned places for the women to work and the children to play. They had to go farther now to get fruit and roots, but it was still a very good place.

Time went by. Daughter towers had granddaughter towers and great-granddaughter towers. The people fought over picking grounds. "This is my picking ground, our people's ground! We've always picked here," the men cried, waving clubs. "Go away."

They went away. They had more and more babies. "We need a new place. We have to make room for more," they said. They followed rivers, they went along shores, all over the world. They had babies, and the babies had babies. The food was far less abundant. Each generation the babies were smaller.

Time went by. A plague spread among the people. Most of them died. The forest recovered. The plague stopped, the survivors went on living. Another plague; again the forest recovered. An asteroid struck. The people lived on.

"Wake up," the mothers said. "Wake up, drink."

"Follow," the children cried. "Right, left, right, left."

"Fruit now," the women said. "Now, hurry."

"Commin," cried the children. "We commin."

"My pick ground," the men said, clubbing one another.

Millennia went by. One night, when all the people were asleep, a Gentheran ship landed on a rocky outcropping where there were no towers. Gentherans in their silver suits came out of it and moved around looking at the towers and the cleared ground. They set tiny mobile recorders tunneling into the towers and tiny fliers hovering over the remaining forest. They talked among themselves and to the large ship in orbit.

"It looks like a total extinction coming!" said a Gentheran. "Can we get genetic samples?"

"Not without the permission of the people if they're intelligent."

"It's hard to tell whether they are or not."

"Leave it for now. We can always come back. You want to leave the monitor ship in place for a while?"

"We've never encountered an extinction in process before. It's certainly worth recording."

Accordingly, the large ship burned a deep, round hole in the rocky area, the monitor ship lowered itself into the hole and buried itself, with only a few well-camouflaged antennae and optical lenses exposed. A shuttle picked up the explorers.

On the planet, the people were so hungry they were eating the fungus that grew on the latrine grounds, down at the bottom of the towers. It was tasteless, but it kept them alive. When they couldn't find food, they would bring dead leaves or bark or bodies to put in the latrine grounds for the fungus to grow on.

Most of the women were no longer fat enough to have babies, so they picked special women to fatten and have babies for everyone. The fungus they were eating was full of their own hormones and enzymes; they became smaller and smaller yet. They no longer had teeth. They no longer had hair. Their ears were longer, their eyes smaller.

"Wakwak," woke the sleeping ones. "Rai lef rai lef rai lef," moved the food gatherers. "Krossagroun, krossagroun," they chanted as they went off into the remnants of the forest. "Mepik, mepik," as they searched for anything organic. They had no names. Each one was "me." At night all the "mes" lay curled against the tunnel walls, in the warm, in the safe. Gradually, words lost all meaning. They made sounds, as crickets do.

Time went by. Sometimes in the evenings a long, fat thing would come down right on top of several towers, squashing many of them. Shiny people came out of the ships to dig up several other towers. The shiny people made sounds.

"How many this time?"

"Whatever we can catch."

"What in hell does d'Lornschilde do with them?"

"How should I know. He pays well, that's all I care."

The shiny people pulled "mes" out of the wreckage one by one, discarding those who were injured or dead. They put the live ones in cages, the cages into the long fat thing, then squashed other towers and filled other cages before going away. In towers not yet squashed, the creatures slept curled against the walls, but the long fat thing soon came back, again and again and again . . .

The last time it came, some unsquashed mes ran away and hid at the edge of the sea in a little cave where they could stay warm. When day came, they stayed there, for they had no tower to return to, nothing to pick, no fungus to eat, and the forests were dead. They were very few, and very hungry. Eventually, hunger drove them to try eating the things that grew in the sea . . .

I Am Margaret/on Phobos

This account of the great task undertaken by the Third Order of the Siblinghood is written for my great-grandchildren. Even though they "know" what happened, children, as I know from experience, always want the details. "What happened next?" "What did he say?" "Did they live happily ever after?" The "I" doing the writing am ... are Margaret. No matter what name I am given wherever I may be, "I" am always Margaret, for this is my story as well as the story of mankind, and the Gentherans, and, possibly, a good part of the galaxy.

When I was about five or six, I liked lying in the window of my bedroom watching the Martian desert move beneath me as the planet whirled. My didactibot taught me how to make a pinwheel out of paper and a pin, and told me to attach it to a railing by the ventilation duct. It whirled and whirled until the hole wore out, and it fell apart. It was the only thing I had ever made, and I wept over it, but my didactibot said in its usual mechanical, self-satisfied voice, that nothing whirls forever, not even planets and stars. At the moment, I thought it was just getting even with me for calling it a diddybot, which it didn't like at all.

That night, on the edge of sleep, however, I remembered that diddybots can't lie or mislead people because truth is built in, and therefore it was true that nothing whirled forever. The end of all whirling meant me, too. Terror grabbed me, and I cried out. Mother came in and comforted me, assuming I was having a bad dream. I didn't know how to tell her I was afraid of being a pinwheel, for she was a pinwheel, too, and someday whatever kept us spinning would wear out, and we would stop.

When I was older, I realized that all sane children come to this realization, but just then it was like a nightmare that I would wake up from. I didn't wake up. It stayed there, that dark hole in the future. Eventually I asked about it. Why did we exist? What were we for? Mother said hush don't think about it. Father said, take care of her, Louise. After a while I realized we never wake up from the nightmare, but we do learn not to think about it.

I watched the Mars surface, near Olympus Mons, where nests of snaky whirlwinds squirmed across the craters. The wind swept the surface all the time, erasing any marks the exploration robots made. Humans didn't do exploration. They stayed in the canyon depths of Valles Marineris except for maintenance trips to the wind generators on the rim. I couldn't see the towers with their huge, balanced vanes from my window, but I knew all about them. I knew about the water mines at the pole, too, where the coring machines chewed the ancient ice into slurry and sent it south, down long pipes to the canyons.

We were on Mars and Phobos because depopulating Earth was urgently important, and Mars was to be colonized as part of Project Compliance, to keep us from being classified as barbarians. I had no idea what that meant, and the didactibot refused to tell me. It didn't lie, but it only told me the things people thought I ought to know, so, obviously, I wasn't supposed to know about barbarians.

I was the only child on Phobos, and most of the things people said to me were politenesses. "Good morning, Margaret." "Too bad, Margaret." "Well done, Margaret." "How are you today, Margaret?" Each of these had an answer I had been taught to give: "Good morning to you, as well." "Yes, it is too bad." "Thank you for noticing." "Very well, thank you for asking." They never said anything different or strange or new.

Besides politenesses, people talked about work. Mother kept records in the hydroponic gardens, and she talked about sorting systems and constructive interfaces. Father worked in the lab, and he talked about new oxygen-creating bacteria and newly constituted biomic-clusters being sent down to the surface. Once I asked Father why they kept on doing it. He said it was to find out what would happen.

I asked if he didn't already know what would happen.

"Tell her," my mother said. "Tell her the way you told me."

Father flushed. "That was private," he said, leaving the room and shutting the door behind him.

Mother shook her head. "He told me about it when we were just getting to know one another. It was romantic and eloquent and non-scientific, so of course he doesn't like to repeat it."

"But you do," I said.

She smiled, a tiny secret smile I had never seen before. "It was a happy time for us, and he was eager about the work. He told me he dreams of creating a paradise down there in the ravines, a world in which all the living things work together to form a functioning mira-cle, something beautiful and marvelous and good. He never told anyone but me."

"But he doesn't know what will happen?"

"Not really, no. Sometimes experiments end up doing the oppo-site of what they intend; some tiny organism is wrong, and everything rots and dies. Other times, the project shows great promise, but it doesn't quite get there. Your father says no one will know for sure until it happens. That's how science works."

The other thing people talked about was the weather down on Mars. Sometimes there were storms that blew up so much sand they hid the planet behind a gray veil. When that happened, I pretended the storm had spun us off into nothingness, and when the dust cleared we'd have gone somewhere else. I didn't tell anyone this. They had been very upset with me when I cried about the pinwheel wear-ing out. I didn't want to upset them again.

The people down in Valles Marineris lived in the "green ravines." That's where the water came out of the polar pipes to be used and collected and used and collected, over and over. Green ravines had transparent roofs. Mirrors on the canyon walls reflected the pale sun-light down through the roofs, and the plants inside produced breath-able air. I thought when I grew up I'd get a job on the surface where

I could live in a green ravine and do something real: run a corer in the water mines or help maintain the wind power stations. Being a child on Phobos Station didn't seem real at all.

Grown-ups on Phobos had regular jobs, but my only job was to be schooled. Each year my didactibot added words to my vocabulary list, and that helped me explain things. I learned that the adults on Phobos were meticulous and painstaking and sedentary. Nobody ever went anywhere or did anything. Everybody had constipation and insomnia. Everyone talked about that, even in front of me. Politenesses, work, weather, constipation, insomnia, and ennui.

The consultants recommended more use of the gym for constipation and insomnia and more attention to hobbies to fight ennui. Phobian hobbies included playing in the orchestra, singing in the chorus, working with the theater group, or joining arts and craft exhibits. Everyone did things or made things fastidiously and meticulously, but not superlatively, so that nobody on station would think they were trying to show off. Showing off or "winning" caused ill feelings. So did criticism.

"But I think his painting is awful," I said once.

"It doesn't matter what you think," my father, Harry Bain, said. "You can find something pleasant to say about it."

"The colors were all muddled," I offered doubtfully.

"Then you say that you appreciate the earthy, organic tones," said Louise Bain, my mother.

One time, when the didactibot and I were getting along better than usual, we decided the wheels on Phobos were greased with meticulous, painstaking, fastidious, and scrupulous insincerity. The didactibot said it could find out if I was musical, or arty, or actorish if I wanted it to, but since no one ever suggested I might be, I assumed children weren't supposed to have ennui and left well enough alone. Diddybot said I was lazy. I don't think I really was.

My pastime was sewing. I did not enjoy it, but it was what Mother did, and Mother felt we should spend time together, "doing something." I actually learned to sew quite well. I made several sets of clothing for myself that were just as good as those brought from Earth on the *Ninja*, the *Piñata*, or the *Santa Claus*. Those were the three ships the Gentherans had given to Earthgov in 2062, shortly after they discovered Earth. The ships were given those names, the Gentherans said, because they had discovered a new world and appeared out of nowhere bearing goodies. It was supposed to be a pun, a kind of joke. I could understand the *Piñata* and *Santa Claus* part but not the *Ninja* part. Ninjas came out of nowhere, too, but they usually damaged people. Anyhow, people said it was nice to know the ETs had a sense of humor. Earthgov couldn't pay for the ships, but the Gentherans didn't mind. They were very helpful. Everyone said so.

Since very few children had ever been born on Phobos, and I was the only one who stayed, no one thought to make provision for entertaining a child, especially not one who was inquisitive or bored, which I was, by age six. By then I had experienced every variation of every possible human encounter—the public ones, at least—and I was tired of them all. I started hiding in corners and behind doors, listening, trying to learn new words and ideas. I became a sneak. My didactibot defined sneakiness as an antisocial adaptation to threat, mostly engaged in by solitary animals. I thought that was right. I was about as solitary as anybody could be. I didn't mean to be antisocial, but at least I learned that adults talked about other things when they thought they were alone.

They had many whispered words and phrases that were evidently not fit for saying out loud. I didn't know what they meant and didn't dare ask anyone, but I used them all the time. In my toy village, I staged plays with my dolls as the actors, assigning them forbidden words and phrases.

"If you don't behave, the proctor will get you," said a mother doll to a child doll as they walked down the tiny business street of the toy village, with its toy houses and toy church and toy trees, even though there were no trees on Earth, for no water could be spared for such things. "I'll tell him you're not two-three-four."

When I was about eight, the didactibot opened a library file for me that had whole books in it, some of it fiction, which is imaginary, and some of it real things I should know about, like history. At first, the fiction confused me. The characters mentioned things the other characters understood but I knew nothing about. The first few times I noticed this, I asked for explanations, only to find that whatever book I was reading immediately vanished from my library file. *Babies* was a bad word; *proliferate* was a bad word. Even my dictionary, though I didn't know it at the time, was carefully pruned to keep inappropriate subjects unthinkable.

All this did was make me determined to learn everything inappropriate in the whole universe, and I spent day after day digging into diddybot's files finding out what people didn't want me to know. That's where I learned about the six human colonies the Gentherans had secretly set up for us on other planets: B'yurngrad, Chottem, Cranesroost, Eden, Tercis, and Thairy. The settlement on Thairy was discovered by the Mercan Combine and the Omniont Federation in 2080, and they traced the people back to Earth, and they'd been going back and forth ever since. The Mercans and Omnionts were bunches of different races, almost all from carbon-based, free-water planets rather like Earth. There were other combines and federations of other kinds of life, too, but I didn't know anything about them.

Sometimes, when Earth was visible, I used my telescope to watch the Mercan and Omniont ships moving between the wormhole and Earth. They were huge ships, the size of little moons, but they might as well have been invisible. No one on Phobos ever mentioned them. The only explanation I could come up with was that all the adults had been on Phobos for so long that they had seen everything, knew what they thought about everything, and didn't need to discuss anything anymore. They were used to exchanging the same greetings many times each day and hearing the same jokes told over and over. I didn't think they realized there were no ideas in anything they said or that every single day they said the same words over and over, like birdcalls: chirrup, chirrup, tweet, tweet chirrup; caw caw cwaup, caw cwaup. Not that I had ever heard a live bird, but my didactibot was capable of vocalization!

Each year more books were added to the library list, and I was careful not to lose any of them. Years later I learned they had been bowdlerized, but the screeners hadn't been attentive or draconian enough to prevent a steady seepage of real information. Ideas oozed out of books like magma out of volcanoes. They solidified into whole, wonderful worlds, and I populated each one with beings and places I read of or invented: flora, fauna, forests, mountains, seascapes, all of them named, though no one knew those names but me, just as no one knew the names of the people I became in my various worlds: here a warrior who led the tribe through many dangers; there a shaman who could send her spirit to far places; here a healer who knew secret ways to cure sickness; there a telepath who could see into the hearts of others and communicate with animals; here a linguist who could understand all languages, ancient and new; there a queen who inspired her realm; here a spy who found out all the things the queen needed to know.

At the time it seemed perfectly normal to be six or seven other people. After all, I didn't have anyone else to play with. I knew, on one level, the different selves were imaginary, but at the same time they felt completely real. "I will be a queen," I told myself, repeating this until it became a mantra. I, a queen will be. Queen Willbea. No. That had an ugly sound to it. It should be softer. Wilvia. Queen Wilvia. That pleased me, and I bowed to myself in the mirror.

The spy evolved very naturally. She was the part of me who hid in corners, who was unobserved, who always listened and picked up information. Someone inoffensive that no one would ever suspect. Just like me. I didn't give her a name. Spies don't have names, just aliases.

"Others have been warriors, now me!" I cried to my mirrored self. I spelled it "Naumi." He was a quiet but very clever one. He wasn't huge and muscular, so he had to outthink other people. He became the warrior who guarded the borders, who protected the queen, and being him was fun because I liked being a boy sometimes. We had no animals on Phobos or Earth, but there were animals on many of my imagined worlds. Yaboons and gammerfrees and umoxen. I talked to them all the time in my guise as Mar, the telepath, who could talk to animals, and humans. I explored things as dark, smoky Margy, the shaman, the one who would travel in her mind. Traveling in my mind was something I did a lot of.

The linguist was going to be me, myself, I decided. I loved words. Learning words was the best part of learning anything, so plain Margaret was the linguist. The healer was young and very kind. She wasn't as clear as the others. I supposed she would come into being later, as I learned more about her particular talents, because a healer would be very useful.

Together, we were friends and companions. Wilvia the queen occupied a throne and meted out justice. Margy sent her mind to distant
places to see what was happening, while the spy sneaked about and
learned specific things about people. Naumi built barricades against
the dreaded mind-worm, a creature I had run across in a footnote
and could define only by implication. Deadly, certainly. Horrid in
some unspecified way, and directed always by some malign and inhu-
man intelligence. This was enough to make me oppose it, or them,
for all my people were on the side of good, always. As warrior, shaman, telepath, healer, spy, linguist, and queen we lived each day among
wonders and marvels and were for the most part contented with
our lives.

Shortly before my ninth birthday, one of those days came along that
goes wrong from wakeup! My hair had horrid knots in it, my clothes
wouldn't fasten, my head hurt, I spilled my breakfast on some of
Father's papers, and he yelled at me. Halfway through the morning,
I grew frustrated over something and heard, with dismay, my own
mouth spewing a few of the words I had always kept secret! The
result was worse than I had imagined. My mother washed out my
mouth with Filth-away and told me I could not go down to the
Mars surface on the birthday expedition I had been promised for
over a year.

That trip had been my beacon, my lighthouse of hope, my only
chance to see and do something new and interesting. I can't explain
what happened then, though I suppose it was a tantrum. I had read of
tantrums, I'd just never had one myself; but this time, I did. I screamed
and threw myself on the floor and shrieked all my hatred and boredom, and I was so completely savage that both Mother and Father
were frightened. They were no more frightened than I was, but at
least they withdrew the punishment. When I got control of myself,
more or less, I was servile in my thanks and fulsome in my promises
of better behavior in the future.

Over the following days, however, my abject groveling gave way
to an unfamiliar resentment, though only one of my people, Queen
Wilvia, felt it deeply. My parents had forced Queen Wilvia to lower

herself, to give in to them, and Queen Wilvia had done nothing to merit it. She didn't like them anymore.

Wilvia didn't hate them. Wilvia knew the word *hate* because I knew it, but experiencing it required a stomach-hurting, churning kind of feeling, the way I had felt during the tantrum. I labeled it carefully. It had been a very strong emotion, the first strong emotion I had ever felt except the arms-from-my-stomach feeling that I got sometimes at night, as though I had arms reaching out of my middle toward something I wanted terribly but had no name for.

Considering the matter calmly, over several days and wakeful nights, I decided what I wanted more than anything was simply to be somewhere other than Phobos Station. I didn't say any of this or even convey it by being sulky. I was docile. My "Yes, ma'am"s and "No, sir"s poured forth with honeyed smoothness. On the promised day, the excursion to Mars took place, beginning with a shuttle ride down into the great canyon, where my parents were welcomed by acquaintances of theirs who worked in the hydroponic gardens. In the gardens, I stood transfixed while a green leaf fell, lazily turning, spinning almost purposefully to land by my foot. I was allowed to take it, a souvenir of all that was alive and lovely-smelling. I saw the commissary, which had thick windows looking out over the dramatically shadowed canyon walls. The shadows moved entrancingly as luncheon and birthday cake were served. Then, while the adults talked (about nothing, using the same words, over and over), I excused myself politely and pressed close to the window. Farther down the canyon stood a magical building where Queen Wilvia might live, the ruby dome and golden towers of Dominion Central Authority, the governing body for all free humans who lived off-Earth: us on Phobos and Mars, the people on Luna Station, and those in the six colonies.

One of the commissary workers happened by and took a few moments to point out several outstanding features in the landscape, including the dome.

"Who's in Dominion?" I asked.

The worker stopped, his brow furrowed. "What do you mean, who?"

"Is it humans?"

"Some," he said thoughtfully. "Some Gentheran, so I've heard."

"What are they like, Gentherans?"

He laughed shortly. "They're little, about your size, and that's all any-body knows. They wear full suits and helmets that cover their faces."

"But they're part of Dominion."

"Well, they found us, and they helped us . . ."

"Why did they help us?" I asked. I'd been wondering about this for a long time.

The worker shrugged. "They told us they owe us a debt, but they didn't go into any detail. Just said they owed us, take what they were offering and be grateful. That's what we're doing, I guess. We are grateful they've kept us out of the grip of ISTO, so far . . ."

"Isstow?" I had never heard it spoken.

"Interstellar Trade Organization," he whispered, with a glance over his shoulder to the table where the adults were sitting. "ISTO has given Earth a provisional membership because the Gentherans asked them to. So long as we have that, the Mercans can't cut up Earth for scrap."

"Margaret," my father called.

The worker hurried away. My brain spinning, I went back to the table to learn that one of the maintenance staff had offered to take me up onto the lip of Valles Marineris when she did her routine main-tenance visit to a wind generator. It took a moment to take this in, because I was still lost in what the worker had told me.

"Well, Margaret?" said Mother impatiently.

"Oh, yes, ma'am, yes, please." I said, daring to say nothing more than that.

While my parents remained below with their acquaintances, I was outfitted for the excursion. I wore the helmet and air supply unit I had worn during the shuttle trip, an item owned by every person on Mars or Phobos, just in case, and I was inserted into a dust suit that was actually quite a good fit, as it was owned by a "little person" on the maintenance staff, one Chili Mech, who had been hired, so I was told, at least partly for her ability to get in and out of tight places. Thus clad, I rode beside the worker in the elevator that took us to the rim.

When we emerged, I followed the worker to the "stem tower," which is what the upright part of the windmill was called, and was told to stay there while the worker climbed the ladder to the rotor. I was not to wander away or go near the rim, even though there was a protective railing along it. Accordingly, I looped my arm through an upright of the ladder and stared ecstatically at the surroundings, relishing the differences from everything I had known before. There was a real horizon; there was distance and perspective; there was wind sound; there were dust storms moving about like whirling dancers. There were colors in the rocks and hills, new colors!

I turned to peer along the length of the canyon to the shining dome. There were Gentherans there, Gentherans who had helped Earth so the Mercans couldn't cut Earth up for scrap. Why would they want to cut up Earth for scrap?

This train of thought was interrupted by a metallic shriek from above, and I looked up to see that the worker had opened a large door into the rotor housing. The door closed behind her with another shriek, and for a little time, I watched the dust devils that formed out of nothing and engaged in wild dances that carried them halfway to the distant mountains before they vanished. The dance was accompanied by soft, barely heard wind song that subsided into a momentary and unusual calm.

Out of nowhere, silent as the dried leaf drifting down in the greenhouse, a whirling thing came out of the sky and landed in the dust not fifty feet from where I was standing.

It looked like a dragonfly, or rather, like the pictures of dragonflies I had seen in my book about the wetlands Earth once had. A hatch opened in the side of the golden thing. A woman came out, unhelmeted, unmasked, her movement stirring the flowing robes she wore into crimson billows.

"You, girl," she called in a glorious, glad voice. "Come with me!"

I felt . . . I felt something I had never felt before. Joy! Ecstasy! I felt . . . I felt the arms-reaching feeling, that this was it, the thing I'd needed, that I must go (that I must obey and stay where I was), that the woman was calling me (that I was probably imagining it). Standing there, with my arm thrust tightly through the stanchion,

I felt my legs pounding, I saw the back of myself running away, not wearing a helmet or a suit, just free as air. I reached the woman, saw myself seized up by the woman, was seized up, saw myself taken, was myself taken into the dragonfly, and felt it go.

Then I swayed with dizziness, my eyes fell shut, and everything slipped away.

I Am Wilvia

Aboard the dragonfly, I was seized with shyness. No one else was there but the red-robed woman and a boy about my age. He was the first young person I had ever seen, and he was looking at me just as curiously as I was at him. His hair was dark as the shadows on the canyon walls. His eyes glittered, as though they had lights in them. I liked the way his lips moved, the upper one curving and straightening, like a bow, I thought, one of those bows ancient desert horsemen had used, that same curve.

The woman lifted me into a seat, murmuring, "Girl, this is Prince Joziré. I am taking him to a place of safety. Joziré needs a companion, and we have chosen you to accompany him."

The boy reached out a brown hand to touch my paler one. I felt . . . I felt the arms-from-my-stomach reaching, and it was almost as though the boy had taken those invisible hands in his own and held them tight. "What's her name?" he asked the lady.

"What is your name, girl?" She smiled at me.

It took only a second before I realized who I was. "Prince Joziré, my name is Wilvia."

"Wilvia," said the boy, returning my smile with a companionable one of his own. "I like that very much." He turned to the pilot to ask, "And where is it we are going, again, ma'am?"

"Look there," said the woman, turning to the controls of her vessel. "Look there, Wilvia. See the road?"

I, Wilvia went to stand behind the woman, looking across her shoulder in the direction they were going. "It is a road," I gasped. There it was, stretching ahead of us in long, curving lines, translucent lines so the ones farther away could be seen through those nearer, the whole reaching on and on into unfathomable distance. "Where does it go?"

"This road goes to B'yurngrad, then on and on until it comes to the center of things and the edge of things. There's a little town on B'yurngrad, so buried in the grasslands that no one ever goes there. It doesn't even have a name. People just call it The Town. Some very wise people live there, and you'll both find friends among them. The two of you will be longtime friends and good companions."

I Am Margaret/on Mars

The next thing I knew, the worker was muttering to herself as she carried me to the elevator: "Never checked the flow valve, stupid people, don't they teach their children that they have to check the flow valve every time they put the helmet on . . ."

When I fully wakened, they told me I had been briefly unconscious because of oxygen deprivation. Momentarily off my guard, I mentioned the dragonfly, only to be told quite firmly that I must have been delirious. I was quite, quite certain the dragonfly had not been the result of delirium, any more than the way my body felt was the result of delirium. I felt as though I had been split in two. I kept reaching in my mind for some other part of me. When I was well enough to stand, I searched the mirror for someone else standing behind or beside me, but there was no one there.

This episode, all of it, beginning with the tantrum and having my mouth washed out with soap, up to and including the departure of the dragonfly, began as simple confusion and ended by changing me forever. From that time on I was absolutely sure of two things: The first one was that somewhere else, there was another me named Wilvia. I knew this because she was no longer with me and because I had seen her go; the second thing was that I had become a mutineer. Until then I had been a curious but customarily compliant child. From that time on, I became a confirmed and silent rebel and simply refused to take part in chirrup tweet caw cwaup. I was determined to learn real language, many of them, all the ones there were! Didactibots were good at teaching people real things. I would get it to teach me the language of the ancient Pthas, a language no one alive spoke anymore!

And that is what I did and it did, except during those times spent in my own worlds, with my other selves. I still had five of them as my companions, all of them but Wilvia, who had gone away and left me behind. Sometimes I thought she had been treacherous or faithless, but I knew that wasn't so. She hadn't forgotten me. Sometime . . . someday, I would find her again.

I was almost twelve in 2096, when the personnel of Mars and Phobos Stations were told the stations were to be closed. For several hours following this incredible announcement, people actually communicated with one another! They disagreed, yelled, orated, hectored, became variously rancorous, anxious, insulting, and grief-stricken. I learned more about them in that brief time than I had learned in the twelve years before. The focus on reality was brief, however. Very soon the Phobos habit of evasive reticence reasserted itself, and everyone turned to their assigned duties. Machinery was wrapped, lines were drained, equipment was secured, personal belongings were packed, and finally the entire staff was shuttled down to the green ravine that held the headquarters of Mars Surface Colony. There we awaited the ship that would take us to Earth.

Oh, how I loved Mars Surface Colony! There were new things everywhere. Despite Mother's sporadic attempts to keep an eye on me, there were simply too many people and too many things going on to keep me shut up. I met Chili Mech, the woman who had lent me her Mars suit for my trip to the rim, and I began to follow her about.

"You're like those old-timey pets," said Chili Mech. "Some little cat or dog. Every time I turn around, there you are. What's the attraction?"

"You know things," I told her. "You talk about things."

"What things?"

"The Gentherans. Tell me about the Gentherans."

"Hasn't your didactibot taught you about the Gentherans?"

"Not really, no."

"Well, let's see. When the Gentherans discovered us, they told us the Earth biome was terminal, they told us how we could save it; but they didn't think we would, so they gave us some spaceships so Earth could set up a few colonies to preserve our species."

"Why?"

"What do you mean, why?"

"I mean, what was their reason for helping us? Did they just like us humans, or what?"

"The Keeper knows, kid, I don't."

"Who's the Keeper?"

"It's just a saying the Gentherans have. Anything nobody knows, they say, 'The Keeper knows.' Then you say, 'Well, ask the Keeper,' and they say, 'You can only reach the Keeper by walking seven roads at once.'"

"Nobody can do that," I said.

"That's the point. It's like saying, when hell freezes over or when pigs fly. Pigs are extinct animals that didn't have wings . . ."

"I know that," I said, somewhat offended.

"Anyhow, the Gentherans insisted we set up one government for Earth, and one government for the off-Earth humans, because if some predatory race found us, all our political subdivisions would get eaten for lunch. ISTO only deals with one government per planet or group of planets, and if a planet doesn't have one government, the Combines just swallow all the local governments up. That threat scared people badly enough that Earthgov got voted in very quickly, and as soon as the colonies were running, they set up Dominion Central Authority. DCA has representatives from each of the six colonies plus one each from the little stations on Luna and Mars, plus a bunch of Gentherans, because they were responsible for helping set up the colonies."

"Someone told me you're the Mars delegate to Dominion."

"I am that. I've been here since the Gentherans picked Mars as the site for Dominion Central Authority and offered to build the DCA structure, around 2067."

"That's the same year my mother went to Phobos, with her parents.

She was ten years old. My father got to Phobos fifteen years later, and I was born in 2084."

Chili Mech shuddered. "Lucky man. He got out just in time. The eighties were bad years!"

"How do you mean?" I sat on the floor and crossed my legs, looking up at the little woman. "I never heard about that?"

"Well, 2080 was the year the Mercan Combine discovered the human colony on Thairy. They showed up in Earth orbit. You've seen the ships. Compared to the little Gentheran ships, they're enormous, like planetoids! They said they were from Interstellar Trade Organization. I can remember Earth people being all bug-eyed like kids at a carnival, here the splendid ETs were, come to solve our problems.

"Well, that didn't last long, just until the Combine and the Federation had a chance to examine Earth and decide it wouldn't be worth their while to negotiate a trade agreement because we had nothing to trade. Earth was falling apart, and it was too late to fix anything."

She pursed her lips, as though about to spit. "Then they dropped the bomb. Since we were out on the edge of nowhere, a very expensive destination to get to, they were planning to hang around in orbit until the imminent collapse occurred and mine the wreckage for scrap after everyone was dead."

My mouth was open, as it had been for some time. "They said it just like that?"

Chili Mech looked over my head into space, slowly nodding. "Just like that, with nine-tenths of Earth's population watching and listening. After we died, their retrieval robots would take the dead humans to make protein meal for their livestock, and their scavenger robots would take all metals."

"What happened?"

"What do you think happened with half a dozen huge ships, blocking off half the sky! Those prancing K'Famir with all the extra arms and legs! The dirty, hissing Hrass, the boneheaded Frossians, the sneery Elos? Arrogant as all hell, while Earthgov's people practically licked their feet! Nobody on Earth had done anything about Earth's situation for at least two centuries, but now everyone was scared spitless."

I waited, finally urging, "Then?"

"Earthgov sent a delegation to ask if there wasn't something, anything the Combine or Federation would do to help us. The Federation and the Combine just hung up there, acting totally uninterested for a while, but finally, when we were just about to give up hope, they offered to stave off our collapse by buying the only surplus produce Earth had: people. They said they'd buy healthy ten-to-fifty-year-old people from us on fifteen-year labor contracts, and they'd even transport them to human colonies once the contracts expired.

"By that time, everyone on Earth was so scared that any way out would have seemed like a good idea. Earthgov consulted with the Gentherans and accepted the offer." She stared at me, really looking at me. "By all that's holy, you've seen their ships going back and forth to Earth, girl. Didn't you ever wonder what the ships were carrying?"

I flushed. I hadn't. It was just about the only thing I had never wondered about. "No. I didn't. What did they buy people with? Money?"

"What good would that do? They buy humans with water."

I thought about that. "What happened then?"

Chili regarded me doubtfully, eyes half-lidded. "Well, that's a touchy subject. You better ask your mom about that."

"She doesn't talk to me."

"Ask her anyhow. You got a right to know."

Later, even though Chili wouldn't say anything more about the eighties, she did talk about other things. She said the Mars program was being phased out because there wasn't enough water on Mars to support a real colony, much less enough to relieve Earth's water shortage.

"Didn't people find out how much water there was when they first came up here?" I asked her.

Chili grinned. "Somehow the Gentherans 'made a mistake' in their calculations. They told us there was a lot more water than we've ever found. Some say the Gentherans always meant to have Dominion headquarter on Mars, so they phonied the data that supported the settlement effort until they got it built. We didn't find out the truth about the water until just recently. In fact, nobody else knows the truth about the water except Earthgov, so keep it quiet, huh, kid?"

Chili's com-link went off with a shrill whine, and that ended the conversation. After that, there were no opportunities for me to find out anything more. The arrival of the *Ninja* was announced, and everyone scrambled to be ready except those few who had volunteered to remain behind to maintain the water and power systems for Dominion Central Authority. I shut myself up in my bed cubicle and cried for hours because Chili was staying, but she'd told me I was too young to volunteer.

On Earth, during the six-month gravitational rehab program, I met quite a few Earthians. They were just like the people on Phobos. The words might be a little different: twitter twitter chirrup, chirrup twitter, perhaps, instead of caw, caw, cwaup, but otherwise, alike. No one said anything real. The daily information services spoke of a decrease in water rations, of the failure of certain algae crops, and the people said chirrup, chirrup, twitter. Or, for those of us in therapy: moan, moan, scream. Rehab was my first experience of real, sustained pain.

"What will we do if our water rations are decreased?" I asked the physical therapist who was helping me learn to walk in gravity.

"Oh, sweetheart, you don't want to talk about that. Let's not spoil the day. Left foot now, step, step, step . . ."

"How much water is a ration?" I asked the technician who was measuring my bone density.

"Honeybun, I just don't think about it," he said with a winning smile. "Measuring it doesn't help anything."

Twitter, twitter, I thought. Caw, caw cwaup. Moan, moan, scream.

The therapy was almost over when Father announced that a proctor would be making a family visit. I had almost lost my trip to Mars over the word *proctor*! I had had my mouth washed out over that word, a dirty word, one no nice child ever uttered. I felt myself flushing red with hostility and embarrassment. I shivered all over and stared at my toes.

"For goodness' sake, Louise," said Father. "That won't do."

"Of course not, Harry," Mother replied, her own cheeks red with chagrin. "It isn't a bad word, Margaret. It's just one we've avoided using until now. You'll have to say it to yourself. We'll have to use it in conversation. Otherwise, the proctor will wonder why his title makes us blush."

I considered rebellion. What had all that Filth-away business been about if *proctor* was not a dirty word? And now I was to use it in conversation? I, who had always been prevented from using any real words whatever? I felt moved to throw another tantrum (it had been over three years since the last one, after all), but I suppressed the inclination. Since I had no idea what this new freedom would entail, perhaps it would be wisest to know its limits before taking a stand.

Instead of a tantrum, I took part in conversations that were scheduled during family dinner so we could discuss the function of proctors and the circumstances which had brought us all back to Earth.

"Do you know what ISTO is, Margaret?" Father asked.

"ISTO is the Interstellar Trade Organization." That was the right answer, but I wanted more. "We have a provisional membership, but I don't know what it means. Provided what?"

It took Father a minute to switch from his usual frown to his recently invented fatherly look. "We have a membership provided the ISTO doesn't declare all Earthians a barbarian people."

"I don't know what that means," I persisted, even though this wasn't strictly part of the subject.

Father gritted his teeth. "ISTO recognizes four types of creatures: civilized, semicivilized, barbarians, and animals. Civilized people know about, care about, and protect their environments. Semicivilized people know and care, but can't do anything . . ."

"Why not?"

Mother said, "Because something prevents their acting in their own self-interest. Public apathy. Commercial interference. Religious opposition. Governmental corruption. The Gentherans say humans have a lot of that."

Father frowned at her and went on. "Barbarians know but don't care about their worlds, and animals don't even know. Animals or barbarians aren't treated like civilized people."

"But what does all that mean? What have we done about it?"

Mother's voice was dead and level. "Margaret, you know we had lakes and rivers once. We had forests once. We had animals on land and fish in the oceans. By the time the Gentherans came, all the freshwater on Earth was confined in pipes, the ice caps were gone, the rivers were gone along with hydroelectric power. All our food came from ocean algae because we had no water to irrigate plants. Our desalinization plants ran constantly, mostly on tidal and wind power. We had nuclear plants, but the Gentherans made us shut them down because the Intergalactic Court doesn't allow nuclear power on occupied planets. We already knew we were in trouble, and we told the Gentherans our problem was a lack of water . . ."

Father interrupted, "The Gentherans very politely told us we were mistaken, the problem wasn't water, the problem was us. The biome was collapsing, everything on Earth would soon die. The Gentherans said too many Earthians were in fact barbarians who didn't care what happened to Earth because they believed they'd be off in some lovely afterlife by that time."

"Would they be?" I asked, wonderstruck at this idea.

"I sincerely doubt it," Mother snapped.

"Didn't anyone listen?" I asked.

Father said, "The Gentherans weren't talking to the people, they were talking to our leaders. The Earth governments went as far as they could when they formed Earthgov and started the colonies, but they wouldn't do anything about depopulating Earth because they thought the public would start riots."

Mother added, "The government decided to break it to us slowly. They told us about the colonies, how colonists had been sent along with all the animals we had left in zoos . . ." Her voice trailed off.

Father sighed. "People were excited about that."

Mother said, "The news programs ran these lovely fantasies about all the people who were crowding us moving away . . ." Her mouth worked. Her eyes brimmed, and she shook her head impatiently. "A silly dream. Even if people shipped out every hour of every day and night, we couldn't keep up with the birthrate. We could never accomplish what the Gentherans said we had to do."

"What did we have to do?" I demanded.

She wiped her eyes and stared at her knotted hands, saying nothing. Father rose to his feet, face twisted in distaste.

"I can't deal with this, Louise. You tell her."

"Harry! Damn it. You're the one who . . . you're her father!"

"You're her mother, and you'll have to. She needs to know, and I can't." He left the room, closing the door behind him.

"What?" I said, thoroughly confused. "What should I know?"

Mother's cheeks were scarlet, and her mouth pursed, as though she had bitten into something sour. Her voice trembled as she said, "The Gentherans told us to apply a numerical rating to every person born on Earth. If a baby is its mother's first child, it gets one point. If the child is its father's second child, it gets two points and adding them together makes the child a three. Only those rated two, three, and four are allowed to have children or any scarce commodity. You're my first child and your father's third child, so you're a four . . ."

I cried, "Father has other children! I have a brother or sister?"

Mother choked. "No. When he was quite young, he had a relationship with a woman. She had twins who died as infants."

"But, if they died, then I'm his first child who lived . . ."

"It doesn't work that way," said Mother, nervously licking her lips. "Any child born alive is counted, whether the child lives or not. That isn't . . . isn't important. The Gentherans claimed it's the fairest way to reduce population. It doesn't cut off any genetic line and it leaves the gene pool as broad as possible." She paused, her hands knotted. "Finally, Earthgov passed the two-three-four laws, but they did it secretly."

Mother wiped moisture from the corners of her mouth with one knuckle of her clenched hands. "Earthgov was debating how to publicize the laws and begin enforcing them when the Mercans and the Omnionts showed up. You know what happened then! The Combine and the Federation said they'd salvage us. We begged for help. They offered to buy our people for water. Earthgov shilly-shallied, as usual. They thought they had a choice.

"They didn't have a choice! They couldn't get it through their stupid heads that there was no choice! ISTO says a living planet is more important than the members of any race on it, and if a race of barbarians or animals threatens a planet, the race has to be 'reduced,' and they were about to reduce us. It couldn't be kept a secret any longer. The story broke everywhere at once: the offer to buy our people, the threat from ISTO, the laws that had been secretly passed . . ." She fell silent, staring at nothing for a time. I waited. "And what they'd been afraid would happen, did happen! The anti–population control people started rioting. Those opposing them began rioting back! Some religious fanatics took advantage of the disorder to start a biowar. That was the Great Plague of 2082 that killed a billion people while those huge ships just hung up there, watching."

"They didn't help?"

"Gentherans help. Omnionts observe. Mercans profit," her mother snarled. "At least that's what the Gentherans tell us."

"That's why . . . it was the terrible eighties?"

Mother wiped her eyes. "That was the start of them. While the plague was going on, all the local wars joined into one big war among former nations and states and tribal areas. That was the so-called Eight-Week War that killed another billion people."

"I wasn't even born."

"No. The war happened right after your father arrived on Phobos. It's a good thing we were there. Otherwise, we might not be alive today." Her voice, already unfamiliarly shrill, went up another half tone. "We might have been just two more of the two billion people the plague and the war had killed, which still wasn't enough to suit ISTO, which started an inquiry . . ."

"Into what?"

"If the plague had been started purposely by Earthgov, ISTO would have regarded it as a good-faith effort to reduce population; if the plague was simply a crime or accident, it wouldn't have helped our rating at all. Everyone knew Earthgov hadn't started the plague, because the fanatics who did it had told the whole world their god had commanded they do it! However, the fanatics were all dead by that time, so they couldn't prove they'd done it, and that gave the Gentherans a loophole through which they *negotiated* with ISTO. They claimed that Earthgov had known the plague was going to start and had chosen not to stop it. That turned out to be 'reasonable grounds' for classifying us as semicivilized.

"ISTO agreed, but only if we immediately started enforcing our own laws by selling all our over-fours to the Combine and the Federation."

"They'd never been enforced."

Mother shrilled: "How could they have been! What with the plague and the war, nobody could enforce anything! ISTO said either comply at once, or the robot slaughterers would start arriving." Her voice rasped, she coughed, before going on in her piercing, unfamiliar voice:

"Earthgov declared martial law and began shipping people out, and that bought us provisional status as a semicivilized and threatened world. We've been shipping people ever since, and we're still provisional."

Mother's tone and expression were forbidding, but I wanted to know! I said, "I still don't understand why we can't talk about it!"

Tears pouring down her reddened face as she grated through clenched teeth, "Have you been listening to me, Margaret? I sound like a—a crazy person! I'm screaming! Even telling you about it makes me crazy! The war happened, and the plague happened, and even in the middle of all that, the proliferators just went on having child after child after child! Other people, those who called themselves the limiters, they blamed the others, the lifers, for destroying the world. If you want to know all the awful details, I'll remove the block on your didactibot and you can look up the Lifer-Limiter Uprising!

"Your father and I weren't here, but we've heard about it from people who were! The hostility was everywhere, in everything. Pregnant women were stoned! Obstetricians' offices were bombed. Hospitals were bombed. Mentioning babies in public could get you killed! We still can't talk about it!"

The door opened, and Father came back into the room, his face drawn. "I'm sorry, Louise. I just . . ."

"I know," she croaked. "I know."

The looks on their faces actually frightened me. I said placatingly, "I suppose if you were somebody with lots of children, it would be terrible to lose them."

Mother and Father exchanged a long look, and when Mother turned to look at me again, her face was gray. "It would be terrible, yes, even to lose one."

I Am Margaret/on Earth

As Mother pointed out, I was twelve years old, a grown-up young woman who would behave herself, who would not blush at the proctor's title when he arrived, for we needed the proctor's approval to get our permanent water ration cards.

"If the Omnionts are bringing water, and we're shipping out the over-fours, why do we need rations?" I wanted to know.

Father looked up from his desk. "Because until the sterilization laws were passed and enforced, every time we shipped someone away, we had two new ones popping up. That didn't stop until the Mercan Combine started buying toilet-trained toddlers as pets for the K'Famir."

Mother turned pale and left the room quickly.

In due time the proctor arrived, a narrow, sharp-edged sort of man who didn't even give us his name. He merely nodded once at each of us as he put his access-and-data console on the table. It clicked and flipped open in several directions, spreading itself across the entire surface before uttering an imperative beep. When the proctor hit a key, its purple screen fetched up a lengthy form.

"Now," the proctor said, drawing a chair up to the table and seating himself at the console. "Let's start with the simple things. Your names. Dates of birth. Identity numbers. Names of all siblings, living and dead. Parents' names and their dates of birth, and their identity numbers, and the names of all their siblings, living and dead. Places of birth, if known."

Mother took a deep breath and started out, "We are Louise and Harry Bain . . ."

Between them they came up with all the names and most of the dates, either from memory or from the family record book.

"Good," said the proctor. "Now, to your knowledge have you or have any of your siblings ever used a name other than the one they were given on their birth registry?"

"Mama's brother Hy," I offered, when no one said anything.

There was a pause. The proctor looked up, as did I. Mother's face was very still, as though she had been paralyzed.

Father said, "Hy wasn't her brother, though he was young enough to have been her sibling. He's Louise's uncle. Margaret's great-uncle."

Mother found her voice. "Hy was named for his father, Hyram, a name he hated. He . . . he doesn't live on Earth, however. Hy has always lived in the Lunar Colony."

The proctor, turning to Father, "And you, sir? Any aliases? Pseudonyms? Noms de guerre?" He winked, making a face, and for no discernible reason, a shiver ran up my back.

"Not that I know of, no," said Father with a frozen smile.

There were other questions, where people had lived, how long they had lived there. Mother and Father weren't always sure about the details, but the database filled in most of the gaps once it had people's identity numbers.

"Now your daughter," said the proctor. "Name, date of birth, identity number? Fine. Now we'll do your DNA."

He took sterile scrapers from a tube, scraped the insides of our cheeks, and dropped the samples into an analysis slot on the console. "All three of your DNA codes will be checked for familial consistency, that is assuming pregnancies were normal and unassisted?"

Father looked uncomfortable. "I don't know."

"You don't know, sir?"

"Twenty years ago my former partner had twins that died at birth. We were separated at the time, and I had no knowledge of them until later. I don't know the particulars."

The proctor said, "If you'll give me the woman's identity number."

Father shrugged. "I don't know. When I learned the children hadn't survived, I didn't even ask for genetic verification. It was a long time ago . . ."

The proctor nodded. "That's all right, we'll find the data on the previous reproductive history and we'll do the GV. Just tell me her name and where she lived at the time."

Father muttered, the proctor nodded and entered the data. "And your pregnancy, ma'am?"

Mother flushed. "Margaret's conception was unassisted."

"Very good. That's all we need. Your family will be filed as a unit. You'll be provided with the code at the time of filing, so you'll have it for reference if it's ever needed."

As his console refolded itself, the man turned to me to ask, "What were you studying on Phobos, Margaret?"

"I started learning ET languages," I murmured. "I know some Pthas, some Omniont, and quite a bit of Mercan Trade Tongue."

The proctor nodded. "I'm impressed. Fluency in ET languages is valuable, but few families are sensible enough to let their children learn them early, when it's easy for them."

I said, "Mother encouraged me. She says she wishes she'd learned languages when she was little."

The machine made a quiet sound, like a hiccup, and produced a screenful of figures. The proctor pressed a button, a machine voice said, "Clear."

"Very well," the proctor said, pressing a button. "We always compare, just to be sure. In your case, everything agrees with everything else. Provisionally, until we receive the information on your previous history, your registration rating, sir, is a two. You, ma'am, are a four. Your daughter a four."

"We're in good shape, then," said Father in a relieved voice.

"You are indeed, sir," said the proctor.

When the door closed behind the proctor, I whispered, "What did he mean, that we're in good shape."

Mother answered. "It means we can have a water ration. It also means anyone who's a five or higher can't."

Father cleared his throat and shook himself, as though to shed whatever mood he'd been in. "Margaret, I think we've had enough of this discussion. We need to take a family walk, get out of here. Right, Louise?"

Mother, looking very pale, nodded. "Yes. Oh, yes. Let's get out of here. Let's give ourselves a treat of some kind . . ."

I looked from one to the other, frightened at their tone. "Is something wrong?"

Her father said, "Everything's all right, Margaret. You can have water, you can even have a family when you've grown up."

"That is, if you pick the right husband," said Mother tartly. "One who hasn't used up all his quota sowing wild oats. No, no, Margaret, don't ask me to explain wild oats."

I felt something squeezing my stomach and farther down, in my belly. As the three of us took our rare, almost unprecedented walk, I looked into every store window we passed while my insides cramped and jumped as though I'd swallowed something alive that was trying to get out, split off from me. My skin felt damp. I thought I saw a shadowy presence moving around, reflected in the window, standing just behind me, but there was nothing there except my own white and frightened face staring back. After a time, I stopped looking and trudged along, eyes fixed on my feet.

Who Is Margaret?

It seemed to me I dreamed the proctor came, just as he had. I dreamed everything he had said and we had said, up until the point where the proctor turned to me to say, "Fluency in ET languages is valuable, but few families are sensible enough to let their children learn them early, when it's easy for them."

"It was Mother's idea," I said. "She says she wishes she'd learned languages when she was little, like her brother Hy."

"You mean her uncle, Hy?" said the proctor.

I stopped. Why had I said that?

Mother said, "My uncle Hy, yes . . ."

The machine interrupted with a harsh, buzzing sound. It spoke: "Duplicated reference to unverified identity, name Hy, maternal kinsperson. Possible data variance. Hold! Hold!"

The proctor sat back, his lips tightly compressed, as printed forms began to flow across the screen. He muttered, "We always compare with former records, just to be sure. There seems to be a record discrepancy."

"Discrepancy?" Mother faltered. Her hand shook on the arm of the chair. I had started toward her, but when I saw the fear in her eyes, I stayed frozen in place.

The flow of forms stopped, leaving only one on the screen.

"A medical record," said the proctor in a chill voice.

"Ma'am, your middle name is, I believe, Hazel? We have a record here of a perinatal death on Mars, specifically on the Phobos Station. Some twelve years ago. To Hazel Bannon, your maiden name, I believe?"

Mother tried to speak and couldn't.

Father said, "It wasn't on Earth. The emigration laws only pertain to Earth."

The proctor shook his head, nostrils pinched. "When the Mars projects were closed, their records were subsumed into ours. During this interview, your daughter twice mentioned an unverified identity. That triggered a universal search by the data system, all medical records and all identity banks."

Mother's eyes were so full of fear that I cried out, "Mother! What's wrong?"

"What's wrong," said the proctor, "is you, young lady. You are not a four. You're the second born of twins. You're a five."

"What does that mean?" I cried.

Mother sobbed, "Oh, Margaret!"

"You could be prosecuted for attempted falsification of records," said the proctor.

"We didn't know," Father cried. "Phobos never counted. We never thought we'd be coming back to Earth!"

"Well, sir. Earth is where you are. You and your wife may remain here, but your daughter, Margaret, will be required to report to the shipping point within the next ten days. The shipping officers will be in touch."

The dream was like watching a play. It was clear. The words were clear. In the dream, the proctor went away. When the door hissed shut behind him, Mother screamed, "I told you they'd find out, Harry!"

Father yelled at me for mentioning Hy's name.

I cowered, wept, then howled, halfway between fear and fury, "You're sending me away!"

Mother shouted, "They're taking you away!"

"You knew about this," I yelled. "You told Daddy they'd find out, so you knew I wasn't a four! Why did you go ahead and have me if you were just going to let them do this . . ."

It was as though they hadn't really thought of me until that moment. Mother fell to her knees and put her arms around me. Father stooped above us both, tears flowing.

I felt something squeezing my stomach and farther down, in my belly. I cried out with the pain, scrambled away from between them, and fled to the bathroom, where I stood, looking into the mirror while my insides cramped and jumped as though I had swallowed something alive that was trying to get out and split off from me. My skin felt damp. I thought I saw a shadowy presence moving around. For a moment I thought I could see it in the mirror, standing behind me, but there was nothing there except my own chalky white, scared face staring back at me.

From somewhere outside myself I heard something, or someone, saying very firmly, slowly, in a commanding voice: "It's all right, Margaret. Just take a deep breath, it's going to be all right."

I don't remember the subway trip to the South American elevator center, I just remember being there. It was huge, surrounded by sprawling dormitory and office buildings and centered on the immense reinforced and raised platform that anchored the elevators, some dozens of them, their transport ribbons virtually invisible, their translucent cargo pods making dotted lines that faded into invisibility, interminate fingers pointed at the silver shimmer of the staging platforms and the geosynchronous shipping station orbiting far above.

The authorities tried to discourage my parents from making the trip, but they insisted. They got no farther than one of the huge intake lobbies thronged with families saying good-bye.

"I'd have thought there'd be almost no one here," Mother murmured. "Surely people can't still be having children that are fives and over!"

"It's the backlog," Father murmured in return. "They're limited by the capacity of the elevators and the availability of transport ships. There are only four elevator terminals, one each in Sumatra and South America, two in Africa. There's been some talk about building more of them as ocean-based platforms, but the last time that was tried, a tsunami took it out. The problem is, building more would be expensive, and Earth can't afford it."

"I thought people would be flowing out," Mother insisted. "This is more of an ooze . . ."

"I'm not in any hurry," I interrupted. My voice didn't sound like me. It was a firm, solid voice, like a shield. Someone else had given it to me. I couldn't have contrived it on my own.

"That's the spirit," Father said, falsely cheerful. "You'll probably be here quite a while. We'll find a room nearby and visit you . . ."

The outposting officer, a tall woman with a shaved head and sharp, black eyes, immediately made the question of visitation irrelevant. "I'm a specialist in colony assignments, Margaret. You've studied ET languages."

"Some," I acknowledged.

"Some is better than nothing. If you ask for a colony posting, we can send you there rather than into bondage. Colony planets are in need of linguists."

Mother ventured, "Would it be . . . someplace where my husband and I could go with her? So we could be together?"

The officer gave her a brief smile, almost a grimace. "Sorry, ma'am. The ships aren't ours, they're Omniont and Mercan ships. Earthgov has negotiated for a few colonist slots on each one; it's the only way we can afford to send additional colonists, and we send no one over twenty-five. Anyone older than that doesn't pay back the shipping costs."

Father said, "A colony would be better, wouldn't it?"

The officer replied, "Most people think so, yes."

"What . . . where is the colony?" I asked. "I mean, what do people do there?"

"All colonies start out as agricultural," the officer explained. "Then we recapitulate the history of civilization, from the ground up, though we cut a few millennia off the process. We go in as agriculturists, build livestock herds, then start prospecting for natural resources. We reinforce the population with additional colonists as soon as the food supply is adequate, then begin extraction of natural resources and get some wind and hydro power plants going. Except for Eden and Cranesroost, we're well beyond that point in our colonies."

"So, why do they want linguists?"

"Trade. As soon as a colony has something to sell, usually agricultural or mining products, somebody has to sell it. The income helps support the inflow of former bondspeople from the nearby Omniont and Mercan worlds."

I found this puzzling. "But, if the colonists have been on Omniont worlds, haven't they learned the languages?"

"Races who buy bondspeople do not teach them the local language. They communicate through interpreters. They find the idea of conversing with their workers repulsive."

"I'd like to use the languages I learned," I said, surprised at a feeling of sudden warmth. I'd felt frozen for days, but this felt . . . it felt right. "Which colony would you send me to?"

"You'll be randomly assigned by a ship assignment computer. It separates bondspersons and colonists, then divides the colonists up by age, sex, skills, and the like, and assigns them singly or in small groups by chance. It avoids favoritism."

Mother cried, "But how will we know where she is?"

The officer started to speak, then looked down and shook her head slightly. I knew she was about to tell a lie. When the officer looked up, smiling, she said, "Your daughter will be able to send you a message after she's settled, but you don't need to worry about her. People her age are always adopted by adults. She won't be struggling on her own."

The words felt like truth, including the encouraging smile the officer sent my way. Something about it had been misleading, however. True, but misleading. I almost asked, "What is it you're not telling us?" but stopped myself. There was no point in drawing out my departure.

The officer had obviously dealt with this situation before. The moment the interview was completed, an usher took me by the arm and led me away as the sounds of Mother's farewells faded into the background. I didn't look back. It was all I could do to stay on my feet.

The first stop was a cavernous dormitory with numbered beds, where I was told to wait. I waited. Within the hour, someone found me there and told me where the toilets were and where the commissary was while attaching an elevator number tag around my wrist and a numbered identity disk around my neck. The fasteners of both items, I was told, were unbreakable.

"These are your coveralls, put them on. These are your shoes. Put what you're wearing into your baggage, put the shoes on just before you move to the pods. These are your baggage tags, attach them carefully. Bags are shipped separately."

I changed into the overalls and packed my clothes. I set the shoes on the foot of my bed, where I wouldn't forget to put them on. I tagged my baggage. Time passed while I sat in a cocoon of fog, too deadened to be afraid. Eventually, a loudspeaker summoned everyone to the adjacent commissary for a meal. The food was like all food, tasteless. No one seemed to be hungry. Back in the dormitory, after slow hours of nothing, I fell asleep, only to be wakened by another usher with a list.

"Ship change," the woman said. "You'll be going up this morning."

I fought down a surge of panic, telling myself it was better to be going anywhere than staying where I was. "Going up" meant putting on the required shoes, making a required trip to the toilets, then joining a queue that wound in a snakelike curve toward the elevator pods. As each one filled, it shifted sideways, locked on to the rising nanotube-reinforced ribbon, and departed, as did the one I was in, packed among hundreds of others, each with an oxygen mask, each in an identical coverall, each with number tags on wrist and around neck.

A voice said: "This stage of your journey will last approximately three days. When we reach the staging platforms at nine thousand miles out, you will have a brief recess while your pod is shifted to the higher-velocity elevators that will take you on the next lap, another twenty thousand miles to the export station. That journey will also take about three days. The officers passing among you will give you a dose of tranquilizers and one of time-release Halt, to shut down excretory function."

There were no windows. There was no wasted space. Rows of heads stretched in every direction. No one spoke. When the pod clamped on to the belt, a few people gasped, but only momentarily. Evidently it didn't clamp on all at once; it slid a little at first, then gradually firmed up so we didn't get jerked around. The feeling of being crushed eased, and after about three hours, I noticed that I felt lighter, though I didn't care greatly. Endless hours passed in a kind of dim nothingness. Orderlies came through, checking pulses. One or two of the people in seats nearby went limp, were unbelted and taken away. I was just starting to feel nausea when the pod abruptly unlocked from the belt and slid off to one side. The doors opened. People stumbled to their feet, out onto the domed, transparent-floored platform where we all stared disbelievingly downward at the Earth, a large blue ball, floating in blackness.

I had to go. So did everyone. As we filed toward the toilets, we were given premoistened cloths to wash hands and faces. There were no mirrors. I noticed men rubbing their hands over their stubbly faces. We were given something tasteless to drink before going into the next pod. The same announcement. The same shots. The same dimness and detachment.

At thirty thousand miles, the doors opened, we filed out. This time the drink they gave us was slightly larger, the time in the toilets was a bit longer.

"Pick up your baggage to your left," we were commanded. Our line shuffled forward, picked up our baggage, joined a new queue.

"Colonist number seven-seven-zero-five-nine-zero-two," said the checker, rubbing his eyes. "That way, to your left . . . To your right . . ."

I was so drugged and distant that when I felt myself split, it didn't seem to matter. One of me turned left, one right, into areas seemingly open to space. Half a dozen ships hung high above, tethered to the station by swaying skeins of boarding umbilici. Five of the ships were immense. The sixth ship hanging above the transparent dome was small in comparison to the others. The access lane leading to it stretched empty across the wide lobby space, while those of the larger vessels held seemingly endless lines of boarders.

"Margaret Bain," said a uniformed officer, glancing from my forehead to his list. "Number seven-seven-zero-five-nine-zero-two." He stepped to the lane divider and opened a gate. "Through there," he said, pointing at the empty access lane leading to the smaller ship.

"But, am I the only one going there?" I asked.

"Your number is the only number going there right now." The officer glowered. "Get over there and stop asking questions . . ."

I stared at the empty lane doubtfully. "Is that a colony ship?"

"Look, little girl. That's the ship you're supposed to be on. Now get over there before I have to call security."

I opened my mouth to say, no, it's wrong, but the officer was red in the face, angry enough to let me know it would do no good to argue. Cowed, I turned into the empty access lane, meeting the glances of those occupying the crowded lanes far to my right, a few staring at me curiously. Among those crowded bodies was another me, walking away, just the way Wilvia had walked away years ago, going somewhere else. I opened my mouth to yell at her . . . me . . . but couldn't think what I would say, even if she, I, looked back.

Before I could make up my mind to do anything, someone put a hand on my shoulder, a tall, robed woman. Her face looked familiar, as though I had seen it somewhere before. Not on Phobos. Not here on Earth. Where?

The woman smiled. "Are you hearing contentious voices, child? It's the place, don't you think? Or the situation? Almost guaranteed to make one question every move. Well, don't let voices bother you. This is where you belong." She took my hand and led me into the boarding tube. "Before leaving Earth, you had begun the study of nonterrestrial languages, isn't that so?"

Perhaps I answered, perhaps not, I don't remember. I do remember turning at the ship's door and looking across the huge lobby. If I was over there, I was lost in the crowd.

In the lock of the ship, the woman turned. "You're extremely young to leave home like this. All I can promise you is that you will not be unhappy where you are going."

"I was told it would be a colony planet."

"Oh, yes. The planet you're going to is called Chottem. It is a colony planet and my home. I know it very well."

"I've heard your voice before," I said, suddenly recalling. "The day the proctor came. Was that you? Telling me it would be all right."

"Did someone tell you that?" the woman asked. "Perhaps it was a friend of mine. We're all inescapable busybodies."

"May I ask your name, ma'am?"

The woman smiled briefly, somewhat ruefully. "Why don't you call me what everyone else calls me. I'm just the Gardener. And since you need a new name to go with your new life, let us call you Gretamara."

New Margarets/Who Are We?

"Bain, Margaret," said the checker, rubbing his eyes. "Number seven-seven-zero-five-nine-eight-two. That way, to your right."

The hallway to the right was crowded, traffic in it made more difficult by the baggage everyone carried. As I moved forward, I heard loud and emphatic voices ahead: "Enter your number, take your chances." "That way." "That way, move it. Wait, you dropped this." "Enter your number." "That way." "Another that way." "Okay, go with your friend there." "Now, you can go this way."

The boarding-tube ports were at a lower level. As those ahead of me moved down the slope, I could see over their heads to the tube ports. Two uniformed men operated a device and called out the results. As I approached, I saw it, some kind of number pad and a lever. Numbers were entered, and arrows lit up, right or left. The line ahead of me shortened, and soon there were only half a dozen left.

"You two together? Okay. Enter one number. Either one." "That way." "You two together?"

"No," a woman cried passionately. "We are absolutely not together."

"Okay," said the bored official from somewhere ahead of me. "Enter your number, sweetheart. Go that way." "Watch it, Bondy! She says you're not together, let her alone. Besides, your number comes up the other way."

I was next. The lever snapped. The arrow pointed right.

"That way, colony girl. Down to your right."

"Where is the ship going," I asked, without any real hope of receiving an answer.

"The colonists end up on Thairy, love. Run on now."

As I turned to my right, I looked back. Another me was standing there, looking at the arrow that had lit.

"That way, bondy girly. Down to your left."

I saw myself turn left, heard myself ask, "Where is the ship going?"

"It's off to Cantardene. Get moving."

Cantardene. What had someone told me about Cantardene? The K'Famir. The dreadful, evil K'Famir . . . somehow, she'd been mixed up. It wasn't a colony planet at all . . .

Margaret/on Earth

So, I, Margaret, dreamed I had been sent away from Earth, split off from myself, not once, but three times! When I woke, it was perfectly clear in my mind, and I wrote it down in my journal, just to remember it. Gradually, as the day passed, the dream faded. I forgot all about it until a long time later, a day when I felt terrible and lay in my bed full of fever and aching. To comfort myself, I did what I had not done for a year or more: I went among my people. The little shy one, the healer, she was gone. The one who had been my spy was gone. My warrior was gone. I took out my journal and read what I had written about the dream. Which one had gone to Chottem? Which one to Cantardene? Which one to Thairy? And where was Wilvia now?

I Am Gretamara/on Chottem

The Gardener called me Gretamara. She took me to Chottem, a blue-and-green planet. We flew across enormous, rolling grasslands into high, splintered mountains near the western sea. We dropped down a valley into a little village, a hamlet called Swylet. We alit near her house and walked to it through her garden, surrounded by a fence with a gate in it. A bell hung by the gate, and she said that people rang it when they needed her help. She was a physician, or perhaps something more than a physician, and she told me my task was to learn from her, to be a healer.

She told me about herself. Everyone in Swylet who had ever ailed knew the Gardener, and even the indomitably healthy had seen her moving about in the shade of the moss-draped trees beyond the fence. Gardener told me about the people, about generations of them, for she seemed to know everything they had ever thought, or wanted, or dreamed of. Gardener said there was always a Grandmother Sage, a Grandmother or Grandfather Vinegar, an Uncle Salt, an Aunt Pepper. The current Grandmother Sage, who was young when she had first sought help from the Gardener, was fond of saying that the Gardener's appearance had not changed over the years, that she was still as young-looking as in Grandmother's youth. Grandfather Vinegar—the current one—claimed that Grandmother Sage had probably dealt with three generations of Gardeners, the current one being the granddaughter of the one Grandma had known in her youth.

"But she's the same, the very same!"

"Ah, no, Granny," said the vinegary one. "It's just the appearance of this latest one has rubbed up against the memories of those others, wearing against one another like coins in a pocket until all the little differences are worn away."

Since the Gardener never left the garden by a route any of them could see, not so much as to step outside the gate, even Grandfather Vinegar could not venture a guess as to how she might have come by a child or a grandchild. Only women and children were invited inside her gate, and they only rarely, and a dreadful penalty was exacted from trespassers. Some of the grandmothers claimed to remember David Highnose opening the gate and walking two steps inside, two steps back out, and falling dead on the path, shriveled as an old leaf.

Aunty Pepper gave it as her opinion that the Gardener was married to the moon, though Uncle Salt said it had to be the sun, for what garden burgeoned by moonlight? Grandma Sage said if she was married to anything natural, likely she was married to the rain, for it was true that sweet rain came to the Gardener's place, even in droughtful times when the rest of Swylet got only the shout and splatter of a thunderstorm traveling through, much noise and little help. Those near the Gardener's fence sometimes heard rain falling, and if a person put a hand on the top rail, that hand would be wet with rain, though not a single drop fell on the dusty road outside.

All Swylet knew how she looked as well as I did: lithe and strongly built, with hard brown hands and a face that seemed to be all bones and eyes until one looked carefully and saw the curve of the lips, the flare of the nostrils, the way color came and went in her cheeks. I thought her very beautiful, though in a quiet way, the way a great tree is beautiful or a mountain. Between the straps of her summer sandals, her feet were brown as her hands. She wore a leather apron with many pockets over ankle-length dresses that were green in spring, gold in summer, red in fall, and blue in winter. Her hair was usually covered by a fine linen wimple topped by a wide-brimmed and battered leather hat. I never saw her wash herself, but she was always clean, and she smelled of flowers.

The people of Swylet also knew the Gardener's cats, very large, round-headed ones who came to the gate whenever a supplicant rang the bell. They were mostly tabby cats, a few black ones, and always at least one with slanting blue eyes in a narrow, speculative face. Each had a name, and the Gardener spoke to them in baby talk as she walked: "There, Bounce, beneath that borage a burrow. See to it tonight. Lightfoot, linger by the lilies. Someone starlit has left them in tangles. Tell me what creature is dancing there, do . . ." Then she would laugh, and so would the cats, in strange high voices, as though they were playing a game. The villagers stated as absolute fact that the cats sometimes danced on their hind legs and spoke among themselves.

I could not tell whether the villagers believed this was truth or had merely invented it for amusement, though Grandpa Vinegar and his ilk never allowed themselves to be amused. Grandpa Vinegar had grown old and sour from loneliness, for his marriage had ended long ago when his wife hanged herself by her neck from the barn loft, despairing over his having brought calamity home to taint her blood and kill the babe in her womb. This calamity came from his chasing after women in the sea cities before he came back to his betrothed in Swylet, barely in time for the marriage feast. So said the Gardener when the woman brought the stillborn to her, begging to know why. The Gardener took the baby to lie among her lilacs. She always took dead babies to lie in her gardens, and certain mothers claimed they could hear their children laughing as they danced upon the Gardener's meadows in the moonlight.

So, they talked about the Gardener, and when they first met me, they talked about me, but no more than they talked about the weather or the crops or the latest scrape the children were into. Generation after generation, the Gardener came down the path among her cats, talking to them as she came, and no matter what the supplicant asked for, the Gardener always gave something that would help. Babies were born and named and taken in their mother's arms to the Gardener's gate to receive her traditional gift of honeycomb on their lips. "That his life may be sweet," the Gardener always said, her voice humming softly among the droning of the bees. "That her life may be sweet."

And there I lived, and I worked hard learning what she taught me. I learned to plant and gather what I had planted and make elixirs from it and to mix them with others to treat specific conditions. I slept well at night because I was tired, and my hands grew callused and hard, like hers. Still, my life was sweet, and she took me on many journeys, including one that was unusual but very important for mankind.

You will need to imagine this:

A volume of amorphous, immeasurable space scattered with stars, singly or in clusters; some bright, some dull; each surrounded by a halo of luminescent mist that swims and wavers, sometimes penetrating the cloud that surrounds another star, sometimes separating from it; everything shifting, neither spiraling nor whirling as a whole but separately erratic, as though each point of light has a different destination.

Or this:

A forest. Here a tree immense past reckoning, its saplings gathered at its feet; there a huge, moss-hung hulk looming lonely at the edge of things; here a copse of fluttering leaves or a brushy labyrinth of old trees, branches intertwined. Imagine the whole underlain with shrubs and ferns over liverworts and fungi, while in the soil below little worms and bacteria writhe and multiply; everything moving slowly, undetectably, chaotically, one part going there, another coming here, all without apparent direction.

Or this:

An ocean inhabited by a thousand life-forms, some solitary, some in schools, some reef dwellers living by twos and threes, here a fanged eel, there a sinuous serpent, here a cloud of clown fishes, striped like a carnival, and over them all the colossal bulks of great basking sharks or whales, they, too, surrounded by clouds of diatoms and krill and bits of floating weed, all moving in separate routes toward indiscernible ends.

Imagine watching any of these for a million years or so as new stars come and old ones die, as old trees rot away and saplings grow tall, as whale bones litter the abyss and young fry hatch, as all the parts within each scene shift in relationship to one another, some touching, some separate, sometimes so remote that the individual seems undetectable by any perception save its own. Imagine that they speak, that space hums and bellows with their voices:

Star calls to star: "Here I am, who is like me?" Tree calls to tree: "I am I, who knows me?" Submarine dweller calls to other dwellers, innumerable calls: some subsonic, some deep, rhythmic pulses, some shrill eeps and squeals. When a response is detected, the thing that uttered moves separately but implacably toward its responder, as by gravity. So equivalence is drawn to equivalence until they are within touching distance.

Gardener took me to this place. She called it the "Gathering," and those assembled there were "Members of the Gathering." She said the place could as well be called Heaven, Valhalla, Olympus, or Glaspfifel, and those assembled could be called gods, spirits, essences. Regardless of title or size, she said each one of them, arose from a mortal source: Human, Gentheran, Quaatar, K'Famir, or any of a thousand others. Large gods arose from numerous sources, and small gods arose from few, size having nothing to do with potency. Any race of mortal beings may give rise to one god or many, and if, by chance or intention, an entire world is struck by a giant comet wiping out an entire living race, the Members associated with that race wink out like blown candles, at once both absent and unremembered.

Each Member, the Gardener said, can think only what its mortal source thinks, and each source visualizes its Member(s) differently. Earthians speaking of their gods: "Him" or "Her" or "Them," visualize very large persons, perhaps of great age, to denote wisdom, or strength, or power. Gentherans visualize kindly uncles and keen-minded aunts. K'Famir and Frossians and Quaatar visualize huge, fanged creatures with curved knives in each of their several manipulators, squatting above bloody altars. Though many mortals speak with authority concerning what their Members want—"Our Father wants us to sacrifice a bullock," "Kali demands we garrote a passerby"—the desires and demands of the gods are always determined by the desires and demands of the people. Whatever the prophet or priesthood comes up with, the gods parrot. The Members of the Gathering think only what their source thinks: bloody, painful, happy, kindly, arbitrary, logical, sadistic, nurturing—every god is always what the people suppose it to be.

Gardener says few mortals have ever seen the Gathering, and those who have seen any of it have seen only a tiny fraction of the whole. Even if mortals could gain access to the place and observe its continuous and eternally erratic movements as it sorts and re-sorts itself, they would be no wiser, for the Gathering is a spiritual mirror of the whole universe in which all mortal races are reflected through their deities.

Whenever a previously planet-bound race achieves space travel, they carry some or all of their gods with them into space. As soon as those deities emerge through the gravitic barrier around their home planet they are drawn inexorably to the Gathering. So when the Gentherans left their original home world, Gentheran Members appeared in the Gathering. So when the Earthians left their world to set up their little colonies, Earthian Members appeared. The Gentheran Members were few, very strong, and mostly cheerful, so said Gardener. The Earthian Members, on the other hand, covered the entire spectrum from horrid to happy, from bloodthirsty to benevolent, from sadistic to solicitous, and were, counting all the little saints of this and that, so very numerous that some of the oldest Members of the Gathering considered the arrival to be more an invasion than an advent.

The Gardener told me that a Quaatar Member, known to his inventors and worshippers as Dweller in Pain, was one of the most annoyed. DIP took an instant dislike to each and every Earthian Member, though it could give no reason for doing so. Members know only what their sources know, and no mortal Quaatarian knew why it disliked humans. It was a received aversion, passed down from generation to generation. Even if no prior reason had existed, the dislike might have arisen anew from the fact that many of the Earthian Members were rather jolly, and the Quaatar, being sadomasochists of the most elemental sort, did not approve of jolly. Pain, honor, blood, and death were the components of their ethos. Agony was their meat and drink, beginning in infancy when baby Quaatar, moving swiftly to avoid being eaten by their elders, often lost body parts in the process; continuing in youth through an endless series of rite-of-passage battles and on to the precedence trials of adulthood, events of ever-increasing excruciation until death intervened. In Quaatar male society, abhorrence of strangers and infliction of pain was the norm. Loathing the foreign or inferior and torturing the loathed was considered the usual thing. So Gardener told me, pointing out, as she did so, a few little Earthian gods with similar tendencies. "That is the god of jihad," she said. "That is the god of crusades. They are identical except for their names."

She explained that the Gathering is a sloshing sea of fluctuating factions, each wavelet betraying an ephemeral or lasting association. By the time mortal races leave their home planets, many of their gods have already amalgamated with one another. Small tribal godlets are often thrust together through shared execrations. All Death-Honor-and-War gods, for example, are identical. The people may fly different flags, but their gods are happy to drink blood from both sides of the battle. All Sun, Harvest, or Forest divinities are analogous. Even when similar mortal races arise on planets remote from one another, similar gods find one another easily.

The oldest deities of the Gathering, those originated by the Pthas, a source billions of years old and wise past belief, had set boundaries for the Gathering: Whatever the mortal races might do among themselves, their gods might not interfere with the sources of other Members. When detected, the penalty for such an attempt was instant eradication.

That "when detected" was a narrow but advantageous loophole, for, as the Gardener said, the right-hand tentacles, palps, or scravelators of the Members of the Gathering were only rarely aware of what the countersegmental organs were up to. Further, no part of the Gathering, including the oldest and wisest, was diligent in finding such things out. Even though the gods of the Pthas had instructed that neutrality or beneficence should govern the Gathering, there was no routine enforcement of that dictum. The Gardener says that mortals often pass laws they cannot enforce in order to be seen as "strong," or "determined," even though they know the laws will not solve the problem.

The Quaatar race was convinced that humans should be eradicated, but they did not wish to be wiped out in their turn, so they conspired in secret, drawing upon the skills of their planetary kinsfolk, the Thongal, the Frossians, the K'Famir.

These races, long separated from Quaatar, were still similar to the Quaatar in many ways. None of them had an emotion equivalent to gratitude, but all of them had a mercantile respect for debits and credits. The Quaatar were credited for having given the Thongal, the K'famir, and the Frossians planets of their own. Winnowed by circumstance, these races were now far superior to the Quaatar, but they greeted their elders with well-feigned respect and rejoiced at joining in vendetta against Earthians. They wished to conduct this massacre without implicating themselves, so, in the Gathering, a similar alliance with similar concerns occurred among Whirling Cloud of Darkness-Eater of the Dead of the K'Famir, Flayed One-Drinker of Blood of the Frossians, and the head of the Quaatar pantheon: Dweller in Pain. As reinforcement of their intentions, the leaders of the four races met on Cantardene, where they sacrificed to their bloodthirsty gods and swore to create a weapon that would seek out and kill humans wherever they were. Cantardene is the home world of the K'Famir, but the Gardener learned of it, and she told me, Gretamara, while I shuddered and wished . . . almost wished I could return to childhood, back on Phobos again.

I Am Ongamar/on Cantardene

During the seemingly endless trip from Earth to Cantardene, young as I was, I served as translator between the cargo and the Mercan crew—an assorted bunch of them: vicious K'Famir, cringing Hrass, sleek and superior Elos, and boisterous K'Vasti. Because I was in a state I can describe only as continuous fury, I did not cringe, and I did not bow. I knew at the beginning of the trip that they had misread my number, that I had been put on a bondage ship rather than a colony one. I had had time to get over it, I thought I had gotten over it, only to feel rage boiling up again the moment we, the humans, arrived and were marched off across a plaza. We were not chained. We had been warned in advance (or, I had been warned and told to warn the others) that acting up by any one of us would result in removing the whole group from sale as light laborers for household use and selling all of us to the mines.

When this warning seemed to have little effect, I then regaled my fellow bondies with stories of the mines. I'd heard a good deal about them during the trip. A few of the bondies had rebelled during the trip. They'd been dealt with publicly and fatally, and I hadn't been so stupid as to try to interfere. That memory and my description of the mines cowed the others into appropriate submission.

Trough-shaped fountains extended along the sides of

the plaza, most of them occupied by naked young K'Famir halfway between gill and lung stages of development. The young were of various colors: black, green, ocher, a few of dull red; all of them sleek and shining, exuberantly noisy, all eight limbs in motion at once as they sprawled and splashed, shrieking at one another in shrill, sibilant voices, conversations that I understood very well, having translated similar ones for what had seemed to be months. The K'Famir had a language of their own, but they used it only during religious obser- vances and on very formal occasions. For commerce and daily life, they spoke Low Mercan, as did most of the vocal populations in the Combine. Though it was an ugly language, I was getting very, very fluent at gargling Low Mercan.

Up ahead of us we could see the bondage-block, a broad, low dais around which each servant offered for sale would be paraded. In a low voice, I reminded the group that we wanted to survive, and sur- vival depended upon being servile. This was the intention I had started with: survive at all costs, do whatever was needful to get through the next fifteen years. I'd passed this intention on to the oth- ers. I'd told them, and myself, that anger could not help and might hurt our chances. We arrived at the block, and I breathed deeply, re- treating into myself as I'd often done on Phobos.

My fellow servants were sold off, one by one, managing to do it without getting themselves whipped or beaten. By the time I was displayed, I'd managed to detach myself from the procedure. I walked about the dais while the auctioneer began the spiel I'd been hearing all morning: Young. Healthy. Strong. Almost immediately a heavily ornamented female thrust her way through the crowd of onlookers.

"I'll see her," the K'Famira called. "She may be what I want!"

"K'Famira Adille," murmured the pitchman. "You need a house servant?"

"I have house servants," she replied, throat pouch turning slightly pink in annoyance as she rearranged her voluminous scarves. "My housekeeper sees to them. I do not waste my time buying house ser- vants. I want a pet."

"Most buyers prefer them younger."

"I don't want one I have to house-train. Humans look like a person cut in half, but they're said to be trainable. Walk it around again for me."

Obediently, I walked, impressions falling into place like coins into slots. When one studied language, one also studied its speakers. The skin around the K'Famira's eye sockets was not wrinkled: She was therefore young. A young K'Famira buying a pet was either a pleasure-female incapable of reproduction or a wife who had been warned not to attempt it. Infertility was a problem among city-dwelling K'Famir, exacerbated by the cultural prohibition against adoption. Male K'Famir accepted none but their own. Returning to the swamps for several seasons was usually an effective cure for the conditions, but that was not always possible.

I knew this in part because the Low Mercan vocabulary reflected the true situation: The word for city included the rootword for sterile; the word for swamp included the rootword for fecund. The word for a pleasure-female was made up of the words *urban* and *k'dawk*, a term for playful congress, indecent when used alone. *Playful* had been the word used in my glossary, but from what I now knew about the K'Famir, I doubted that any interchange between male and female could be playful. I now knew things I had not known I knew, for until now I'd had no mental hooks to hang them on. After a long voyage of listening to K'Famir talk, I had acquired hooks in plenty.

Because many K'Famira were sterile, pets were common. Any small, biddable creature would serve. Pets could be brought up in the family and kept for an unlimited time, or, when they reached adulthood, the pet could be freed to a colony. If the family didn't free it, the pet could be sold again for fifteen years of labor. One of the more discouraging facts I had learned on the ship was that time spent as a pet did not count against the term of bondage unless the family wished it so. The one encouraging thing I had learned was that K'Famir males did not find Earthians sexually attractive or at all interesting.

So, I focused on these trivia, standing very still and ignoring the manipulators running over my body.

"What's your name, human-female-young," Adille asked in Mercan, waiting for the translator to convey this to me.

"Margaret," I said, without waiting for the translator. "And I'm twelve Earth-years old."

"You speak Mercan?" Adille sounded almost outraged.

"I do, Great Lady," I said, focusing all my attention upon Adille's speech in order to blank out her smell.

"Well, then. You would be a bargain, wouldn't you?"

"I would seek to please the Great Lady," I said.

The cargo manager on the ship had been kind enough to instruct me in what to say. Great Lady. Great Lord. My only desire is to give good service. What does the Lord require? And so on. I had taught these same phrases to those in the cargo, though only a few of them had learned to say the words in Low Mercan. The cargo manager had told me he much regretted that he could not buy me for himself, as an assistant during future voyages.

"And your name, again?" Adille demanded.

"Margaret."

"Margaret. What a strange name, and yet, I suppose you're used to it. We'll keep some of it for you, wouldn't that be nice? My last pet's name was Onga. Suppose we call you Ongamar?"

And Ongamar I became. Ongamar who found her role not unfamiliar, for she fetched and carried, grateful to be frequently ignored, reconciled to being occasionally petted and fussed over, meantime listening to every word spoken in her presence and, when possible, those uttered behind closed doors. Thus I, she, expanded my Mercan vocabulary while learning a great deal about the K'Famir race and the Combine of which it was a member.

In general, I, as Ongamar, found the situation tolerable. The Mercan people were uniformly disagreeable, but simple pleasure-females—as distinguished from the breeding consorts of males in the hierarchy— had no dynastic ambitions and shared few of the more deadly K'Famir attributes. Though vicious if provoked, females were not routinely cruel; their interests were narrow and restricted to their own comfort; their servants and pets did not find them hard to please.

The males, however, were uniformly sly and vicious, even before they were sent to their male-only religious schools. By the time they left those schools, they were sufficiently menacing that pets, servants, and children stayed out of their way, and even consorts and pleasure-women were careful of their demeanor. There was no K'Famir law against the negligent or purposeful slaying of children or wives by male K'Famir, or the slaying of male K'Famir by male K'Famir, though penalties were exacted for slaying the mates or children of other males, which was considered to be theft.

As Ongamar, I was allowed to take my own exercise unsupervised in the walled gardens, which were extensive. My usual food was a tasteless kibble, made especially for pets of several humanoid races, but I was also fed scraps from the table, many of them delicious, though some were revolting. Adille's previous pet had been of another race, but Adille learned which foods were acceptable while I invented ways to avoid being stuffed with foods that made me ill. Vomiting on the carpets resulted in a beating with one of the special slave whips made of flemp hide. The skins had microscopic, hook-shaped scales on them that tore the flesh and prevented the wounds from healing. Pets were beaten for any "dirty" behavior such as tracking in soil or leaves or failing to put clothing away, or spotting anything with blood, which occurred when I began to menstruate, some little time after arrival.

The first bleeding upset Adille, and I was taken to a K'Famir veterinarian, who explained the biological function to Adille, not to Ongamar, and gave a kit of supplies to Adille, not to Ongamar, that Ongamar was to be trained to use. Thereafter Adille speculated from time to time whether it might not be fun to breed Ongamar and raise a litter of little ones. When she mentioned this in her current patron's presence, however, his throat sac bulged to its fullest as he bellowed that one animal in the house was barely tolerable and there were to be no more.

The semiaquatic K'Famir wore clothing as protection when outdoors, or as adornment. While at home they were constantly in and out of the fountains with which most of the rooms were furnished, Clothing for pets was allowed. When my own clothing began to wear out, I begged Adille for fabric to make simple, long-sleeved shifts. In public, K'Famir and pets without fur or scales wore voluminous scarves to prevent sunburn.

During the first year of captivity, I accompanied Adille and her current patron, Bargom, to the pleasure quarter to meet some old friends. They stopped at various stalls, including one tiny one where

Adille saw a kind of bib lying under a glass bell. Made of many tiny beads, it created pictures.

"Bargom!" Adille cried. "Look at this! Doesn't that look like you?" As it did, the bead colors shifting suddenly to create the very likeness of Bargom when he was startled, side-eyes very wide and angry.

"Nonsense," he said. "It looks like your mother."

I stepped a little to one side and saw what he meant. It did resemble Adille's female parent, who from time to time cohabited with Adille.

"How does it do that?" cried Adille. "Oh, Bargom, look at the tag. It's only twenty mantrim. You promised me something fun to amuse me during my molting. Buy it for me."

"Surely it's only a trick," he said.

"Not at all," murmured the stall owner, who had appeared from behind a curtain as they stared. "It portrays memories, which it captures from the minds of those who confront it. Each owner helps it develop more complexity. Here on Cantardene, K'Famir images mostly, though on occasion it will portray events."

I recognized him as a Thongal, a serpentine, periodically sexless race that was occasionally seen in the Cantardene markets. I had been told of this race at school. This particular Thongal had tattered ears and abraded hollows below his eyes where his heat sensors and rudimentary sex organs should have been, routine punishment on the home planet. It lifted the glass bell so Adille could see the necklace more closely while she stroked the shining surface of the minute beads.

"A strange thing to be so cheaply priced," said Bargom, peering at it but coming no nearer.

"A strange thing is not always much desired," the Thongal said, with a deprecating snarl. "K'famir prefer the familiar."

"Is it a necklace?" cried Adille.

"It could be, if one wished to wear it, though I am told it may become too heavy to be worn comfortably."

Adille reached forward and picked it up from the velvet pad, hefting it between her palps, laughing. "Not heavy at all! Oh, Bargom, do get it for me."

I reached up to stroke the glowing beads, running the tip of one finger over them, looking up to catch the Thongal's eyes fixed upon me.

"Pretty pet the lady has," said the Thongal. "May one ask its name?"

"Ongamar," said Adille, casually. "Though it had another one. What was it, human?"

"Margaret," I murmured, catching a peculiar expression in the Thongal's eyes. Amusement? Glee? Satisfaction?

"Margaret," it purred. "From Earth, no doubt."

Bargom had found a forty-mantrim note in his pouch, and the Thongal took it with a gloved hand, passing the necklace and the change back to Adille in those same gloved hands. Adille waited while I fastened the clasp around her neck, then we went on to the evening entertainment: dinner at a restaurant, where I stood beside Adille's place to cut her food, meantime watching her necklace shifting and changing, sometimes somber, sometimes violent in color and action.

After the meal, Adille and Bargom had front-row seats at a pouch-howling concert, while I waited in the "servant races" section, just far enough off the lobby to be spared the worst of the cacophony. When we reached home, the necklace was taken off and laid upon the ledge of Adille's grooming trough.

"You know," said Adille, rubbing her throat pouch, "it really is heavier than it feels. My neck is quite weary from it."

I stood beside the trough, examining the necklace without touching it, for when I had touched it before, I had felt a threatening emanation, tangible as a smell, as though something dangerous had wakened and looked at me with recognition. As the Thongal stall owner had done. As though he knew of me, which was an unpleasant thought.

"Great Lady," I murmured, "perhaps it might be best not to wear it very often."

"Nonsense, Ongamar," said the K'Famira. "It's just that we've had a long day, and I'm a bit tired."

I was unconvinced. To all the regrets I had brought from Earth,

I now added one more: a deep regret at having touched the thing at all. Somehow, though Adille had received the gift, I felt it had been intended for Margaret-by-any-name, as a trap intended for a particular victim might allow someone else to fall into it first. So Adille had been caught, but the trap was not dissatisfied, for it had caught me as well.

I Am Naumi/on Thairy

The ship bringing me from Earth landed on the colony world of Thairy. A door opened from the ship into a somewhere outside, a place full of mist, an impenetrable nothingness. Voices echoed, but they made no sense. Words were meaningless. I was moved here and there. I had a sense of motion but not a sense of being, as though it happened, had happened, was happening to someone else. I was aware, but not sensible of. I laughed quietly to myself, finding this all most amusing.

Then suddenly, not. Something reached inside me and pulled. It wasn't pain, one couldn't call it pain, but it was not something one wanted to happen, it was a strangeness one wanted desperately to stop happening. I cried out. There was an abrupt sound, as though someone spoke angrily in an unknown language, and a dark curtain came down.

When I, Naumi, wakened, I found myself in a narrow bed in a small, very clean room. Very clean, I thought, and empty, for it held only the bed, a stool beside the bed, and a few pegs with clothing hanging on them on the far wall. Above the pegs was a label: Naumi's clothes. Below the peg, a shelf, a label: Naumi's shoes. I read this with some concern. Who was Naumi?

The sound of feet outside somewhere, then a white door opened through a white wall and someone came in.

It was the very nice old man who only had one eye. His name. His name was . . .

"Mr. Weathereye," I said.

"You remembered," the man chuckled. "Very good! You see, I told you it would all come back to you. What else?"

"My . . . my ma. She was killed."

"That's right. And your father, also. But that was a long time ago. Since then, you've been living . . . where?"

"With . . . Pa Rastarong. He took me in."

"Exactly. You see, you knew all this. It's just that bump on your head that made you forget for a little while. You live near the town called Bright on the colony world of Thairy. You live with your pa, and your name is . . . ?"

"Naumi Rastarong," I said.

"Exactly. What else?"

I frowned.

"Reach for it!" demanded Mr. Weathereye.

I reached. There was something there, just out of reach. Ah. Well. What was it?

"Some other language," I said. "I know some other language!"

"You do indeed. Several, as a matter of fact."

We fell silent, the man smiling, humming quietly to himself while I was preoccupied with something else. "Mr. Weathereye," I said at last, "I don't feel like my skin fits!"

"That's natural," the old man said. "Any time you get a good bump on the head, that's natural. You'll feel a little strange for a while, but you'll get used to it."

We fell silent again, and this time I drifted into what was almost sleep. An elderly lady and a lanky, lazy-looking fellow came into the room and sat on chairs near Mr. Weathereye.

"Rastarong," he said. "Lady Badness."

They nodded. The woman asked, "How is he?"

"Ah," replied Mr. Weathereye, "feeling a little strange, as who wouldn't. All that long journey."

"Does he know his name?" asked the other man.

"Naumi," said Mr. Weathereye. "I asked him, the way we do, when he was half asleep, 'Hey, boy, what's your name,' and he said Naumi."

"What does it mean?" asked Lady Badness.

"How in galactic parlance should I know?" Mr. Weathereye said in a testy voice, running his finger around the edge of his eye patch, as though it itched him. "It's his name. I asked, and he told me."

"When can I take him home," asked Rastarong.

"Soon. Just don't hurry him."

"I have fostered before," said the other, slightly peeved.

"Of course," soothed Mr. Weathereye. "Haven't we all."

They rose and departed. Behind them, I was surprised to find my face wet with tears, my heart swallowed up in a sorrow I couldn't or identify or connect. Mama and Papa, dead and gone? No, not that. That was long ago. This injury they said I'd had. I couldn't even remember that. No, it was some word, some label that lay within reach of my tongue but not within reach of my mind. Who was that? And why was I grieving for her?

I Am Wilvia/on B'yurngrad

Joziré and I sat on a haystack above a town with no name, the remains of our picnic luncheon scattered around us. I was chewing on a straw and making pictures out of clouds when Joziré asked, "Willy, do you know when your birthday is?"

I thought a moment. "I don't even know how long a year is, here. I'm not even sure how long we've been here."

"Here is somewhere on B'yurngrad, and we've been here about three school years," he said. "I know because I'm working on volume three of the history of governance."

"I'm still reading about laws." I sighed. "The sisters at the temple say I have to learn all about laws before I can study justice. I think it ought to be the other way around, but they say not."

"It's the same with the brothers at the abbey. I have to learn all the stuff that didn't work before I can study the things that did. They say if a ruler doesn't know what didn't work, and why, he'll waste time, treasure, and lives learning it the hard way." He stared at the sky, cleared his throat, chewed his lip.

I made a face at him. "What are you so twitchy about?"

"Lady Badness says I have to go away to school next year."

I sat up, horrified. "Just you? Not me? Where?"

"Just me. Maybe it's only for boys. She didn't say where."

"I guess that's how Lady Badness got her name," I said angrily. "She's all the time bringing bad news."

"It's not bad, exactly. It's just . . . troubling. Lady Badness says I can't come into my full powers until I'm well schooled, and I can't be king until I come into my full power. . . ."

"What powers?"

"I have no idea. Something Ghossy, I guess. She says when I'm well schooled, I'll know, and if I don't get well schooled, it won't make any difference. I'm sure she's right, but . . . I don't want to leave you, Wilvia. Four years is a long time." He turned his head to stare sightlessly at the two nameless hills that rose gently above rolling grasslands, each bearing a school on its crest: the gray-towered abbey for boys, the white-domed temple for girls. His school; my school. Between the two, the town straggled down into the valley on both sides of a boisterous, nameless river crossed by half a dozen old stone bridges. From the hayfield where we sat, we could see the whole town: gardens, farmlands, orchards. For all we knew, it could be the only town on B'yurngrad.

"It'll probably be just as remote as this is," he said. "My mother sends me letters by couriers, telling me I have to stay hidden."

"Because of the Frossians trying to kill you."

"Well, they killed my father, they've tried three times to kill my mother, they've been hunting for us ever since we left Fajnard. Mother's spies on Fajnard say the Frossians want to wipe out the royal house before they invade, so our family won't be a center of rebellion."

I whispered, "The sisters told me about it, and I've studied all your mother's writings. I know she was the one who established the Court of Equity on Fajnard. Think of that, Joziré! A court dedicated to pure justice, one that can overrule the law! They didn't even have one of those back on old Earth!"

"I know." He fidgeted. "Willy . . . ?"

"What, Jos? Don't fidget."

"When I go away, will you wait for me until I come back?"

"Unless they send me somewhere else. Of course."

"I don't mean that. I mean, will you not get too friendly with any other boy until I come back."

I felt myself turning red. "You mean wait for you . . . that way."

He sighed deeply, running his fingers through his dark, curly hair. "You're really too young to make a promise like that. You're probably about thirteen, developmentally speaking, and I'm probably about sixteen. I know I have to go to this school, but I don't want us to be separated. That sounds soppy, but I don't want us to forget one another . . ."

I took his hand. "Jos, I'll wait for you forever. My stomach won't let me forget. No one else in the world can make a fried garlwog sandwich the way you can."

He aimed a blow at me. I blocked it and aimed one at him. I didn't dare let him go on talking that way, or I'd start to cry, and I didn't want to cry. We tumbled into the hay and came to rest, me with arms pinned at my sides, him above me, nose to nose.

"Promise!" he demanded. "Or I'll leave you here for the big wild garlwogs to make dinner of."

"They don't eat meat." I tried to laugh.

"You," he said, fixing me with his eyes. "You, they'd eat. Now promise."

"I promise Prince Joziré, heir to the throne of the Ghoss, that I, Wilvia, will not . . . get friendly with any male person until said prince returns."

He let me go suddenly and turned away to hide his face before he got up to gather the remnants of our picnic lunch into the basket. I had promised, but I could see it hadn't helped much.

"Jos," I whispered from behind him. "I really mean it. I will wait."

He forced himself to grin. "I know you will."

We walked back along the farm road, each of us thinking of all the wrong things we could say and do. At least I was. I was having other thoughts, too. Old ones. As we came near the town, we saw Lady Badness sitting on a waystone.

"There you are," she cackled. "I'd about given up on you. If you don't mind, Highness, I must speak with Wilvia."

He was Highness instead of Majesty because he hadn't been

crowned king, yet. And he did mind, but he gritted his teeth and plodded on.

"He told you he's going away," said Lady Badness, after he had gone halfway to the town. "You've promised to wait for him, but . . ."

I felt the words leave me like a gush of water. "I've promised. But is it because I really want to wait for him, or is it because I'm supposed to be a queen, and the only way I'll ever be a queen is if I marry Jos." I put my hands to my face, which was burning, wishing to call the words back. They had been true, the words, but I hadn't meant to speak them out loud.

"Ah," said Lady Badness in a satisfied tone, "that's the true question, isn't it. One you have to answer, Wilvia. Do you want to be queen?"

I stared at my feet, unable to answer.

"You see yourself with a crown. I know you do. You see yourself being gracious and wise. Isn't that true."

"Yes," I said grudgingly.

"Are you gracious and wise?"

I desperately wanted to lie, knowing it would do no good. "I . . . I don't . . . No. I'm not."

"Well, no matter how much Joziré loves you, he will not marry you unless you are gracious and wise, for the Queen of the Ghoss must be both. Becoming a queen is extremely hard work, and why would you want to do it? To be queen? Or to be with Joziré? Or because it is a worthy thing to be? If Joziré were gone, dead, would you go to all that work, just to be queen?"

We went up the hill together with the questions unanswered. I couldn't answer them. Not then. Not for a very long time.

I Am Gretamara/on Chottem

The Gardener told me that Swylet had been founded by several wagonloads of malcontents who, tired of being told what they might and might not do by the Lords of Manland, had set off westward in search of a place where they might do as they pleased. They left the coastal cities of Manland, Chottem's only human-occupied continent, and turned west, through the surrounding orchards and vegetable plantations, the dairy farms, the estancias with their horses and herds of cattle and haylands and grain-fields, then left settled people behind as they moved into endless plains, where flocks of purple-feathered jibbernek bruised the sky at midday and whole villages of skritchers pranced on their rock-mounds, screaming alarm in the voices of old women. They climbed slowly into rolling hills, thence to a high tableland from which people could see for the first time retreating ranges of mist-valleyed mountains: indigo on azure on sapphire on ice.

Moving into those mountains they had arrived at last—and purely by fortune, so they thought—at a well-watered valley, hidden and protected by ramparts of immemorial stone. There at the end of nowhere they found an area fenced off, grown up in shrubberies and trees, and occupied by the Gardener. She welcomed them and told them to build beside the flowing river and to name their hamlet for the small, swift birds that nested there, the swylets.

Every now and then, a man or two from the village might back-track into the world on an urgent errand, to obtain breeding stock, or seed, or certain tools the settlers could not make for themselves. Sometimes they brought new settlers with them when they returned, though, as time went on, such additions became extremely rare. No one ever found the place by accident, though Swylet-born folk who went adventuring could always find their way home.

One such adventurer was the young artist Benjamin Finesilver. He had wandered the land with hunters, climbed the mountains with miners, sailed across the great freshwater seas of the north with fishermen. He had spent a season following the herds across the grasslands with the nomadic Skellar people, humans drawn from an ancient itinerant culture on Earth to inhabit the endless northern plains. From the black city of Bray he had sailed eastward toward the sunrise land of Perepume. The ship had anchored far out and discharged its trade goods into small boats crewed by little people no taller than his waist, who wore veils and talked a strange language in the high, sweet voices of children. They did not show themselves to strangers, the ship's captain told him, nor did they allow visitors.

To Benjamin, this was a great disappointment, but he was not long downcast. Since he had no way to see the farther side of the world, he would forget about Perepume and concentrate upon Manland. Though the eastern half of the human continent was flat, fertile, and relatively boring, the west and north held innumerable wonders in their broken, mysterious lands. Blue butterflies the size of a man's two hands. Beetles with gemmed carapaces that fought battles with the spears on their noses. A little fox the size of a kitten, which crept about the houses at night, crying like a baby, then laughing as it ran away when people came out. And the k'yur, which were rather like large cats but more like very thin bears, who stood atop the hills on three-moon nights and sang with the voices of angels.

Benjamin Finesilver talked with printers and booksellers and found them eager to help him. The people of the sea cities had plenty of time on their hands and plenty of money in their pockets, and though they were far too complacent and indolent to seek the marvelous for themselves, they were mightily amused by seeing or reading of anything wonderful and strange. The printers introduced him to people who published books, and the people who published books introduced him to people who financed such things, and thus Benjamin was brought to the attention of Stentor d'Lorn and his daughter, Mariah.

It followed that after ten years absence from Swylet, Benjamin returned with Mariah d'Lornschilde as his wife. She was lean and disdainful, with hair black as a traveling tinker's pot and blue eyes that silvered like swift fish in shallow water. She was taken aback some by Swylet, for it was smaller and slower than she had imagined. Still, she thought she loved Benjamin Finesilver, both because he adored her and because he had given her a way out of a sore predicament, and she was willing to spend a year or two in a dull, bucolic place if it pleased him.

Gardener knew this, as she knew everything about everyone in the place. She told me that even as a boy, Benjamin had been so eager to leave Swylet that he had paid very little attention to the place. Even had Mariah been interested in the hamlet, he could not have told her anything important about it, and he would never have thought to mention the Gardener to his new wife, even if he had remembered that the Gardener existed.

So, when the Grandmas came to welcome the bride, she was astonished when the first thing they said was, "You must go along to the gate and speak with the Gardener."

"And why must I do that?" she cried, laughing and shaking the ribbons in her hair so they danced on her head like butterflies. "In my home, my father speaks to the gardeners, and that is quite enough attention paid to them."

The Grandmas shared swift glances, some puzzled, some amused, a few even angry. "It's a custom," said Grandma Vine. "One we have. You might like to share our customs."

The others nodded, making light of it, saying yes, yes. Do share our customs.

"Well then, I will," said Mariah. "When I have time."

When they talked with her after that, time and again they would bring the Gardener into the conversation, for more than one had noticed the bride's waist was thickening and her steps had slowed. "A good time, now," said Grandma Bergamot. "Especially with your first."

Mariah, who felt nauseous most mornings and out of temper most afternoons, turned the talk to something else: the carpenter's newly built shop on the green, the plethora of lambs in the meadows, the way the cats kept on crying so strangely outside her window, keeping her from sleeping.

"Those are the Gardener's cats," they said. "Inviting you to visit."

"Nonsense," she said. "If the woman wishes to meet me, let her pay me a call." Indeed, she regretted mentioning the cats at all, for when she had peeped out the window to see what cried there, the moonlight had disclosed a crowd of furry, prick-eared animals dancing a gavotte. Mariah had a strong appreciation of her noble lineage and costly education. She was quite sure that if dancing cats existed anywhere in Chottem, her highly regarded professors would have told her of them. Therefore, she had simply been dreaming.

What could the women say? They had said no less than they had said to any of their own. They had suggested, invited, encouraged. If she had been of Swylet, they might have surrounded her, swept her away, and not let her go until they were outside the Gardener's gates, but she was not of Swylet. Who knew what family she came from, or what power it might have to upset their lives? Who knew what she thought or meant or intended with that easy, scornful laughter and superior mien that just missed being contemptuous. All very mannered, nothing to complain of, but very much as though they were *merely* a group of well-meaning ewe sheep while she . . . she was something else.

"Let her be," said the newest Grandma Vinegar. "She'll come to us soon enough when she needs to."

"No," said Grandma Bergamot. "I'll plead some tea for her. That much I can do, at least."

It was soon after my arrival on Chottem that Grandma Bergamot came to our gate and rang the bell. The Gardener and I went to the gate, the cats trailing around us.

"This is my ward, Gretamara," said the Gardener. "She has come to live with me while she learns to be a healer."

Grandmother Bergamot bobbed a curtsy, said a how-dya-do, and I greeted her with a smile. She glanced from me to the Gardener and back again, and I knew she was thinking we were kin, for we had the same tawny hair and green eyes, the same golden skin. Only our eyes were different. The Gardener's eyes were full of wisdom, but mine could have held only an endless list of the questions I had been asking since I arrived.

Grandma Bergamot recalled her errand and pled some tea for the new woman, who had come from far away.

"What is she like," the Gardener asked.

"Tall and dark, with silver eyes and a proud walk," said Grandma Bergamot. "She was Mariah d'Lornschilde in a sea city called Bray, and our Benjamin brought her home as a bride. She does not nest well here. It's as though she's counting the days until she can . . ."

I could see Grandma Bergamot hadn't known this until she said it, but it was right. We had seen the proud, dark woman. To us, too, it had seemed she was counting the days until she could . . . what?

"See my proud cock, there," said the Gardener, pointing at a peacock beneath a willow, tail and wings spread wide, quills rattling an accompaniment as he pranced before three inattentive hens. "See how he dances. He would dance to the cabbages if there were no hens about, but his joy would not be in it. Perhaps the people of Swylet are only cabbages to Mariah d'Lornschilde, and though she dances, joy is not in it for her."

"If her heart does not dance for Benjamin, then for what?" whispered Grandma Bergamot.

The Gardener shook her head. "Who knows. Gretamara will give you tea for her, Grandmother Bergamot, but I do not think she will drink it. Come back just before sunset."

I made the tea myself. The brew, heal-all, was the first brew I had learned, and when Grandma Bergamot came, I was waiting at the gate for her.

"I thank thee, Gretamara," said Grandma Bergamot.

"I will take your thanks to Gardener," I responded.

"Do you plan to visit long?"

"So long as the Gardener wishes," I said. "I am learning a great deal from her."

"And do you like it here in Swylet?"

"I have heard the history of Swylet and its people," I admitted. "And I like it very much where I am."

Grandma Bergamot took the tea. Gardener told me she had probably spent the day devising some way to get Mariah to drink it, and so she had. Grandma's own house was on the street where Benjamin Finesilver lived, and Mariah walked down that street each afternoon with a market basket in her hand and a parasol over her shoulder. So, next afternoon, when Mariah went by, Grandma Bergamot was sitting beneath her grape arbor, tea things set ready on a little table, and she invited Mariah in. "Do come. Have a cup of tea. I'm feeling lonely today."

Such a plea could not be politely refused, so Mariah came in and drank a cup of tea, while Grandma Bergamot only pretended to join her, for everyone knew the Gardener's gifts were for the intended ones alone.

"Odd," said Mariah. "An odd taste. Lovely, rather . . . what? Like rose petals but with something else. Where did you get it?"

"It's a brew gathered hereabout," Grandma replied. "If you like it, it would please me to make you a present of the packet."

Mariah started to refuse, then realized it would be rude to do so, and while she was often thoughtlessly haughty, she was never wilfully rude. She accepted the ribbon-tied packet with gracious words, picked up her basket and her parasol, and went off down the street. Though it had all worked just as Grandma Bergamot had planned, something about it had not been satisfying.

The Gardener stood on the stoop of her house, eyes fixed on the treetops as she spoke to me. "I see the packet of tea is going home in the marketing basket. It is sliding down as Mariah walks, and there it is beneath the apples and potatoes, the honey and the flour, the fresh eggs and the cut of lamb for Benjamin's supper. With most women, this would not matter, for she would see it when she put away the foodstuffs. However, Mariah is no cook, so Benjamin has hired one. There is Mariah, giving the basket to the cook, ah, yes. And the cook is putting the packet away in the cupboard."

"Won't Mariah ask for it?" I asked.

"No." The Gardener shook her head. "Tomorrow she will feel

well, very well. She will not think that it has anything to do with the tea she drank. In a day or two, the effect of the tea will wear away, but she will never think of it again."

Benjamin Finesilver, meantime, was getting on with his work. He had finished a good many paintings of places he had been. He had a comfortable study in which to work and sufficient funds to live decently for a year or so; he had written a good deal about the areas he had traveled through. He had not bothered to write anything about Swylet; he seemed scarcely to have noticed it since returning there. I saw him go by, several times. He did not even glance across the fence.

It was not long thereafter that Mariah considered it best to stay at home. She told Benjamin that the village women might show themselves swollen as melons as, indeed, most of the younger ones did at intervals, but Mariah's people did not do that. When one became ungainly, one stayed home with the front curtains drawn. One sunned in the garden and read books and sewed clothing for the baby, or so Mariah's aunts had instructed her. Mariah obeyed faithfully, though her days were so boring that she prayed for the baby to come quickly so her visit to this provincial backwater could be over.

Grandma Bergamot tried once again. She called on Mariah and was admitted if only because she broke the boredom of an endless afternoon.

"Our Gardener is a healer, you know," Grandma Bergamot said. "I know you've had the midwife here, and she's skillful, but when one has one's first, it does no harm to have a little something extra. Wouldn't you visit her, Mariah? In your carriage, just to her gate?"

"What is all this nonsense about the Gardener," cried Mariah in a temper. "I have written to my father in Bray. He has sent word that his doctor is coming to tend me, all the way from Bray, where my father is Lord Governor. When the baby comes, I'll be well enough provided for."

And that was that. The Gardener knew this as she knew everything that went on. She could stand in thought for a moment, staring into nothingness, then be able to tell me what everyone in Swylet was thinking or doing. This time, she stood outside the door, and her mouth was sad, for she pitied Mariah.

"Can you go to her?" I asked.

"I can do nothing out there. Only in here, which is why those in need come to the gate."

"I could go for you," I suggested.

She shook her head sadly, and I knew I could not do anything out there either.

Not long after, on a dismal morning with rain beating from a sullen sky, the baby announced its desire to be born weeks early, long before the doctor was expected to be there. The midwife was fetched. The labor went on. The midwife, in some agitation, suggested that someone go to the Gardener for Mariah, who was having a very difficult time. Benjamin Finesilver, who knew no more about childbirth than he did about Perepume, said nonsense, send for the village healer. This was done without improving the situation. The midwife again said someone should go to the Gardener, and this time Mariah screamed from her bed, yes, yes, go get someone, someone to help me . . .

Benjamin came himself, feeling a fool. Few men ever presented themselves at the gate, but he vaguely remembered having been taken there a time or two as a child, so it held no fears for him. He rang the bell, as the Gardener had said he would, and we went down to the gate. Benjamin begged something to ease his wife's pain. The Gardener asked him to put his hand over the gate, which he did, and she took it in her own while looking into his eyes. With a gesture, she summoned me to look at him also, and I saw what she had told me I would see.

After a long moment, she nodded and told him to wait. We went back into the house, and shortly she sent me to the gate. I told him, "Make a tea of this and have her drink a cup every hour. It will ease her pain."

"Will the child . . . will the child be all right?" he begged.

"You must bring your daughter here," I said, as I had been told to say. "To receive the Gardener's honey on her lips."

Thus somewhat comforted, he went back the way he had come, to brew the tea and make Mariah drink it and to see the pain leave her eyes, though the labor went on. After several more cups of tea and as many hours had passed, the baby girl was born.

"All's well, then," cried Benjamin.

"All's well with your daughter," said the village healer, turning back to the room where Mariah lay amid the crimson flood neither he nor the midwife had any way of stanching. "And your wife is in no pain."

All night Benjamin sat at the bedside holding Mariah's body in his arms. He would not look at the child the midwife brought to him, not until dawn came—clear, cloudless, hymned by birds— when he took the sleeping baby wrapped in its blankets and came down the street to the Gardener's gate. He rang the bell and waited, the tears still flowing down his face. By the time we reached the gate, Grandma Bergamot had come up from her house, for she had heard the bell.

"I've brought you the child," Benjamin cried, tears flowing down his face again. "Her mother is dead. You did not save her!"

"You did not ask me to save her," said the Gardener in a stern voice that cut through the fog of grief he was in. "You asked me to ease her pain. I did so. Grandma Bergamot asked me to save her some months ago, and I sent a medicine for her then."

Grandma Bergamot called, "Oh, she's right, Benjamin, she did, indeed. I sent her home with the tea myself. We tried to get Mariah to come here herself, but she wouldn't hear of talking with the Gardener . . ."

Benjamin gasped, recalling how Mariah had laughed about the Gardener. And he, he himself had not asked the Gardener to save her. Why? Why had he not? Sobbing, he thrust the child across the gate and into the Gardener's arms. "She's yours. Take her. I must take Mariah's body back to her people. I do not know how I will face them, and it is likely I will never in this life return to Swylet." He turned away, stumbling off toward his home, and by nightfall he was gone. The people of Swylet never saw him again.

Grandma Bergamot came to the gate, whispering, "Do you want me to take her, Gardener? I've raised five and helped with as many more." She peered at the baby, crying out a little. "Oh, but the wee thing, born far too soon!"

The Gardener shook her head, the silken folds of the wimple moving like grass in a wind, reflecting glimmers of light to play across her face. "Her father was one who looked so far he could not see a treasure lying at his feet. Her mother was one who looked so close, she could not see anything outside herself. The child was given to me. I will keep her and teach her how to see."

"But she's so tiny, so frail. Have you . . . I mean, do you know . . ."

The Gardener turned her eyes on the old woman and smiled until Grandma Bergamot flushed in confusion. "Do I know how to raise up a child, even one born too soon? Why, Grandma Bergamot, I knew you when you were Dora Shingle, a red, wrinkled squaller. I put honey on your lips. I gave your mother a galenical to cure your diaper rash. I fed you herbs for the summer fever and strong tea for the winter chills. I cured your earache and your sore throats and your belly cramps when the womanlies came upon you. Why would I not know how to raise one small babe who cannot be as troublesome as you were? Come in a moment and see for yourself."

Grandma looked around. No one else was about except two small red dogs chasing one another down the street. The gate was opened, and Grandma walked in, following us down the path, around the corner, through the shrubs, across the little lawn kept grazed short by fat ewe sheep, and through the door of the Gardener's House. The kettle was already hanging over the fire, and the cradle had been set beside it to warm, for we had known what was to happen. There was honeycomb on a plate, some of which went on the child's lips and some on Grandma Bergamot's and some of which was given to me.

"What will you name the baby?' Grandma asked, licking the sweetness from her mouth and wishing she were a child again, with no manners to keep her from begging more.

The Gardener smiled. "There's much thinking to do about that. Too small a name makes a person smaller than need be. Too large a name makes life a struggle to live up to. A name should fit, you know. It should be the size of the life it will signify."

Grandma wondered briefly how large a name Dora Shingle had been, before it occurred to her that now would be a good time to ask the Gardener some of the things she had long wanted to know.

"Gardener," she said, "since you're being so kind, would you tell me please where the cats come from?"

"Ah," said the Gardener, "well, where do cats come from? From kittens, no doubt."

Grandma Bergamot chuckled. "Oh, mayhap they do, or mayhap not. These cats of yours are no ordinary cats, Gardener."

"True," she replied. "Well, there's no reason not to tell you, Grandmother Bergamot, for your heart is good and you mean no ill to them. My cats come from the far side of Chottem, far east from the sea cities, where lies the blessed land of Perepume. There the cliffs rise from the sea to prevent invasion by ship, and great ragged continents of perpetual cloud prevent invasion from the air. Now that men have come to Chottem, however, it will not take them forever to find a way past these barriers. That means the people who live there may need to find a new world, though it will be a time before it becomes necessary for them to go." Then she turned to the cat at her side and said, "Isn't that true, lovely one."

"Oh, very true," said the cat, with a wide yawn as it stretched itself into a bow from tail-tip to tongue-flip. "As far as it goes."

Grandma put her hand on the cradle, which felt silky smooth under her hand. "This cradle is old," she murmured.

"Many children have used my cradle," the Gardener agreed. "Including some even smaller than this one." Then the Gardener said something else, then something else again, and before long, while I watched from the gate, Grandma was walking out and the busy dogs were in the exact same place they had been when she entered that gate. Though she felt she had been inside for a very long time, the sun still stood in the eastern sky as it had when she had entered.

She resolved to tell her friends about the cats from Perepume, and about the time standing still, for it explained so much that they had wondered about. The Gardener stayed young forever, because . . . because . . . Why was that?

Wonderingly, still licking the honey from her lips, she went off home, unable to remember anything except that Mariah d'Lornschilde had died in childbirth and Benjamin Finesilver had given his girl baby away to the Gardener and she herself had seen the child being rocked in its cradle by a girl called Gretamara.

Inside the Gardener's House, we sat sharing fragrant tea, the steam wreathing our faces and moistening our cheeks.

"Was there anything in what just happened that you did not understand?" the Gardener asked.

"I understood very little of it," I said. "I know you could have saved the woman's life but did not do so . . . I don't understand that. I know you are keeping the baby here, even though several of the women out there would care for it well enough for it to grow fat and healthy, and I don't understand that, either."

"This child," said the Gardener, laying her hand on the cradle, "is now the heiress of Bray. The previous heiress of Bray, her mother, was a foolish woman, a self-centered woman, family-proud and accustomed to the servitude of others. What reason might one have for wishing her daughter to grow up here instead of in the House of Bray?"

I thought that over. "Perhaps to let her learn of other things than she would learn there?"

"See, you do understand the answer, both to your first question and your second."

This was a troubling thought. "Then this child must learn to value things other than those Mariah valued."

"Yes," said the Gardener. "You and I must make sure of that. She will be high-spirited, I know, but she has no taint of evil. She will accept tutelage if both she and we are wise. We will court wisdom on her behalf by naming her Sophia. Sophia is the spirit of wisdom." She sipped her tea. "Are you happy here, Gretamara?"

I thought about this for some time, for I wished to say nothing to the Gardener that was not the truth. "I am often very happy here, Gardener. Your gardens fill me with such joy that it sometimes hurts. I value the ways of healing that you teach. Still, I think there is pain in much of what you do, and I do not understand why you changed my name or why we stay here, behind the fence, always alone."

The Gardener sighed, rising to look out the low, many-paned window that gave upon the garden. "As a young child, you had several people you enjoyed being, a queen and a warrior and a spy, this one then that one. Many children have such selves, harboring all kinds of possibilities within themselves. Each person contains the seeds of several persons. I have named one such person Gretamara to distinguish her from the rest. Gretamara is a healer.

"As for being alone, I am accustomed to solitude. My friends and I have a job of work to do. If it is to be done well, we must reduce distractions and interruptions . . ."

I interrupted, "But you're always being distracted and interrupted."

The Gardener laughed, "As you have just done! Not always interrupted, Gretamara, as you will learn. And, as I was saying, distractions and interruptions must be reduced without cutting ourselves off from one another or the daily lives of the people who have chosen and created us to care for and defend them. Our task must be accomplished without anyone noticing what we are doing. So, my friends and I live a compromise, sometimes meeting, sometimes separately, but always near a gate and a bell to summon us into ordinary life."

I asked, "Am I . . . one of your friends?"

A shadow crossed the Gardener's face. I thought it might be an expression of sorrow, but if so, it soon passed. The Gardener said, "Unlike ordinary people, Gretamara, we cannot choose what or who we will become: We are as we are made to be. You cannot choose to be one of us, but you can choose to be of inestimable value to our work. That choice is not to be made today, however, not even very soon. For the time being, your task is only to stay contentedly here, learning to heal those in need and whatever else I can teach you."

"May I learn another thing, then?"

"What thing is that?"

"Your stories, Gardener. Please, may I learn all of your stories."

"My stories?" The Gardener smiled. Outside the garden grew, the cats strolled, the sky paled, pinked, darkened. It wasn't a bad time for stories. "I will tell you a very old story about the angry man and the fish . . ."

Which she told me. A story that I heard again and again, later, many times, in many places.

I Am Margaret/on Earth

It did not take long to find out that Earth was no different from Phobos. People on Earth engaged in ritual repetition; most of them thought as little as possible; most of them occupied themselves with things and events that were not very important. Amusement stage dramas were the same as the ones I had seen on Phobos. All music had been so extensively filtered, corrected, and augmented by technology that it all sounded alike. Singing voices were improved by electronic means, as were the faces, the bodies, and the dramatic ability of actors and actresses. No one was plain; no one was allowed to be ugly; no one was very different from anyone else. In school, the stupid students got the same grades as the smart ones except for the tiny secret marks the educational archivists made in their records—in case a VIP needed a truthful reference.

I took my usual refuge in books, finding escape easier now that I had books written in other languages. No one had the time to sanitize books in Omniont or Mercan tongues, so Omniont peoples were allowed to be weird and eccentric, Mercans were unremittingly repulsive and violent. That most ancient of people, the Pthas, were enigmatic and profound. Their language was one of the most beautiful to hear, but the Pthas themselves were gone. They had ruled our galaxy for a billion years, fostering young races, helping people rise from barbarity to civility, but in the end, they had left our galaxy to explore the mysteries of the universe. The Pthas had taught that merely speaking their language would mold the mind toward truth. For that reason, so much as any human could learn to speak their language, I learned to speak Pthas.

The Quaatar were another story. They considered their language too holy for anyone except a Quaatar to speak, but I (along with two others in my class) learned to read and speak it. Out of bravado, I suppose. Showing off.

Each of the races whose languages we learned had different notions of good, bad, honor, dishonor, truth, or justice, a bewildering but marvelous array: more fruit for supposition and interpretation in one volume than in everything I had read until then. The K'Famir had no word for truth or justice; they had over fifty for degrees of torment and at least that many for honor, divided into classes, depending upon whose honor had been defiled, how grossly, and by whom. The Frossians had no words for good or bad: things were either edible or nonedible, profitable or unprofitable. The Quaatar had no words for equality, fairness, or impartiality. To each of them, every other Quaatar was either above or below them, while every thing or trait was either Quaatar or filth. The Quaatar word for filth was the same as their word for food: it applied to all non-Quaatar races except the K'Famir and the Frossians, who were called *gvoiup*, a collective noun meaning "morsels saved to be eaten later." Of course, as the didactibots never tired of reminding me, books were only books. Only long experience could truly teach translators how to interpret and explain these exotic beings.

When I was eighteen, I was admitted to the Advanced College of Linguistics and Policy from among whose graduates most of Earth's diplomats and ambassadors were selected—that is, those persons that Earthgov titled ambassadors or diplomats. What they were called by the other races involved was known only to a few, who thought it wisest not to publicize the matter.

ACoLaP, as the school was called, was one of the few educational institutions with a permanent exemption from the nondiscrimination rules. In all Earthian, nondidactibot schools, exceptionally bright students could move no faster than the slowest in the class in order that no lazy or inept student be left behind. It had proven easier to slow down everyone than to speed up the laggards. Earthgov, however, felt this rule should not apply when Earth's planetary security was involved, which gave my admission a definite éclat. Both my parents basked in the glow generated by this accomplishment, and I was trotted out on various occasions to meet my parents' friends, rather as a prize cow might once have been.

Since neither Mother nor Father had been at all helpful in my achievement, I rather resented their gloating. I had to give myself a good talking-to in order to let it go. They were not bad people; they were as they were. If they had been different, probably so would I, and I rather liked the way my own life was tending, for I had met someone.

Sybil, one of my classmates, was the daughter of a largish clan of professional people, and Sybil invited several of her classmates, including me, to dinner at her family's home. I liked Sybil far better than the other students she had invited, for they were among a small elitist group at the college, about a dozen sons and daughters of extreme wealth and power. Though two of the young men had condescended to honor me with their attentions a time or two, I had not been interested, but my indifference did not extend to Sybil's brother. He was Bryan Mackey, young Dr. Mackey, currently established in the extended residency program of a premier and respected hospital.

Young Dr. Mackey had a mop of sandy hair, amber brown eyes, a wide mouth, and a disconcertingly penetrating look, which he focused on me the moment we met. We sat next to each other at dinner. He asked me out. I agreed, somewhat nervous at having an actual date, and even more nervous on finding the experience enjoyable.

Thereafter, whenever he had a few hours off duty, he asked to see me, usually for dinner, where he very shortly fell into the pattern of complaining throughout the meal about problems in his professional life.

"The man doesn't know medicine?" he said of a superior.

"He's an administrator," I said, in what I hoped was a soothing voice.

"Yes, but he's a *medical* administrator. How in heaven's name can a man administer a program he knows nothing about?"

A week or so later it was something else, and something yet again the week after that, a whole chain of somethings I could identify very readily as "annoyances": directors who knew little but directed much; decisions that favored ease over idealism; rulings that frustrated his skill; orders that wounded his pride. I had seen it all on Phobos, where it had been decently hidden by custom. Here, his bleeding resentment was ripped out and laid before me in all its blatant gore.

"There's a better way to do that procedure! The damned rules were written twenty years ago! Mortality is a lot higher than it needs to be, if they'd just let us treat people the way we've been taught to . . ."

Slightly irritated, I said something I'd thought of many times but had heretofore refrained from saying. "Have you considered that they may want to keep the mortality as high as possible?"

He turned, eyes blazing, only to pale as though he had been slapped in the face by an icy wind. "You mean . . ."

"My father says population numbers aren't dropping fast enough. Desertification has eaten too much cropland there's no way of replacing. Look at how hard they're pushing emigration."

"Emigration! Call it what it is: providing slave labor for the Omniont Federation and the Mercan Combine."

I said, "It's not really slavery. It's bonded labor for only fifteen years. It's better than dying, Bryan."

"Have you ever seen a settlement planet?"

I shook my head, worried at his tone, which was more hostile and furious than usual, even for Bryan.

"Well then, don't be so damned sure it's better than dying."

I felt myself getting angry. "Do you enjoy being with me?"

"Margaret! You know I do!"

"Most times when we're together, I go home feeling . . . as though someone had been beating on me." Actually, I usually went home full of such vicarious anger on his behalf, such overriding animosity against those who were frustrating him, that I lay awake most of the night explaining to them what stupid people they were. I had little experience with violent emotion, and that little had been troublesome. Even on Earth, I had seen little or no emotion displayed until I met Bryan, who was looking at me now with wrathful exasperation. I spoke through gritted teeth:

"Could we . . . could we just have dinner together sometimes without your being . . . so furious about everything?"

He gaped, then closed his mouth with a snap, turning red, breathing heavily. I was about to get up and leave him there when he said through his teeth, "You're right! Father tells me the same thing. He says I mustn't take the day's frustrations home with me. Good heavens, Margaret, you must think I'm a . . . well, I don't know what. Rude, certainly."

I smiled in relief, demurred, insisted it wasn't all that important, just that I thought we would digest our meals far better (tasteless though they were) if we were less overwrought.

Once in a great while thereafter, he would begin a tirade, only to shake his head at himself, and say, "Forget it, it isn't important." Instead we talked about books, about an experimental theater movement, about music. One night, I went home with him for an hour or so, leaving him breathlessly to return to my parent's apartment. The next time I told Mother I was spending the night with friends. Neither parent questioned this. Both of them had fallen back into the Phobos habit, speaking constantly of work or speaking of nothing at all.

When Bryan and I could take a panting moment from our lovemaking, we decided, quite independently, that we were perfect for one another. Preoccupied by sensations that were completely new to us both (since early youth, Bryan had been kept far too busy to get sexually involved with anyone), fearful of saying, feeling, or doing anything that might threaten our delight, we played with one another very carefully, avoiding anything that might be in the least annoying. With Bryan, I felt complete. Those strange splittings-off that I had imagined happening on Mars when I was nine and here on Earth when I was twelve seemed to have healed. I didn't have that arms-reaching-out feeling with Bryan. My arms were delightfully full.

The fact that we didn't speak much about our relationship seemed natural to me. It was the way things had been on Phobos, it was in keeping with my upbringing. To Bryan, I realized it was purposeful, the result of continuing resolution, his perseverant gift to me, not to involve me in his rages, disappointments, frustrations. For this honeymoon of time, we rejoiced in one another, avoiding all irritating subjects, each of us remaining blissfully unaware of the other's true desires or plans or hopes for the future.

I Am Naumi/on Thairy

On Thairy, during dry-time's height, I spent a lot of time at the swimming hole by the river. Every year the wet-time runoff dug the hole anew; each year a deep spring welled a fresh coolness from beneath it; each year it stayed icily fresh, even when the sun-scorched riverbed mummified under its wandering wrappings of sand. I swam by myself sometimes, and sometimes Mr. Weathereye or Lady Badness went with me. Mr. Weathereye was forty at least, maybe older, and Lady Badness was variable, depending on how she felt: sixty-two on a good day and a hundred-two on a bad one. I called her Lady Badness because Mr. Weathereye called her that, and because whenever she talked about her life, she always said, "Ah, but there was so much badness then."

A school of tiny snout fish lived in the pool, along with a tangle of slimy green noomis and every wet-time a silver-scaled gammerfree spawned a litter of pups in a hollow at the bottom of the tree. The mother gammerfree sat on a protruding root and talked to me, or so I thought, at least, and it occurred to me that since I knew several languages, I should be able to decipher what the gammerfree was telling me.

She greeted me with a lilting whistle. Pursing my lips, I did my best to copy the sound. "Pheeeew," said the mother gammerfree before repeating the whistle again.

This time I did it better. "Pheeet," said the gammerfree, going on to another whistle. By the time the gammerfree was tired, I had several words I was sure of. *Pheeew* meant no good. *Pheeet* meant all right, or passable. Another whistle meant something to do with food, and that first whistley bit meant "Good day." Or maybe "Hello."

Lady Badness and Mr. Weathereye wandered by, she to soak her shins from the diving rock and Mr. Weathereye to study the botany of the area. Not long after, looking for trouble, here came wandering an ineradicable lout—which is what Mr. Weathereye called the type. He saw me sharing my sandwich with the gammerfree pups and promptly shied a stone at them while demanding I get out of the way so he could kill them. I jumped up when I first saw the lout, putting myself between stone and gammerfree pups and receiving a nasty cut on my chest for my efforts. When I said the lout should go away, he threatened to beat me flat. I braced himself for battle, but just then Mr. Weathereye came tripping up behind the lout and hit him across the butt with his walking staff. It was a long walking staff, and the far end of it achieved a considerable velocity during the swing.

"Why'd you do that?" screamed the lout.

"Why'd you threaten to beat my friend?" asked Mr. Weathereye. "Why'd you throw a stone at those little creatures?"

"They're vermin, stonin's all they're good for," cried the lout. "And he wouldn't get out of my way."

"What if I think you're vermin, and beating's all you're good for and you're in my way?" asked Mr. Weathereye, advancing as the lout withdrew in some confusion.

I settled back on the stone, and shared out what was left of my lunch with the frightened pups, all huddled together in fear. The mother gammerfree nuzzled me and gave me a quick lick with her rough tongue while I stroked her from her scaly nose to the tip of her scaly tail.

"Will the lout change his ways?" I asked around a mouthful of egg salad.

"They seldom do," said Mr. Weathereye, adjusting the patch over his bad eye, caused by an accident in the long, long ago when he was a mere youth. "By the way, Naumi, the schoolmaster's looking for you. I meant to tell you earlier."

School was out for the dry season, and since I had concluded the term satisfactorily, the schoolmaster had to be looking for me for some other reason than schoolwork. I put my clothes on and set out to find the schoolmaster, Mr. Wyncamp, knowing he kept office hours even during summer when school was out.

"Naumi Rastarong," he said by way of greeting when I entered his office, staring at nothing and pushing the papers on his desk around. Looking uncomfortable, he pushed his glasses up on his nose. "I have here a communication from the Dominion. It says that you have been selected to provide life-duty to the Dominion, and your escort will arrive on Valstat's Day with all the paperwork your pa will have to sign." Mr. Wyncamp chewed his lower lip and put the paper down as though it had burned him.

I didn't notice, for my brain had gone dead at the words *life-duty*. No one from the town of Bright had ever been selected for life-duty, at least not in the lifetime of anyone still living there. I knew about duty, of course. In school, everyone learned that submission to the Dominion brought with it the onus of taxes paid by everyone, and short service paid by some. Being picked for short service wouldn't have surprised me at all, for lots of young people were chosen to spend two years as child minders, cooks, builders, or crop harvesters. When somebody got selected for short service, well-wishers always said, "Two years is short stay for no more tax pay!" Two years of service did bring a ten-year exemption from taxes and interest-free loans for education, so it wasn't that rare or fearsome.

But life-duty, that was another thing altogether. It meant forty years in the service of the Dominion itself. The things people said when they heard about life-duty were usually of the very small comfort variety: "Well, look at it this way. It's better than dying from the pergal pox." Which was true, but so what? Though I had no way of knowing it, most youngsters, when advised they had been chosen for life-service, did exactly as I was doing: They sat with their mouths open, too stunned to object even if there'd been anyone to object to. The notice came from Dominion Central Authority; there was no mechanism for appeal.

After a while I looked up to see Mr. Weathereye standing in the hallway, leaning on his cane. When he saw me looking at him, he beckoned. I took the letter that Mr. Wyncamp had given me and trudged out into the hall.

"Life-service?" whispered Mr. Weathereye.

I could only nod. I was trying to recite the words of the Thankfulness Pledge that we said every morning at school, the one that went, "We thank those in the service of the Dominion at the sacrifice of their own ambitions . . ."

"I didn't even have any ambitions yet," I confessed.

"I think they try to catch candidates before they have many," opined Mr. Weathereye. "But I thought you wanted to be a warrior?"

"Well, I did, do. Mr. Wyncamp said I'm so good at battle games, it was likely I'd become a warrior. But, you know, I thought Thairy Guard is where I'd serve, at the very most." Thairy Guard was what Mr. Weathereye called Men Minus Mission. There wasn't much use for warriors on Thairy.

"Do you want me to help tell your pa?" asked Mr. Weathereye.

I said, "Y'know he's not really my pa."

"Yes, I know that."

". . . 'F I go alone, he'll think I'm making it up," said I. "He usually does, if it's anything out of the ordinary."

"That's what I thought," said Mr. Weathereye.

Outside, we met Lady Badness, who fell in beside us without even asking what had happened, so I figured she and Mr. Weathereye had had their suspicions all along.

Pa Rastarong's house was outside the town of Bright, a smallish place, set at the eastern feet of the Lowering Hills.

"Why'd they choose me?" I mumbled to himself.

Lady Badness said, "Some professorial type did a study, long time gone, trying to determine similarities of character among those chosen for life-service. Only thing similar among 'em all was nobody wanted to go."

"That's me, right enough," said I. What was I good at? Nothing much except school and battle games. Didn't much like team sports, though I was very quick on my feet and agile in getting up perpendicular sides of things when pursued by one or more ineradicable louts.

Mr. Weathereye had always advised that getting away from a lout was in most cases preferable to killing the lout, which I was perfectly capable of doing, because I was really *very* good at battle games, including the art of unarmed combat, though none of the louts knew it.

"They don't even know I could hurt them," I'd said.

"How would they know?" asked Mr. Weathereye. "Louts don't study battle games, and your teachers don't make a habit of talking about it."

"My name has been on the battle game roll of honor in the hallway at school," said I. "Four years running."

"The only thing rarer than louts who think is louts who read," said Mr. Weathereye.

"I'll miss people," said I. I'd always thought the people in Bright compensated for the fact my foster pa was kind of strange. The citizens of Bright considered friendliness toward children a duty, even when it wasn't a pleasure. Amiability was part of the effort good citizens put forth to get all seven-year-olds through their dozen-years, that period beginning at literacy and culminating (when it did at all) in passing the adulthood examination and receiving a citizen's ID. It took about twelve years to get there, starting between age five and seven, though some took more or less, and a few never reached it at all.

On entering the dozen-years, people gave up baby clothes and baby behavior. They put on the bright red tunic of students, which I had just set aside, and they behaved appropriately, or at least tried to give that appearance. It was appropriate to be willing to learn and to be respectful of elders; but whether one did or not, one had to achieve mastery of the essentials. Once that was done, and the adulthood examination was passed—I had passed—one took the oath of citizenship and became a member of society. One could then wear adult clothing and engage in adult behavior: One could marry, beget children, drive a flier, operate heavy machinery, or conduct business. One could even stay out all night and engage in lechery and sottishness, with no one to forbid it.

No one knew anyone who had failed the adulthood exam, though everyone remembered certain people who hadn't taken it but had been called to life-service and were not heard from thereafter. Their fate, whatever it may have been, was Dominion business and nobody else's, though family members had been known to kick up a fuss when Sonny or Honey disappeared, at least right at first. Fuss always resulted in a visit from a Dominion agent, who came to remind the family of their own oaths of citizenship, and after that, the families always settled down or pretended to. It was rumored that certain people might have been transported to Tercis, but no one knew for sure.

All this was on my mind as we turned from the cobblestone thoroughfare onto the graveled stretch of road that led to Pa Rastarong's house, an overgrown and ramshackle dwelling standing amid a clutter of what Lady Badness called lost opportunities and ill-starred innovations: the rusted model of a grebble thresher that had worked quite well until actually tried on grebble; the remnants of an all-sense information grabber with the unfortunate penchant for grabbing everything except the item desired; and the automatic power legs for fruit pickers that had on at least two occasions lifted their wearers into near-Thairy orbits.

"Pa's got a new invention," I offered.

"Ah," said Mr. Weathereye unencouragingly.

Undaunted, I continued. "He says it'll make our fortunes, mine'n his both. It's a kind of all-round rain deflector. If somebody wants to play ball at night, for example, or if somebody's having a wedding or a parade . . ."

"They rent a rain deflector," said Mr. Weathereye tonelessly. "Before I buy shares in it, I'd like to have one question answered. Where does the deflected rain go?"

"Pa's working on that," said I. "What he wants to do is just send it back up and back up, bouncing around up there, until people are finished with their party, then it can come down."

"The result could be a deluge," said Mr. Weathereye. "Perhaps an inundation."

"There's that," admitted I, kicking the front door, which opened with a protest of moisture-swollen wood and the crack of an already split frame.

Pa Rastarong was fast asleep on the living room window seat, the only place in the room sufficiently upholstered with pillows and padding to make a comfortable resting place. Mr. Weathereye sat down on the nearest stool and waited patiently while I shook Pa awake. When he was sitting upright, bleary eyes fastened on his unexpected guest, Mr. Weathereye told him about the letter.

"They can't do that!" spluttered Pa. "He's the only one I've got here at home!"

"It doesn't matter," said Mr. Weathereye. "Think about it. You learned the rules in school, just as we all did, now think about it."

Pa probably had learned the rules, but I doubt he'd thought about them since. He screwed up his face, trying to think. "Three categories of service," he said finally. "That's all I remember. And nothin' was said about life-duty when I took him on!"

He glared at Mr. Weathereye, who cocked his head and said soothingly, "You're right, of course. That's why I came along to tell you about the letter, because it sounds so unbelievable that Naumi could have been selected. It is true, though, and if you have questions about it, you can talk to Mr. Wyncamp."

"The teacher," said Pa in disgust.

"He sometimes is, yes," agreed Mr. Weathereye. "The Escort will be here on Valstat's Day with the papers for you to sign."

" 'Nif I don't?" Pa said, working up a semblance of mule-headedness, as he sometimes did.

"I suppose they'll disappear you," said Mr. Weathereye without emotion. "That's what usually happens to people who forget the oath of citizenship." He stood up, bowed briefly over his cane, then stumped to the front door, where I let him out.

"What do I need to do?" I asked, as I followed him down the path. "Like, pack things up? Or not?"

"Not," said Mr. Weathereye, examining the far horizon as though something very important might happen there at any minute. "Everything you need will be provided. You may take memorabilia that will fit into a box no longer, wider, or taller than the length of your hand from tip of middle finger to wrist, not counting fingernail if it protrudes."

The days went by all in a rush. The Escort came to the house.

Mr. Weathereye and Mr. Wyncamp attended as witnesses. The Escort paid over a lump sum to Pa, to compensate for the loss of my company, and Pa signed the papers saying he'd been properly informed of the legality of the selection. He even wept a bit, surprising himself almost as much as it surprised me and Mr. Weathereye. Crying wasn't Pa's kind of thing at all.

The Escort had a flier waiting outside the door, and as soon as the papers were signed, I took my box and my jacket and left, leaving the two witnesses to comfort Pa. I thought Mr. Weathereye would probably comfort him in no time by investing in the rain deflector. He'd invested in the information grabber, the elevator legs, and the grebble thresher before, so it was likely he'd stay in character.

I Am Margaret/on Earth

One morning I arrived at the college to find a note saying the Provost wanted to see me. Though I had no reason whatsoever to think this boded anything but good, I confess to an attack of the frets, and I took an extra five minutes to comb my hair and put on a face that wasn't apprehensive. The Provost's name was Dione Esedre, and I had met her at gatherings of the college: a very cool person, very efficient.

"Margaret Bain," she said when I entered, just a tiny hint of question in her voice, as though to make sure she had the right person.

"Yes, Provost," I said.

She gave a little sigh and riffled through several papers on her desk. It was one of the conceits of ACoLaP that the people there, both teachers and students, still read words from paper; it was a truism that very few other people did.

"Four members of your class have been selected to attend a meeting that's being held at the local Dominion Offices. It's a meeting of diplomats, high officers in Earthgov, plus a few Gentherans. They want a few advanced students to sit in, on the theory that you'll all be working for them in the next few years and will do a better job if you know what's going on. Not sure that I agree, but it's not my place to argue." She emitted a smile brief enough to indicate she might be jesting, not long enough to indicate real humor.

"I'm very flattered," I said.

"Don't be, not yet. Here's the secrecy oath you'll be required to sign. Don't think it's just a matter of routine. It's deadly serious, and unless you're absolutely sure you can abide by it, don't sign it."

I remember clearly only one phrase from the document, which was ". . . on penalty of death," but that one was enough to make me look up, startled.

"I said it was serious," she remarked with another of those lightning smiles, a mere lip-writhe of amusement.

"I . . . I'm pretty good at keeping my mouth shut," I said, thinking twenty-some years of perfecting the trait had succeeded remarkably well.

"If you're sure you can, go ahead and sign it. I confess, I'd love to attend myself. I've never seen a Gentheran."

"You probably wouldn't," I said without thinking. "They wear suits and helmets. Nobody ever sees them."

She looked momentarily offended, then relaxed. "Of course. I'd forgotten that you were on Mars."

The upshot was, I signed, and she gave me an identity card that had a password under a seal and told me where to go on the following day and not to mention it to anyone, not my parents, not my boyfriend, if I had one, or anyone else. I really would have loved to tell Bryan, but he was working that evening, so I was saved from temptation.

The following day, I went as directed, presented my card, seal intact, and was fed through a whole series of identification procedures involving eyes, fingers, biometric, physiometric, how I smelled, and the like. Finally, I was shown to a seat at the back of a windowless room containing a large conference table and chairs plus the usual side table holding drinks: nova-coffee, nova-tea, bottled Swish in three flavors that differed only in color. Each chair was equipped with a full-sense viewer, very advanced technology that I'd been exposed to only a time or two. I was gawking at the viewers when three of my fellow students came in, we nodded to one another without speaking, and they sat down at some distance. At first I was surprised to see them, for these very elite students were not particularly good at their studies. They made error after error in class (many of which our teachers simply ignored); on written tests they always scored incredibly well (adjective chosen for precision, in that no one believed the scores were real). They had a sneering attitude toward students from less exalted backgrounds than their own very moneyed ones. All of them had family members among the Directors of the College, and that probably explained why they were here. I had bested all of them scholastically, which had led more than one of them to advise me, sneeringly, that my test scores didn't matter, for the "way things were," they would succeed, and I would fail. So far as I could tell, none of them had any experience whatsoever with the way things really were, having been untouched by reality since birth.

Within moments, doors at the other side of the room opened, and several humans and Gentherans (small, as I'd been told, and in suits and helmets) filed in and were seated. I was so amused to see that the Gentherans were seated in elevator chairs, permitting them to rise to the level of the table, that for a moment I did not recognize that one of the ascending chairs held someone I knew: Chili Mech! She was staring at me.

I grinned and waved. She said something to her neighbor, lowered her chair, and came over to me. "Margaret, is that you?"

"Chili. It's so good to see you! I had no idea you'd be here."

"You must be one of the ACoLaP students! Good for you. You always said you were going to learn every language in the universe."

"If I said anything that egotistical, I was very young and foolish."

Chili said, "I must get back. They're going to convene. In case you didn't know it, Margaret, this is a meeting of both Dominion Central Authority and Earthgov Executive Council. You'll understand why when you hear what's going on. Can we get together during the break?"

"Certainly," I said. "I'd love to."

When the roll was called, I noted there were representatives present from the colonies, Chili being the one from Mars. The Gentheran names were real tongue twisters, the first speaker being named Sister someone. It sounded a little like Lorpa, if one accepted that there was something subtly wrong with both the L and the R. We were not allowed to record or take notes, but nothing had been said about not remembering, and I have a very good memory.

Sister Lorpa spoke Earthian very clearly, in a high, sweet voice, starting without preamble to describe something called the "ghyrm." I recognized this as a Cantardene word meaning "eater." She said Gentherans and Earthians had become aware of these creatures when several hundred human bondslave miners on Cantardene were killed by them.

"At the time," she said, "we considered this to be some kind of plague that would affect only people on Cantardene. We were shortly disabused of this idea when several humans in transit to Chottem from bondslave planets farther into Mercan space were also slain by the ghyrm. Since that time we have bent all our resources toward discovering what the ghyrm are and where they come from. Thus far, we have had virtually no success in answering the latter question."

She went on to tell us what her people had learned about the ghyrm. It was not a bacterium or virus, it was an organism that could take various shapes or appear to do so. Genetically, it was all one creature, and perhaps it had been cloned, though it appeared and acted differently in different circumstances or, possibly, when directed by some outside agency. It could take over a person or invade a small area and move rapidly from person to person to wipe out all human life as it had done on Cranesroost, where Settlements Two, Five, and Six were wiped out.

We students were not the only ones who exclaimed at this. Evidently, almost no one in the room had known about Cranesroost. The speaker asked us to put on the viewers, which we did. Silence fell. Someone, somewhere, turned them on.

The technology was beyond anything I had experienced. I actually became the person on Cranesroost. I was a settlement captain who knew all about the place. The settlement lay just within a hillside grove of miraculous trees, huge as cathedral towers and as bulky, effective barriers to wind and the worst of weather. Just outside the grove, the glittering sand of the lakeside sloped toward silver water, placid in moonlight, riffling recurrently as though from something breathing on the farther shore, perhaps something very large, one titanic arm pillowing its head as relaxed lips puffed, and puffed, and puffed, touching the quivering surface with the gentlest of exhalations.

I was the captain of the settlement, standing at the edge of the lake near a roost of cranes that appeared almost real in this quiet light. I knew the children had built them out of bits of wood and pipe, an evocation of times long gone, a time when cranes really lived, danced, mated, hatched, brought forth young. Seeing them in the moonlight, I, the captain, almost believed in them, or something like them. The Cranesroost settlement had seen birds, or things like birds. They didn't fly, but they ran very fast, and they ate the fishy things in lakes as cranes no doubt had done. We settlers called them fishers and hadn't learned much about them yet, for winter was pressing, and shelter had to come first. Observing birds would no doubt be a pleasant pastime in later years.

Unknown things were worrisome, the captain thought, even though the Gentherans gave the planet a good bill of health. There were native creatures, yes, some of them poisonous but none of them ferocious or sneaky or particularly intelligent, being more of the "I'll leave you alone, you leave me alone" variety. The captain relied on this when he had sent the scouting team out early that morning, but if there was nothing dangerous out there, they should have been back.

So he stood watch, waiting for three men and one woman who trekked around the lake to the north. Their orders had been to go as far as they could go by noon, then turn around and come back by suppertime. Suppertime was over hours ago. Suppertime was a dimming memory.

"Captain?"

"Who?"

"Me, sir. Gruder."

"I haven't seen a thing, Gruder."

"This isn't like Kath."

The captain snorted. "It isn't like any of them. You should be getting some sleep."

"The little one keeps waking, asking for his ma. I keep telling him she'll be home in the morning. Do we send out a search party, or not?"

"I don't know. I thought four of them was enough to be safe, you know. Four pairs of eyes. Eight strong legs and arms."

"What are you thinking?"

"I don't know what to think. Maybe they saw something a little farther off and kept going after noon. Then, coming back, the dark caught up to them. Maybe they're lying up there along the bank, just waiting for light."

"Let's hope so."

"Let's, and if they did, damn 'em, they can stand watch for the next hundred nights. Worrying us like this . . . what's that?"

"Where?"

"Down there, north. Along the lakeside. I saw light, fire. Like a torch. See it, there it goes again!"

We watched, nearly hypnotized as the one spark was repeatedly occluded by trees, then steadied, became two, then four, moving slowly in a line along the shore. The captain sighed. "I guess they got tired. Decided to rest before they made the trip back. Or maybe they're carrying something. Go on back to bed, Gruder. She won't be here for another hour, at least."

The other man yawned widely, took a deep, relieved breath, and returned to his cabin, one of the first ones built, the nearest to being finished. In the little paddock alongside the house a goat bleated, briefly disturbed in her rest. The captain stayed where he was, though he sat down on a stump to rest his legs. The sparks continued their arc around the edge of the lake, growing in brightness, then disappearing behind the nearer trees and emerging again, four of them, bright as stars.

"Welcome," he said at last, when the missing four stumble up from the shore.

"Captain?" said Kath.

"Yes. And Gruder's been up, too, waiting for you. Where in the hell did you all get to?"

"Brought you a present," said Kath. "Something we found." She approached, holding something out in one hand. We all peered at it.

"What's that? Beads? On a thong or a thread? Now who in heaven's name put that together on this world?"

Kath shrugged as I took it from her. "It was just lying there, on the bank, on top of a rock. Like it had been put there for us to find. Red bead, yellow one, blue one, a couple black ones. Funny, huh?"

"So, what kept you?"

She rolled her head on her neck as though it hurt. "We just . . . I guess we lay down for a while. Must have fallen asleep. We're really tired." She yawned, her eyes rolling away from me in the torchlight, whites showing all around like a frightened animal.

"Kath?" I said urgently. "You all right."

"Oh, sure, Captain. Sure. Just tired. See you in the morning."

I, we, the captain, glanced once more at the thing in our hands. A mere thread, like a bit of string, with half a dozen beads on it. Now who in heaven's name . . . Well, it didn't matter. Let it go. We could talk about it in the morning . . .

We felt only a few moments of what followed before someone, blessedly, shut off the viewer. There were exclamations, cries of distress, a general murmur that slowly quieted.

Sister Lorpa was still on her feet. "The beads were actually a ghyrm, perhaps more than one. We have established that the ghyrm take over the minds of the persons who carry it or them. We infer the ghyrm are directed by a reasoning force that may be a part of the ghyrm race or something quite outside it. This is pure speculation. We don't know."

Someone asked how the Cranesroost infestation had been discovered.

"In settlement Six, the last person infested woke to find everyone dead and the thing around her throat. Though close to death, she was able to com the neighboring village, to describe the thing, to say she could not get it off her and that it was killing her. The person she reached followed standard emergency procedure: That is, he made no effort at rescue and informed Dominion immediately. Dominion personnel in noncontact suits found everyone in the three villages dead. They scouted the areas around the surviving villages and found nothing like the necklace of small beads mentioned in the com. From the captains of the destroyed villages, they retrieved the sensory recorders, one of which you have just experienced."

Someone said indignantly, "Cranesroost was off the wormtrails!

Its location was known only to the settlers and to Dominion! How did the ghyrm find it?"

This led to charges and countercharges, back and forth, much heat, little light, and the Chairman put an end to the discussion.

Sister Lorpa concluded, "We have had some breakthroughs. We have succeeded in capturing ghyrm, caging them so they cannot escape, and habituating some of our members to their presence. These captive ghyrm are infallible locators of others of their kind. Certain members of the Siblinghood have been trained to hunt ghyrm, using a captive ghyrm as 'finders.' They are very successful on a planetary surface, though all efforts to use them in space have failed."

That item disposed of, the Chairman introduced an elderly woman as "a member of the Siblinghood, Lady Badness." I saw one of my fellow students silently convulsed at this introduction, though from the look of the lady's face, amusement was not appropriate.

She introduced herself as the chairman of a biracial committee of Gentherans and Humans that had spent some forty-odd Earth-years trying to devise a nontraumatic method of depopulating Earth in order to prevent the final collapse of the biome on the one hand and a visit by ISTO slaughterers on the other. She spoke of the colonies as "emergency, last-ditch attempts to guarantee human survival and the survival of thousands of species of Earth organisms in case the slaughterers could not be forestalled."

She said she had several points to make. I set myself to remember them.

Firstly, she said Earth's governments had been warned that depopulation was an absolute necessity for Earth's survival. Secondly, she said the government had justified its inaction by quoting the standard statistical projections indicating that population growth was slowing, that as soon as all parts of the world had equal economic opportunities, population growth would stop, and total population might even drop. Thirdly, she admitted the standard projections were irrefutable but totally irrelevant, as human population had exceeded the number Earth could support over a century ago. Even while ice caps melted, while prehistoric aquifers dried up and the lands over those aquifers began to subside, governments had refused to acknowledge that humans were responsible. Only when aliens arrived in starships to tell them the end had come did governments try to deal with the situation, and by then, it was too late.

She said, "Outshipment, as you know, has slightly slowed but failed to stop the process."

Several people around the table uttered angry variations on "We know all that," rather loudly and, I thought, rudely.

Lady Badness merely stared at them until they subsided. "Of course you do. So do I, but we're putting it into the record one more time, just in case at some future time someone questions what we've said and thought and decided. This brings us to the fourth and final point. We must choose between two repellent futures:

"A, we do nothing, and the ISTO slaughterers will kill over ninety percent of all of the people now alive on Earth. I have seen records of that process. The best one can say for it is that it doesn't take long. It is both quicker and bloodier than the demise of Cranesroost. It is not a process I wish on any population, however, no matter how pigheaded that population may be.

"B, we impose the solution Dominion and the Siblinghood have been working on since Dominion was formed: the sterilization of ninety-nine point something-or-other percent of Earth's population."

I happened to be looking across the table at Chili. I saw her shoulders heave as she took a deep breath. I glanced at my fellow students. They looked outraged. I had been numb since the Cranesroost experience, and I stayed that way.

Lady Badness went on:

"Gentheran Research Laboratories has completed testing of the planetary sterilant. It will kill no one. It will simply make ninety-nine-plus percent of the fertile persons on Earth live out their lives without progeny. A small, random fraction of human beings has a genetic resistance to the sterilant. This genetic resistance is found among all subgroups of the population. There will be no genocide of any cult, culture, or coloration."

I sat with my mouth open, unable to believe what I was hearing. Around the table were murmurs and outcries. My fellow students were now whispering to one another.

"Those affected by the sterilant will produce a pheromonic by-product attractive only to other sterilized persons. There will be no other changes. People will continue to 'fall,' as they say, in love, but it will be the sterile with the sterile, the fertile with the fertile. Natural life cycles will go on, but very few people will have children.

"Today our only decision is to choose: A or B."

The Chairman spoke: "We will have no more discussion today. We act, or ISTO acts. Suffering is minimized if we act. Slaughter is certain if we do not. Will someone move the question? . . . I recognize Maintainer Chili Mech."

Chili moved that the Gentherans be directed to go ahead with the sterilant. The Chairman called for a second and got it. The vote was yes. Someone asked when it would take place. Sister Lorpa said within the year. Then nobody said anything for what seemed to be a very long time, and the Chairman announced a break for refreshment.

Chili came over and led me to a little table against the wall. All three of my fellow students had Lady Badness trapped in a far corner and were talking at her, too volubly, I thought, too disrespectfully. Chili followed my line of sight and shook her head, very slightly. "That's not a good idea," she said.

"I know," I murmured. "But it's very much in character for them. Usually, if they don't like something, the something ceases to exist."

"Really," she said. "Wait for me, Margaret. I'll get us something to drink."

I saw her speaking briefly to a couple of guards, who went to Lady Badness's rescue. Chili returned with the Gentheran, Sister Lorpa, whom I recognized by the insignia on her helmet. I rose and gave the half bow that is considered polite among Gentherans, saying, "It is rude of us to drink when you are denied refreshment."

"Not at all," she said, in that high, sweet voice. "Our suits provide whatever hydration we need. I understand you are here as an observer, under a vow of silence. You were much surprised by what you heard?"

I said, yes, I was, though I understood the reasons. What I was actually thinking at that moment was whether it had ever been important to me to have children.

She sat down with us, and Chili asked her what the next step would be.

"It's all been planned," she replied. "First, we'll mount a saturation publicity campaign announcing that population stasis has been reached. Since this has been forecast by politicians and proliferators for the past century, it will surprise no one and mollify many. We will announce that the population has crested and is now beginning to decline, very slowly. Newssheets will cover this event. There will be interviews with prominent pronatalist officials and religious leaders telling us how gratified they are. Our polls indicate that virtually all humans will be delighted with the news.

"At the end of the first year, population will indeed have declined by between one and two percent. We will issue frequent glowing reports on how well this is going. We do not plan any outreach effort among those who are infertile, but every childbirth will serve to identify those who are immune. The immunes must be provided with intensive reeducation. Meantime, the two-three-four rule will continue to be observed. Outshipment will continue."

"Must it?" I asked, a little fretfully, I'm afraid.

Sister Lorpa's faceplate turned toward me. "Your government has contracts with the Federation and the Combine. Unless you want a war of retribution, those contracts must be honored . . ."

"Well then, if outshipment is to proceed, will intensive education really be necessary?" I wondered aloud.

She did not answer, for we were being approached by a tall, dark man dressed in velvets, brocades, and gems.

"Sister Lorpa," he said, half bowing.

"Delegate from Chottem, Von Goldereau d'Lornschilde," she said, turning toward me as if to introduce me.

He did not wait for this. "May I once again plead with your people to find my kinswoman, the heiress of Bray! She would be an adult woman now, some twenty Earth-years old! She is needed in Bray, and if she no longer lives, then evidence of that is needed in Bray! Our economic future depends upon it!"

Sister Lorpa said expressionlessly, "We are aware of your concerns, Delegate. Be assured, if we can assist in finding your kinswoman, we will do so."

He half bowed again and nodded to Chili, totally ignoring me.

"You asked about the need for education," Sister Lorpa said, when he had departed. "Delegate d'Lornschilde is from Chottem. He is a descendent of the founders of that colony, and he is claimant to the estate of Stentor d'Lorn, which, in truth, represents a large part of the gross planetary wealth. He pretends he doesn't care about the estate. At every meeting he urges us to find Stentor's grand-daughter and return her to Bray! It is all pretence and bluster; his real interest is in finding evidence of her death so he can claim the estate, for, like the rest of his family, he is interested in nothing but money and power. Despite the fact that he and all his kinfolk had to leave Earth because Earth had been destroyed by money and power, he has already asked the Dominion Central Authority for permission to exceed the population limits set for Chottem, excusing this on the basis that construction creates many of their jobs, which means more profit for him.

"Earth listened to that 'we have to make room' kind of nonsense for hundreds of years, and look where Earth is now! That man has taken no lesson from it. Human beings are incapable of learning any-thing outside their own lifetimes! We fight against this disability con-stantly! Oh, if only . . ." She sighed. "Well, 'if only' butters no beans, as you humans used to say."

"Sister, you're not going to tell the people of Earth about the ster-ilant, are you?" I asked, unthinking. I put my hand over my mouth. "Oh, forgive me . . ."

"There is nothing to forgive. No. We will not tell them. Sibling-hood has a definition of evil that our group has tried to keep in mind during our deliberations. *'To cause any creature willful pain is evil; to pretend that another sentient creature cannot feel pain is evil; to enjoy the pain of another, sentient or insentient, is ultimate evil.'* We would be causing willful pain if we told them; we would be committing evil if we allowed the slaugh-ter of mankind through our own inaction. The population drop will not be sudden. Those who die will be those one would expect to die, the aged, victims of accidents, the chronically ill. The human popula-tion will dwindle gradually over the next century, slightly over one percent of the original population per year, with only a tiny fraction of that number being born. At some point, when living conditions have improved, we will set the record straight for future genera-tions."

I asked, "What about those who want to have children and can't?"

The mirrored hood turned in my direction, showing me my own troubled face. "Some couples may be disappointed not to have children, but in most cases they will not speak of it, and neither will anyone else. It has been a long time since any pregnant woman showed herself in public on Earth. Since the plague, the war, and the Lifer-Limiter uprising of '81 and '82, people on Earth have not spoken of reproductive matters except behind closed doors, and very rarely even then."

She was perfectly right. People would not speak of it. They would be glad to have a little more water in their ration, a little different food to eat. Perhaps two "admit-to-the-park" permission slips each year instead of only one.

Sister Lorpa left us, and I asked Chili something that had been on my mind since the session. "What is this Siblinghood everyone refers to?"

She frowned, shaking her head. "They don't define it. One gets the impression it's a kind of lodge or secret society that does very technical, scientifically advanced work. It has both humans and Gentherans as members, and it is alleged to have members from other races as well. Their financing is secret. Their work is secret. When they have something to offer, they offer it. They're the ones who found out why mankind always destroys his environment . . ."

"What?" I demanded in astonishment. "There's a known cause?"

Chili gritted her teeth. "Margaret, forget I mentioned it! Remember, you're under a vow of silence. Yes, there is a reason, but it's not to be mentioned. You may learn of in time."

She returned to the table as the group reconvened, and several Gentherans spoke of the plans for rehabilitation of Earth. Much of it would be done by the Gentheran-Human Rehabilitation Corps, a body organized by the Siblinghood (here they were again). As soon as five percent of housing space opened up in any city, people would be moved into that space from suburbs of that city. The suburbs, when emptied, would be razed, highways leading to them would be removed, the land would be reseeded and reforested. These would be enormous jobs, so we were told, that would offer full employment to anyone wishing to work. Merely replanting desert provinces such as those formerly known as Brazil, Canada, Central Africa, and Indonesia would occupy several centuries' worth of effort.

Since cities were more efficient and easier to maintain as habitat than extensive, land-consuming suburbs, they would continue to absorb smaller urbs until all of them were gone. As space opened up in the cities, dwellings would be consolidated, and buildings would be razed to create parklands within the cities themselves, so that no dwelling would be far from open, green space. Outside the cities, reclaimed land would not be farmed until the population had dropped to the point that some or all of the algae factories could be closed.

Eventually, dairy animals would be returned to Earth, they said, and the seas would be restocked with fish and other living things. "It is possible even whales may be restored in time," a Gentheran said, visibly moved by the idea. "We have the genetic information, and it is not beyond our capabilities. When natural space is restored, human people will be allowed to wander through it at will, so long as they do so on foot or on muscle-powered vehicles, taking with them only what they can carry. The use of destructive, noisy machinery for recreational purposes must become anathema to humans, as unthinkable as eating one's young."

We were referred to the reports and studies supporting the plan, and to the specifications for each separate area, available in the document department together with a timeline of the expected stages of rehabilitation. I was not allowed to see or receive the documents, of course, just as I was not allowed to take notes or speak with anyone about what I had learned. All very strange and frightening.

The most frightening part, however, came the following day. The other three students who had attended the meeting were not in class. It took me only a split second to decide it would be inappropriate to ask where they were. Later that day, the Provost sent for me, and I found her sitting at her desk, looking rather pale.

"You wanted to see me, Provost?"

"We have had a ... great loss," she said. "I wanted you, particularly, to know of it. It seems the others of your class who attended yesterday's meeting announced to one of the participants that they intended to tell the media what had occurred there."

I started to exclaim, and she put up her hand. "Please do not inadvertently mention anything that did occur."

I swallowed. "I would not do so, Provost. Perhaps my classmates thought the secrecy agreement did not . . . apply to them."

"No rule or standard has applied to them since birth," she said. "Great wealth breeds great arrogance, Margaret. Some months ago, each of the three was handpicked by the Directors to take junior but very important posts at Earthgov after graduation. If I were of a suspicious nature, I might guess that those three were picked to attend yesterday's meeting in order that their arrogance could be assessed under . . . controlled conditions."

"But . . . surely I wasn't picked for that reason."

"No," she said. "Someone else picked you, and before you ask, I am not to say who it was."

Though I had imagined Bryan's face if I told him what had happened, I was not about to commit suicide. I would, however, have given a great deal to have been enlightened. The thought that I, Margaret, had been picked by someone(s) to attend a meeting I couldn't talk about, that I, Margaret, knew what was going to happen to Earth, a secret known only to a handful of other people, was terrifying, and not the least of the terror was that there was no possible, ascribable reason why I should be involved at all!

I Am Ongamar/on Cantardene

Adille, the K'Famira, had said she would not wear the necklace again, yet it hung across her throat pouch the next day, seeming rather larger than before. She wore it the day after that, also, moving restlessly about the house as though something troubled her.

"Let's go for a walk," she demanded. We went out into the city, and I followed Adille's restless feet here and there, without direction, pausing wherever voices were raised or threatening gestures were made. A few days later, Adille dragged me to a public execution, which Adille had always sworn was only for rabble. I hid my face in my lap, winding my arms around my head to keep from hearing the accused screaming as his lower arms and legs were lopped off. It was not mere horror I was hiding from, it was the pain itself that I felt, no matter how I hid my eyes. The day after that we attended the baiting of a dozen traitors' families by wild klazaks, the sand of the arena running green and a dozen or more young K'Famira ululating from quivering pouches as the klazaks tore first the traitorous parents, then the young . . .

"Please don't make me go," I begged her the following day. "It hurts me, Great Lady. It hurts me to see people killed." I was taking a risk in saying it wasn't mere dislike, that it was torment? "I feel it . . . it hurts . . ."

"I know, I know," Adille said distractedly. "Of course,

yes, but I must . . . I must see it. Or something. Something different. Something new. I must . . ."

"You always said the executions were for the rabble," I cried. "Are we not rabble if we watch?"

"I don't know," Adille said, her mouths set in ugly lines. "But I must. I must. And it wants you with me."

Bargom disapproved of her wearing the necklace. He told Adille it was ruining her appearance, making her look old and tired. Several times he tried to take the necklace away, but he could not approach it. Each time he tried, he found himself headed out the door, away from it. In the end, he went out the door and simply kept going. During all this time, Adille complained that the beads grew heavier, until they achieved such a weight they could no longer be worn.

Then the sharing began. Adille explained it. She had to go out and find the things the necklace wanted to see, always in my company, then she had to return and lay hands upon the necklace to let it see the horrors through her memory. Mornings we went, and nights. Adille grew too weak to force me to go with her, but still she went alone, returning to lay hands upon the necklace, to which I was now inexorably drawn so that I, too, heard, saw, smelled everything. Years went by as Adille wandered, coming home each night to fall exhausted into bed, eating little, growing thinner with each day, while I eked out our existence by selling the ornaments of the house, then the furniture. The time came that Adille was seen watching something that should not have been watched by anyone. She had warned me that this might happen.

"It sends me places people aren't supposed to be. It makes me hide and watch, when no one is supposed to watch. It makes me climb walls, hide outside windows. I saw what my clan leader, Draug B'lanjo, did to the Omniont Ambassador. They sent his body to the Federation, claiming it had been done by the Hrass. I heard them talking. They want to stir trouble between the Omniont and the Hrass so they can take over the Hrass shipping routes."

"Doesn't that disturb you, Great Lady?" I asked. "The thing that happened to the Ambassador?"

"Him. Oh. I suppose it might have disturbed me if I hadn't been so worried about being seen."

I had always wondered if Adille felt anything at all for the victims she saw tortured and slain. Seemingly not.

She went on, "Someday, they will see me. Someday, I won't come home . . ."

And one day, she did not. Counting over the seasons I had been with Adille, I estimated it at somewhere between three and four Cantardene years. I myself was then seventeen, or eighteen.

The K'Famir who came to the house some days later told me to clean the house before Adille's father, Progzo, arrived to dispose of Adille's belongings. The necklace box lay on the dressing trough, and when I reached out to close the lid, the thing inside lashed out at me like a whip, wrapping itself around my arm. Frantically, I tried to pull it loose, to no avail, as it crawled across my body to plaster itself against my breast, seemingly rooted into the flesh. I could not escape the thing that had killed Adille. Because I had touched it, because I had lived in proximity to it, it had the same power over me it had had over her.

I was young and strong, however, which was lucky, for it took all my strength to bear the thing. Adille had made no provision for me, and her family did not want me. When the bondservant agency reclaimed me, the thing was wrapped against my skin, under my clothes, a bead or two showing at the throat or poking through a buttonhole. I wore a high-collared dress to hide it, and for a wonder, the bondage merchant did not require me to strip. I soon learned why. I had already been sold to House Mouselline as a seamstress, a creature to alter lingerie, a fitter who could work quietly and virtually unnoticed. I had had much experience at being unnoticed. Afterward I gained more.

The fitters, mostly Earthian, wore wigs of short gray hair that covered the lobes of their ears. The thinner of us had our bodies padded, and we were clad in sensible dark dresses, high-necked, ankle-length, and long-sleeved. Our feet were shod in shapeless shoes. We carried pincushions on our wrists and a measuring rod in one hand. It was claimed by House Mouselline that we were the heirs of an ancient Earth guild that had borne these symbols of craftsmanship through the centuries. Though rough and callused hands would have matched the rest of the image, our hands were, in fact, kept as soft as the fabrics we touched, for House Mouselline dealt in ultrasilk and vivilon and mazatec, all produced, so the labels said, on the Isles of Delight. At 250 credits or more a span, no one, not even Ephedra Mousselline herself, could afford their being snagged by some fitter's abraded knuckle.

Those Mercans who saw us, or more likely looked across us, saw human bolsters with lowered eyes and mouths full of pins: Miss This; Miss That; Miss Ongamar. The "Miss" was a courtesy title, a calculated oddity. Titles were not usually given to bondspeople, but in the intimacy of the fitting room, one did not want to disturb the mood of serene luxury by kicking or hitting a servant or even commanding them in the ugly lingua Mercan of the plantation. Fitters, therefore, were selected from among the few bondservants who were skilled at sewing and understood the language. They were spoken to with condescending politeness.

"Miss Ongamar, the Lady Mirabel wants three of the vivilon chemises, in violet and puce, and they need just a tuck under the lower arms." "Oh, Miss Ongamar, Princess Delibia has ordered the gold-mesh games gown by Verdul, and it needs an underdress by tomorrow afternoon. The Princess is green-fleshed, about a number four shade, so be sure you pick fabric to match." "Oh, Miss Ongamar, the Baron's plaything has ordered twelve pair of vivilon pantaloons, and they must be monogrammed with the Baron's crest over all four orifices."

Miss Ongamar's fingers nipped and pinned and basted. Her, my, hands darted. This to be seamed invisibly. That to be embroidered, very visibly. This to be let out just a bit, to drape a touch better over Dowager Queen Dagabon's ever-enlarging pouch; that to be taken in to fit the young neuter the Baron was currently amusing himself with. And when the showroom was closed and the workroom silent, even then I might be there, finishing up this little task or that one before going home.

Home. I actually had one.

One of the few privileges of being employed by House Mousselline was the housing allowance, actual money, to pay rent, to buy food. House Mousselline had no interest in maintaining a bondslave dormitory and kitchen. Those who worked for the house were expected to fend for themselves. The allowance was small; for the innovative, it was sufficient. So it was I went out the back service door into the Baka Narak, which I translated to myself, "Allee Sensual," and turned left to the corner. Another left would take me into the turmoil and clutter of Bak-Zandig-g'Shadup, "Street of Many Worlds," which was thronged with people of many races at all hours of the day and night. If I turned right, however, the way led down a short block to the service tunnel, and down the tunnel to the Crafter's and Seamer's Residential Compound for Bond and Free, where most of the employees lived. I, however, did not enter the compound. Instead, I went along the narrow service walk that ran beside it and into the cobbled courtyard at the rear, where the refuse bins were kept. Past their lidded bulks, next to the rear wall and the alley gate, a narrow door opened into home.

This had been space no one else wanted: unrentable, unusable, exactly the kind of space I had searched for since my bondage to House Mouselline. I had heard two fitters speaking of it, regretting that it would not do, for it had no heat, it had no light. I had made a modest offer for it, and the offer had been accepted. Within the limits imposed by my circumstances, the place was perfect. Inside were stone walls worn smooth by centuries and a stone floor old as time. Huge, ancient pillars supported the crushing weight of the upper floors. This had been the stable of a castle once, a monstrous fortification that had guarded the coast of a planet-bound people in the days of the last Regency, before the K'Famir had conquered the Welbeck people, slaughtered them (when they proved to be reluctant and untrustworthy as slaves), and taken over their world. Now the ocean had receded some distance, and the stable was almost a cellar, though it had kept a tiny window overlooking the enclosed garden. The grille allowed only an obstructed view of fruit tree branches, but the fresh, flower-scented air was welcome.

I shook my lantern to be sure there was fuel in it before lighting it. The place had at one time had water piped in for the animals. I had found the pipes, had worked away at them for a season with twists of wire, dragging out the rust and scale, making them workable again. I had found an old coal stove in an alley, had taken it apart with chisel and hammer, had carried it to my lair piece by

piece and put it together again. It sat under the round hole where
the flue of one just like it had no doubt inserted itself a hundred
years before. Best of all, the place had a little, low, windowless
room, no more than a closet, with a door that locked. The closet
room was where I left it in the evenings, when I had to go out. If I
carried it all day, I could not carry it all night, and the thing seemed
to realize that. This evening I went to that room first, took off my
outer clothing and detached it from me, shutting my mind against
the sound, half growl, half sucking whine, when I pulled it away. It
writhed into the darkest corner and did not move, even when I
fetched water for it, for if it grew dry, it chafed me, and the abra-
sions burned like acid.

I poked up the fire in the stove, filled the kettle and set it over the
flame, dragged the washtub into the middle of the floor, and took off
my daily disguise. The gray wig first, then the padding around my
body. As soon as the water was hot, I poured a sufficiency into the
tub, stepped in, and gave myself the nightly sponge bath that washed
away its residue, a slight stickiness that smelled of mold. When I had
emptied that tub down the floor drain, I heated the kettle again, and
yet again to give me enough water to sit in, legs over one towel-
padded side, head leaning against the other. It was the best time of
day: the feeling that time had stopped, the warmth of the stove on my
skin, the softness of the perfumed water. House Mousselline sold essences to put in bathwater; Miss Ongamar had become an expert
petty thief.

Bathtime was also time to review what I had heard during the day:

A neuter talking to another as it tried on ribbon trousers, discussing its patron's purchase, from the Omnionts, of new technology that
detected ship-shields. "They're giving him an award for inventing
it?" Crow of laughter.

A sterile female speaking of the breeding wife of her consort.
"The stupid plassawokit can't do a thing but lay eggs! It's a wonder
she doesn't drop them in the public street."

A trader's wife telling the delightful story about her husband completely fooling buyers and charging them triple for merchandise. "Ridiculous Gentherans in their shiny little suits. No more brains than a
glabbitch."

I remembered everything, making cryptic notes so I would not forget. The cracked mirror I had taken from a trash bin let me examine my face, running my fingers along the pain lines, noting the dark circles that surrounded my eyes. I bore no scars, but there were other signs of the burden I had carried all these years. Even now, while I sat here in the comfortable warmth of my own place, it could reach out to touch me, its touch like fire.

When I was ready to leave my lair, I appeared much thinner. My hair was now curled at the sides of my head, like a mane. I had sprayed my legs in one of the currently fashionable colors, and they peeked seductively from the slits in the long, full trousers, topped with a multicolored, sparkling jacket discarded by a humanoid patron, expertly mended by myself. My face was entirely different, the eyes wider and brighter, the green-painted lips much fuller, while across my forehead and back across the center of my skull extended the bony protrusion of the K'vasti people, a humanoid race akin to the Frossians, who frequented the pleasure quarter both as buyers and bought. House Mouselline sold clothing, but it also sold cosmetic prostheses, and I had acquired an armamentarium of parts: noses, ears, forehead and jaw growths, mouthfuls of various teeth, as well as mittens and gloves that counterfeited the hands of a dozen races. I could make myself up to be a K'vasti, a Frossian, a Hrass. I had been all of these and a dozen others. I had found it necessary to be each and every one of them to find the things it wanted.

Sometimes I became virtually invisible, a nonentity clad in gray robes, my gray skin marred by oozing eruptions caused by exposure to the charbic root used to fumigate dwellings. Sometimes I emerged as a creature anatomically unlike myself, the effects managed by prostheses and skillful dressing. Sometimes I went out as myself, or almost myself, a humanoid that got itself up to appear attractive in order to be an acceptable client in the places I sometimes had to go. Or, as tonight, a K'Vasti who would be welcome in the secret quarter, where creatures with certain tastes congregated, where tonight, as every night, something quite dreadful would likely happen within my sight and hearing.

From the courtyard the alley gate gave access to one of the twisting, narrow streets that tunneled toward the pleasure quarter. I walked freely, as might any one of the various races who thronged the area, four or five different sexes, some who had no gender at all, some bond, some free. Half a hundred eating houses were scattered on the near edge of the quarter, serving the foods of a hundred planets, several of them not only edible by humans and K'Vasti but deliciously so. Eating was my first intention. I would enter the quarter after I had eaten, but only as a last resort, if I could not come up with something to share with it in any other way.

Ahead of me, back against the wall, a Hrass huddled, the way they did, always appearing frightened to death. Possibly with good reason. Moved by an inexplicable urge, I went to stand behind it.

"You are Hrass," I said in the creature's own tongue.

"Soooo," it replied, noncommittal.

I shifted to the K'Vasti dialect. "Can you understand me?"

"Soooo!" An affirmative.

"I have something to tell the Hrass. Earlier this year, Draug B'lanjo of the K'famir killed the Omniont Ambassador. He sent the body to the Omnionts, saying the Hrass had done the killing. Draug B'lanjo did this because he wants to take over the Hrass shipping routes."

I turned on my heel and left him. If he talked to the wrong people, they would be looking for a K'vasti. Therefore, I must remember to burn the K'vasti prosthesis as soon as I got home, but not before, for the sharing had to be done every night before midnight, and today had produced nothing usable: no new scandals murmured across my bowed head, no crimes of violence or passion described while I stitched. No corruption uncovered or pretenses betrayed while I listened. So far as Bak-Zandig-g'Shadup was concerned, today might almost have been Eden, and therefore useless to me. Any daytime Eden had to be followed by a nighttime hell, with me doing as Adille had once done: walking the pain path, the horror road, the tortuous routes toward the terrible.

The thing fed on blood, pain, and death. If it knew where these things were, or would be, it would send me there. Sometimes, in the middle of the day, it would squeeze me, tighter and tighter, until I could not breathe, bringing me to the very edge of suffocation, in order to relish my panic.

"Miss Ongamar, are you quite all right?" Lady Ephedra would ask.

"Oh, quite, Lady Ephedra. A spasm of indigestion, I think. Nothing severe."

"You looked quite ashen there for a moment. Would you like to go home?"

I could not afford to lose a day's allowance, as Ephedra Mouselline knew very well. The words seemed kind, but the intent was unmistakably minatory, and the thing relished this as well.

In those short times, each day when I was not at the command of it or Lady Ephedra, I sometimes thought of my own life and future. The time would come when my years of bondage were completed. Release from the thing was probably not possible after so long a time, but as my time of release approached, if I could encounter someone human or Gentheran, I could warn them. I had seen humans and Gentherans in the pleasure quarter. They were always closely watched by steel-helmeted security officers. I could not legitimately speak to a human as a bondslave, but I could, perhaps, as a K'Vasti, assuming my disguise would fool the officers.

If such an opportunity ever came, I would not ask for help for myself. I was as guilty as the worst of those I had observed. I knew that purposeful watching was in every respect as evil as the torture itself. Peering into the darkness of pain was the equivalent of inflicting pain. Watching torture was the equivalent of agreeing to torment. Making a spectacle of it was equivalent to doing the torture oneself. Yes. Whether the torture was real or only apparent, the watcher was guilty, for the watcher chose to see it, thereby creating an appetite. My pursuit of agony made me as heinous and depraved as those who committed it. No matter that I did it to save my life, or perhaps only continue what passed for my life, it was evil.

It would be better for me to kill myself than to continue as I was. Of all the choices I might make, that was the only good one, and I was determined to take the thing with me when I did it. I did not have the right to leave life with this duty unperformed, but I would hang on only until I could warn someone.

I Am Gretamara/on Chottem

One evening, as we sat on the porch of the Gardener's house, watching the Gibbekot playing with Sophia, I wondered aloud what had happened to Benjamin Finesilver, her father.

The Gardener shook her head slowly and sadly. "You know that Mariah expected her father to send a doctor from the city of Bray. D'Lorn had hired a guide, a man named Bogge, who actually knew the way here, but shortly before the doctor was due to leave Bray, Benjamin Finesilver arrived at Stentor d'Lorn's door. His carriage contained Mariah's body, wrapped in cerements.

"Benjamin was sobbing, Stentor was blind with fury. Had Benjamin not been so obviously torn by grief, Stentor would likely have killed him on the spot.

"'Was there no help for her?' Stentor cried out.

"'Only the Gardener,' said Benjamin.

"'The WHAT?' demanded Stentor.

"'The . . . local wisewoman, midwife kind of person,' Benjamin said. 'Everyone told Mariah to go to her, but Mariah wouldn't go. She said you were sending a doctor from Bray . . .'

"'And what had this woman to say?'

"Benjamin looked up, confused. 'To say? Nothing. Mariah never went to her.'

" 'Wasn't she summoned when Mariah was giving birth?'

" 'The Gardener can't be summoned, sir. She is not . . . not a mere person. One has to go to the Gardener, not the other way round.' " The Gardener fell silent, her eyes following Sophia.

"I am surprised Benjamin knew that much," I said.

"I doubt that Benjamin did know it until after Mariah was dead. Certainly it was more than Stentor could accept," said the Gardener. "Benjamin tried to explain that the women of the town had tried their best, but Mariah would not take their advice. Then Stentor asked about the child. Benjamin had no more wit than to say, 'I did not wish to endanger a newborn upon the road, so I left her in safety with the Gardener, sir . . .'

"And that was the end of Benjamin Finesilver, Gretamara. His departure from life went unnoticed save by several faithful and tongue-less servants of Stentor d'Lorn who were ordered to see him on his way. The following day, while Stentor was locked in his chambers, raging with grief, Bogge, the wanderer he had hired to take the doctor to Swylet, came to the palace and was turned away by the gateman. 'He doesn't need you to take the doctor. It's too late for the doctor. His daughter's body has already been placed in the tomb of her family.'

"Bogge was uncertain what propriety demanded of him in such a case. 'Should I speak with the Lord? I have already spent some of the money he paid me . . .'

" 'If I were you, I'd stay away for a time,' said the gateman. 'Likely the Lord doesn't want to be reminded of it. As for the money, it was probably little enough. I'll tell him you came and offered.'

"And so the gateman did, sometime later, after Bogge had departed for some other place. Only then did Stentor d'Lorn realize the consequences of his haste in disposing of his daughter's husband. Benjamin would have known the way to Swylet. Bogge had claimed to know the way, but the gateman knew neither where Bogge had gone nor when he would return. None of the wanderers currently in Bray knew of Swylet or Bogge.

"Since that time, Stentor has sent his agents here and there in fruitless searches for a mountain place known as Swylet. The name does not appear on any map known to the archivists; it is not mentioned in any account cited by explorers-cum-amateur-geographers."

"How do you know this?" I asked.

"I was there," said the Gardener. "I needed to know, for Sophia's sake, and I could not know truly unless I was there."

"You could not know what he was thinking?" I asked.

The Gardener shook her head. "Except as his actions betrayed his thought, no. Almost all humans are at least partly my people, but not he. He is as dark to me as a K'Famir or a Frossian. I do not know what he thinks or feels, but I know he has not given up the search. He has willed everything to his granddaughter, setting aside only a sizable reward for whatever person shall return her to Bray."

I shivered at the fate of Sophia's father and the darkness that dwelt within her grandfather, and I thought it was as well that only the Gardener and I knew where the heiress of Bray might be found.

I Am Naumi/on Thairy

When I was taken for life-service, the Escort helped me aboard a small flier and directed me to take the seat nearest the single window.

"Flown before, boy?"

"No, sir."

"Well, first time is always memorable. From that seat you'll get a good long look at Thairy from the route we're going."

"Where are we going?" I wondered, as the words left my lips, if I was even allowed to ask questions.

"Academy," the Escort replied. "You're being taken directly to the academy at Point Zibit. That's across Gentheren country from here. You ever met a Gentheren?"

"No, sir."

The man laughed. "Well, of course not, and neither have I, nor are we likely to. You just settle yourself back there. If you start to feel sick to your stomach, tell me right away."

"Yes, sir."

The flier went gently upward, the Escort glancing back occasionally to see whether I was going to be all right or not. Not that he'd hold it against me if I wasn't, but I supposed washing out the flier wasn't one of his favorite ways to end the working day.

I amazed myself by feeling exhilarated. Excited, in a nice way, and eager to look down on Bright, so tiny, like the little toy village I remembered having . . . no, seeing somewhere. No, it was one I'd imagined, when I was a child. Strange. I didn't really remember having it, just . . . knowing about it. The toy village moved away from beneath us as we followed the road, the one I had never followed farther than the quick route to the swimming hole. It wound over little hills, past tiny farms with toy barns, and as we climbed higher, whitish dots appeared in the fields. Cows, maybe, though they seemed too large. After a while the road began to twist back and forth like a serpent, we went steeply upward, and I was looking down on mountains. Every now and then a house roof winked sun in my eye or a stretch of narrow river glinted silver amid the endless carpet of trees.

We went higher yet, crossing a great cracked slab of red cliffs onto a tableland even more thickly forested than below. There the trees were interrupted by wide streams, sizable lakes and towns where piers thrust out into the water. Suddenly there was only water. What I'd seen earlier hadn't been lakes at all. They'd been . . . inlets, that's all, inlets. This was the lake. Or maybe it was a sea. Only seas weren't high up, like this. Seas were down in bottomlands.

"The Upland Sea," said the Escort. "Impressive, isn't it. This mesa is huge, the size of a continent, and it's higher at the edges than in the middle. They say it's what's left of a caldera, the edges are the rimrock, the middle had a lot of ashes in it. Water filled it up, then ate waterfalls down the edges, washed out some of the ash after every rain, every snow, gradually wore it down to where it is now. Gentheren country. There's the city."

He turned the flier on its side, so I could look down. A city made of glass and trees, a wide grove of trees, monumentally tall and joined together with spider silk bridges and canopies.

"It's beautiful," I said. "Can we go closer?"

The Escort laughed. "If you want to be shot out of the sky, maybe. We're as low as we're allowed to be."

"They don't let you land there?"

"I told you, it's Gentheren country. Humankind stay off. Entry by invitation only."

"I thought Thairy was a human colony," I protested. "They told me in school it was."

"It's a human colony, down below, off the mesa. Plenty of room down there. The Gentherens don't bother us, and we don't need to bother the Gentherens."

Soon the city was behind us, though the forested height went on for hours. I yawned, stretched, yawned again, fell into a doze. Later I woke and looked down to see the far edge of the continental mesa approaching. On this side it ended abruptly in a sheer cascade of black stone that flowed all the way down to the sea.

There, on the narrow shore between precipice and beach, was a town, a ribbon city only two or three streets wide but endlessly long. Directly below us, a hook of land extended into the sea, a curving extrusion covered with walls, squared-off fields, streets, structures, all of them as rigidly angled and paralleled as ruled lines.

The Escort pointed down. "Fort Point Zibit."

"The academy?"

"Right. Now, Naumi, that's your name, right? Naumi, I'm going to let you in on a secret. When you get there, some snotty cadet is going to ask you your name. You say, 'Naumi on X, sir.' The joke is, while you're on Academy grounds, you're 'on X-zibit.' That's because the upperclassmen watch everything the younger ones do and the officers watch the upperclassmen. Every cadet is somebody on exhibit."

"That's silly," said I, flushing.

"Well, do it or don't do it," said the Escort. "But if you don't, you'll wish you had. Weathereye said you had louts back there in Bright."

"Yes, sir."

"Well, Naumi, there's louts here, too. The difference is, these louts have to play by rules, but sometimes they make the rules, and they can lout you to death if you don't play by the same rules they do, silly and otherwise. I'm telling you this because that friend of yours, Weathereye, asked me to."

The flier landed on a strip of paving by the sea, and when I stepped down onto it, the sun made a glittering road of light stretching from the sea edge at my feet to the great orange orb hanging only a finger's width above the ruled rim of the horizon. I had left in the morning, without breakfast. I had come all the way west to the sea, and now I was hungry. It had been a long day.

"You Noomi?" called a voice from beyond the fence.

I started to say yes, then stopped. The person there had an unmistakably loutish look to him. I picked up my light pack and plodded across the yard until I was only an arm's length away.

"Nah-ow-me on Ex," I said very quietly.

"What kinna name's that?" the stranger asked.

"Any kind at all," said I.

"Well, I don't like it," said the other. "I think I'll rename you noomi. That's a kind of worm."

"That could work both ways," I offered, with a level stare into the other's eyes. "Them as names, get named."

"Grangel!" someone yelled. "Quit slopping about and bring the new cadet over here."

Grangel turned slightly red and spun on his heel. "Yes, sir," he called, then, over his shoulder, "This way, noomi."

I followed him at a sufficient distance to avoid being either tripped or elbowed. As we approached, the uniformed officer at the controls of the hovercar got out and stood erect. Though I was untutored in what might be expected, Mr. Weathereye had always said that civility could not possibly be resented by any civilized person; that if resentment were offered, it was a sure sign of loutdom.

"Naumi Rastarong, sir," I said, bowing slightly.

"Welcome, cadet," said the officer. "I'm Captain Orley. Pile yourself in the back there. You've had a long trip, and I imagine you're hungry."

"Yes, sir," I replied, salivating. "Very."

"Then we'll leave the civilities for another time. Grangel, you have post duty this shift."

"Yes, sir."

"Well then, I'll let you go on over to the gate. No need to go all the way back into the Point, then turn around and come back. You did have early mess?"

"Yes, sir," grudgingly.

Grangel was left to plodding while I was whisked, the captain giving a running commentary as we went. "These are the main gates. Post duty is guard duty, standing watch at the gates. All cadets do it sometimes, but most of the time it's done by what we call black-checkers, those who accumulate black checks on their record for fighting, harassing, disobeying orders, or showing disrespect to officers."

The gates fled by, huge stone pillars flanking metal grilles on wheels—open—and half a dozen statue-stiff cadets standing guard. "Sometimes the black-checkers get tired of being idiots and shape up. Sometimes they get tired of being punished for being idiots and quit. We don't care which, quite frankly. Too many cadets are children of privilege who think we're here to serve them instead of the other way round. I know you're not, so I can say this without fear you'll quote me to your parents." The vehicle turned into a wide street that ran straight toward the sea. "This street is called The Parade. That's the armory to your right, to your left is the officers' residence, then the officers' dining room. Right is the cadet mess. That means dining room, too, but officers get to use fancier words. Same food, both places. Now, that's First Cadet Row going off to the right, men's and women's houses on the left, classrooms on the right. Four streets, First Row for first years, Second Row for second years, and so on."

By the time we reached the fourth street, I could see that it was shorter by far. "Not as many fourth-year cadets, sir?"

"Not so many, no. The big break comes at the end of years one and two. Most everyone who gets into third year goes on to finish, including some of those children of privilege I mentioned earlier. People send their children here because they can't do anything with them, then they act surprised when we can't either—though not as surprised as we are when we can do something with them. Off to the left are the sports fields. You like sports."

"Not much, sir. I'm better at other things."

"What things would those be?"

"Battle games, sir. And academics." This was Mr. Weathereye's word. Mr. Wyncamp just called it schooling, but this place seemed to call for Weathereye kind of language.

"That's interesting," said the captain. "A word of advice, if I may."

"Of course, sir."

"Pick some sport, don't care what. Something you hate the least, maybe. Claim it. Make that yours. It's useful to have while you're here. Something you can do in the games for your Row or your House, whether it does you any good or not. Understand?"

"Swimming, sir?"

"Of course, swimming. You like that?"

"I'm fairly good at it, sir. And mountain climbing."

"When you say mountain climbing . . ."

"Cliffs, sir. Straight-up places. Places other people don't usually go."

"Hmmm," said the captain, swerving the vehicle to head back the way we had come. Outside the cadets' mess, he beckoned to a tall, bearded fellow who was lounging by the steps and called, "Sergeant Orson. Here's the one you've been expecting." Then, to me, "Sergeant Orson is a good man. Pay attention to him. Tell him your troubles, if you have any. If you don't, tell him you don't. Understand?"

"Yes, sir, Captain Orley."

Then I was standing on the roadside, smelling food as the man approaching me grew larger with every step until he loomed like a tree. "Cadet Naumi," he purred from a truly overwhelming loftiness. "Welcome to Point Zibit."

The seventh morning after my arrival, the sixty male and female residents of Houses 4A and 4B ran up the side of a mountain. I was accustomed to running, though not on an uphill track. Still, I acquitted myself fairly well, coming over the last rise and down into the final clearing slightly ahead of the middle of the pack. Stamina, Mr. Weathereye had always told me, is half attitude and half practice. I had the attitude, and the practice would no doubt come.

Sergeant Orson stood at the entrance to the clearing, pointing across it to the large commissary wagon, already thronged by earlier arrivals. I joined them, noting the wide choice of foods, including several things I would eat only if I were starving. I took a modest plateful of the tastier stuff and wandered about the clearing as I ate it.

East of the wagon, a section of cliff had fallen to create a vast pile of scree. Behind the wagon, north, the road continued upward along the cliffs, separated only by a narrow strip of sloped woodland from the seaward precipice to the west. The south side of the clearing held the road we'd come in by, as well as a picket line where eight huge horses were tied. As I passed, I stroked all eight enormous soft noses and leaned my head against one or two huge, silver-maned shoulders. The horses' feet were feathered with brushes of silver hair above hooves as big as dinner plates.

Grangel, the cadet who had renamed me Noomi and whose cronies had helped in making it a universal term of ridicule, dragged in close to last. He was loud in his outcries of displeasure at the food choices left for the laggards until Sergeant Orson silenced him and climbed into the wagon bed, calling for attention. Reading from a prepared list, he divided our group into teams of six and told us we could take a short rest, after which we were to collect stones from the scree along the base of the cliffs and use them to construct drystone walls "this long . . ." displaying lengths of cord, ". . . and this high . . ." displaying shorter ones, ". . . in the areas already staked out west of the road.

"I'm going back to Zibit with the wagon," he cried. "We'll return with your supper about sunset. Have the walls done by then."

The hostler and the sergeant busied themselves stowing the mess wagon and hitching the team. I, who had decided it would do no harm to get a good look at everything, picked up two measuring cords from where they'd been dropped, strolled over to the staked area, and looked it over, then walked over to the edge of the scree and looked carefully at the stones there. What seemed at first glance to be a mountain of raw material would actually yield a much smaller volume of usefully flat and stackable rock. A much better selection of flattish stones lay above my head to the left, where a narrow shelf extended above and along the upward road. What stones had collapsed there had not fallen as far, and less stone had fallen on top of them, making them less splintered than most, though the shelf would take some climbing to get to. On my way back, I saw the hostler remove a number of shovels from the wagon and lay them under the thorny growth at the foot of the trees, where they were easily visible to anyone who was using his or her eyes.

I returned my plate to the wagon and sat for a few minutes, taking deep breaths. Sergeant Orson bellowed at us to start work, and the horse-drawn vehicle rolled slowly away down the hill. I stared after it, feeling the rumble of those wheels up through my feet and legs. We had flown over the high mesa to Zibit in a flier. The officer who met me had used a floater. The obviously heavy commissary wagon was drawn, however, by eight huge horses. All very interesting.

My team was number six. The other five members of it, two girls and three boys, immediately began rushing or staggering back and forth as they fetched stones to the assigned site. I went a bit farther up the road, thrust my fingers into a few narrow slots, found a few almost invisible footholds, and worked my way up to the shelf where the flat stones had piled. I began dropping the stones onto the roadway beneath, taking care not to drop them upon one another. When the largest one of my teammates came near, I said over my shoulder, "Hey, Ferni. I'm picking flat ones for the bottom row. If I drop them down there, can you help me carry them over? It'll go faster if somebody picks and the other people carry, you or me, one or the other?"

Ferni, a generally affable cadet, took a look at the wall I had ascended and said, "Go ahead. It's easier to take them from here than dig them up out from under all the little ones anyhow."

Within a very short time, Ferni was joined by the other two boys, Caspor and Poul, and the girls, Jaker and Flek, who also found it easier to take the stones I dropped down than to dig them out of the general rockfall, especially with all the squabbling over territory that was going on. Meantime, I mentioned quietly to Ferni that one of them should always stay by our stone pile to prevent it being borrowed from by neighboring teams, and Ferni quietly passed the word to the others.

I, meantime, was counting to myself: so many stones to the row, so many rows to the layer, so many layers to make the wall. Mid-afternoon came, and team six had not built a foot of wall while some of the others had sizable structures. Grangel, working with one of the fastest teams, was loud in his mockery and direct in his abuse.

"Look at the noomi bunch!" he cackled. "Buncha real slow worms!"

"We better build something," complained the smallest of the group, Poul. "Everybody's ahead of us, and they're calling us names."

"Good enough," I conceded. "I think we have almost enough stone to complete the job. We'll start with the largest flat ones we have, but let's grab a couple of those shovels over there to level the soil first."

We leveled, to cackles of derision, particularly when I poured a thin stream from my water bottle at various spots on the leveled area to see if it went anywhere.

"They think old Orley told them to dig a latrine!"

"Ho, Noomi, you puttin' in a swim pool?"

The leveling process uncovered several jutting stones, the smaller of which I insisted we remove. We bridged the larger ones when we set flat base stones around them. The big, flat stones were laid up quickly into courses one and two. As we were midway through the third course, cries of dismay erupted from the neighboring group five, whose quickly built wall suddenly collapsed in a cloud of dust when one hasty rock carrier tripped and fell into it.

"Slowly," said I in a low voice. "Don't look at them, look at what we're doing, starting on course four. Make sure every stone is level and wedged to the next one. If it teeters, it's in wrong!" With no comment, the other five went on building while I fished my coil of twine from my pocket, one of the things I'd brought in my memorabilia box, tied one end of it around a small stone, and heaved it over a low branch that jutted just above where we were working, lowering the stone until it hung just above the earth alongside their wall.

"What are you doing?" demanded Ferni.

"We did our best to level the bottom," I replied. "Now we have to be sure it's rising straight, otherwise it'll topple over like that other one. Point your fingers, lay your palm where it just touches the string and your middle finger just touches the wall, move it up and down and you can tell whether the wall's going straight up. If we had some really straight sticks, we could put in some stakes, but there aren't any."

"There's shovels," said Ferni. "Nobody's using them."

I grinned at him, and together we brought over the shovels and made a line of them, each handle adjusted by plumb line to be straight up and down. No one had watched us doing this because all eyes were on group two, where Grangel was summoning attention by showing off what heavy stones he could lay in place. As he heaved an especially large one atop their structure, I clenched my teeth and held my breath. The rock immediately below the space Grangel was attempting to fill was roughly spherical, wedged into position with small, also rounded pebbles. When Grangel's burden hit the wall, the round rock slipped sideways, the smaller pebbles shot out of place, and half the wall collapsed as the spherical stone bounded across the space between walls two and three, hit wall three a resounding blow and destroyed a large part of it.

Groups two and three began to direct their scorn at Grangel instead of at me.

"Pay no attention," said I. "Caspor and Ferni, we're going to need more middle-sized and small flat rocks to finish off. You'll find the best ones right under where I was getting them. The four of us will go on building if you'll gather more stones for us, and don't waste a trip. Pick them carefully."

The wall went on growing. Almost flat, it rose regularly equidistant from the vertical shovels, needing only a final layer to reach the required height. Each layer contained stones of varying thickness, but all were leveled and interlocked, with no rounded ones used at all. While Jaker, Poul, Flek, and I leveled the course for the last layer, Caspor and Ferni moved back and forth with the smaller flat stones I had asked for.

Only four teams were still building. Teams two and three were madly piling rock, making up for lost time; five had not yet totally recovered from its collapse, and six was still leveling its last course while the teams that had finished amused themselves by insulting those who had not. "Noomi" had become a favorite word, and I noticed our team looking sideways at me. "Don't expect me to notice that nonsense," I said quietly. "We're all too busy doing what we're supposed to do: build wall." When team six laid the last few stones securely on the layer beneath and took the shovels back where they'd been found, the sun was sinking beneath the sea, its rays penetrating the western fringe of trees, turning our work into sharply contrasted shapes of shadow and brilliance. Around the clearing, the teams were lying about, their backs against convenient tree trunks.

Ferni murmured to me, "The more even the walls are, the fewer shadows on them, did you notice that?"

"Enough to decide where I want to sit down," said I, leading the way to a large tree, well away from the building area. The others assembled around us, sprawling around the tree's roots. Lying as I was, my eyes fixed on a shadow above the shelf I'd climbed earlier. "Ferni, Jaker," I said. "What's that up there on the rock wall?"

"It's a bush," said Ferni.

"Above the bush," I said.

"A shadow," said Jaker. "But see the way the light goes into it. It could be a cave."

I started to stand up, so I could get a better look, when I felt a premonitory shiver in my feet. "Listen," I murmured to the group. "When the wagon gets here, no matter what happens, just don't say anything. No yelling or jeering."

"But I'm hungry," whispered Caspor.

"We all are, but we're not going to yell about it."

"Wagon coming," called someone from team two.

The team nearest the road got to their feet and began cheering.

Our team six remained where we were, sprawled around the tree as the horses came into view at the top of the rise sloping down into the clearing. By now, most of the cadets were on their feet. The driver clucked to the team, the horses bent to their collars, jerking the wagon over the top, and down they came at a gallop, thundering, the stones echoing the noise. The ground shook. The walls shivered. Small stones popped out here and there; minor avalanches began. The horses kept coming. One by one the walls slumped, tottered, fell.

"Ours stood up," whispered Caspor, sitting up. Then more loudly, "Ours stood up!"

"Shhh," said I, loudly enough that all five of them could hear me. "Don't you dare cheer or yell or anything."

There was a good deal of shouting going on as blame was assigned and denied, resulting in several bloody knuckles and at least one split lip.

The wagon came to a halt. Sergeant Orson jumped from the wagon seat and moved among the collapsed heaps.

Our group got up, everyone yawning and stretching, making good theater of it, as Lady Badness used to say back home in Bright. The other five were giving me little looks, grinning.

The side of the wagon went down. Food smells drifted out.

"Well," said the sergeant. "You bunch, team six, there by the tree. Come get your plates while I walk around and inspect the others."

We were back under the tree with highly piled plates on our laps by the time group four, with two-thirds of their wall still standing, went to eat. Teams one, eight, and nine each had half a wall standing, and they ate next. Five, seven, and ten had some wall standing, though not much, but still, they got to eat before groups two and three, who were sullenly watching others enjoying their supper.

When all had been fed, the officer strolled over to our tree. We put our almost empty plates aside and stood up.

"Good job, cadets. Who's the leader here?"

"It was a group task, sir," said I. "I think we all worked equally hard."

"Built rock wall before, have you?" the officer asked, moving his gaze across us, receiving several no sirs, including one from me.

"Hmmm," he said, turning to look at the newly built wall behind him. "You leveled the soil?"

"Yes, Sergeant," said three or four voices.

"I don't see a large pile of unused stone. Selected the stones carefully before you hauled them over here, did you?"

"Oh yes, Sergeant," said Caspor and Ferni.

The sergeant turned to Caspor. "I'd have to swear somebody knew what he was doing. What is it you're best at?"

"Not much, Sergeant, except numbers. I do real well with them."

"And you?" to Ferni.

"I'm good with animals, Sergeant. Like those big horses."

Jaker, Poul, and Flek disclaimed any abilities whatsoever. Sergeant Orson frowned.

"And you," he said to me.

"Battle games," said I without expression. "I'm very, very good at battle games, Sergeant."

"You mean strategy, Cadet?"

"Of course, sir. What else is there?"

One day, just for exercise, I decided to run up the track along the cliff to the clearing where we had built the walls. I had some free time, and though the shadow on the cliff side was only a tiny mystery, I never did like mysteries, especially ones that might be solvable in an hour or so of free time.

Getting up the wall was only a minor problem. There were a number of grips and good places to put one's feet if one had the wits to see them and remember where they were when the time came to climb down. The shadow was indeed the very narrow entrance to a cave, one that would show up only when the sunlight hit it at a particular time of day. I climbed onto the lip of it with some elation. Since it was morning, there was no sunlight to fall inside the west-facing entrance, but I'd brought a torch, just in case. It lit a level floor that went straight in, past a dark recess to the left, then bent around a corner to the right. I walked it quietly, just in case there was something in residence, though it didn't seem likely. Unless it was something with wings.

I had no sooner had the thought than the torch was knocked from my hand by a flurry of wings, headed out. Birds! Rather large birds. They circled over the clearing, complaining loudly at my intrusion. I looked up to see nests stuck tight to the walls, visible even without the torch in a flickering blue light that came from farther in.

The light was just around the corner in a section of tunnel that looked just like any section of tunnel except for the light itself, a whatever that I couldn't really see. It was more a blue shivering in the air, an evocation of some other . . . what? Without thinking about it, I took two steps into it and found myself somewhere else. Though I couldn't see where, not clearly, it was very definitely somewhere else.

I held very still for a long moment. This was not something I wanted to do right at that moment. Some other time, maybe, but not right now. Carefully, I stepped back, one step, and two, and was back in the tunnel once more, with the very strong feeling I had just avoided some very great danger.

Watching my feet carefully to be sure I didn't stumble into some other unsuspected threat, I climbed carefully down the rock face and jogged back to Zibit, all the while reviewing what I'd seen and felt in the cave, saving it, as it were, in my mental memorabilia box. Something to take out and look at from time to time. Something to keep for the future.

♦   ﹡   ●

Occasionally, as time went on, and only when I was out of sorts, I regretted having been so successful in that first cadet exercise, for it had an unanticipated result. I had ended up with Caspor, Ferni, and Poul as constant companions in the dormitory, and with Jaker and Flek tightly attached to the group during field exercises. Ferni, I really, genuinely liked. It was a feeling I couldn't really identify, one I'd never had before, an internal heat, a wanting feeling. It wasn't an appropriate feeling. Or maybe it was an appropriate feeling but not . . . not for an appropriate person, even though something inside me felt Ferni was . . . completely appropriate. More likely I felt this way because he and I were so much alike. We were both orphans. Both reared by foster parents. Both, surprisingly, with vacant spaces in our memories, and both of us ending up at the academy without warning or provocation. After some thought, I decided it would be best for me just to set the feeling aside and enjoy working with him.

As for the others . . . Jaker and Flek could have been sisters, both quiet, both unexpectedly strong and very determined in everything they did. Caspor and Poul had been sent by their parents. None of them seemed to have particular skills except for Caspor's uncanny mathematical abilities and Flek's mysterious affinity for armaments— she could break down and reassemble the model RB27 faster than the rest of us could decide how to start.

"What they're like doesn't matter," I told myself sternly. "It's just like building rock wall. You don't complain about what you have to work with, you just make it work!"

I set out to learn everything I could about each of the five, so we could knit together to stand strong and indivisible. It turned out, the best way to do this was by involving the whole group in solving problems. It let us see everything from as many points of view as possible. Even though Jaker didn't usually solve problems on her own, she always saw something in them the others had not seen, and the same was true of each of them. I began to see things differently myself. Here was the problem, and there was the way it went, and it swerved around Caspor and fled toward Ferni, then Flek, then went on, touching each of them, sometimes circling back, until suddenly, one of us saw it! There it was, the route laid out as if in flashing lights, an avenue so well marked that we could not possibly mistake it. A high road, paved and guttered. We had only to point it out to the others, lead them down it, and at the end, there was the solution, right where it should be.

"The talk road," Ferni called it. "Let's help old Naumi find the talk road." And help they did, to their own benefit no less than mine. It was a new experience, this having friends and working together. I hadn't realized until then how lonely my life had been before.

Neither Sergeant Orson nor Captain Orley seemed to take any notice of this. Several dormitory mates did take notice of this to their dismay, for we had become so tight that bullying any one of us brought a quick and unpleasant retaliation.

A plump, gray-haired woman who worked in the kitchen had taken a bit of liking to me. She thought I looked like her son, long since grown and gone away, so she sneaked me extra cookies that I shared with the others, and she kept me up-to-date on the local news, like who was dropping out and who wasn't. So, one evening I went to see if she had anything for us. She told me to go through into the kitchen next to the officers' dining room and wait for her while she finished putting tomorrow's loaves in the oven.

I went where she told me, quietly, as was my habit, though not with any idea of sneakiness. I heard people talking in the dining room. One of my professors said, "Cadet Poul. You know the boy, Captain Orley."

"Of course I know the boy, the son of . . ."

"Very much the son of the largest import-export firm on Thairy, right! I didn't think he'd last out the year."

"You mean he will?" asked the captain in amazement.

"He will. It seems a trio of his dormitory mates plus a couple from the women's dorm have a study group led by young what's-his-name, the foundling boy from Bright? Ah, Naumi."

"A study group?" in a tone of slight dismay.

"It's not unheard of, Captain. We even suggest it."

"I wasn't saying it's a bad idea. I was just surprised. Poul's actually learning something? He'll pass?"

"Better than merely pass, by a good bit. So will the others. It seems Caspor is in charge of things mathematical. Ferni is in charge of things biological. Flek, it turns out, has a family interest in armaments . . ."

"I didn't know that!"

Well, neither had I known it, and I found it very interesting indeed, so I went nearer the hatch between kitchen and dining room and sat down quietly on the floor.

"Surely you know of Flexen Armor. Flexen Magma Canon, FMC? Her grandfather is Gorlan Flekkson Bray. Originally from Chottem."

"She's that family? I had no idea."

"Cadet's the offspring of one of the daughters, her surname isn't the same, and the mother didn't make anything out of it when her daughter was registered. She's been wandering around the factories with her maternal grandfather since she was old enough to walk. She chose to come here, and her grandfather recommended her to the academy. She's packed to the gills with engineering information she has no idea she knows, or knows the usefulness of."

"I suppose the rest of them have hidden qualities as well?"

"Not that we know of. Jaker is a quiet, self-contained young woman from another extremely wealthy import-export family. The Jakers and the Pouls are linked, matrimonially, with cousins in common. She has no outstanding abilities, but she, too, is learning. And Naumi . . . well, he doesn't shine in any particular class. He doesn't attract attention. That pack that follows Grangel—all of whom will be dropping out any day now, one fondly hopes—harassed him a bit when he first arrived, but that's dwindled off to nothing . . ."

"But he leads this group?"

"Oh yes, sir. He wouldn't say that, of course, but he does. That's his outstanding quality, I guess. That and something else . . ."

"Which is?"

"You know we give the cadets problems to solve. Tactical problems. You know. We're looking for optimum, seventieth, eightieth percentile answers. Most cadets are lucky to rate over fifty percent with a solution. Naumi and his group come up with the optimum answer nine times out of ten. The tenth time, they come up with an answer we've never received before, and when we give it to the battle simulator, it comes back as an even more highly rated response, one that the simulator hadn't thought of. He always says it's a group effort, what he calls a talk-road effort, and from what we can learn, it is, but he's always the one that pulls the group together."

This was news. I knew we'd been doing well, but not that well.

"It seemed to us," said a professor, "that is . . . we all thought he should be recommended to the war college, at once. Why wait four or five years with ability like that?"

There was a long pause, then Captain Orley said, "I objected to the boy being admitted, nobody that he was, late in the year as it was. I thought it would be a handicap both for the boy and for his house. However, I'm a man who can eat my earlier opinions for breakfast without choking on them, which is a good thing. This boy got in because he was recommended."

Mr. Weathereye. I knew it!

Someone said "Every cadet who comes to Point Zibit is recommended by somebody!"

The captain said ruefully. "Oh, he had that sort of recommendation from his schoolmaster and friends back in Bright. That's not what I'm talking about. Naumi was recommended by the Third Order of the Siblinghood."

Someone, I think it was Professor Hilbert, the mathematics man, said something in a harsh voice. "The Order. I find a great deal wrong with that, Captain Orley. First, though I know the Siblinghood is real enough, I find some difficulty in believing the Third Order actually exists. Secondly, if it exists, why is this supposedly all-powerful, all-knowing group interested in a schoolboy? And finally, assuming such an organization does exist, how does one verify that any information comes from that organization and not merely some clever-cock who wants to pull strings?"

Captain Orley murmured a reply while I was wishing I could have seen his face, to know how he felt about it. "It's a bit like discussing God, isn't it? Is there one? If there is one, how do we know it is speaking? How do we know what it wants?"

"Exactly," snapped Hilbert.

"The eternal questions," the captain went on. "Which always come down to the same answer. One has to trust the interface between oneself and it. The prophet. The sacred writing. The beatific visions. Then the second prophet who clarifies the issues. Then the new writing, and the new visions. Then a declaration of heresy and a reformation. Then a schism. Then a sect. Except that with the Third Order there is no writing, no visions, no prophet that we know of . . ."

"Then how in the name of all good sense . . . ?" yelled Hilbert, while two or three other people said, "Shhh, shhh."

Captain Orley raised his voice. ". . . how does the lowliest member of the selection committee, myself, wake up one morning to find the message pinned to my shirt, which was in my locker, which was locked, which was inside my room, which was locked, which was in the officers' quarters, which are guarded. A real message, which I read half a dozen times before it disintegrated into shiny dust."

Hilbert huffed. "Ascribe it to whatever you ate and drank the night before, Captain. You were seeing things."

"I could tell myself that. There are five of us on the committee, however, and we had not dined together for a long time. Nonetheless, it happened to all five of us. Same message, same location, more or less, all in places protected against intrusion, all signed, 'The Third Order.' I'll be glad to give you the names of the other four if you'd like to hear it directly from them."

I noticed I could see them reflected in the side of one of the big pots hanging on the wall. I saw them glancing at one another. I wondered if they were reviewing everything they had said, wondering if maybe this Third Order might be listening.

"Tread carefully, gentlemen. If what you tell me is true, if what I have told you is believable, it is likely Naumi will come to us, or someone will come on his behalf, if and when he, or they, consider the war college is a good idea. If Naumi chooses not to stand out, then I would suggest you let him . . . stand in, just where he is, where the Third Order recommended he be."

I told Ferni about it, back at the dorm. He asked what the Third Order was.

"I never heard of it," I said. "Honest, I never. But I was called for life-duty, so maybe . . . maybe it's just something they want me for."

"That makes you out to be pretty important," Ferni said with a lofty look. I swear, sometimes the way he drew himself up that way you'd swear he thought he was king of the world.

I said, "Not necessarily, Ferni! A squirt of axle grease can be important if that's what you need. That's probably all I'm supposed to be. Something to help turn a wheel."

We left it at that. I think Ferni forgot all about it. I put it away among my mental memorabilia and tried not to think about it, though sometimes I did, wondering what it all meant.

I Am Margaret/on Earth

Except for the rumors and whispers that followed the disappearance of our three classmates, college life was undisturbed for a time. I was fully focused on the final section of my "lateral studies," those intended to broaden understanding of linguistic development. Everything known about the Pthas and their linguistic survivors had been reviewed; the aeon-long changes in the Quaatar language likewise; along with the accepted works on dialect development among Mercan and Omniont planets. The last thing on the list was to consider a speaking race that had lost its use of language, as recorded by a Gentheran exploration ship. My friend Sybil, Bryan's sister, had made a vomit face when mentioning it, so I'd been putting it off.

Still, it was a required thing, so I settled my earpieces, keyed my didactibot, and faced a barren planet dotted with tall, irregular lumps. With a hiccup and purr, the lecture began in the same sweet, high voice I had heard at the meeting, Sister Lorpa's voice. Or one of her kin.

"While on a routine journey of exploration, the Gentheran ship *Pendaris Kuo* happened upon an uncharted system with one live planet. Since the planet was occupied by a previously unknown race, a monitoring shuttle was implanted into a rocky area to provide a longitudinal recording of the inhabitants.

"The earthen towers you see are the homes of the only

land animal living on this world. These clay mounds are analogous to the termite mounds found on Earth during the multispecies ages. Since there is no evidence of a precursor race on the planet, Gentheran historians researched the archives to determine how these creatures may have arrived there. An ancient Quaatar logbook entry may have described the ancestors of this population stowing away on a Quaatar ship, then fleeing the ship on this planet, 'Into the thick vegetation that covered the world.'"

The point of view receded. "Assuming that one tower was built initially, and extrapolating from the growth rate observed by the buried ship, we see here how the towers spread, resulting in the complete deforestation of the planet. There is evidence of several natural disasters that virtually eliminated these creatures on this world, but each time forest growth returned, they also returned to destroy it.

"Gentheran researchers picked a tower at random and fed audio-optical leads and chemical sensors into it, using the ordinary micro-burrowers used by xenoarchaeologists. These fibers provide sufficient light to permit a pictorial record of life inside. Only the various types are distinguishable from one another. Members of each caste or type are identical.

"The first recording begins at dawn. The creatures you see before you are curled against a tunnel wall, sleeping. To give human students some sense of scale, each creature could easily be held in your cupped hands."

I could see why Sybil had been disgusted by the creatures. So was I. They were naked and gray. They had large ears that were folded against the head, each head pillowed on one skinny arm. The legs were short and almost as thin as the arms. They had no noticeable sexual organs. The faces had a common bilateral pattern, one shared by many races: sight and scent organs grouped at the upper end above the ingestion aperture. These mouths were toothless, the creatures had no chins and no appreciable necks.

A second type of individual appeared, slightly larger, with a larger mouth. As it passed along the line, it uttered a sound, *wakwak wak-wak,* as it kicked the feet of each sleeper. Those kicked stood up, each in sequence, as room was made by the previous riser. Uttering this continuous *wakwak wakwak,* the kicker went up the tunnel, while behind it the wakened creatures made a half turn to face the direction it had gone, moving their two legs in a steady rhythm while making a continuous sound: *railev railev railev*. The line began to move, slowly at first, then more quickly as space opened up between the awakened ones.

I yawned. Bryan and I had been together the night before, and I was sleepy. Covertly, with a guilty glance at the monitor, I keyed the lecture to fast-forward, stopping shortly before the end. ". . . the protolanguage these creatures may once have spoken has not been identified. The Gentheran expedition did not take genetic samples, since sampling of speaking races is forbidden by IGC rulings without the consent of the individuals. The Gentheran research team was unsure whether this population was or was not a speaking race, though their opinion was that language had once existed but had been lost, and the current sounds made by the creatures were mere flock-murmur, the sort of recognition noises made by birds. The researchers chose not to presume what the IG might rule on the matter, and as yet, no researcher has been sufficiently interested in this oddity to return to the world in question. The buried Gentheran survey shuttle is still there, however, recording the passing of the race and the probable reforestation of the planet, which has been labeled in Gentheran, 'Drdpls,' or, in Earthian, 'Hell.'

"For students, the importance of this report lies less in what it tells us about this race than in what it tells us about language. We believe that at one time, this creature had language formed and ramified by experience. Brought to a world with no inimical organisms and plentiful food, it expanded endlessly until it occupied the entire land surface of the planet. As food became scarce, the creatures became progressively smaller, eventually reaching the stage we see now.

"Along the way, all meaning was lost except for verbal signals, the kind of signals any animal species develops in order to stay in touch with its own kind, call others to a feeding spot, or alert others to danger. Every linguist should know that language must be used to be retained, and the compilers of this report have warned that human language on Earth is also being reduced. As humans become more crowded, they become less tolerant of variety. To fit into a crowd, people must be similar, and Earth's population today is a vat of homogeneity with only a pretense of choice remaining. One may pick model x with one curlicue or model y with three, the tasteless brown cracker or the tasteless yellow cracker, the actual difference in either case being nil. Any real choice among things of unlike value might lead to disparity, which leads to conflict. Ideas also contribute to disparity, and therefore in crowded populations, ideas must be restricted to the least controversial, the least interesting. Children all receive the same grades in school. Workers all receive the same pay. Clothing is similar; foods are identical; and with the passage of all distinctions, the words for them also pass. Who now knows of oranges, whale blubber, corsets, chopsticks, panty hose, nutmeg? What is a cable knit? Where might one find a T-bone? . . ."

I pushed the stop and reversed, listening to this last bit again. What was a cable knit? Or a T-bone? I had known for years that people didn't say anything, but I had never considered that they might actually be losing language! Suddenly interested in this, avid to learn more, I keyed the machine to play it over. My intention was interrupted by a crash as the rear door of the classroom was banged open.

Around me the whispers fell into silence. The man in the door was a black-clad proctor. During the last ten years, proctors had become both ubiquitous and universally dreaded. He spent only a moment scanning the room before striding directly toward me. He leaned down, spoke quietly, waited while I stood and started to gather up my study materials.

"Leave them," he said. "You won't need them."

I saw a dozen pairs of eyes on me, some of them curious. I shrugged, hands out, obviously as ignorant as they were, trying desperately to look nonchalant. What had I done? Or more likely, what did they think I had done? Did this have anything to do with that meeting? Did they think I was involved in what my fellow students had said . . .

The monitor spoke from the front of the room. "Settle down. Get on with your lessons, please."

Outside in the hall, I asked, "Where are we going."

"To the Provost's office," the proctor replied, not breaking his lengthy stride. "Stupid woman insists on seeing you." I trotted to keep up with him, readying myself for a considerable walk, only to be surprised that a car driven by one of the security staff awaited us at the main corridor.

Cars were silent and fast. The driver, an expressionless woman with her clearance code tattooed on her forehead, left us at the Provost's office, where I stood just inside the anteroom door, watching the car dwindle down the hallway, trying not to huddle under the watchful eyes of the proctor.

"Do you know what she wants me for?" I asked.

"I don't answer questions," said the proctor.

It was a threat. There was just time to realize that before the Provost's aide came for me and took me to into her office.

The Provost looked up. "Margaret."

"Yes, Provost."

She rose. "Margaret, I'm sorry about this. If you were not a party to this deception, you will be shocked at this news." She walked around the desk.

"A party to what? I have no idea . . ."

"You are seemingly a student here under false pretenses." She shut the door between us and the proctor.

My mouth dropped open momentarily, before shame and anger snapped it shut. "I am a four, Provost. I am my mother's first and my father's third child."

The Provost nodded, saying more softly, "That was thought to be true ten years ago when you received citizen's approval at age twelve. Two years ago, however, as you are no doubt aware, it became apparent the planned population cuts had not been deep enough, and the selection criterion was moved back another generation. Only twos to fours from two to four parents are now approved."

"Yes, ma'am. Of course I know that."

"All over-fours were instructed to report to the local emigration office?"

"Yes, ma'am."

"Interesting, because it appears that your mother's older brother was born as a twin. Your mother is, therefore, at least the third child of both her mother and her father, a six."

"I don't understand! My mother didn't have an older brother. She had an uncle almost as young as she was, but . . ."

"The medical records establish that your mother had two older brothers. Twin boys were born to your maternal grandparents."

"Uncle Hy?" I murmured, completely lost. "He's Mother's uncle, and he lives on Luna!"

She shook her head. "He may well live on the moon, if he chooses, but he and his brother were born on Earth, and they were your mother's siblings, not her uncles." With a sorrowful expression she reached across the desk and took my hand. "I have seen the records, and this is true, Margaret! You must accept that it is true."

"But . . . but, Provost, that would have been recorded! It would have been in the . . . in the files . . . I would have known . . . Mother would have known . . ."

She shook her head, patted my hand, and said compassionately, "You really didn't know. I'm so sorry."

"Mother thought Hy was her uncle!"

"She may have been told he was. The record of your family's enrollment session is in the permanent files. This year, when the emigration rule was moved back a generation, all the modules were instructed to fact-check and recompute. The module noticed an anomaly, a person named Hyram living on Luna. Original records established that Hyram was a twin of George, who died at birth. Your mother was a six, therefore neither you nor your mother may be registered among two-fours any longer."

"But . . . I'm still a four."

"Though it makes no difference, you really aren't. You were also a twin, whose sister died at birth. It is very rare to have twins in successive generations on both sides of the family, and your father begot twins, which means you're a three on your father's side, a two on your mother's, so you yourself are a five, the child of a two and a six." She looked at the papers in front of her. "Strange. If you hadn't mentioned the name of Hyram during your registration session, no one might have caught that part of it."

I had mentioned it? I sagged, catching myself on the edge of her desk. She rose, put her hand on my shoulder, whispered, "There's nothing I can do, Margaret. There is no appeal. But I insisted they bring you here because I want you to know something. I said you were selected to be at that meeting, and you were, by the Third Order of the Siblinghood. I doubt you've heard of it, and I know nothing more than the name, but that very fact may be important to you in the future. Say it?"

I gaped. "The Third Order of . . . the Siblinghood?"

She opened the door, saying brusquely, "Proctor? Take this woman to the Resources Office for outprocessing."

I was driven home in a Resources floater, black, with the gold symbol on the doors: a stream running down a hill, a tree on the hill, above that a cloud, a sun, the words ENOUGH FOR ALL. That symbol always reminded me of that historic educational effort called "No child left behind," which actually meant "No child gets ahead," for compliance meant dumbing everything down so no one would learn more than the least capable. "Enough for all" really meant "Too little for everybody." As we went, the false windows displayed pictures of tree-lined streets, the vents emitted the smells and sounds of summer: flowers and cut grass, birds singing, children playing. All false. All mere pretense. There was no water for trees, grass, flowers, and solar radiation would kill any child who played outside.

Halfway home, I suddenly thought of Bryan. Bryan! What could I say to Bryan! Sybil was in the class the proctor had just taken me from, and she would tell him! Bryan was a third generation two, a first child of first children, so he might feel that I was too shameful to . . . He might even think it best not to tell me good-bye . . .

In that, I misjudged him, for he arrived at my home almost immediately after I did.

"Margaret, I just heard. Sybil told me. Where's your mother? Did you have any idea about this?"

"No," I had said, tears streaming down my face. "I hadn't. Mother is already gone. She left me a note."

"What did they tell you?"

"Seventy-two hours to prepare for shipment out."

"I had no idea it would happen that fast! Listen to me, get your things together, but don't sign any bondage agreement or do anything until I get back to you . . ."

He was abruptly gone. What did he mean, until he got back to me? What on earth did he think he could do? The agreements were pro forma. They would take me regardless. Still, it was typical of him to try fixing things. He had become a doctor because he had always wanted to fix things. Well, this wasn't something he could fix, and I wished he had stayed with me, held me close, pretended for a little while this wasn't happening.

In the meantime, I stood in the middle of the room, tears streaming down my face as I told myself what I had to do. I had to pack. I couldn't go off without anything to wear. At least I was strong and healthy. At my age I would live through the fifteen years. Mother, though. Mother had never done a day's hard labor in her life, and she was . . . what? Fifty. I moved witlessly around the apartment, into my cubicle and out of it. I opened the closet door, took things out of drawers, put them back, thinking distractedly that Bryan needn't have ordered me to do nothing, for nothing seemed to be all I was capable of. I focused on what I was doing for all of thirty seconds, then forgot whatever it was. I found myself sitting, unable to react in any way to the chaos going on inside me.

In early evening my father came home and fell crying upon my shoulder.

"She told them I didn't know," he said. "I did know, Margaret. I just never thought it would make any difference. On Phobos it didn't make any difference, and we never planned to come back here . . ."

I put my fingers over his mouth. "Don't tell them that, Father. If Mother told them you didn't know, she did it for you. Let her do it. Let her at least feel good about that."

"I should be with her!" he cried.

"You're thirteen years older than Mother is. They won't take you on a labor contract, you're too old. Concentrate on what you can do to help her. Send packages, maybe . . ."

He seized upon this idea and fell abruptly into the old Phobos habit of saying the same things over and over with minor variations. He would do this, she would do that, they would stay in touch, he would provide, she would reply, he would find out, perhaps he could visit . . . then, starting over, he would do this, she would do that. I nodded, responded with monosyllables, let him talk until exhaustion took over and we both slept.

On the second day, Father left to say good-bye to Mother at the assembly point where she was being held.

"Do you want to come, Margaret?"

"I'm not allowed to leave the house."

"But surely . . . not even to say good-bye?"

"Not even that." It was true, but also, I preferred not to go. I had no idea what I could say that would not be hurtful or accusatory, and neither of them deserved that. They'd raised me with all the affection and care Phobos thought proper. The rules were made by whom? Dominion? Earthgov? ISTO? Certainly my parents had had no control over that. But still . . . still . . . Father said they had known! If they had known, why hadn't they at least warned me? Let me get used to the idea . . .

I resolved once more to focus on packing. Sturdy clothes, shoes, warm things in case my destination would be cold. One could always strip down to almost nothing if it were hot. I caught myself folding and unfolding, taking out and putting away, accomplishing little.

And then, unexpectedly, Bryan arrived. He tugged me toward a chair, made me sit down, and took my hands in his.

"I've been finding out about a colony planet called Tercis. It has a subdivision, rather like a state or province, called Rueful . . ."

"Rueful!" I cried.

"Don't interrupt with questions, Margaret. We haven't that much time. Rueful has very few doctors. Doctors and some other professions are allowed to volunteer for places like that." He gazed at me expectantly.

What did he want me to say?

"Why would you volunteer, Bryan? You're in your last year of the specialized training you've always planned on. If there are few doctors, it must be primitive! You wouldn't want to go there! How could you practice medicine there?"

"We've talked about how I feel about practicing medicine here, Margaret. Over and over . . ."

Well, of course we had at one time, before we had agreed not to, but why bring that up again now? "Yes. So?"

He took a deep breath, and blurted, "And if I volunteer, I can take my wife with me . . ."

I stared at him, unbelieving. "You would never volunteer for something like this on your own, Bryan, and if you're doing it for me, I can't . . . can't accept it."

He drew me into his arms, spoke into my ear, urgently, roughly. I must accept it. He loved me, he had loved me since his sister had first introduced us. He had always intended to marry me. No, of course he hadn't spoken of marriage, it hadn't been the right time, but that didn't make it less true. He couldn't, absolutely wouldn't, lose me!

I tried to reason with him, without success. He wouldn't let up. He went on arguing, demanding. Over and over, becoming more intense with every repetition.

Finally, in acute misery, I cried, "Oh, Bryan, if you really do love me, then leave me alone for a little while and let me think about it. I can't stand any more of this."

Bryan went away. When Father returned to the house, I did not mention Bryan's visit. I hoped Bryan would have second thoughts and give it up. I was shamed enough. I couldn't bear to carry any more humiliation than I already felt, and if Bryan made such a sacrifice, he would hate me, and I would spend my life regretting it. It was absurd, preposterous.

I went on packing and repacking, finally achieving the best arrangement anyone could achieve who had no idea where she was going. Bryan did not return, and as I wiped tears from my face, I gave silent thanks for that. In the morning, however, as we were about to leave for the assembly point, he came back, a pack on his back, traveling cases in both hands.

Father blurted, "Bryan, what are you doing here?"

"Came to get Margaret, sir."

"To get . . . you've volunteered for bondage?" It wasn't unheard of, but it was exceptionally rare.

Bryan turned and grasped my hand. "You didn't tell him what I've decided?"

I cried, "I wanted . . . I hoped you'd change your mind."

"I haven't." Without releasing his grip, he turned to face my father. "I love Margaret. I've volunteered to provide medical service on Tercis. Margaret and I will be there together. It's not a high-tech civilization, but it's far from bondservice. I have the authorization papers with me. All Margaret and I have to do is com the Bureau of Volunteer Services to record a contractual union, then she can go with me."

I stood dumb, incapable of words or feeling.

Father broke from his astonishment to ask, "What colony, Bryan? Do you know anything about it?"

"It's a good-sized planet, one the Dominion has divided into sections for human populations of various types. The place that most needs a doctor is called Rueful." He laughed briefly. "It's also inhabited by the Rueful, who practice a religion called Rue."

"Who are 'they'?"

"Just an ordinary human population, rural, needless to say. Rueful has a few small towns, half a dozen middle-sized ones, one small city, a lot of open country. Almost entirely agricultural. Fewer than a million people in the whole place. The Dominion Settlement Board provided the original supplies: seeds, domestic animals, the usual settlement stuff. According to the Board it's very natural, trees, rivers, some local wildlife, birds, that kind of thing."

"What technological level?" Father asked.

"Three," Bryan said, flushing a little.

"Three! So they have electricity."

"That's about it. Horses for transportation. Actually, you can go all the way across the settled area in a couple of days on a horse. It never gets really cold on Rueful, and they heat the houses with stoves burning wood or coal. There's a coal mine and a lot of forests."

"What language do they speak?" I asked.

"Regular Earthian standard plus some Mercan or Omniont jargon the ex-bondspeople have picked up. We'll understand one another. The area we'll go to is called The Valley. It has no doctor. No hospital. Not much of anything in the way of health care." Bryan's brows pulled together, making a deep furrow between his eyes. "We'll have to build something, a clinic, a small hospital. But I can practice medicine the way I need to, without all this damned bureaucratic red tape! And Margaret will make a good nurse . . ."

Which would have been the last thing I would ever have considered being! Even as a child, I, Margaret, hadn't played at being a nurse . . . a healer. The healer part of me had been totally . . . separate. I wasn't interested in people's bodies. The very idea was appalling!

I tried not to let my dismay show on my face. The whole universe was conspiring to make my education useless.

He pleaded, "Margaret, we don't have much time!"

"Margaret?" urged Father.

I cried frantically, "Father, I tried to talk him out of it. This isn't fair to him . . ."

I was talking to his back. He was leaving, saying, "I can't offer anything to this discussion!" The door shut behind him.

Bryan stared after him.

"My father . . . often . . . departs when things are difficult."

Bryan took my hand. "Margaret, we'll be together, you'll have a job to do that needs doing, your life expectancy ought to be the same as on Earth or better, you won't be eaten by some ET monster or worked to death in the fields by some ET slave driver."

I drew away from him. "But you were so enthusiastic about your new residency . . ."

He almost snarled at me, face darkened with passion. "Damn it, listen to me, Margaret! I've given it up. No matter what you say, yes or no, I can't get it back. It's gone!"

The words clanged at me as though I were inside a huge bell! Something inside me snapped. If I had to be dragged away against my will, at least let it be by someone who cared about me.

"All right, all right! I suppose it's for the best. I'll go with you."

Bryan seized me in his arms, laid his cheek against mine, then released me. There was no time for talk, he said. No time for anything but continuing the process, getting to the assembly point. It took only moments to make the com contact with the Bureau of Volunteer Services, to give my identity number to the authorization clerk, and the whole thing was done.

Rather than drag my father back into the situation, I did what I knew he would prefer. I added a postscript to the note I had already written, saying Bryan and I were going together. I was numb, in the grip of that same, weird vacancy I had felt on the day the first proctor came, as though I had been split in two, as though some monstrous cleaver had irrevocably sliced me apart from myself.

And yet, when I turned to Bryan, ready to argue once more, I saw on his face an expression of exaltation. He clasped my hand between his and smiled gloriously at me. I bit my lips, choking back what I'd meant to say. If this was how he felt, it had to be all right. It would turn out to be the best thing I could do. He had given up . . . whatever he had given up, but I would make it up to him. No matter what it took. I told myself this, over and over again. A mantra. I will make it up to Bryan.

At the assembly point, we were taken aside by a young usher who led us to a smaller area set aside for volunteers. There our papers were processed by an efficient woman who, when she saw we were headed to Tercis, shook her head and bit her lip.

"Are you leaving anyone here on Earth that you hope to communicate with in the future?" she asked.

"My father," I said haltingly. "Bryan's family," turning to him, only to find him staring, red-faced, at his feet.

"You weren't told that will be impossible?" she asked.

I shook my head.

"There's a time anomaly on the Tercis route. The way around it is too expensive to consider. You'll arrive on Tercis . . . sometime before you leave here."

I thought of the international date line on Earth and nodded, showing I understood. I thought I did.

"The difference is about fifteen to twenty years," she said. "Any message you sent might arrive before you were born."

"You knew this?" I asked Bryan.

He confessed that he did. For a moment I was furious, then I wondered what difference it actually made. The Gentherans were the only ones who could travel among the stars without losing their lives to time. Bryan and I had known we would not see our families again. In fact, it made no difference at all.

"You should have told me," I said. "But it doesn't matter."

In the dormitory we sat for most of a day and a night, silently holding hands. I repeated the mantra to myself whenever I began to get edgy, echoing it again as we queued for the subway. Once we were seated, exhaustion took both of us, and we slept all the way to pre-shipping.

Anxiety didn't return until we actually boarded the elevator. We stood at the mouth of the pod, confronting all those heads, like beads, like bubbles, a pavement of heads, all going away, to where? To what? Was it even certain there was a destination at the other end? Then we were seated; officers came through with their calming sprays; and all my concerns were temporarily put to rest.

I remember turning to Bryan, and saying dreamily, "Bryan, do you know anything about the Third Order of the Siblinghood?" His eyes were shut. He didn't answer. I went back to the mantra. We were going up to the shipping station, to Departure. We would be put aboard a ship. We would go to Tercis. Bryan and I would live on Tercis, together. All I had to do was just . . . do what I was told to do, go where I was told to go. Everything . . . everything would be all right. I would make it up to Bryan.

I Am M'urgi/on My Way
to B'yurngrad

... I drew away from him. "But you were so enthusiastic about your new residency!"

Bryan almost snarled at me, face darkened with passion. "Damn it, Margaret, listen to me, I've given it up. It doesn't matter what you say, yes or no, I can't get it back. It's gone!"

The world clanged at me as though I were inside a huge bell! Something inside me snapped. If I had to be dragged away against my will, let it be by Earthgov, by the Dominion, by someone I could hate. Let me not be eternally burdened with someone else's sacrifice! "No, Bryan. No," I screamed at him. "You had no right to do this without my agreement. I will not."

Brian turned white, stared at me in disbelief, then turned on his heel and left me without another word. Numbly, I took up my pack, waiting only a moment to be sure he was gone. I would leave now, while Father was out of the room. I would find my own way to the assembly point and avoid his reproaches for not accepting Bryan's offer. During the previous sleepless night I had written a farewell note. Let that suffice.

At the assembly point, the usher led me through vaults sonorous with regret. "What do they call this place?"

"We just call it the separation lobby. People from their kin. Earth people from their planet. The optimistic from their hopes, and the pessimistic from their estimations of how bad it can be. The answers are always *none* and *worse*."

I was stunned. "You don't try to be comforting, do you?"

"If we're honest, there's nothing comforting we can say. Some of us lie. Some of us don't, like me. I have to put it into words I can handle or the scope of it swallows me. We see millions go through here, and damn few of them go smiling. Today it'll be a bit easier on you. Several ships have come in for immediate loading, so we're sending people directly to the subways. Here's your check-in pass, follow the red line down that way. It takes almost a day to get there, use the toilet before you go, don't drink anything after."

I stumbled away amid others, to join the long queue of émigrés lined up to board the continental subway that would move us a day-long journey to the elevators. Away. Going away, and I couldn't feel anything.

When I arrived at preshipping, one of the ubiquitous ushers saw me standing alone, and said, "Down that hallway, that's your dormitory. Lately we've sped up the process. You shouldn't be here more than a day."

"And then where?"

"You'll probably be in the third or fourth ship out. Either way, you'll be going to B'yurngrad in the Omniont Federation. Actually B'yurngrad is an Earth-colony planet in Omniont Fed space, but it's also a transshipment point for the Omniont worlds in the area. You'll probably change ships there."

"Probably?"

"To smaller ships that'll take the cargo to various Omniont planets. You should be glad it's Omniont space, by the way."

"Why is that?"

"Omniont Federation is marginally better than Mercan Combine."

"How do you know that?"

"We know how many ships go to bondslave worlds, and how many go from those worlds to the colonies. Omniont and Mercan get about equal numbers of bondspeople to start with, but more of those from Omniont worlds survive to go on to the colonies later.

"Don't let it get you down. You look strong. You'll make it. And don't think about sending messages. Travel through space is also through time. Bondspeople are always asking us how they send messages back to their people here on Earth. We tell them, don't bother. More likely it will get here after your people are all dead."

"But . . . representatives from our colonies have meetings every year, on Mars!"

"Sure, and the Gentherans provide the travel on little ships that go point to point with a technology no one else has. No one knows how they do it but them. They say it wouldn't help the trading races, because trading ships are too huge to use it, though the time problem is one reason the ET long-distance ships are so huge. They carry whole families aboard. Toward galactic center, among the crowded worlds, time is less of an issue. You can actually travel among them without losing all your friends every time you leave one world to go to another."

I gaped at him. No one had ever mentioned this.

"You probably haven't slept much lately. Go that way, then right to section ninety-seven, row eighty-eight's at the back, bed five-A will be extreme left, here's your bed ticket. Get some rest."

Wondering how the usher expected anyone to rest, I plodded into the cavernous dormitory. Though almost every bed had an occupant, it was almost frighteningly quiet. I found the row and section without difficulty, thrust my bags under bed 97-88-5A, and fell onto it. I was exhausted, I was frightened. I admitted to myself that I should have gone with Bryan. Finally, I told myself I had the choice to cry about it or throw a tantrum or to go to sleep. Of the three, only one would do me any good, so I turned on my side, shut my eyes, and concentrated my whole attention on not screaming. Eventually, I actually did sleep.

Later, how much later I have no idea, I was awakened by a loudspeaker. "Any outshippers able to speak any Omniont or Mercan languages, please report to your dormitory office at once."

I heard it perfectly well, but decided it was part of the frustrating dream I'd been having. They damn well had my records, and if my language skills had been any use to them, they should have let me know before now. Without opening my eyes, I turned over and kept on dreaming.

I Am Mar-agern, Going to Fajnard

"Outshippers, attention. If you speak any Omniont or Mercan languages, please report to your dormitory office at once."

I heard it perfectly well. I sat up, stood up, paused, looking at my bags for a moment, then collected them and trudged down the long aisle toward the distant office. The sleepy-looking officer inside looked up when I entered.

"I speak some of the Omniont and Mercan languages," I said.

"I'm sure that's a great comfort to you," snorted the officer. "Why tell me about it?"

Angrily, I snarled, "Because there's a loudspeaker announcement that anyone who speaks those languages is supposed to report to the dormitory office. Is that here, or somewhere else?"

He sat up, shook himself, and went to his com, where he spoke in muted tones for some little time. "Come with me," he said over his shoulder as he headed out the door. "They're sending transport to take you to the elevators. Oh, by the way, what's your number?"

"All I have is my bed number?"

"That'll do. Give me your bed ticket. We can cross-check it to your identity. A Mercan ship was delayed here when their cargo translator for the voyage took sick. They can't wait any longer to leave."

"A Mercan ship?" I whispered. "Their cargo translator?"

"Mercan, right. When they say cargo translator, they mean the person who translates commands to the cargo, the bondslaves, the outshipped."

I could not reply. Seemingly, all the fates in the universe were stacked against me, and I was absolutely incapable of making a beneficial decision about anything at all. The choices that had seemed best to me, possibilities that had shone with hope and encouragement, if only slightly, always turned to shit. Perhaps it would be better simply to take what came, refuse to choose anything, leave the choosing to others who were not damned as I was to do the wrong thing at every opportunity.

I Am Ongamar/on Cantardene

I, Ongamar the spy, was kneeling between the left feet of a K'Famir pleasure-female, pinning up her skirt so the gold-plated graspers above the pads would show seductively, when I realized I could hear the chatter from an adjacent fitting booth through the floor-level ventilation duct. The pleasure-female had been drinking xshum all morning, provided by House Mouselline. She was barely able to stand and would not have heard an earthquake, so I had no need to ask many loud questions about the fitting to disguise the fact I had heard what was going on. Human hearing was far better than that of the K'Famir. To normal human ears, they always sounded as though they were shouting.

"Tonight there will be a midnight sacrifice on Beelshi," squealed the customer in the next booth. "I asked Wonbar to take me, but he said no females. I think they sacrifice females, that's why they don't want females watching."

"Surely not," said Lady Ephedra in a conciliatory tone. "We would hear of such a thing. People would disappear."

"Pocomfis disappear all the time," said the first voice. "They have no place to live, they work at ugly things, who cares if they disappear."

"What God would accept the sacrifice of a pocomfis?"

asked Lady Ephedra chidingly. "Sacrifices must be worthy, which means expensive. Half a flibit would buy a pocomfis. There now, move your upper arms, now the lower. Ah, it doesn't bind, does it. Good. If you'll take it off, I'll have it ready for you by closing time tonight."

Pocomfis were the maimed ones, those who had lost an arm, a leg, an eye, a sexual organ. If the lack could not be effectively disguised with a prosthesis, then one was an outcast. Being maimed was shameful, for it meant the gods had decided one was unnecessary, disposable, unimportant. What Lady Ephedra had said was quite true: pocomfis were cheap as dirt; cheap things were not a worthy sacrifice. A worthy sacrifice had to be expensive, very expensive: both vulnerable and without a family that would retaliate.

Beelshi was a low hill just outside the town, its slopes covered with the large earthenware jars in which the K'Famir dead were interred. Adille had attended a funerary ceremony there and described the place to me, her pet: a hilltop crowned by an ancient plaza, somewhat cracked and weedy, surrounded by temples and mausolea. A huge rounded boulder stood at its center and was stained, so Adille thought, with blood offerings people had made to Whirling Cloud of Darkness-Eater of the Dead, chief god of the K'Famir pantheon.

If true, such sacrifice would feed the thing for me! I could arrive at Beelshi early enough to hide among the funerary jars. Likely the sight would be enough to please *it* for some time. Though *it* had become too heavy for me to carry, *it* still insisted that I find something new every day, even as the number of unexplored sites and events grew smaller. I would go in the guise of a Hrass. I had the lengthened nose, a wrinkled protrusion that was almost hoselike. I could emulate the squinted eyes of a creature that avoided the light, the gray skin, the slightly scaly long-fingered hands. Add to this the voluminous dirty robes usually worn by Hrass, and I would be Hrass so far as the K'Famir were concerned.

Early that evening, I left my place through the alley gate, scurrying tight against the wall, the way Hrass usually moved. When they ate, walked, talked, bargained in the market, they always tried to have a solid wall behind them, and when they crossed open space, they moved as fast as possible. In general, the K'Famir disregarded them, for most of the Hrass on Cantardene were crew members of those disreputable ships that carried necessary but disgusting cargo: uncured flemp hides, for the making of slave whips; bathrop manure for the mushroom farms; dried charbic root to be ground into powder as a poison for vermin. The robes I had procured were authentic, both in fabric and in odor, thereby guaranteeing I would be overlooked and ignored.

I went through alleys, as Hrass would go; I muttered to myself, as Hrass invariably did. I gained the foot of Beelshi before it was totally dark and found, as I had hoped, that it was as yet unguarded. I climbed the hill, not by one of the main paths or the stairs, but by edging slowly among the jars until I reached one of the smaller mausolea surrounding the hilltop plaza. The building had a decorative lattice around it, one easy to climb, even burdened as I was by my garments, and the roof of the place was above the head level of any K'Famir.

Once atop the roof, I found it had a massive parapet penetrated in several places by rain spouts, wide metal troughs, the outer ends shaped into gape-jawed monsters. The troughs were large; one of them emptied into the plaza; the parapet was half my height thick, certainly wide enough to hide me from above. If I crawled into the trough, I could remain there, invisible to those below but able to see the altar area through the downsloping jaws of the spout.

When I had hidden myself, I examined the surroundings carefully while there was still enough light to do so. Many of the temples and mausolea shared common walls, and those that did not had only narrow spaces between them. They made a complete wall around the plaza, broken only by the wide flight of stairs that extended down the hill to my left. The plaza itself was made of large slabs of flat stone, cracked by age, with small, dusty plants growing in the cracks. At the center was the great stone Adille had spoken of, equipped with metal eyes around the upper surface, and beside it, another stone Adille had not mentioned: an irregular pillar, buried for part of its length in the soil. The pillar seemed to be uncut, and yet I had the strong impression that the upper end of it had a face. Perhaps it was only that the side nearest me was slightly hunched, like a shoulder, making the upper part appear headlike. A broken line of jaw. Two hollows that might be eyes. Altogether, a sinister-looking thing.

I turned my eyes back to the flight of stairs. At the very bottom, a company of guards was being posted around the hill. Within the next hour, two other rows of guards were posted, one midway up, one just outside the buildings that edged the plaza. If I had delayed my arrival, it would have been impossible. I curled into the smallest possible compass, cushioned my head on one arm, and actually dozed off, pillowed and warmed by the many folds of the heavy, malodorous robes.

I was wakened by the shriek of metal, the boom of a drum, the growling chant of many voices. Below me, lit by cressets, the metal door to the mausoleum shrieked against the stone of the threshold as it was drawn open. Peeking over the edge, I saw several K'Famir as they went in and returned carrying cages that were set at the edge of the plaza. In the flickering light, I could see they had small creatures in them, the size, so I thought, of a rat, perhaps. I had never seen a rat, but they had figured in the stories I had read as a child. Small enough to be held in two hands, large enough to be frightening if a lot of them came at you. These creatures were not coming at anyone. They were crouching in the cage, their large ears flared, their large noses quivering. No tails, I told myself. Not rats, because they have no tails. They looked like frog dolls, except for the ears. I concentrated on the chant, recognizing many of the words but not all. A hymn to their god, Whirling Cloud of Darkness-Eater of the Dead. The chant mentioned an offer of sacrifice, something, some quality that was to be . . . credited? The words fell into place. An offering would be made that was to be credited to the account of those who made it. This struck me as funny, and I almost forgot myself enough to laugh. What a strange mixture of worship and accounting. I amused myself with the idea until the first small creature was laid upon the round stone, tied to the metal eyes, and selected members of the group began applying blades and heated irons to its body. The creature screamed. Oh, by all that was holy, I heard words. It spoke words.

Not understandably, but unmistakably! I buried my head in my arms, pulling my robes over my ears, but nothing prevented the shrill screaming from going on, and on, and on . . .

When the torture ended at last, I looked up. A netted cage was being placed over the mutilated body. The chanting resumed, urgently. The tall pillar of stone wavered before me, actually seeming to look downward at the circling fog that had materialized inside the cage. The stone spoke. I heard it, not with my ears but with some deeper sense of recognition. The fog swirled. Solidified. I could not see what had materialized inside the cage, but whatever it was touched a deep well of revulsion. A knife was thrust into the small creature, which emitted one final shriek, then the cage was removed from over the corpse and carried away, down the hill while another victim was selected to receive the attentions of another group of K'Famir. After that, another, and another after that, and another. Each time the torture, each time the death, each time the stone looked down, something solidified inside a cage and was carried away. I lost count. I stayed curled tightly, head buried, until at last a silence came and dragged on and was finally broken by a familiar voice, someone I knew, someone I had met. I looked up, listened. It was Progzo. Adille's father!

"This was the last of the sacrifices we bought from the supplier who trades with us through the death-house. Some time gone the supplier warned us these sacrifices were becoming few; the place that bred them was empty of them. The supplier sent us a sample of another sacrifice, one that could be provided in unlimited numbers. Then that supplier ceased dealing with us.

"These new ones will work very well," he trumpeted. "We have found a new vendor to provide them through the death-house. We have the original sample here. Others will soon arrive from the new vendor. Bring it!"

From the temple beneath me a K'Famir emerged bearing a child in its arms, a human child of perhaps nine or ten. At the altar, the child was asked his name.

"Fessol," he said, shyly. "I am Fessol."

They were the last words the child uttered, but they were not the last sounds he made. He was larger than the small creatures, and the torture was done carefully. It went on until dawn. The cage was set in place, a larger thing materialized within. The tall pillar almost seemed to bend above it.

"Too much light to carry it into the city," Progzo said. "It might be seen. Put it into the place and lock the door."

The cage was put in the mausoleum below me. The K'Famir and their guards departed. Only Progzo and two other K'Famir lingered on the step.

"Will this kind work as well on humans as the others do?" one asked.

Progzo answered. "Our supplier sent me a few of these a long time ago. They were much more expensive than the other kind, the little ones, so I tested one myself. I arranged for it to fasten on my daughter's pet, a human. It was my daughter it fastened on, but she did not live long. Her pain was amusing."

"I, too, find females' pain most amusing," the other answered.

"Adille's pain was not worthy. She was sterile. A mere plaything. Of no value. The ghyrm feeds on the human pet now."

Some time after they had gone, when the plaza was completely empty, I struggled down from the temple roof and went into the plaza itself. A few torches still burned. The bodies of the victims were nowhere to be seen. Had they been taken away? Perhaps eaten by the K'Famir? Perhaps by Progzo, who had arranged for the death of his daughter, and for my continuing pain. Progzo, who had spoken of a human child as a new form of sacrifice?

I had thought I was past any anger, but what burned in me at that moment was too hot to be anything but rage. A torch burned beside the door of the mausoleum, which had been locked with a length of chain threaded loosely between the door handles, loosely enough that I could push one door open to make a sizable crack for the torchlight to fall through. The cage was just inside, and in the cage was a creature I knew all too well.

"Come," it whispered. "Come here. Feed me."

The crack was too small, and the cage that held it was of too small a mesh for it to escape. I was about to turn away when something behind the cage caught my eye. A pool of light held between the massive, uncut stones of the far wall. And not far from it, a pool of dark among the boulders of the adjoining wall. Between them, a machine of some sort. A very strange machine. I stared, stared, almost too long, for the thing had extended a tentacle and was feeling its way toward me through the crack. Only its little gasp of anticipation alerted me. I turned and struggled witlessly down the hill, through the alleys. I had seen nothing during the night that I had not seen the K'Famir do before. All male K'Famir seemed to be experts in torture; perhaps it was something they learned in their malehood school, but this was the first time I had seen it used against an absolutely helpless victim instead of against an adversary, or against a female consort or daughter they wished to be rid of.

I dreaded the fact that *it* was waiting for me, eager to make me relive it all, to drain me of everything I had seen, felt, heard, smelled. Well, *it* must not learn what I had heard! *It* must not know that I knew how its kind were made! Without at all understanding why, I knew without any reservation that the thing must not know of it.

Past experience helped. I had learned that if I concentrated on the pain and the blood, *it* would pass over the specifics of surroundings and torturers. Particularly . . . yes, particularly when *it* was very hungry. I delayed feeding *it*, therefore, until after I had eaten and had arranged my thoughts carefully. Then I fed *it*, concentrating on the little creatures, on how they had writhed and cried out and screamed, playing the scene over and over in an endless loop, until the thing drew away, satisfied.

As I dressed for work, my mind was busy sorting out what I had seen, putting together all the clues and sayings gathered during my time on Cantardene. On my walk to work, I fit everything into a scenario that was consistent with what I had learned and observed, not only last night, but all during my enslavement.

Male K'Famir prayed to Whirling Cloud of Darkness-Eater of the Dead, personified by the standing stone. The sacrifices acceptable to the Eater of the Dead were pain, terror, panic, horror. All these were bankable, and the aim was to build up a credit account with the god. If Adille's father, Progzo, had a large credit

account with the Eater of the Dead, the god would not eat Progzo
when he died. Perhaps the Eater would even allow Progzo to feast at
the god's table. Moreover, the god was not a myth. There was actually something there, in that stone!

I had been only twelve when I had arrived on Cantardene. Things
I had learned before that time were indistinct in my memory, but I
recalled reading of a human tribe who had had such a god, such a
worship, such an obsession with blood and pain. They had built high
temples, they had torn out the hearts of their victims, cut off their
hands and feet, let the blood flow until the temples were red with it.
Even so late as the twenty-first century, only shortly before my own
time, there were makers of films and plays who had rejoiced in gore,
who had made suffering an object of prurient amusement for desen-
sitized audiences. Some such were even produced in the name of religion, as though cruelty could ever elevate mankind! Viewing cruelty,
religious or not, only did to the viewers what it had done to the
K'Famir. It helped create new torturers.

The gods of the K'Famir, however, went further. They took pain
and horror and created from it creatures like the one to which
Adille had fallen prey. Every time the ritual was held—and this was
just one city of Cantardene, there were many other cities, probably
many other hills and rituals—living persons were tortured to death
and *things* were produced. Did anything of the victim live on in the
horror in the cage? I thought it unlikely. Only the pain and horror
were embodied in something that lived to create more pain and
horror.

And was the god really a god, or was it some other kind of life-
form? Some other, unknown race of beings? Though, of course, such
life-forms might be considered gods, of a kind . . .

And where had the strange sacrifices, those little rat-sized beings, come from? Where had the little boy come from? The pools
of light and dark inside the mausoleum, how had they come there?
A mausoleum was a death-house. Progzo had said he obtained it
through the death-house. Traded for it? If the pools of light and
dark were gates into other places, could trade pass through them,
even of living things? Perhaps the strange machine was some kind
of control . . .

I could do nothing about it. Not yet. All I could do was go back to work.

"Are you well, Miss Ongamar. You look quite pale."

"Quite well, thank you, Lady Ephedra."

"We have much work today."

Much work indeed. I took my place in the fitting room, my ears alert as I listened, listened, listened.

I Am Margaret/on Tercis

As I well knew from my eighteen years on Tercis, residents of the Rueful Walled-Off (officially listed as *Tercis, Expiatory Sect 909*) are expected to be at services each Rueday morning. In The Valley—as the southern, sloping, arable half of Rueful is called—Ruehouses are found even in small hamlets, such as Crossroads, Sorrowful, and Repentance. Contrition City, supporting its own notion of its importance, has a dozen or more, as does Deep Shameful, and others are found in every town in the northern, more mountainous half of Rueful, the Heights. In Rueful, on Rueday, one goes to services unless one is bedridden, witless, or dead.

Around Crossroads, attendance is expected even of the walking comatose, a chronic condition afflicting several local residents: Hen Kelly, for example, or the Johnson brothers. Bodily present, spiritually and cerebrally nowhere, they let their heads fall back onto the edge of the pew while their sagging mouths exhale vapors strong enough to stupefy any congregant within breathing distance. Ma Bastable from Ma's Kitchen and Ms. Barfinger from the Boardinghouse, both very high-chinned and solemn in their Rueday lace collars, always sit behind these miscreants, glaring at the back of their heads from opening prayer right up to the end of services when the pastor says, "It is time to rue."

Ceremoniously the two Keepers open the Ruehouse doors to let the penitence flow down the hill into River Remorseful while all of us stand perfectly still until the last person finishes ruing. However long it takes, no one moves or makes any kind of noise until the pastor speaks the words of forgiveness. When something really bad happens in Rueful, it will always be blamed on an interrupted ruing that's risen up to become a contumacious influence. Well, no. What they actually say is, "Damn rue-bug is loose amongst us!"

On this particular Rueday, Bryan and I and our twin daughters, Maybelle and Mayleen, were almost last to leave the Ruehouse, walking slowly and solemnly to give all that contrition time to get well away, so we wouldn't step in it and track it home. Truth be told, both of us were so weary we couldn't have walked any faster if we'd tried.

"Pastor," said Bryan on the front stoop, gravely nodding.

"Doctor," the pastor returned, with the same nod, and a slightly less formal one to me and to the children. "Missus Margaret. Miss Maybelle, Miss Mayleen."

The other congregants had scattered, some to the northern road, some to the road that led across the river bridge, some to the streets of the little town of Crossroads, at the south end of which stood the clinic and the doctor's house, our house.

"Well, even though I didn't get enough sleep last night, I still stayed awake," said Maybelle with a sigh.

"You were very good," I told my sixteen-year-old daughter unnecessarily. Maybelle was sometimes wakeful at night, possibly because of her heart condition, not immediately dangerous, Bryan said, but one he would keep an eye on. "Thank you for not snoring during services."

"She wasn't any better than I was," said Mayleen angrily. "I was just as good, better even."

"You were very good," I said wearily. "No one said you weren't, Mayleen."

"You and Maybelle are twins," said Bryan in his falsely jovial, 'speaking to Mayleen' voice. "Equally good, equally pretty, equally smart, in everything."

I found myself thinking desperately, Oh, dear God, if that could only be true! Some days I wished Mayleen had had the heart trouble so she'd have less energy to devote to dissension, dissatisfaction, or to discovering new injustices she had suffered. Some days I thought Mayleen was sixteen going on two, and Maybelle was sixteen going on fifty.

Bryan stopped and turned toward us, asking, "Who's that man staring this way, Margaret? Is he staring at the girls?"

"Billy Ray Judson," I said quietly. "You know his parents, Bryan. Judson owns that farmland north of the Conovers' place. We've met them and the younger half brother and sister several times. They were at the Ruehouse Festival last month."

Bryan nodded, forehead furrowed as he dredged up the memory. "Oh, yes. James Joseph is the boy, the girl's name is Hanna. James is a nice, polite boy, but even if we know the family, his brother shouldn't be directing that sort of stare at a schoolgirl."

"I'm not a schoolgirl," said Mayleen. "He likes me, that's all. You don't think people should like me?"

"Of course people should like you," I said with a degree of desperation, wagging my eyebrows at my husband, who ignored me in favor of returning the Judson boy's stare with a slightly censorious one of his own. "Your father just means you're a little young to get involved with someone Billy Ray Judson's age."

Maybelle started to say something, thought better of it, and tugged her sister by the hand. "Race you to the house," she said.

"I'll just walk," said Mayleen, sauntering slightly away from our family group to smile enticingly at the Judson boy.

Bryan started to say something, and I snarled, "Don't," in my firmest voice, locking my arm through his and speeding my footsteps to abbreviate the whole encounter. Maybelle moved along quickly at my side, asking her father a question about the clinic, thus deflecting him from saying, thinking, or doing anything about Mayleen. Meantime, I considered for the thousandth time the subject of twins. Twins should be similar, and identical twins should be identical; but Maybelle had all the goodness and good sense of any two normal people, and Mayleen had none at all. That fact was both frustrating and painful, for in any future I could imagine, Mayleen would carve out a hard and unrewarding life for herself.

This line of thought led inexorably to another: It was probably best that my first babies, the twin boys born soon after Bryan and I arrived on Rueful, had died at birth. Mayleen and Maybelle had been the second set, and we'd stopped there. I no longer grieved over the two dead children. Though Maybelle was a kind, good girl, if the two who had died had followed the girls' pattern, there might have been at least one like Mayleen. Having even one more like Mayleen would be insupportable. I simply could not have managed.

This little exchange had hooked me on one thorny link of an endless chain of interlocking memories, all of them embarrassing or hurtful, all of them inappropriate for a woman who had just been to the Ruehouse! I made myself look at the clinic up ahead, pure white, shining like a beacon, without a spot on it. Wrong word. I derailed again, wishing my life could be that spotless, gritting my teeth in fury and ordering myself, STOP THINKING. Stop regretting. Stop chasing yourself around like a dog after its own tail! The memory chain went only one place! Back to Earth on the day the proctor came, never anywhere else!

During our first couple of years on Tercis, while Bryan was teaching me to help him in his work, he had told me I was a natural healer. Since virtually all of what Bryan called "healing" I found intensely embarrassing and distasteful, I'd choked on that accolade. Sometimes I thought my repugnance was some failing in myself, other times I wondered if any solitary child reared without intimacies on Phobos, as I was, could grow up to be comfortable with the duties "healing" required. Doing it for sixteen years hadn't made it any easier, but the bargain I'd made with myself required that Bryan and the children never know how difficult and disgusting I found it. I'd kept that bargain! They didn't know, but I did. I'd found no way to keep myself from knowing it, hour by hour, rue it on Rueday though I would. I sometimes felt it would have been easier to labor in a Cantardene mine with a whip at my back than to do the things Bryan expected of me.

As we mounted the porch, I glanced back to see Mayleen flirting and giggling with the Judson boy. The Judson man. He had to be at least in his midtwenties. I stared, openly disapproving, until he shrugged and turned away. Mayleen waved and called after him before unwillingly joining the rest of us.

"It's nice to have paint on the house," I remarked in the complacent, calm voice I'd practiced until it became second nature, the one
that carried just the right message of *everything's lovely, everything's just fine*
I ran my hand along the door molding. "It really looks wonderful."

"Never saved the life of a painter's son until this spring," said
Bryan, with a wry twist to his lips. "So this is my first paint job as a
fee. Pity the boy didn't get sick a decade or so ago."

"Better late than never, Daddy," said Maybelle. "You always say so."

He did always say so. He always said a good many things: that
every day was a beautiful day; that our troubles had all been worth
it; that each year would get easier; that we had a good, pleasurable
life; that we'd done the right thing; that he was better off here than
on Earth. Maybe he really believed it, but I'd been too busy atoning
for Bryan's self-sacrifice to have entertained the notion it had been
anything but a martyrdom for him. No matter what he said, I knew
what he'd sacrificed.

"Where's Daddy, Mom?"

"Out back, Maybelle. Don't bother him."

"What's the matter?"

"Hen Kelly's mother died."

"She's been dying for years. Daddy shouldn't feel bad. It isn't his
fault."

"He thinks . . . he knows he could have cured her back on Earth.
It makes it hard for him."

It was hard for him, and what could I do to make it up?

He'd ask, "Where did you get this piece of equipment, Margaret?"

"I think someone brought it in from the next Walled-Off, Bryan.
Is it something you can use?" He'd been grieving over not having it
for two years, and it had taken me a year and a dozen broken regulations to get it smuggled in.

"Of course it's something I can use! But it's not a technology
we're permitted to have yet. The Walled-Off Inspectors . . ."

"Let me worry about the Inspectors," not mentioning the valley
grapevine I had tapped into, the informants I paid off with eggs or
fruit or other barter that patients had offered to meet their bills.

"I didn't think we could afford a larger furnace for the clinic,
Margaret."

"Bryan, it's one that was taken out of a building being remodeled up in Contrition City. It didn't cost anything." It really hadn't cost anything: except the time spent in cultivating Billy Ray Judson's father, who did a lot of remodeling in Contrition City; except for the pies I baked every few weeks for the wagoner who brought it down to Crossroads; except for the winter's worth of preserves I'd given Abe Johnson, who had put the boiler and pipes together. Most of the clinic improvements came about in similar ways: the windows, the added room, the shelves in what Bryan was pleased to call the pharmacy.

"I saw Daddy out back again, and I think he's crying!"

"I know, Maybelle. The little Benson boy died."

"I thought Daddy knew how to fix his back."

"Daddy did know, dear. Daddy just didn't have the special medical equipment he needed in order to do it."

Every day I told him that I loved him, though I'm afraid my love weighed light on the scales, particularly as lovemaking became infrequent, then rare, then extinct, killed off by unending exhaustion.

Still and all, I had seldom seen him lose his temper, and never as badly as he did a week or two later when Maybelle said to us quietly, privately, while Mayleen was somewhere else, "Daddy, Mom, I'm pretty sure Mayleen's pregnant by Billy Ray Judson."

As the words left Maybelle's mouth, Bryan turned as red as an apple, and his face swelled. "Get your father a glass of Hen Kelly's best," I demanded. Maybelle darted toward the kitchen, and I seized my husband's shoulders and pushed him into a chair.

"She's not going to marry that ne'er-do-well," he grated. "That . . ."

"Bryan, hush. Listen to me. I know you're angry. I'm angry. But I'm not surprised." He erupted under my hands, and I thrust him down, hard. "No, don't say anything, just listen. I'm not surprised. It's exactly what we could expect from Mayleen. She isn't Maybelle. She's another person entirely, and nothing I do or you do is going to make her grow up or become sensible. Now listen to me!"

He stared at me, amazed. In all the time we had been on Tercis, it was only the second time I had raised my voice to him, and it was definitely the first time I had openly acknowledged Mayleen's particular . . . difficulty. Maybelle came in with a glass of Hen Kelly's five-year-old best. I put it in his hand, and said, "Maybelle, close the door and watch out the window to be sure nobody's out there listening."

I leaned over Bryan once more: "Billy Ray's father has built up a good construction business in Contrition City. Judson was married twice. His first wife got herself killed in a drunken brawl in the tavern where she evidently spent most of her time, and it's doubtful whether Billy Ray is actually Judson's son, though he's always treated the boy as his own. It was the second wife who reared Billy Ray, along with Hanna and James Joseph . . ."

"I'm really not interested in their damned family history," snarled Bryan, lowering the glass.

I laid my fingers on his lips. "Bryan, the family history is important! Judson still has title to the land he was awarded when he first settled here, near Crossroads. He built a house on the piece across the river and lived there for a few years, but he never farmed it because by the time the population built up to the point market farms made sense, he already had his construction business well established. Now lately, Billy Ray's been talking about farming. His father told him it was a hard life, and he wouldn't advise it . . ."

"Advising Billy Ray not to do something is absolutely guaranteed to make him want to do exactly that!" opined Maybelle from the window. "Mr. Judson should have begged him to be a farmer and forbade his joining the army!"

I shook my head in reproof, but I was smiling a little, and Bryan was staring at both of us as though we'd lost our minds.

"How do you two know any of this?" he demanded.

"Maybelle and I go shopping, we listen. We have the quilters over, and we listen; we go to the Ruehouse, we listen. And Maybelle is right, it might have prevented a lot of misery if Judson had forbidden Billy Ray to join the army, because he'd have done it, just to upset his father, and that would have at least removed him from Rueful. Now listen to what I say, Bryan! Mayleen's exactly like him. If we say black, she says white. Our opposition would only make both of them that much more determined. That's by the by, however.

"What's relevant is that Mr. Judson has already given property to the three children. He's given Hanna some income property in Contrition City, and he's given half the farm to each one of the boys. Billy Ray is eldest, he picked the land across the river with the house on it. It's his, and the farm is big enough to support him and Mayleen."

"When did this happen?" Bryan demanded.

"Billy Ray getting the farm? Over the past few months. Mayleen wants to marry him—no, I haven't heard her say so, but I'll wager Maybelle has."

"She's right, Daddy. It's all Mayleen talks about."

I nodded. "And if she's pregnant, which I have no doubt she is, unless you're capable of forcibly aborting her, Bryan, then locking her up in the attic for the next ten years, she's going to manage being with Billy Ray, one way or another."

"And you accept this?" he asked angrily.

"Accept it?" I, sighed, at a loss. As I'd accepted Rueful? As I'd accepted becoming his nurse? As I'd finally accepted that one of my children was born to misery. "What are our choices, Bryan? Tell me if we have any. I'd love to know."

He mumbled and grumbled to himself, gradually losing steam as his kettle cooled.

I said, "There's one good thing, Bryan. Our family here, Maybelle, and you and I, will be much, much happier with Mayleen married and living somewhere else. Ninety-nine percent of our upsets and problems are Mayleen."

Bryan said plaintively, "God, Margaret, she's only sixteen!"

"After the number of years we've lived in The Valley, you should know every man here believes if a girl is big enough, she's old enough, and the ruing can come later!"

Bryan, deflated, rubbed his forehead. "I didn't foresee my own daughter being considered big enough."

"Well you can rue that come next Rueday. Maybelle and I'll stand right beside you and rue it double."

"No, I won't," whispered Maybelle. "Because you're right, Mama. We'll be so much happier if she's somewhere else. She just makes our lives a misery."

It was a mistake, of course. I had forecast Mayleen's life, but I had not considered Mayleen's children, all ten of them. Yet another mistake to add to the endless chain. Still, as I often tried to console myself years later, it was quite possible, given Mayleen's stupidity and Billy Ray's pigheadedness, nothing could have prevented it, even if I had known where it would lead.

I Am Wilvia/on B'yurngrad

On B'yurngrad, my years of study had come to an end. I was congratulated by my instructors and was honored by being summoned by the High Priestess for an interview concerning my future life. I had never been to the High Priestess's office, which was known to be high in the dome of the Temple, between the outer shell of stone and metal and the inner shell of plaster and gilded tiles. One of the novices offered to guide me up the endless stairs that spiraled through echoing spaces above the Temple vault.

"Does the High Priestess climb these stairs every day?" I asked, puffing slightly.

"Wilvia, we don't know," said the novice, a woman even younger than my twenty years or so. "When she summons us, we climb up, and she's there. If she doesn't summon us, we don't go, and we have no idea where she is."

We climbed farther. The stairs leveled into a ramp that curved gently upward to a wide door.

"In there," the novice said. "Knock first."

I knocked. A voice bade me enter, which I did, struggling with the weight of the door. The room was empty except for two chairs, one of them occupied by Lady Badness.

"Well, come in, Wilvia. Don't stand there gawking."

"I didn't know you . . . how long have you . . ."

"How long have I been head of this agglomeration? A very long time. Is it rewarding? Yes. Does it take a lot of my time? Not really. Your teachers are pleased with you."

I flushed. "They seem to be, yes. I'm surprised. The final examination was not at all as I expected it to be."

"The judging of cases. No. It's never as we expect it to be. That's why we train women judges here at Temple. It is the nature of men to make rules for everything and to play complicated games with them. For them, the game is more important than justice.

"Ordinary people prefer justice. They prefer that things be taken case by case, they prefer an attempt at justice over the rules of law, for they know that pure law is often used by the clever to victimize the innocent. Sit down, child."

I lowered myself into the other chair. In the center of the room was an open well surrounded by a railing. I could hear the shush of footsteps and the murmur of voices far below in the Temple. Above, a similar hole pierced the dome to show the sky, where white birds darted across an infinite blue.

Lady Badness spoke: "You have done what was required, learned what was necessary, and I have come to take you away."

"Away?" The word, leaving my mouth, sounded bruised and tentative. "But . . . Joziré will come here to find me . . ."

"Joziré is waiting for you on Fajnard. His mother, the queen, has died, not at the hands of Frossian assassins as was feared, but from sorrow, an illness we do not know how to cure. Joziré must now take the throne. He wishes to do so with you at his side, *if* that will be good for his people. Will it, do you suppose?"

"He never sent me word," I cried angrily. "Never once . . ."

"He could not have done so without risking his life and yours. Would you have wished him to do that?"

I bit my tongue. "Lady Badness, no. I didn't think."

"You will have to think if you marry Joziré, will your marrying him be good for his people?" repeated Lady Badness obdurately. "You marry them when you marry him."

Over the past five or so years, in those few moments when I had had time for reflection, I had asked myself this question many times.

"I believe I will be good for his people," I said firmly. "I will love them as I do him, and they will be my people."

She nodded, looking at me with what I thought might be sadness. Not joy, at any rate.

"Then I must tell you what is forecast for the lovely lands of the Ghoss. They may soon be threatened, probably by either the Frossians or the Thongal. If that happens, you may need to leave your people, your country. You may need to leave Joziré, for his sake. You may have a long, troubled time in your life. You may know sadness, and sorrow, and loneliness. You may have to work very hard just to stay alive. Or, you can forget Joziré. You can stay here. It will be safer. You will be among friends. I think it is only fair to give you warning before you put your foot on the path . . ."

She stared at me, into me. I know what she saw, a kind of whirlwind, doubts and sorrows and joys all spun together like the whirlwinds on Mars. Joziré's face, his eyes, the feel of his hands. The dragonfly ship. The woman in red. What I had left. What I had promised.

I heard myself say, "Even if all that is true, every word of it, I still choose Joziré. I still choose to be queen, to rule justly, to do what he would have me do."

And that seemed to be answer enough. She stood up and gestured. A ship edged its way over the window in the dome and dropped a ladder down. Old as she looked, Lady Badness went up the ladder like a tree rat, and I went after her. The ship was piloted by the same woman in red who had brought me here with Joziré all those years ago. She smiled at me, indicating the older, one-eyed man with her. "Mr. Weathereye, Wilvia." I bowed, he nodded, the ship moved away.

I was not conscious of time passing, which it must have done, before we saw an enormous highland centered upon a tall, white palace. We set down in the paved courtyard.

"These are the highlands of Fajnard," said the one-eyed man, turning toward me. "Much work awaits you here. Do you think you're up to it?"

I simply stared at him, my mouth open.

Lady Badness said, "I have seldom seen anyone work as hard as

Wilvia has done. I have faith in her." She leaned forward and pointed through the open door of the ship. "See, there!"

A man was approaching. I looked, and looked again. He was taller, and stronger-looking, and even more handsome, and . . .

"Joziré," I cried, and went running toward him.

Behind us, the ship left very quietly.

I Am M'urgi/on B'yurngrad

I found my first housing on B'yurngrad in a hostel kept by the Siblinghood of Silence. The first person I met there was a tall, dark-haired, lean-faced fellow named Fernwold, who stared at me as though I was long-lost kin. He was, so he said, the sorter-out, the questioner and annoyer who fitted awkward pegs into weird-shaped holes wherever that was possible.

"First thing," he said, looking me over from head to toe, "is for us to learn how you came here to B'yurngrad?"

I gritted my teeth and prepared to be terse. "I was twenty-two years old, on Earth, recently identified as an over-four, being shipped out. I might have ended up on a ship that went into Mercan space if I'd told them I speak Omniont and Mercan languages, so I kept my mouth shut. I was put on an Omniont ship that was scheduled to stop here on B'yurngrad to transship its cargo to various Omniont worlds."

He cocked his head. "You stopped at this transshipment point, and ..."

"... And the ship unloaded the bondspeople onto three smaller ships that had come to pick us up. Two ships left. I was on the last one, and while it was still sitting in the port it developed something called a core resonance. Does that happen?"

He nodded. "Often killing a lot of people."

"The repairs were going to take a long time. The shipmaster was told to get rid of his cargo, as feeding us was expensive . . ."

"How did you know that? Did the shipmaster tell you?"

"Of course not. I heard him talking to his superiors, whomever. They said sell us if possible, but get rid of us. I inferred that meant kill us. It seemed logical."

"So when you said you spoke alien languages, you meant you really speak them, not just know a few words?"

"I really speak them, yes. That was to have been my lifework. Translation. Diplomacy. Understanding. And why are you staring at me, what did you say your name was?"

"Fernwold. Ferni, for short. A good friend at the academy called me that. I'm staring because you look like him."

I discounted this as unlikely. "Fernwold. Some person or group bought us or ransomed us—at least they paid something to get us released, or hosteled, whatever. The next person I met was you."

"The Siblinghood of Silence ransomed you," he said, looking thoughtful. "Thus moving you from bondservice into sibling service. What's that old saying, from the roasting spit into the fire?"

I stared at him, openmouthed. "The who?"

"The Siblinghood of Silence. You haven't heard of them?"

"I've heard of something called the Third Order . . ."

He put his finger to his lips, eyes conveying a definite message. "No. You haven't. No matter how well you remember it, you haven't heard of it, but you do remember the Siblinghood."

"A bi- or multigender fraternity of some kind?"

I thought his responsive smile rather wolfish, hearkening back to my childhood love of animal books. His eyebrows were dark and extremely mobile, two physiognomic punctuation marks that leapt about to mark each utterance, parenthetical or exclamatory. Just now they were tented, conveying amused disbelief at my ignorance.

"Rather more than that, Salvage. It is on behalf of the Siblinghood that I am here to find out what each member of the ransomed cargo may be fit for. Some of them will be easy. They'll be kitchen help. They'll go to the workshops of the building crew. The High-house of the Siblinghood here on B'yurngrad is always in a state of reconstruction. Its work changes minute by minute and hour by hour.

"They'll tell us to build a dormitory for fourteen Thrackians found floating, because maybe the Thrackians can give us some information about this, or that, or something else. Or they'll say they need a new kitchen for the Pfillians who have ritual requirements for their food. Or, as now, they'll tell me you Earthians habitually segregate by sex, so we need two temporary dormitories, please . . ."

He touched my shoulder lightly. "Of course, such segregation is fully voluntary. I have very nice quarters if you're not intent on that old Earth rule."

"I am quite intent on obeying all such rules," I said, resentfully intractable. "Who are they, the Siblinghood?"

"What do you care, Salvage? Fate has dropped you into kinder hands. No real bondage for you."

"My name is not Salvage. It's Margaret. And I love it, the way you say no real bondage?" I laughed. "I don't know what you call building walls and laying floors, Silencer, but bondage isn't far from it."

"So, give me a reason to assign you somewhere else, pretty one. I'm not hard to get around. Anyone with a warm heart can do it."

I took a moment to think. "I've already said I know languages, Sibling. Several. Even many. Surely among all this important work your Siblinghood is busy doing, there must be a position open for a translator."

"Hmmm." He stood, stretched thoughtfully, glanced at the barred windows and doors, said, "Don't go away," in an amused voice, and left.

I was there for several days while all those around me were assigned here and there. I sat. I borrowed a book on the language and customs of the Hrass and read it cover to cover. When he returned, it was with a different demeanor. "I have your assignment," he said. "Eventually, your language skills will be of great use. For the time being, however, you are to be trained by a shaman who has sent word you are to be renamed. This is necessary, I am told. You are to be called M'urgi." He wrote it down for me. "It means 'explorer' in a dialect spoken here about. Pronounced as I did, MAR-gee."

"Gee as in game," I said witlessly. Something in what he had said had rung a bell in my brain. The reverberations made me tremble. "As in gossip, gamble, garden, or even Mar-gar-et, which is what the

Mercan crewmen on the ship called me, with a giggle and a slither when they did so! Why must my name be changed?"

"Shamans on B'yurngrad always name their novices, and it's customary to do it in advance of training so the novice can get used to it. That's what we'll all call you from now on . . ."

When I started to speak, he shook his head at me. "Don't ask. I am as surprised as you are, and anything I might tell you could be wrong. You're to wait here until your . . . ah, 'mentor' gets to someplace where you can safely be handed over to her. Meantime, you're to learn your new name and report to the supplies officer to be fitted out with clothes."

"I have clothing with me," I said.

"Not the kind you'll be needing," he replied with a wry, sideways grin. "Yours don't smell right. Not smoky enough."

Before I could ask what he meant, he was gone.

A shaman. Shamaness. Shamana. What was the female version? Did it matter? Why did it sound so very, very familiar?

It wasn't until that night, when I was just falling asleep, that it came me with such force that I sat up, fully aware. A shaman. Of course. That was one of my people. Margy! M'urgi? Close enough. I lay down again in the quiet darkness, mind spinning with something weirdly like hope.

The next day, he came back.

"It will be a while, M'urgi," he said. "Your future teacher is off on the edge of nowhere, seeing what the tribes are up to . . ."

"Tribes?"

"Bondsmen from Mercan planets who arrived here in no mood to settle down. Wildmen. They kidnapped a few shiploads of females, and they live out in the grasses in skin-covered huts, taking their herds north and south with the seasons and practicing a strange, violent, blood-and-honor religion. They come into the towns maybe once a year to sell their wool and hair and cheese. They learn nothing, for they're convinced they know everything that matters. They're boring. Even hearing about them is boring, so why don't we relieve your boredom. And mine."

We did so, finding much to talk of, much enjoyment in the talk. When I asked him to tell me about the Siblinghood, Fernwold said:

"Since you're to be a shaman, I can tell you this, though we don't speak of it usually. The Siblinghood is an organization of humans and Gentherans and a very few persons of other races. Most of the humans are a different kind we call Ghoss, though some of them are ordinary people, like me. Along with the humans and Gentherans are some extraordinary members who have strange and wonderful capabilities, men and women who are . . . something else."

"And what does it do, this organization?"

"It helps out here and there, when the human race itself gets into trouble. Which we inevitably seem to do. And the Third Order is trying to achieve some other grand vision . . ."

"And you're a member of this group?"

"A very, very minor member, yes."

"If there's a Third Order, I suppose there's a first and second one."

"Not any longer. Both existed; both were destroyed. The only thing I know about the Orders is they're attempting to find a unique spacial configuration, some esoteric galactic connection. What they call a 'cluster.' The First Order found one, the Second Order found one, and both times it promptly broke apart and killed a lot of the Siblinghood people who were exploring it."

"Someone broke it?"

"Maybe, or it may have just happened. The configurations they're looking for are only temporary. Finding them is like finding dew on the grass. Just because it's there at dawn doesn't mean it's going to be there ten minutes later. The Second Order operated much more secretly, just in case the first configuration was purposefully destroyed. They found over fifty partial configurations, but some of them were traps and others were just blind alleys. They discovered who set the traps and removed them, but by that time, they'd been delayed too long, and the cluster was gone again. The Third Order is being extremely security conscious. No one outside the Siblinghood knows who's part of it, or what it's found out, or even what it's looking for, and even we insiders know almost nothing, and if you're smart, you'll keep your mouth shut about the nothing you know."

The few days turned into twenty. By the end of the twenty, Fernwold and I were closer than friends. On the twenty-first day, I was sent away, to spend the journey time wondering who it was I had thought I loved, back on Earth, and why it was I thought I had loved him. Strangely enough, though I grieved to lose Ferni, I had gained a certain peace of mind. For Margaret, I had probably decided badly, but for M'urgi, the decision about Bryan had been the right one.

I Am Mar-agern/on Fajnard

When I arrived on Fajnard, in the Mercan Combine, I was still well shy of my twenty-third birthday. On arrival, our group of bondservants were chained together, though lightly, and escorted on foot across the port, which swarmed with races I had read of or heard about, and as many more I had never known existed. Our destination was a warehouse where a group of Bondsfolk Relief workers fed us and gave us bondservant clothing: trousers, shirts, long vests with pockets, a light jacket with pockets, a heavy, waterproof jacket with pockets, and a wide-brimmed waterproof hat, plus some softer material from which to make our own underwear.

Prior to our being sold, we were examined by two human doctors from Medecines Sans Limites who explained that they had volunteered to work on Mercan planets in order to care for those in bondage. Their existence in this far-off place brought Bryan vividly to my mind. Seeing my distress, the doctor asked me if I was injured or ill, I blurted out Bryan's name, and what had happened, while the doctor regarded me, unmoved.

"Though I can understand your reluctance, from my point of view, you were a fool," he said calmly. "None of us want to start a life from a position of indebtedness, even though everyone alive profits from the past. You're here now, however, and if you're to have any kind of life after you leave here, you must forget the past. Regret and nostalgia will result in depression, which is fatal on this planet. Pay attention to what I'm about to say: The most important rule is to repress how you feel about things and be supremely alert to what is happening around you. How you feel, what you think isn't important. What you do, how you act, is important! Don't act or speak until you have some inkling of what the result will be.

"I'm picking the first part of your own name, Mar, and I'm adding the suffix 'agern' to it. On Fajnard, long names are indicative of aristocracy or nobility. Bondsfolk are allowed the shortest possible names, and the suffix 'agern' means 'slave.' Your tag says Mar-agern! That's your label! Repeat it over and over to yourself, keep it in mind so you can be quick when some Frossian utters it. When a Frossian yells 'agern,' it means whatever bondsfolk are closest, so be alert for that, too.

"Sleep whenever you can, wherever you can. Try to stay as clean as possible. The purchase contract specifies bathing facilities, but that doesn't mean your buyers will have them, or that they'll be sanitary, or that they won't be frozen in winter. That means you sometimes use your drinking water to wash with, or the water that's used to water stock, usually umoxen. Since they produce the finest wool among the known worlds, the Frossians are careful of them, and their water is probably kept clean. If you have any difficulty staying clean, cut your hair off, all of it, everywhere on your body, as that will reduce infestation.

"Frossians are a three-sex race. All the queens are on one planet, elsewhere. Never ask where. That question can get you killed. There are a few hundred breeding males on Fajnard, the workers and soldiers are neuters, and they're the ones who'll be ordering you around. They're touchy, easy to anger, preoccupied with their own status in their own particular work crew. Anything you do wrong reflects on them, so don't do anything wrong.

"Eat sparingly and save the least perishable of what you're given in a pocket. If you don't have a pocket, use the materials we gave you to contrive one. You may be given three meals today and only one or none tomorrow. If you feel just slightly unwell, don't let it show. Even if you feel quite sick but can put on appearance of working, do so.

This marks you as a noncomplainer and builds a store of tolerance among the overseers. Then, if you think you're dying, kick up a real fuss, and if you're loud enough, they'll probably send for one of us, particularly before they've had their value out of you, that is, during the first ten to twelve years you're here."

"They send for one of you?"

"There are several MSL doctors here, male and female, and we've trained some helpers who've worked out their bondage. The Frossians tolerate us because they get more work out of healthy servants. We're certifying that you're healthy to start with. If you're careful, you may stay that way."

That was my last earth-human contact. On the following day, our shipload of émigrés was sold. I had dreaded the poking and prying that I expected to accompany this process, but seemingly the buyers were not interested in touching the merchandise. A scaled, bone-crested, tailed, four-legged, two-armed Frossian emerged from a crowd of similar beings, put a rope around my neck, and led me and two others to a weirdly ornamented wheeled vehicle that lurched as though it had no gyros. We went through the city into the country-side, grasslands on all sides, occasional copses of strange, bulbous-trunked trees with horizontal, cylindrical branches from which huge straplike leaves hung like shutters, turning as the sun moved. The end of each branch ended in something that looked very much like an eye, and the eyes followed the progress of our vehicle.

At the end of the journey, a cluster of shabby buildings in the midst of endless grass, another Frossian led me, still roped, to the barn. The ceilings were low enough that I knew I could touch them by reaching up. I did not reach up, for I had already learned that any voluntary motion on my part brought a choking jerk on the leash. A long aisle ran down the center of the building between open pens on either side, pens without fronts, just three walls dividing the structure into equal areas filled by huge animals.

They were furry . . . no, woolly. Enormous brown eyes peered at me with unmistakable intelligence. The ears were long enough to be amusing, even funny, and the horns were long enough to be danger-ous. And the tails! Curving upward and forward, each of them spread long, fine wool in a perfect parasol above each animal or, when lowered, a blanket, so evenly distributed it might have been spread by some domestic who had just changed the linens. I could not see their feet, for the hind legs were bent under their bodies and the front feet were curled against the ponderous chests. Four-legged. Not unfamiliar, as though I might have seen their like in a book, or more likely their attributes. Horns like cattle. Faces like buffalo. Coat and ears like poodle dogs. Those marvelous umbrella tails? Giant anteaters came to mind, though as I recalled, their tails had been more brushlike. Of course, I knew them only from books.

The Frossian spoke in his own language. "You are responsible for feeding them, and watering them, and cleaning up after them and taking them to pasture and bringing them back. Any one of them gets hurt or dies, you get hurt or die. You stupid humans don't understand anything Frossians say, but the whip will teach you."

"On the contrary," I said in only slightly halting Frossian, "I understand very well."

The Frossian's eyes widened momentarily, before his arm lashed out, clubbing me across the face as he hissed, "I explain! We don't talk to slaves, and we don't want them talking to us, especially if they contradict what we say!"

He left me lying in the straw, facedown, half-stunned, realizing suddenly that the word for *contradict* in Frossian was the same word as *insult*, that the word for *explain* was from the same root as the word *demean oneself*. From the umox nearest me, a strange, whistling call rose up. Still dazed, I looked at the creature and saw that it fluted the sound through its nose. Within moments, I was surrounded by a group of people who looked so like me, I would have sworn they were family. They were Ghoss, they said, speaking to me in Frossian.

"Oh, girl, umox say you spoke to overseer. Such a bad idea to speak where any overseer can hear you!"

"Why did you do such a thing?"

"Didn't they warn you. The doctors? Didn't they say not to speak? Not to move or speak? Surely they warned you!"

"Ummm? Here, let us see your eyes, let us see your arms."

"Not too bad. You'll have a strange-colored face for a few days."

"Now you can count on that one's enmity so long as you are here."

Finally, then, I remembered the doctor telling me not to speak, and I cursed myself silently. So proud of my ability to speak, I had to do it! Pride. Rotten pride. Obviously, pride was something to be forgotten.

"Who are you?" I asked.

One of the women spoke. "I am Deen. We are Ghoss, dear girl, as you no doubt are yourself."

"I'm not Ghoss, whatever. I'm human."

"Well, of course, Ghoss are human. Tsk. Here, let me put some salve on that. Don't worry, the doctors gave it to us. It won't harm you."

And so my servitude began with the first lesson: Do not speak unless among the Ghoss and where no Frossian could hear. With the Ghoss I spoke Frossian while I learned their own language, one with strangely familiar words in it, an old language, they said, dating back to the time they had been brought from Earth by the Gentherans and given to the Gibbekot, the indigenes of Fajnard.

"The indigenous race? You mean, this isn't a Frossian home planet?"

"The Frossians have no home planet except one place where the queens live. Frossians eat up planets as a plether of umoxen eat a field of hay." Deen snorted her derision.

"What's a plether?"

"So many as will fit into a pen, Mar-agern. A plether of umoxen is fewer than a plether of Gnar, but both take the same barn space. As I was saying, the Frossians take everything they can take without triggering action by ISTO, then they go ruin some other world. When they came here, our Gibbekot friends went into the mountains, but some of us . . . well, let us say we do not hide as well as they. The Frossians forced us to stay here and work for them."

I thought this last was less than truthful. The Ghoss had nothing about them of abasement or servitude. I conjectured that they might be here for some other reason. What that reason might be, I had no idea, and it wasn't explained, even though I became woven into the life of the Ghoss, almost one of them.

I would have been quite content to be Ghoss if I could have managed it, for they had invisible networks of solidarity and succor that prevented even the least among them from being trod upon and broken. If you were Ghoss, you just knew when help was needed, but I had no such connection. For me, help did not come unless some Ghoss actually saw my trouble or the umoxen let them know. Either way, they would arrive with salve for the welts, with painkiller, with soft words, with behind-the-scenes string-pulling to save me further punishment. They claimed me in kinship, even though I knew I was not kin.

"You always claim not to be Ghoss, but you obviously are!" said Rei-agern, a middling old one, with an interestingly ugly face.

"I am a bondservant from Earth. None of my family ever were Ghoss, there are no Ghoss on Earth."

"Well, there obviously were sometime, because that's where we came from originally, some thousands of years ago."

"Captured and enslaved," said I sympathetically. "I'm sorry."

"No such thing," cried the other. "We were never slaves of the Gibbekot! We were their friends, their coworkers. We stayed at their invitation, true, but it was not into slavery! Many of us went with them when the Frossians came, and those who did are still with the Gibbekot, back in the hills."

I thought the talent they had might have been a gift from the Gibbekot, for they were something other than merely human now. Perhaps they had mutated, or evolved.

I soon learned the routine. Rise early, go to the privy, wash in the bucket, go to the kitchen, take whatever food was offered, return to the barn, open the big door, and urge the plether to get up and move. The umoxen seemed to take a perverse pleasure in being difficult to rouse, and it was days before I realized they were playing with me. When I stopped chivvying them and took to leaning on the doorpost, chewing a straw, careless of whether they moved or not, they moved. The same ones always led, the others followed with one small, brown one at the rear, and I walked by that one, soon enough with my arm across the creature's shoulder, feeling through the wool for any sharp seed or spine that might fret an umox.

As I walked I watched everything, looked at everything, attentive to the presence of continuous miracle. There had been no grass, no fog on Earth. I had suppose these things to be of one kind. Grass was green. Fog was gray. Instead, neither was ever a single color, ever a single thing. The umoxen relished the fog, murmuring their way through it, the moisture condensing on their wool so that when the sun broke through, it lit a procession of jeweled chimeras, garbed in rainbow.

Sometimes an umox would come up behind me, so softly I did not hear it, then suddenly *whuff* at me from behind, frightening a yelp from my throat, and at that they laughed. I knew it was laughter, though silent, for their shoulders shook with it.

"You are naughty animals," I told them. "Shame on you." At which they laughed the harder. They had voices that ranged from that same high, fluting call I had heard the first time I met them to a low, satisfied rumble I could hear through the soles of my feet.

"Can you get me some brushes?" I asked the Ghoss. "Some brushes, a pair of pliers, maybe a large comb."

"We can," they said. "But the herdsman won't let you keep them."

"I'm going to hide them in the pasture," I confessed. "In a hollow fence post."

So equipped, I began grooming my charges. First the little brown one that I walked with to the pasture each day. I worked the comb through its wool, slowly, carefully. I brushed the long wool of its tail, strand by strand, not hurrying. It was a way to pass the time, not something I had been told to do. Soon the little umox began to rumble-hum, the sound of a deep-toned stringed instrument, stroked with an endless bow. The next umox added a tone, then the one next to it, and soon there were twenty humming, one vast, endless harmonic chord that sounded upward, through my bones.

When I had finished with the little brown one, I turned to find my next victim and was confronted by the leader of the plether, who looked at me significantly and turned, offering its tail. From that day on, I spent my days grooming the plether, two days per umox, strictly in rotation. I hid my implements in the hollow post each night. Before long, I was telling them stories of Queen Wilvia and the nazeemi and the yaboons while they rumble-hummed along, not only my own plether but all those within hearing, a vast harmonic sound that continued until my brain sang with them, and time went by without my noticing it.

The pliers the Ghoss had found for me were useful in reaching seeds that had worked their way back inside the long, sensitive ears or pulling thorns from their strange feet: an almost complete circle of hoof surrounding a soft center made up of four stubby fingers that curled up, out of the way. Usually they could pull thorns from one foot with the fingers of another, but sometimes, especially among the old ones, their ankles had stiffened, and they could no longer do it for themselves. They came to me from all the plethers around, flopping down on their sides with a great whoosh of expelled air, holding up the painful hooves. Sometimes, also, they caught something in their teeth that their long, flexible tongues could not retrieve: a piece of fencing wire or a short length of the cord used to bind the hay. I asked the Ghoss to get me scissors and pliers that were more pointed. Time went on as I told endless stories of my worlds, of Naumi the warrior, and Margy the shaman, of the nameless spy and of Queen Wilvia, who ruled a far and wondrous land.

It had been summer when I arrived, and I had slept on a pile of hay beneath the shelf where the water buckets were kept. When the nights grew colder, the overseer told me I was to sleep in the same place, though he knew it was exposed to every current of air from above and below, a place where it was impossible to stay warm.

"The better to keep her wakeful," the overseer laughed to his cronies. Since the Frossian knew well I was always wakeful from first light until the night bell, expecting me to remain wakeful through the night was mere persecution.

Deen-agern said so. "Mere persecution, Mar."

"What's mere about persecution, Deen? If you live under it, it's not mere, believe me."

"Well," the older woman huffed, "we *all* live under it. All us Ghoss."

"They don't treat you like this, and I'm not Ghoss." By this time, I spoke in the language of the Ghoss, not fluently, but understandably.

"The overseers think you are."

"Well, they're wrong, and so are you."

The Ghoss had been right, however, about the enmity of the Frossian herdsman. He remained implacably hostile. He began by stealing my clothes, piece by piece, until I had only one set of trousers and shirt to cover me. In the summer, it didn't matter, but now that it was winter, the absence of cover was long torture through every night. The Frossians didn't like the cold. According to the Ghoss, the Frossians preferred warm planets with high heat and humidity. In summertime, there were often only a few guards left on the place; their overlords were somewhere wet, basking in the sun.

The first wintry night below the bucket shelf, I stayed awake while cold breezes caressed my backside through the cracks and another ice-wind hand played its fingers over the rest of me. My second night, I dreamed of fire. Fire on hearths, fire in forges with hammers ringing, bonfire on the heath with people dancing, fire on eastern mountains glowing against the clouds in a false dawn more feverish than rosy. Fire anywhere, anytime, so long as it was warm.

During the day that followed, I decided to weave a thick blanket for myself from discarded rags, all wound about with tail wool from the umoxen themselves, tail wool I gathered from hedges and fences about the place. I would have to hide it somehow, so the overseer didn't take it. If I had been Ghoss, the overlords would have been more cautious with me, but evidently they knew I was not, even though I looked just like them. No true Ghoss would have been ordered to sleep below the bucket shelf, so someone, or some set of someones, obviously regarded me as neither one thing nor the other. I myself had heard the least overlord, him of the twisty mouth, with nasty words dropping from it like spit, describing me:

"She's an abomination, a *Mar*. The *frumdalt* want to get rid of Mar. We should get rid of it now."

"Merely an aberration," the middle overlord had replied on hearing this muck. "We haven't enough bodies to do the work, surely not enough to go about killing this one and that one until nearer their time. We can get rid of it later, but not now. It still has work years in it."

The word the least overlord had used, *frumdalt,* was unfamiliar to me. *Fruma* was the name of the carrion birds who frequented the river bottom. *Dalt* was one word used for a hilltop or tower. I asked the Ghoss.

"*Frumdalt?*" said Rei-agern. "I think it means 'god,' or perhaps something else to do with their religion, but we don't pay attention to their religion."

"A frumdalt might be something on high that eats dead things," I suggested.

"Ah," said Rei-agern with a puzzled look. "On Cantardene they have a god called Eater of the Dead."

Next night I lay down on my bucket shelf, curled into a tight ball, waiting for the herdsman to make his last inspection, which he did, coming in to poke me in the process, to be sure I wasn't asleep. Then, he went off to his warm bed in the snug quarters in the loft, leaving me to stand shivering by the shelf, pulling my scant wrappings around me. I dozed, fretfully, coming fully awake to find the little brown umox lying next to me, warm as a little furnace.

"Don't," I told it, looking into its eyes, deep and dark as those forest pools I had dreamed of as a child. "The herdsman will take it out on you. He wants me to suffer here. He mustn't see you here, he might do something dreadful to you."

The little one went back to the other umoxen where they lay tightly together in deep bedding, covered with their great, fluffy tails. It took a lot of cold to chill even one umox, much less a plether. I sat shivering as I heard the little one talking to the others, knowing its voice, slightly higher than the big ones, slightly sweeter.

"Mar-mar," said a large umox, one or several of them. "Come here."

"I'm dreaming," I thought to myself. "I've been frozen under the damned shelf and now I'm dreaming."

"Here," said a deeper voice, joined by several others to make a low, harmonic sound in my head, as though great chimes were ringing there. "Here, young one."

I rose like a puppet and staggered toward the plether bedded in the hay. As I came near, one shifted, then another, letting me fumble my way to the center of the plether, where a nest of hay was waiting, already warmed by the huge body that had lain there. "No need to go to the cold far," whispered the voices. "Warm is here. Lay self down . . ."

Which I did, though it was more a stumble-flop than a graceful recline. The warm tails of half a dozen umoxen moved slightly to cover me from head to toe, leaving only a little space around my nose and mouth so I could breathe. "I'm dreaming," I advised myself. "I'm in my own hay nest, and I'm dreaming."

"Dream then," whispered the umox. "Dream a thing we have meant for you and made for you. Dream what you will do when you wake."

For the first time since winter came, I was comfortable. The thick tails of the umox were blanket-warm though light as air, feathered from tip to rump with the finest wool in any world known to man or Ghoss.

"Why didn't you invite me before?" I murmured, half asleep.

"Why didn't you tell us you were cold before?" the umox murmured in return. "You tell us stories of Queen Wilvia, you tell us about the nazeemi, you tell us many things we already know very well, but you do not mention to us that you are cold. If you cannot tell the whole world simply by being, as the Ghoss do, then you must tell us. Little one saw you shivering and went to warm you. You feared for her. She came and told us. We do not let those who care for us come to harm."

"I'm sorry," I murmured drowsily. "I'm sorry I'm not Ghoss."

"Even if you are not Ghoss, you are quite likely our good friend."

I did not try to decipher this, for I was already asleep. In my dream, I wandered with umoxen, walking beside them as they trekked over vast green plains below ranges of snowcapped mountains, while high above us a golden bird cried strange words from the roof of the sky. I knew I was in an umox dream and had no wish to leave it.

Early in the morning, the herdsman came through with his staff, prepared to poke me again, but he found my space already empty. I, meantime, peered at the taskmaster through a fringe of tail wool that hung over my eyes. When the man moved away, gone to breakfast, the great bodies shifted again, making a way out. By the time he and I encountered one another, I was on my way back from the privies.

He stared at me with some suspicion, noting, perhaps, a certain unwarranted rosiness in my cheeks, a certain rested look around my eyes. "Cold last night," he muttered in an evil tone, obviously hoping I would answer.

I pretended not to hear him, merely standing where I was with my jaw sagging witlessly until he moved away.

He said nothing more, though I noted several questioning glances during breakfast lineup. When I had eaten, I returned to the barn and my winter chores, forking down the fragrant hay into the long troughs that lined the day barn before letting the umox into the day barn and starting the long job of cleaning out the night barn. Fine, rich hay for eating was the guarantee of high prices on the wool market, and there was plenty of it to be had on Fajnard. All the lowlands were grassland, all edible, sweet-smelling, and useful, and it never rained during haying season—so said the Ghoss.

As I had begun to do on my first day in the barns, I accompanied the rhythm of the pitchfork with a silent chant that kept my mind away from the past as the doctor had suggested. "Fif-teen" pitchfork into the haystack, "more" pitchfork raising hay, "years" pitchfork tossing hay, one step along the road to understanding how I had come here and what it all meant. One step, then another, and another, and another, three steps more along the road to discernment. Fifteen long, long years.

Eventually, it was spring. Fourteen ... more ... years, I chanted to the pitchfork. And then fall, winter, and spring again. Thirteen ... more ... years. And so on, and so on, and only a few more years.

I Am M'urgi/on B'yurngrad

Night on B'yurngrad. A steppe wide as an ocean, rustling with grass. Far in the night a broken horizon surmounted by a toenail of moon and a spear blade of dew-bright stars, pointing downward at the cleft between two hills.

"See," whispered the old woman, reaching to untie the long plait in which her hair was usually confined. "See," fingers moving upward through that hair, casting it forward, letting it move in the wind to blow like a veil before her eyes. "See, there, where the spear points downward, where the lance falls to reach the heart of water . . ."

"I see," I, who had been Margaret; I, M'urgi, whispered.

"This is the sign of the hunters, the skull-faced ones, who go wandering in the night. When this sign comes, they come eastward, running in the grasses. In this time when there are no wolves, they are the wolves of the night, they the tigers, the leopards, the swift-footed hunters. Prick your ears to the wind."

I listened. At first I heard nothing. The old woman's hand touched my ear, featherlight, and I heard. Through the wind-rustled grasses came the pant of breath, the fall of foot, the small rattle of bone beads strung on thong. One, at first, then several more.

"I hear," I murmured.

"How many?"

"Five, maybe six, but if six, the other is far off, following."

"If six, he is the one we want. Find him."

I closed my eyes, laid my hands palms upward on my knees, straightened my spine as though it were a cannon barrel, and shot my perception upward, through the top of my skull. Looking down, I saw myself, the old woman, the tiny fire before us, the circle of amber light that ended just beyond our haunches. I laid myself forward upon a dark pillow of air to follow the night road, the road of discovery, sending my thought in the direction of the sound, swooping along the dark air to meet it, even as it moved to meet me.

I came first upon the five skull-painted ones, panting down a narrow cleft between two hills, feet thudding on the soil, one well in advance of the others, a long pole carried over his shoulder with a pouch of something at its tip, then three more men, then a laggard. The sixth was farther back, nearer the place they had begun, and I flew toward him, sensing the old woman at my side.

Almost we missed the child. A boy, perhaps ten or eleven. Not yet come to strength, certainly, howsoever he burned with purpose, the hard red glow of it easily visible, even from our height.

"M'urgi, if this one lives," the old woman whispered, "over a thousand will die, for he will betray them and their good purpose. I have seen it."

"How many times?" I asked.

"Ten times watched, five times seen."

"Then it is equally likely he will not do the thing."

"I will be dead before the time comes," whispered the old woman. "I pass the burden to you, M'urgi. It lies before you."

I shivered in the chill dark, in fear of night, in grasp of bloodshed, in danger of being mistaken. A long moment went by before I said, "I accept the burden."

The night road retracted beneath us. The sky opened and dropped us beside the dim coals of our fire, which we covered with ashes before sitting down once more.

"What did the lead man carry," I asked, "at the end of that long pole?"

"Ghyrm," replied my teacher. "Ghyrm to use against another tribe, one he wants to do away with so he can take the women."

"Will the ghyrm take only men?"

"The ghyrm will take those they are purposed to take."

"Where did he get it?" I whispered.

"He bought it with pain, from someone who sells for pain. From Cantardene, most likely. Hush. They come."

Five runners approached, darting past not far from us, eyes set on their own road, sparing no glance that might have discovered two smoke-faced, black-garbed women hidden downwind in the dark. The air moved to me, and I smelled their sweat. When they had gone, I built up the fire once more. Much later, another footfall, this time interrupted.

"Hey, boy," I said. "Where you goin' in the night?"

He spun, frantic, relaxing when he saw us women sitting there, amber light reflecting from our faces. "Find m'dah," he said wearily. "I trail 'm this fah."

"And where's he gone, then?" I asked.

"Dunno. D'wanna be lef wit de women. No more."

"Ah! Fahr sure." I patted the ground beside the fire, inviting him. "He'll be mazed, he will, come back this way and find how far you come! That's a clevah idea."

"Is't?" he asked doubtfully. He had not considered whether it was clever or not. He had only thought of his shame, being left behind with the women, the babies. "Yeah," he claimed, inflating his chest as he approached the fire. "Is clevah. D'you hab watah?"

"Hab tea," I murmured, seating him by the flame, guiding his hands to wrap around the crude mug. "Y'know, some dahs don tell reasons propahly. You dah tell you his reasons, leavin' you?"

The boy spoke from inside the teacup. "Nah."

"Thot so. Prob'ly somethin goin on back in camp, your dah, he wants to know 'bout it. He wants to know do you keep you eyes open, you mouf shut. He can leave no mahn dere, for watchin. He can leave a son, though, son old enuf, smart enuf to watch. Thas prob'ly what he thinks."

The boy put the cup down, obviously in the grip of unaccustomed thought. "You spose? An I muck it all?"

I, M'urgi, shrugged. "You make it back in time, he nevah know. An, if he ast, did somethin happen, you say nothin happen or somethin happen, jus the way you see it."

I was speaking to the air. The cup lay empty and the boy was gone, back along the trail. The old woman said, "He may not make it back, tired as he is."

"He'll make it back," I said. "I've seen it."

"Ah. And when did that happen."

"Last night. You took us along the night road to the north. I saw the encampment there, saw the coming shadow cover it, heard the second wife buying poison from a traveler, saw the boy lying behind a bush, listening. Same boy."

The old woman smiled, though wearily. "I didn't see it."

"You were far ahead, scanning for whatever it is we're always looking for."

"It's ghyrm we're always seeking, and those who sell them," the old woman said with a touch of annoyance. "And you didn't mention the boy."

I nodded, familiar enough with her to be unmoved by her irritation. "It meant nothing, until tonight. Who are they, Wolf-mother?"

"The hunters? Followers of the ghyrm-way since the first bondsmen came from Cantardene. On that planet some evil creature taught them this way they follow: brother against brother, family against family, tribe against tribe, never a peace long enough for them to grow numerous, but with strong taboos on killing the women so they can always recover their strength. Faces painted like skulls to show they fear no death, for he who dies for honor goes to the place of Joy. Death and honor lovers. That's what moved the boy on the trail, honor."

"He will tell his father about the second wife. What will his father do?"

"Fly and see," the old woman whispered. "If you care enough to spend yourself on them. If you ask only for my guess, well then, the father will watch to see what she does. And she, she will try to poison him, so her own son can take that boy's place. And the man, he'll be so angry, instead of crying her crime aloud and sending her back to her family in shame, he will forget the taboos and will kill her. Her family will kill him for breaking the taboos. His brothers will kill her brothers. They will be much preoccupied with killing one another, and larger conflicts will pass them by. The boy will not be responsible for a thousand lives. Perhaps."

"To what purpose?"

The old woman shook her head. "We can see tomorrow, even next season or, for some things, a year. Farther than that, the road of discovery becomes a path of shadows, mere shades of portents of things uncertain. I saw that boy lead a raid a year from now, down from the hills into a village. I saw everyone in that village dead. Ten times I saw, five times I saw them dead. Perhaps in that possibility, the wife had killed her husband, the boy had laid blame and sought revenge. Whatever. It is your burden now, your duty to crouch over the fire and see."

"Is this why they sent me, Wolf-mother? Is this my life?"

"Only those who sent you know why, M'urgi. Only they know what your life will be, though I have seen a shadow on it . . ."

"What sort of shadow?"

"One that kills. Someone wants you dead, M'urgi. Sometime. Not yet, but sometime. In the meantime, there are more chants for you to learn, and more herbs for you to pick, and many futures for you to see . . ."

I laughed, without rancor but without amusement, either. My hands and face were black with soot from the fire. My hair felt as though several generations of birds had been nesting in it, leaving their lice behind. The hides that warmed me stank to high heaven. I had been with the old shaman woman for almost ten years. Whatever my unknown benefactors might expect of me in the future, I sincerely hoped it involved bathing at more regular intervals.

And, ah, it would be nice to see Ferni again.

"You're thinking about him," said the old woman in a minatory tone.

"I have seen myself with him elsewhere, Wolf-mother. In a dream I saw myself among the tribes, many tribes, all gathered together. And he came out of darkness into light, carrying something mysterious. Then I blinked, and when I looked up, I saw my own face, three times. One me a lot like me. One me much older. And one me looking out of a man's face."

"Thinking of him, dreaming of him, that'll get you killed," said the old woman.

"How long since you've had to warn me of that, Mother."

"A year or two," she replied grudgingly. "Maybe more."

"Maybe many more. You speak of dying. I have sworn to fulfill your burdens. When I have done so, then, perhaps, I may think of him? Find him in that place I dreamed of, among the tribes."

"Then," came the reply, a whisper in the night. "Only then. Perhaps."

I Am Margaret/on Tercis

On Rueday, all the Judsons are present in the Ruehouse, from me, Dr. Bryan's widow, Grandma Mackey, right down to Mayleen's daughter, Emmaline, youngest of the fourteen who'd been born to Mayleen, the ten who had survived. Though I have been Ruing for close to forty years now, I am still unable to confine my ruing to Rueday. Ever since Bryan died, I have stood here each Rueday, between my daughter Maybelle and my granddaughter Gloriana, eyes tight shut, hands twisting at one another, body trembling like a branch of autumn leaves in a chill wind while I rue having let Bryan sacrifice himself for me. Not that Bryan is the only thing I rue. I rue the twins, oh, the twins, my two sets of them, Maybelle's one set, Mayleen's seven sets—not even including all the ones miscarried or born dead. Oh, for how many years have I rued, and still I wish I could go back and undo it all.

In the pew behind me, Mayleen was ruing having a sister and a sister's family who were so rotten to her. Marriage and motherhood had not changed Mayleen; they had merely confirmed her misery. Billy Ray Judson was probably ruing that his brother had ever been born, for Billy Ray was as Billy Ray had ever been, jealous and hateful.

The seven Billy Ray Judson children who still lived in Rueful would be spending their ruetime as they did most of the rest of their time. Each Rueday I told their names over to myself. The eldest, Joe Bob, had left home to work on the Conover Farm, down The Valley. Perhaps he was ruing the fact he had not joined his twin in volunteering for the army. The second oldest twins had left years ago. Ella May had applied for membership in the Siblinghood of Silence and been accepted. Janine Ruth, her sister, had also applied and been refused, so had moved up to Repentance, which had more scope for her talents, which I refused to think about. Only one of the third set of twins had lived, Benny Paul, who was probably spending ruetime planning how to get Jeff, Gloriana's brother, into trouble. Trish, the survivor of the fourth set, who was simple but not asexual, was probably thinking of whatever boy was currently making use of her. Sue Elaine and Lou Ellen had made up the fifth set, and Sue Elaine was without doubt ruing the existence of her cousin, Gloriana Judson; while little Orvie John and even littler Emmaline, each sole survivors, rued the fact they had been given no breakfast this morning and probably no supper last night and were so hungry it was very hard to be quiet. The moment I laid eyes on them this morning I knew the money I had most recently given their mother had not been spent on food! Poor babies.

I knew them so well. I did not know them at all.

Next to me, I knew that Maybelle was resolving to be more patient with her twin. James Joseph Judson, Billy Ray's half brother, Maybelle's husband and Gloriana's father, was probably ruing not chastising his son Til, who was becoming more and more like Benny Paul. Til's twin, Jeff, was conscientiously ruing whatever iniquities Til and Benny Paul had got him into most recently. He always rued saying yes; he always said yes because Til was his brother.

Maybelle's daughter, barely pubescent Gloriana, usually had a lengthy list to rue, I'd seen her look up attentively when Pastor Grievy asked us to rue ". . . the great failing of our people in the long ago . . ." and I wagered with myself she was trying to figure that out. Gloriana was a great one for figuring things out.

I knew them so well, and I really did, even Til. They were family, while Mayleen's husband and children seemed more foreign than a tribe of Frossians. Or yaboons.

The choir voices began a slow diminuendo.

In the next pew, Abe Johnson had his eyes tightly closed. He usually spent double the average time ruing his mail-order wife, who had vanished, leaving him with her son, Bamber Joy, an event Abe would never understand if he rued the whole matter for a hundred years. Even he, however, eventually felt Pastor Grievy's tightly focused gaze boring through his eyelids, and with a sigh, lifted his head. The words were spoken, and we slowly left the Ruehouse.

People walked to and from services on Rueday as a minor religious thing, only faintly colored by notions of expiation or propriety. Most people who felt reasonably well did it out of habit unless the weather was intolerable, which it rarely was. All Tercis's extremes, either icy or furnace-hot, had been reserved for the coldhearted and the hot-tempered; the Rueful had been granted a Walled-Off with a pleasant climate.

The Judson clan gathered briefly at the Ruehouse steps. I touched Mayleen's shoulder. "Have you heard from Ella Mae, Mayleen?"

"Of course not." She shrugged my arm away. "She's in the Siblinghood of Silence, so she's silent so far as her family is concerned."

"I thought she might have a furlough this summer."

"Not with us, she won't. Last time was enough." She stalked off after Billy Ray, while I furtively gave the two little ones the cookies I had brought in my pocket. As quickly as a squirrel hides nuts in his mouth, they hid the cookies in their raggedy clothes. As Billy Ray led his brood westward on the highway toward the bridge that would take them across to their farm on the west side of the river, I saw them breaking off little pieces and taking sneaky little mouthfuls.

"Oatmeal," whispered Maybelle. "And raisins, and eggs."

I nodded as I cast a glance southward where my old home stood, now an addition to Ms. Barfinger's Boardinghouse. "And sugar," I whispered. "And butter."

Jimmy Joe and Maybelle led us toward the road that wound down sloped meadows and northward on the river's near side, strolling hand in hand, as if they were courting instead of having been married practically forever. Til raced on ahead as though eager to fit a whole day's devilment in before sunset. Gloriana ambled along beside me, stopping when I stopped to admire a flower or a fluttering bee-bird, and Jeff trailed behind, probably still trying to think of a way to keep Til from getting him into any more trouble.

By the time our family neared the bottom of the hill, other people had turned off, and we were alone, moving north along the pasture road.

Gloriana whispered, "Grandma Meg, what did Aunt Mayleen mean about the Siblinghood of Silence?"

"It's a kind of organization," I said. "They don't accept just anyone as a member. Only men and women who really want to spend their lives doing good for people. They call it the Siblinghood of Silence because they're not allowed to talk about what they do."

"I hardly remember Ella May."

"She's strong, and has a rather plain, pleasant face, and she's a good person." Unlike, I didn't say, her twin sister.

"That's why she left, I guess. Daddy says the only way you can give Aunt Mayleen and Uncle Billy Ray anything without their being nasty about it, is drop it off after dark and hope the dogs don't drag it away before morning. Probably Ella May tried to do them some good."

Which was one of the more perspicacious things Glory had said recently. Mayleen and Billy Ray would definitely resent any effort to do them good. "I think Ella May tried very hard to help them the last time she was home," I said. "I think they told her not to come back."

I saw her tuck that away, probably to think about later.

"Grandma, what was the great failing Pastor Grievy always talks about?"

Aha, I'd been right. "Probably something that happened a long time ago, before your Grandpa Doc and I came to Tercis. It might have been something that happened to cause the Walling-Off, when all those bondslaves were being dumped here, ready to kill anyone who looked at them crosswise."

"You and Grandpa Doc came later."

"We came here directly from Earth without any bondage in between. I was twenty-two, he was thirty."

"And Grandpa Doc talked you into coming here."

I pinched my lips and clenched my hands. "In a manner of speaking I suppose he talked me into it, yes. It was come here or go elsewhere, and this seemed appropriate at the time."

"Tell me about him."

"Glory, for heaven's sake. You remember him!"

"Not really. He died six years ago, when I was only six or seven. I wasn't grown enough to . . . to know what he was really like. As a person, I mean, not as a grandpa."

"Well, when we get home, come on up to my house, and I'll show you some views of him and tell you about him."

I stared resolutely ahead, down the road, wondering when, if ever, I would be finished with trying to explain Bryan Mackey. How could I explain him to Gloriana when I couldn't explain him to myself after all our years together? And when, under heaven, was I going to be able to stop trying to make it up to him and let him go?

After he died and I decided to sell the big house in town to Mrs. Barfinger, Jimmy Joe built what was locally called an "old-mother house" for me, up the hill behind his own place. The house wasn't so far away as to be troublesome going back and forth, but it wasn't so close as to infringe upon my privacy, or his and Maybelle's. The house was surrounded by trees and set at the back of a wide, rocky ledge that gave a view across most of the valley. I had grown to love the place more than I had ever loved the house in town, perhaps because I could be alone there, and loneness was comforting to me. When we got there, Gloriana echoed my thoughts, saying as she usually did, "I like this better than your other house. The other one was too big."

"It needed to be big," I told her, as I rummaged through my desk to find the viewcubes of Bryan. "We had three children, and Grandpa Doc was always bringing home stray cats."

"I don't remember lots of cats," said Gloriana doubtfully.

"It's just a way of speaking, Glory. I mean stray people. People in need of a bed or a bath or a meal."

"So he was nice to people."

I found the viewstage and set it on the window seat while considering this. Yes, on the whole, he had been nice to people, sometimes even those he was furiously angry with. Glory came to stand beside me as I flicked through the views. Bryan, a sandy-haired young man smiling, his arm around a young, pregnant Margaret, who had drawn cheeks and dark circles around her eyes; Dr. Mackey, a man thinner and older, still smiling, with a strained-looking Margaret at his side and teenaged Maybelle and Mayleen at his feet. That was taken just a few weeks before Mayleen got married. Then Grandpa Doc, a gray-haired old man seated beside light-haired Grandma, smiling, always smiling.

"He doesn't look angry," Glory said. "You tell it like he was always angry." She sat in the old rocking chair and touched her toe to the brick floor to make it sway. "I don't remember Grandpa ever acting angry."

"He almost never let it show," I admitted. "When we lived in the big house in Crossroads, he used to go out back and chop wood until he calmed down. One of the Walled-Offs here on Tercis is called Hostility, you know? Grandpa claimed to be afraid he'd be sent there, and he said there was nothing better for getting rid of hostility than an hour with an axe and some very resistant wood." I put my hand-kerchief to my face, stood up, and walked to the window, where I stared out, my back to Gloriana.

Gloriana knew I was crying. She changed the subject. "Grandma, whose fault is it that Lou Ellen's family's so poor?"

I cleared my throat and dabbed at my eyes. Whose fault indeed? "Start with the fact Billy Ray never really worked his land. He was too busy chasing your Aunt Mayleen, who was sixteen at the time! They got married because she was pregnant. Your mother met your father at Mayleen's wedding, so some good came of it, even though that's where being poor started. Since we couldn't have stopped it without chaining Mayleen to the wall, it's nobody's fault."

"Aunt Mayleen and Mama are different."

"They have different lives. There's a difference between having a very large family starting when you are sixteen, or having a small family after you have both an education and a livelihood."

"Billy Ray always talks about being a farmer," said Gloriana. "But he doesn't even know what kind of a farmer he is. It's always some-thing different that doesn't work out. But Mama and Dad are farm-ers, too. Sort of."

"Your mother and dad aim lower. A few chickens for eggs, a little garden for summer vegetables, a few fruit trees for preserves and jelly. And even if they had none of that, their jobs over in Remorseful would support you and Til and Jeff."

"So, if it weren't for the money you give Mayleen, they'd go hungry?"

"Even with it, they go hungry," I said angrily. "I give it for food, but they don't spend it on food! Did you see Emmaline's face this morning? That poor baby! I'm going to stop giving money and concentrate on cookies! Oatmeal cookies keep really well!"

"Couldn't Uncle Billy Ray get a job that would support the family?"

"He doesn't want a job; he wants to farm. He says he can support the family farming if things would just go right. If the universe would just cooperate, he'd make a living. Since it's the universe at fault, nobody should blame him."

Glory chewed on that for a while. "Anybody could say that about anything."

I murmured, "I give thanks every day that I ended up in such a cozy little house as this one in such a lovely place as The Valley, even if Ruers are mostly a little sad and not all that interesting."

"We've got some interesting people. Bamber Joy's stepfather is sort of interesting."

"Abe Johnson? Well, advertising for a wife isn't all that interesting, but getting one with a half-grown boy-child, a wife who pretty soon runs off, leaving the boy-child behind, that's rather interesting. And where in heaven's name did she go? Rueful isn't that big! She should have turned up somewhere."

"Bamber Joy says he's going to find her someday."

I shook my head at her, warningly. "Bamber Joy. The name alone is enough to guarantee he walks a hard road, Gloriana."

"He didn't pick his name. I like him."

"Your mother and I don't mind your liking him. We just object to your getting into fistfights on his behalf."

"He never starts them! Somebody needs to fight for him."

"Well, you're two of a kind."

"Objects of derision, you mean," Glory snapped.

"That wasn't what I had in mind, no. You're simply taller and a lot smarter than most of the local residents."

Gloriana flushed. She always flushed when someone said something complimentary about her. "I have to go," she said, getting to her feet and giving me a peck on the cheek. "I promised Lou Ellen a picnic down at the ferry pool."

"Oh, Glory . . ." I said.

"Well, I *promised,* and she's probably waiting for me."

She turned and fled, out the door and away down the hill before another word could be said. I went to the door, still blotting my eyes, watching the girl going away, always going away to something else, somewhere else, restless as a fleabit cat, just like me, restlessness chronic and exhausting to control, constantly throwing shovelfuls of activity over my wretchedness, trying to bury what wouldn't stay buried.

It had been a battle that took its toll on flesh and spirit, but I had not let Bryan see it. All my youthful dreams had been lost. The doubts had begun to circle almost as soon as we'd arrived, like those ancient carrion birds, scenting the rot that was setting in. And for what? If we could have made a real difference in Rueful, I would have been proud of our struggle, but all we really did was exhaust ourselves to keep a few pigheaded people alive a year or so past their time. Not a great achievement. If it hadn't been for the idyllic fantasy Bryan had woven for me during the few days before we left Earth, I wouldn't have been hypnotized by his exuberance, caught up in his certainty that love would see us through life, that it was a fair bargain for both of us, that it would all work out well.

"I've loved you since I first met you, Maggie. You were worth every year." He had told me that, time and again. I wish he hadn't said it. If he'd been angry with me, just a few times, I could have given myself some room. As it was, I had to be as faithful and helpful as was humanly possible. Even so, I never honestly felt the scales were balanced. All the good times we planned were things we would be doing now, and he was gone. There were more doctors in Rueful now, things would have been easier. We could have had time together. My fault. I shouldn't have let him bring me here. I should have taken my chances like everyone else.

Instead, here I was, grandma to a very troubled brood. What the proctor had said back on Earth was true: my family did indeed run to twins, lots of them, and of them all, only Maybelle, and Jeff and Gloriana seemed capable of love and joy. No, that wasn't fair. Probably Joe Bob, which is why he'd left, and Ella May's joining the Siblinghood of Silence meant she had it in her to be happy and good, or the Siblinghood wouldn't have taken her. And little Emmaline and Orvie

John? They might turn out all right, too, if they didn't starve to death first. The others though, well, they were fruit of a blasted tree, born because of bad choices I'd made, one after the other.

Likely, if I said any of that to Gloriana, the girl would say, "Well, Grandma, if that's so, here's right where you belong! You sound mighty rueful to me."

And, as Gloriana all too often was, she would be right.

All of which was fruitless and melancholy. I needed to get out of the house and do something. I knew the way to the ferry pool, where Gloriana was going, and I decided to join her there.

I Am Margaret/on Tercis

Sparkle in the noon-light, river running, road dust fluffing in a teasing wind, grass bending and swaying, Gloriana on her way to the ferry pool. From the road, I saw her running through the meadows down toward the river. Ahead of us, the Great Dike ran east to west, a wall of black stone, onetime southern edge of a mighty water that had covered a great part of south Rueful to a considerable depth. The water had worn its way through the top of the dike and begun chewing a channel all the way to the bottom. How many millennia it had taken to gnaw its way down, no one in The Valley knew, but we all gave thanks for the wide-cupped plain of loamy soil it had left behind. This was fat soil, coveted by anyone who knew how to farm.

The day had warmed, and my face was wet, though it would be cooler near the river. Something was pushing the season. Every weed patch had turned into a jungle, every garden was sprouting a thicket, and each day was already full of lazy stupefactions from noontime right up 'til supper. I watched as Gloriana crossed the grassy riverside, eaten into a lawn by the Birkin's geese, who honked at her querulously as she went by. "Glory, why such a hurry, have some nice grass."

"Thank you, no," she said. "I'm meeting Lou Ellen, and I'm already late." That's what it sounded like to me, at least. Not that I spoke Goose. Not that I spoke anything much anymore. Sometimes I lay in bed at night thinking in Earthian, then translating those thoughts into Gentheran, or Pthas, or one of the other tongues I'd taken so much trouble to learn. I grieved over that. I grieved over the possibility I was losing my mind, too. Sometimes lately I had thought something was being said when there wasn't a sound; sometimes I had known something had happened even though I hadn't seen it. Senility. The madness of the old. I had gone so far back in time getting to Tercis that I was probably older than my own father right now. And thinking that, madam, I said to myself, will drive you bonkers.

Gloriana climbed down into the river bottom to walk under the high arch of the bridge. Dominion had built the bridge to speed transport of materials quickly from Walled-Offs in the west to Walled-Offs in the east. Some nights we could hear the trucks roaring far across The Valley, growling and echoing as they crossed the bridge, then fading to a distant beelike hum among the mountains. They never came the other way, so we supposed they must return through other Walled-Offs, north or south, taking export stuff to the spaceport near the Western Sea.

I didn't follow Gloriana's route. Under the bridge, the river bottom was scattered with rounded black boulders separated by narrow lanes of sand. Gloriana could swivel her way through them, but I no longer had hips hinged like that. The pool where the old rope ferry had been, prebridge, was on the far side of the dike, a circle of dark water with green rushes all around it, quiet as a dream even on noisy days. That's where Glory said Sue Elaine's sister, Lou Ellen, was waiting.

When Lou Ellen was tiny, she had been very frail and had spent more time at Glory's house than she had at home. It was easier on her to be in a quiet place rather than in Mayleen's house with its cold drafts in winter and swarming flies in summer, where rackety, quarrelsome people were always going at it hammer and tongs. Besides, Mayleen didn't have the patience for helping Lou Ellen eat, and Sue Elaine had said right out loud it would be better if she just starved to death and got it over with. Lou Ellen ate very well if the food was mashed up soft, and Gloriana was good at doing that. The two of them had spent hours playing card games on Glory's bed, upstairs, where no one would bother them. Lou Ellen was a good player; there was nothing wrong with her mind even though her body had been fragile as a sooly leaf eaten away by worms until nothing was left but lace.

One day I heard Lou Ellen ask, "Glory, are you my friend? Sue Elaine says I don't have any friends."

"Of course I am, Lou Ellen. What you think I'm doin' here?"

"I thought maybe it was just you're my cousin."

"That too. If you'd rather have me for a sister, I could be your blood sister, just like the blood brothers in those stories Aunt Hanna tells us when she comes visiting."

"I'd like that," Lou Ellen whispered. "Oh, I'd like that."

Through the slit in the door I had watched while Glory got a darning needle and cooked it in the flame of the coal stove so it wouldn't have any germs on it, then pricked their fingers and pressed them together and swore to be blood sisters forever.

"Not just for this year or next year or the year after that, but blood sisters so long as I live," Glory said. Glory was only in first grade then, but she could already write pretty well. She and I had taught Lou Ellen to read and write. The two of them wrote the promise out together, very neatly, and put their names on it. Glory put the folded-up promise in an old lozenge box, wrapped the box in a piece of oil-cloth, and buried it at the foot of the tall, standing stone halfway up the hill toward my house. Glory had always said the stone looked like a huge, armored person, standing guard over the valley. I saw it all, and the place by the stone was a good place for a promise to be protected and safe. The whole thing was so dear it made me cry, but I never let on I'd seen them.

Instead of going below the bridge, I went up to the near end of it, toward town, crossed the road, and went down the other side on the steep path through the woods. When I got to the bottom, deep into the shadows of the trees, I saw Glory coming out from under the bridge, looking toward the old, splintery pier, gray as a goose feather. She smiled radiantly, raised her hands, and called, "Lou Ellen!"

I stopped. I was intruding on her. Everyone, even young people had a right to their private time. Still, I didn't feel like going home. I sat down with my back to a tree and thought about having a nap. I shut my eyes.

"How long you been here?" Glory called.

I think my eyes must have opened, just a slit. I saw Lou Ellen on the pier. She shrugged waveringly, almost like heat waves rising. Her voice came like a whisper of wind.

"Don't know," she murmured. "A while. You look all hot. You bothered by something?"

"Me? Not much." Glory felt her face. "Well, yes, I am. Here it is summer again, about time for me'n Sue Elaine's birthday party, and as per usual, nobody's invited you."

Lou Ellen smiled, then whispered in a soft little voice I could barely hear, "Do you want to go to the birthday party?"

"Ballygaggle no, Lou Ellen! I don't even want to *have* a birthday party unless I can have one of my own. I'm tired of sharing my birthday with somebody I don't even like just because we were born in midsummer. It's the same dumb thing every year. Grandma and Mama make a big fuss over it, and everybody gets their feelings hurt, and Grandma goes around all sad and doesn't talk to anybody for days and days afterward!"

"Then why should my feelings be hurt not being invited someplace I don't want to go anyhow? It's nice I don't have to."

At which point I should have picked myself up and gone home, but I didn't. I was asleep, so I couldn't.

Glory asked, "You going to help fish?"

Another of those wavering shrugs. "You do it, Glory. You like catching them."

Glory opened her pack and got out her fishing gear, a string tied to a piece of stinky meat, and lowered it into the shallows near some rocks. Within two minutes, a big crawdad grabbed it with his claws. Tercis crawdads weren't earth crawdads, but Earthians had given them the same name because they had pretty much the same look to them, claws in front, legs behind. She pulled it out and put it in the bucket.

"You're sure lazy," murmured Gloriana

"I know." Lou Ellen sighed. "I've been like this lately."

Lou Ellen went on dreaming, Glory caught crawdads, the sun slipped down from the top of the sky.

"I've got twenty-one," Glory said, yawning. "That's ten each. What do you think's better? Should we flip for the extra one, then maybe have hard feelings, or should we just toss the littlest one back?"

"Throw it."

"You pick which one."

Lou Ellen drifted over to the bucket and pointed, but as Glory tried to toss it, it nipped her, pinching like crazy. She danced around, waving her arm and yelling ow, ow, leggo, leggo, her eyes so scrunched up it took her a moment to notice the two people who came out of the reeds across the pool and walked across the deep pond toward her, their feet leaving not so much as a ripple in the mirror surface of the water. In my dream, I had seen them coming.

Glory's eyes flew wide, and she forgot about the crawdad, which hung twitching on her finger while she stared at the impossible people. To me they looked to be partly silver and partly blue, as though extremely cold people were contained inside coats of clear ice, but they didn't look at all frozen. Their eyes and arms and feet moved, their huge, furry ears twitched back and forward, and their little pink triangle noses wrinkled at the corners, just like cats. They had that same sort of upper lip, too, split just below the nose and curving up on either side to make a rounded W shape. If cats could smile ingratiatingly, that's what these people were doing.

Glory said something like How do you do, or Hello there.

Lou Ellen said, "Who you talking to?"

Glory looked down where Lou Ellen was sitting at the end of the pier and said, "Them."

Lou Ellen looked all around. "Who's them?"

Glory turned toward the smaller cat-person, and said angrily, "Now, that's not fair! You're going to get me locked up again, everybody thinking I'm crazy, and that's not a nice thing to do. You let Lou Ellen see you, too."

The bigger one remarked, "Of course. How thoughtless of us," and he cast his eyes over toward Lou Ellen, who immediately screeched and grabbed at Glory, getting the crawdad's other claw instead. It pinched her, and she howled.

"What is it your intention to do with these creatures?" asked the bigger one.

Glory said, "We'd planned on eating them."

"Are they edible?" the smaller one asked. "They seem to be quite barky and fibrous."

"The tail meat inside the shell is very nice," Glory said, self-consciously shifting herself into politeness mode. This meant doing what I had told her, over and over. Concentrate on good grammar, speak quietly, without expletives—even silly ones, like "Ballygaggle" instead of her daddy's "Balls!"

"Then you're carnivores," said the bigger cat-person.

"No, we're Judsons," Glory said. "Gloriana and Lou Ellen Judson."

"A judson is . . ." said the smaller one, leaving it hanging like it was something she didn't know what to do about.

"A family," Glory told them. "It's a family. Like, we're related. Lou Ellen and me, we're cousins. Her daddy and my daddy are half brothers, Billy Ray and Jimmy Joe Judson, and her mama and my mama are twin sisters, Mayleen and Maybelle Mackey."

"Sisters who are very like one another, perhaps?" asked the smaller one, her eyes glowing.

Glory took a long breath before she said, "Not all that much, no. Aunt Mayleen thinks my mama's cornered the market on selfishness, and my mama thinks Mayleen's too lazy to breathe on her own, but it makes no nevermind because Lou Ellen and I are best friends, no matter what."

"It's good to have friends," said the smaller one to the bigger one. "No matter what kind they are . . ."

"Besides," Glory interjected, "I didn't catch on to your asking about carnivores right at first, because I was thinking of the Conovers, the folks on one of the farms down the road. But I do know what a carnivore is, and we're not quite. There's another word for what we are . . ."

"Omnivores," said the smaller one in a satisfied voice, like she'd been planning a dinner and had been worrying what to serve. "No, we're omnivores, too, so I wasn't worried about our having a meal together. My companion's name is Prrr Prrrpm by the way. I am Mrrrw Lrrrpa, and since you have called your cousin Lou Ellen, you must be Glorrrr-iana."

In my dream I said their names, over and over, the *r*'s rolled like an engine running, and when they used Gloriana's name, her jaw dropped, and it took a minute before she could say, "I'm Gloriana, but how come you know that?"

"We were given directions," said the larger one. "We were told to find Gloriana Judson at this river, by this pier, early summer, period two, day ten, at twelve-forty-nine in the afternoon local time. We have a locator." He removed a gadget from his belt and held it out: an egg-shaped, translucent blue thing with a silver handle.

"What does it say?" she asked.

"It says you are . . . who you are."

"And why does it say that," Glory demanded.

"Because," said the littler one more softly, "you, no other person, are the optimum person to help us with our task."

Gloriana considered this. She looked baffled. They just stood there, as though they expected her to do something, and in the dream, I could see her considering what might be proper.

"We were about to have our lunch. You're welcome to share it, if you like. We've got enough crawdad tails for five each and enough potatoes and bacon and apples for everybody."

"What fun," said the smaller one. "What can we contribute?"

"There's that roast pleckle leg," he said. "And a whole basket of whalp berries. And those preserved grum stalks the trader gave us when we visited on . . . somewhere."

Or something similar. The two cat-people walked up onshore as if it was all decided, shedding their ice coats as they came, and almost immediately the two of them had a fire going, the groceries out of their bags, and water boiling a lot faster than water ever behaved for me when I was in a hurry!

Glory wrapped the potatoes. "We'll prob'ly have to have 'em for dessert," she said, as she buried them in the fire. "They'll take a lot longer to bake than the crawdads will to boil."

The food the cat-people had taken out of the bags seemed more voluminous than the bags themselves, but Glory didn't comment on that, which was dreamily appropriate. When the crawdads were cooked, the four of them took the shells off and ate a bit of them and a bit of grum stalk, which Glory said was spicy and tart and a little peppery, and then a whalp berry or two, very sweet, then a bite of apple, and then some more of this or that while the little wind sent wavelets clucking around the splintery lopsided pier and terci-crows cussed at each other in the trees.

The two cat-people were full of questions about the Judsons and the farms and what they raised and what did best, like turnips, and what didn't do so good, like anything fancy they might get more than fifty cents for. Glory waded out into the pool to get the jar of kinda-lemonade she kept there, where it stayed cool, and when she came back, they passed the drink around, and along about the third drink, the smaller one wiped her mouth on one paw—it did look like a paw, but it had fingers like a hand—and looked Glory straight in the face.

"Gloriana Judson, could you find the goodness in your heart to do us a favor?"

Glory looked suddenly skeptical, and I knew she was thinking of Bobby Duane Hansen's Crusade of Help. Bobby Duane lived over in Repentance, but he was always crisscrossing The Valley in a wagon, suggesting very strongly that people find it in their hearts to help him out. Pastor Grievy thought Preacher Hansen was a poor excuse for a Ruer since Ruers weren't allowed to connect their religion to money, and it was usually cash money Bobby Duane was asking people to help him out with.

"What's the catch?" Glory asked.

They looked confused, so she said, "Usually, when somebody asks you to find it in your heart to do something, it means the heart's going to find heartache right soon in the doing. At least that's what my daddy says."

"Heartache?" said the smaller one to the big one.

"Displeasure," he said, trying it out. "Pain, suffering. No, no. No suffering, no expense, no pain or adversity."

Lou Ellen was looking at Glory sadly, as though Glory had done something really unpleasant, slapped a baby, or kicked a puppy.

"It's no nevermind," Glory said, catching sight of Lou Ellen's face. "I'm just shooting off my mouth. Grandma says I give the wrong impression because I do that all the time, and it's a defense mechanism from being teased for being a mutant, and it's one I should grow out of. You go ahead and ask your favor, and I'll let you know can I do it."

The two cat-people exchanged looks, then the larger one asked, "Why are you suspected of being a mutant?"

"Oh, because I'm taller than any girl my age, and I've got this hair so black it sometimes looks blue, and my eyes are a weird color. I don't look like any of the Judsons, not any of 'em."

"I believe you are within the range of human variation," said the smaller person. "I, personally, know several people much like you, and it is unlikely you are a mutant."

The larger one was silent for a moment, nodding quietly, as though to affirm his companion's judgment. Then he stood up very straight and said, "We have a girl-child, very young. Though she is scarcely more than a baby, a great mission is foreordained for her, a duty to perform when she is a little older. Others, our enemies, will seek to prevent her doing this. Since our child must be old enough to walk and talk, at least, before she can undertake this great duty, she needs an unlikely place of safety and warmth in the care of an improbable custodian."

Glory looked at Lou Ellen, who whispered, "Why didn't they leave this baby with her grandma?"

Soft-spoken as she was, they heard her fine. "Our enemies would think first of that. She would not be safe anywhere our people are known to live or in any district where we are known to visit. This is a place we have never been before and may never come again, and this will assure she is well hidden."

"Isn't there anybody else to do this thing you're talking about her having to do?" asked Glory.

The little one reached out for the big one's hand and held it tightly. "When a task is unequivocally assigned by great wisdom, there is no point in complaint or argument. It will be done by our child, Falija, or it will not be done at all. We hope only that she will be staunch-hearted and that we can return to help her when the time has ripened."

This was said with terrible sadness.

"You're going away?" Glory asked. "You're leaving her?"

"We must. To protect her, by leading our enemies away," said the littler one, with a strange, choked sob.

Lou Ellen whispered: "How old's the baby? Is it weaned yet? Is it potty-trained?"

Her question made perfect sense. Glory's brothers, Till and Jeff, were sixteen, so she'd never had any experience with potty-training or baby feeding, but after Lou Ellen there'd been Orvie John and little Emmaline plus several babies in between who'd lived a little while before they died. Lou Ellen knew all about babies.

"Weaned?" said the smaller one. "Oh. Mammalian feeding of infants, yes, no, that is, Falija is old enough to eat food such as we have just eaten. She is also omnivorous. She can drink water from a cup. She can digest milk, but she prefers meat or vegetable things. She is still very little, not yet knowing how to ... read? Write? Or speak very much. Our babies are ... potty-trained almost from birth, and we use a low sandbox for the purpose."

"How long you figure you'll be gone?" Glory asked.

The bigger one shook his head. "We cannot see the future."

"And what if you don't come back?"

"What we can do, we will do, and if all goes well, we will return in time. Will you keep her for us?" The larger one sighed. In my dream, for it was a dream, the sound came to me half through my ears and half through my heart, like the grieving wind of late autumn that pulls the last leaves down, or the dark breath that gasps at the light when a deep old cellar is opened. The sigh fluttered wearily inside me, finding no rest, and Glory's face held an expression that must have been like my own. She couldn't say no.

"You know," she said, "some people don't like anything that's any different from what they're used to. I've got some personal experience with that, and I wouldn't want this little one to come to any harm ..."

The smaller one whispered, "If you will love her, and keep her warm, and feed her, and clothe her and teach her as she grows, she will be able to keep from harm. Our people have their own ways."

"Feeding people isn't always easy," Lou Ellen commented. "Last winter, my folks didn't eat all that regular ..."

The cat-people nodded, like they'd already figured that out. The bigger one took a little pouch from his pocket and handed it to Glory. She opened it and looked at what was inside. All I could see was a vagrant sparkle. "This is a connection to something like . . . a bank," said the big one. "When you need money for Falija, for her food, or clothing, or whatever she may need, you speak the need into the bag. Then set the bag down and leave it for a time, and when you come back, you will find what you need beside it."

"Well," said Gloriana. "That's something."

The smaller one whispered, "It will not provide forever. It is tied to us, and what happens to it, we feel. It can be broken, and we with it, so hide it away from anyone greedy or wicked or silly. It is better kept a secret thing."

Glory ducked her head. I knew she was thinking, of course it would have to be hidden away because Jeff couldn't keep anything from Til, and Til ruined everything he was a part of, and next thing I knew, they reached up into the air and pulled the baby out of nowhere as though she had been there the whole time, in an invisible crib, just floating along behind them.

She looked like the pictures I had loved in my children's books, so long ago on Phobos. She was definitely a kitten, but the size of a big-gish cat, like the pictures of Earthian tiger or lion cubs, only more slender and delicate. She had big eyes, tall, tufted ears, and a triangu-lar face pointed at the chin. She looked fragile, like something made of glass and covered with satiny golden fur, with the same curved mouth and the same pink nose as her parents. She yawned, showing elegant fangs in front and a line of chewing teeth at the sides.

Glory reached out to take her. The cat-baby looked up at her doubtfully, but when Glory cuddled her, one of the little paw hands came up to pat her nose, and Glory looked down at her in absolute adoration.

Lou Ellen said, "You're holding her wrong. You should support her head."

"It's all right," said the little cat-person. "Falija is already very strong. You don't need to worry about her neck or bones or muscles. Just . . . treat her gently and lovingly, will you, please?"

Evidently their kind of people didn't cry, because from all the sadness I could feel emanating from them, if the smaller cat-person could have cried, she'd have flooded the place.

"One more thing," the littler cat-person said, taking a little green book out of her pocket. "When Falija begins to speak, read this book to her aloud, several times. It is the key to her learning. Promise?"

"I promise," Glory said, reaching out for the book without taking her eyes from the baby.

"Good-bye," they said, and they were gone, just like that.

Later, I woke up, still under the tree, thinking what a lovely, silly dream that had been. I was stiff from sitting on the ground so long, but the remembered dream resonated happily all the way home.

Next morning I went down to get a few eggs from the chicken house, pick up my milk and paper, and maybe have a cup of tea with May-belle while she got ready for work. I heard her moving around up-stairs, and when she came down she was shaking her head the way she did when Gloriana did something weird.

"What now?" I asked

"That silly child has promised some woman she'd take care of the woman's cat while the woman is on some kind of pilgrimage to the Shrine of Sorrow over in Deep Shameful. Says the woman gave her money to do it."

I'm sure I looked at her witlessly. A cat. "When did you find this out?"

"Just now! I went in to wake her, and here in the bed is this cat. Big one, and not full-grown yet. She'd already made it a little sandbox by the door, so I can't get angry about it."

All I could think of was the strange dream I'd had the day before. "It wasn't dressed up, was it?"

"What wasn't?"

"The cat?"

"The cat was in its fur, like all cats are. What's the matter with you, Mother!"

"Sorry," I said. "I guess I'm not awake yet."

Glory came into the kitchen as her parents were getting into the carriage, plopped herself down across from me, and asked, "Any-thing interesting in the paper?"

"Some tragedy, some comedy, nothing that'll matter in a hundred years," I said. "I understand you've got a cat."

"It's not mine. I'm just taking care of it for somebody."

"So your mother said. Why don't you come on up to my house and be my company for breakfast?"

"I'll have to get the cat."

"Well, get it. Bring it with you."

Glory got the cat. Without clothes on it, I couldn't tell, really, whether it was like my dream cat or some other cat. We walked up the hill to my house. Billy Ray and Mayleen always fussed about my living where I did. I had told them, "Joseph built the little house for me, Billy Ray. You build a similar house over on your side of the river, I'll split my time fifty-fifty."

"I'm safe," I told Maybelle. "I told him that five years ago, and Billy Ray's still working on the plans."

When we got into my house, I got the kettle started on the wood cookstove. My little kitchen was squeezed in between the big cookstove and the sink, just big enough to turn around in, a one-person-only space. The rule was if I cooked, Glory cleaned up, and vice versa. The only other rooms were the bedroom and bathroom at the back, next to the warm closet behind the stove that held the big water tank. James pumped it full each morning, and the cookstove chimney went up through a smaller tank to make hot water.

When I put our forks and mugs on the table, I asked, "What's the cat's name?"

"Falija," Glory said.

I couldn't remember whether that name had been in my dream or not, and it didn't bear worrying about. I said, "It's time for strawberry jam. Are you going to pick for me this year?"

"Sure. Lou Ellen'll help." Glory set Falija on her lap and scratched her fur around her ears.

I continued my examination of Falija. "That's a very strange cat. Could be a Manx, since it doesn't have much of a tail."

"It's a new kind," Glory said.

I supposed she was right. It was a new kind to me, at any rate.

"It's more . . . omnivorous, like people," Glory said. "The . . . lady told me so."

Falija was standing on her hind legs with her front ones on the table, making the little prruup prruup noises. "She's hungry," Glory announced. "Can I fix a plate for her?"

I nodded, fascinated by this little animal. Glory found some left-over oatmeal in a pot on the stove, an apple in a bowl, and a chicken leg in the refrigerator. She cut everything up in pieces and put it on a plate. The moment Falija saw it, she jumped off the chair and cleaned the plate, including the pieces of apple, eating slowly and neatly, while I scrambled eggs and made toast.

When the cat had finished eating, Glory fetched a little bowl of water and Falija washed. First she took a little drink, then she dipped her paw in the water and washed her face, and dipped and washed down her neck and around her ears, and then she dried off the paw on the rug.

"That's not any ordinary cat," I said around a mouthful of scrambled eggs. "Gloriana, tell me truthfully, where did you get that creature?"

Glory looked out the window for a while, then she looked me in the eye. "A lady gave me some money to take care of her for a while and keep her safe. She's very smart, Grandma."

"She's a mutation of some sort," I half whispered, as though I were afraid someone would hear me.

"That's what everybody says I probably am, because I don't look anything like all the rest of the Judsons. Every single one of them has light hair and blue or green eyes but me, including you, and Aunt Mayleen and Mama, and they're only Judsons by marriage."

I stared out the window. "Oh, somewhere in the line, there's always a dark-haired ancestor."

"Well, it's nobody recent," said Gloriana. "And nobody else is my size, either."

Falija climbed onto my lap. She had claws, but when she climbed, she just barely caught the clothes. Her claws didn't touch the skin, and there she was on my lap, turning around and around, and settling down to have a nap, still going prruup prruup prruup and opening those huge eyes to stare at me. I stroked her, very softly, while her little pawlike hands pressed and released against my leg, kneading and kneading.

"She certainly acts like a mammal," I said. "That's what kittens do with their feet at the mother's mammaries, pressing and kneading that way. It's like baby goats and lambs and calves, butting at the udder. But, Glory, those paws, those eyes, she's not a real cat. Some kind of marsupial, maybe? Her hind legs and pelvis aren't built like a cat's, and neither is her head. She has a much higher skull than a cat . . ."

"Maybe she's just a newly discovered species."

"No species I ever learned about while I was at school. No kind I've ever read about, either. Of course, there's no special reason she should be terrestrial." I gave Glory a hard, searching look. "I'd be inclined to say she's neither Tercian nor Earthian."

"I've told you the truth," Glory said, turning red. "And you can see for yourself she's just a baby and needs taking care of. And that's what I'm going to do."

"All right," I said, "But Gloriana, you promise me something. If you need help with this little one, you come straight here to me! Promise, now."

Since I was already the one Gloriana went to when she was in trouble, I figured it would be an easy promise.

When Glory had finished with our dishes, Falija was asleep, so we sat out on my little porch while Gloriana went back to wondering why she was so different from all the other Judsons.

"And something else," she said. "How come my mama and Lou Ellen's mama don't look alike when they're identical twins?"

"They used to look alike," I said. I fetched the album from the bookshelves inside. "See there, that's when they were babies. You couldn't tell the difference between them." The picture was of Maybelle and Mayleen as babies, sitting back to back on a picnic bench, like a pair of bookends. "It wasn't that they were born looking different, Glory. It's how they've lived their lives."

"They have different personalities," Glory said. "You'd think that should be the same, too."

"One would expect so," I said, for hadn't I expected just that? Time to change the subject. "Your mother says you have a litter box for Falija."

"Yes. And she knows how to use it."

"She has a very short tail. Hardly as long as my thumb. She has a poophole." That's what we all called it. It isn't polite, but the more common words are abusive and contemptuous, and the correct terms occasion intense embarrassment among the Rueful, as though they referred to something esoteric and possibly blasphemous.

"Poophole is at least a specific vulgarity rather than generalized lewdness," said Glory, grinning at me. She sometimes quotes me word for word. She remembers a lot of things people say, whole paragraphs that seem to stick in her mind like a caramel on teeth. Funny child. I loved her very much.

"Lou Ellen was with me when the lady gave me Falija," Glory said, not looking at me. "I asked her to stay last night, but she wouldn't. Whenever I ask her to stay, she says, 'No, no, Glory. It's all right. It's a pretty path along the water and through the fields, and I keep looking for . . . things.'

"Grandma, what do you think she's looking for? It's a mile up to the notch where the bridge is and three miles from there, by the road, to Billy Ray's farm. Lou Ellen says it doesn't take her any time at all, so she has to have a secret way to cross the river. She never shared it with me, and we share everything, absolutely everything, but not that, and it hurts my feelings."

I didn't have to answer, because Falija had wakened. She reached up with a little paw and patted Glory's chin, wiping off a tear. Then she licked the paw, and that made Glory smile and forget about Lou Ellen.

I didn't forget, however, because I'd seen her in that weird dream yesterday. On the pier. Talking to the strange people, Falija's parents. I didn't believe that dream had been real, not at all, so perhaps I was going absolutely mad, instead of simply partially mad, an idea that for some time had seemed rather convincing.

I Am Naumi, with Fernwold

"I knew a woman, Naumi," said Fernwold, who was sitting in hot water up to his chin. "Years ago."

"Ah," I replied, opening one eye. "And you're just now remembering her? Why?"

"You just reminded me of her, somehow. Perhaps it's the way the steam curls your hair around your ears. Hers did that, too. Or maybe I was just thinking of hot pools, and it reminded me of B'yurngrad. That's where she was . . . is."

I gritted my teeth at the thought of Ferni and his woman, reminding myself sternly that this obsession was a private one, never mentioned, never to be shared. Ferni had every right to be attracted to some woman, damn her, whoever she should be. "Who is this woman?" I asked, managing to sound interested.

"Set out to be a translator for the Diplomatic Corps. Got detoured into being a bondslave. Freak accident marooned her on B'yurngrad. Siblinghood picked her up, sent her into the wastelands to learn shamanism."

"Did she have a name?" I asked, merely to show I was listening.

"M'urgi," Fernwold said. "That's what the shaman named her. I forget what it means."

"Something mythic, no doubt." I sat up a little so I could see the arrival and departure board by the door. I liked very much being with Ferni, but if he was going to talk about women, I would just as soon be somewhere else. Besides, nonplanetary transshipment points had a reputation for last-minute changes in boarding times.

In this case, it was no help. I still had entirely too much time. I let myself slip into the wet once again. This particular transshipment point, Gilfras Station, had been established by that ancient and honored race, the Pthas, only they knew how long ago. Its current crew mined comets for water and made a very good thing out of it, that is if everyone paid what Ferni and I had paid for a private bath, and why in heaven's name had I done that!

Ferni mused, "A name that's mythic? I suppose that's possible. Last time I was among other Siblings, I heard the shaman died, and M'urgi was called to active duty, still on B'yurngrad."

"How long since you've seen her?" I asked.

"Been with her? Oh, ten, eleven Earth-count years, I suppose. Maybe more."

"Not unusual for you. I didn't see you for a full five years after we left the academy."

His forehead furrowed as he said tentatively, "I was busy, running about. That whole time is hazy."

"And you're wanting to go see . . . what? If you remember her correctly? If she remembers you?"

With a great thrashing of water, Fernwold sat up.

"There was something about her, Naumi! When I first saw her, I felt I'd known her for years. When we talked, I could have been talking to you, she was so familiar. She could have been your identical twin."

"No she couldn't!" It sounded rude even to me. I amended, "That is, not if she was female."

"I don't mean biologically." Ferni subsided, letting the water flow over his chin once more, stopping just short of his lips. "Psychologically, maybe. Maybe nothing, just an addled mind seeking connections." He stared moodily into the water, seeking answers. "I applied for some leave to go find her a few years back. They said no. She was busy, too busy to be interrupted. The Siblinghood is worse than the

Omnionts, I swear. At least the Omnionts let you go after fifteen years."

"Do you want to be let go?" And oh, wouldn't I bless and curse the day that happened. If Ferni were just . . . elsewhere, where he could be remembered with joy and without this constant internal battle not to get personally involved!

"That's not what I meant!"

Silence except for the soft plutter of wavelets against the sides of the tiled pool, the shlush of the water running away to the boiler, the gurgle as it returned.

"If you can get your shamanistic friend off your mind for a little while," I said. "I asked you to meet me here because I need your help,"

Ferni looked up, lips curving. "I have more to say about her, but I can give you a few minutes, Noomi."

Ignoring the slur, I explained. "The Siblinghood has given me a problem." I paused to think, rubbing my face with the back of my hand. I needed a shave. At age thirty-six, thirty-seven, maybe it was time to grow a beard. Which was simply a divagation, putting off the ridiculous, or the sublime, I had no idea which. I said as quickly as possible, "Somewhere within our reach there's a being no one has ever seen, and this being knows everything."

"What did you say?"

I repeated myself.

"The Siblinghood knows this?" Ferni, incredulous.

I sat up, removed the wet towel from around my head, and said, "I'm told the Siblinghood presumes this to be true."

"Why, in the name of Chamfalow's chief cook?"

"Well, this is the way it was explained to me: Mankind is in a very dangerous situation regarding survival as a race. Unlike every other presumably well-intentioned race, we do not have a racial memory . . ."

"You're joking! The Gentherans have a racial memory? The Pthas had a racial memory? And the Garrick?"

"According to what I've been told, all of them do or did, yes."

"Since one already knows a good deal of human history, one expects there must be a catch in there somewhere."

"Isn't there always? As I understand it, the memory in question would include everything back to the time our parental primate stepped down out of a tree. Maybe even farther back, to the first time we crawled out of the ooze. And, we must know it, not learn it. Know it so we feel it in our bones. Or membranes, if we didn't have bones at the time. We have to remember war, not merely think about it. We have to remember struggle, and pain, and having beasts eat our children. Presumably, this inner knowledge would halt our tendency to do the precipitous, silly, and often very dangerous things that people reared in relative safety often do for stupid or prideful leaders, like sheep running ahead of a purposeful, nipping dog.

"The only hope of finding such a memory lies in our finding someone or something who knows everything, including the true history of the human race. The solution also requires that this thing or creature exist within our reach, since if it doesn't, its mere existence is of no consequence to mankind."

"Ah," said Ferni, wiping steam out of his eyes. "And?"

"The problem they've given me is to find the being."

"To *presume* there's a being, then *find* it."

"More or less, yes."

"I presume there's a pot of universal elixir sitting on the bench in the changing room; I think I'll go find that." Ferni snorted, getting water up his nose.

I didn't reply.

Ferni said, "You're serious?"

"Deadly serious. They told me it is likely the penalty for not finding it will be our own extinction, sooner or later, and not much later at that. Have you ever . . . have you ever seen recordings of the planet they call Hell?"

"Ugh." Ferni ducked under the water, came up spluttering. "I'm a member of the Siblinghood, Naumi! I've never heard of any of this! Unless . . . could it be a Third Order thing?"

My eyebrows went up at this. "This plan or plot or whatever one may call it, is being implemented by a small secret group within your organization. Is there a secret group called the Third Order? If so, very interesting, because it's not the first time they've fiddled with my life. They had something to do with my being at the academy in the first place."

After a considerable silence, Ferni offered, "I know the name. Is it possible some kind of . . . spatial anomaly is involved in all this?"

"Well, if the thing exists, it has to exist somewhere. An anomalous location might explain why no one knows where."

"I wonder if the old talk road would come up with anything?"

"The other four are meeting me on Thairy. That's why I asked you to meet me here. There's a quick route from here to Thairy. And to B'yurngrad, if you're wanting to look up your shamaness. Just think, one day there from here, one day to Thairy from here. No lost time. Lucky Pthas to find the wormhole to end all wormholes . . ." I realized I was babbling and fell silent.

Fernwold steamed. "All this vapor is doing nothing for my powers of ratiocination. Assuming I have any. Do we know anything at all about this being?"

"The Siblinghood archives have several ancient stories that involve something or someone called the Keeper. Many of them were preserved by the Pthas, and that fact lends them additional credence. Some of the stories drop clues to the Keeper's approachability. The number seven figures prominently. There are a few phrases common to most of the stories. 'One person walking seven roads at once finds the Keeper.' Or, 'Seven roads are one road.' Most of the stories are about untangling a difficulty or solving a problem . . ."

"And we want this Keeper because it, or he, knows everything?"

"It, I think. Knows everything. Yes."

Ferni emerged gradually from the water, heaved himself out of the pool, and reached for a towel. "Tell me one of the stories."

I gawked at him, then averted my eyes.

"Come on, Noomi! Presumably they told you some of the stories. Tell me one!"

"I can tell you one about a man and a fish," I said.

Now it so happened that a man of Dabberding was walking along the River Rush one day when a fish spoke to him from the shallows along the bank.

"Hi there, you, man," said the fish. "How is the world treating you?"

"Not well," growled the man of Dabberding. "My wife is ill, my children need shoes, the cow went dry, my donkey is lame, my old dog is on her last legs, and a fox is eating my chickens, one after the other."

"Ah," said the fish. "That must make you very angry."

"It makes me boil," said the man of Dabberding. "My wife is sick because my neighbor dragged her out in a rainstorm to help him gather up his geese. My children need shoes because they went to help their mother and ruined the shoes I'd just bought them. The cow went dry because my neighbor said his bull would breed her for less then I usually pay. The bull was no good, but my neighbor wouldn't give me my money back. The donkey is lame because my wife had to ride her in the mud, into the village, to see the healer. My old dog is on her last legs because she caught cold for trying to bring the geese in, and the fox is eating my chickens because my neighbor's no-good bull bashed a hole in the coop, and I've no wire to fix it with."

"So you're angry," said the fish.

"Oh, if my neighbor were here in front of me, I'd bash him bloody," said the man of Dabberding. "This is all his fault."

"Is there anything you're angry about that the right information wouldn't fix?" asked the fish.

The man of Dabberding thought for a while, then he said, "I would know how I could heal my wife, how to make shoes for the children, where I could find a good bull, where I could find a little money to rent another donkey to let my donkey rest until his leg gets better, who's giving away a good pup so my old dog could lie contented in the sun, and how to keep the vermin out of my chicken coop."

"Then the problem is solved," said the fish. "I will tell you where to go."

So the fish told him to go down a certain forest road, and up a certain steep hill, and through a long thicket, and out onto a precipice where a little temple stood all by itself, and inside the temple was an altar, and on the altar was an image. "That little image has all the information in the universe," it said. "There's nothing it doesn't know."

So the man of Dabberding set off down the forest road. As he went, he thought about his encounter with the fish, and as he thought about that it gradually came to him that the little temple the fish spoke of might possibly belong to King Frum the Furious, and a bad-tempered, ill-natured king he was, too.

Still, the fish hadn't said anything about it, so the man from Dabberding went on until he came to the steep hill, which he climbed, and into the thicket, which he fought his way through, then out onto the precipice where the temple stood. Sure enough, inside was an altar stone, and on the stone was an image, a statue of a little old man with a long beard and a wrinkled face and squinched-up eyes, sitting cross-legged and peering at a golden book in his lap, a book with writing that flowed across the page like water.

Well, the man from Dabberding didn't even pause for thought. He took the image, wrapped it in his jacket, and went across the temple to look over the cliff edge to see where he was in relation to the river and the places he knew. He had just located the river when he heard loud voices coming from below. He looked around, and there was a path coming up the cliff from one side with men on it, and there was another path leading along the cliff with more men on it, both headed in his direction. He couldn't get back to the thicket without being seen. He couldn't even get into the temple without being seen. If they found him with the little image in his shirt, they would kill him for sure.

So the man sobbed silently, threw the image far out into the air, watched it fall partway, then he sat down on the precipice and waited.

The men arrived, among them King Frum the Furious, and they found the image missing at once. They surrounded the man of Dabberding and asked him where the little man with the golden book was. "I don't know," he said truthfully, for he hadn't seen it land. "Who was it an image of?" he asked, because he didn't know that either.

They knocked him down and searched him, but he had no statue. They searched the edges of the thicket, but there was no statue. And all the while the king lamented and lamented that his luck was gone, the pride of his lineage was gone, the image of the keeper was gone.

"Keeper?" asked the man from Dabberding. "What's a keeper?"

"It's a thing that knew all the king's secrets," whispered one of the men-at-arms. "That little statue knows everything that has ever happened in the whole world."

"In the whole universe," whispered another man-at-arms. "Where could it have gone?"

"An eagle, perhaps," said the man from Dabberding. "Or a large raven. Ravens like sparkly things."

"That's true," said the first man-at-arms, and he went to tell the king, who was still lamenting. After a time, the man-at-arms came back and told the man from Dabberding to get himself gone before the king remembered he was there, which the man did very quickly, fading himself into the thicket like a rabbit into a burrow.

The man got himself through the thicket, down the hill, back down the road, and again to the riverbank where he'd met the fish. "Fish, fish," he called. "I'm very angry. I barely escaped with my skin."

The fish came up to the bank, and when the man told him what had happened, the fish asked, "Is there anything making you angry that can't be solved with the right information?"

"Probably not," said the man.

"Well then, go get the information," said the fish. "It must be lying along one of the seven roads that lead to the bottom of the cliff."

"Seven roads," cried the man. "It's already getting along toward evening."

"Then you'd better hurry," said the fish.

Since the man had seen the riverbank from the top of the hill, he figured the roads must come from the river, so he walked along the bank in the proper direction until he came to a road that turned toward the cliff he could see through the trees. He ran very quickly along that road, stopping only once when the sun caught something shining in the undergrowth that turned out to be one of the legs of the image he had tossed from the top of the cliff. Well, one leg was one leg, but a leg wouldn't help him, so the man went on down the road until it came right to the foot of the cliff and turned back toward the river at an angle.

So he ran and ran along this road, stopping only once when he saw something lying on the path, which turned out to be the other leg of the image he had thrown from the cliff top. Well, two legs was two legs, but the whole statue was better, so he went on running toward the river, where the road suddenly turned back toward the cliff again. On that road he found an arm, and on the next turn, another arm. And on the next turn, which was number five, he found the body, and on the next turn toward the river again, he found the head, which was all very well, but the book with the letters running across it was still missing.

It was almost dark when the man started on the seventh road, going toward the cliffs for the fourth time, and he was actually at the cliffs when he saw it, shining at him in the last of the sunlight. So he sat down and put the statue together, and when he put the book into his lap, he saw words there.

"How to cure your wife's illness," he read. And this was followed by a recipe for a medicine made out of very common plants that the man found on his way home.

That night, after he had given his wife the medicine, he looked at the book again. This time it said, "How to cure lameness in a donkey," followed by a recipe for a poultice made out of very common things he happened to have around the house. And when he had done that, he looked at the book again, and saw the words "How to make ruined shoes like new again," followed by a simple procedure the man was able to manage before he went to bed.

In the morning, the book told him of a widow living just down the road who had a pup she was giving away and who also had a bull she would let him use in return for the resultant calf. Then the book told him where he could find some discarded fence to mend his chicken coop. And last of all, the book told him what to do in order to be rid of his neighbor, a few very simple words having to do with misdeeds discovered and forces of law on the way, whispered in the neighbor's ear.

The neighbor packed his cart and moved out before lunchtime. The man from Dabberding watched the cart go off down the road, the useless bull hitched to the back. Then the man from Dabberding remembered what the man-at-arms had said about the Keeper knowing everything in the whole world, so he knelt before the image and said, "Keeper, you have been very kind to me, and I'm not angry anymore, and I want to do for you whatever you most desire. Please tell me what that is."

Then he looked at the book, and the words ran across it, saying, "Roads out, roads back, seven roads was one road. Cow, donkey, dog, wife, shoes, fox, neighbor, seven cures was one cure. Two arms, two legs, body, head, book, seven parts was one Keeper. Let one person walk seven roads at once, go where they meet and find me there." And with that, the Keeper vanished, leaving only the story behind.

"That's the story," I concluded.
"Sorry, Naumi, but it doesn't tell me much."
"It didn't me, either," I replied.

"When did you say the others are getting to Thairy?" he asked after a few moments.

"They'll ostensibly come for the class reunion, but they'll arrive several days early."

"Well then." Ferni dried his legs, saying thoughtfully, "I wish M'urgi were here. She had a very good head on her shoulders."

I frowned, for the name teased at me. "M'urgi. Interesting name. Why don't you go find her, Ferni?" I took a deep breath, managing a casual tone. "We have quite a bit of time before the reunion. Bring her along."

Fernwold, wrapped in the towel, sat down on the stone bench beside the pool and fixed me with his "This is important" stare. "I was going to locate her anyhow, because of this other thing I wanted to tell you about. It happened a day or two ago. I was sitting in a tranship-tavern waiting for departure time, the way one does, not thinking about anything much, when I overheard someone saying, 'The word came down all the way from the top.' Someone else replied, 'That doesn't make sense.' The first voice said, 'Sometimes it doesn't make sense, but the orders are, she's got to be killed, and it has to be done soon.'

"That got my full attention. The second voice said, 'Why her? Why some smoke-flavored old shaman's hag from the steppes of B'yurngrad.' The first one said, 'No hag, she's young yet.'"

I frowned at him. "So, you put shaman, smoke-flavored, B'yurngrad, and suchlike together, assuming they meant your friend?"

"Exactly. I casually looked at the people around me. A dozen races at least, most of them speaking interlingua . . ."

"Any accent?"

"No lisping, so not K'Famir. They didn't curse one another, so probably not Frossian. There was no discernible stink, probably not Hrass." He paused. "There were a few elder races there, too, very strange old ones, the kind that make you go elsewhere when you see them coming, you know . . ."

"Quaatar? Baswoidin?"

"Quaatar? Yes, now you mention it. There were a couple of them." He sighed. "You're at least taking me seriously."

"It could be serious. Why, precisely, do you believe so?"

"Some time ago, the word filtered down through the Siblinghood that the leaders wanted to be informed if any of us caught wind of 'Top-down threats to specific and seemingly harmless humans . . .'"

"If you've quoted the conversation correctly, the threat was definitely top down. It may be be smart to check on her, my friend."

"She probably won't even remember me."

Oh, she'd remember him! "Come now. Unforgettable Ferni?"

My friend laughed ruefully. "Meantime, I'll keep your puzzle in mind. Will the others be with you for a while?" As he dressed himself, he seemed to forget whatever the strangeness had been. He looked more like himself.

I said, "All during reunion. I'll be there for even longer, because I've agreed to teach a course at Point Zibit."

"Professor Noomi," drawled Ferni. "Why, I knew him when he was only a worm."

I Am Mar-agern/on Fajnard

As the end of my years of bondage approached, the enmity of the Frossian overseer increased, and its verbal hostility toward me became more frequent. It had not forgotten I could speak and understand Frossian, so I knew these open threats were part of its general plan of harassment.

"We agree," said Deen-agern, the Ghoss, when I mentioned it to him. "Frossians do not forget much. They are completely ignorant of enormous areas of knowledge, but they don't forget things that happen to them. It's time we got you out of here, Mar-Mar."

"I have less than a year of bondage left!"

The Ghoss raised a nostril. "You have only as long as they want you to have. Fifteen years is enough for most slaves: the bones are weakened, the back is bent, the strength is exhausted, and the Frossians are willing to let them go. Only draining the last of a slave's strength at the end of its bondage proves they have gained their money's worth: a full fifteen years of labor, with the least possible strength left over to go elsewhere, often just enough for the ex-slave to totter across the landing field to the colony ship. This is so well known that we counsel bondspeople to pretend greater and greater weakness during their last several years."

"You've never told me that!"

"We had no reason to, even though you've stayed strong, and the Frossians have felt they weren't getting full value for their money. Now, however, something new has happened. We've heard the Frossians talking. Some very important breeding male has communicated with the planetary leader here on Fajnard. It, in turn, has informed the least overlord that a bondswoman who speaks Frossian is to be killed, quickly and without delay. The least overlord has told the overseer, the one who keeps threatening you."

"Why?" I cried. "The only Frossians I've ever seen are here, here on Fajnard. Why would some overlord care about me?"

"You don't know; we don't know. Certainly the least overlord doesn't know or care, and the overseer doesn't care because it was going to kill you anyhow. You'd be dead by now except for the umoxen. We know they warm you in winter, protect you at all times. They prevent the Frossians from stealing your clothes and food and from fouling your water. Is this not so?"

"You know it is."

"Well, depend upon it, the overseer also knows it's so. Very soon now, some Frossian or other will separate you from the umoxen, take you elsewhere, and you will not return."

"The overseer hasn't said this."

"Of course not. The overseer knows you understand what it says. It says only what it means you to hear. To make you look in the wrong direction."

I frowned, saying hesitantly, "Where am I to go? This is the only place on Fajnard that I know."

"There's a better place, and we'll take you there. It's the place we Ghoss go, when we are weary of serving the creatures."

"Why you serve them at all is more than I can understand!"

"True. It is more than you can understand, at least for now. After a time in the hills, you may understand it."

The next evening, when a plether of umoxen were pastured in the fields with only me to watch them, several of the huge creatures wandered over and began to hum at me. "Mar-Mar, time to go away."

"You've been talking to the Ghoss," I said.

"Ghoss been talking to us," they remarked. "Time. You stay until tomorrow, something bad will happen, so, we go tonight. Get on up." It knelt on its front legs, giving me a foreleg to step up on.

It was the first time one of them had offered to carry me, but I did not hesitate. The small group of them started for the fence between the pasture and the river bottom, all the rest of the plether following along. At the fence they simply leaned against the posts until they broke off, then amused themselves by trampling vast lengths of fence into the ground and crossing them with trodden umox-paths, back and forth, humming as they went, finally splitting in a dozen different ways, one of which led through the riparian woods and into the wide but shallow stream of late summer. Here the umox knelt again as I splashed into the water. I saw the umoxen distributing themselves widely among the stream-side woods. The umox I had ridden touched my cheek with its tongue and went to join them.

"Mar," said a familiar voice. "Over here."

Rei was standing in the stream, a pack on his back.

I went to join him. "I didn't bring anything with me."

"You didn't have anything you'll need," he said. "Come, we go upstream. Stay in the water."

The water was cool but not icy, coming only to our ankles. I put my head down and waded, occasionally turning aside from a large stone or dead tree that had been washed down during flood. The journey was hypnotic, the water gurgling around my feet, the plethers humming in the pastures we passed, the small creatures cheeping and chirping in scattered reed beds. I lost track of time and did not think of it again until I looked up through the branches of a shutter-leaf tree to see the sky growing light. The branches creaked, the leaves turned to face the sun, an eye at the end of a branch winked at me.

We had entered a low-walled canyon. Rei said, "Far enough! We will sleep through the daylight."

"Where?" I asked wearily.

"My customary wayhalt. Up there." He turned between two massive tree boles onto an almost invisible trail that led up the canyon wall to a small cave, well hidden behind a protruding outcropping of stone. We sat, Rei took food from his pack and handed it to me. We ate without speaking, and I fell into sleep the moment I lay down.

Rei's hand over my mouth wakened me. "Shhh," he whispered. "We have searchers down in the stream."

Together we crawled to the mouth of the cave and peeked around the outcropping that hid the entrance from below. I saw torches and smelled their smoke. I heard the angry jabber of irritated Frossians.

"There's no trail."

"If there was a trail, we couldn't see it in torchlight."

"Better go back, get some provisions, come back and try again in the light."

"The least overlord will kill us!"

The voices continued their jabber, becoming softer as they retreated, back the way we had come. Rei stood at the opening of the cave, reading the air as the Ghoss often did, for it was full of messages from their kinfolk, who might be anywhere on the planet at all.

"Deen says the Frossians are angry," he reported, with an air of satisfaction. "They had a great deal of trouble rounding up the umoxen. Some of them think you were probably killed in the stampede. The least overlord, however, insists that they find your body. He has to tell his overlord that he has seen you dead with his own eyes. Your enemy, the herd overseer, thinks you have slipped away in the confusion. He has sworn to hunt you down. We must hurry to reach the falunassa."

I puzzled at the word as I translated it into Frossian. *Those in the faraway.* "Is that their name?"

"It's a descriptive term for people in hiding. Here, they are the Gibbekot. If humans live on a planet, the Gibbekot become falunassa in faraway mountains perhaps, or deep deserts, or great canyons, always in the most secret places. They are not fearful. They simply prefer not to have the problems that result from unlike creatures housed too closely together."

I stared into the distance. "Won't the Gibbekot object to my coming?"

"No. You've been described to them. We told them the umoxen had adopted you. That was sufficient endorsement." He returned to the cave and picked up his pack. "Let's put space between us and this place before those Frossians return."

Luckily, we had a moon providing enough light to let us see our way on up the canyon, past confluences with other small streams, the wash growing narrower, shallower, and rockier the farther we went, at last dividing itself neatly into two tumbling brooks, left and right, both leading up stony channels.

"Here we go," said Rei, as he turned to the right and began climbing up the stream, from rock to rock.

I followed. There had been a time, I reflected, when this journey would have been impossible for me. On Earth I would have been too weak and too flabby to have walked any distance at all carrying a pack. My flesh had grown hard during the years of bondage. Perhaps I should thank the Frossians for that.

During the next few hours, as we passed several other places where streams or dry washes came in from the sides and as the stream we followed became a mere trickle, I became less sure I should thank anyone. "Rei, how much farther do we climb?"

"Not far. You're doing well."

It still seemed a great distance. The sky was growing light when a breeze from behind us carried a great uproar to our ears. Shouting. Something mechanical, roaring.

"Aircar," said Rei. "Hurry."

I managed to be close behind him as he climbed the last plunging stretch of piled stone and stood erect at the top. "There," he said, pointing. "Gibbekot country."

We stood on a natural dike. The source of the stream we had followed was a small lake stretching from the dike at our feet eastward toward green pastures sloping upward to gently rounded hills, these backed in their turn by receding ranges of blue mountains. Umoxen grazed in the valley, but there was no sign of other inhabitants.

Rei moved to one side, thrust his hand into a crevice in the rock, and pulled. Somewhere wheels turned and creaked. Somewhere a valve opened and the lake before us developed an eddy that spun itself into a vortex. Below and behind us, a spate of water boiled out of the rivulet to gush wildly over the rocks we had climbed, the soil where we might have left tracks, any surface where any trace of us might have remained. Rei stood for some time, watching the water wash away all traces of us, and when he was satisfied, he thrust his hand into the crevice once more and shut the water down. As it silenced, we heard the roaring again, nearer.

He plunged into the shallow water and began to wade around its edge. "There are a dozen sizable streams entering the river we walked in. After rain, any of them might be in spate. There are about fifty little canyons and washes on this upper stretch, where we climbed, and the same is true of the other forks. Even if the Frossians have the patience to search them all, they are unlikely to get this far, and if they get this far, they will get no farther. Frossians like dampness, but they're afraid of open water." He raised his head and called across the valley. The echoes returned, amplified. An umox, the nearest, turned ponderously from its grazing and came toward us, down the left side of the lake. Rei plowed through the shallows to intercept it, with me close behind. The umox waded out to meet us; Rei grabbed handfuls of the creature's long hair and pulled himself onto its back, then tugged me up beside him. The umox lumbered out onto the meadow and across the grasslands toward the nearest grove of trees. It did not speak to us, at least, not in any way I could hear.

"Scenters won't be able to smell us," I said.

"Not over the smell of the umoxen, no," Rei agreed. "Here. Pull the back of my cloak up over yourself. It's unlikely they will see us, and we will be under cover soon."

I covered myself. Rei lay flat on the broad umox back, and I lay on his back, both of us covered in a cloak very much the color of the umox's wool. The roaring came close, closer. The umox stopped, grazed, took a few steps, grazed again. I was about to panic when Rei murmured, "From above, the umox is one of a herd, all grazing. Hear them?"

I did hear them, all around us. Our own umox was working its way steadily through the herd toward the edge. Peeking from below the robe, I saw trees not far away. The herd leader snorted, and all of them moved into the trees, quite quickly, as the machine roared directly overhead, turning to return, even lower.

By that time, we were on the ground, lying in a hollow beneath a fallen tree, and the herd was moving into the open pasture once more. Rei said, "Anyone searching along the ground will find valleys full of umoxen on every side, streams everywhere, many little canyons and tricky places easy to get into and hard to get out of. Frossians have explored here from time to time, but none has ever left here to tell others what he may have found."

"Why did you bring me here?"

"We Ghoss were told to bring you, reason enough."

"Told by whom, Rei!"

He shrugged. "Those who have the authority to do so."

I gave up in frustration. Be thankful, I told myself. Be damned thankful you're here instead of down there. The words resonated, bringing a childhood memory. Be thankful we're up here, on Phobos, not in that windstorm down there on Mars. Be thankful you survived your bondage. Be thankful for your strength, your endurance. Be thankful you didn't go with Bryan, wherever he ended up going. Be thankful you didn't run off on the dragonfly, when you were a little girl. Be thankful the woods are all around us, for the aircar circled endlessly above us.

Be resentful about all those years of language study, however, for all they did was get you into trouble with the Frossians. Of course, I wasn't dead yet. Language might still have some use.

"Here," said Rei, pointing ahead once more. "Here is the Gate of the Gibbekot, and through it is the way to your freedom."

Our way led into a shallow valley grown up in forest. On both sides the trees marched up slopes that grew gradually steeper. This was a new thing for me. I had labored for fifteen years among the riverside woods that drained the pastures of the umoxen: a few large purple-leaf trees, widely separated, with thin saplings and brush between, and never any feeling of being cut off from the light. Here, the darkness was a palpable presence even at the edge of the forest, a deepening reality as we went farther to be surrounded by many kinds of trees: the shutter-leaf, which seemed ubiquitous; silver-leaf, columnar black-bolled trees with leaves that were silver on the bottom; parasol-trees, with huge, tall green-gray trunks culminating in a flat canopy well above the general forest, some dark green, some laden with brilliant red fringes. We could see perfectly well, it wasn't a question of being unable to see, but it was like seeing in late evening, bulks and masses of shadow, movement rather than form, a muffling of sound along with nose-filling, palate-touching smells, mostly resinous, occasionally threatening. I shuddered.

Rei patted my shoulder and pointed to a tree we were passing. "That's what's making you shiver. We call that Fros-bane. Take a good look at it. You don't want to touch it, ever."

The bole was a pale green, smooth as my own skin, with tiny beads of amber upon it, evenly spread as dew.

"See those drops? That's the bad stuff. Like an acid. Eats your skin, gets into your blood, you end curled up in a circle, screaming at the pain. The Gibbekot have planted them all through the woods, along here. They're immune to the stuff, but the Frossians aren't."

"The trees might work better if they didn't smell so bad," I opined. "I'd avoid them just because of the smell."

Rei grinned. "Frossians have no sense of smell. Didn't anyone ever tell you that?"

I glared at him. "They've been saying I stink for the better part of fifteen years!"

"They say it because we say it. If the hay is moldy, we say it stinks. The Frossians think it means rotten, evil, malign. They can see in the infrared, but they have no sense of smell. Ghoss do, however. Umoxen do, and the Gibbekot don't want to hurt Ghoss or umoxen."

I thought about this. "Is this tree natural? Or was it genetically created by the Gibbekot?"

"Why do you ask?"

"Because poisons and thorns and other defenses usually evolve against a particular life-form. The Frossians aren't native here, so it wasn't against them. What kind of thing threatened these trees to make them develop this defense?"

Rei said over his shoulder, "The Gibbekot got them from the world where the Frossian queens live. It's the only world that's truly Frossian, the great hatchery from which they all come, and there are deep valleys there full of trees that had already evolved defenses. The Gibbekot just sent for them."

"The Gibbekot are spacefaring?" I asked in amazement. "You never said they were spacefaring."

"I still haven't. I said sent, not went. Now hush. You're making too much noise. That aircar may be carrying listening devices, and we need to keep our eyes and ears open."

To me, whatever path we followed was indistinguishable from any other way among the trees. The forest floor was covered with a thick blanket of leaves, needles, mosses, all held together by the wiry stems of ubiquitous creeper that grew only a finger's width high but unendingly wide. When I turned to look back, the way we had come, I couldn't see a footprint anywhere. The creeper simply flattened beneath our feet and sprang back once we had passed.

I whispered, "How are you finding your way?"

"Ghossways," came the reply. "Now hush."

I hushed. We heard the aircar behind us, in the direction of the lake, I thought. It came a little closer, then turned back the way it had come. We walked for an hour or more, then began to climb as the floor of the valley climbed. By this time, evening had come, all aircar sounds had ceased, and the darkness beneath the trees had increased enough that I was eager to emerge from the gloom. Within a few hundred yards, we came from the shadow into the red light of sunset, the sky scattered with clouds ranging from gold to crimson to violet-gray. Before emerging, we scanned the sky carefully to be sure it was empty. When we were sure, we climbed a slanting ledge to an outcropping of stone that jutted from the hilltop, a narrow slot in it leading to another small, sheltered cave.

"How many of these places are there?" I asked.

"Enough to hide us, whatever direction we go. Tonight we stop here," said Rei, gesturing to include sandy floor, smooth walls, a store of firewood stacked high against one wall, a water jar, sacks of food. "They know we're here. When they're ready, they'll send for us."

"And until then?" I asked.

"We can build a fire, heat some food, talk about the weather, read a book—I brought one for you . . ."

"A book," I breathed. "I haven't read anything for . . ."

"I know," he said. "I brought you a book written by a Gibbekot. We'll read it together, and that will give you a taste of their language."

I warmed myself at the fire, ate the food Rei provided, drank the tea he gave me, something new, something with an oddly attractive taste. I started to look at the book, a simple collection of words, one to a page, but was too sleepy to go on. Yawning, I curled up beside the fire.

I was not asleep. It felt like a dream while asleep, but I knew it wasn't a dream. Rei watched me. When I was totally relaxed, he reached out to shake me. I tried to speak, couldn't speak, tried to move, couldn't move. I should have been afraid, but I wasn't. It was peaceful where I was, a firelit bubble of complete tranquillity.

"She's sleeping," he called.

The two beings who materialized at the entrance to the cave spoke to Rei with soft voices as they carefully unwrapped something they had brought with them. Rei turned me onto my stomach and applied whatever it was gently to the base of my skull. I felt something there, a kind of creepiness, as of something settling into place.

"How long will she be like that?" asked Rei.

One of the beings said, "Until it's completely absorbed. It grows up under the skull in back, very thin, very flat. Then it has to connect to the rest of the brain, and that takes a while."

The other said, "It takes a good while, actually. It could take as long as a season . . ."

"She'll go on sleeping all that time?" asked Rei, with a furtive look at the stack of supplies.

"Yes. She's profoundly asleep, though a dream state sometimes occurs, and she may be aware this is happening. Don't worry about the process, it's always successful. All her body functions are slowed down, as though she were hibernating. She won't need to eat or drink. Just send an emanation if you need more supplies, and someone will bring them. Keep her warm."

"We'll be safe here?"

"Completely," said the larger one, with a lick at his fangs and a twist of his furry ears. "You may depend upon it. When she wakes, there will be a period of confusion. Just ease her through it, and don't forget to read her the book."

"But she already knows her language."

"She doesn't know ours," said a visitor, departing.

Rei took the book from my hand and put it safely with our packs before covering me with a blanket. I remember thinking how thoughtful they had been, but then, they had known we would be coming.

I Am Wilvia/on Hell

On Shore, which is what the water people call their world, little towns have been built all up and down the sea's edge, many of them on stilts above the water, and waterside property is already filled. Some of the people have moved back into the forest and built mud houses there. It is warmer in the forest, where the trees break the sea winds at night, but the people come back to the shore in the daytimes, to fish and gather seaweed, while the children race up and down the sandy beaches, in and out of the warm, rolling sea. Most of the females are pregnant most of the time, and there are many, many babies.

Through sensors planted here and there, I, Wilvia, watch, I, Wilvia, listen. Half insane in my solitude, I have memorized their faces and names, have learned their simple language. I understand when one tribe of the people talks of starting a new village. The old village is getting crowded, they say, and they think it would be good to go up the river a long way. The good food of the shore can be found up the river, too, where there is room to spread out. Also, the biggest trees grow along the river, the best ones for boats! They can build boats and trade the boats for things to eat.

"Maybe we should leave big trees," says one of the males. "Takes a long time to grow a big tree."

"There's more," says another one of the males. "There's plenty of big trees. They'll never run out."

"I guess you're right," replies the first one. "We do have to make room for more of us all the time."

"Oh, yes," the other replies. "We always have to make room for more."

"Fools," I say, thrusting my forehead against the screen I am watching, reaching out to turn off the sound. "Oh, fools, fools."

Perhaps I should go outside. Perhaps I should show myself to them. Become their queen, perhaps, if they don't kill me first. Rule them as Joziré and I ruled the Ghoss . . .

We had a Trajian juggler at the court. The Trajian are long-lived but few, inveterate wanderers, often abused and abased, seemingly unable to settle in any one place. Their females command a very high bride-price, as there is only one of them for every two or three males. My juggler, Yarov, was a solemn little long-armed fellow with no assistant, no mate, for he had been unable to raise the bride-price necessary. He had stayed with us for a surprisingly long time. When I knew we might have to flee, I gave him a box of gold and gems, things he could use to travel, to keep himself, to buy a wife, for I knew how lonely he was. He stood before me, his little mouth open, as though he could not understand kindness. I told him it was not half what I owed him for the pleasure he had given us.

I wonder about him often. He did a wonderful trick, tossing a little carved king into the air, which separated and came down, arms, legs, torso, head, crown, seven separate pieces that were miraculously reassembled and tossed skyward again. I took it as an omen. Though our reign might be broken, we would reassemble and reign again . . .

So, should I reign over these creatures?

No, and no, and no. Those who brought me here said both my life and the future of mankind depends upon Queen Wilvia staying hidden! Hidden on this virtually unvisited planet called Hell, buried in this ancient Gentheran ship, only its sensors connecting me to reality, only its maintenance system keeping me alive. Only this stale tragedy to occupy me: these fools . . .

So, I am in hell, Wilvia is in hell. But, oh, my children, where are they? Beloved! Where is he? Where are those I love while I cower here, of no use, no use to them at all.

Joziré and I ruled the Ghoss, and we did it well. I was pregnant, expecting our first child, when the Thongal came. Joziré was taken off in one direction, I was taken in another. For a while, I was hidden in a Walled-Off on Tercis. It was a strange place, but better than this. The hunters followed me there, so we went to Chottem, to live among the Gentherans. There, the Gardener visited us from time to time to reassure me that Joziré was well. That was far, far better than this. Then hunters came to Chottem, so we returned to Tercis, only for a little time, and my protectors brought me here. My guides said no one would find me, and they would be my companions.

But they had to leave. Just for a time, they said. They planned to return. Perhaps they were caught, killed . . .

Patience. Patience. I say the word over and over, accompanying each thud of my forehead against the steel. And how long will patience alone keep me relatively sane? Is it even important to be relatively sane? I wait, and weep, as I watch the little creatures outside begin the destruction of their world yet again.

I Am Gretamara/on Mars

Under the dome of Dominion Central Authority on Mars, Sophia and I sat among a scattering of people, Human and Gentheran, most of them chatting quietly among themselves. Later in the day most of them would attend a meeting of Dominion Central Authority. This earlier gathering was by invitation, in order to hear a report on the effect of the general sterilant, and on Earth's rehabilitation since its application. Sophia had come to Dominion headquarters to conduct certain business before she descended upon Bray, and the Gardener had thought I would be an inconspicuous companion.

"Sophia," I murmured. "Your business here on Mars is completed, and strictly speaking, we are not invited to this gathering."

"Let us stay until they throw us out," she said, her eyes bright. This was her first trip away from the Gardener, away from Chottem, and she was excited by everything. "Tell them that as the heiress of Bray, I am interested in the work of the Dominion."

"Actually, only a few members of Dominion were invited to be here," I whispered. "However, if we are very quiet, and if you keep your cloak around you and your hood shadowing your face, they may not notice us."

She giggled. If she removed the cloak, both of us knew very well they would notice her, whether they noticed me or not.

The Gentheran laboratory representative was as Gentherans always are, fully suited and helmed. He spoke Earthian, as any Gentheran did who had anything to do with humans. "Out of respect," the Gardener had said, though she had not explained respect for what.

He introduced himself as Prrr (rolled *r*'s) Tgrr (a great many more rolled *r*'s.) "Our cooperating contractors and researchers have asked us for an update on the Earth rehabilitation situation. You will recall that during the first Earth-year after the sterilant was applied, the population, exclusive of those outshipped, dropped by slightly over one-point-one-nine percent. It was predicted that between point-nine and one-point-two percent of the population would die naturally in that time, so we are well within the estimates.

"The task of consolidating the population into smaller areas met resistance only during the fifth and sixth year, when the first consolidations took place. There is still some complaint, but it is generally pro forma griping that precedes orderly acquiescence. We make no attempt to remove outlying population centers until the nearest city has lost at least five percent of its population. Only then are outlying populations moved into the vacated housing and the empty nonurban communities razed. Though the process is slow, it is happening everywhere, which makes it an enormous undertaking. We have enlisted all human construction industries to help us in rehabilitation, and all children over the age of ten are required to assist in restoration of grasslands and forests.

"We have replanted five percent of the Brazilian desert where at one time jungles grew in leaf mold containing thousands of microorganisms atop hard, infertile soil. When the trees were burned, so was the leaf mold, along with the microorganisms. The stony, sterile ground was barren. On these barrens we have planted hardy 'starvation'-type coverage: many thorns, few leaves. When these have had a few decades to accumulate organic detritus, we will plant slightly less hardy things at their roots. After another few decades, we can plant the next generation, and so on. It will take over two hundred years for each acre to achieve fifteen percent of the organic mass it once held. It will take a millennium or more for each acre to achieve anything approaching the fertile growth that was its glory as one of Earth's chief oxygenators."

The listeners murmured at this.

"I have said nothing about fauna. Earth fauna was almost totally destroyed long before the sterilant was applied. We have genetic materials from the creatures that were typed before the forests were destroyed, but the typed ones were mostly larger animals that made up only a tiny percentage of the total life-forms. Many bacteria, for example, were never collected, never known to exist. The people of Earth did not understand that humans were part of a worldwide organism, that something as tiny as a cluster of bacteria could mean the difference between life and death for every living thing, the difference between a functioning, flourishing planet and a desolation. We Gentherans believe, as did the Pthas, that this is also true on a galactic scale: Very small things make very large differences, and we must be careful about destruction, even of things that seem useless or evil. We are experimenting with biotic clusters that are functionally parallel to the lost ones, but we cannot expect to achieve a total replication unless we find a pocket, somewhere, of the original forest. Such miraculous finds have happened during reconstructions of other planets, in the mouths of caves or in narrow canyons. We might be lucky enough to find one.

"It is too early to discuss any rehabilitation of the oceans. Perhaps in three or four hundred years, that process may be begun. Are there any questions?"

We listened to the ensuing discussion, some of which reminded me quite a bit of conversations I'd heard on Phobos, as a child. It was concerned with rehabilitation contracts and with the imposition of sustainable economic models. Earth had always operated on a continuous-growth model that requires a poverty class. Sustainable models require productive work by all members and are quite different.

When all the talk was over, the Gentheran thanked them for their attention and the audience, chattering, rose and dispersed. In the doorway, Sophia and I lingered.

Sophia said, "Why didn't the Gardener tell us about planetary economics? I shall have to read up on it. To tell the truth, Gretamara, I'm a little frightened of going on to Bray."

"I know, dear. The unknown is frightening, but you have always known it was what you had to do."

"Yes, but it was always some time in the future. Now it's immediate, isn't it. If it were not to be today, surely I would not be here, arranging all the legalities."

I grinned at her. "Oh, that's true enough, Lady. If it were not today, you would not be here, nor would I. I hope you feel the Gardener has taught you well."

"Both of you have taught me to hold my tongue," said Sophia meaningfully. "I have given you my oath to do so."

Most of those who had attended the brief meeting had gone even as other delegates to Dominion began to arrive. Two Gentherans came toward us and introduced themselves as Mwrrr Lrrrpa and Prrr Prrrpm. I identified them to myself as smaller one and larger one.

Smaller one of them said, "Von Goldereau d'Lornschilde has just arrived. He's over there by the door. He's been badgering us for years to find the heiress of Bray, and we're told she is here." She turned her mirrored helmet toward Sophia. "We are told you have grown up in a little town on Chottem, in the care of our friend, the Gardener. Would you mind dreadfully if we made the introduction?"

Sophia turned to me with a slight, wicked grin. We had planned for her to meet Von Goldereau, either here or in Bray, so I said, very seriously, that the Gardener and I would both be delighted. The two Gentherans turned and went toward d'Lornschilde purposefully, while Sophia and I walked a less direct route that brought us up behind him just in time to hear the Gentheran crow, ". . . but now we have great news to impart, Delegate Von Goldereau d'Lornschilde! You may rejoice, Delegate. The heiress of Bray has been found!"

We could only see the back of Von Goldereau's neck, which turned a peculiar ashen shade. "Found?" he choked. "Where did you find her?"

"Precisely where she has been all along, in the little village of Swylet-Upon-Sea, on Chottem, in the care of the Gardener."

We had edged around a little so we were able to see that some color was returning into Von Goldereau's face. "In the care of a gardener!"

He sneered. "She'll be completely unschooled. She'll be a bumpkin, a rustic, a peasant! Totally unable to accept the great responsibilities she will have to shoulder. It's best that I take her in hand, I think. See that she's educated properly . . ."

"Oh," said the other Gentheran, the larger one, "we think that will be unnecessary, Delegate. She has been reared by a great friend of Genthera."

The delegate's skin fell back toward its former ashen shade. "Genthera? What had Gentherans to do with her?"

"Enough to assure she would be no bumpkin."

"But she was left with some herb grower? Some vendor of vegetables?"

"Yes. With a great friend of our people."

He could find nothing to say, not a word even when the smaller one nodded to us. Sophia threw back her cloak and hood and moved around in front of the man, so he could see the loveliest woman he had ever seen, the perfected image of Stentor d'Lorn's daughter. She was dressed in the most recent style adopted by the wealthiest class in Bray, her hair tumbled about her head in a black cloud set with diamond stars, and when she offered her hand, the sparkle of stones from her fingers and wrists almost blinded him. Quite perfect! Just as the Gardener and I had planned it.

"Delegate," she said in the cool, careless voice she had inherited from her mother and had long practiced to perfection, "I understand you have been looking for me."

Von Goldereau found his voice, the upper register at any rate. "Only to offer any assistance I can." He bowed low over her hand and would have kissed it had she not withdrawn it quickly. "May I offer to escort you to your home?"

"Thank you, no," she replied. "Here at Dominion headquarters, I have been arranging for various things to be done in Bray. We have sent people there to attend to my business. They will see that the local legalities are taken care of, and they will offer proof of my identity. I will be returning there very shortly."

"The Great House has been largely untenanted," said Von Goldereau with a note of desperation. "Surely you will allow me to hire servants for you, to see to its being readied for your arrival."

"Kind of you, but unnecessary, Delegate. Workers have already been dispatched, people I know and trust. Even as we speak, they are opening the house my grandfather built."

He was at a loss, and I knew why. The Gentherans had been making unscheduled visits to Bray for some time, and it had become much harder for Von Goldereau d'Lornschilde to keep the family business operating in the way Von Goldereau, and Stentor d'Lorn before him, had preferred. There were things going on in Bray that he did not wish Dominion to learn of, that Dominion had not learned of, yet, however diligent its search. Certainly he didn't want the heiress to know of them until he was sure where her allegiance lay. With Stentor d'Lorn, he would have been on solid ground, but with my friend, he was at sea.

I could read his thoughts on his face. He was thinking it might be best to miss the meeting of Dominion and hurry back to Bray. He was also thinking that, on the other hand, something might occur at the meeting that was important, and the other delegates from Chottem might take advantage of his absence. His eyes, his hands betrayed his thought. So caught between two fires, he saw Sophia's amused expression, the look of one who read a clearly written book.

She said, "Von Goldereau, we are kinfolk. Please do not upset yourself over my return. Be assured that my friends throughout Dominion have the matter very well in hand. I am at the age of reason in Earth-years, the age we humans seem to feel appropriate for the acceptance of responsibility. At this age, we need no regents, no guardians, no overseers or protectors except those we have selected to oversee and to protect. Do not trouble yourself on my account."

And with that she turned and swept away, glittering like a fountain, with people bowing as she went and me hurrying after her, trying not to laugh. It wasn't funny. I knew that there was really nothing funny about it, and yet, for just a moment, I was delighted.

From behind me I heard the deeper-voiced Gentheran say: "Bumpkin, I think you said, Delegate d'Lornschilde. Or was it peasant?"

Von Goldereau did not reply. When we reached the door and looked back, we saw that he had gone. We both knew he was returning to Bray as quickly as possible.

Meantime, the heiress of Bray put her arm around me and said,

"That was interesting, don't you think, Gretamara? The man is up to something."

"If what the Gardener has told us is correct, Lady, we know the man is usually up to something, and something well beyond a bit of thievery or corruption. We will need to watch him."

"When do we leave?"

"Now," I said. "She's waiting for us now."

We went down to the smaller landing lock. There were several Gentherans standing about, staring in astonishment at the great golden dragonfly piloted by a woman in red robes, apparently a human woman. For many reasons, mere humanity seemed increasingly unlikely to me.

In the ship, the Gardener spoke softly. "The Gentherans back there are a bit confused. They have seen the ship; they have seen me. Among the cognoscenti I am rumored to be a member of the Third Order of the Siblinghood, as I was of the First and Second Orders. They saw me come to transport the heiress of Bray and her companion. Now they are retelling old tales in which my arrival always presaged great events. They are saying my arrival today cannot be coincidental."

I asked, "Are there to be great events, Gardener?"

She said, "It is time you knew: The Third Order of the Siblinghood, as did two Orders before them, has been trying to solve the 'human problem' for a very long time."

"The human problem?" I asked, somewhat offended.

She put her arm around me. "Forgive me, Gretamara, but your race as a whole has the unfailing habit of fouling its nest, ruining its environment, killing its original planet, and doing its best to kill any others to which it is moved. Because we love and admire the human race for its many good qualities, we call this not 'the human condition,' meaning an irrevocable state, but 'the human problem,' one we wish to solve. The effort has gone on for some millennia, without result, and some of those involved in the effort are beginning to believe it is a waste of time and treasure.

"In searching for the solution, the Siblinghood has relied heavily upon on its Gentheran members. The Gentherans have traditionally been supportive. Now, however, many Gentherans are questioning whether a solution is possible. Also, they complain that the Third Order has kept the work so secret, even from most of the Sibling-hood, that no one knows what's going on."

"I presume you kept it secret because some evil fate met the First and Second Orders," I said.

"Evil fate, yes. To our surprise, our plans were betrayed to unex-pected adversaries twenty thousand Earth-years ago, and again ten thousand years ago. After each of these failures, we waited until all memory of the events had been lost by the opposing races before we began again. This time we have worked in almost total secrecy, but secrecy loses friends. People are reluctant to trust that things known only to others are worth the effort, and also, they've begun wonder-ing if the antihuman feeling on the part of other races may not be well deserved."

"Weariness and lack of support I can understand," I said. "But why do they care what others think or feel?"

Gardener shook her head. "If a widespread, mercantile race feels intense enmity toward another, both trade and travel are affected. Those friendly with the enemy are also considered enemies, some-times to their loss. If humans were hated only by one or two races, as during the other episodes, it wouldn't be so troublesome, but this time at least three or four other races are involved. The Quaatar. The K'Famir. The Frossian. And the Thongal."

"Quaatar?" said Sophia. "From what you've taught me, they're not even in contact with humans! They don't buy bondspeople. Their territory is astronomically remote. How could they be bothered by humans?"

"The Quaatar bother easily. Some time in the remote past, they may have encountered humans under adverse circumstance. Perhaps a Quaatar tried to eat a human and got an upset stomach. That would have been enough. Every sentient race in our galaxy knows how easy it is to anger the Quaatar. We aren't sure what happened; we only know something happened, for the Quaatar hate humanity with all the viciousness of hundreds of generations, one piled upon another, and they have recently influenced others in the Mercan Combine, notably their congeneric races—Frossians, K'Famir, and Thongal—

to feel the same way. At a psychic level Quaatar, Frossian, and K'Famir interests and opinions have coalesced into a metaphysical force directed against mankind. If they are aware that the Third Order is trying to help humans, they will do whatever they can to thwart us, or kill us."

I said, "But they don't remember the last time."

"No. We waited until they had forgotten, until the records had fallen to dust."

"But you say 'if they know.' You aren't sure that they know."

Gardener almost whispered, "We are not sure if they know, or how much they may know. This time we have been diligent in spreading what is called 'disinformation.' If they are aware of false stories we have spread, they will intervene by destroying certain refuges and seeking for certain fictional agents. This will tell us that they suspect. If they are aware of the truth, they will pick a different set of targets. By their actions we will see what they know, but at what cost? Our plans will be in ruins. A dilemma, isn't it?"

Sophia stared at her. "The real refuges and the real people must go unnoticed."

"Exactly. If they are suspected, they may be harmed."

"But," I said, "if you seem to protect them, you draw notice to them."

"Yes. And that is why we are taking great pains to protect surrogates for both. But, are the vile races fooled, or not?"

I thought on this for a time. "You have taught me, Gardener, that elevated and powerful creatures usually do not carry their own garbage. They tell others to do it, and the word is passed down the chain to underlings. As the command travels farther from those on high, the less secret it becomes. Do we have people who listen for such things?"

Gardener nodded. "Oh yes, we have listeners, Gretamara. Disaffection is not so far advanced among the Gentherans that they have abandoned us. They listen, a great many of them, in many, many places." She laughed, something she did seldom. "And now, we three are about to be become listeners by doing something we do very rarely, lest we be discovered."

I looked out the front of the dragonfly ship and saw that it followed a shining road that seemed familiar to me.

"When we arrive at a particular place," said the Gardener, "I will take a shape that's not my own. You will hide inside my skirts. You won't make a sound, you won't ask a question. When we leave will be time enough for questions, but for now, you will listen. All the pieces of our puzzle are in motion, the time approaches, and we must know what our enemies are planning. We will risk ourselves to see if they will tell us."

Sophia had turned quite pale, and I took her hand in mind. "I was here once before with the Gardener," I said. "Years ago. We will be all right." She clutched my hand strongly. After a time the ship seemed to stop moving toward the space ahead that was cluttered, scattered, littered with blobs, clusters, clumps, bunches and sprinklings of ... somethings.

Slowly we floated nearer, hearing as we did so a great murmur, as of waters washing endlessly against the edges of the galaxies.

The Gardener whispered, "This is the great tree where all mortal created deities roost, all the Gods from every-place, every-race, every-time. Look to your left and down. Those are the Earthian Members. Do you recognize any of them?"

When Sophia did not answer, I said, "I see an old man with an eye patch," I said. "I forget his name. One of the gods of the people of the north that I read about as a child. And that very strong one with the hammer. That might be Thor."

"Actually," the Gardener murmured, "he is Thor, Hercules, Apollo, Gilgamesh, Adonis, Osiris, Krishna, virtually every young male deity known for strength, beauty, and intrepidity, just as my colleague, Mr. Weathereye, is Odin, Jupiter, Jove, Allah, Jehovah, or any other ancient male deity known for wisdom, power, and prescience. And the old woman there, Lady Badness, is Erda, Norn, Moira, Sophia, the wisewoman who can detect the pattern in the weavings of happenstance before mankind hears the shuttle coming."

"I'm named for her?" asked Sophia.

"For her, yes. And I, Gardener, am also Demeter, Cybele, Freya, Earth Mother, Corn Goddess, a thousand names of female deities wise in the ways of growing things, solicitous of women and children, caretakers of the beasts of the field and the woods. Some of us Members are sizable, for many mortals, including humans, believe in strength, and power, and nurture, and wisdom."

"What are all those hunched-up things?" asked Sophia.

The Gardener shook her head. "Sophia, those are the gods many humans prefer. They are hunched from ages of sitting on people's shoulders, whispering encouragement."

"But they're *tiny!*" she said, in disbelief.

"Many humans prefer tiny gods," said the Gardener. "Tiny gods of limited preoccupations . . ."

"Limited to what?" I demanded.

"To mankind, of course. And to each believer, particularly. Each human wants god to be his or her best friend, and it's easier to imagine god being your best friend if he is a tiny little god interested only in a tiny world that's only a kind of vestibule to an exclusive little heaven."

"Some of them are yelling," said Sophia.

"Oh, yes. Those are hellfire gods. Since there is no supernatural hell, they never really send anyone there, but their sources get enormous pleasure, thinking about it."

"And those," murmured Sophia. "Off to the side, all together?"

"I know what those are," I said. "Gardener told me those are dead people whose spirits have been imprisoned here. Some group or other on Earth has deified them or sainted them and claimed they can do miracles, so instead of passing on, humans hold them here, at least until they're forgotten."

"Can they do miracles?" asked Sophia wonderingly.

Gardener murmured, "We only know what our Sources know, we can only do what they can do. Many times persons actually heal themselves, or their bodies do it for them, but they prefer to believe one of us did it."

"What do you mean, you can only do what men can do? Men cannot fly about the universe in dragonfly ships," said Sophia.

"The Gentherans can," said the Gardener. "And long ago I melded with Sysarou, Gentheran goddess of Abundance and Joy, just as Mr. Weathereye down there has melded with Ohanja, Gentheran god of Honor, Duty, and Kindness. Gentherans have much the same needs mankind has; they have created similar deities, and we of Earth have melded with all the more accepted ones."

"You can do that? Meld with the gods of other species?" I asked, astonished.

"If we are similar enough, yes, which is a good thing, for Gentherans remember far, far into the past, and since we have melded with them, we, too, remember far more than do the gods of mere Earthians."

In the little silence that followed, I thought to myself that even if these gods could do nothing their people couldn't do, the Gardener, no matter how she disclaimed it, had powers they did not have.

She whispered, "I am looking at that mob of little Earth gods, hoping to find among them a disguise I can use."

The dragonfly ship came closer. "There," Gardener said, pointing. "That little female one. Its name is Oh-pity-me. It cannot see the sun for the daylight nor the stars for the darkness, and it is worshipped by a surprising number of people. It is not fierce enough to be interesting to the K'Famirish Members, and they will find it utterly unthreatening. I choose that one. Now, come with me and be very, very still."

The ship moved and unbecame. The Gardener was a small, dark cloud that hid us within her robes of dripping sorrow. We could see, we could hear, and we could understand everything we saw and heard, including the conversation of the three dark shapes nearest us, each lit by sullen fire.

"These are Dweller, Darkness, and Drinker," the Gardener spoke without sound. "Dweller in Pain, of the Quaatar. Whirling Cloud of Darkness-Eater of the Dead, of the K'Famir. Flayed One-Drinker of Blood, of the Frossians. Listen!"

Dweller snarled, "Look who is near to us. An Earthian Member. This is not your locus, Member. Yours is over there, among that shabby pile of Earthian trash."

"I am where I am," the Gardener whispered. "I am weary of them. They are noisy sometimes. I like it better here."

"Why, it's a little weeper," sneered Darkness. "Not like the rest of them."

"Not like them, no," whispered the Gardener. "They want only to go on. I want to end."

"Soon you may have your wish," giggled Drinker.

"Oh, if only that could be," murmured the Gardener. "Can you make it happen?"

"Ah, yes," chuckled Dweller, emitting a belch of fire. "We intend to make it happen."

"But Earthians don't want to die," the Gardener persisted.

"They'll try to stop us," sniffed Darkness. "They and the Gentherans . . ."

"The Gentherans?"

"Dweller has seen Earthian Members mixing with Gentherans. This means they are plotting together," said Drinker.

"They're always plotting," breathed Gardener. "I want to destroy them, and myself . . ."

Drinker whirled slowly, a ragged spiral of torn skin, dark with bruises, wet with blood. "We have learned that Gentherans watch intently over certain people . . ."

"Our Sources hired Thongals," giggled Darkness. "Very sneaky Thongals to find out what people the Gentherans are watching over. The Thongals found two of them among our people: one feeding a ghyrm on Cantardene, one feeding the umoxen on Fajnard. They are dead, or will be soon. Perhaps you can find others for us . . ."

"What are the Earthians and Gentherans plotting to do?" moaned Gardener, in the little god's weary voice.

Drinker gaped hideously. "Whatever it is, we'll stop it."

The three turned toward one another, put their heads together, murmuring. Gardener drew apart. Soon we found ourselves a distance away, the dragonfly around us.

"They suspect," said the Gardener. "And it seems they have identified some very important people."

"Are those gods real?" I demanded.

"I am one of them, Gretamara. We exist, but we are not real in the sense that a tree is real or a rock is real. If all the people in the universe were gone, the rock or tree would still be there, but we deities exist only while our people do."

"My parents believed there is only one god," I insisted.

"Oh, I believe there is One," the Gardener agreed. "A being larger than any mortal god; a being that encompasses the universe without being dependent upon it, preexistent and postexistent, a being so vast only a fool could claim to know its purposes, One who sets all into motion, then waits . . ."

"Why did it create the K'Famir?" I interrupted angrily.

"I did not say 'create.' The K'Famir are not a creation, they are a consequence, as are we all, Gretamara. Health or disease, pleasure or pain, joy or grief, all are consequences of the creation of life: All are possible. If no room is left for the possible, it is not life, it is mere repetition. Within our race, we encompass the scale from great good to absolute evil; we have had great leaders and philanthropists, and we have had serial torturers and killers. These last, mankind has regarded with sick fascination, trying to understand them as human beings. They should not try, for they are not human beings. Body shapes are only that, a shape, but when evil inhabits us, it is the same evil that inhabits the K'Famir. If you believe all humans have a capacity for good, then you must identify those who have none as something other than human. Only death ends them.

"The One god does not meddle in its creation, but we mortal gods often pretend it is our business to do so. We cannot move a straw upon a mortal world, but we can move ourselves from place to place . . ."

I asked, "How did we get here if you cannot move a straw?"

The Gardener smiled. "Where is here? Did I move you? Or did I merely whisper in your ear to see what I see? Now I shall whisper again, and what wonder! You will somehow be moved to Chottem, to Bray, to the house of Stentor d'Lorn, to find whatever secrets it holds and whatever darkness it hides."

I Am Margaret, at a Birthday Party on Tercis

On the day of the birthday party, we loaded the food into the wagon and drove across the bridge toward Billy Ray's farm.

"How many of 'em this year?" Jimmy Joe asked me.

I sighed. "The only ones left at home are Benny Paul, Sue Elaine, Trish, and the two little ones, plus Mayleen and Billy Ray."

"Humph," said Jimmy Joe. "Seven of them and six of us. Thirteen. Suppose that's an omen? I suppose their contribution to the festivities is hamburgers? Someday I must taste one."

When Mayleen and Maybelle were little, I had mentioned that hamburgers were an old Earth tradition for summer gatherings. I had never tasted a hamburger on Earth, nor had I at Mayleen's, even though she provided "hamburgers" at every birthday party.

This year would be no different, I saw as we approached, for Billy Ray was lighting the fire, using lots of coal oil. Mayleen, standing among billows of ugly, smelly black smoke, slapped the meat patties on the grill. They both came over to help us unload the food we'd brought from home, leaving the smoke and the flames to sort it out between them. Later, we each took one of the resultant "hamburgers," covered it with a bun, then lost it over where Uncle Billy Ray's dogs waited with their tongues out.

Maybelle had made salads; I'd brought fried chicken and two birthday cakes. The two little ones ate like starving creatures and went to sleep under the picnic table, icing all over their faces. As soon as the food was gone, Benny Paul pulled Til away, and Jeff followed them, his feet dragging. Trish and Sue Elaine sneaked off after. I watched the departure with some anxiety. The hangdog look on Jeff's face did not bode at all well.

Billy Ray started his usual after-food tirade. It seemed Joe Bob, the oldest boy, had threatened to call the placement people and get Benny Paul sent to some other Walled-Off. "Got no right to do that," Billy Ray shouted. "There's nuthin wrong with Benny Paul!"

Except killing the Conovers' prize bull out of meanness. Except pimping his sister, Trish. Plus many other barbarisms I only suspected.

"You gotta go speak to Joe Bob," he said to me. "Get him to tell 'em there's nothing wrong with Benny Paul."

I said. "I wouldn't feel right getting involved in a family argument, Billy Ray. That's between you and him." I got up and went over to the picnic table to pour a glass of berryade.

I heard Maybelle say, "Please don't get Mother involved."

"I just said . . ."

"We know what you just said," James interrupted very quietly. "Just please don't fuss Grandma over it."

Billy Ray gave him a nasty look. "This is my place, and I'll fuss who I damned well please, Jimmy Joe. You all don't like it, you can leave." He got up and stamped off to the house before I got back with my glass full.

Glory was peeking through the branches, waiting for the usual sequence to play itself out. Since Billy Ray had stomped off mad as soon as he'd stuffed himself with food, it was about time for Mayleen to do likewise.

"Don't see why Mother ought to be left out of family things," said Mayleen in a nasty voice. "It's her fault, all these Mackey twins. It's bad enough being pregnant all the time without having two babies to bury or take care of at the end of it."

Maybelle said sharply, "Mayleen, I know Papa talked to you just like he did to me. You didn't have to get pregnant all the time."

"That's my business! And I don't thank you for butting in!" She got up and stamped back to the house.

James looked at his watch, the little muscles at the corners of his jaw jumping around like water on a hot skillet. He walked off and came back with Jeff, who looked relieved to be going.

"New record for the shortest time," said James, as we drove off. "Total elapsed time, arrival to departure, including the unpacking of and setting out of food and the collecting of leftovers, one and one-quarter hours, not counting travel. Half an hour shorter than last year. Keep workin' at it, we'll get it down to where we can just drop off the food and turn the wagon around in the driveway."

Since our teatime had been cut short, when we got to Maybelle's, I went into the kitchen to put the kettle on. Outside, Jeff was giving Glory the ringroot bracelet he'd carved for her birthday.

"What was Benny Paul up to?" Glory asked him when she gave him a thank-you hug.

"Him and Trish," he said, making a face. "They were going to do a sex show for us, and Til said we'd get to . . . take part."

"Jeff, you've got to stay away from him."

"We're brothers, Glory."

"You'll be roommates in another Walled-Off if you're not careful! Billy Ray said Joe Bob threatened to call the Placement Board about Benny Paul, and if Til's been part of his nastiness, Til may have to go, too."

The shock on Jeff's face as he went by the kitchen door told me he'd never thought of that. The look on my face, mirrored in the door, said I'd never thought of it, either. I stood there, dazed, wondering what other important things I'd missed.

I certainly wasn't missing anything about Falija, for by this time, she was staying at my house most of the time. Glory came up to see her and said her living with me was a good thing, to keep her away from the boys.

"But I like Jeff," said Falija.

Both of us froze. I thought I had misheard, or maybe Glory was playing a trick on me, but Glory was staring at Falija, as surprised as I.

She said, "You're talking!"

"Umm," said Falija. "Yes. But it's not quite right."

"It sounds perfectly fine to me. How long . . ."

"Oh, a while. I practice at night when everyone's asleep."

Well, there was no nonsense about my being asleep this time! Fully awake, I'd heard it with my own ears. I heard more of it after Glory left, so it was no trick of hers. I had to believe it. By late summer, Falija was talking a lot, though only to Glory and me, and she was walking on her hind legs whenever she couldn't be seen.

"It's a good thing nobody else sees her," Glory said. "It's getting harder and harder to believe she's just a cat." She looked up to find my eyes fixed on her, but I forbade myself to ask the question. Glory shrugged, as though to say, "Either you believe me or you don't, and so far, you haven't."

James came home from work one night, shaking his head. "Grandma, where'd you tell me Billy Ray's oldest girl went?"

"You mean Ella May? She joined the Siblinghood a long time ago, when she was only about fourteen. Why?"

"I just wondered if we ought to let her know . . ."

"Know what?"

"Her twin sister, the one who moved up to Repentance last year . . ."

"Janine Ruth." Somehow, I knew what was coming. Ella May's twin was Mayleen all over again. "She hurt somebody."

He nodded. "Placement Board sent her to Hostility. I thought somebody ought to tell the family . . ."

"James, if you don't want to be blamed for causing it, you forget you ever heard about it."

He thought about it for a moment. "You're right, Grandma. They'd figure someway it was my fault, or Maybelle's."

Falija talked more clearly every day. She was able to get out of sight very quickly, so I stopped worrying about her going places with Glory. Whenever Glory went fruit-picking, Falija helped her. There was scarcely a branch too thin for her to climb out on and scoop fruit off the tree quick as anything. Glory could spread out a blanket and Falija would drop the fruit onto it fast as Glory could put it into baskets.

One night the two of them wakened me in the middle of the night. Glory said, "Falija found something she thinks we ought to see, Grandma."

"Fine," I said. "We'll go see it in the morning."

"No," she said. "Falija says it has to be now."

I wavered between outrage and curiosity. Curiosity won. I put on shoes and a big sweater. Falija led the way down to the road, up the valley, until we got to the rise before the cemetery.

Glory said, "I don't go in there, Falija."

Falija said, "I'm not taking you in there. We're going up the hill."

So we clambered up the ridge of the rise, past the cemetery fence, and onto a big flat rock between two thimble-apple trees. Beside the rock was some deep grass where we could sit in the moon shadow of the trees, and the fiddlebugs were making a noise so much like a ringing in the ears you couldn't tell if it was inside or outside your head.

"There," whispered Falija.

Down the hill two little girls were running stark naked, hand in hand, along the meadow, and behind them some other children, all naked, some of them paired off and some alone. Along behind them came Lou Ellen.

That's when I realized I was dreaming again. I had that same, misty feeling I'd had down at the ferry pool. The naked children gathered around Lou Ellen. Glory started to get up, and Falija put a claw into her arm. "Don't," she said. "They'll run away if you go down there."

Some older, familiar-looking children came through the trees. They were as tall as grown-up people, but they had no breasts, and there was no hair on their bodies. I thought I should know them, but I couldn't remember who they were.

"They're all children," Glory said in confusion.

"Well," Falija said, "not so much children as just young, and they're all the same person, really. Some grown larger, some not."

"Why not?" Glory whispered.

"Oh," Falija whispered. "Where they are, they don't need to be old. They've already learned everything they can."

I was dreaming again. I had to be. A woman wearing red robes that billowed and flowed around her like a rosy cloud came out of the woods. She stood for a time, watching the children until they wandered into the trees on the far side. Lou Ellen was with them. I had never seen her with that expression of joy on her face. Bliss, I'd call it. Absolute bliss.

"Who is that woman in red, Grandma?"

"I can't quite remember," I said.

I remembered when I wakened in the morning, though. It was the woman who had taken Wilvia away, and it had all been a dream. Even after I found my big sweater there on the bed, I told myself I'd just been chilly in the night, that was all.

School started the next week. Glory, Bamber Joy, and I went down to Ms. McCollum's store to buy school supplies. I always went in first and paid Ms. McCollum for the children's supplies while he and Glory sat on the stoop enjoying a cold drink. This time, I heard heavy footsteps coming onto the front stoop, and two men came slamming in, walked up to the counter, and asked Ms. McCollum if there was anybody in town who had a new cat.

Ms. McCollum looked as though she didn't know whether to laugh or get angry. It was a silly question, but at the same time, it sounded threatening. She had to swallow before she answered, very slowly. "I guess everybody in the valley has a new cat at least once a year. There's kittens everywhere you look."

"Not a kitten, ma'am. This is a dangerous kind of cat from another world."

"There's a lady over in Remorseful who sort of collects cats, but they're just ordinary cats. I sure haven't heard about anything like that."

I knew she meant Dorothy Springer, a retired schoolteacher who had a barnful of cats and spent her whole pension feeding them and having the vet fix them. The two men didn't react; they just stood there for a minute, silent. They sounded so mechanical, I had the strange idea that maybe they were shifting gears, or waiting for instructions. Then, with not so much as a thank-you, they turned around and left.

When we got home we told Falija about it, and the hair on her neck rose until she looked like a lion.

"They didn't come from your people," Glory said to Falija. "Your people know where you are."

"Her *people*?" I asked, with lifted eyebrows.

"She means my parents," said Falija firmly. "Anyone sent by my people would know exactly where I am."

"We've got to be sure no one else in the family says anything," Glory said in a worried voice.

All this was extremely upsetting. I had spent months sorting out what I chose to believe was real from what I had dreamed from the fictional stuff that was left over. At least, I thought I had. Now this new thing! A threat from who knows what from who knows where against someone who shouldn't exist in the first place!

I cleared my throat, turned toward Glory, and said in my most portentous voice, "You had a cat earlier in the summer, but it went away some time ago, didn't it?"

Glory stared at me for a minute before she caught on. "Yes. Of course. The lady who left it with me came and got it."

I said, "The family hasn't seen it for some time."

Glory shook her head and grinned at me. "No, ma'am."

I was invited to supper that night, and at the table, Glory said, "I kind of miss the cat I was keeping for that lady. None of the barn cats are very friendly. Maybe Ma Bailey'll give me one of her kittens."

I said wonderingly, "The cat you were taking care of. Is it gone?"

"The lady came along the road when I was riding my bicycle. She told me thank you and let me keep the rest of the money."

"I thought it ran off," grunted Til.

"You gave it enough reason to," muttered Jeff.

After the dishes were done and the chickens shooed in, Glory walked back up the hill with me. We sat down on the porch, and I said what I'd been thinking about for days, "Glory, I've cultivated blindness as long as I can. I've always congratulated myself on being a realist, but it's getting so I can't tell the difference between what's real and half real and mostly supposition. I want you to tell me everything, whether you think I'll believe it or not."

Glory gave me a look.

"I won't doubt you," I said firmly. "Whatever you say."

She took a deep breath and started in. The cat-people. The money bag. I have never believed in telepathy, not really, even though one of my childhood imaginary people was supposed to be a telepath, and the only alternative to having seen it myself was to think I had read it from Glory's mind. Believing I had seen it was easier. It had not been a dream, it had been real, but I had suppressed the reality of it.

Surprisingly, to me at least, when I finally took it in, things made more sense than they had up until then. Falija was not just an anomaly. She really was a treasured creature of some other race, and we really had to keep her safe.

Glory said, "I never fed Falija cat food any more than the barn cats get cat food. They eat what they catch. Falija eats what I eat. There's no cat-food trail anybody can follow, and Falija doesn't even associate with other cats. She won't go into the barn at all. Whenever she sees a barn cat, she gets all strange."

"How do you mean, strange."

"All sad, upset, silent. So I don't take her in there."

"What about the money bag?" I asked her. "The one the people gave to you to pay for Falija's needs." Glory had given me the money so Sue Elaine couldn't borrow it without asking, which was one of Sue Elaine's many unattractive habits.

"It's in my boot," Glory said. "With some dirty socks shoved down on top of it."

I mused, "It has to have a power source. People use detectors to find metal and things like radioactivity."

We went down the hill together and up the back stairs to her room. She shook the bag out of her boot, and something else fell out with it: the little book Falija's mother had given Glory, which Glory had told me about. We had both forgotten what the person had told Glory to do with it. Glory stared at it with her face all knotted up. I felt absolutely idiotic. Here between the two of us we'd forgotten the one thing we were supposed to do for Falija, even though I hadn't really believed it until tonight!

We talked about a safe place for the little bag, and we eventually decided to bury it next to metal, not as easy as you'd think on Tercis, where metal was rare and expensive. We finally thought of the cemetery fence. Glory got a trowel out of Maybelle's gardening basket, and we hiked over to the cemetery to bury the bag next to a fence post. If anyone used a metal detector, they'd think it was reacting to the post, though I thought it likely that the bag was of a technology far, far beyond metal detectors. Chances were, whoever might look for it would be equally sophisticated. Nonetheless, we scattered the place with rocks, weathered side up, then we went up to the thimble-apple rock to be sure we hadn't left any sign of being there.

When we looked down the meadow, there they were, all Lou Ellen's friends with Lou Ellen among them, moving out into the moonlight on the meadow, dancing like leaves dance on the wind, almost weightless, floating up and down, free and glorious, as though they had forever to dance in. They sang, too, with Lou Ellen's voice among them, joyful and blithe.

I looked down at Glory. She was gazing down the hill with such longing that it almost broke my heart. She wanted to go down there with Lou Ellen. I started to say something, then stopped. Some things couldn't be fixed with words. She wiped her eyes on her sleeve, then stared, way across the meadow. I followed her gaze. There was the woman in red, looking straight at us from the edge of the trees. I could feel the woman's eyes on me, almost stroking. I lifted my hand; the woman smiled and waved and disappeared into the forest.

"Who is she?" Glory asked.

"A dream from my past," I said. "A woman who flies a dragonfly ship. Everything down there in the valley is a dream."

Falija wasn't around when we got back, but the next morning, Glory came up to apologize for forgetting about the book.

"I forgot what your mama told me to do, Falija. I was supposed to read it to you when you began to talk."

"I've been talking for a long time," Falija said, with a little frown between her eyes.

Glory flushed. "I know, Falija. It's my fault. I'd forgotten it until last night. Now listen." She opened the book. On each page there were only a few words. The first page started out: 'Our word for insight is ghoss.' Ghoss was spelled out as guh-HOSS, so the reader would know how to pronounce it. The next page had another few words, and so on, a few hundred of them altogether.

Then I took the book to look at it, and Falija stared at me in a funny way and said, "Please, read it to me again, Grandma." I did. When I'd finished, Falija went off in a corner by herself after putting the book on one of my bookshelves, hidden behind some other books.

That night, Falija came into my bedroom and climbed up onto my bed, digging her claws into my shoulder. I woke to see her frightened face inches from my own, eyes as big as moons. I held her while she curled up on my chest, shivering as though she'd been frightened half to death.

"What is it?" I whispered. "Falija, what is it? Tell me."

"In my head," she said. "There's a whole world in my head, and I can't shut the door in between . . ." Then she said something in another language that went on and on, and she shut her eyes and just lay there, shivering like an abused animal. At first I didn't realize what she'd said, but then it came to me. She was speaking Gentheran. I wrapped my arms around the little person, to comfort her, and we stayed that way for a long, long time. Falija would shiver, then she'd calm down, then she'd make this pitiful little noise and shiver all over again.

"My home," she whispered. "My home is the land of Perepume on the world of Chottem. I can see the cliffs of Perepume, where the spray from the green ocean smells like spicebush and pine. I see the forests, where the wind sings in the boughs. I hear the tongues of Perepume, lilting and laughing through the long nights. They were there, inside my head, in my mother-memory. The words you read to me opened the door to the mother-memory all at once, and it scared me. I didn't know where I was!"

I held her tight. "That must be how your people pass on information," I said, trying to sound very calm, as though it wasn't anything unusual or strange. "I wish our people could do it that easily. I'll bet you know all the history and geography now, without even having to read a book or study about it."

Falija looked confused for a moment, but then her ears came forward, and she did her cat smile. "I think I do. I really do."

"That would be wonderful," I said enthusiastically. "Gloriana will be so jealous! Just think, no homework."

"What's homework?" Falija asked.

I explained about school. It seemed to soothe her to hear me talk, so I went on about being in school myself, when I was younger, and how difficult some classes were. "But your way, you just have one sort of scary night—and that's our fault for forgetting the book until now. But, you have it! It's all right in there. Oh, Falija, I really envy you." And it was true, I did.

Falija curled a little tighter against my chest and seemed to doze off for a while. Then she woke up, and said, "Grandma, they have human people in my world."

I half opened one eye and said sleepily, "Do you suppose that's why your family left you with Gloriana? Because they already knew about human beings?"

Falija looked puzzled. "Maybe. They're in my world . . . no, a special few of them live among us. And there are bad creatures, Thongals. They were on Fajnard, too. They tried to capture the king and queen of the Ghoss, who barely escaped . . ." Her eyes got big, and she didn't say anything more for a long while. I slept.

"It's part of a story," said Falija loudly enough that my eyes snapped open. "It starts at the beginning, and it goes on to the end. Shall I tell it to you?"

"You can't just pick out the important parts?" I suggested sleepily.

"No. One tells it all, or one doesn't tell it. I think Glory should hear it, too. It's a long story . . ." She stood up. "I'll go get her. We'll come back here."

And she was out the door, silent as a shadow.

They came back up the hill together, Falija draped over Glory's shoulder. I turned on the light as they came near, the light scoring deep shadows into the ledge before the house and throwing an amber glow on the bottoms of the branches.

Glory opened the door and yawned. "Falija says you have something important going on here."

I was at the stove, putting on the kettle. Falija jumped up on the sofa while Glory came to set out the cups and get the sugar and tea out.

"What kind of tea, Grandma?" she asked.

"Oh, that strong one I use to wake up with," I said. "I'll never get back to sleep, after, but never mind."

Glory measured the tea. The kettle boiled, the tea was steeped, and we moved over to the sofa, where I put my nose in the steaming cup and felt better immediately.

"All right," I said to Falija. "What is it?"

Falija said, "I now have the memory I got from my mother before I was born. It just didn't open up until tonight."

"How did this mother-memory get into your head?" I asked.

Falija got wrinkles between her eyes, looked puzzled for a moment, then said, "In early pregnancy, our females duplicate a certain part of their brain, and the duplicate moves down what's called an epispinal duct to the womb, and this mother-brain part connects to the baby's mind before the skull grows around it. Then, after the baby is born, that mother-mind gradually makes connections with the baby's brain, and, when the child learns to speak our language, the words link up and open the way to all that information."

I chewed on this for a while. "Not until the child learns to speak?"

Falija said, "That's why the book was so important. Ideas are expressed in words, and even the ones that are thought of in pictures or feelings need words to decode them, so babies have to have words in our language to tie them to the mother-brain. If I'd grown up among my own people, I wouldn't have needed the book, because I'd have heard the words from the first. It's very interesting, isn't it? There's so much of it, it will take a long time to absorb it all."

I said, "You already know some things, though. You know where you're from."

"From Perepume, yes. I know there are humans on my world, and the humans call the planet Chottem. Perepume is a separate part, a . . . continent. I have memory of a world called Thairy and one called Fajnard. My people live on both of those as well, and so do humans. I know the names of a lot of other worlds, all of them occupied by different people, all spread out and joined together by . . . channels, ropes . . ."

"Wormholes?" I offered.

"Spcc'ci in my language," she crowed. "Yes, wormholes. The whole network is huge. Almost none of the people in it know about all the other people in it, but my people know secret ways to get from place to place very quickly. And I know the story, the one I said both you and your grandmother should hear."

"The one you woke me up about," I said.

"That one. Yes."

"Well, nighttime is a good time for storytelling. Let me turn out some of these lights. Open the stove door and bring the teapot over here, Glory. We'll sit in firelight."

And then, to Falija, "Tell the story."

"In the long, long ago, the Gentherans came to Earth the very first time . . ."

"Not that long," I said. "It was only a century or so."

"No." Falija's eyes glowed in the light of the stove. "You mustn't interrupt the story. The first time Gentherans decided to visit Earth thousands and thousands of years ago, they discovered your people living in caves and making crafty things with their hands and thinking crafty thoughts. Your people fought with each other quite a lot. The Gentherans are a curious people, very interested in other beings, and they thought your people were intriguing, so they took some of them to Fajnard, near where a lot of my people, the Gibbekot, live. They gave the humans a place with caves to live in, near good soil where they could plant crops. After that it seemed like no time at all, they were overcrowded and began to fight with one another.

"So, the Gentherans decided to change the humans a little, not so much as would make them unhuman, but enough to make them less likely to overcrowd and fight. Sometimes a Gibbekot baby dies before the mother-mind leaves the mother's head, and when that happens, our doctors can take the partial mind and give it to other creatures. So the Gentherans obtained an unfinished mother-mind from my people, one that had our language in it and some of our other talents, and the Gentherans cloned enough of these mother-minds to give them to all the humans.

"In the humans, it had an unforeseen side effect. Some Gibbekot are almost telepathic, and the partial mind that they cloned for humans had that quality, and in the humans it was stronger! Suddenly, the humans understood one another better, they stopped lying and cheating and fighting each other, their lives became much more contented, and remarkably, they passed the mother-mind on to their children! They named themselves the vabil ghoss, which is to say *those having insight,* in my language. 'Enlightened ones,' I guess you'd say.

"Both the Gibbekot and the vabil ghoss still share the highlands of

Fajnard very happily. In time, they dropped the vabil part of their name and were known just as the Ghoss. Ghoss do some things better than we do, and we do some things better than they do, and Ghoss went with my people when colonies were established on Thairy and Chottem."

I frowned in concentration. "Your people must have liked us a good deal!"

"The Gentherans had a special reason to be interested in humans. That's why they're so set on helping you. Gloriana, you know your cousin Trish? You've told me about her, and I've seen her because I was curious. She's not quite complete, and I've even heard you, Grandma, feeling sorry for her."

"So?" said Gloriana.

"In time long past, an armada of Gentheran ships was traveling near a variable star, and the radiation caused a mutation in all the un-born babies. They were born physically deformed and mentally lim-ited. Their fingers never developed, they couldn't stand erect or learn to speak, and because of that they couldn't access their mother-minds and were forever trapped in babyhood. Even though they couldn't mature into true Gentherans, they did mature sexually and were able to have children. Because they were mute and crippled, our people called them, 'the afflicted.' Our people grieved over them just as you do over Trish, Grandma.

"When the Gentherans found your race, oh, many thousands of years ago, they had some of the afflicted ones with them. Your people were . . . silly about them. They just loved them. Your people, espe-cially your children, were just delighted with these poor, handicapped Gentherans, and the poor, handicapped Gentherans liked them just as much.

"As soon as this was known, Gentherans began bringing their handicapped ones to Earth. Your people adopted them. Some of them lived with you, some moved out into the wild, some even evolved into other types, but they were all . . . happy, as they could never have been among Gentherans . . ."

Into the silence, I said, "She's talking about cats, Gloriana." I stared at Falija, trying to figure something out. "Falija, your people are the Gibbekot, right? Then who are the Gentherans?"

"The spacefaring moiety of us," she said. "Half of us are spacefarers, the other half are settlers, but we're all one people." She sighed. "The afflicted were no longer such a great sorrow to our people because they were happy. Everywhere there are humans, they're still happy, and we owe their happiness to you."

"Anyone would have loved them!" cried Gloriana.

Falija replied, "Not as you do. Gibbekot are not perfect. No creature is perfect. Gentherans expect their children to be like themselves, and they grieve when that is not so. Seeing the unfortunates still makes us uncomfortable. Ever since then, the Gentherans have felt a debt to humans, and they've kept in touch with Earthian people, even though they're not happy about the way humans behave.

"Up until meeting humans, our race believed that each intelligent race was either ethical or vile; either it had evolved a moral and ethical system or it hadn't. The K'Famir and the Frossians are vile races. They take what they want, they kill when they feel like it, they're amused by torture, and they never identify with their victims. Some humans are exactly like them.

"The Gentherans and the Gibbekot have an ethical system, along with rules of morality. They try to be fair to all thinking beings as well as some or all living beings that don't think. Some humans are exactly like them, too.

"Before that time, we thought every species had one kind of mind or the other, but not both. Except for you humans. Human politicians brag about the good they're pretending to do while they take bribes not to do it. Human commercial interests talked about helping people while they destroyed all the fish, trees, and clean water on Earth. The Gentherans know a lot of evil races and a lot of good races, but the human race is the only hypocritical race we've ever encountered.

"The only race that espouses virtue and can't practice it?" I murmured.

"Exactly, and our people wanted to know why. When they investigated, they found there was a physiological difference. They learned that every ethical race has a racial memory, and every vile race has none. Ethical races are fully aware of their own history. We Gibbekot have millions of years of increasingly intelligent, purposeful being in our minds along with all the happenings and all the consequences of those happenings along the way.

"But humans don't have a racial memory, and neither do the K'Famir or the Frossians, or the Quaatar, or the . . . well, a good many others."

I was dumbfounded. "You can remember everything?"

"Yes. We really can, though it's not so much remembering as it is just knowing. You don't have to remember which way is up or what green is, you just need to learn the word for it. Even though my people were very fond of the strange humans, they were upset that every generation of them made the same mistakes. Instead of knowing what war was by remembering their own children screaming as their entrails spilled out and their skins burned off, your people talk about patriotism and bravery. Which is more real to you? If it's been twenty years since your last war, humans don't recall the reality, so if some not very bright leader yells, 'If you're brave and patriotic, you must defend our cause,' off you march.

"Imagine that you remembered being the very first premammal, and remembered being various primates, and remembered being every kind of prehuman. My people thought humans needed that, in order to stop making the same mistakes over and over."

"Real do-gooders, the Gentherans," I muttered. "We have written histories, after all!"

"Oh, yes," said Falija, twitching her ears. "The smarter ones of you can read about the past, and you can record what you see, and you have retained enough information between generations for science to develop, but few people pay attention to history. If some powerful person wants to do something history says is foolish, he just claims what is written isn't true, or doesn't apply to the present, and since most of you haven't read it, you believe him. You have improved, that's true. You finally learned that human sacrifice didn't do any good. You finally learned that slavery was evil; that is, most of you did, for a while, but not all of you forever. Some races would have tried selective breeding at some point, but you cared more about being unique than you did about being good. My people think you'll go extinct soon if you don't have a racial memory. I guess that makes us do-gooders."

I stared at her a long time. "Perhaps your people were thinking of giving us the kind of minds you have."

Falija said slowly, "It would be logical, wouldn't it, but there's nothing about that in my mind, and I can't imagine how it would be done. Where would they get one? You don't remember your first ancestors. You have no memory of ninety-nine percent of what makes you what you are! Instead you have comfy baby-stories you tell yourselves to explain why you're not good people. What sin you committed or how you didn't do what this god or that god told you. Instead of learning how not to be bad, you learn how to be forgiven and carried off to heaven. Most of you find it easier to believe the baby-stories than to learn from history and science, because it takes brains and hard study to understand history and science, but the stories are simple and comfy. People who want things easy and comfy resent people who study things. They teach their children the comfy stories and tell them not to worry about studying, just buy a ticket to go to heaven, and gradually, everyone becomes as ignorant as everyone else. It's happened time after time on Earth."

From what I knew of Earth's history, she was right. "Yes, Falija, I know how that works. And I have never until this moment been envious of cats." I picked up my teacup, found it empty, and poured a bit more. "What else do you remember?"

Falija nodded. "There's another group, the Siblinghood . . ."

I snorted. "Even I know about that! You remember Ella May, don't you, Glory? Mayleen's second eldest, Janine Ruth's sister? She was accepted by the Siblinghood, and more power to her!"

Falija went on, "The Siblinghood helped the royal family when Thongals attacked on Fanjard."

I said, "If I remember my studies, Fajnard was overrun by the Frossians."

"That was later. The royal family was attacked by Thongals twice. The first time was thirty-six or -seven years ago when they killed King Joziré the First. His wife fled into hiding with the crown prince, who was only a baby. The Siblinghood helped hide Prince Joziré, while he grew up and was educated.

"Meantime, the Frossians stayed in the lowlands of Fajnard while the Gibbekot and most of the Ghoss fortified the highlands. A few of the Ghoss always pretend to be slaves on the lowlands in order to keep an eye on the Frossians. Peace was maintained, and after a number of years, the Gibbekot and Ghoss thought it would be safe for Prince Joziré to return to Fajnard.

"He was about twenty then. He married his childhood companion, and they were crowned as King Joziré the Just and Queen Wilvia the Wise . . ."

"Wilvia?" I faltered. "Queen Wilvia?"

"Why?" asked Glory. "Is there something wrong with that name?"

I shook my head. "No, child, it's just a case of imagination meeting reality head-on. I used to play dress-up as a child. Most children do, I suppose. I often played I was a queen, and that was her name, Queen Wilvia. I can't believe it."

"The young queen became pregnant," Falija said. "And then, suddenly, with almost no warning, a group of dissident Thongals invaded the highlands, and again tried to capture the king and queen. Well, the queen was taken into hiding at the first sign of trouble, and the king was smuggled off Fajnard in another direction."

"Does this have something to do with the great task your parents said you were to perform?" asked Glory.

"I believe so," said Falija, ears forward and eyes slitted. "I have a story in my head, about the man who talked to the fish. I remember a saying. 'Who knows? The Keeper knows. Well then, ask the Keeper. Where do I find it? All alone, walk seven roads at once to find the Keeper.' If my mother memorized all that and put it in my mothermind, it had to be important, didn't it? And all that about young King Joziré and Queen Wilvia. The threat against them hasn't stopped! Some race or group is trying to kill them!"

I asked, "Do you have any other languages in your head?"

"P'shagluk khoseghu bahgh," said Falija. "Ephais durronola."

I gasped. "Quaatariis. Pr'thas!"

"What?" cried Gloriana.

"She speaks Quaatar," I cried. "And Pthas! Oh my blessed soul. We only studied Quaatar because it was a precursor to an obscure Mercan tongue. It's a foul language, full of nasty words, and only the Quaatar could consider it holy. As for Pthas, well, they were the ancient and revered ones, the only people, it is said, who knew the name of the Great Experimenter . . . don't ask. That's just what was said. We have much of their language preserved, but of course it's not spoken anymore. Oh, I wish I'd known about this earlier."

Glory's face went red, all the way back to her ears. "If I'd told you, you'd have accused me of making it up!"

I stared at my shoes, ashamed. "You're right. I would have. I humbly beg your pardon. You'll have to forgive me without holding a grudge, Gloriana, because you and I must share this secret cooperatively, to keep Falija safe."

I Am M'urgi/on B'yurngrad

I entered the oasthouse through the summer door, which would have been enough to make those inside dislike me even had I not brought sleet gusting in to make a brief fog above the hearthstones. Their thoughts were on their faces: icetime was hard enough on the men, offering few and seldom comforts, without having them sullied by some fool southlander woman who couldn't tell a summer door from an icelock.

High-booted and wrapped in heavy furs, burdened with a high basket securely strapped to my shoulder, I stood for a moment in seeming ignorance of their hostility, though the lack of any greeting confirmed I had set myself wrong with them. B'Oag, the oastkeeper, made the matter clear, snarling, "Dja ne'er see an icelock where'er in devil's keep yah come from?"

The chill voice that came from behind my thick scarf was well practiced to have all the power it needed. "The summer door was nearest, Oastkeeper, and I have come too far to consider niceties." I unwound the scarf from my mouth, then from my neck and shoulders, and finally from around my head to display the golden diadem banding my forehead. At once the oasthall was murmurous with contrived conversation, all the men staring intently into one another's faces, talking of the season, the temperature, the monotony of the winter diet, anything except me. Even

B'Oag's eyes darted toward his other guests, as though to anchor his intention elsewhere, before reminding himself that he was, after all, on home ground, his name on the oasthouse sign, and not, therefore, required to give way.

"I'll be needing a room," I said. "Supper, also. Wine if you have it, or cider, or tea, if that's all there is."

The oastkeeper's eyes roved quickly over the company in the room. That meant his rooms were all filled. I saw his assistant, perhaps his son (they resembled one another), nod covertly from his chair in the corner, indicating he would take care of it, and B'Oag nodded shortly in return. "M'boy Ojlin'll have a room made up, mistress."

"Envoy, Oastkeeper. My title is envoy. One who wears the circlet has that name and no other outside the Siblinghood. I am come for a reason you already know. Let us not fence with one another. The night is too long and cold for that."

He flushed and fumbled while I regarded him with level, amber eyes. He, like many others, was fascinated by my eyes. He considered them catlike. These people told stories of us. They said it was something we ate off there in the badlands that made our eyes glow. Or if not something we ate, some dreadful thing we did. They were only lenses of a particular kind, which anyone should have been able to figure out. Human worlds are always awash in superstition, only a stubborn elite proof against it.

"I'll also need a lockroom," I murmured, easing the straps over my shoulders and putting an end to his speculation.

At this he paled, his nostrils pinched shut, as though to shut the very smell of me out. "Ask Ogric there." He nodded toward a dwarfish man near the stair. "Ogric keeps the key. I'll be putting your supper on the table by the copper."

Ogric did indeed have the key, though we had to go out into the storm to use it, for the lockroom opened onto the oasthouse courtyard. Still, it was in a sheltered corner, so I did not bother rewrapping myself before opening the door and peering into the closetlike space, floored and walled with square stones, a handspan to a side. "Is it sound?" I asked, holding out my lantern to survey it.

"D'rocks tall as me, everone in wall, everone in floor. Top slab, d'tooken ten umoxes lif' it."

I nodded, half smiling to myself as I calculated mentally: each rock a handspan square, each one a man's height long, laid so that the walls were a man's height thick, the interior space two man's heights high, one wide, one long, the slab on top a veritable mountain. It had taken only fear to move these northerners to this prodigious labor and only stupidity to go to all that trouble, then put a wooden door on the place.

"Ah," I murmured. "So it's tight, is it?"

"Aye . . . ma'am, dad'is. Comes ere ragin' crazies mid ice, we drow'm in dere. Dey stay. Dairn'd nodin geddin ou'vit."

"I'll take the key," which I did, from a hand that trembled slightly before Ogric turned and fled back to warmth, leaving me alone in the dim light of the lantern. I stepped inside with my basket, shutting the door behind me. A short time later I stepped out without the basket, shut the door firmly, and locked it behind me, then put my ear to the heavy, ironbound planks to listen for what sound might come from within. Hearing none, I took a deep breath, and another, pushing all the stench of it from my lungs, gasping as I replaced foul air with clean. Finally, I picked up the lantern and made my way back to the oasthall, now bereft of the greater number of its former occupants.

"Ruinous on business, envoys," B'Oag was saying to his son when I entered. He looked up and flushed. "Meaning no disrespect, ma' . . . that is, Envoy."

"I take no offense, Oastkeeper. We are not good for business. We are not supposed to be. Comfort yourself with the knowledge that if I find what I seek, I will not be here long."

"And that would be . . . ?"

"Do not trifle with me, Oastkeeper. You know what I'm here for and probably where it is and who has it. It's likely everyone in the district knows, including the children in their cradles. I have no doubt the whispers began the day he or she brought it home, whoever that person may be."

B'Oag mimed innocence, widening his eyes and pursing his lips. "Envoy, I have no idea . . ."

I turned away from him impatiently. "I left my burden in your lockroom, Oastkeeper. When my task is done, I'll go my way, taking it with me. If my task is weary and long, it will grow tired of its imprisonment, and then . . . then you will wish you had made it easy for me."

Without waiting to judge the effect of this threat, I went to the table by the wide, bell-shaped copper that hung over the heat source: a hot spring, a little fumarole, maybe a boiling mud pot, though it didn't smell like a mud pot. The copper funneled the heat upward into coiled flues that ran first through the oasthall, then into the rest of the place, including the spaces for animals. The laundry probably had its own source, preferably a hot spring that provided hot wash-water for clothes and linens.

The cider was already on the table, along with a plate covered by an overturned bowl to keep warm a dish of stewed meat, legumes, grain, and herbs. I took off the scarf, then the coat, hanging them on the back of a nearby chair. I wore boots to my knee, and trousers above that, thick with padding to keep out the cold. I stripped off my gloves and my padded jacket, becoming smaller as each layer was removed. At last I sat down in my shirtsleeves. I knew what they saw. A slender woman not yet of middle years, pale brown hair in many tiny braids making up a complex pattern that ended in a beaded knot at the nape of the neck, golden eyes glittering in the firelight, skin reddened by the unaccustomed heat. I must have looked quite ordinary, except for the eyes and the gold Siblinghood diadem with its jewel blooming upon my forehead as though it carried fire within itself.

Something moved at my throat, and I took it from beneath my shirt, a tiny feathered thing that blinked in the firelight before settling itself on the table beside my plate. I beckoned, and B'Oag came to my side. "A pinch or two of raw grain, Oastkeeper. I found this little one in the snow, barely alive. Do you know what sort it is?"

"Chitterlain: one that waited too long to go south."

"Well, I am of no mind to let it freeze."

He fetched the grain, a small handful, and scattered it on the table where the chitterlain lay. It stirred itself to peck at the offering, at first doubtfully, but then with renewed energy, stretching its four wings, first one pair, then the other. I poured a bit of water into a saucer and put it where the creature could drink from it.

B'Oag whispered to his son while I ate, the others in the room kept their voices down. Several times, all speech stopped when sounds came in from outside, a ragged howling, a snuffling at the summer door, a low growl, almost like a purr, a shrill yap or two followed by shriller yips. Dire wolves and their pups. Ice cats and their kits. The great ape-bears had already gone deep into their dens. All feathered creatures except the thunder-buzzards had fled south long ago. Now there were only the winter beasts, the winter men (for their women-folk stayed home in snowtime), and one envoy from who knew where.

"What's in the basket?" the boy asked B'Oag, in a voice I could hear clearly, his curiosity overcoming his prudence.

I saw B'Oag go white again, lips pinched. "Ojlin, hush, or I'll hush you! We don't mention it! We don't question it! We don't know about it! It's not of us, it's of them!"

The opening of the icelock door went unnoticed among the howling and growling outside until a chill draft announced the cracking of the inner door to admit a tall form, as thickly bundled as I had been. From the corner of my eye I saw him removing his gloves one finger at a time, slapping them against his thigh to remove the ice crystals, laying them on the nearest table while he unbuttoned the thick coat, furred outside with a shag woven of the long, curly winter locks of adult mountain gnar, furred inside with the soft woven fleece of the young. Beneath it were seemingly endless layers of other clothing, which he merely unbuttoned in series, all the while looking about himself, ceiling, floor, shuttered windows, the hot copper with its armspan wide coil of metal flue above it, both hood and flue radiating welcome heat.

I ignored him and went on with my meal.

"Oastkeeper?" he asked at last, through the scarves still hiding his face.

"B'Oag Thenterson," he said. "An 'ow may we serve you, sir?"

"Food. Whatever she's having smells good. And a pitcher of cider, if you have it."

"This early in the icetime, we've got it," said B'Oag, as the stranger paced slowly across the floor.

Before I realized what he was doing, he was at my shoulder, leaning above me. "Envoy?" he whispered, almost in my ear.

I turned, startled, looking up into a face I remembered as in a dream. "Fernwo . . ." I breathed. "Where did you . . . what are you . . . ?"

"Hush," he murmured. "There's a roomful of ears about us, don't you know? Ears ready to mishear, noses to smell conspiracy where none exists, mouths to twist good intentions into evil certainties. We know all about it, Envoy. We were told often enough."

"Sit down," I quavered, taking a deep breath. Then, more evenly, "You're being conspicuous."

"Thank you, yes. I'll sit here next to your friend. Chitterlain, isn't it? A bit far from its kindred. But then, so am I. It's been a long road, finding you."

I set my spoon down, lifted my glass to sip at the cider it contained, willing myself to appear impassive. Envoys were always impassive, facing life or death with the same quiet comportment, the same emotionless mien. This wasn't death. It was suddenly too much life, but appearance could be everything.

B'Oag arrived with plates, bowls, a pitcher of cider, another glass. He stood uncertainly nearby.

"Put it here," said the new arrival. "The envoy is an old acquaintance, and I'll sup with her."

The oastkeeper had only waited for the word. The plates came down with purposeful clatter, Fernwold pulled out a chair and sat facing me. I had again dipped my spoon.

"Good?" he asked.

"Passable," I said. "Anything made with smoked or salted meat is passable at best. This is dried in the smoke, not too salty, and the oastkeeper has traded for seasonings, too, which some of them up here don't bother to do. They figure people get hungry enough, they'll eat anything."

"Including envoys?"

"I doubt they consider envoys among the general run of people who frequent oasthouses."

"And you're here for . . . ?"

"In pursuit of duty, Fernwold . . ."

"Ferni," he suggested, smiling. "You called me Ferni."

"Fernwold," I said again firmly. "Why are you here?"

"I learned you were sent. I had some time and a reason or two. I decided to offer assistance to my old friend, Margaret."

I shuddered, only slightly. How long had it been since I had heard that name? "Say it as B'yurngrad says it, if you say it at all. I am M'urgi, shaman of B'yurngrad steppes. You are Fernwold, seeker and assessor. I am, from time to time, given the crown of an envoy—as are you, I've been told—and we're not allowed assistance."

"We're not allowed to ask for it. It can be given, and it often is."

"By whom?" I whispered. "I've never had help!"

He shrugged, took a great gulp of the steaming cider, belching slightly as it expanded the cold air in throat and belly. "Perhaps they never thought you needed it until now. No. Perhaps I knew you never really needed it until now. Don't go all proud on me, love. We know one another too well for that."

"Knew," I breathed. "Once."

"We need one another's help, whether you know it yet or not. And everything we knew of one another, we still know, Shaman, and it was a good deal more than can be dismissed as 'once.' I told you then what I tell you now. I knew you the moment I saw you. We are mates, M'urgi, whether we meet once a lifetime, once a decade, or every day. Nothing changes when we are apart."

My hand on the pitcher trembled only slightly. "Some of that is right."

"Which part?"

"Nothing changes when we're apart. It's when we're together things must change. Ferni, where have you been!"

He gritted his teeth. "My recent life has not been one I wanted to drag you into. Or thought I had the right to. I worry about the parts of my life I don't remember!"

I paled. "The Siblinghood wiped your mind?"

"Perhaps they. Or someone, something else that's left me missing a few years here and there. I remember everything since meeting you, however. And before that, the academy, I remember that." He drank again. "Are you carrying?"

I bared my wrist, letting him see the round sucker marks where it had drunk my blood, not much of it, just a little every day, enough to keep it from going dormant, but not enough to give it the power to overcome my will, so long trained and tried, like steel forged, folded, beaten, and hardened, over and over again. I pulled the sleeve back into place. "They have a lockroom. Built of stone, a maht thick."

He touched the marks gently with a fingertip, erasing them and the soreness that had accompanied them. "I'll never understand northerners. It's carried in a basket woven out of reeds or straw. Any latched closet would hold the crippled ones we carry, but they build a lockroom thick enough to hold the devil."

"They've never seen one, Fernwold. I have seldom seen one. We take some pains not to look at them until we have to, don't we? Fear and superstition always follow the unseen, the unknown, the whispered of." I sighed, wiggling my fingers, now free of pain. "I would have healed me after I'd eaten, when I felt warmer, but thank you." They taught us this healing of the ghyrm wounds. It took only concentration and a little strength. A little more than I had had when I came in.

"I know," he said, returning to his supper. The chitterlain moved over near his plate and regarded him with beady eyes, then began preening its feathers as though it had decided he was harmless. He smiled. "They talk, did you know that? The chitterlain?"

"I did not," I said. "You mean like a . . . what was it, a parrot? A mimic?"

"No, no. They talk. There's a one-eyed old fellow, a member of the Siblinghood, I think, hangs about from time to time. He says they're the last remaining of a race of creatures that once were starfarers, city builders."

"This little one?"

"Yes." He leaned down close. "You understand what I'm saying?"

"Sooor," it trilled. "Loor ti ellld."

"Which means?" I asked.

"Which means, 'Yes, I speak of old times.' They live in colonies, the chitterlain. They spend the winters in the south, getting fat and telling stories to their children. In the spring, they fly back to the northland."

His voice was weighted with sadness, and he turned back to his meal. When the soup and cider had warmed him somewhat, he turned to the more substantial and savory stuff. "Are you here on retrieval?" he asked between bites.

"I thought you were told where I was."

"I was. I didn't ask why, for my errand had reason enough."

"And what was that?"

"First to find you, then warn you, then to protect you. There's a threat against your life."

I shrugged. "That's been the case since I left Earth."

"This is specific, but I don't think anyone's followed you here. What's the situation?"

"The Siblinghood tells me they have a ghyrm here."

"Recent enough that nobody has . . . ?"

"We're never quick enough to prevent somebody from playing the fool!" I snapped. "Otherwise, this retrieval could have waited until the thaw."

"When are you going to find it?"

I shook my head, looked around the room, where this chair and that had been emptied since his arrival. "Not here. This isn't the place to discuss any such thing. Let's talk about something else."

"Very well. Have I told you it's a good thing you stayed out of Mercan space. I've been on a few of those worlds recently. Rinwall. Bonxar. Fajnard." He dropped his voice, almost to a whisper. "I've gone into the mountain fastnesses of Perepume a few times, visiting the Gibbekot, who say revolution's brewing on Fajnard: Gibbekot, Ghoss, and umoxen on one side, Frossian overlords on the other."

"You go spying for the Siblinghood?"

"The Siblinghood is merely keeping an eye on what's happening. They haven't offered the Gibbekot any help as yet. You'd have known if they had."

"I've been away from the news for some while," I said. "Are the Frossians involved in this supposed threat to me?"

"It's possible. Their nature is to be loyal supporters of whatever demagogue has the most power, and though there are no Frossians on B'yurngrad, the threat could come through them to someone local." He frowned. "You're thinner, M'urgi. You look well, but thin. It's strange, when I see you I think how well you've taken to the discipline of our calling. Most women don't like the solitude."

I considered this. "Most *people* don't, male or female, but people who grow up as solitary children already know the eremitic life. We find it more comforting than onerous. The work is easy enough, except when we're carrying, and that isn't often."

"True. This one you're hunting, any idea where it came from?"

"The wild tribes have been using them as weapons for as long as I can remember."

"None reported on Chottem," he murmured. "None on Thairy. Fajnard is suspect, of course. Frossian society would be meat and drink for the ghyrm-things."

"Except among the tribes, we've heard of few on B'yurngrad. Not here, not yet."

"Except for the ones in our keeping, no?"

I made a face. "Let's not talk about them. I have far more than enough of them. What's the news?"

So we talked: of the legal maneuvers in the city of Bray, on Chottem, to have the heiress of Bray declared dead so the ancillary branches of the family could claim the fortune; how the sudden arrival of the heiress had thrown all that into a heap; of the most recent results of the Great Walling-Off, Dominion's social experiment on Tercis; of rumors that the Queen of the Ghoss, Wilvia the Wise, who had disappeared from Fajnard long ago, had been seen on Tercis some years before; of the Reunion of Academy Alumni that was to take place at Point Zibit on Thairy and of Ferni's friends who would be there. Inconsequential talk, as the chitterlain ate and drank its fill; casual talk as the chitterlain flew to my collar and burrowed into the warmth of the scarf about my throat. All the time, Ferni's eyes never left my face.

When we had finished our meal, he asked, "Have you a room here?"

I slanted a sideways look at him, deciding whether to admit it or not, deciding I really had no choice.

"May I share it?" he whispered.

"Ah, Ferni," I murmured, half to myself. "After all this time. Over ten years! Sometimes I thought I'd only dreamed you, now here you are. Why now?"

"Couldn't help myself." He smiled as he started to reach for my hand but stopped, aware of the eyes and the ears still in the room. He stood and went to the counter where B'Oag stood. "We'd like another pitcher of cider, Oastkeeper. Is there a heating coil in the envoy's room? If so, we'll talk out our business there, rather than ruin your trade for the whole evening."

"I thank you for your consideration," said B'Oag, glancing around his nearly empty oasthall. He turned to his son. "Ojlin, be sure the steam coil is turned on full in the envoy's room, and take up a pitcher of cider."

"That's all right, Oastkeeper," Fernwold murmured. "Here's your pay for our dinner tonight and for the room. I'll carry the cider and set the coil myself."

B'Oag, bewildered at the largess on the counter before him, made no objection to this at all.

I Am Ongamar/on Cantardene

On Cantardene, years had passed since I, that is, Miss On-gamar, had witnessed the sacrifice on the funeral hill. I had fed the thing with parts of that happening, fed it to such satiety that it hadn't bothered me for several days. Then came rumors of the population crest on Earth and the accompanying restoration of the planet, fed day after day by statistics showing that Earth's population was actually and consistently falling. Within a century, so it was whispered, the population would be reduced from eighteen billion to the tenth of that advised by Dominion as a sensible maximum human population for the foreseeable future. On hearing of this, the K'Famir threatened to sue for damages in the Interstellar Trade Organization. If Earth's population fell, there would not be enough surplus humans to provide slave labor, and the K'Famir had contracted for slave labor!

Responding to the suit, the Dominion announced that humans would continue to be shipped as bondslaves into both Omniont and Mercan areas of influence for the term of the contract, which was fifty Earth years. The Mercan Combine, and its K'Famir representatives, immediately accused the Dominion of restraint of trade and threatened various unpleasant consequences, such as tariffs, raids on colony worlds, and the like if the downward trend were not immediately reversed. To all of these the

Dominion replied that Dominion business was Dominion business, not subject to Combine or Federation demands.

The matter had then been appealed to the ISTO, who referred it to the IG Court of Justice, where the Dominion view had recently been unanimously sustained, the court holding that habitable planets, being few and extremely valuable, were more in need of protection than was the provision of cheap labor on planets with an enormous population of an idle elite, and further, that the welfare of the planet must always take precedence over the greediness of its inhabitants or, in this case, their purchasers; and, yet further, that a decline in the population of a previously highly proliferative species, if indeed this had happened, was more a matter for celebration than harassment.

The most recently circulated rumor was that Dominion Central Authority had recently disappeared from its usual seat on Mars and left no word as to its whereabouts, thus forestalling forcible retaliation by the Combine. Dominion had, at least for the time being, vanished in the smoke.

"What will we do for fitters?" Lady Ephedra demanded. "All our fitters are Earthian slaves. Tell me, Miss Ongamar! You are Earthian! What will we do for fitters?"

"I suppose you will have to pay them, madam," I said, through a mouth full of pins. "There are always Earthians willing to work if the pay is good."

"Pay fitters?" Lady Ephedra was shocked into silence. "I've never heard of such a thing."

"Pay workers? Not for the next few lifetimes, at any rate," I heard a K'Famir crew boss telling his friend. "They're still bringing shiploads of them out from Earth. By the time we've used them all up, the Earth colonies will be overpopulating, just as Earthians always do, and we'll buy up the excess. Just wait and see!"

I acknowledged to myself that it was selfish to feel so, but I was grateful that Earth had been struck by salvation, despite itself! Not that Earthians appreciated that fact, according to the K'Famir, though that may have been wishful thinking. All this babble continued to feed *it*, day after day, and thankful as I was, I detected something worrisome in the thing's appetite, a nervous undercurrent that reminded me of a childhood time when I had stuffed myself with candy, each mouthful creating a need for another mouthful, so that no amount of the sweetness satisfied me. I had been very sick, very sorry, and so the thing in its stone closet seemed almost to sicken as it gorged on the talk about Earth.

Could one imagine that *it* felt anxiety? Or, more likely, that the creature or organism that directed the ghyrm and its appetites was feeling anxiety. Something I might turn to my advantage? Now that my contract as a fitter was drawing to a close, was there a way I could escape from *it*? Though the years on Cantardene were longer than Earth-years, I believed that less than half a year remained before my official enslavement would be over. I could look forward to being taken to one of the colony planets, and I had applied to go to Chottem, with B'yurngrad as a second choice. Even Thairy or Tercis would be acceptable. I had been twelve when I arrived on Cantardene, twenty-two when Adille had died, I was almost thirty-seven now, actually older than that, if one figured in the relative length of the years. If I could leave the planet without the thing, distance would surely attenuate its influence on me, or so I prayed. If I could not escape *it*, would *it* expect transport to an Earthian colony? I had not, myself, committed any evil yet, and was determined to avoid doing so.

I tried not to think of the possibility that I would not be allowed to go at all. My hands busied themselves with a vivilon chemise, setting in a gusset without a moment's thought while my mind remained caught in its web of anxieties. I knew things about the K'Famir that I should not know. I knew things about the Mercan Combine that I should not know. Creatures of various kinds had talked back and forth over my stooped body, giggling over pillow talk, telling secrets. I knew that the Mercan Combine planned to take over Chottem, that the Omnionts intended to annex Thairy and Tercis. Oh, not right away. Not until all the servants on Earth had been pumped into the system. The thing had sucked up this information with groans of pleasure, but still I had felt its underlying dissatisfaction, its barely sensed agitation.

This morning I had told *it* I would not return until late, for I intended to go into the pleasure quarter to hear what other races thought of the news from Earth. It had hissed at me, as it always did, a threat, a certainty of death if I did not return timely. How *it* would accomplish this, I didn't know. Adille had simply died of weakness, for *it* had drained her dry. I felt no weakening as yet. My mirror showed no dissipation of strength or premature aging. The thing didn't want to weaken me. It wanted to go on using me.

I bent over to pick up a few spilled pins and once again heard conversation from the neighboring fitting room.

"I'll have Miss Ongamar take care of it. I never have any complaints about her work." It was Lady Ephedra's voice.

"She's been with you quite a while," said a languorous, uncaring voice. "Not cheating the decree, are we, dear?"

Shrill squeals of laughter. "Aren't you dreadful to say such a thing! She's been with me for a long time because she's very good. Quite the best I've had. A decree is a decree, but I confess I shall hate to turn her over to the males up there on the Hill of Beelshi."

I stopped breathing. Lady Ephedra's voice went on. "I don't know why they always want humans. They don't use any of the other slaves as sacrifices, only humans."

I gritted my teeth and breathed lightly, lightly, they mustn't know I was listening. In case someone peeked in, I had to keep my fingers busy, but that voice could only belong to one of the baron's neuters. Of all the K'Famir, I hated the neuters the worst. At least the others seemed to know they were being cruel, the neuters did not even realize it. They had no minds at all.

"How much longer does she have?" asked the languorous one.

"I may be able to stretch it to a year," said Lady Ephedra. "For some reason, they wanted her dead several years ago. Someone, somewhere ordered it. I misled them then, telling them she had died, and I have lied to them several times since, extending her term of bondage. Very soon, I shall not be able to lie to them anymore."

"Do you always obey the decree and let the males kill your fitters?" the neuter asked.

"Oh, yes," said the Lady Ephedra. "Stretch it out as one may, one must obey, eventually. One doesn't know what they may have picked up in the fitting rooms. They always die on the hill, shortly before their terms expire."

In the neighboring room, I straightened, my hands still working as I finished the chemise and set it aside, momentarily amazed at how easily I had done the task, created a piece of clothing for a creature more like a spider than a human, a creature with eight extremities, with two mouths, four eyes, no visible ears, and several sets of copulatory organs, some of them used only for pleasure.

So they did not intend to let me go. Though it was likely Lady Ephedra didn't know precisely how her fitter was to be killed, she knew it would happen. I was suddenly very warm, almost hot, the fury rising in me like a wave. I would kill them all, I would burn down House Mouselline. I would . . .

I would do nothing precipitant, I warned myself. I had been fortunate to overhear. It gave me time to make a plan. Time perhaps to get away. Time certainly to arrange that someone in Dominion would learn of all the things I knew.

"Are you finished, Miss Ongamar?" asked the Lady Ephedra from the doorway of the little room. "Everything completed."

"Oh, yes, Lady Ephedra," I said, bowing humbly. "Just straightening up before I leave."

I Am M'urgi/on B'yurngrad

Ferni rose early and quietly from the warm bed where I lay, still half asleep. He left the door ajar, and I heard him speaking to B'Oag in the oasthall below.

"You're putting a fine polish on that copper," he said.

"Been rumblin' at me," B'Oag complained. "In the night. D'ja hear it?"

"Once or twice," Ferni said. "It didn't sound like an imminent eruption."

"Yah, well, last time it went, it didn' give any warning atall. Never hurts to check, see all the seams're tight."

"You have a relief valve, don't you?"

"Be a fool not to, wun I?"

"Any chance of getting some breakfast? Do you have a henhouse here?"

"Oh, sure. Sev'ral nice little vents comin' off this spring, 'ere. Got one of 'em cased up through the henhouse 'fore it warms the barn. Keep a lantern out there, so eggs we got. Hens won't lay 'thout light, 'thout heat. I got jibber sausage, too, smoke or plain. The bread'll be baked another little while. Y'wanna take it up?"

"Good idea. The longer she rests, the quicker her job will be."

There was silence for a few moments before B'Oag remarked, all too casually, "I heard somethin' a few days back. Mebbe somebody's got one a those, like she has."

Ferni said, "I'm sorry to hear that. People who happen on those things usually don't live long after."

"Thing is, this person has a fambly person sick, like to die. This person knows the . . . the thing takes souls to Joy."

Ferni made a sound of rude derision. "Oh, again I'm sorry to hear that. That story is put about by the things themselves, so people will let them in, let them near. I've met with teachers, wisemen. The creatures don't take the soul to Joy. They just eat it until nothing's left. Envoys like her upstairs are sent to stop the soul-eating, to trap the evil thing and see it's put where it can do no harm."

"Y'mean there's no Joy? No bein' took up?"

"Who would say the good are not taken to Joy? They may well be, but not by these things. The person who found this one was worried because his dear one is near to dying?"

"She," B'Oag corrected. "Where's these things come from, then, these evils? Did a man make them?"

Ferni said, "They're parasites, Oastkeeper. Like a louse or a flea, only more deadly. We don't know who makes them, but we will find out!"

"You're one a them, then. Them silence people."

No sound. Ferni didn't agree or disagree. Perhaps he only waited, his nose full of the same wonderful smell that had opened my eyes wide. Someone had opened the oven door and filled the oasthouse with the aroma of new-baked bread.

"I'll see to breakfast," said B'Oag. "Ya'll wait?"

"I'll wait," Ferni said. "No need for you to make the trip upstairs."

I dozed, only a moment until I heard the thud of Ferni's step on the stair, and I grinned when he came in, unable to help it.

I sat upright, pulling the blanket around my shoulders. "By the Ghost of Joziré, that smells edible."

He set it on the foot of the bed, turning a troubled face toward me. "By the Ghost of Joziré? Why's he a ghost? I thought . . . I thought he was just hiding out somewhere."

I examined his face. "It bothers you to think he might be dead? Did you know him?"

"Of him, yes. A good man, so I've been told."

"It's just something people say, Ferni. What did you bring for breakfast?"

"Eggs," he said. "Sausage and fresh bread and tea and what looks like"—he uncapped the small stoneware jar to see what it held—"honey."

I made a lap and beckoned for the tray.

"I have news," he said.

"The oastkeeper decided to speak of it, eh? I thought he knew where it was."

"Well, he hasn't told me where, yet, but he's told me why. Somebody's on death watch."

"Then we'll hope we're not too late."

"After breakfast," he agreed. "And, by the by, what's this oath on King Joziré's ghost?"

Spooning honey onto fresh bread, I said, "I've seen it, the ghost."

His mouth fell open, and it took a moment for him to latch it up again. "Come now."

"You're the one sent me to that shaman, Ferni. What'd you think she'd teach me? How to make tea?"

Now it was his turn to think. "Quite frankly, I didn't think about it at all. At the time, I was just told to do it, send you, I mean, and I thought you'd be safe there."

"Safe I was for a time. Then safe I wasn't, but I was less fearful than previously. You say you've heard a threat. Well, I've seen one. Someone does want me dead."

"What did the shaman teach you?"

"She taught me ways to fly, to escape, to die, if necessary. To see spirits and converse with ghosts. To speak at a distance to someone receptive. Though she seemed to think I knew most of it already. It was in my bones, she said, else all her teaching would have done naught."

Ferni asked, "So what did the shade of King Joziré have to say for himself?"

Around a mouthful of egg, I said, "When I saw him on the night road, he said he was wandering, seeking Wilvia and his children . . ."

"His children?" Ferni gaped at me, forehead furrowed.

"Twins. A boy, a girl."

"What makes you think Wilvia and the children died?"

"I didn't say they did!" I snorted. "I didn't say he did."

He muttered, "Well then, what you saw wasn't a ghost. What you saw was a night wanderer, a spirit: alive, asleep, dreaming."

This was perfectly possible. "He seemed so familiar to me that I didn't even wonder. I didn't think of him being a spirit wanderer, though I do that myself."

After we had eaten and put on multiple layers of additional clothing, I put the chitterlain in a cage Ferni had borrowed from the oastmaster, set it in a warm place with food and water inside, and went to retrieve the basket from the lockroom. Then we heard B'Oag's reluctantly given directions, which concluded with: "She's only a lass, Envoy. Go easy with her."

"Easy as I can," I replied. "If it's not too late to go any way at all."

The ice storm had given way to frigid calm. The road was only a shadow-edged depression that curved around the snowy hillocks before us. Ice lay beneath the thin layer of new snow, too slippery to traverse until we strapped thorn-feet over our boots. The world was painted in shades of metallic gray, silver where weak light struck it, pewter where shadows fell, iron beneath the cover of ice-laden trees. When we had gone far enough to be out of sight of the oasthouse, I gave Ferni my tool kit to carry before opening the coin-sized window in the basket. It had to be held well away from me as the questing tentacle emerged hesitantly into the cold. It squirmed, then slowly flailed the air, up, down, right, left, suddenly becoming rigid as it pointed in the direction we were traveling.

We held our breaths as much as possible, for when the ghyrm were not well fed, they stank, sending out their smell to others of their kind, calling a gather of the hungry. Alone, ghyrm were weak, easily crushed, burned, poisoned if one had the right tools, and thus unlikely to survive long treks in dangerous country. A gather of them, on the other hand, stank with a feculent rot that made creatures emerge gasping from burrows or plunge unconscious from the skies. Both of us had seen records of tribal settlements ravaged by ghyrm in which nothing was left alive beneath, upon, or above the soil.

The tentacle began to swerve slightly to the right of our line of travel. Shortly, we came to the narrower lane that went in that direction, a barely shadowed trail around the breast of the hill. The tendril quivered.

"When will you basket it?" asked Ferni, observing the questing tentacle with disgust.

"As soon as I'm sure we have the right place," I replied.

The house lay just behind the hill, dug in for more than half its height, small, shuttered windows high upon its walls beneath the deep eaves of the high-pitched roof. The door was set at the inner end of a roofed tunnel that led through the hill to the house wall. The tentacle quivered its eagerness. Before we entered the tunnel, I took my tool kit from Ferni, opened it, and fastened it around my waist, where I could reach it easily. I slipped the killing knife from its sheath and put it near the tentacle, which shrieked as it lashed back into the basket. I shut the opening and set the basket on the snow.

"What makes them yell like that?" asked Ferni.

"I don't know any more than you do," I retorted. "The Siblinghood doesn't tell us. I've always supposed the blades are poisoned because they make ulcers on our skins if we touch them."

The latchstring was out. Ferni released the inside latch, letting us into a long, ice-cold room, ashes on the hearth, an inside door standing ajar. We peered through the crack: a bed, a body lying on it, another beside it, no movement in either. I stepped back.

"It's loose in that room," I said. "Probably on the girl."

We pushed the door open and went to the side of the young woman lying beside the bed, pale as the snow. The woman on the bed was long dead. Ghyrm-kill were often virtually mummified, making it impossible to learn when they had died. We did not see the thing itself.

The girl's chest moved in a shallow breath. I said, "She's still alive, so it's on her somewhere, under her clothes. They can sometimes move quickly. There are too many hiding places in here, including us. Take the girl's feet, I'll take the hands. We want her outside on a nice, empty, hard-packed snowbank."

We carried her out through the doors and the tunnel to lay her on the snow some distance from the house. I returned to the basket and opened the porthole once more, carrying the basket near to the girl, watching the tentacle as it quivered, quivered, stretched itself to the maximum length near the girl's breast. I set the basket a safe distance aside, took my killing knife in one hand and a cutting tool in the other, starting at the girl's throat and slitting her clothing as far as her waist.

"There," whispered Ferni, pointing with the tip of his knife at a pulsing red mole on the girl's breast, a mole with legs that trembled as it sucked her life into itself.

"How long does one of them take to kill a person?" he asked.

"If there's only one small one, half a day or more. Lend me your knife."

He held out the sheath, and I drew forth a twin to my own, a broad, curved blade with a slightly hooked end. With a knife in each hand, I bent forward, catching the thing between them like grist between grindstones, mashing and twisting the flat sides of the blades to pulverize what lay between.

A scream came from between the blades, impossibly shrill, barely within the limit of hearing, and was echoed by a howl of fury from the basket as the tentacle turned toward the house, quivering, quivering.

"More of them in there?" asked Ferni.

"If the tentacle stays rigid, yes," I said, scrubbing the blades in the snow to clean them. "When they kill someone, they sometimes split into buds. The buds don't always grow, but sometimes they do."

"The Order wants us to capture them . . ." he said doubtfully.

"I know," I said, returning his knife carefully. "Several times I've tried, but it's impossible to capture the tiny ones. There's no way to hold them securely outside a laboratory. We have to put everything that may be contaminated in that building, then we have to burn it."

"What about her?"

"We strip her bare, shave her head and body hair into her clothes, throw them into the house along with that spot on the snow, which could conceivably have buds in it, search her body, wrap her in one of our coats, and take her back to the oasthouse."

"She'll freeze!"

"It's partly the cold that's kept her alive so far. The things aren't as active in the cold. She won't freeze in the time it will take us to get her back. I've done this before, during even colder times. I'm quick at it."

Under the clippers from my tool kit, the girl's clothes and hair fell away like wool from a shorn sheep. I scanned every intimate part of her, an inspection that Ferni regarded with discomfiture.

"I violate her no more than needed," I explained. "I look only in the creases. The creatures do not enter the body orifices. They have gills, and they need air. Here, wrap her in my coat, I have four or five layers on besides it. They'll keep me warm enough until we get back."

"How do we fire the house?" he asked.

"An incendiary in the pocket of the coat. Pull the lever and toss it inside."

I checked to see that the tentacle still pointed rigidly at the house, forced the tentacle into the basket, and closed it, then put the bundled girl over my shoulder and started back the way we had come, leaving the basket for Ferni. From behind me came a sudden whoosh, then the crackle of flames and the sound of curses. He caught up to me where the lane joined the road.

"Let me take her."

"When we get halfway, you can have her."

We went on trudging toward the steam plume above the oast-house, sun breaking through the clouds above us in momentary encouragement. At the halfway mark, we traded burdens, arriving finally at the oasthouse under B'Oag's accusatory frown.

"We committed no violence on her," I snapped from behind my colleague. "The thing was killing her. It already took the woman. Was that her mother?"

He looked down guiltily. "Her ma, yes."

"Well, she didn't get to Joy, Oastkeeper. She's simply gone, erased from existence. That's what the creatures do. You should talk to your neighbors and let them know the facts."

"What about her?" he grumped, pointing at the girl.

"I'm taking her to your baths, where I'll search her skin, to be sure there are no more." I would do it, though I was positive there were no more. My "finder" should have reached for her if there had been. However, I remembered too well finding a bead of a thing on my clothing one time when I undressed for bed, and I'd been positive that time, too.

"What about her ma's body?" B'Oag asked Ferni.

"We left it in the house, and we had to burn the house behind us, for there were more of the creatures inside."

The oastkeeper grumped, "Thought what you were for was to catch 'em, take 'em away. That all was a good house."

"You can't catch the tiny ones," Ferni told him sternly. "Some are too small to see. And, since you knew about all this, now we'll need to know who may have brought it here and who else knew about it besides you."

B'Oag scowled. Ferni scowled back at him, a look that transformed his normally genial face into one of threatening ferocity, threatening enough, at any rate, to result in a less overtly hostile conversation.

I left it to Ferni and lugged the girl off to the baths, where I stripped off even the silky shirt and trousers that served as a warm bodysuit by day and decent sleepwear at night. During a northern winter on Fajnard, one got bare only in the tight oasthouse baths with their deep tubs of steaming water, constantly draining back into the stone basin they came from, constantly renewed and reheated. I took the girl into the tub with me, held her nose, and submerged her for a long count of thirty. No ghyrmlets surfaced, gasping for air. I dragged, her out, wrapped her warmly, got myself dressed, and took her to a warmed bed. Her body was alive, but only time would tell if her mind still was.

It was some time before I returned to the oasthall to find B'Oag looking haggard and ill-used, ostentatiously avoiding my eyes as he attended to business. Ferni sat waiting by the copper, a steaming cup in his hand. Seeing me approach, he set out another and poured from the pot. "Well?" with raised eyebrows.

"She's clean." I took a grateful sip of the hot tea. It had honey in it. "The basket?"

"Back in the lockroom. B'Oag says the girl, G'lil, and her mother worked with the weavers' guild in the nearest town south, place called Vaccy. Summers, after shearing season, the local women weave at the mill; winters they weave with small looms at home, piecework, special commissions, fancy stuff they've no time for in summer. When the weather permits, they pick up supplies at the mill. Not long ago, the girl came in here, wanting to talk to B'Oag about Joy, how people got taken there when they died, what could be done to assure it happened.

"Finally, she admitted it was her mother who was dying. The doctors in Vaccy said there was nothing more they could do. B'Oag says he told her to take the doctors' word for it, just keep her mother warm and well fed. The girl asked him if that was true even if someone had found a Taker. That's what they call them around here. Takers. He told her all that was foolishness. This is what he tells me now, which may well be a lie. His excuse was that he didn't think she'd actually found one. Then you arrive, making him believe she might actually have done so. We discussed where she might have found it, and he said the only place the girl ever went was to the mills and provender stores in Vaccy."

"The mills import raw material and export fabric?"

"They do, yes." He turned back to his tea. "They buy wool and hair from the farms around here that were started when the colony was founded: sheep, camel, goat. The mills import down from Choubirds raised somewhere in Omniont space, and umox wool from Fajnard. The fiber for ultrasilk and vivilon comes in as cocoons, great sacks of them." He laughed. "According to B'Oag, the mills label the fine fabrics as coming from the Isles of Delight." He laughed. "Seemingly the K'Famir merchants don't want it known their underwear is woven by dirty humans."

I shook my head. "This girl didn't weave vivilon, her hands are hard as rocks. Nonetheless, she was there, at the mill. Your mentioning cocoons makes me wonder . . ."

He nodded. "When B'Oag mentioned it, it struck me that cocoons with something live inside could make an excellent hiding place for vast numbers of infant ghyrm."

I thought about this for a while. "It doesn't answer the question of how she knew what she'd found, or thought she knew. The things are repulsive in their own shape, but they usually pretend to be something else."

"I've heard that."

"This search-and-destroy business we accomplished today is new to you, isn't it."

He nodded again. "So?"

"So what have you been doing during your years with the Siblings? I thought all of us were out seeking ghyrm."

He shook his head at me. "There are more things than ghyrm threatening the Siblinghood. There's the question of the survival of the human race. There's exploration for new colony planets, and from time to time certain people need to be located, which we also do. That is, those of us who are not, like you, busy killing ghyrm as a full-time job."

"What people do you locate? And for whom?"

He merely smiled at me.

"Oh, right. You're a Sibling of Silence. Very well. We won't talk about that. What shall we talk about?"

He mused, "I was interested in your story last night, about how you got here to B'yurngrad. You said you could have gone on a ship into Mercan space. Any idea where it was going?"

I shook my head, still annoyed by the memory. "I found out later, yes. It was headed for Fajnard. Where the Frossians are. How about you? How did you get into the academy?"

"I don't know, and they don't say. They just tell you you've been recommended, and that's it. Many of the cadets were from well-to-do families, and heaven knows I wasn't. I got in with the group I told you about the other night, Naumi and the others, and we all did well through our fellowship, six of us, all of us helping each other when needful. When I graduated, I was sent on one of those 'can't remember' missions . . ."

"Which is . . . ?"

"One I literally can't remember. They take the memory away, so no matter what some inimical force might try, they can't get it out of me. I don't even know if I joined the Siblings before or after, but I've been with them ever since."

"At least you've traveled. Except for my youth on Phobos and ten years or so on Earth, I've spent my whole life here on B'yurngrad, and I spend too much time regretting all those years of school, learning languages I've never used. When the shaman died, I fulfilled her burdens, which I'll tell you about another time; and then I was briefly apprenticed to a full-time ghyrm-hunter. That's when the Siblinghood made me a member."

"B'yurngrad isn't a bad world. It has some really beautiful places on it."

"Unless ghyrm have been reported at one of them, I've never been there."

"No vacation?" he asked, seemingly astonished.

"I've never asked for one," I said, somewhat surprised at my own admission. "I didn't know it was allowed."

"It's a rule that we're allowed to have vacations. You're probably entitled to at least a year's off-time by now." He mused, staring at the still-steaming cup before him. "Tell you what. There's something happening, something I think you'd be helpful at. Let's arrange for some vacation, and we'll do some traveling together."

The idea was attractive. I could not remember being so taken with an idea for many years. Not since . . . not since childhood. Not since the visit to Mars.

"Mars," I murmured. "The dragonfly."

He looked at me wonderingly. "Is that where they are? On Mars?"

"Where what are?"

"The dragonfly ships. The ones the . . . person pilots. It was a kind of vision or dream Naumi had, at the Academy. I don't really remember what he said." He laughed ruefully. "Do you ever get these weird memories? As though you've been somewhere or done a particular thing before?"

I could only nod, yes, indeed, we all did.

In the morning, the sun came out, the day warmed. The girl, G'lil, who had spent the previous night bundled up next to the coil in my room, began to moan and quiver. At noon, she awoke, and I fed her soup, as much as she would swallow.

"Now," I demanded, "suppose you tell me where you got that thing that we stopped from killing you."

"What thing . . . you mean the Taker. Ma . . . where's Ma?"

I took several deep breaths and told myself to be patient. "G'lil. Your mother is dead. She was not taken to Joy, she was eaten, and you came very close to being eaten, because that is what the ghyrm do. They are parasites, like leeches, they live off other creatures' lives."

"But," she cried, "but Ma said, but the man said, they said she'd go to Joy, it would take her there."

"It didn't take her there! It didn't take her anywhere."

"I don't believe you," the girl cried. "I won't!"

From the doorway, Ferni spoke. "She has too much invested in pretty lies, M'urgi."

"I know," I said grimly. "So, we do this another way." I put both my hands on her shaved head, closed my eyes and chanted. The girl quivered, tried to squirm away, then went limp, eyes wide open, seeing something. She moaned, cried out, then began to scream.

Below us, in the oasthall, furniture tumbled, boots thundered up the stairs. B'Oag came down the corridor bearing a truncheon, his face red with anger.

Ferni held up his hand, stopping the big man as though he had run into a wall. When Ferni beckoned, B'Oag came to stand beside him in the door. The screams were subsiding into moans once more. I removed my hands and stood up, staggering a little. G'lil's eyes opened. "Aaaah," she cried. "Dead. All dead."

"Right," I snapped rather weakly. "All dead. As your mother is dead. As you would have been dead."

"What did you show her?" Ferni asked in an awed voice.

"I showed her that little colony from Earth, Cranesroost. I showed her in lengthy detail how that looked, before and during."

"What?" demanded B'Oag.

Ferni said, "The envoy showed the girl a memory of a human colony that was eaten by the ghyrm, Oastkeeper. When the ghyrm were through with them, nothing human lived in those places at all. Not a hair. Not a cell."

"He said . . ." The girl wept. "He said it would take her to Joy. The man said it would."

"Now we get to it," I growled. "What man?"

"The man at the mill. I was there to get supplies for the winter weaving, and he was delivering sacks of cocoons to the mill boss. He heard me telling my friend how bad off Mama was, and he said he had something that would help her. He said he couldn't give it for free, but he gave it to me for a half jig-bit, for almost nothing. He said it was a Taker."

"What did it look like?" asked Ferni.

"Like a few beads on a little string of vivilon. One red one, one blue one, two yellow ones. He held it to my ear so I could hear it sing. He said put it around her neck . . ." The girl shuddered. "Oh, Ma, Ma, what did I do to you?"

I sat down on the bed, suddenly exhausted. "Do we have to burn the mill, Ferni?"

B'Oag began to rumble threateningly, like his own heating system readying an eruption.

Ignoring him, I continued "It's within our authority, but I dread the upheaval that will cause. These people have little else to sustain them."

"There may be an easier way," Ferni replied. "Let the girl rest, and come with me. And you, Oastkeeper, don't get in an uproar over something that may not happen."

We went outside, some distance from the oasthouse, where I sat wearily on a wall.

"I've never seen that done before," said Ferni.

"It seems to be a talent I have," I said. "The ability to see other worlds, to take a spirit shape and go into other worlds. My shaman had it, too. It was she who taught me. Once I have seen something, I can show it to someone else . . ."

"How did you see that destruction?"

"I had seen a little of it before, on Earth. For the rest, I reached out to some creature that had seen it all: not with human eyes, but good enough for all that. It may have been a horse, or a dog, or even a goat. My shaman taught me to connect with the minds of animals. That's why the chitterlain is content to stay with me. She knows I'm taking her south, where her kindred are."

He muttered, "Since the mill is all that sustains these people, I believe we can ask our Siblings to exterminate any pests that may be sheltered there without harming the mill itself or the people thereabouts."

"They can do that?"

"I'm told so, yes, on a small scale. There's been some recent technological advance among my old academy friends that give them the capacity to disinfect one building, more or less, though not yet a city, and certainly not a planet. I can't make contact from here, however."

"How did you get here?" I asked, amazed that I hadn't wondered this before.

"There's a flier, hidden over behind one of those hills."

"Well, go then. Find out about it."

He gazed at me thoughtfully. "M'urgi. While I'm at headquarters, I'm going to arrange for some time off for both of us. Whether they approve the strike or not, I'll be back here within the next few days to get you . . ."

"You're taking a lot for granted," I half snarled.

"No. I'm not taking anything for granted, and you know it! This is important, and I can't even take time to explain it to you now. Just remember, I'll be back within a few days. Stay here. If they approve the strike, it will happen during the next few days. Tell B'Oag he has to get everyone out of the mill who may be working there or maintaining the place. If anyone lives close, they should go away for a few days. May I rely on you for that?"

"Of course."

"Then you may expect them to send the machine, unless I bring word they can't when I return."

"They, being who?"

"Dominion or the Siblinghood. One or both."

"Ah yes." I shrugged. "One or both. Or as we in the field say, one is both. Sometimes they seem joined at the heart."

We returned to the oasthouse. Ferni packed up his belongings and departed. I explained in some detail to B'Oag that he had to see to emptying the mill.

"They won't do as I say, Envoy!"

"Tell them they may do as you say in comfort, or I will come down there, and they will do as I say with pain. I will lay my hands on them and show them! You saw how that girl suffered. Do you want it for them as well?"

When he had grumbled his way onto the road, I returned to the girl, who grizzled at me lengthily about her bare skull before demanding sulkily to be taken to her home.

"No home there anymore, girl. The thing you brought into it multiplied like weeds in the spring. We had no way to get them out of your house, so your house had to be burned."

The lamentations started afresh. I hadn't time to wait them out, so I told her, "B'Oag will give you a job here for the rest of the winter. You will have company here, including B'Oag's son, Ojlin, a marriageable young man. By spring, I have no doubt you will have a new home of your own to worry over."

This seemed to be a new thought, and she perked up. "Ojlin, he wunt look at me, all bald like this."

"Tie a scarf around your head until it grows out."

The idea of having a future was interesting enough that she stopped crying. That evening B'Oag returned to report. "The envoy wanted the place empty, and I done that all, and what in billy-be-drat is that girl doin' behine my counter with my son?"

"Helping you, Oastkeeper. She needs a job, you need the help. Your son needs a wife."

"Now you just wait, woman . . ."

"Envoy," I corrected him with a steely voice. "I will not wait, B'Oag. I have come, I have found what I was sent to find, killed what I was sent to kill, sorted out the results of both finding and killing, and the job seems well done to me. I have thus far made no fuss about your part in the matter. Do not cause me to choose otherwise." I fastened my eyes on his, my hands slightly outstretched as though at any moment I might lay them on some part of him.

B'Oag gulped, breathed heavily, gulped again, and said no more. By evening's end, he was showing G'lil how to tally up the day's receipts.

I spent two more days at the oasthouse, feeding the chitterlain and sleeping, mostly. On the third day, a strange machine came out of the western sky, hovered over the mill at Vaccy for some time, then went away again. Those of us who ventured into the mill the next day found a great many dead mice, rats, spiders, and other vermin, along with a scattering of strange-looking creatures the others could not name. Like squid, I thought, recalling pictures I had seen as a child. A pulpy and bulbous thing with tentacles and suckers on it. I named them and kept talking until everyone knew the name and the danger.

The following morning, when I woke, I found Ferni waiting for me in the oasthall. Wordlessly, he took my pack and tool kit, tucked the chitterlain into the collar of my shirt, where it would stay warm, and led me out of the place to be half blinded by the sun on the snow.

"Where are we going?" I asked him, as I put on my goggles.

"Someplace south and safe," he replied, then, seeing my skeptical look, "Well, someplace safer than this, where your chitterlain will find its kindred. Then . . . a little later, we're going on to Thairy."

"To see your old friends at the academy?" I asked.

"To see old friends," he agreed. "And perhaps new ones."

I Am Margaret/on Tercis

Glory and I were sitting on my porch, mending underwear.

She said, "Bamber told me his mama left a note when she went away. He couldn't read yet, but Abe read it to him."

"I didn't know that. I thought she just disappeared."

"His mother said she was in danger, and so was he, so don't attract attention."

"Could she have been an escaped bondswoman?" I asked.

"Bamber honestly doesn't know, but Abe kept the note, and when Bamber learned to read, he read it for himself."

"I remember you two helping one another learn to read in first grade. Does he know you tell me about him?"

"I wouldn't tell you unless he thought it was all right. Bamber doesn't mind your knowing, Grandma. He says he thinks you're a lot like his mother."

"I hope not," I snorted. "Leaving a child like that!"

"Bamber says she must have had reasons, and Abe isn't mean to him or anything." Glory knotted her thread and bit it off. "Bamber's funny about a lot of things. He's just as smart as I am. In school, he knows all the answers, but he just gives enough right ones to get by, then he puts down wrong answers for the rest."

"Why does he do that?"

"What the note said. He doesn't want to attract attention."

"I suppose his mother might have had reasons for wanting him to be unnoticed," I admitted grudgingly.

"Abe Johnson's still a peculiar choice. I wish we could adopt Bamber," Glory said.

"We've already half adopted him," I replied with some indignation. "We see that he has clothes, even if some of them are hand-me-downs. We pay for his school supplies. And between your mother and me, we feed him about five times a week. Considering everything, I think we're being very helpful."

The conversation stuck in my mind, though. There weren't many diversions in The Valley. Any little irregularity was food for surmise, so why had I ignored the mystery of Bamber Joy's abandonment? Whatever the reason, it wasn't the boy's fault!

A day or so later, I recruited the two of them to help me pick up chicken feed and groceries. At the store, I treated the young ones to the bottles of sweetberry drink they liked, and they sat down on the steps while I went inside. I was barely through the door when a car came booming across the bridge like a thunderstorm on wheels, more noise than you'd ever hear in Crossroads, and of a particularly irritating kind. The only vehicles we see in Rueful are driven by sedate officials on Dominion business, so the minute I heard the sound, I thought of the men who had asked about the cat.

The machine slid sideways into the turn, kicking up a cloud of dust as it kept right on coming, a danger to every child and chicken in the neighborhood. It didn't slow down until it was almost on top of the store. The two men got out, looking like they were headed to a hanging.

I got over by the potato bin just as they banged their way in. One of them said loudly to Ms. McCollum, "Have you found out anything about a new cat yet?"

Ms. McCollum came right back at them. "What's its scientific name? One of the people here in The Valley wanted to look it up. She wanted to know was it Earthian? Maybe an ocelot?"

The taller one said to the other, "Did the people at the office tell you the scientific name of the cat, Walter?"

Walter said, "No, Ned, they did not. We will have to get that information."

The taller one continued, "So, you have not heard of anybody with a strange sort of cat, ma'am?"

"Most everybody has one or two ordinary, everyday cats."

"Has anyone been buying unusual amounts of cat food, ma'am?"

"Only Ma Bailey, because her mama cat had kittens that're starting on solid food."

"You have seen those kittens yourself, ma'am?"

"Everbody in town has seen 'em. Just step down the street to Ma's Kitchen, and she'll try to give you one, and another to keep it company."

The two men turned to go out, and I followed them to the door. On the porch, Walter stopped and glared at Glory. "Little girl, do you know anyone around here who has a strange cat?"

"First off," Glory said, "I'm not a little girl. Little girls are younger than ten, and I'm considerable older than that. And no, I don't know anybody who has a strange cat."

The man stared through her as though she weren't even there. I shivered, for Bamber was looking up at the man with eyes so blank they could have been cut out of blackboard. He stood up slowly, getting himself between Glory and Walter.

"My steppa, he shoots cats. Can't abide 'em. Maybe he shot the one you're lookin for."

The two men blinked slowly, then got back in their car and went tearing back up to the bridge, where they turned east and kept going, raising more clouds of dust.

Bamber turned to me, and said, "Grandma, whoever sent those two sure didn't intend anybody to look at them close."

Glory said, "You mean the way they talk?"

"They talk like the machines talked in the place we were before my mom came here and left me with Abe."

She cried, "Bamber, you just remembered something. You had a memory!"

His mouth dropped open. "I guess I did. That's funny."

He took a slow swallow of his drink, then shook his head. "You know that stuffed turkalope the sheriff hangs out in the trees at our place? Every year he hangs it there?"

Turkalopes are large Tercisian birds that run quite fast and don't fly very well. Some people raise them for meat, though I've never cared for the taste.

"Why does he do that?" I asked through the screen door.

"Because it's illegal to bother or kill the wild ones, so the sheriff hangs up this stuffed one, then he hides until some idjit tries to kill it, then he arrests them."

"Why are we talking about stuffed birds?" asked Glory.

"Because those two guys are like that stuffed bird."

I realized what he meant. "You mean a decoy! Hold the thought while you load that chicken feed, Bamber. Let me get the groceries."

I picked up the few things we needed, paid Ms. McCollum for it and the sacks of feed the young ones were putting in the wagon, and we started for home. As soon as we were out of earshot, Bamber whispered, "If decoy's the right word, then there's somebody we can't see watching those two decoys to see if anybody's interested in what they're saying or doing."

That was more talk out of Bamber than I had heard if I had put his whole year's conversations end to end.

"Because . . ." Glory whispered.

"Because," he said, "if somebody takes an interest in those two men, that person may know something about the cat." He turned that blackboard gaze of his toward me, a tiny smile on his lips. "But we're onto them, aren't we, Grandma!"

Bamber unhitched for us at Maybelle's house. We left the chicken feed in the barn and carried the other stuff up the hill to my house. Falija wasn't there, though Glory and Bamber said hi to Lou Ellen.

I made chicken sandwiches with pickles for them while Glory and Bamber discussed what the men might really be up to. As usual, Lou Ellen didn't want all her sandwich, so Glory split what she didn't eat with Bamber.

"Should we do something about those men?" Glory asked. "Or would that just get us arrested for shooting at the decoy?"

"The safest thing to do with bait is pretend you don't notice it," I told them. "Sniffing at it might be even more dangerous than trying to eat it. Glory, I do wish mightily we knew what this is all about."

Bamber gave me a very straight look. "You can trust me to look out for Glory, ma'am." Then he ducked his head as though he'd scared himself, speaking up that way.

"Well." I grinned at Glory. "It seems we have an ally."

"I'm glad," said Falija, suddenly appearing on a chair nearby. "Allies are good things to have."

That startled Bamber, and he stood gaping as though he'd lost his wits.

"Falija, what do you think about those men?" Glory asked.

"Grandma's right. We should take no notice, not even if ten more of them arrive and dance across the bridge waving large tambourines."

"Tambourines?" I said.

"Isn't it a word? I learned it just this morning. A festive instrument to accompany dance. Can't you visualize those two men with tambourines?"

This set Glory and Bamber to snickering, and even I had to laugh. When the children left, they stood for a while on the porch. Glory said, "I really don't know that much about her, Bamber."

"Her suddenly showing up that way! I seem to remember something about cat-people who do that," he murmured. "They live on Thairy, and Chottem, and Fajnard, and they're called the Gibbekot."

They went on down the hill, their two dark heads almost level with one another, their long legs moving easily. Glory and Bamber Joy. Maybelle didn't encourage the friendship because she felt Gloriana shouldn't be particularly friendly with any boy until she was quite a bit older. Knowing what I knew about Gloriana, I thought friendship, boy, girl, or animal, was what she needed, and the two of them were good for one another.

A couple of days later The Valley grapevine spread the news that Dorothy Springer had been found murdered in her house. The sheriff had called the Rueful Public Safety officers for help, because there hadn't been a murder in Remorseful in anybody's memory. I wondered if this were another decoy. No one in Rueful would kill someone else to find out who cared or who didn't, and I had to remind myself that Ned and Walter weren't from anyplace as simple as Rueful.

"What are they saying at school?" I asked.

Glory stared at her feet. "Mary Beth Conover said it had to be a crazy person, but others said no, if the person was crazy they'd be in Schizo-ville, the Walled-Off for crazy people."

"You didn't take an unusual interest, did you?"

She shook her head no. "You think it's another decoy?"

I told her I didn't know. The presence of Ned and Walter here in Rueful, where they didn't belong, had mostly annoyed me, but now, I felt frightened.

That night Glory and I hiked over to the cemetery and pretended to pull weeds along the fence—just in case someone was watching us—while she dug up the little pouch the cat-people had given her. It was the only connection she had to them, and she'd told me if she needed something from them, she might need it in a hurry. Back at the house, we folded it flat, ripped a seam in the lining of her jacket, and put the bag inside. Then I restitched it, almost invisibly, so no matter what happened, she would have it nearby.

Half the town went to Dorothy Springer's funeral. Everyone was sorry she was gone, particularly the local folks who'd taken it upon themselves to feed her forty or fifty barn cats until they could find homes for them. School let out early in the afternoon, and the Remorseful Ruehouse was full of young people and their families. Bamber and Glory went with me, and we were just part of the crowd, which was a good thing because Ned and Walter were there, sitting in the back row, scanning the congregation.

We saw them on the way in. When we came out of the church, they were gone, but they were out at the cemetery when we arrived there. I had brought a bouquet, some wildflowers and some from my little garden. A lot of other people had done the same, and from under my lashes I watched the two men focusing on every person who laid flowers by the grave, trying to find something unusual. Glory started to cry, but by that time most of us were a little tearful.

"The Remorseful cemetery isn't as pretty as the one near Crossroads," I said when the burial was over. "But it does have a nice view of the mountains. Here, take my handkerchief, Gloriana. I didn't know you knew Dorothy."

"I just knew her to say hello to. It's just . . . just . . ."

"I know. The minister enjoyed himself, didn't he. Made a real three-hanky affair out of it."

"He did. Sort of."

"If it's any comfort to you, I have a friend in the sheriff's office, an old patient of your grandpa's. She told me Dorothy was dozing in her chair, the way she did of an evening, when someone hit her on the head with something heavy. It was very sudden, and she probably didn't even feel it. Also, she was well past ninety, and beginning to show signs of failing. She actually told me she wished she could just die quickly, in her sleep, and that's almost what happened."

"Was she a friend of yours?"

"Oh, for about forty years. She was one of Grandpa Doc's patients, too. Well then, most everybody around here was! You don't need to grieve over her, Glory."

"It wasn't grieving so much as thinking I could have caused her to die, Grandma! Even though it was Ms. McCollum who actually mentioned Ms. Springer to . . . you know who . . . it could just as easy have been me."

"Death usually makes us feel guilty," I told her. "As though those of us still living are part of a conspiracy. Let's not brood on it, Glory. Til and Jeff are spending the night with friends, and your mother suggested that she and your dad would relish an evening to themselves, so I'm inviting you and Bamber to have supper at my house."

I'd made a big pan of what farm folk called "all-in," meat, cheese, beans, grain, and spicy sauce. Different kinds of peppers grew well in Rueful; almost everybody used them, red, green, or yellow, plus the tiny purple ones that set your mouth on fire.

Bamber ate three helpings of all-in and two of dessert. He was apologetic about it until I told him he was a growing boy, and if I remembered rightly, they ate all the time. Bamber flushed and looked pleased, as though he'd received a compliment, as perhaps he had. He'd been told he was normal boyish, and Bamber probably didn't often get to think of himself that way. After dinner, Falija, Bamber and Glory did the dishes, and I sat on the porch, watching the battle-bats skydiving for bugs until the dishwashers joined me.

Glory asked Falija if her new brain had told her anything new and helpful.

Falija smiled a cat smile. "As a matter of fact . . . it's still light enough for us all to see. Let's take a walk in the woods. Maybe we'll find something interesting."

Since Bryan had died, I often went woods wandering in the dusk or moonlight. I knew Falija saw well even when it was quite dark, so we wouldn't get lost. She led us up the hill, past a huge chunk of black rock that went up like a steeple, then up a steep slope—me scrambling, with Bamber boosting me from behind—that ended against two huge boulders separated by a narrow slit. Following Falija, we squeezed inside. The opening split in two, and Falija led us to the right. Directly ahead of us was a screen of some kind, a wavering light, as though someone had turned a breeze-riffled pond on its side. I would have stopped right there, but when Falija plunged right through it, the children went after her, so, naturally, I went after them.

We stood in a tunnel of wavering light. To our right was a line of squared-off boulders that made a low barrier between us and the drop beyond. Bamber went to the gap between two of the stones and peered downward while I tried to figure out how we had possibly climbed this high! We were on a ledge, out in the clear, high above the nearby hills, with a view that went all the way to the next Walled-Off, but nothing looked familiar: no town, no pottery chimneys, no notch where the river flowed. On our left, the cliffs went up into the sky where the last lavender clouds of evening floated in front of a full moon, just rising over the mountains. I stared at it, and it at me, and its expression was completely different from any moons I knew.

I whispered, "What do you call this place, Falija?"

"I guess I'd call it a very good place from which to watch what goes on down there," Falija said, pointing through the gap in the stones. The ledge followed the half circle of the cliff; directly across from us water poured from the cliff top into a pool far below, where a wide green lawn was edged by young trees. The trees were horsing around in the wind, like boys at a school dance, pretending not to notice there were girls there—and there really were girls there, though it took me a little while to see them, for they were pale as moonlight, their skins shining firefly green and their eyes glowing like lamps.

If they had clothes on, they were transparent, but clothes or no clothes, they looked nothing like human schoolgirls. I wasn't sure they were girls at all. They could be . . . just themselves, not male or female.

"What are they?" I asked.

"They're nyzeemi," said Falija. "At least that's what they are in our language. I just found this place this morning, and when I got back, I looked in your encyclopedia to see if you had anything like them. You don't. Nyzeemi aren't human, or female, or mythical."

"Where did they come from?" Glory asked her. "I've lived here all my life, and I've never seen them."

"You've lived back there, but never here, in their world," Falija said. "Though we're not actually in their world. We're just inside a way-gate. It's something like the window above the cemetery, where we went to see the dancers. You get to that one by jumping off the rock between the thimble-apple trees."

Bamber shook his head. "Falija, how did you know about the gates?"

She said, "My people use way-gates to go back and forth. They're instantaneous. If you can see way-gates, you can move around the galaxy like moving around your house. My people came here through a way-gate. It was all in my mother-brain."

Glory blurted, "You didn't come in a spaceship?"

Falija laughed, a kind of purr-hiccup, a prrrit prrrit prrrit, with the pitch going up at the end of each syllable. "From Chottem, where my parents came from, it would take several years to get to Tercis in a spaceship. Spaceships go through wormholes to get from one planet to another, but not all places are connected by wormholes. Really big spaceships, with lots of power, can generate their own wormholes and the protective field that lets people go through without getting scrambled.

"Way-gates are different. There's no other kind of space involved, they just step across folds, if you know right where they are. My mother-mind remembers hundreds of them. Why did you think they came in a spaceship?"

"I just supposed it," Glory told her. "Your people sure didn't come from anyplace on Tercis that I'd ever heard about."

"No," Falija admitted. "And neither did those men who are hunting for me. They probably came through a wormhole, and something evil sent them after you three."

"Me!" Glory squealed like a snared gaboon.

"Glory?" I blurted, sounding just as surprised.

Falija nodded seriously. "I think so," she said. "Maybe it's more like a feeling because you and Glory and Bamber . . . all three of you are part of my duty."

I, of course, with my usual arrogance, had been assuming that Falija was part of mine, so this set me back on my heels.

"Why me or Bamber?" Glory asked.

"I don't know why," Falija said. "Do you know why, Grandma? I've seen you biting your lips a lot lately, as though you were thinking."

I shook my head. "I have no idea, Falija. And since I'm usually thinking something or other, lip-biting is more or less a constant."

She turned and pointed to the trees below. "It's selection time. The nyzeemi are picking their trees. They have to do it while the trees are still young, so they can grow old together . . ."

Behind the young trees, the forest stretched endlessly away in ranks of hills before jagged lines of mountains against blue distances. Some little way back from the clearing, at the end of a glade, a grove of huge old trees towered above the others, only their leaves shivering, for the branches were too huge to be moved by the wind. I happened be to be looking at them as several old nyzeemi melted out of the bark and wandered out into the clearing, followed by others. They weren't as thin as the young ones, they moved more stiffly, they were wrinkly and aged, with twisty arms and long, long fingers. The old ones spoke to the young ones, pointing at the trees, their clouded heads nodding.

"They're advising the young ones whom to pick," said Falija.

"All the trees I see are from old Earth," I said. "Earth sent tree seeds with our colonies, so it must be a colony planet down there."

Falija considered this. "I suppose that could be, but considering the size of those trees down below, it's more likely the seeds came from Earth thousands of years ago, when there were still forests on Earth."

"It's so beautiful," Glory whispered.

Falija whispered, "There's an ubioque down there who keeps the moss soft and the waterfall beautiful, just to attract nyzeemi for the trees."

"There's an ubi-thingy for every place?"

Falija shook her head. "Only beautiful, natural places. There were ubioques on Earth, but once their habitat was gone, they died . . ."

She stopped suddenly, her ears pricking. All the wind and murmur sounds from below had stopped. We heard something approaching: loud, inappropriate, a hideous clamor like rocks bashing together. Falija whispered, "It can't see us, but it might be able to hear us. Be still."

The nyzeemi vanished. The wind dropped. The trees drooped in absolute quiet. The soft purling of the waterfall was lost in the clamor as a long, gray thing like a huge, lumpy snake came bashing through the trees.

"The people here call it a gizzardile," whispered Falija. "This is a huge one, and those lumps are the stones inside it that it uses to mash up the creatures it swallows."

The gizzardile attempted to coil itself into a circle, a task made more difficult by the many unyielding lumps inside itself, which the gizzardile seemed to be working back toward its rear end. When the heavy rear end was bunched together, the more sinuous front part began to rise, much like the pictures I have seen of cobras rising out of snake charmers' baskets, except that this creature's rising seemed to have no upper limit. We held our breaths as it came ever higher, stopping with the top of its head no great distance below us, facing into the waterfall, where it dipped its huge, fanged mouth with loud slurping sounds.

I couldn't take my eyes from it, from the multiple pairs of bowed legs along its sides, the spiny extrusion that might be a dorsal fin, though just now it lay in a wrinkled pile along the creature's spine. I am not usually afraid of serpents, knowing as I do that most of them are harmless and useful in keeping vermin in check, but the look and smell of this thing could have been designed to instill fear.

It had a stink peculiar to itself. If malice smelled, it would smell like that.

After slurping at the falls for what seemed an interminable time, the creature lowered itself, redistributed its lumps, and moved away through the trees with the sound of a retreating avalanche. It left a slick gray-slimed trail on the ground. As the end of the tail disappeared, a crowd of tiny people came out of the woods pushing barrows and carrying shovels. They dug the grayness up and carried it away. Immediately, the green mosses moved back into the places the slime had been, and the little people followed the slime trail back into the trees.

"Where are they taking the stuff?" Glory asked.

"They probably know of a way-gate nearby, one that opens into a fire pit or a volcano or even into a little sun, and they'll dump it to be burned."

"And what are those little people?" Bamber demanded.

"I'm not sure," said Falija. "In your world, little people are mythical, and they're called different things. These are quite real. In their language they're called a word that means filth-carriers. They have no sense of smell and no aesthetic perceptions, they aren't bothered by nastiness, though they themselves are quite clean, so they make their living cleaning it up when it intrudes on special places."

"So that's a magical world down there?" asked Bamber

Falija replied in an astonished voice, "No, of course it's not magical. It's completely real. It simply has a lot of life-forms that you're unfamiliar with."

Glory asked, "What do you mean, it's not magical, it's real?"

"It's a real world. It has real qualities. Up is always up and down is always down. Fruit falls from a tree, it doesn't float to the sky. Creatures are born in this world, and grow up and eventually die. What's true today is also true tomorrow.

"If this were a magical world, all those things would be subject to change by anyone who had power or could command it by spell or enchantment. Magical worlds can't exist in our universe because their rules change constantly, and there's no difference between evil and good. Power is power, and everyone does whatever they can get away with."

"I always thought magic was sort of nice," said Glory.

Falija's ears drooped. "Humans are fascinated with magic. Your people like to believe in powers that will break all the laws of the universe, just for you." Falija shivered. "My bones feel it's getting really late back home. It's time to go."

So we went back through the shimmering gate, down to my house, all of us silent and full of wonder. Falija and I stopped off while the other two went on down the hill. For a moment I wondered if I should call them back, tell them not to mention what had happened tonight, not even to Maybelle or James. I decided they knew enough to keep their mouths shut, and in fact, they did.

The first day of the following week, I drove Bamber and Glory over to Remorseful to school. Some of the people who had been taking care of Dorothy Springer's cats were interested in setting up an animal refuge in her memory, a place for stray cats and dogs and whatever. They'd asked me if I would help, and I'd said I'd talk with them about it that morning. School hadn't started yet, and most of the students were out on the lawn when we arrived. The children got out of the buggy just as a series of unusual noises came from the main street, down the hill, where the stores and bank and offices were, like a huge door slamming repeatedly. Everyone jumped up, peering down the street and jabbering. Before anybody could move in that direction, the head teacher came out of the school and told everyone to get inside until we knew what had happened.

I hitched the horse and went inside with the children, thinking how ridiculous this was, in Rueful, of all places. Bamber went out the back door of the school before I had a chance to ask where he was going. Inside the doors, the head teacher was telling everyone the Dominion Alarm system had already summoned Dominion officers, and everyone was to stay inside with their belongings at hand, in case they needed to be sent home.

A moment later, a Dominion Police flier buzzed up over the hills and headed for the downtown, and only moments after that, Bamber Joy sneaked back into the school and came to find Glory and me. He said he'd sneaked over to Main Street where supposedly armed men had robbed the bank. He'd seen Ned and Walter in front of the bank, waving their arms and claiming to have seen the robbers running off into the woods. Since woods covered most of the mountains around town, the alleged robbers could be anywhere. That's the way Bamber said it, alleged robbers. The police had already sent for scent-hounds and fliers and heaven knows what else.

Not long after that, a Dominion Officer arrived to tell everyone to go home and lock themselves in. Bamber disappeared. Glory, Til, and Jeff got into the wagon with me, and we were just at the edge of town when we saw Billy Ray's wagon with him and Benny Paul in it, recruiting people for search parties. They yelled at Jeff and Til to get in the wagon, and Til was over there before I could say a word. Jeff said he'd wait and go with his dad, which was quite sensible of him.

We left Jeff unhitching the horse at Maybelle's, while Glory and I went up to my house to discuss the matter.

"I think this is another decoy," she said. "Even if the bank really did get robbed."

I said, "Real or not real, when a so-called robbery scatters every able-bodied man and boy from The Valley into the mountains, it makes me a little nervous, doesn't it you?"

Falija's eyes were as big as teacups, and her ears were back.

"There," Glory said, stroking Falija's head. "That's exactly what Bamber thought, especially since Ned and Walter were telling the sheriff where the robbers went. But, Jeff isn't gone, and neither is Bamber. His stepdaddy probably went with everyone else, but Bamber will show up here just as soon as he finds out what's happening."

And he did, a fairly short time later, sticking his head in the door, panting like he'd run five miles, which likely he had.

"Ned and Walter are back," he said. "They've got four or five other guys with them, and they're going house to house down the valley road, coming this way, waving fake badges and saying they're deputized by Dominion to search every house for the bank robbers."

"They'll find me," said Falija, sounding a little panicky. "They will. They'll sniff me out."

"Then we need to go somewhere else," Glory said in a determined tone. "Don't we, Falija?"

Falija looked at her, and the creases between her eyes went away. "Of course! Up the mountain! Where I took you the other evening!"

"Right," said Bamber Joy. "Through that gate! Maybe we could even close the gate behind us. Glory and I'll come along to keep you company."

"Glory, and you, and I," I said. "Unless Falija would be safer going alone."

"Grandma," said Falija, "there's no time to explain now. They're looking for me, yes, but they're also looking for anyone who helped me, and that includes all three of you. I wouldn't be safer alone, and I'd have failed my duty."

Glory said, "They were asking for scent-hounds to be brought in . . ."

Falija said, "In that case, they'll find me or anyone I've been with or anyplace I've been lately . . ."

"Should we take Lou Ellen?" Glory asked, sounding worried. I started to say something, then bit my lip.

Falija gave Glory a troubled look. "Glory, Lou Ellen will be all right. She'll either meet us on the way or she can visit her other friends, and they'll keep her safe."

A few more words bubbled up among us, and we confused each other for a few minutes with ifs and buts, but the upshot was that I wrote a note saying I had the notion to go camping up the river over the next few days, and I was taking Glory and Bamber Joy along to fetch and carry. Glory took the note down to her house, put it on the kitchen table, dumped her books and stowed a few things in her backpack, grabbed her bedroll and jacket, and rejoined Bamber and me, who were making up a couple of packs and bedrolls ourselves.

I said, "Spare socks? Underwear?"

Glory said, "I brought some of Til's clothes for Bamber, since he didn't have time to collect anything."

I locked my door behind us but left the curtains open so anybody could look in and see nobody was home. Just about that time, Bamber saw two cars coming along the road from the bridge. If they got to the Judson house, they'd see the note, but since we weren't really going where the note said we were going, it didn't matter much if Ned and Walter followed the false lead.

We went uphill, walking on rocks so as not to leave a visible trail. Bamber came last to be sure no one had made any marks or dropped anything. We reached the spire of black rock, and from there we could hear men yelling down the hill. Glory climbed halfway up the rock to get a better view and reported there were two cars in the driveway as well as her daddy's buggy, her parents, and Jeff, along with several other people.

When we got to the slit rock, Falija told us to help her make a rock pile right beside it. Bamber and Glory fetched some bigger ones while I gathered small ones. Glory went into the slit in the rock, took my hand, and helped me over the pile. Falija and Bamber came through and reached back to arrange the stones into a teetery heap that looked as if it had fallen that way, a perfect place to break a leg. They topped it off with a few broken, dried branches that pretty well filled the crack between the stones.

This time we went straight through the watery tunnel and out the other end onto the ledge. It was daytime, and the nyzeemi weren't there. When we looked back, a black pool filled the whole width of the ledge behind us.

Falija said, "Get up on top of the railing stones."

"On top?" I said, shocked. We were quite high enough already.

"It's the only way down," said Falija, climbing onto a stone herself.

Bamber and Glory climbed up, each took hold of one of my arms and pulled me up between them. Falija said to shut our eyes and jump, and that's what Bamber and Glory did, dragging me off the ledge with them. I thought of screaming, but by the time I'd decided on it, we were floating. We landed soft as featherweed floss. Bamber and Glory let go, and I stood there trembling. After I decided I was all in one piece I took a deep breath and asked Falija, "What was that?"

"My people put a kind of elevator there. It isn't magic. It's just a force field. They sometimes put them in places like this where the way-gates end up in difficult places. I knew the field was there. I could feel it."

"The people can't follow us?"

Falija shook her head. "Not unless they know precisely where this way-gate is, because if they are what we think they are, they can't smell it or see it, the way my people can. Each gate creates an aversion field so nonsensors walk on past it without even noticing."

"Well," I remarked, with a glance at the ledge we'd jumped from, "we probably shouldn't go too far. We might get lost, and we'll want to be able to go back . . ."

Falija was shaking her head. "Grandma, I'm sorry, I thought you understood that the gates go only one way. There are ways to get back to Tercis, but the closest is five worlds away from here."

I felt my face go dead. All my blood drained to someplace below my feet. For a moment I tottered there, feeling lost and out of place. I thought about fainting and decided not to. As I'd learned so long ago on Phobos, what was, was. All fainting did was delay dealing with the inevitable. "Well then, just in case you're not totally correct about their coming after us, let's get out of the foyer of this place and into some part that's not quite so exposed from above."

That seemed sensible to everyone, so we moved off quietly under the trees, hearing nothing at all from behind us or even around us. A few bird sounds. A tiny breeze. That was all. After a time we came to a trail and turned left along it, simply because leftward ran downhill and it seemed easier. I was breathing very hard.

"Are we moving too fast?" Falija asked, concerned.

"It's not the walk, it's the . . . what, Glory?" I asked her.

"The difference," Glory said. "The strangeness. The not knowing whether they'll catch up to us and what they'll do."

Falija said, "I'm certain they won't catch up to us. Not now. Not today. Not here." She took my hand and caressed it. "Nobody expected us to come here, so we don't need to worry about dangers coming after us, just the ones we may happen on."

"Which isn't likely," said Gloriana quickly. "Is it?"

Falija shook her head. "Not around here, no."

When we had gone about a mile down the trail, we heard voices coming in our direction, people singing, a clinking noise, a strange sound halfway between a whinny and a moo, then the crunch of wheels. We left the trail and went back into the trees to lie down and peek out without being seen. In a few minutes a wagon appeared, hitched to two large creatures covered with close, curly hair like a sheep's. Their tails arched forward over their backs and head, the long, silky hair making a parasol over the entire animal. They had horns like cows, single hooves like horses, plus long, silky ears that extended almost to the ground.

The people in the wagon looked rather human, if one could accept green humans somewhere between Falija size and human size. Those with ribbons tying up their dark green hair were on one side of the wagon, and those with kerchiefs around their necks were on the other.

"Let's try that last chorus again," said the right-hand animal, speaking perfectly intelligible Earthian. "One, two . . ." and they all began to sing, girls high, boys medium, the team of animals, baritone and bass.

> "The right time of day
> For raiding hay
> Is three o'clock in the mornin'.
> The world is asleep
> and the birds don't peep
> so the farmer has no warnin'.
> We can cut, we can bale
> with a sharp toenail
> and an energy that's unflaggin',
> And the entire crop
> fits under the top
> of our 'inside-out' hay wagon . . ."

"What are those people?" whispered Bamber.

"The team are umoxen," said Falija thoughtfully. "And the people are hayfolk. All winter they let their toenails grow. By summer they're as long as scythes, then they hitch up their wagons and go dance through the hayfields at night, cutting enough hay to get them through the winter."

"What do they do with it?" Gloriana asked.

"Eat it," she said. "That's why they're green. They call themselves hayraiders, but they only take the first cutting, so the farmer doesn't lose everything."

"Except the fruits of his labors," said I disapprovingly.

"Not exactly," Falija told me. "The farmer depends on the hayraiders to do the second and third cutting for him, and there's some other kind of arrangement as well. It's fair to both."

"Then why are they called raiders?" I asked, outraged.

"Because they like it. It makes them sound adventurous and bold. It's a lot more fun to dance in the moonlight than it is to work in the noonday sun, especially if it's illicit."

"What's an inside-out hay wagon?" asked Bamber.

"One that seems bigger on the inside than it seems on the outside."

Glory asked, "Why do they speak Earthian?"

Falija said, "A surprising number of worlds do, particularly worlds where Gentherans have been. Gentherans call human language one of the two great gifts from Earth. Earthian is a lot easier to read, write, and speak than most languages, as well as having an enormous vocabulary. So, whenever you find several races living together, chances are they'll speak Earthian. The hayfolk and the umoxen also have their own languages, of course. Shall we ask them for a ride?"

I shook my head doubtfully. The wagon did look filled to over-flowing with creatures. Suddenly, however, the left-hand umox called, "Who's out there? I hear you thinking! Come out now, before they come slishing and slashing after you!"

Falija led us out onto the road as the hayfolk came down from the wagon. Their toenails were longer than my forearm, gently curving out to the sides. I supposed they had to curve that way, or they'd have to walk with their feet far apart. The biggest one came forward, stopping far enough away that he wasn't threatening to cut anyone off at the ankles.

"Well, Gibbekotkin, and where did you pop from?"

"Here and there," said Falija. "Is there room in the wagon for passengers?"

"Depends on who's asking," said the nigh umox.

"And where they're coming from," said the off umox.

"And where they're going," said the largest raider.

"Falija is asking," she said, "for her friends, who are coming from danger and going toward refuge, so far as is possible."

"Who's after you?" asked the nigh umox suspiciously.

"Don't know," she said. "Just know they are. Human-type men . . ."

"Who sound like robots," Glory offered.

"Lurking and lying," said Bamber.

"Up to no good," I supplied.

"The unmentionable's creatures," said the largest raider, nodding vigorously. "We've seen 'em here and there in their great, smelly wagons. Very good description. Climb up on the driver's seat, you two ladies. Gibbekotkin in lap, brother in back. My name's Howkel, by the by."

Glory and I climbed onto the seat, and Falija settled across both laps while Bamber Joy squeezed himself among the raiders. When the wagon started to move, I thought Bamber probably had the best of it, because the hay was soft but the seat certainly wasn't.

The banks of green moss on either side of the road were so clean they looked freshly vacuumed. The only fallen leaves in evidence were brightly colored, unbroken, and set out in artistic arrangements. Now and then the wagon passed a little pile of twigs and branches set by the trail, as though waiting to be picked up by something.

"Have you any new stories?" one of the girl hayraiders asked. "We usually tell stories on long rides."

"I have one you might like to hear," said Falija. "It's about a villager who talked to a fish."

"Oh, tell it please," said the Hayfolk.

And as we rolled along, Falija told a strange tale about a fish who helped a man out of his difficulties by directing him to the Keeper of all information. It was interesting, but rather complicated. I'm afraid I dozed a little, waking up just as Falija said, "And so, since that day, whenever the man has a difficulty, he has walked seven roads at once, for only in that way can he find the Keeper again . . ."

I said to Falija. "If that whole thing was in your memory, Falija, maybe it's important."

"Some stories are very important," said Howkel. "Specially in the summer grasslands of Fajnard."

"This is Fajnard?" I cried. "Fajnard is under the rule of the Frossians. This isn't a good place to be!"

Howkel snorted. "The Frossians think they run the world, but they actually only occupy about a tenth of it, around the lowland cities. They're used to rampaging onto a world, digging up the ore, cutting down the trees, moving on. They have a chant, 'Move in, dig up, cut down, move on.' No ore here. Trees are poisonous to 'em. The wealth here's in grass after it's fed to umoxen to make wool, but that's slow work, year after year. Frossians aren't used to patience. They're already getting itchy and neglectful. Pretty soon they'll decide they'd rather be somewhere else. While there's Frossians here, hayfolk have nothing to do with them! We stay far from the cities, up here in the highlands."

"Wind coming," said the off umox.

They stopped the wagon, all the hayfolk got off and went into the woods. The long-haired umoxen lay down and tied their ears under their chins with the four stubby fingers in the middle of their hooves. When the fingers were folded up, the hoof part hit the ground, but when they wanted to, the umoxen could use those fingers almost like hands.

Very shortly we heard the wind, and we all lay down as well. It came louder and closer, then it came down the trail, a whirlwind that went past us like a train going full speed, and when it was gone, so were all the little twig piles along the road.

So the moss beds had been vacuumed.

"What kind of world is this again?" Glory asked Falija, who was grooming her whiskers back into shape.

"A natural world," she said. "One where certain creatures are embodiments."

"Embodiments do vacuuming?" Glory asked.

"The embodiment of order might, or the embodiment of beauty."

"Is this where your people live?"

She shook her head. "Some of them, yes, but I don't know what direction they might be in. I do have an anticipatory feeling, though. As though enlightenment may be around the next corner."

Glory sneaked a look at me. I was chewing my lip.

"You know, Grandma," Glory said, "you might as well tell us now. There's something bothering you."

I shook my head, then looked at Falija, then looked up at the sky. Maybe I was asking God for a sign.

"She will," said Falija. "But not now, not with all these hayfolk about."

The hayfolk came out of the woods as the umoxen untied their ears and got to their feet, making harrumph, harrumph sounds. "Where are you headed?" Falija asked the nigh umox.

"The Howkel Farm. Just outside the woods. Dallydance is just down the road, if you're looking for a town."

"Are there humans there?" Glory asked the umox.

"Like you? No. A few of the ordinary sort, though. Like her," and he pointed at me with one leg.

Glory tried to sort that out. "She's my grandmother. We're the same kind of people."

"Humph," said the off umox. "Tell that to the gizzardile. You don't even smell alike."

"That's enough of that," said Falija in a commanding tone. "We don't discuss how people smell, and umoxen aren't the best judge of odors, anyhow."

It was true they had a decidedly barnyard smell, which all of us present were more or less used to, but the umoxen took it as an insult.

"Oh, isn't it a commanding Gibbekotkin! Doesn't it have qualities of leadership! Pardon us, your royal sagacity, but those two, the boy and the girl, are alike, and that one, the old woman, is something else again. And anyone who says different is blind as a battle-bat, smell or no smell."

"Here, here, what's this," said Howkel, who was the last to emerge from the woods. "Controversy? Argument? On such a lovely day? What are you umoxen up to?"

"Harrumph," said the nigh umox. "Nothing at all. Except having my intelligence insulted and my fragrance referred to in a tone of derogation."

"Tsk," said Howkel. "Well, folk, you've lost your ride for sure. I never ask the umoxen to haul anyone who's insulted them. If you get so far as our farm, though, do drop in for a meal and a bed. Dame Howkel is a fine cook, if I do say so myself."

And with that, he and his tribe leapt upon the wagon, dumped our backpacks onto the road, and trundled off, leaving us standing there with our mouths open. I felt I'd done nothing but gape for weeks.

"Now what?" I asked, simmering.

"Now," said Falija very softly, "now that our curious hayraiders have departed, it's time Gloriana knew the truth."

I could feel myself turning red, then white, then gray before my legs went out from under me and I was suddenly sitting on the grass, not knowing how I got there. Glory got her water bottle out of her pack and moistened a clean hanky to make a coolness for my forehead.

Finally, I murmured, "It was twins, Glory. All those twins."

"What was?" Glory asked. "What about it. I'm not one!"

"I know. I know. I married your Grandpa Doc, and I had twins. Conjoined twins. They died almost as soon as they were born. And we thought, well, it's probably for the best, it happens sometimes, next time will be normal. Then I had your mother and your aunt Mayleen, and they were joined, too. Grandpa Doc had to cut them apart because they were joined at the back of the head. That was the end of having babies, so far as I was concerned. We figured, it was just me, you know. Some mutation that happened on our way to Tercis. Years went by. Then Mayleen . . ."

"Mayleen was only seventeen when she had Billy Wayne and Joe Bob, and they were joined, but Grandpa Doc separated them all right except for the terrible scars. After them, two or three sets died, then it was Ella May and Janice Ruth. Then Benny Paul and his brother who died. And more dead ones in between before Trish survived. Then Sue Elaine and Lou Ellen. We'd already realized, by then, that every time Grandpa separated twins, one of them was . . . wrong, somehow.

"Your mother, Maybelle, is sweetness itself, but Mayleen . . . And Joe Bob is a sensible, kind person, but it's good Billy Wayne went into the army, because he's as bad as Benny Paul. It was the same with Ella May and Janine Ruth. Ella May applied to the Siblinghood because she couldn't stand it that her sister was a really vicious person. It was as though only one out of each pair had any goodness. Trish is like an empty bottle. Nothing there at all but babble and bubbles. And it went on and on, sometimes one lived, sometimes neither, five times both. And you know what happened to poor Lou Ellen after she and Sue Elaine . . ."

I saw Glory's face change, saw it convulsed with fury, and suddenly she was screaming, "It wasn't fair letting Sue Elaine have legs and not letting Lou Ellen have any!" Then there was a vast quiet, as though the whole world was waiting for her answer.

I whispered, "The nerves to the legs were connected to Sue Elaine's brain, not to Lou Ellen's. There were only two legs, only one spine attached at the pelvis. Actually, Lou Ellen didn't have any legs, Glory. You know that. Grandpa Doc had to separate them. He waited until they were three. You used to play with her on the bed for hours, and you knew . . ."

"She got well. She does too have legs now," Glory said. "She does. She goes everywhere with me!"

Falija put her paw on Glory's hand and let the claws out, just a tiny bit. "Glory, Glory, Lou Ellen is dead. You know that. You saw her dancing with all her selves. You know she isn't really alive. In your heart you know that."

Glory's hands went to her throat, as though she were choking, but still she cried out, "Bamber's seen her! Tell them, Bamber!"

"Well," he said in a sad voice, "I've seen her ghost, Glory. But then, I can see people's ghosts, and I guess you can, too."

"She's buried in the cemetery," I said. "I know you wouldn't go to her funeral or even into the graveyard to see the stone, but her grave is there, Glory. Really."

Glory looked around, trying to find something else to prove Lou Ellen was still alive. "You make her sandwiches," she said frantically. "You say hello to her."

"Just to keep you contented, Glory, so you won't go back into the state you went into when she died. You end up eating the sandwiches yourself. And nobody says hello to Lou Ellen until you look at her and show us where you think she is. Except Falija says you really can see her, and now Bamber says he can, so you're not . . . you know, what we thought you were . . ."

"You all thought I was crazy. Mama and Daddy and you!"

"Well," I cried, "I beg your forgiveness for that, but there was just no end to the tragedy and the loss and the pain. And when your mama had Til and Jeff, it was the same thing. Jeff is a wonderful boy, but Til . . . Til's another one like Benny Paul. When your mother got pregnant the second time, Grandpa Doc knew the babies wouldn't live, because a friend of his had sneaked across the Walled-Off to lend him some other medical machine that The Valley doesn't have.

"I . . . I went up to Contrition City and I went to the refuge there, the one for pregnant women who want to give up their babies for adoption. Women sometimes come to Rueful just for that reason, you know. I asked for a woman who would have a baby about that same time Maybelle would; Grandpa arranged for a private place for the birthing. Maybelle's babies were born dead, all scrambled together. We never told her. When she woke up, you were there, and she and your daddy have always thought you were theirs. Nobody knew you weren't except Grandpa Doc and me and the real mother."

"And Mama got her tubes tied," Glory said in a dull voice. "But Aunt Mayleen didn't."

"Not right then. She and Billy Ray were dead set against it, but Grandpa did it the year before he died. He told her she had an infection he had to clear up, but what he really cleared up was her having any more babies. He just said it was the infection did it, and that's what he told Billy Ray."

"I can't understand how you kept all this quiet," said Bamber. "That many conjoined twins would have been on everyone's tongue."

I said, "If my husband hadn't been a very fine doctor, if he hadn't had a few advanced medical devices that he really shouldn't have had in Rueful, and if he hadn't had me to help out, it would have been a circus. But Billy Ray's farm is away from everyone, and so is Jimmy Joe's. We never allowed anyone to see the babies until they were apart. Later, when they went to school and played with other children who saw the scars, we had stories to explain what happened. With Til and Jeff, it was an accident in an old barn. With Maybelle and Mayleen, the scars were small anyhow, just at the back of their heads, mostly covered by their hair, and we just told them they were born that way . . ."

"How did you keep Mayleen quiet?" Glory cried. "When she started having twins, she'd have screamed about it."

"Not Mayleen. You know what the folks in Rueful would have thought about it and said about it. She didn't want that. She'd have died before she'd have admitted it, and Billy Ray likewise."

Everyone was still. I was watching Glory, thinking she'd break out any minute with tears, howls, accusations, but she seemed more . . . interested, or troubled than outraged.

"I don't know what this means," Glory complained. "I feel like

I'm lost. Not . . . not orphaned, exactly. I know that Mama and Daddy love me and that you do, too, Grandma. But I feel like there's part of me floating free, like a wood chip going down the river, turning around and around, with no idea where it's going . . ."

"Which means the umoxen were right," said Falija. "Glory and Bamber are a different sort. What did the woman look like, the one who gave up Glory?"

I wiped my eyes with the wet hanky. "I never saw her. She sent an old woman to bring Glory to us, a very old woman. Budness or Bodness, she said her name was. She said the mother was too broken up to do it. Well, I understand that. No woman gives up a child unless things are terrible for her. As for Glory, well, even as a baby she had dark, dark hair and brown skin, and when I commented on it, the old woman said the baby's father was very tall, and very dark. I asked her what had happened to the father, wondering, you know, why the mother was giving up her child, and the old woman said he had disappeared and the mother couldn't raise her little girl alone."

"Why didn't you just tell Mama the babies died?" Glory asked, still in that curious, almost uninvolved voice.

"Because your mama has a heart condition, Glory. You've heard us mention it. She almost died when Til and Jeff were born. And she almost died again when she saw them, and again when they were operated on. And she's fretted herself for years over the fact that they aren't . . . equally endowed. Grandpa Doc didn't realize how serious your mother's condition until after the Til and Jeff were born, but after that, he just couldn't let her go through all that again."

Glory turned to stare at Bamber, her eyes moving from his hair to his eyes to his height. Like hers, all of them. He had an arching nose and a wide mouth, like hers, one that always looked like it had too many teeth in it. Dark, vital, lean, and fit. I felt soft compared to both of them. I could have howled.

"I knew we were alike," Glory said very softly. "More like family. I never looked like the Mackeys or the Judsons. Do you think we have the same parents?"

He thought about this, troubled, as she was, but not angry. "It's possible," he said at last. "I don't remember what my mother looked like. I don't remember anybody before we came here to Rueful. It would explain her leaving me with Abe Johnson, because she might have wanted us to grow up near one another . . ."

I was listening to this with continuing amazement. I had known about Gloriana's birth mother! Why hadn't it occurred to me that Bamber might have had the same one?

"What about when Til, and Jeff, and Trish, and all of the rest of Mayleen's children start having babies?" Glory demanded.

"Grandpa Doc fixed them all, before he died, even Emmaline, when she was just a baby. We had quite a plague of appendicitis among the girls and hernias among the boys, but none of them will have children, not even the nice ones, and that's another reason why your cousin Ella May joined the Siblinghood. She and Joe Bob were old enough and sensible enough that Grandpa told them the truth. Oh, Glory, it was such a burden for your grandfather. I know he felt he'd been cursed. I felt I was a curse to him. . . ."

Glory murmured, "Then I'm glad I wasn't Mama's baby, really, but I'm glad I'm her child."

I broke down then and cried, while Bamber and Glory tried to comfort me, though every now and then Glory would mutter that it would have made so much more sense if we'd just admitted it to one another instead of trying to keep it secret. Perhaps later I could explain that both Grandpa Doc and I had been from an older time on Earth, when things like that couldn't be talked about at all. Maybe he had been ashamed of it. I *had* been ashamed of it. Maybe he'd had dreams of his family going on, down the generations, and he just couldn't admit to the world that they wouldn't. And then, too, I knew Bryan hadn't struggled to keep life in some of those babies, when he'd seen how awful their lives would be. Like Lou Ellen. That poor baby had whispered to me that she prayed to die, so the pain could stop. Glory had just been so generously accepting that she'd never realized how dreadful Lou Ellen's life really was . . .

Glory stood up, her jaw set. "I think I've had about all the emotions I can take for one day." She took a deep breath and helped me get to my feet. "If we're going to find someplace to sleep by sundown, we'd better get started."

I Am Margaret, with
Hayraiders on Fajnard

We reached the gate of the Howkel Farm at nightfall. While Falija and I waited at the gate, Glory and Bamber went to the door and knocked politely. Dame Howkel answered the knock.

"So you've arrived!" she said. "Good enough. I always say to Lafaniel, that's my husband, Lafaniel, that he truckles too much to them umoxen. Nice creature, true, polite in their habits, but set on having their way! Beckon your folk in, now, and we'll see about supper."

The two beckoned as instructed, I thinking meanwhile that I'd never imagined anyone quite so round, green, and cheerful as Dame Howkel. Once inside, however, I forgot about the probability of eating hay, for the aroma was of something very savory. Dame Howkel bobbed a curtsy toward Falija.

"Welcome, ma'am and Gibbekotkin. Howkel'l be along shortly. Our young have had their supper, us oldsters waited for you."

She showed us the way out back, where a washbowl sat on a table next to the well beside a stack of towels and a steaming kettle. Once back inside, we were given mugs of fragrant green tea, and by the time Lafaniel Howkel showed up, we were deep in conversation with the Dame concerning the plight of Fajnard.

"I was speaking of the Frossians," said the Dame to

her husband. "I was telling how the Gibbekot planted those acid trees all along the valleys to stop the Frossians coming."

"I would've warned you of the same," Howkel said, pouring himself a mug of tea. "They smell very pungent, so they're easy to avoid. You'd think the Frossians'd learn to look at the trees to see which ones do it to 'em, but they never do."

He turned toward me and said pointedly, with a sidelong glance at Falija, "Since you're Ghoss, you'll be going to the Gibbekot, won't you? They'll be wondering where that child is, wanderin' off and findin' the comp'ny of strangers."

"I'm not from Fajnard, and they're not Ghoss," said Falija, in a lofty tone. "We came through a way-gate from Tercis."

"Not Ghoss? Then what are they?" demanded Howkel.

"Same race," said Falija. "Not the same . . . talents."

"You say a way-gate," breathed the Dame. "I didn't know we had a way-gate anywhere near here."

"Never seen fit to mention it to you," Howkel said, fixing Falija with a doubtful eye. "We have a pair of 'em, one that comes in from Tercis, and one that goes out to Thairy. And right now, there's gizzardiles lyin' both ways like sentries!"

"We saw one," said Bamber. "Very ugly."

"Supper," said Dame Howkel in a peremptory tone. "Let's not upset ourselfs with gizzardiles right afore supper."

We sat down at the long, wide table, the Dame at one end, Howkel at the other, his feet neatly crossed so his toenails curved inward before him, making floor space for the feet of those at his sides. Each place held a large bowl of stew, which had a certain verdant leafiness about it, but also bits that crunched or melted. We talked about food, the Dame ticking off many kinds of nuts and roots and seeds that made up hayfolk meals. "Along with hay," she said, listing the kinds of hay, each with its own taste and texture.

"Have you always been hayraiders?" Gloriana asked.

"Hayfolk," said Howkel. "Not raiders 'til the umoxen came, and they was brought from the plains below by the Gibbekot. They was the ones started cuttin' hay from the grasslands, not knowin' we was countin' on it for winter food for ourselfs. Generally nice folk, the Gibbekot. We told 'em we needed it, and they worked it out right away. We get first cut. After that, we cut hay for the umoxen, and we get umox wool from the Gibbekot in return. Hayraidin's just doin' what we always did."

"You always cut the hay at night?" asked Bamber Joy.

"Oh, sure. Nicer, cooler at night, and there's usually a moon, since Fajnard has five of 'em."

"Did you always have those remarkable toenails?" I asked.

"Our people say we always did," said Dame Howkel. "Course, I cut mine, now I'm past dancin' the hay, and we all cut 'em off after the hay's in for the season and sell 'em in the market for sickle blades. No better edge nowhere than Hayfolk toenails. Besides, it's warmer in the winter if you can keep your feet under the blanket 'stead of lettin' 'em hang out the foot of the bed. Now, suppose you tell us where you're headed. We can tell you the safest roads, depending on where you're going."

Falija, who had been rather quiet since Grandma's revelations on the road, made a little annunciatory noise, then: "My duty is to guide these folk in walking the seven roads of the Keeper. It is a task I was given by my people."

All of us turned to her in amazement, Bamber and Glory with their eyes wide, the Howkels with their mouths wide, me with both eyes and lips shut tight, afraid to say the wrong thing.

"When did you decide that?" cried Glory.

"It came to me while I was thinking of the fish story," Falija said. "You remember what I told you about my language and my mother-mind. I said you sometimes have to hear a word in context before you can understand what it really means. I had the seven roads in my mother-memory. It's my job to help the walker walk the seven roads. I knew the story of the fish, but it didn't connect to anything in my mind until just a few hours ago. All seven roads are one, and they must be walked simultaneously by one person." Her voice faltered. "There's nothing in my mind about how that's to be done."

"What is it, a riddle?" asked Bamber.

Falija shook her head. "All I know is, we just have to keep going."

"On this road?" I demanded. "In front of the house?"

Falija dropped her head, shaking it slightly, saying in a sorrowful voice, "I don't know."

"Road you came by was a way-gate road," said Howkel, pushing his chair back and honing his toenails together with a sound like steel on whetstone. "That road out front just goes to Gibbekotika by way of the mountains, that's all. So, likely it's a way-gate road that's meant."

"And there's one that goes on to Thairy," murmured Bamber Joy. "You said."

"Well, yes," mused Howkel. "A way-gate road as well."

"That's two roads that are one road," said Glory.

I took a deep breath. "Are all the way-gates one-way roads?"

"One way," Falija murmured. "I remember that someone long ago invented a machine to reverse them; but when they're let alone, they're always one way."

"My oh my," the Dame said, shaking her head. "That's a lot of confusion and supposition, that is. Seems to me you'd be better off finishing your supper, having a good night's sleep, then deciding what you're going to do next."

"Dame's right," said Howkel. "Never make plans when you're weary, and I'm weary. Been cuttin' hay the last eleven nights."

"There, that's so," the Dame said, nodding to her husband. "No more talk of roads tonight."

Glory and Bamber agreed, though Falija looked slightly mutinous. I reached out and petted her between the ears. Falija sighed and settled to her supper.

"There, now," said the Dame. "That's better. You're a dutiful Gibbekotkin, the more credit to you, but even the dutiful have to eat and rest." She turned to her own bowl, raising her spoon with a little moue of discomfort.

I saw that her arm was bruised. "What have you done to yourself there?" I asked. "That looks painful!"

"And so it is," said Howkel. "And it's gettin' no better, neither. It's a summer bruise, and it's been there a time now."

"Let me see," I said, taking the Dame's arm in my hands. Indeed, there was a darkness, like a bruise, except that on the green flesh it looked more like a crushed place, one that was not healing. "Tell me," I said, after some thought. "When you are ill, does your body get hot? Do you run a fever?"

"A fever? And what is a fever?" asked the Dame. "When our people are ill, they get cold."

"But this place on your arm is not cold. The tissue there is ruined. It needs to die and fall away, so the good tissue underneath can heal. Isn't that what usually happens?"

"Oh, aye, it does," said Howkel. "When Maniacal's toes were cut to pieces on the sharp rocks, they got cold and fell off, and the new ones grew. Thankful it was wintertime, we were."

I nodded. "But in summer, warm as it is, it would be hard for a bruised place to get cold enough to fall away. Well then, I would put ice on this. Is there any ice about?"

"Close enough," said Howkel. "And where did you learn such thinking out, ma'am?"

"My husband was a doctor," I said. "He always said, find out what the body does for itself and help it along."

"Think of that," said the Dame. "Just think of that, Howkel." And, with a smile of great sweetness, she reached up and kissed me on the cheek.

I Am M'urgi, with Fernwold on B'yurngrad

Once we were in Ferni's flier, I demanded to know what he meant when he said he was taking me somewhere safe.

"I overheard something," he said. "Perhaps meaningless, perhaps not. It made me believe you might be in danger."

"From whom?" I demanded.

He shrugged. "From someone who wants you dead, my love."

I laughed. "That's fairly indefinite."

"M'urgi. Listen to me. I was in a crowded place, waiting to take a ship from one place to another. Somewhere close to me a deep voice says, 'The word came down, all the way from the top. The orders are she's got to be killed, soon.' Second voice asks, 'Why some smoke-flavored old hag from the steppes . . .'"

"Old hag!" I interrupted angrily. "I am not an old hag!"

He said harshly. "I'm not finished! The first voice says, 'No hag, she's young yet.' Now, you tell me. Is there anyone else working here on B'yurngrad that answers that description? 'Smoke-flavored, steppes, young yet,' says you to me."

I couldn't answer. The words described me, and me only. "Who?" I said finally. "Who wants me dead?"

"I don't know. I couldn't find the speakers. I stayed there listening for a long time, no luck. I have no idea who or what they were. What enemies have you made while here?"

"Enemies made as whom? As the night flier, the shaman's girl? As the shaman herself after the old woman died? Since then, being a ghyrm-hunter? That last one we can answer. The ghyrm distributor probably wants all hunters off the job."

"There are a dozen hunters, at least. You're the only one fitting the description. Why only you?"

I shook my head at him. "I'm baffled, Ferni. If I've learned anything on this job, however, it's that a workman never knows how the work looks to people who see it from the outside. We carry ghyrm. That makes us devils to some. You saw how that oasthall emptied out when I was there."

"I imagined as much. That's why I said I was taking you someplace safer. Everyone around here knows who you are, what you are. They'll talk: 'Yes, the woman was here, she went off in that direction.' That's why I've gone five directions since taking off. If anybody's watching, we'll hope we lost them."

"And what is there, where we're going?"

"A lake. A forest. A waterfall. A little inn, where the Siblinghood sends people who need a long rest. A view over the grasslands. Horses."

"Horses?" I said doubtfully.

"Yes. The innkeeper keeps horses, for people to ride."

"That's new!"

"It is new, yes. Five or six years new. The Siblinghood brought in the original stock from Tercis, where they had too many. The grasslands are perfect for them. They actually eat plants the umoxen don't like, so they fit."

"Can I ride one?" I asked wonderingly.

"I should think so," he said, grinning at me.

I turned from him to look out the window of the flier. Below, the grasslands extended beyond the range of vision, a wave-rippled ocean of green, blue, silver, and almost yellow, with here and there a patch of vivid red and once in a while a copse of towering trees. I felt tears in my eyes and wondered why. It came to me after a while. Death threats or no death threats, I couldn't remember ever being this gloriously, miraculously happy.

I Am Margaret/on Fajnard

Glory, Bamber Joy, Falija, and I spent the night in the hayloft of the barn, where sheets and blankets had been laid atop the hay, and we awoke early to hear Howkel whistling as he milked Earthian goats down below. Now, where had they come from?

While combing hay out of her hair, Glory remarked, "One of the things Falija's folks said to me was that Falija would not be safe anywhere her people were known to be or known to visit. And Howkel says her people live here, so she's not safe here!"

"You haven't seen fit to mention this until now," I growled.

"I didn't remember it until now," Gloriana cried. "It never made any difference until now."

We told Howkel our dilemma at the breakfast table. He thought about it for some time before saying:

"There's a shortcut to the Thairy way-gate without going through Gibbekot country. Suppose I send a couple of the youngsters with you as guides. Good at sneakiness, youngsters. Never known one that wasn't."

"Send Maniacal and Mirabel," said the Dame. "They're sneaky, that's certain, and the longer the journey the better."

"Them's the oldest," Howkel confided. "My Dame's purely weary of wishin' they'd move on and set up on their own."

"Breakfast first," said the Dame. "Haycakes and syrup."

Midway through breakfast, Glory leaned toward me. "Did you know your face has turned a little green?"

"Did you know all your teeth were the color of grass?" I returned, without easing my pursuit of the last of the haycake around my plate. "Mighty peculiar-looking."

"You two stop it," muttered Bamber. "One of you'll say something, and the other one will pounce on it, and then no matter how high our mission, it'll all go to nonsense."

"Quite right," I agreed. "Your teeth are only slightly green, Gloriana."

"And your face hardly shows it except around your ears," Gloriana conceded.

Maniacal and Mirabel brought a wagon around to the front of the house, one seat in front and hay deeply piled in a short wagon bed behind. The three creatures pulling the wagon were leaner and taller than umoxen, with great, muscular hind legs.

"Gnar," said Maniacal. "Not as strong as umoxen for the long haul, but very fast when they need to be."

"You think they'll need to be?" asked Bamber John.

"We won't know 'til it happens, but if it does, you just burrow down in that hay and leave the rest to Mirabel and me."

We took the precaution of burying our packs in the hay to start with. Falija had said nothing all morning, and I didn't like the way she looked, her eyes unfocused and the fur on her face every which way.

"Did you have bad dreams, Falija?"

Falija nodded slowly. "I think I must have. I remember running as fast as we could away from something."

"That's a happy thought to start the day," I remarked, punching the hay to make a larger pillow. "Maniacal, where is this way-gate to Thairy?"

"First there's a long stretch of grass, then a bit of forest and a little climb. Pa Howkel told us how to find it. We won't be going near the Ghoss and Gibbekots, but we'll likely pass a few hayfolk farms. When we do, just hide 'til we get on by."

So the morning passed, us mostly lying on the hay, occasionally napping, sometimes burrowing while trying not to scratch or sneeze.

Noon came and went, as did a good part of the food Dame Howkel had packed for us.

Late afternoon had come when Mirabel said urgently, "Get down into the hay. Somebody coming."

We burrowed. Mirabel got into the wagon bed and carefully covered any parts we'd left showing. The wagon moved along, easily, not fast, then suddenly Maniacal let out a whoop and we began to clatter along the road at very high speed.

Mirabel leaned down and said, "Two humans in some kind of machine. Maniacal is heading for the woods."

"I'll bet it's Ned and Walter," mumbled Bamber Joy, around the wisps of hay that kept creeping into his mouth and nose. "Or somebody just like them. I need to see."

He tunneled through the hay until he was under the wagon seat, then pushed his head up under it where he could look out through a crack. "Not the car from Tercis," he cried. "Another one that smokes and snarls, but it's not catching up yet."

Time went by as we rushed and clattered.

"Now they're catching up to us," cried Mirabel.

"Look up there ahead," growled Maniacal. "What do you see across the road?"

"Oooh," she said. "Gizzardile. Oooh, Manny, that's the biggest one I ever saw!"

"Hold on tight," shouted Maniacal. "Go, gnar, go . . ."

Our speed increased, the rattling turned into a chattering hum, the vehicle behind us sped up as well as we flew down the ruts. I had tunneled up next to Bamber Joy, and we both saw the cylindrical something or other, like a mighty tree trunk, down across the road. No forest anywhere near, and the buggy was flying toward it, was going to hit it at full speed . . .

"Fly, gnar, fly," yelled Maniacal, and the buggy flew, or at least it leapt, following the trajectory of the three animals that took off as one in a long arc across the gizzardile, landing beyond it with a great swaying and crashing as though the wagon were falling apart.

Bamber and I quickly looked behind us. The pursuing vehicle was closing on the gizzardile, which suddenly and quite quickly, considering its bulk, reared its forward end and turned it to face the noisy machine. The fin that had lain along the creature's back rose into a huge fan, numerous legs stretched out on either side, and before the vehicle could stop, turn, or maneuver in any way, the gizzardile chunked its huge, lumpy lower part directly into its path, and when the machine struck, collapsed its higher parts on top with a great shriek of rending metal.

"Whoa, gnar," said Maniacal.

"They were after me," Falija remarked. "That must be what I dreamed about, but they didn't catch us after all!"

Maniacal was out of the wagon, unhitching the Gnar.

"Don't we still need them?" Bamber asked.

"When good creatures do a great good thing," said Maniacal, "we don't ask them to spend their strength doin' more when our own strength will suffice. So Pa Howkel has always told me. They jumped their weight, and ours, and the wagon's over that critter. That's a story for tellin' at the Haymeet, many a year from now . . ."

"Nobody'll believe it," remarked Mirabel.

"Not if you tell it, but they know I'm no tale maker. See yonder? Just above those trees? That's where we're going, and these good creatures can find their way home by theirselves while that gizzardile is occupied. Since gizzardiles eat most everything including rocks, it'll be a while."

"We won't make it before night," I said.

"No," said Mirabel, "but there's a little cave up there, above the lake, where Pa's camped out many a time. We can get there by full dark, and there's both late and early moons." He pointed high above us, where a half-moon was in bud, to the west, where a crescent sailed like a little boat toward the horizon, while far to the east an almost full moon blossomed over the hills.

"How'll you get your wagon back?" I asked. I had been thinking to myself that for a wagon that looked as rattletrap as this one did, it had held up extremely well: more to it, perhaps, than met the eye—just as with Pa Howkel.

Mirabel said offhandedly, "Pa'll bring an umox team to get the wagon when the gnar get home without it."

And with that, we shouldered our packs and made for the line of forest, which was now no great distance ahead. Behind the forest lay the mountains, slowly thrusting up to cover the last of the sunset yellow sky while rosy clouds gathered like bridesmaids, and a diamond star pulsed against the high blue, like a signal light someone had lit in a window.

"What star is that?" asked Bamber Joy.

Maniacal looked up at it, cocking his head. "That's the summer star. That's the star that shines on Thairy."

I Am M'urgi, with Fernwold on B'yurngrad

The inn was very much as Ferni had described it. The rooms were very simple, paneled in smooth, aromatic wood. In our suite, I luxuriated in a hot, foamy bath that smelled of flowers and found myself becoming somewhat resentful toward the Siblinghood.

"They never mentioned this place. They never told me I was entitled to a vacation. They never suggested I might need a rest. I'm still digging soot out of the creases in my skin!"

"I can't see any," remarked Ferni from the other end of the tub. "Not anywhere. I'm looking very closely."

I flushed and submerged. When I came up again, I grinned at him. "Behave yourself, or I'll do a chant on you."

"What is that?" he asked.

"What is what?"

"I've never understood that shaman business. The chants, what you did with the girl at the oasthall. What they call night flying. All that."

I twisted my wet hair into a knot atop my head and let the water lap at my chin. "You really want to know?"

"I don't suppose I can *know*, but I'd like to understand."

I sat up a little. "All right. The first lesson the shaman taught me was belief. Before I could do anything I had to believe that here, around us, is an insubstantial entity that senses everything. It wraps around stars, it surrounds worlds, moons, comets, all the trash and dust that's out in space, encompasses all races of creatures no matter how small, is everywhere. It pushes things together to separate one thing from another; it forms boundaries. The shaman calls that entity Kuzh. We'd say 'the Holder.' "

"The Keeper?" murmured Ferni in a strange voice.

"The Keeper? Yes, that would convey the same meaning. The shaman taught me to believe by showing me that the existence of the . . . 'Keeper' was the only explanation for what she could do. Once I'd really perceived what she could do, once I'd tried to think of anything else that would explain it, I believed, I learned to touch it, go into it, move inside it, not with my body, just with my senses. Kuzh is insubstantial, so bodies can't move in it, but senses can. Whatever senses you have, you can use them there to learn what's going on. The shaman and I used ours to prevent as much slaughter as possible among the tribes. We nudged them gradually toward something less violent. The shamans call it night flying because it's easiest to do when sensory stimulation is decreased, when it's dark. The Kuzh, the Keeper around you is not only sensing, but also reflecting the patterns of what's going on, sensing what each pattern will lead to and how long it will take. The closest times are the most accurate. That's the way we foretold and prevented massacres."

"How?" he asked.

"Sometimes just by whispering a word in someone's ear. Sometimes by asking the nearest settlements to make a raid just before war was to break out. Different ways."

"How long did it take you to learn to do that?"

I sighed. "It took me three years just to make the first contact. Another year to learn to lie on the night and go with it. Maybe two more years to pick up the sense of what was going on around me. The old woman said I was way too old to learn easily, a child of three or four is better at it. Still, she got four good years out of me. Enough for us to prove that some of the tribes were running ghyrm into the settlements."

"Did you find the source of the ghyrm?"

"We came close. All we had was the pictures they had in their minds. They went down into a darkness. Someone gave them the ghyrm, and they were paid in weapons. We tried again and again to follow them when they went wherever it was. We were never there at the right time."

He laved his arms. "Do you miss it? That work?"

I felt my brow furrow. "Well, Ferni, I was generally very dirty, very stinky, no baths out on the steppes, our clothing was mostly un-cured hides, we slept itchy, we had bugs and what not. Do I miss it? Not the doing of it, no. The feeling of it, yes. That weightlessness. That was a nice feeling. But, so is this."

He grinned at me. "What do you want to do today?"

"Horses," I cried. "You promised me horses."

We rode, later on, down a forested valley where a bright, tumbling river spilled a lake into the grasslands at the foot of the hills. I ex-perimented with my posture, the saddle, the animal, trying to figure out what was possible, what was comfortable, what was least painful. Ferni had picked up considerable skill, which he patiently passed on. By noon, we were well out into the grasses, the hills some way behind us. We stopped among a scattering of small trees by the river, tied the horses, and spread out our lunch.

"I'll never get back on that animal," I snarled. "You didn't tell me it hurt."

"Only the first few times. Walk around a bit. That'll help. Have some wine. That'll help even more!"

"Oh, I'm sure being sotted would enable me to ride like the wind, for all of two steps before I fell off!" He hadn't brought enough wine to made me insensible, but he was right, it did dull the pain.

I lay back on the grasses, head propped on one hand, admiring the velvety turf and the herd of gnar some little distance away, peacefully grazing while their young leapt and pretended to fight with their front feet. We watched them for a long, contented time.

"Are they native here?" Ferni asked drowsily.

"Umm," I replied, lying back on the blanket. "What? The gnar? Yes. They're native here, but they've been transplanted to several other grassland planets. The closest one I know of is Fajnard. Only on the highlands, though. They won't stay anywhere near the Frossians."

"They're kept for wool?"

"It's more hair than wool. In the winter they grow an undercoat that's warmer than any other natural fiber known. It's not as fine as umox hair, but it's hollow, and that makes it a marvelous, lightweight insulator. The herders pull it out in the spring with combs shaped like little rakes."

"Can they be ridden?" he asked sleepily.

"No. They're very good at pulling light wagons, but their body proportions are all wrong for carrying people as horses can, or as umoxen will, even though they're very slow."

The herd went leaping away, toward the hills, in great, ground-eating bounds, and I, half asleep, wondered what had spooked them. All was silent except for the horses' teeth, chomping grass, the twitter of some small creatures in the reeds along the water, the deep breathing of us two drowsers.

The tribesmen came out of the grasses fast and low. Four of them leapt upon Ferni and held him down, tying his hands behind him, his feet together, blindfolding him. Four of them seized me up, gagged me, wrapped me in a net, and ran off into the grasses. The horses jerked wildly at their reins, whinnying and screaming.

From the net that held me I thrust my mind back to the place Ferni was. He was pushing his face against the ground, shoving the blindfold away to find himself alone. "Stupid idiot," he raged at himself. "Promised her horses. Promised to keep her safe. Damn! Where did they come from? No tribesmen nearer than a three-day ride, they told me! No danger! Don't worry!"

While he railed at himself, he was working his hands as far apart as possible so he could sit on them, work his way back, move the hands forward, damn, damn, nearly dislocated a shoulder there, never mind, go ahead, dislocate the damned thing, get the hands in front, in front, pull up the knees, get his feet through. He was thinking he had done this before, but it had been a long, long time. Now the thongs were at mouth level and he chewed them, slobbering as much as possible to get them wet, stretching the wet leather, more, more, one loop between his teeth, up and over, another loop, up and over, now loosen the whole thing. Off!

I watched him as in a dream. His hands were numb. He had to wave them, yell at them before they'd stop pricking and work. Now.

Leave the clutter by the river to mark the place. Get on the horse and follow . . .

I saw him searching, read his face: Where? No sign. No sign at all. Not a trail through the grasses. He couldn't follow a trail if he wasn't high enough to see a trail!

I sensed his frustration, fury, grief. He mounted one horse and grabbed the other's reins to lead it as he raced back the way we had come to get help.

I Am Margaret/on Fajnard

Even though we had ridden in the wagon all day, we were tired, and the moonlight was not restful. Romantic as all get-out, probably, but not helpful, except as it kept us from stumbling, falling, or running headlong into one another. Even the young ones were weary, though the hayfolk young were more accustomed to the light and the terrain than we three from Tercis. Falija was by now resting on Bamber's shoulders like a fur scarf, head hanging, half asleep.

We had been walking for some time on a trail that ran along the side of a rocky hill—one of the Mountains of Mupple, Maniacal claimed—heading toward a comfortable cave, though what made a cave comfortable had not been explained. I was second in line. Ahead of me, Maniacal was pointing at something.

"There's a light there," I said stupidly. "Is there supposed to be a light there?"

Mirabel's voice came from behind us. "The Ghoss use it sometimes."

"But not the Frossians?" I asked hesitantly.

"Never the Frossians, no," said Maniacal. He moved slowly forward, the rest of us following, our eyes darting back and forth between the rough footing and the distant flicker of firelight, crossed by a walking shadow that went, then returned in the opposite direction.

"I'll go on ahead," said Maniacal, when we were only a

short distance from the cave opening. He edged away from us and went more rapidly, stopping a few paces short of the opening to creep forward slowly, extending his neck like a telescope to peer around the nearer stones.

"What's he doing?" whispered Glory. "How does he do that?"

"We all do it," said Mirabel. "It's how we keep track of where we are in the deep grasses, put our heads up when we need to. You bony people can't do it, and I've never figured out how you manage without."

"You don't have bones?" asked Grandma.

"Only a few," said Mirabel. "Here and there, and they do wander about."

Maniacal was returning. "It's a Ghoss," he called. "He's got another Ghoss there, sleeping, but he says come ahead."

We went on. Inside the sandy cave an elderly man stood to welcome us, bowing, introducing himself. "I'm Rei. The one sleeping over there is Mar-agern. Come in, sit down. I was just heating water for tea. I know you raiders can't go long without your tea, and I happen to have some." He stopped in some confusion as he got a good look at me. "Excuse me. You're not all hayfolk. Ma'am. Ah, well. Not Ghoss, then. Not you, not the young ones. Escaped bondspeople?"

"No," I said with some asperity. "I'm Margaret. This is my granddaughter, Gloriana, and her friend, Bamber Joy. And this is Falija."

Rei bowed deeply to Falija, still curled around Bamber's neck. "Gibbekotkin," he murmured. "Welcome. Do you come from the city?"

Bamber squatted to let Falija jump down. She sat on her haunches, eyes moving around the cave as though to penetrate its stone walls before she turned her gaze back to the man who had welcomed us. "We thank the Ghoss, Rei," she said. "These people came with me through a way-gate from the planet Tercis. We are bound for the way-gate that leads to Thairy. We were pursued, our lives threatened. A gizzardile intervened and saved us inadvertently. We are very weary and grateful for your help."

The Ghoss bowed again. "As our ancestors promised yours, we will do whatever we can do."

"A little rest would be most welcome," I said, trying to swallow a yawn.

We sat around the fire. Tea was poured and another pot heated and brewed. Maniacal distributed the food we had left, but we only nibbled at it, too tired to be hungry. The Ghoss did not question us, but he stared at me with particular intensity.

Finally, intercepting this gaze, Falija said, "We are on a quest, Ghoss Rei. There are creatures about who don't want us to make it. They were on Tercis, they are here on Fajnard, possibly they will be on Thairy. The quest is to walk the seven roads that are one road."

"A riddle?" suggested Rei.

"You could say that, yes," I said. Some color had returned to my face, and I felt both slightly strengthened and in need of going someplace private. I shifted uncomfortably.

"Around the corner, there," suggested Rei. "You'll find what you need."

Seeing my startled look, Mirabel said, "They're telepathic, the Ghoss. They can tell what you're thinking or needing."

"Ah," I said, at a loss for any real words and not at all sure I liked people being aware of when I needed to pee. Around the corner was a wooden seat over a crevice in the rock as well as a waist-level stone hollow constantly filled by a seep from above. I washed my face and hands, feeling somewhat refreshed.

When I returned to the others, I had to pass the sleeping person very closely, and I looked down, to avoid stepping on him, her. I looked down, and stood, looking down, not moving, not moving at all.

"Grandma?" cried Gloriana. "What is it?"

"It's me," I answered, eyes still fixed on the sleeping form. "For the love of heaven, Gloriana, it's me."

Gloriana came to stand beside me, gaping, moving about to get a better look. "She's . . . she's younger than you, Grandma."

"She's me, the way I looked in the mirror, not all that long ago." I turned to face Rei, demanding, "Who is she?"

"Mar-agern was a bondslave sent here to Fajnard," said Rei, glancing back and forth between us. "You're right. I saw the resemblance when you came in. She came from Earth when she was about twenty-two."

"I came from Earth, when I was twenty-two."

"And your father's name was . . . ?"

"Harry Bain. And her mother's name was . . ."

"Louise Bain," said Rei.

"How did this happen?" I cried, looking from face to face. "How did this happen?"

"Shhh," said Rei. "We don't know how. Perhaps we know why . . . Gibbekot?"

"Her name?" I cried. "What's her name?"

"As I said, her name is Mar-agern," said Rei.

"Not quite close enough to be Margy," I laughed. "Or maybe it is? One of my play people. Margy. First Wilvia, then Margy. Is there to be a Naumi as well?"

"Sit down, Grandma," Glory urged. "You're very pale. This is all very weird and strange, and you're allergic to strange."

Bamber took one arm, Glory the other, and they sat me down near the fire, where I shook my head silently, slowly, hoping to negate the existence of everything in the neighborhood, perhaps myself included.

"Gibbekot?" asked Rei, again. "Do we know why?"

"Yes," whispered Falija. "Yes, of course. That is, perhaps, though as yet there are only two of her, and the story would demand at least seven . . ."

A low, continuous moan came from the sleeping woman. She rolled restlessly to one side, then the other, exposing the back of her head.

"What is that on the back of her head?" I demanded.

"That is a mother-mind," said Rei.

"Where did you get it?" demanded Falija harshly.

"I didn't," Rei replied. "The Gibbekot got it from the same place they got the ones they gave our ancestors. They grew them. With grown-up humans, the network just works its way up inside the bottom of the skull. The one on Mar-agern is almost absorbed. She'll wake within another few hours." He sighed deeply, tiredly. Evidently he had been under as much stress as we had.

Falija spoke to Glory and me. "It's as I told you. Nothing to be afraid of."

Rei said, "You said there was a story about seven?"

"There is a story about a man who spoke to a fish," said Falija, beginning the tale.

I lay down, all at once, before I simply collapsed. My eyes flickered. "Excuse me if I don't listen, Falija, but I've heard the story, and I am very tired."

"Sleep," said Gloriana. "It's okay. We'll keep an eye on things, won't we, Bamber, Maniacal?"

They spoke together. "Oh, yes." "We will."

I heard Falija's voice going on with the story, saw the light of the fire flickering on the cave wall, saw Maniacal and Mirabel curl up against the wall to sleep, later felt Gloriana and Bamber Joy lie down on either side of me, probably to keep me warm. Then I didn't see anything or feel anything for quite some time.

I Am M'urgi/on B'yurngrad

I woke to the terror of being blind and speechless, or, as I admonished myself after a moment's panic, blindfolded and gagged. Nothing wrong with my senses, just my surroundings. I was being carried in some kind of sling or net through grasses that rustled. I had seen tribesmen carrying butchered game this way, all the meat piled into the hide and slung on a pole between two of them. Were these tribesmen? Probably. The danger Ferni had warned me of? Probably not. If the goal had been to kill me, they could have done it at once, while I was sleeping.

So, what did they want?

I took a deep, deep breath and let it out slowly. Then another, and another yet. I was not in pain, which made it easier, though I had learned to do it even when in pain. The jostling didn't help, but I could overcome that. Stillness. Inside, the stillness. I straightened myself in the sling and brought my head forward, onto my chest. Now, now, now let the spirit find the knowing cloud, the being, the great register, the omnipresence, the all, now, now, now lie forward upon the cloud and look down . . .

Five of them. Two carrying, two running alongside to spell them when they were tired, one in front to lead them along the back trail through the grasses which led, led, led there, inside the forest, a temporary camp. Small huts covered in hides. A campfire circle with a spit above it. No women. One of the huts new, the scraped hides bright and clean, and a narrow bed and chair inside. They didn't use chairs, or beds. The furnishings were for me, as were the chains attached to a stout pole that ran up the middle of the hut, buried at the bottom, tied to the framework at the top. So. If I proved unwilling, they intended to keep me by force. For someone? For something?

Back, back to the five runners, skulls painted on their faces, death-and-honor tribesmen. Each face, carefully, carefully, not that one, nor that, nor either of these others. The one in front. Yes. Very possibly. He had changed a good deal in the intervening years. He was no longer a boy. Now he was a man, scarred from battle.

Could I find the time trail that led to him? I drifted, searching, there he was, there the woman who had tried to poison his father. There the woman was, slain, as the old shaman had foretold. There was the father, slain in his turn, and others, over and over, leaving only this one and a scatter of other youngsters. He took them. He wove them. He made them a tribe. They captured women. They fathered children. Here he was, planning this raid. The ghostwoman, he said to them. The ghostwoman who saved the life of my father. She is here, nearby. All the tribes know I want her, that I will pay for her. Someone has seen her. He will lead us to her, for gold.

Where did a tribesman get gold? I flew on the word, on the image, the warm gleam, the soft shine, searching, finding it at last, an ancient place, buried under a landslide, tunneled now by avid hunters, guarded now by members of the tribe . . . So. They had found some ancient, wonderful city here on B'yurngrad, where no city had ever been found, and they had burrowed into it like rats. He had paid someone to find me, and he himself had come to get me, and his motive was not murder.

I looked around at the landmarks, the mountains, where the stars stood, then fled back, back to my body, which had by now been carried near to the forest camp. The bodiless search had taken hours.

They entered the camp. I was untied, unblindfolded. I stood up arrogantly. "Bring me watah," I demanded. "I will go in mah own place." And I strode into the hut I had seen, finding it as I had seen it.

When they brought the water I sneered. "Wahm it. I will not wash myself in cold watah." And, when they returned with warm water, I said, "Go away. I am mos angry!"

Each time I was obeyed without question, but still there were five guards set around the perimeter of the hut, still there were half a dozen others a bit farther out, keeping watch. And he who had paid for me squatted by his campfire, watching the door of the hut as a starving man might watch the prey he needed to keep life within him. Something deep and terrible was happening, and every man here knew of it.

I stayed inside long enough to make it clear I did only what I willed to do, then came out of the hut and went to the fire. "Bring my chayah," I commanded.

Someone brought the chair. I sat down, looking down on him. "Sssso," I hissed. "You clevah boy, save yr dah, ya did. Then he go muck it all, fahget taboos. He get kill fah nothin. Now you here, now you lay hans on ghos-woman, make all tha ghos angry wit you. Whas in you head, runnah?"

He ducked his head, rolling it on his neck as though it hurt. "Don wan muck it all. Din take hohses. Din hahm man. Mean no hahm. Mean no blood. Need . . . need somebody hehp us."

It was the face I had seen years ago, determined yet unsure, concerned not to make a mistake, meaning no harm, threatening no blood, no theft of horses. Ah, well, only a matter of time until the tribes got their hands on horses. Then things would become interesting.

"Tell me!" I demanded.

"Cahn you see?" he cried.

"I tiahd," I exclaimed angrily. "I soah! Ya haul me lahk meat and spec me to see? Ya tell it, den I see."

He leaned over the fire, stirring it with the stick in his hand. "I got woman," he said. "Chil'ren, l'il ones. We all got women, chil'ren. We talk to tribes, here, there. They dyin'. Dis thing comes, kills 'em."

"Ghyrm," I breathed. "You speak of ghyrm!"

"Yesss . . ." Like the hiss of a serpent, eyes wild.

"Some tribes carry ghyrm! Your dah, he carry ghyrm!"

"All," he whispered. "All tribes carry, like spear, like arrow, not hurt dah one dat carry. Now . . . now it hurt dah ones dat carry . . ."

"Tuhned on you," I said. "Evil tuhns on da one who use it, no one evah tell you dat? You not lissen to dat?"

"You a huntah," he said in accusation. "They say, you a huntah, findah. You kill the things."

I stood, thinking furiously. Yes, I was a hunter, yes, I could kill the things, but if they were widespread among the tribes . . . then all of B'yurngrad was in danger. "Not alone," I cried. "I mus bring moah my people! Moah huntahs!"

"Nah," he said, face obdurately set. "They say ahl righ one huntah. No danja foah owr folk in one huntah."

I sat down. "Yoah name?"

"Dey call me Dahk Runnah."

"Dahk Runnah. Yah go to hunt meat, yah go alone?"

"Go wit men in tribe."

"I hunt ghyrm, I hunt wit folk, mah tribe. Alone, I cahn do no good."

"Iz lie!" he said angrily. "You go alone mahny times. Mahny times!"

"I go find alone," I said. "Suah. Find one, mebbe can kill if I have special knife. Moah dan one, no. If many, cannot kill alone."

"You find. We kill'm."

"Dahk Runnah, you no can kill'm. You think you kill'm, but they still alive, on you body, tiny, so tiny you no can see'm. I need special stuffs, special folk to kill'm wit."

"Nah," he said, scowling. "Jus you. Nobody moah."

"Tha mahn," I suggested. "The mahn, he a good huntah. Wit the mahn?"

He turned from me and stalked away. Several of his men gathered around him, talking urgently, throwing angry looks in my direction.

I took up a brand from the fire, gathered wood from the pile, returned to my hut to make a tiny fire in the circle of stones. I sat beside it. They would do as they would do. I could find the ghyrm for them, but I could not kill the creatures without sanctified instruments or the machines the Siblinghood had to offer.

There was one thing I could do. If I could still do it, out of practice as I was. If Ferni . . . ah, if Ferni was only receptive.

I Am Gretamara/on Chottem

The Gardener had asked me to accompany Sophia to the city of Bray, as otherwise the heiress would be without friends or confidantes. It became obvious that more than mere friendship was needed as soon as we arrived at Stentor d'Lorn's mansion. Even though workmen had been sent ahead, we knew it would take both of us to deal with the mess.

Battalions of men and women with shovels and buckets and washtubs were still laboring to erase what a few decades of leaking roofs and inattention had allowed to accumulate. The carpets, which had been thickly strewn with Cantardene charbic powder to keep them safe from vermin, were rolled against corridor walls. These had to be taken out of doors on a day the wind blew toward the sea and there well beaten before anyone could breathe in the same room with them. Many of the furnishings were simply falling apart. The walls were mapped with continents of mildew crossed by wandering tributaries of cracks. While the entire planet of Chottem was still relatively primitive so far as plumbing and sanitation went, the mansion had been built before even that low standard had been achieved.

Sophia and I took up residency in a small house at the back of the property that had been occupied by a watchman's family, a place to which we could retreat from the stench of sewers, the reek of paint, and the chatter of hammers.

There were also interruptions. Von Goldereau d'Lornschilde dropped by frequently, usually to be told we were not home. We heard it rumored that he had challenged Sophia's identity, on the grounds that Stentor's granddaughter should be older than Sophia appeared to be. Hearing of this, Sophia summoned an attorney and sent him to Von Goldereau with a message saying that friends of the Siblinghood were granted the favor of youth, as indeed, we were, and members of the Siblinghood would be glad to testify for us. She and I had aged mostly on the Gardener's time.

A day or two after we arrived, a strange old man came with a bunch of keys, which he said Stentor d'Lorn had put in his keeping with instructions they were to be given to his granddaughter and none other.

"There's a man been looking high and low for these," the old man said. "Name's Von Goldereau d'Lornschilde."

"He didn't know you had them?" I asked him.

"No. He looked among the mighty, never thought to look among us, the little folk."

"Why did d'Lorn leave them with you?" I asked.

"Oh, I owed him a favor, ma'am. He took my son, Fessol, his name is, when he was only six years old. Stentor d'Lorn took a liking to him and sent him to another world to be educated and made into a fine gentleman. Told me if I'd keep these keys until his granddaughter came to reclaim them, she'd see I got to go there, see my boy, how wonderful a life he has."

I shivered when I heard this, for no reason except that such an act of charity was out of character for the man who had brooked no opposition from anyone during his life, and who had killed his son-in-law out of hand—as was well known in Bray. Sophia, however, took the keys without comment, asking only for the oldster's name and where he might be found, that she might properly reward him when she learned where his grandson had gone.

A goodly number of cooks and butlers and other assorted functionaries were hired and let go again before the heiress had assembled a staff that could, in her opinion, acquit itself well in opening the house to guests.

"Anytime soon?" I asked in dismay.

"Not soon, no," said Sophia almost fretfully. "I want to be an influence for good on this world, and this house . . . it works against me! I'm not comfortable in it."

No more was I. Shadows swallowed the corners; sounds chittered along the ceilings; a foul smell which was not sewers came and went at intervals. The place displayed luxury without comfort, ostentation without art. I hated it. Each day saw the arrival of people paying calls, not only people from Bray but from all the cities up and down the shore. Some of them, who hinted to Sophia's butler that they had handled her grandfather's business (wink, nod, wink), she declined to speak with personally, leaving it to the servants to put them off with evasion or hauteur or whatever worked best.

Sophia learned of a man in Bray who located people, and she hired him to find any still living who had served the house in Stentor's time. When they were ferreted out, she spoke with them, giving them generous gifts in return for information. From one of the former gatekeepers, she learned where Benjamin Finesilver's bones had been hidden. She sent for them to be moved into the tomb of the d'Lornschildes, directly above the tomb that held Stentor himself, but she planned no vengeance on those who had followed her grandfather's orders. We had both learned from the Gardener that old vengeance is like old cake: still seeming sweet, but so dry that one invariably chokes on it.

Some days, I simply had to get away from the place, and since there was always marketing to do, I took the basket and strolled down into the town to spend a few hours among the sellers of eggs, fruit, vegetables, fish—many of them things I had eaten in Swylet—and in the little alleys where stilt walkers and fire-eaters, fortune-tellers, magicians and jugglers amused the populace. One I most enjoyed was a Trajian, long-armed and long-legged, with a furred little body and a face like a sloth, a visual cross, I thought, between that animal, a teddy bear, and a monkey. He always finished his act by putting out a little table and two chairs, then seating a doll in one of the chairs, a doll dressed as a crowned king. The Trajian juggled the table, the chairs, the king, who promptly came apart in the air, arms, legs, body, head, crown, all seven parts spinning off in different directions, only to be skillfully gathered on the fly and reassembled.

Each time I saw the performer, he looked directly at me and smiled. This confused me a little. Trajians, so the Gardener had told me, kept themselves at a distance from people of other races, for they were a people many times unjustly accused of everything from laying misfortune to the spread of dread diseases.

Knowing this for the nonsense it was, I smiled at him in return, and dropped a coin in his bowl each time I went. On the fourth or fifth such occasion, I turned from leaving my gift to confront a bulky man in the livery of Von Goldereau's house, obviously drunken and belligerent. "Yul bring bad down on us," he growled, laying his hand on my shoulder, to push me back. "Y've no right smilin' at the likes of that!"

"Oh, sir," cried the Trajian. "She was only being amused at the juggling . . ."

"And y'filth, y've no right speakin' to me at all," said the ruffian, flinging out one huge arm that caught the juggler across the face.

I heard his neck snap. I felt the juggler die. Everything became very still and very hot. "You," someone cried in a great voice that echoed down the street as though a cataract had shouted in a stony canyon, the reverberations continuing as in a monstrous bell. "You have brought down bad fortune upon yourself and your house. You will leave no child; you will gain no profit; you will taste no food. From this moment, your body will shrink into nothingness, for I, the Healer, take life from you to restore what you have unjustly taken!"

And I laid my hands upon him. For one instant he looked surprised, then horrified. His eyes rolled up into his head and he fell, gurgling, his face turning white. The crowd drew away from me as I knelt beside the juggler, putting my hands on him. I felt the life flow into him, the life I had taken from that other. I felt the bone knit. I felt the heart beat beneath my hands, like that of a bird.

He opened his eyes. He said, "You look so like her, so like sweet Queen Wilvia . . ." And then he fell into sleep. He had healed completely; I knew it to be so.

A female of his kind, dressed like a princess, came from the wagon with several other of her kind. "I am the wife for whom Yarov, Juggler to the Queen of the Ghoss, paid a great price," she said. I knew it was the way of Trajian women to introduce themselves so. I nodded respectfully to her, and her people picked the juggler up and took him away.

Only when I felt the pain in my throat did I realize that great voice had been my own. When I went through the marketplace on my way home, people stood aside and lowered their heads. One or two, I touched, for they were in pain, and the anger that had moved me was still strong enough in me to heal them. The Gardener had told me of this, this avenging fury, but I had not known I could feel it. I was not sure I ever wanted to feel it again, though I knew I would not be able to withstand it.

Gradually, the workmen at the mansion accomplished their tasks. Outbuildings filled up with leftover lumber, tools, ladders, and paint. One old stable held enough powdered charbic from Cantardene to mothproof ten mansions. In time each problem was solved, each bit of wreckage was removed or repaired, each group of workmen was paid and went away. The place became orderly, clean, and quiet, and for the first time, I thought we might have time to reflect upon why Sophia had returned to Bray, what we would do about the mansion, and what she might accomplish here. Sophia, however, had a remaining concern that she mentioned to me over breakfast:

"I've been considering this discomfort we feel. You know, we haven't even looked in the cellars."

I shuddered, thinking first of the effusive old man who had brought the keys. The cellars could not be in any better condition than the rest of the house and might be worse. Sophia ignored my shudder and went to get the keys, which were heavy and unnecessarily intricate. Or so we thought until we had penetrated past the second door, at which point we went back and quietly closed and locked the doors behind us in order to prevent inadvertent interruption.

"Where did he get these?" demanded Sophia, holding out a ruby the size of a pigeon's egg, the topmost from a keg of similar stones. "I've never seen jewels like these."

"There's a world's ransom here," I replied, wishing desperately that the Gardener were with us.

"Let's just look quickly, then close it all up," Sophia urged. "This isn't something we can deal with now."

Even our quick look disclosed endless stores of treasure, none of it in the least corrupted, not even the fabrics: cloth of gold embroidered with emeralds, cloth of silver dotted with sapphires, cloth of diamond in the original bolt, woven from crystalline thread as made only by the Pthas and never by any race since.

"An old city," I mused, on recognizing this latter fabric from a sample the Gardener had once shown me. "Someone has found a great treasure-house of ancient times."

Beyond the last door, triple-barred, triple-bolted, triple-locked, we came upon an unlit tunnel where a lantern was set upon a table next to a stoppered bottle of lamp oil and a cane with a protruding sword tip. This last, I picked up as I followed Sophia, who carried the newly filled and lit lantern. The tunnel had not been formed by men. It was part of a natural cave, with stalactites hanging from the ceiling.

"He found this place," I said with certainty. "He had the rest of the cellars dug around it, but this one he found!"

"Yes," I said sadly. "And he had the doors built, then closed in the men who built them." I followed her pointing finger to the cluster of desiccated flesh and protruding bones against the wall. Four men, or what had been men. They wore the shackles of bondsmen, and they had written their fate in their own blood on the floor beside them. *"He does not want anyone to know what is here."*

Turning aside from this pathetic message, we stopped momentarily, for the cavern split into a Y, each arm blocked by an iron grille before a viscid, quivering curtain. To the left, the curtain was pale, lit with rainbow gleams. To the right the curtain was obsidian, not quite opaque, with shadows moving in it. Scattered folds of yellowed paper and the dried corpses of weirdly shaped creatures had penetrated the grille and were stuck to the walls and the floor before the dark curtain, some of them outside the grille. Moved by an instinctive revulsion, I used the tip of the sword to flick the creatures through or into the curtain of light, only to see them flair and vanish into nothing. Meantime Sophia picked up one of the papers, unfolded it, and read:

"'Four thar of gems for each little human male.'" And another. "'A qualux of woven gold for half a dozen children, very young.'

"What was he doing?" cried Sophia, a whispered cry, full of horror. She picked up the other papers and unfolded them, reading them out:

"'Why don't you answer! Five thar of gems for each little one. We need many!'

"'Why don't you answer!'

"'Why don't you answer!'

"'We don't have enough little human ones! We must have more! Answer or we will seek business with humans elsewhere on Chottem! We will send *them* to suck you dead.'"

I put my hand on Sophia's arm, silencing her. "Shh, look there!"

Sophia looked at the dark curtain where a deeper shadow was being cast by something passing there, a thing with several legs, at least four arms, and a limber body that writhed like a snake.

I took the papers from Sophia's hand, picked up the others that were scattered about, and said, "We are in danger here. We must send word to the Gardener! And we must relock all these doors and hide the keys, for what may come, indeed, what may already have come through this gate is something that must get no farther into the house."

We passed the old bones on the way out. I did not mention the message written in blood, which Sophia had not seen. Stentor had not merely left his workmen to starve. He had beaten them first. Both of us were pale and shivering when we returned to the upper floors of the mansion. "This is an evil house," said Sophia. "I thought so when I saw it, telling myself that it was only because it was dirty and unkept. Well, we have cleaned it and mended it and set it in order, and it remains evil. What am I to do?"

"For now, nothing," I said, though my aversion was as great as her own. "I agree, it is an evil place. Instead of moving into the mansion as we planned, you and I can continue living in the little house in the back garden. Let us hide these keys, and meantime I'll tell the Gardener what we've found."

That night I sat up very late writing a long letter describing what we had found below and enclosing the strange notes we had picked up from the floor. I knew that when she left us in Bray, she had planned to go on to many distant places, seeking information. I knew she could not keep close watch upon us at the same time. Still, I hoped she was within reach. I went to a back gate that opened upon the graveled alley used by tradesmen and collectors of trash. A horseman waited there, and I put the letter in his hand, whispering, "Quick as may be." He was her messenger. She had told me he would be there in case of emergency.

The next day Sophia told the housekeeper we would not be moving from the little house in the garden. The housekeeper bowed politely and said nothing. What difference did it make to her where the mistress slept or dined? If truth be told, the servants probably thought it spoke well of her, for all of them disliked being in the house of Stentor d'Lornschilde after dark.

I Am M'urgi/on B'yurngrad

When Ferni could not find my trail, he returned frantically to the inn where we had been staying and sent messages off in six directions asking for aid from the Siblinghood. He had returned his borrowed flier to the Order after we arrived at the inn, so he spent the rest of a frustrating day attempting to locate another one, meantime assuring himself that if the abductors had wanted me dead, they would have killed me where I slept at the riverside. He concluded, as I had done: They wanted me for something else; therefore, I was alive.

By the time he found an available flier, it was already dark. Since he would not be able to see the trail until morning, he ate a tasteless meal and lay down, requiring of himself the long discipline that would clear his mind and let him sleep. Not long into that sleep, a dream insinuated itself, a dream of me standing before him, taking his hands in mine, chanting. In the dream, he concentrated upon that chant, listened to it with all his attention.

"I am well," I sang. "I am here, not far away. They who hold me are tribesmen. They believe I alone can kill the many ghyrm among them. I have told them I need help, but they say no, so you must summon the help I need. Go to the Siblinghood. Tell them. Get from them all the things I will need, including a finder. Be sure you bring knives. Fly here at dawn tomorrow, bringing help. Now waken and remember!"

And with that he awoke, the whole thing clear in his mind: how I sounded, what the camp looked like and where it was located, what I needed, what he had to do! "Bless you, old shaman woman, wherever you are now," he muttered as he dressed himself. "You taught her well!" I was still there, watching, when he said it.

It was not long after midnight. We had not brought ghyrm-hunting supplies to the inn with us, but a Siblinghood outpost was only a short flight away. When he arrived there, however, it did him little good, for a very junior member was in charge who seemed to know little or nothing about where anyone in authority might be or when such a person might return. Ferni passed on the new ghyrm information to be added to that already in the file, then he requisitioned everything useful the more helpful supply officer would let him have, including a finder, though Ferni himself had not been certified to use one.

"Don't you even try to use it," the supply officer instructed sternly. "They do wicked things to the minds of those who are not inured to them. Leave the cover on the basket port. Land as near to her as you can get, put all the stuff out of the flier, then get out of there. Don't try to rescue her. Wait until we get set up to do that. I know M'urgi, and she can take care of herself. She knows the tribes as well or better than anyone else in the Siblinghood."

All this I saw, heard, knew of while lying on the bosom of the night. By dawn he had packed my personal belongings from the inn and was already hovering over the grasslands by the river. At first light, the shadow trail showed dark among the grasses, and he had not followed it far before he saw the smoke of our campfires. He hovered, waiting. I emerged from a hut, tribesmen gathered around me. I pointed upward at the flier, then down at the nearest clearing, and beckoned.

He put the flier down, took the supplies out, and laid them at the edge of the clearing. The last thing he moved was the basket with the finder in it, setting it carefully among the other tools of the ghyrm-hunter's trade. He returned to the flier, saw me come out of the trees among the tribesmen, saw me wave at him with a lifting motion, which he obeyed. As he turned the flier away, he saw the men carrying the supplies back toward their camp. He was wondering, I think, whether they would move the camp at once to keep him from finding it again. No doubt he knew I would lead him to them again if they did so.

On the ground, I supervised the arrangement of my supplies.

"In my own place," I demanded, pointing to the kit that held my personal things. Then at the basket, "That! Don touch that. I move it ovah on rocks, away from us. Don go near that!"

"I wahn see," said their leader, reaching for the clamps that held the lid. "I see firs, no hahm."

"Ssssss," I hissed. "You see, you die! I see, I die. You wahch!"

I opened the port on the basket. The tentacle came out, reaching, moving side to side with a sound like the slithering of snakes. The men backed off, muttering among themselves. The smell reached them, and they went farther away. After a long minute, I took a newly delivered knife from its sheath and held it toward the tentacle, which screamed an ear-shattering sound and retreated into its basket. I closed the port and turned, hand on the lid clamps of the basket. "Now you wan see?"

Though the leader shook his head, he was obviously not content. "You hab this why?" he demanded.

I smiled sweetly at him. "Is findah, Dahk Runnah. Is findah ob ouder ghyrm. You say I find, you kill'm. Ah don dink so. I dink when ah find, you *dry* kill'm, dey kill you."

"What we do?" he cried. "Mus do sompin!"

"We mus do sompin, yea, yea, sompin. But you wahn muck it? No? Den we dalk. We plahn. We dalkin' much by the fiah. Now you go, get yoah people. Bring dem heah. I look dem ober, see dey hab no ghyrm, show you how knife wuk, an we make plahn."

After more discussion, more argument, finally settled by Dark Runner, the tribesmen agreed to do as I asked, and two of them set out across the grasses to fetch the rest of the tribe. I, meantime, with a fine display of hauteur, told the ones remaining I was not to be disturbed, retired to my hut, rolled myself in the blankets provided there, reminded myself of a shaman's discipline, and fell instantly asleep.

Meantime Ferni—as I learned later—though less worried than formerly, was no less agitated, for he had run headlong into an uncommon and frustrating blockage in the normal operation of the Siblinghood. He had visited two other posts, saying he needed help, but the only people on duty were people who couldn't authorize it; the people who could authorize it were somewhere else, having a mysterious meeting with someone or something important; they would get back to him.

In a fury of stamping about and muttering, "Well, if that's the way they're going to be, the hell with them." His thoughts turned, as they frequently did, to Naumi. He would give up on the Siblinghood, for the moment at least, and go to Thairy for help. As Naumi had pointed out, he was only two days away, and Ferni knew I would be quite safe for two days, or for ten times that. Which did not mean he would put off rescuing me any longer than necessary, but which did mean he could take the time without feeling he had forsaken me.

By midafternoon, he was on his way. Half a day later he was at the transshipment point, where he rented a bed for a few hours and caught the earliest possible ship that would drop him at Point Zibit at noon, midnight, dawn, he didn't bother to find out which. He did, however, have a hope that not only Naumi would be there but also the rest of the talk-road crew. Ferni had a high opinion of their joint abilities, and just maybe, they could come up with something new about the ghyrm.

I Am Margaret and
Mar-agern on Fajnard

On Fajnard, when I, Margaret, woke in the morning, warm between Gloriana and Bamber Joy, I sat up to confront a younger self who was crouched at my feet, staring intently into my face.

"Margy?" I said.

"Mar-agern," said the other, in my—our voice. "Who're you?"

I looked around. Rei, the Ghoss, was rolled in blankets, sound asleep next to the wall. Maniacal and Mirabel had already gone, probably back to Howkel's house. Gloriana and Bamber still slept. Among all these sleepers, my other self had wakened and found herself duplicated. She was younger, thinner, and more muscular than I. Her skin was darkened by the sun, her hair bleached almost white and cut very short. Her hands were a laborer's hands, hard and somewhat gnarled.

"We," I said carefully, slowly, "are both Margaret. I don't know how, or why. We both left Earth at the same age, we both had the same parents. I assume we will both remember the same things, up until the time we left Earth."

The Mar-agern one of us thought. What thing might two of us have shared? Well, one at least this other would not have forgotten. "Who was my . . . our lover?"

"Bryan," I answered. "He volunteered to go to Tercis if I would marry him. I accepted his offer."

"I refused him," Mar-agern said. "I didn't think it was fair to him."

"Neither did I," I replied, "but I accepted and spent my life trying to make it up to him."

"I was shipped as a bondslave, here, to Fajnard. Among the Frossians."

"We speak Frossian," I said. "Fairly well."

"I speak it a good deal better than fairly well," said Mar-agern, her lips curving into a wry smile. "I'm also quite an expert on umoxen."

"I know nothing about them," I confessed. "You seem to be younger than I am."

"They told us about that," said Mar-agern. "It's the wormholes. Different ones take different amounts of time. Some even go back in time, getting there."

"Yes," I said. "Tercis is one of those."

We sat for a while, staring at one another, wondering.

Gloriana rolled over, and said, "Good morning, Grandma." Then, to Mar-agern, "You never were my grandma, so I'll just call you by your name. Good morning, Mar-agern."

"Mar-agern," said Bamber, sitting up and yawning. "The Gibbekot gave you a mother-mind, did you know that?"

"Know what?" Mar-agern asked in surprise.

"You don't know yet?" came a voice from above—Falija. She had been curled up on a rock shelf some distance above our heads, and we had not seen her until that moment. "Well, there will be a book here, somewhere. Glory, I think it's over there in that pile of things by the wall."

Gloriana went to find it, brought it back, and handed it to me, and I looked Mar-agern in the face as I read the first page. "'Our word for insight is *Ghoss*.'"

While I read to Mar-agern, Bamber and Gloriana chopped kindling, raked the ashes from the coals, added splints of firewood, and blew the flames to life before hanging a pot of water on the spit above it. Rei, awakened by the noise, got up, folded up his blankets, went around the corner, and emerged moments later with his hair combed and his face washed. By the time the three of them had breakfast cooked, I had finished the first reading of the book, and Mar-agern was reading it again to herself, myself, on the ledge outside the cave entrance.

"Will it be as hard for her as it was for you?" Gloriana asked Falija.

"Probably not," Falija said, bounding from stone to stone down the wall. "She's spent a lot of time with the Ghoss, and they've got mother-memories, though theirs go back only to the time they received them from the Gentherans."

Outside, Mar-agern laid the book aside, put both arms around her knees, and rocked to and fro, making an unpleasant grating sound in her throat.

"On the other hand," said Falija from behind me, "I suppose it might be harder."

"Take her this," said Rei, handing Gloriana a mug of tea. "The Gibbekot who brought the mother-mind said it might help."

Gloriana took the tea to Mar-agern and coaxed her into drinking some of it before sitting beside her to talk about nothing in particular until Mar-agern stopped rocking and moaning. Falija came out, sat down on Mar-agern's other side, and said, in her own language, "You're doing very well. Much better than I did."

Mar-agern responded in the same language, "Really! I feel like a plether sat on me!"

Gloriana sniffed, saying, "Well, if you two are going to converse privately, I'll just have a bite more breakfast," as she returned to the cave.

I greeted her with a question. "I don't suppose I'm just dreaming, am I?"

"Sorry, Grandma. No. She's really you. And she isn't. She doesn't know me or anything about me, so she isn't Grandma. But she's like you, like a sister, maybe."

"Our . . . mission? Our quest? Is she part of it?"

"Falija thinks she has to be. Remember, she said something last night . . . that there had to be seven of you."

I felt myself turn pale, and I whispered, mostly to myself, "Seven. I can't believe it. Where could they be? Who would they be?" And even then, I knew who they would be. There had always been seven of me, of us.

"Maybe where we're going," Gloriana answered. "Where the way-gate goes, to Thairy."

"And the way-gate is where?"

"Rei says Maniacal told him where it was before they left early this morning. Not far from here."

I said nothing more, just put my nose in my cup of tea and kept it there, using the fragrant steam as a barrier between myself and whatever was going to happen next. Eventually, I said, "Gloriana, I thought you told me Falija's people sought you out by name. How did I get involved?"

Bamber Joy looked up from his pack. "Probably Gloriana was just the door that led to you. She'd be more willing to take on a pet cat than you would, Grandma. She'd be more open to strangeness than you would. If whoever set this up wanted to get to you, they could do it best by going through Gloriana."

"Falija didn't even ask me to come along," I said.

Gloriana grinned. "Falija is smart. She knew you'd offer. If you hadn't, she'd have made some reason you should. Something inside would have rung a bell or set off an alarm, and she'd have made sure you were with us. Are you scared or something?"

"Scared. Yes. Not frightened out of my wits, as I was yesterday, but quite apprehensive. Aren't you?"

Gloriana shook her head. "I don't see why! We escaped from Ned and Walter. We avoided the gizzardile. We met Howkel's people, and that was fun. So far nothing awful has happened."

I shook my head, drawing a deep breath. "Child, if someone set this up, all this weirdness and marvel, believe me, they weren't doing it just so we could meet the Howkel family, amusing though they may be! The reason has to be a big reason, and big reasons in my limited experience almost always mean very big risks. I remain apprehensive. Now, I'm going to wash my face, then I think we'd better be going. If my other half wants to go, that is. She may not, you know."

Indeed, Mar-agern did not.

"I know nothing about this," Mar-agern said. "Rei said we were going to Gibbekot country."

"I am Gibbekot," Falija said firmly. "I was sent to gather you people up and solve a great riddle. You wouldn't be here, right in our way, if you weren't meant to come with us!"

"I don't see that at all," Mar-agern said, with a shrug. "As a matter of fact, I can't think at all! My head is suddenly full of things I seem to know without ever having known them. It's very difficult, very strange."

Falija frowned for some time before saying, "Mar-agern. Let us sit out there on the ledge in the sun and talk. There are things you need to know, stories you need to hear. Then, when we have talked, you will be more comfortable with your situation. It really is a far better one than you were in just a few days ago, marked for death, as Rei says."

Rei, who had been outside for a while, came in to add his own point of view. "By all means talk with the Gibbekot, Mar-Mar, but the Ghoss say the Gibbekot here on Fajnard want you to go with the travelers. They have omens of consequentiality."

While Falija talked, Mar-agern simply sat on the ledge, umoxlike, head shaking as the umox seemed to do when they didn't like a situation. I knew how she felt, as though she, I, were being stretched in several directions at once.

I went out to put my arm about my other self, saying, "Surely it's better to move toward something than to run away from something."

Rei said, "She's right, Mar-Mar. The way-gate is only a short way. Take the things you need from here, and we'll go."

"You're coming with us?"

"No. There's a party of Frossians coming up the canyon where we walked. Some of our people are going to lead them astray. You should be on your way before I leave."

Though Mar-agern was still unconvinced and certainly unwilling, there was no more argument. We collected our belongings and set out upon a narrow path up the mountain, Rei in the lead, a coil of rope over his shoulder.

To me, Margaret, rope meant climbing or some other unpleasantness, and my already glum mood deepened considerably. When we reached a fork, Rei stood for a moment, recollecting what Maniacal had told him before choosing the route. This happened twice more, on increasingly faint trails, until we stood at a narrow cleft in a rock wall that we edged through one by one . . .

. . . and came out on a rock ledge edged by a line of stones. Near enough to wet us with spray, a waterfall plunged into a lovely pool among green mosses. Dead ahead was another rock cleft holding a black, wavering pool.

"We've been here," cried Glory. "We came in this way."

"And there's the way we go out," said Bamber, nodding to our right where a pale light pool glimmered at the back of a rocky recess. "I didn't see that the last time we were here."

"We never came this far across the ledge," said Falija. "We jumped down below." She turned to Rei, asking, "How did we get back here?"

"If you went down there," he replied, pointing below, "you must have taken the lowland road that leads in a long curve east and north to the hayfolk. When you left there, you took a road that went straight across the curve you'd made before, like the string of a bow."

He turned to Bamber, taking the coil of rope from his shoulder. "I'm told it's narrow in there. You'll need to remove your packs and drag them through. The Gibbekot say you'll need this rope at the other end, where the gate comes out in Thairy. They also say their people live on the heights in Thairy, but the people you need to connect with will be down by the sea."

He waited while we filed in, Gloriana first, then the rest of us.

I came out into a sandy cave, on Gloriana's heels. We stumbled just far forward enough to escape being knocked down as the others came through behind us. Birds murmured above our heads, drowsy sounds, as though settling for sleep, and the light on the cavern wall glowed red. Behind us, the way-gate we had just left was black and ominous. To our left, the tunnel curved around a corner, and there was another light-filled gate that went on to somewhere else. The two were really only a few steps apart, as they had been on Fajnard.

The cave entrance was the other way, a narrow slit facing west where a red fire of sun hung above a glistening sea. The cave entrance was midway up a sheer drop of stone that ended below us in a tree-edged clearing with a road running across it and upward to the right.

"Without wings, we won't get much farther," said Gloriana.

"That's what the rope's for," Bamber Joy explained. "Though I don't know how the Gibbekot knew about it."

Falija said, "They probably use this way-gate all the time. We have people here on Thairy."

"Of course," I said, in a falsely pleased voice. "Isn't it nice to have one thing make some sense!"

"Tie the rope to that rock pillar," Falija directed. "We can lower Grandma and Mar-agern, then we'll knot the rope so Glory and Bamber can climb down."

"I do not need to be lowered," said Mar-agern, rather offended. "I can climb down the rope."

"Well then, you can help the children lower me," I said crisply. "I do need lowering."

When all of us but Falija had reached the clearing, she untied the rope and leapt from one invisible foothold to another, joining Bamber and Glory, who had already penetrated the thin line of trees at the edge of the clearing to look down another precipice to the sea.

"Town down there," cried Glory. "Looks like the road goes all the way down."

Falija was staring longingly at the upward road, as though trying to find some excuse to go in that direction. Her people, at least her kind of people, were up there, but I could tell she was being urged away from them just as she had been on Fajnard. With a tiny whine of frustration, she turned toward the downward road. I put my hand on the little person's shoulder. "You must be as confused as we are."

"It would be nice to rest," Falija said. "It would be nicer to talk to someone who really knows what's happening."

"Perhaps no one knows, and we have to figure it out for ourselves. At the moment, I'm thankful there's a town down there. Maybe we can sleep in beds tonight."

"If the people there are hospitable," said Mar-agern. "I haven't any money. We don't even know what's used for money here."

I exchanged glances with Gloriana, who felt for the money bag in the lining of her jacket, and said, "I'm sure we'll think of something."

The road rose to a shallow crest, and from there went steadily downward in an easy, curving, unwearying slope that turned sharply to the right at the bottom. From there it went only a short, straight distance toward a pair of open gates guarded by uniformed young men, stiff as broom handles. Nearby stood a cluster of older people, three men and two women, talking among themselves.

As we came closer we heard one of the women crying out, "Look there." She was pointing upward along the coast at a far-off speck against the now-crimson clouds. "That must be Ferni's flier! He'll be here very soon, Naumi."

"Now me?" I said. "Naumi? Wasn't that what we called . . ."

Mar-agern nodded. "I remember. It was indeed."

The two of us walked toward the group, I called out, "Naumi! Is that your name?"

The person I was hailing turned with a polite smile and froze, as though he were seeing a ghost. "My name is Naumi Rastarong." He paused, swallowed. "And yours and your sister's, ma'am?"

"Margaret," I said. "This is Mar-agern."

"Are we related in some way?" Naumi asked.

One of his friends came up beside him, and Naumi said, "Caspor, they look like family, don't they?"

Caspor said, "I could work up the odds on their not being, but the resemblance is astonishing. That dip in the upper lip, and the slant of the eyebrows!"

"And their noses," said another friend. "Even the same color eyes!"

Naumi said, "Jaker, let's introduce you four. Flek, Jaker, Caspor, Poul."

We all nodded somewhat distractedly at the two men and two women, and I asked, "Do you remember coming from Earth?"

Naumi cocked his head, obviously wondering at this. "No. As a matter of fact, my earliest memories start at about age twelve, when I survived some kind of accident and was put in the care of my foster father, here on Thairy."

"Age twelve," said Mar-agern. "When the proctor came."

"And nothing happened," I replied, "but I . . . that is, we always felt something had."

"Maybe something did happen," Falija offered, "and you just didn't know about it." She looked up to find five pairs of eyes staring at her as though she had grown another head. "Did I say something odd?" she asked.

Flek stammered, "It's just . . . we've never seen . . . we thought you were . . . I mean . . ."

"They thought you were somebody's pet," said Gloriana indignantly. "This is Falija, our guide. Her people are called the Gibbekot. A great many of them live up there, on the heights, or so she tells me."

"We thought that's where the Gentherans live," said Jaker. "And we've never seen any of them. We have no idea what they look like."

"Rather like me," said Falija. "Only larger." She turned toward Naumi. "Excuse me if I am impolite in not using your correct title, but you must be one of the people we're looking for."

"What people are those?" Naumi asked.

"The people who began life as Margaret Bain, who were split off from her in some way, at some time in her life, and who seem to be scattered across a sizable chunk of the galaxy. Margaret and Mar-agern were split at age twenty-two. You, Naumi, were evidently split off at twelve."

"But he's male!" Mar-agern snapped.

Falija said soothingly, "My mother-mind tells me that in all gendered races, one sex always shares some of the traits of the opposite sex. Perhaps he, Naumi, was split off from among the most male traits Margaret Bain possessed. Or maybe it really doesn't matter very much."

"This all seems very unlikely," I growled peevishly. "Just when I get used to something, the ground shifts."

A noise from above attracted our attention to the flier, which was approaching a landing pad not far from us. Naumi beckoned everyone to follow him, and we arrived just as a lean, dark-haired person came from the flier, threw his arms around Naumi, smiled across his shoulder at the others, and froze at the sight of Mar-agern, just as Naumi had done.

"Margy?" I thought he said.

"Mar-agern," she corrected him.

"But you . . . she . . . Naumi! Except for the hair, she looks exactly like M'urgi! They could be twins! What's going on?"

Naumi held up his hand, hushing him. "Ears are quivering over there at the guard post. Let's find somewhere less public. May I suggest the dorm common room? Plenty of room for the . . . ah . . .

people who have joined us. The reunion doesn't start for two more days, so there'll be no one there but us."

Chatting over his shoulder about the weather, the beauty of the sunset, how wonderful it was to see everyone, Naumi led our group past the guards at the gate. We went down a central road and turned right to enter one of the large buildings facing the side street. Inside, Naumi took us straight back through the building to a large room opening onto a central courtyard.

"All right," Naumi said. "Somebody tell me what's going on."

We looked at one another. Gloriana took a deep breath, and said, "This all started when Falija's parents left her with me . . ." She went on to describe briefly how that had happened. Falija, dutiful as ever, picked up the story from that point: her fostering on Tercis, her acquisition of the mother-mind, the threat on Tercis, our travels to Fajnard, where we had picked up Mar-agern, and our trip to Thairy. She said we had learned that the way-gates go one way in pairs, one coming in, one going out, and had verified that in the cave we had come in through.

"You came through that thing up on the cliff," Naumi said. "So that pool of light is a way-gate! I found it the first year I was here, but I'd never heard of way-gates, and it seemed a bit dangerous to try on my own. I'd almost forgotten about it!" He turned to Margaret. "But you called me by name. Both of you."

I said, "When I . . . that is, when we were a child, I, we invented imaginary people, roles to play, fantasies to act out. *Now me* was a warrior. I said to myself, 'I will be a queen,' and 'will be a' turned into 'Wilvia,' and there really is a Queen Wilvia, but we don't know where she is. Margy was our shaman . . ."

"That's M'urgi," cried Ferni. "The woman I'm in love with, the reason I came to Thairy! She's a shaman! She's been captured by tribesmen. They won't hurt her, at least not for a while, but . . ."

"Shhh," Naumi said. "Just a moment." He turned to me, I suppose because I was the eldest of the group. "I've found it isn't smart to believe or disbelieve too early in any situation, but one thing we need to know immediately: Are any of you in immediate danger? Are you being pursued? Is there an emergency of some kind?"

I turned to the others, who looked quite blank. Even Falija shook her head, no, not right now.

Naumi turned back to Ferni, took him by the upper arm, and sat him down. "Now. Everyone sit. Flek, will you and Poul get us something to drink? How about our visitors? Are you hungry? Well then, just something to drink while Ferni tells us whatever he has to tell us, because that does sound like an emergency."

Ferni, openly staring at me-Margaret and other-me-Mar-agern, began his story with the arrival of another Margaret on B'yurngrad. "Her name was Margaret," he said. "She was twenty-two. She was from Earth."

"So were we," Mar-agern and I said simultaneously.

Ferni went on with M'urgi's name change and education by the shaman. "I wasn't with her again, not for years," he said. He told of his search for her, of their ghyrm-hunting in the northlands. "I love her," he declared almost defiantly. "We love each other, and they took her! The tribes are being eaten by ghyrm, and they want her to kill them all, which she can't do by herself!"

"The Siblinghood won't help?" Naumi asked.

"I can't reach anyone above midmanagerial-not-allowed-to-decide-anything-unless-it's-in-the-book!" cried Ferni, pounding the table with one clenched fist. "Which makes me think there must be some great crisis going on somewhere. Someone may be available when I get back, two days from now, but I knew our old talk road was assembled here, and I thought we might come up with some answers."

"Talk road?" asked Falija.

Caspor laughed. "We used to call it that. When we had a problem, we'd talk about it, sometimes forever, and eventually we could almost always figure it out. Ghyrm infestations of tribesmen on another planet are a little outside our expertise, I'm afraid."

"Possibly not," said Flek. "The company has been working on a weapon."

"May I ask, what company?" I asked.

"My grandfather was Gorlan Flekkson Bray, originally from the city of Bray on Chottem. He didn't like some of the family ways, as I understand it, so he moved here, to Thairy, to start a company he later called Flexxon Armor. In Bray, he'd traded with the Omniont races for technological information. Here on Thairy, he recruited some very bright young people who developed their own refinements, and he began by manufacturing high-quality armor for the colonies . . ."

"Are the colonies under attack?" I demanded.

Flek shook her head. "Not yet. Everyone knows what the Mercans are like, though, and we're right in the middle of Mercan space! So, while we publicly supply armaments for the colony police and the frontier scouts, we're also developing and stockpiling very-high-tech arms and armament to help the colonies resist invasion. Gorlanstown, up the coast a way, is the only city large enough to furnish our work force. We have twenty different buildings there, under twenty different names, so that almost no one knows the full extent of what we do."

"Are you sure you should be telling us?" I asked.

Flek smiled, a surprisingly wicked smile. "I would tell Naumi anything. You either are or are not Naumi. If you betray us, you're not Naumi, and you're stupid, besides."

Glory choked back a giggle, but Mar-agern laughed until tears ran down her cheeks. "We're being tested, Margaret! What about the others who obviously aren't Naumi. Glory? Bamber Joy? Falija?"

Caspor said, "We've been told the Gentherans are completely honorable. If this young . . . Gibbekot is related to them, we may trust her honor. If these are your grandchildren, reared by you, then they, too, should be completely honorable."

I thought of explaining that neither of them was actually my grandchild, but let it go. It didn't matter. I trusted the boy at least as much as I trusted Gloriana. "You imply you have something to kill ghyrm."

Flek nodded. "We developed a metal that kills them, and we've been providing the Siblinghood with knives made from it. Recently, we've developed a machine that kills ghyrm in confined areas. The Siblinghood sent you one, Ferni, not long ago. Did it work well?"

"So I understand," he replied.

"That's good, because the first few models killed humans and a lot of other creatures as well. The problem was that the genetic code of

the damned things is very similar to the genome that ninety-odd percent of all Earth mammals share, including humans."

"As though humans were the intended target?" Naumi asked.

"We've considered that possibility. The rest of the genome is a
weird amalgam that no one has been able to identify! We've improved
greatly on that model, however. What we have now is a small prototype of a weapon that, when we enlarge it, can wipe ghyrm off whole
worlds without killing people or umoxen or whatever. The prototype
only covers fifty square jorub."

"Jorub?" I asked.

"Thairy measurement," said Caspor. "A jorub is ten taga, which is
roughly three miles, old Earthian. Say four hundred fifty square
miles. But how high?" he demanded of Flek.

Flek said, "The dimensions of the field, length, width, height are
variable. Since ghyrm don't fly, the fifty-jorub figure has a low ceiling,
to cover more ground. It would have to be set higher for mountainous terrain, of course. At this point we're sure it doesn't kill Earth
animals or any creatures native to any of our colony worlds, but
there's always the possibility it will kill some essential something that
we aren't aware of. Eventually, if we can locate the place where the
ghyrm are coming from, we plan to drop some really big machines on
that location and wipe them out at the source. Anyhow, it seems relevant to our discussion."

Ferni said earnestly, "For my situation, it would be helpful if we
could give the tribes a lot of those knives you mentioned. M'urgi and
I both used them when we went ghyrm-hunting. We have to give the
tribe something to make them let M'urgi go."

Caspor had been staring at the ceiling, his lips moving silently,
and suddenly he demanded, "Where's the star map we used to have
in here?"

Naumi looked up, puzzled. "Behind the screen, over there. It's a
new one. The old one's display circuits were so worn, no one could
read it. Why do you want a star map?"

"This way-gate business interests me. I'm wondering what the underlying logic of all this business may be. Margaret—if you'll excuse
the familiarity, ma'am—came from Tercis to Fajnard. Then the group
came from Fajnard to Thairy. They tell us the gates are one way, that

each place has one gate coming in and one gate going out. It would be interesting to know where all the gates are . . ." He went to the screen, moved it aside, and stood before the map pedestal, mumbling to himself and switching it back and forth among view planes.

All of us newcomers were staring at Caspor wonderingly. Ferni said, "He'll do that for quite a while. Caspor has to figure everything out. If it doesn't have a logical, mathematical solution, he drives himself crazy."

"If he wants to know where the way-gate is that leads away from here," said Gloriana, "it's up in that same cave, just around another corner."

"There are two of them?" Naumi was astonished. "When I discovered it, I thought there was only one."

"You saw the outgoing one. The incoming ones are black," said Falija. "Don't try entering them from that direction."

"But I stepped inside the light . . ."

Falija said, "Yes. And then what?"

"I stepped back out."

"Then you never went all the way through. You were just inside the gate. If you'd gone on through, you couldn't have come back. Not the way you went."

Naumi furrowed his brow, staring at the ceiling as he tried to remember. "There was a dark recess to the left when I went in. The way in must have been in there . . ."

"We were discussing weapons," reminded Falija.

Flek nodded. "We have the next model of the machine in the final stages of assembly."

"Is it something you could do in a hurry?" asked Ferni. "I'm not worried about M'urgi, not really, but—"

"Well, I'm worried about her," I interrupted. "If she's one of us. It seems that seven of us may be necessary in order to do something important, and if M'urgi is one of the seven, she's probably irreplaceable." I thought about this for a moment, saying with surprise, "Any of us are!"

"Why seven?" demanded Caspor, from his position before the star map.

"It's a story," Falija responded. "About a fish and an angry man."

"Can you tell it briefly?" Caspor asked, turning toward her.

Falija said, "There's also a saying, and it's shorter. 'Who knows? The Keeper knows. Well then, ask the Keeper. Where do I find it. All alone, walk seven roads at once to find the Keeper.' The story repeats the phrase 'Seven roads are one road.'"

"What's a keeper?" asked Jaker.

"In the story, it was the little statue with a book in which everything in the whole universe was written," Falija said.

"The Holder," cried Ferni. "The . . . rememberer that fills the universe and senses everything that happens. M'urgi knows about that!"

"Ah," said Caspor, turning back to the map. "Seven. Seven directions. Now, how would that work out in pairs? Divided into our customary three hundred sixty degrees would be fifty-one-point-four-two-eight-five-seven-one and so on, more or less forever."

He punched keys on the map control and spun Tercis toward the top, another key and a line down from Tercis, slightly to the left. "Margaret came from Tercis to Fajnard," Caspor said. Another line, upward to the right, "Margaret and Mar-agern came from Fajnard to Thairy. If I come away from Tercis at the same angle . . ." One more line off at a weird angle. Caspor fiddled with the controls, spinning the line into a cone. "It ends up in the nowhere," he said.

"Let me try it," said Falija. She went to the map and stared at it for a moment before entering the next line. "I seem to recall that from there . . ." The line bounced back from nothingness and hit a star. "Chottem. Where my people are!"

"That's a colony world," said Margaret. "Where from there?"

"From Chottem . . . Cantardene."

"There's no colony on Cantardene! That's a Mercan world."

"We have people on Cantardene," said Naumi. "Bondspeople. The Margaret there may be a bondsperson."

"We have an import-export office on Cantardene," said Jaker. "That is, Poul-Jaker Import-Export does. There's a freeport area, Crossroads of the World, they call it. The bondservant market is there, and so is all the gossip twenty races can spread around. By wormhole, it's only a couple of days from here."

"We can send someone," said Poul. "That salesman of yours, Jaker! We could get him on the next ship out. You know who I mean, the one who seems to be able to talk anyone into anything, what's his name?"

"Stipps," said Jaker, grinning. "Stipps the Lips."

"I've met him," said Ferni. "On B'yurngrad somewhere. Do you have an export arm there?"

"We have an export arm everywhere," replied Jaker.

"Aha!" said Caspor as he spun the lines from Thairy and Cantardene. "They don't intersect anywhere. They come close at B'yurngrad. No, they don't. Yes, they do . . . didn't . . ."

"What?" blurted Naumi.

"I mean, let me play with it a while. I need to update the galactic shift . . ."

We turned our eyes away from the chart, unable to keep them away for long. Ferni said, "Flek, will you help me?"

"Ferni, I'll do everything possible. I'll see what knives we have in stock . . ."

"Can you lend us the prototype?" asked Naumi.

"If we can think of a good way to use it, sure. We can disassemble it so you can carry it. Jaker, you'd be welcome to go with me."

Jaker shook her head. "I'd just be in the way, Flek. I think Poul and I'd be more useful getting one or several spies into Cantardene and seeing if we can find the other person we're looking for. The K'Famir are among the universe's most despicable creatures; but they do business, and when creatures do business, they have to make deals, and you can't make a deal without betraying something of your nature. We're accustomed to snooping around to ascertain what people will buy or sell.

"I saw Stipps this morning, here on Thairy. He's one of those cocksure, egocentric people you love to hate, a very youthful arrogance for a person that age—and with only one eye, at that—but at least ninety percent of his opinion about himself usually pans out . . ."

"One eye?" asked Naumi. "How old?"

"Oh, middle years or more, and yes, one eye. Some kind of accident in his youth, he says. Why?"

"No reason, except that I knew, know someone like that, though I haven't seen him in years."

Jaker gave him a questioning look, but when he said nothing else, she continued. "If no one has any objections, we can get Stipps on the ship tonight, though . . . the task is a bit vague. Who are we looking for?"

"For me," said Mar-agern and I, as with one voice. "It would have to be a bondslave who looks very much like us," I continued. "Could be older or younger . . ."

"Younger," said Falija. "Somewhere around Naumi's age because they split off at the same time, and Cantardene isn't that far from Thairy."

I nodded. "She'll speak several of the local languages. Can't be too many women like that among slaves."

"What other skills will she have?"

Mar-agern and I looked at one another. "If she was only twelve?" I said at last, shaking my head.

Mar-agern said, "She would probably sew quite well. I did."

"Of course," I agreed. "She would sew well."

"Aha!" shouted Caspor. "Yes! Ferni, until this very moment that link didn't go to B'yurngrad! It's a new link."

"What?" "What do you mean," cried several voices.

"I mean, if we start on Tercis, it goes from Tercis to Fajnard, from Fajnard to Thairy, from Thairy to B'yurngrad, from B'yurngrad to Cantardene, from Cantardene to Chottem, from Chottem to that point out in nowhere . . ."

"I know what's there," said Falija. "My people found it ages ago."

". . . and from nowhere back to Tercis. One way. The whole way. Seven roads is one road, but it's only been one road since the last automatic update on galactic shift! B'yurngrad wasn't in position until very, very recently."

"How long does it stay in position?" I asked.

Caspor turned back to the map, whispering to himself, "There has to be some stretchiness in the connection, something that holds on for a while . . ."

Falija said into the silence, "This means the configuration is not a permanent one. We know some parts of it have been in use for some time. The one from Tercis to Fajnard and Fajnard to Thairy, for instance. Howkel knew where those roads ended up, so people came and went through them. Other points have come into contact more recently. And this last link . . . has only very temporarily completed the one road."

Caspor had been playing with the star guide, rotating the strangely angled image. Now it bloomed on the screen as a seven-pointed star. "From this point of view, it's a septagram, but all the end points are in motion. I postulate that once the connection is made, there's enough stretchiness to keep it in contact for a while, probably not very long. In a few days, the whole thing should fall apart."

Falija said, "So the seven roads are one road now. Seven Margarets on seven planets with one road among them . . ."

"And everything dependent upon time," said Ferni. "I wonder if that's what has the Siblinghood in a furor . . ."

Flek, Jaker, and Poul had risen, and they were gone almost before those of us remaining had digested what had just happened.

"I'm suddenly hungry," Mar-agern said. "Would it be possible to have something to eat?"

"Certainly," Naumi replied. "Especially if, during supper, we can hear more about this mother-mind business."

The eight of us, including Falija, dined alone in a small dining room at the officers' mess, an exceptionally good dinner, as the academy cooks were trying out the menus they had selected for the reunion. As we ate, we decided what else needed to be done before we could go to B'yurngrad. When we had freed M'urgi from her captors, we would continue through the B'yurngrad way-gate to Cantardene (assuming Caspor's map of the way-gates was accurate) to find another of us, if and only if Jaker's one-eyed egotist hadn't found her first.

"The gates on Cantardene may or may not be close together," I remarked. "The ones here and on Fajnard were. I never saw the one that enters Tercis . . ."

"I did," said Falija. "It was very near the one we used, hidden back in a cleft in the rock where most of them seem to be. It makes sense that each pair would be close together."

I murmured, "I should mention that we left Tercis because a couple of pseudohumans were chasing us. Or trying to. On Fajnard, they were definitely chasing us."

"Robots," said Bamber Joy, who, while eating enormously, had said very little up until then. "Acted like robots, talked like robots. Might have come from some technological Walled-Off on Tercis."

"What Walled-Off did you come from?" Ferni asked curiously.

"Rueful," I answered. "The name says it all, and it's too long a story for tonight."

"Not a high-tech place, though?" asked Naumi.

I shook my head. "No, Naumi, not a high-tech place. We had electricity, and that was about the extent of it. No powered vehicles except for those from Tercis Central we occasionally saw, plus the one Ned and Walter drove."

"Let's leave it until morning," Naumi said. "Our minds will go on worrying at it overnight, and they may give us a head start after we've slept."

We finished our meal and trooped back to the cadet house, where Mar-agern and I were given rooms down the hall. Falija, Bamber, and Glory took their pick of bunks in a nearby dormitory.

I returned to the common room, needing to sit quietly for a time before attempting sleep, but I found Naumi, Ferni, and Caspor still there. When I came in, Naumi rose, went to a low cupboard along the wall, and took out a bottle.

"Caspor? Ferni? Margaret? Yes? Me, too." He poured, distributed, and sat down opposite us, turning the glass idly in his hand. "Have any of you ever hear of a planet called Hell?"

"Yes," I said. "We learned of it in school, back on Earth, and Falija mentioned it to me just a few moments ago. The native race has almost gone extinct several times. By now, they probably are."

"That seventh star-point, hanging out there in the nowhere. That's how someone described that planet, Hell, to me."

"That's what Falija said. That's a seventh planet."

"We're a long way from walking road number seven," said Caspor. "Right now I'm a good deal more worried about a place like Cantardene in the known-where than anyplace in the nowhere. And there's always the possibility I'm totally wrong about this whole thing."

Naumi emptied his glass, yawned, rose, and bid us good night, concluding, "You're usually right, Caspor. I don't see we have any choice but taking a chance on it."

They went off to bed. I sat there for some time, thinking of that seven-pointed star, wondering about Hell, and what one of us could be doing on it, out in the nowhere.

I Am Gretamara/on Chottem

The Gardener arrived in Bray late in the evening. She found Sophia and me sitting on the terrace beneath the tree. As we rose to greet her, she said, "You've found out what was rotten here on Chottem!"

Sophia said, "Gardener, you knew something was wrong!"

"I'd smelled it, Sophia. This is too recently settled a planet to permit any legitimate accumulation of great wealth, not in one lifetime, not in several, yet Stentor was a rich man, and Von Goldereau grows richer by the hour."

"Slaves," I said. "Men grow rich selling slaves."

"Yes, selling slaves, including children, has always been a quick way to riches."

I said, "The children don't come from this world, Gardener. They have to come from somewhere else."

"An old man brought me the keys to the cellars," said Sophia. "He said he'd given his grandson to my grandfather to be sent to another world to be educated as a gentleman. I'm afraid this was a cruel and vicious joke. What world needs human children to educate and make gentlemen?"

"There is no such world. There is a world, however, where children are surplus, and another where children are bought and sold."

"Earth," I said. "And Cantardene."

Gardener nodded. "Yes. Anyone needing a guaranteed source of children would deal with Earth."

"Would any parent sell . . . ?" I breathed.

"Earthians have sold their children for thousands of years," said the Gardener. "Surplus daughters have been sold as prostitutes, surplus sons to the army. Among the sterile castes of K'Famir, human pets are common, but that does not account for the numbers necessary to have amassed this fortune."

I was gripped by the memory of my own feelings when I had been ripped away from my home. Through tears, I said, "With riches like those in the cellars, Stentor must have brought enormous numbers from Earth. But how? On what ships?"

"Omniont or Mercan captains wouldn't transport cargoes to Chottem that would sell for more on Cantardene," mused Sophia.

"True," Gardener agreed. "But the Lorn and Bray families were wealthy on Earth, and they bought ships to bring settlers from Earth. The wealth in these cellars could have purchased an armada!"

I thought out loud. "Stentor could have claimed the children were to be colonists, but where did he keep them?"

Sophia gestured widely. "Manland is vast, and mostly uninhabited. People have come here since we arrived, winking and nodding to say that they did business with him, Von Goldereau among them. Perhaps he knows."

"We know none were sent through these cellars since Stentor died," I said. "The notes we read make that clear. If Von Goldereau is in the same trade, he has another route."

"You left none of the dead creatures down there?" the Gardener asked. "I would like to have seen one."

"I left none, but I can describe them for you," I offered. "The size of my two hands, clenched together, with ten or eleven arms or legs or tentacles . . ."

"Ghyrm," said the Gardener. "Well, that's what I thought they must be. When Stentor did not reply, they were angered, and they sent ghyrm through the gate to destroy him. He was too wily to be taken so. Tomorrow we will go down there, Sophia, and have a look at this place, this doorway. Whoever is buying these children has access both to great wealth and to ghyrm, and I need to send word of that to my friends. Also, if your cellar can spare some of its riches, we may use some of it to pay for what we must accomplish next."

"I have never known you to buy anything," I cried, astonished.

The Gardener replied, "Warriors like to be paid, even those of the Siblinghood, who are choosy about what they fight for. We will have need of more than a few of them."

"Would my grandfather have approved of this expenditure?" Sophia asked with a sly smile.

"Almost certainly not." The Gardener grinned.

"Then you may use as much as you can, with my blessing," said the heiress.

I Am Ongamar/on Cantardene

In House Mouselline, I, Miss Ongamar, pinned and basted, seamed and embroidered, and each day my escape plans ripened. Those plans, almost a year in the making, were now complete. I had pulled together all the notes I had made, put them in order, and transcribed them all in minuscule script on the inside of my Hrassian robes. I had recently stolen money from House Mouselline, not a difficult task, since Lady Ephedra trusted Miss Ongamar to tally each day's receipts and make up the transfer document for House Mouselline's banker. These accounts would be audited, of course, but I had begun after the last audit and still had time to spare.

Disguised as a Hrass and using the stolen money, I had purchased a go-pass on an outgoing ship that was to leave during the anniversary celebration of the Great Leader's accession to power, tomorrow. House Mouselline would be closed, today was my last day, so I took my self-allotted share from the cash box and tucked it under my padding, totaled up the transfer document and laid it atop the box, then began tidying the little cubby where I worked, paying no attention to the clamor in the showroom, until I heard my own name.

"Miss Ongamar, yes. If you don't mind." I was stunned by the voice, a human voice, male, very firm, a little amused.

"This shop is only for the *tamistachi,* the elite of

K'Famir," shrieked Lady Ephedra. "Dirty human slaves are not welcome."

The man laughed, a deep, truly amused chuckle. "Ah, but Lady Ephedra, I am not a dirty human slave, I am a diplomat from the Dominion. Here, my diplomatic pass. Here's identification, see, my likeness without a doubt, resembling no one else."

"It doesn't matter, it doesn't matter, someone may see you here, someone may smell you here . . ."

"Then it would be wise to let me see Miss Ongamar so that I may go away the sooner, would it not?"

I heard the scuttling feet and stood with my back to the wall. The curtain that enclosed my cubby was drawn aside with a rattle of rings, and Lady Ephedra pointed toward me with both left arms. "She is here! See her and go!"

The man stood politely aside while the Lady departed, then slipped into the cubby, looked me over from head to toe with one eye and one eye patch, whispering as he did so:

"Gather up what you need and come with me."

"And who are you," I grated, halfway between anger and terror. I had needed only one more day! If anything was guaranteed to make the Lady Ephedra my enemy, this was it.

"I am sometimes called Stipps, sometimes Mr. Weathereye," he said, bowing slightly. "I often work with the Dominion and the Siblinghood, which group tells me your term as a bondservant was actually fulfilled some time ago. I have the documents here, as approved by the K'Famir official for this sector, and if you will be kind enough to take me to your living quarters, we will discuss your future plans."

I dithered. If . . . if what he said was true, then I needn't fear the retribution that Lady Ephedra would exact. On the other hand, if it wasn't true, I was in trouble up to my eyebrows. On the one hand, the man seemed very sure, but on the other hand, people were often very sure about things that had no truth to them whatsoever . . .

He leaned forward. "Please, Margaret. Just release your hold on the back of that chair and come with me."

"Ongamar," I corrected him. "Miss Ongamar."

"Yes, Margaret. I know."

Somehow, he managed to convince me. Somehow he managed to

dissuade Lady Ephedra from making a fuss as we went out of the building to the street and down the narrow way to my rooms. When I reached out to put my key in the door, he whispered, "Where is it?"

My throat froze. I shivered in terror, trying to speak.

"Point," he said in my ear. "Just point."

I did so. Mr. Weathereye said, "Ella May?"

"Here," said a female voice, the person herself coming through the alley gate, a sturdy woman with a case in one hand. We went in. The woman opened the case, empty except for a small set of implements, which she removed before she went to the closed closet door.

"It's in here?"

I nodded. The pair went in. I heard a scuffle, then a scream so shrill it made my ears hurt, then a panting sound, another scream and silence. The woman came out, wiping a peculiarly shaped knife on a piece of glowing fabric.

"Now," Mr. Weathereye said cheerfully to me. "Do you have anything here you want to take with you?"

I begged, "Where are we going?"

"Off Cantardene, my dear. My claim of signed release documents was a false one, for which I apologize. By this time, Lady Ephedra will have summoned the K'Famir, who will shortly assault this dwelling with the aim of killing you. We suggest you quickly put all necessities into this case, and we'll go."

I was jolted into movement. I had already set aside a folded change of clothing and shoes. My Hrass robes and disguise lay ready, and if this man could not do what he told me he could do, I might still use these to escape. I saw his eyebrows rise when I put the disguise into the case, filling it completely. Ella May dropped the implements atop the Hrassian false nose, and we went out the door.

The gate through the wall was open. In the alley outside a dark, smooth vehicle hummed quietly. Its doors opened, Ella May climbed inside and extended a hand to help me inside, where I collapsed onto the seat with an abrupt sense of mixed elation and horror. Either I would wake up and be back in Lady Ephedra's fitting room, or I had escaped. I had no intention of finding out which. If this was to be a temporary ecstasy, I would not abbreviate it.

The vehicle rose soundlessly except for an almost subliminal hum.

Mr. Weathereye touched the door and it became transparent. We looked down on K'Famir wearing the straps and weapons of police massed at the street opening of my little alley, then pouring down it in a flood, blocking both door and alley as a dozen or so of them rushed into my dwelling.

"Why?" I cried. "Why do they want to kill me?"

An old woman seated in front next to Ella May turned and said, "The orders came from the palace of the K'Famir Chief Planner. Next to the Great Leader, that's as high as K'Famir go. Some long time ago, he gave a Thongal spy a few ghyrm to be fastened upon certain human bondslaves on Cantardene to see if these bondslaves were part of a conspiracy. You were one of them. Lately, the Chief Planner learned that the Siblinghood had been looking for you, watching for you. This was taken as proof you were part of a conspiracy, so he ordered that you be killed now, tonight, instead of later, which Lady Mouselline preferred."

"Why?" I whispered. "Why would he even know about me?"

"Perhaps he doesn't. He probably takes take his orders from someone else," said Mr. Weathereye. "We don't really know what creature may be at the top, but if it isn't K'Famir, then it's Quaatar or Frossian."

"Or all three," said the old woman. She turned toward me once more. "I'm Lady Badness. We had already planned to come for you. Such badness here among the K'Famir, always such badness. Lady Mouselline always has her fitters killed, but she has delayed your execution several times, and we took advantage of that, not wanting to . . . betray ourselves beforetime. When we learned that the Chief Planner's office wasn't going to wait any longer, we moved quickly, as we are moving to find out who the creature at the top of this evil pyramid may be."

"Who told you that they wanted me killed?" I cried.

"Someone who listens for us," Lady Badness replied. "We have people who listen for us. The K'Famir walk in the Bak-Zandig-g'Shadup, their clothing brushes against one of our listeners, they walk away, but now their clothing listens to what they say and tells us about it."

"I guess I'm one of your listeners, too," I said. "That's what I did, there in the fitting room. I listened."

Below us, the K'Famir were coming out of the house. One of them waved something to another.

"What's that thing he's waving?" asked Ella May.

I looked down, uncertain. Suddenly the image magnified, and I saw what it was.

"Oh, no," I cried. "My go-pass. I was going to leave Cantardene tomorrow . . ."

"Will they know the pass was sold to you personally?" Lady Badness asked sharply.

I shook my head. "I bought it in the guise of a Hrass, for they're always coming through Bak-Zandig-g'Shadup . . ."

"You left most of your belongings back there," said Mr. Weathereye. "They may assume you plan to return. In any case, unless they've recently had a great advance in technology, they cannot see this flier, even if they are looking directly at it."

This rang an alarm in my mind, but for the moment I could not think why. "Where are we going?"

"We have a place here on Cantardene, a very safe place, we hope, and just until we can figure out a way to get back to . . . where do we want to get back to?" he asked the old woman.

"Thairy, I believe. That's where we started from . . ."

"But the others were going to B'yurngrad . . ."

". . . or B'yurngrad. I imagine either would do."

I murmured, "What do you do there, or here? I mean, what is your work?"

The man laughed. "Rescuing maidens. Not without self-interest, you understand. Since the K'Famir kill anyone they suspect of knowing something touchy about the K'Famir, and since you were scheduled for killing, we assume you have something that will prove to be very useful to us."

"Oh," gasped I with a spurt of pure joy. "Oh, after all these years, I do have something for you!"

Their ship sped across the pleasure quarter to the outskirts of the city, passing above Beelshi. I shuddered.

"What is it?" asked Mr. Weathereye.

"I saw them . . ." I began, stopping, gulping, my throat blocked by swallowed tears.

"Tell us," Lady Badness said firmly.

"I don't want to talk about it. I wrote it all down."

"Which is why you must! We haven't time for documents."

I started haltingly, finally letting it all spew out: the little creatures, the little boy, the creation of the ghyrm, the pools of light and dark I had seen in the mausoleum, the strange machine. Gasping, my face wet, I concluded, "The K'Famir worship the Eater of the Dead. Torturing living things turns them into what you killed back there."

Ella May cursed under her breath. "Lady Badness! Look there, ahead. They've found our ship!"

"How could they?" demanded Lady Badness. "It was shielded. No one comes out here!"

Below us the K'Famir swarmed over the ship like ants.

"They can't get into it," said Weathereye.

"Unfortunately, neither can we," said the old woman.

"They have shield detectors," I said, coming out of the spell of my narrative to realize what was going on. "One of the customers at House Mouselline was talking about its patron being honored for inventing it. The K'Famira laughed a great deal. He hadn't invented it, only bought it from the Omnionts."

"Now the woman remembers!" grated Weathereye. "We don't dare go down there. If we do the correct thing, we blow the ship right now and let them think we're in it."

"Too late," cried the pilot. "They've detected us!"

"Do the correct thing, then," cried Weathereye. "At least take some of them with it."

The ship below us went up in an enormous billow of smoke and fire that threw some hundreds of the uniformed K'Famir through the air like windblown leaves. "That should distract them for a time," growled Ella May.

"How does it work?" Weathereye demanded. "Their sensor. Does it detect the veiling system, or does it penetrate the system to detect the ship?"

I gaped, trying to remember what else they had said. "It detects the system," I said at last.

"Turn the system off in this ship, Ella May," Weathereye ordered. "Get down as close to the ground as you can. Night is coming. Set us down in the shadows somewhere, among these hillocks. We're trapped here now. Have to figure out something . . ."

"The gates," said Lady Badness. "She told us about the gates on the Hill of Beelshi."

"She didn't tell us where the hell they go," snapped Weathereye.

"They don't both go," the old woman snarled in return. "One goes, one comes. Remember!"

"What I remember is the genetic work the Siblinghood has done on the ghyrm," Ella May said as she searched for a place to set down. "And what you told me of the armaments research they're doing on Thairy. Whatever they came up with to kill ghyrm also killed humans. It finally makes sense!"

"It's true the closest tissue match to ghyrm is human," said Lady Badness, turning toward me. "Weathereye and I belong to a small group of interested bystanders, well, not always just bystanders, obviously, since here we are, not just standing."

"What do you mean, the ghyrm are human?" I cried.

"No, no, dear. Not human. Humans are the closest genetic match. What you saw there on the Hill of Beelshi makes it clear the ghyrm are manufactured from humans."

"But the little creatures I saw weren't human. I could hold one of them in my hands!

"They must have once been human, genetically speaking. The human genetic dictionary contains many words, perhaps whole paragraphs, that are not usually expressed. Under certain conditions, however, the genetic vocabulary changes. If the environment is impoverished, much of what is thought of as human is simply repressed, letting simple, earlier processes take over. Language is reduced, then lost. Argument is replaced with violence. Symbols and repetitive chants replace art and music. Minds are reduced in complexity, reactions are simplified. Reproduction may be limited to certain castes. So with the little ones you saw. Genetically, they must still be human, however. Torture simply removes the remnants of humanity— pain does that, you know. It destroys the higher centers of the mind, leaving only the screaming hunger that lies at the center of all ancient life."

"Leaving, also, genetics sufficiently like yours that your immune system does not react to them," said Weathereye. "Your bodies do not reject them, as they would anything foreign. Which means they can take their time to feed on you quite nicely."

"You say, 'genetics like ours,'" said I. "Your genetics aren't human?"

"Like, but unlike." Lady Badness laughed. "We're mere meddlers, my dear. Doing what we can for those we depend upon."

"There," said Ella Mae, indicating a fold of land now dark in shadow. The ship descended soundlessly into its depths.

I offered tentatively. "We are not far from the outskirts of the city, and we're on the Beelshi side. I can lead you to the mausoleum and the gates."

"I would feel better about that if I knew where the gates go," said Weathereye. "I should have asked. Still, since we have no way to get you and Ella May off this planet otherwise . . ."

"I have my own disguise," I said. "I don't have enough for all of us . . ."

"Quite all right, my dear," said Lady Badness. "Take your shape, and we two will copy you. We're quite good at that. We make our living at it, one might say."

I opened the case and took out my Hrassian garb, the nose, the paint, the wig, the dirty robes, the little mirror that let me see myself as I changed. "Now," I murmured as I worked, "the Hrass keep a solid wall to their backs whenever possible. Crossing open ground, they hurry, frequently glancing behind them. They mutter constantly. I think the real Hrass utter prayers, but I have had good experience with the phrase 'Old rhinoceros my brother will you have some bread and butter.' This phrase has in it many of the Hrass phonemes, and it avoids sounds they do not make. Please remember to start the phrase at different intervals and do not say it in unison." I stopped, for all three of them were grinning at me.

"You were on your way to becoming a translator, I believe," said Weathereye. "A woman who spoke many tongues."

I blushed. I had been going on and on, sounding like my own didactibot! "That was long ago," I said. "Some days it is hard to remember. I apologize for seeming imperious. You probably know all this far better than I . . ."

"Not at all," said Lady Badness. "We know little or nothing about the Hrass. We are human followers, our fates inextricably interwoven with your own."

"Do I set the destruct?" Ella May asked.

"I should think so," said Lady Badness rather sadly. "If they find it, we can't get it back."

I said, "We can work our way up the hill among the tombs, those big pottery jars that contain the bones of the dead. That is, I suppose they are bones by now. There's been no room on Beelshi for new ones for a very long time, or so I've heard. They chain the door to the room, so we'll need something . . ."

"I have the proper tool," said Ella May. She turned with a grin, displaying a small tool clasped in one hand. "Are we ready?"

"Just have to fix my nose," I commented, doing so and with quick strokes of my fingers blending the paint around the edges. "I can see you're amused by this, but I can't tell why. Beelshi is terrible and full of pain. I don't like going back there."

"We are not amused, dear lady," said Mr. Weathereye. "We are simply delighted with you, which is quite another thing. Your resourcefulness, your determination, both do you credit."

The four of us left the ship with me leading. When I looked back, it seemed to me two Hrass followed me, muttering, scurrying, glancing around quite as authentically as I could have desired. Ella May stayed between them, making do with a long cape and a scuttling walk. The Hill of Beelshi was to our left, across a well-traveled road and an open area of fields that might be fenced. If so, I would rely upon whatever tool the young woman carried to get us through.

We waited for the road to clear, then scurried across it without incident.

"Who is Ella May?" I panted to Lady Badness.

"She's a member of the Siblinghood of Silence. Have you heard of that?"

"I don't think so, no. What do I call her, Sibling?"

"That's considered quite proper, yes. But she would probably prefer to be called simply Ella May, since you're probably related to one another."

I had time for only one astonished look at the elderly person before resuming my scuttle. Beyond the road were fences, quite a number of them, but Ella May had only to touch them with the tool, whatever it was, and a sizable hole appeared.

We approached Beelshi on the side opposite the one I had climbed before. There were no guards. Presumably, all the guards were out hunting for Miss Ongamar, which thought offered fleeting amusement. Once among the funerary jars, I paused, allowing us all a brief rest. The distance had not been far, the terrain not challenging, but the skittering mannerisms took both concentration and energy. We worked our way upward, pausing outside the upper ring of temples and mausolea while I located the building I had spied from before.

When I pointed it out, Ella May whispered, "Since there's no one here, I suggest we go straight across. It's quickest."

I hesitated, my agitation no doubt plain on my face.

"What?" demanded Mr. Weathereye.

"You see that tall stone, the one that looks like a person hunched over the stone of sacrifice. I've seen its eyes. I got the strong impression that it could see."

"And you think it might utter an alarm?"

"I don't know. If I were here alone, however, I would work around behind it to the place I want to be, then go in very quickly, closing the door tightly behind me."

"I see no reason to doubt your counsel," Mr. Weathereye murmured. "Let us do so."

We were stopped in our tracks by a cacophony of shouts from the foot of the hill behind us. Ella May slipped away to a vantage point and returned almost immediately. "They have mechanical scent detectors down there, they've picked up our trail. I suggest, watching stone or no watching stone, we run for it!"

We did so, rushing across the rough pavement like so many cockroaches, I thought, harkening back to what vermin were left on Earth. Humans and cockroaches. As we crossed before the tall stone, I glanced up to see the red glare of its eyes fastened on me. The creased rock ridges of the mouth opened to emit a huge, stony voice. No one needed a translation, though I made one automatically. "Here, here, here it is!"

Within moments we were up the steps of the mausoleum, Ella May applied her tool to the chain, we pulled the door open, closed it firmly behind us and bolted it with the three huge bolts that were obviously well and frequently used, for they bore no rust and slid into their sockets with a satisfying thwack.

Ella May was facing the shimmering pool of light. She went toward it, thrust her hand in, drew it out again, then tried the same with the black pool, only to leap back with a choked oath.

"Way-gates," said Ella May. "One comes in, one goes out, and the black one is obviously the one that comes in."

The other gate, the shimmering one, had great stacks of empty cages beside it, along with heaped kegs of treasure.

"Read the meaning of this," demanded Weathereye of his female companion, gesturing at their surroundings.

"It says trade," said Lady Badness. "Treasure sent through this gate, creatures returned through this gate. What Miss Ongamar has seen is the key: The K'Famir were paying for human beings to be sent through this gate."

"Were paying?"

"Look at the dust, heavy years of dust. Nothing has come through here for a considerable time."

"But they used this one gate, both ways?"

Ella May said, "Nothing is stacked conveniently next to the other one, and that machine with wheels is an odd thing to find here..." She went to look it over more closely. "Phase transformer! Look at the size of it. It has to be salvage, because no one has used anything like this for years."

"Used it to do what?" Lady Badness demanded.

Ella May nodded. "The fields of these gates are obviously oneway. This thing, if started up inside it, or in contact with it, is probably designed to reverse it."

We turned toward the door as it clattered with a hammering of spearpoints.

"The K'Famir police don't carry energy weapons," said I. "But it won't take long to get them from the armory."

Ella May said, "I suggest we push this machine into that light pool and turn it on. It seems to have its own energy source."

"Don't push it all the way in," I cried. "Push in the front end, but leave the end with the controls out, so we can see what happens."

"An excellent suggestion, my dear," said Mr. Weathereye, applying his shoulder to the machine, which seemed reluctant to move in any particular direction. The clatter outside grew louder, and there were coordinated calls.

"They're bringing up something to batter the door down," I translated. "We have to make it move."

We managed to get it turned around, though it seemed to me that only Ella May and I exerted any real force upon it. With a last, desperate shove, we thrust the end of it through the glowing gate. When Ella May pushed the button, the shimmering pool turned abruptly black as air smelling of dust and damp rushed around us. When she pushed the button again, it reversed.

"So they were trading with one source," mused Mr. Weathereye. "I wonder where the black one goes."

I had gone to peer through the crack along the hinge side of the great door. "They're in the plaza. They're bringing up some huge . . . looks like a log?"

"Battering ram," said Ella May. "We don't have much time. I suggest we go through there"—pointing at the shining gate—"and take the machine with us."

"When we get to the other end, we use it to seal it off behind us," said Lady Badness.

"Exactly," said Ella May.

"This road, rather than the other one?" I asked.

Ella May shook her head. "We don't have time to move it to the other one. This one smells fairly clean."

From outside came a chant, "Hrnah, cush, hrnah, cush." The battering ram had arrived and was thundering against the door. The metal shrieked as it bulged inward in a huge, swollen carbuncle. Crates toppled in a cloud of dust. Ella May and I thrust the machine ahead of us.

Voices outside built to a bellowed unison: "Hrnah, cush, hrnah, cush!"

The door screamed, the hinges popped, long metal screws flew across the room, one striping my cheek with blood. Over my shoulder I could see the bolts bending slowly, a little more with each crashing blow. We pushed, grunting, sweating, the others swearing words I had never heard before, thrusting through the shining disk only moments before the great metal doors came off their hinges.

The heavy machine was moving more easily, as though downhill, and I glimpsed the room behind us as it filled with K'Famir who were obviously unfamiliar with the gate. Some of them approached it cautiously, some searched behind the crates, some approached the other gate and were shocked by it, as Ella May had been. We were still pushing when the machine reached the end of the way we were in and protruded into somewhere else. Several of the K'Famir tried reaching into the light gate, discovered it did not hurt them, walked boldly through and began to pursue, spears waving.

"Turn it around," I cried, shoving at the nearest exposed surface of the device with all my strength. The bulky device was now moving fast enough that the momentum carried it around and let it come to rest with the four of us in the clear while the front of it remained inside the gate. I was nearest to the control and I slammed my fist down on it, holding it down. From inside the gate we heard the high, ululating screeches of K'Famir voices just as we, ourselves, were thrust hard against the machine by a gust of air that came from behind us. It rushed away into the opening, then stopped.

"It's closed," said Lady Badness. "I hope whoever was in there was blown out. Now it's black at their end, just like the other one. They can't use either gate, unless they have another machine."

"Were the soldiers pushed back?" I whispered.

"The sounds of pain receded," said Mr. Weathereye. "I think it likely they were more than merely pushed. Flung, perhaps."

"It's dark in here," I said. "The only light is from the pool . . ."

"I have a light," said Ella May, turning it on. We looked around ourselves, trapped in a short tunnel, blocked at one end by the shimmering gate and at the other by a locked iron grille. Beyond the grille was a huge, heavy door.

Ella May asked, "Shall I see if I can cut through the grille?"

Weathereye shook his head. He sat down and leaned against the wall. "There's no hurry," he said. "We're not trapped. Cantardene can't follow us. While we have a moment, I'd like to sit here quietly while Miss Ongamar tells us what she has learned over the last decades she spent there."

To their manifest amusement, I took off my Hrassian nose, turned my outer garment inside out, and began at the left side hem to read them everything I knew about the K'Famir.

I Am Gretamara and
Ongamar/on Chottem

When the Gardener joined Sophia and me as we break-
fasted under the flowering tree, she seemed distracted.
While we ate, she merely sat, eyes half shut, obviously
troubled.

"Gardener," Gretamara said at last. "Something's
wrong?"

"Something's happened, but I can't locate it. I knew
something was going to happen, but I don't know what!"

Gretamara looked up, suddenly alert. "It's the cellars,
Gardener. Sophia and I had the same oppressive feelings
about the house, and they came from the cellars. This
morning I had the feeling that a wind had swept through
them . . ."

"But it was not something dreadful," the Gardener remarked. "Perhaps that's why I'm confused about it. If it
had been dreadful, I would have thought of the cellars,
but this . . ."

"Let's go look," I said, rising from my chair. "We'll stay
behind the iron grilles, just in case."

We made our way down the many stairs, beyond the
first, second and third doors, coming at last to that final
door, triple-locked, triple-bolted, triple-barred. As we approached it, the Gardener held up her hand, tilting her
head. "I hear a voice!"

We laid our ears against the crack where the door met

the jamb to hear a voice murmuring, or perhaps reciting something, for it went on and on, uninterrupted.

"It sounds like you, Gretamara," said Sophia.

The Gardener stood tall, eyes gleaming, her teeth showing between her lips in what I thought could be either a grim smile or a snarl. "Of course!" she said. "Unlock it!"

Sophia did as she was bade. The first bolt drawn silenced the voice beyond the gate. Moving the second bolt caused an eruption of noise, as if something on wheels were being moved. The third bolt and bar met only silence, as did the rusty squeal as the door was cracked open.

The Gardener spoke through the crack. "Is there someone there who has a name and a number?"

After a long moment, a male voice responded, "Is that you, Gardener?"

"What name and number have you, Weathereye?"

"I have Ongamar, and she is number four. What number have you?"

"I have Gretamara, and she is number three," said the Gardener, pulling the door wide open. Inside, facing us, were an old man with an eye patch and three women: one quite old; one middling young, stocky and healthy looking; the other smaller, thinner, more sallow and bent, but bearing a definite resemblance to me.

"Lady Badness!" cried the Gardener. "Weathereye! What brings you by this route?"

"We accompanied those for whom it was the only route," said the old woman. "You know Ella May, of the Siblinghood, and this is Miss Ongamar. You must hear what she's been telling us!"

"Who are they?" asked Sophia in wonderment.

"Old friends and a new one!" said the Gardener, as she signaled Sophia to unlock the iron grille. "One devoutly wished for! What is that machine you've brought?"

"A device for changing the direction of the way-gates," said Ella May, bowing to the Gardener and receiving in return a kiss on her cheek. "We believe there was a thriving trade going on through this gate, with goods passing in both directions. The machine made it possible."

The other woman was standing very still, her feet apart as though to brace against shock, as she stared into my face. "Who are you?" she asked at last.

"I . . . was Margaret," I said. "Now I'm Gretamara. And you?"

"I was Margaret. On Cantardene they called me Ongamar."

"When did you . . . when did you become someone else?"

"I was twelve."

"So was I, twelve."

"You're little more than that now?"

"I'm a lot older, really. I just haven't . . . aged much. We were split when the proctor came, weren't we?"

"Yes."

"Why?" we both said at once. "Why?"

"Because," said the Gardener. "It was necessary, for a very good reason, and it actually happened some time before that." She turned to Weathereye. "Was she in some kind of danger?"

"Oh, a very definite kind," he said. "Someone has found out too much and is trying to kill any or all of them."

"How?" the Gardener whispered. "How could anyone have possibly . . . ?"

"How could anyone have possibly what?" cried Sophia. "Gardener, what's going on?"

"Shhh," she replied. "Not here." She unlocked the grille, beckoned the others through it, relocked first it, then the heavy doors, and led us out the cellars, locking each of the doors behind us.

As we reached the ground level, Lady Badness said, "For all we know, there may be listeners down there. After all, the other end's in Cantardene."

"Which is a pesthole," remarked the Gardener. "If anything found out, I'd guess it was something from there . . ."

Miss Ongamar said, "The stone. The standing stone. They call it Whirling Cloud of Darkness-Eater of the Dead."

Sophia and I exchanged a horrified look. I murmured, "We saw it, didn't we, Gardener?"

Gardener said, "I took them to the Gathering, Weathereye."

Ongamar said, "The stone called out, 'It's here.' It meant me, didn't it?"

"Probably," said Mr. Weathereye. "As I said, the order to kill you came from the very top levels of Cantardene."

"The very top levels were present when they made the ghyrm," Ongamar said. "Anything any of them knew, that stone knew. What is that stone?"

"Ah," Lady Badness murmured. "What a good question. What would you say, Weathereye? Not merely K'Famirish, is it? Something of the slaughterhouse added? The torture chamber? The mass grave? One, or more, of the ancients in the Gathering?"

"Quite possibly," said Mr. Weathereye crisply.

"Quite possibly what?" cried Sophia, stamping her foot.

"Quite possibly an amalgamation of K'Famir and Frossian gods along with something a good deal older," the Gardener answered crisply. "You and Gretamara were there, Sophia. You saw the Quaatar."

"You said they couldn't do anything . . . by themselves," I cried.

"They can't," said Lady Badness. "Just as a battery can't do anything by itself. Attach a wire to it, however, and current flows. We gods are like that. We accumulate energy, feelings, emotions, needs, wants, hopes, dreams, hatreds, everything. Normally, most of it cancels out: Love balances hate, hope balances despair, joy balances sorrow. If you get a god that's only one thing, however, only pain, only hate, only death, with nothing to balance it, then it accumulates. Attach a mortal to it, and you've got a lynching, a crusade, a clinic bombing, a jihad, an inquisition, an assassination. Those three, Dweller, Drinker, Darkness . . . they've set up a hate-and-horror generator! I would like to know how they found out about our plan, though. I thought we'd done an excellent job of hiding our traces."

"Did the plan have anything to do with me?" asked Ongamar, tears gathering in her eyes. "If it did, they've found out from the ghyrm. I saw the ghyrm being created, and one of them has been feeding on me for years, using me to spy out horrors. I tried to keep some things to myself, but it knew me. It knew all about me . . ." She looked imploringly at the Gardener. "I know it doesn't keep information to itself, I know it doesn't. That . . . that stone probably knows everything the ghyrm does, everything *every* ghyrm does . . ."

"But what does it know?" the Gardener asked. "That you are Earthian? Everyone knew that. That you are female, sick of the place? Obviously."

"I saw them being created. I don't think the ghyrm learned that from me, but I can't be sure."

"Ah," said the Gardener. "Well. Would it know there are more than one of you? You didn't know that yourself . . . unless . . ."

"Of course," said Mr. Weathereye, scowling. "Unless another one of the seven is also in contact with a ghyrm! Well, I was sent to Cantardene to find someone who had been Margaret. Aha. Yes. And why was I sent? Because there were already three Margarets on Thairy and another one on B'yurngrad who was in danger, and the one on B'yurngrad is a member of your Siblinghood, Ella May, and she's a ghyrm-hunter, like you, who usually carries and feeds a finder. Which is, as we all know, simply another ghyrm.

"So, if we have one Margaret on Cantardene, known to a ghyrm, and another Margaret on B'yurngrad, also known to a ghyrm, and if those devils in The Gathering know everything the ghyrm know, then it would not take them long to figure out there was at least one more Margaret than there should be . . ."

"They identify us?" Ongamar asked. "Individually?"

"Oh, I imagine they can," said Lady Badness. "At least the ones they don't kill."

"There are such things as identical twins, or even triplets," I said indignantly. "Don't they know that?"

"Of course there are," said the Gardener. "But if a monster is several million years old and has survived enough extinction episodes to become completely paranoid, one is not averse to killing a few twins to eliminate a possible threat."

"Several million years old!" whispered Ongamar. "Who?"

"This is not the place nor the time," said the Gardener. "We must move very quickly before they know we've been warned . . ."

"Where are we?" asked Ongamar

"On Chottem. Weathereye, you say there are three already assembled on Thairy? What are they doing?"

"Going to B'yurngrad to pick up a fourth one," he replied, with satisfaction.

"Two here, four there, leaving only one, and we know where she is. So, Weathereye will take Ongamar to B'yurngrad, where she'll tell them about ghyrm. Then they find transport . . . Not a way-gate. No! The way-gate's reversed. We can't leave it that way!"

Weathereye frowned, eyes suddenly widening. "Of course! We need to change the gate so it goes from Chottem to Cantardene, the way it was, then we have to hide the machine."

"There will be guards posted at the far end, on Cantardene," said Ella May. "If you turn it around, they'll come through."

"Do you have charbic?" asked Ongamar. "They grow it on Cantardene for export to Chottem. Charbic is lethal to the K'Famir, so they use slaves to work the fields."

"Charbic?" mused the Gardener.

"Sometimes called mothbane," I said. "The carpets here were adrift with it when we arrived."

"So they were," cried Sophia. "There are still sacks of the stuff filling up one of the stables."

"Ah, very well," said Mr. Weathereye. "Do you have stout retainers, Sophia? Stout enough to lug the stuff down below?"

"I don't want them to see . . ." Sophia said.

"They won't see," said the Gardener. "Lady Badness can arrange that your men see nothing but floors and walls." She stood, beckoning to me. "Gretamara and I will go just before the way is locked. Weathereye will precede us, with Ongamar and Ella May, continuing through the way-gates to Thairy, then on to B'yurngrad if that is where the others have gone."

"You're leaving me here alone?" asked Sophia in panic.

"I'll stay with you," said Lady Badness. "I'm really quite useful. Don't worry."

The Gardener stayed above while the rest of us returned below, and into the right-hand branch of the tunnel.

"If the K'Famir get through the grille, they'll go through this gate, too," whispered Sophia.

"It will do them no good," said Lady Badness with a peculiar, almost anticipatory smile.

"We're off, then," said Weathereye, patting Sophia's shoulder.

"There are four gates between us and Thairy, but it will take us very little time." He bowed the women through, then followed.

Sophia took a deep, shuddering breath.

"You feel adrift," said Lady Badness, patting her hand.

"Gardener has been . . . my mother, my family," said Sophia. "I know all about my real mother. I know what kind of family she had. I think the Gardener is a lot harder to live up to."

"She is only what our source is, and you're part of that."

Sophia was not cheered by this, as it seemed only to deepen her responsibility, but she resolutely sent for men to fetch sack after sack of powdered charbic root, then led them below to dump them just inside the gate.

"All kinds of vermin come through here," Sophia said loudly, with a convincing shudder. "The charbic root will kill them, and we'll shut this entry down."

"Entry, ma'am?" asked the most forward of the men.

"A way my grandfather used to get down to the harbor," she said. "He bought it from the Omnionts, but it lets rats in."

When everything was prepared, the four strongest were told to stay by the machine while she pushed the button. Then they pulled the bulky thing back through the grille door, the sound of shrieking wheels covering the faint, distant howls that Sophia heard. She locked the grille and the gates behind her, then pointed out a dusty corner where the machine could be hidden under a pile of old sacking.

I watched them as they crossed each of the cellars, looking around with great curiosity. Everyone had heard the rumors of Stentor's great hoard, but all I saw, all they saw was stone, dust, and cobwebs, with not so much as a scatter of coins on the floors. None of them noticed the old woman sitting quietly in a corner. When they had finished, Sophia thanked them for a job well done, paid them exorbitantly, and told them to take the day off.

"Now what are we to do?" Sophia asked Lady Badness.

Lady Badness turned toward me and asked, "Are you and the Gardener ready to go?"

"We are," said the Gardener, coming down the stairs.

"It will be frightening, just waiting to see what happens," said Sophia.

"We will stay busy," said Lady Badness with a somewhat-gloating look. "Since the K'Famir may actually try to come through the way-gate, you and I, Sophia, must be ready with a proper welcome."

The doors and the grille were unlocked only long enough to let the Gardener and me into the tunnel. We heard them being locked again, behind us.

We emerged from the way-gate into darkness. Light bloomed slowly around us. We were in a cube, a gate in the wall behind us, another in the wall ahead, an uninterrupted wall to either side, a ceiling, a floor.

"Do you have a name and a number?" whispered a mechanical voice.

"The name is Wilvia, the number is two," said Gardener.

The wall to our left slid open, making a slender opening. We squeezed through and it shut behind us.

"It's a Gentheran survey ship," remarked the Gardener. "It's been buried here for a very long time."

We moved down the dimly lit passageway and came to a view-screen that looked across a clearing into a forest. Through the trees we saw a shoreline and an expanse of water. Along the shoreline was a village swarming with very small people, somewhat humanlike in appearance.

"Where are we?" I asked.

"At the far end of nowhere," replied the Gardener. "A place that interests no one, a place visited only by accident. The Frossians were determined to kill Wilvia, Queen of the Ghoss, so we kept moving her about in order to keep her safe."

"When we were children," I said, "we invented Queen Wilvia, and Naumi the Warrior, and all the others. There was a spy, too. I suppose Ongamar was the spy. I wonder if they found a warrior . . ."

A door opened at our approach to disclose a courtyard garden with flowering trees grouped around a burbling fountain. Cushioned chairs were set around it, one of them holding a slender, careworn woman, who rose, startled by our arrival. She wore a simple white robe and a diadem. The glowing gem at the center of her forehead was her only adornment.

"Gardener," she said, but she was not looking at the Gardener. Her eyes were fixed on me.

"Wilvia," the Gardener cried. "You're pale, tired. Why are you all alone? Where are your companions?"

"They had to go," she gestured, her eyes still fixed upon Gretamara. "A long, long time ago. Who . . . how . . . ?"

The Gardener motioned to me to be seated, remaining standing herself to observe the two of us. "You recognize yourselves?"

"Myself?" Wilvia stood. "She's younger than I."

I shook my head. "I've been living with the Gardener since I was twelve. People who live there don't age very fast. One named Ongamar has been a bondslave on Cantardene since she was twelve, and bondslaves do age. There are four more of us."

"As I told you," the Gardener said to Wilvia.

"I know you told me!" Wilvia took a step away, her cheeks burning with quick, hectic color, her eyes shifting restlessly, her voice shrill. "Being told is one thing. Confronting oneself, after all these years . . . Oh, Gardener. When I saw you, I thought it might be my children! Or Joziré!"

"You know your children are well, for you and your friends left each of them in a safe place, did you not?"

"Yes," she whispered. "My friends and I . . ."

"But where are your companions? They should be here."

"Gone," said Wilvia, taking a deep breath. "They had to go to Tercis to take their child. They weren't supposed to be gone for very long, but when they started back, they realized they were being followed. They sent a message here, to the ship, to let me know why they hadn't returned."

"I need to see," said Gardener, moving through the garden. I rose to follow her, but Wilvia stayed where she was.

"Gardener, there's something wrong with her," I said, as we went from the garden into another ship corridor.

"Isolation is wrong with her," the Gardener said angrily. "Isolation, and grief. Her children were taken away for safekeeping, her husband also, a pair of Gibbekot were her only companions. We didn't mean for her ever to be left alone!"

A door opened, and we went through into a control room. The Gardener turned to the right, to the communications room. "Access message from Prrr Prrrpm and Mwrrr Lrrrpa."

"Message accessed." Two faces appeared on the screen.

The Gardener said. "Prrr Prrrpm and Mwrrr Lrrrpa. Message!"

The larger Gibbekot said, "Wilvia, we can't come back to you just now. We have placed Falija in foster care, as planned. As we were leaving Tercis, we detected someone following us, which means we have to lead the followers away. We knew it was a risk. Have patience. We will return to you as soon as possible . . ."

The screen went blank. We returned to Wilvia.

"You've been alone since they left?" cried the Gardener.

"Alone, yes. I know it seems longer than it really has been. I still have books to read. There's plenty of food. Sometimes I spend days just watching them, out there, wondering at them. They've been almost wiped out over and over, but they don't remember a thing . . ."

"And no one has come here at all?"

"Sometimes in the nights, I've wakened, thinking I've heard the gate. It makes a kind of liquid sound, you know, like water, flowing, but nothing happened except for the sound. I'm sure you're right, that no one knows the ship is here." She sat down again, closing her eyes and trembling. "Tell me it's time to go?"

I got up and sat beside her, putting my arm around the queen. "You will not be left here alone again," I said, staring directly at the Gardener as I said so.

"Quite true," said the Gardener. "If the two of you will give me just a day or to so I can make sure everything is . . ."

"No," said Wilvia. "Enough, Gardener. Years in the first place I was taken, years in the second and third. Almost a year, maybe more, in this place. I am beginning to think I have died and am only imagining being alive! I'll go where you go, or I'll go through the way-gate to Tercis."

The Gardener sighed. "No doubt that will do as well, though by this time the way-gates may be swarming with K'Famir."

"We can be sure there's no one in the gate-room," said Wilvia. "You put a sensor in there."

"And you left Lady Badness behind on Chottem," I said. "I doubt she's let anyone come through."

"Lady Badness?" asked Wilvia.

"Lady Nepenthe, Mistress of Forgetfulness," said the Gardener, with a twisted smile. "A talent we share. Mankind gave us that talent, they wanted us to have it because they needed it themselves. I have used it regularly on the villagers in Swylet. Lady Badness will have used it on the men in the cellar who saw all that treasure and forgot it even while they were looking at it. But it's a human thing, and it's not likely to work on K'Famir, though . . . who knows? Very well, we'll go to Tercis, and you two will wait for me there while I go to B'yurngrad by other ways."

Wilvia stood, shaking her long garments down around her. She stood proudly erect as though stretching herself upward.

"Don't you need belongings of some kind?" I asked.

"I need nothing," she said, with a smile that trembled into tears, "save to leave this dreadful place."

She followed us back the way we had come. The door opened on an empty room. The door slid open. We moved quickly to the shining gate and went away.

We Margarets Assemble/
on B'yurngrad

I, Naumi, was at the academy when Jaker commed me
from the office of Poul-Jaker's import-export company,
to say their sales rep Stipps had returned with the bondslave they wanted. Her name, he said, was Ongamar. She
did speak several languages, and sewing had indeed been
her livelihood. Though he had been directed only to find
her, matters on Cantardene were extremely volatile, and
since her life was at risk, he had taken the liberty, which he
hoped would be forgiven, of rescuing the poor woman.

"Where is she?" I demanded, after a moment's awed
appreciation of this folderol.

"He brought her here," said Jaker. "But we can be
with you shortly. It seems appropriate to let her rejoin
her . . . other family members."

I set out to report this development to everyone else,
wherever they were, just getting out of bed or bathing or
having breakfast, and in a very short time they commed
from the gate to tell me we had visitors. When I arrived
there, so-called Stipps bowed, saying:

"You're looking well, Naumi."

"Thank you, sir," I replied. "I rather expected to see
you. Just at the moment we're very busy. Is this the lady?"

"Ongamar. She has important information about the
ghyrm. I know you're very busy, but do you feel it would
be worth your while for the two of you to find out

precisely what our enemies are up to just now? I know the Gardener and Lady Badness have been otherwise occupied. It would only take us a moment."

I laughed, not from amusement. "If the lady is willing, I am willing, Mr. Weathereye. Flek, Jaker, will you be host for me? See that everyone has breakfast, and we'll be back shortly."

"You *know* him," said Jaker. "What did you call him?"

"A nickname. From my youth. I'll tell you all about it when we return . . ."

Ongamar was small and somewhat bent, as though by habit, but her eyes snapped as she looked at me. I hustled the other two past the gate guards and returned. Mr. Weathereye took us each by the hand and we . . . traveled somewhere.

We very gradually coalesced not far from a trio of towering . . . what? Smoke. Fire. Sullen darkness lit with livid flame. Dweller, Mr. Weathereye told us without words. Drinker. Darkness. They were immense, and we were nothing, a huddled, small, muttering form. Ongamar and I knew that humans spoke many languages: dead ones, live ones, artificial ones, extraterrestrial ones. Mr. Weathereye had a wide variety of mutters to pick from, and esoteric nonsense in several tongues slipped from his mouth.

"What is it saying?" demanded Drinker of Blood.

"Just babble," replied Dweller in Pain. "Some prelinguistic source has been carried into space by a more advanced race, and their Members have ended up here. Ignore it. You were telling us about Cantardene . . ."

Darkness replied, "We found the copy! The one to be killed. It got away through a trade duct! I howled for the source to come, but the copy got away and took our machine with it!"

"It doesn't matter, does it?" said Dweller.

"What do you mean, it doesn't?"

"You don't need the machine because you don't need the duct. You're getting the raw material directly from Earth through Chottem, aren't you? That supplier, what's his label?"

Darkness snarled, "D'Lornschilde. And he overcharges us."

Dweller continued. "That doesn't matter either. When our people conquer Chottem, as we will, we'll get it all back."

After a pause, Darkness muttered, "I suppose you'll say it doesn't matter that the copies are named Mar Gar Et. A ghyrm told us about the Mar Gar Et on Cantardene, one coded On Ga Mar. The ghyrm said there was another Mar Gar Et on B'yurngrad, one coded Mar a Gi. They're copies, and copies are dangerous."

"That is dangerous," admitted Dweller.

"Why? Why dangerous?" asked Drinker.

"Dangerous because of ancient oracle!" cried Dweller in Pain. "All Quaatar know when seven roads are walked at once, Quaatar end. Frossians too, most likely. And K'Famir. This oracle goes far, far back in history of great Quaatar race."

Darkness nodded ponderously. "This is why we look for copies. We found more! One Mar Gar Et in Fajnard. One Mar Gar Et on Tercis, where Gentherans were seen! That's four."

"Four can't do anything," said Dweller.

Darkness said sulkily, "The Mar Gar Et that got away on Cantardene knows about ghyrm. If she talks to Gentherans, she'll tell!"

Dweller laughed, a fume of smoke and licking blue flame. "Even if she tells Gentherans everything, I say, again, again, it doesn't matter! Five copies, six copies, doesn't matter. It's too late to help the humans, because very soon there will not be any humans. There are enough ghyrm piled up on Cantardene that we can start dropping them on Earth right after we test them on B'yurngrad."

Our substance became rigid and manifested a foggy mass rather like a huge ear.

"B'yurngrad is our test. We will drop enough ghyrm to kill every human there. If one of your Mar Gar Ets is on B'yurngrad, there will be one less copy. When B'yurngrad is dead, we scoop up the ghyrm and take them to Earth."

Our muttering little form eased away, losing shape, losing substance, becoming nothing. Ongamar and I felt solid soil beneath our feet, looked up to see the sky, the building where we were all staying at the academy.

"You will be going to B'yurngrad almost immediately," said Mr. Weathereye in a strange, far-off voice. "Perhaps I will see you there."

"Where did he go?" asked Ongamar in a strangled voice.

"God knows," I said, then surprised myself with a blat of nervous laughter. The episode had been ridiculous, but I was sweating, my teeth were clenched, my stomach felt as though I had swallowed an anvil. Ongamar was gray, shuddering, tottering. I took her arm to support her, and she leaned as though to hold me up. Perhaps I needed it. So propped, we entered the building and found the common room where Flek and Jaker were with Mar-agern and Margaret. Gloriana, Falija, and Bamber Joy arrived almost immediately. Margaret provided us with cups of strong coffee—from the new coffee plantations on the Southern Isles—and we made halting conversation while we waited for Ferni. When he arrived, I introduced Ongamar, adding, "Mr. Weathereye says she has vital information."

"He thinks so," Ongamar said. "I have seen ghyrm being made, and he thinks I should tell you about it."

Then she told us a story. It was obviously one she had told before, for she told it without hesitation, almost matter-of-factly, while giving us far greater detail than I, for one, felt was necessary. Several of us had to leave the group to stand breathing deeply in the open window.

"That's why the genetic match," cried Flek. "They're made from human beings."

"Assuming the little creatures I saw were a kind of human, yes," Ongamar agreed.

"At least the ghyrm bodies are," said Ferni.

"Is there anything to them but bodies?" Caspor asked.

Flek said, "Something, yes. Something that processes information, remembers, reports. Not a brain, exactly. More of a computer with only one program."

"So if the flesh is mostly human," said Jaker, "where does it get its motivation? That has to come from somewhere else."

I asked, "Ongamar, did you ever detect anything from your parasite that felt human?"

She considered. "Not really, no. If I delayed giving it what it wanted, it punished me. I suppose humans might have that reaction, but the ghyrm was that way all the time. It wanted blood and pain, only that. It didn't eat, smell, touch, or look at anything else. It wasn't interested in anything else. If it had been human, surely it would have . . . wanted some variety, wouldn't it?"

We spoke of this for some time. I did not want to discuss the other thing. I did not want to think about the other thing, but finally we ran out of anything more to say about the ghyrm, and I could not hesitate any longer. I told them what the cabal planned to do, first on B'yurngrad, then on Earth. "When they have killed every human on B'yurngrad, the Mercans will scoop the ghyrm up and repeat the process on Earth itself."

There was a long, deadly silence before Flek cried, "But that's ludicrous. This cabal—it sounds like monsters out of a fairy story! Shadowy beings of total terror. Surely they have families, children that they care about. No living thing could be that . . . that uncaring. That bloodthirsty."

"You would not say that if you had been there," said Ongamar harshly. "If there was anything but cruelty inside the K'Famir on Beelshi, it didn't show. And they don't care about their own families. Their women are for amusement or breeding; their daughters are for sale or disposal; their sons are turned into copies of their fathers. Living creatures are valued only for their usefulness, and if they aren't useful for anything else, they become useful for the young males to use in perfecting their skills of torture in their malehood schools."

"But we don't understand why," I said, sounding plaintive even to myself. "We feel we need to understand why."

Margaret responded. "Naumi, I strongly suspect they don't need a why. When one considers violence and cruelty, the whys seem to get lost. During my studies on Earth, I had to watch accounts of human history, and I can't count how many times I saw and heard some human cry out, 'But why do they want to kill us?' People of one color killing another. People of one religion killing those who followed another. People of one language killing those who spoke another. Sometimes just people rioting, killing anyone, because they couldn't stand the lives they had . . ."

"We don't do that," cried Flek, obviously distressed.

Margaret said, "You personally may not, but humans do. The only difference between the human race and the Quaatar is that humans in general believe those who do so, do so in error, and they urge penitence. When I studied the Quaatar language, I learned they believe avoidance and regret are signs of weakness. You can't convince them they're wrong because right and wrong aren't part of their vocabulary. Male Frossian and K'Famir are like that, but so are some humans."

A silence fell. My old friends gathered around me.

"Remember Grangel," said Caspor. "He was sort of Frossian."

"He was," said Flek, beginning a chain of reminiscences. I knew what she was doing. Trying to talk us into calm.

I said to the others, those still strange to us, "Why don't you go on over to the commissary and get something to eat? Ongamar looks like she could use both food and a lot of sleep."

Margaret and Mar-agern chivvied them out. Though Glory and Bamber Joy looked rebellious, they were too well mannered to object. The six of us continued talking. The others returned and scattered in various directions to take naps. Later that afternoon, when Ongamar and Margaret came back into the common room, they found me sitting there alone.

"Was your discussion valuable?" Margaret asked.

"Possibly," I said, feeling a quick, almost furtive smile cross my face. "Our old talk road has yielded a plan, and Flek has made certain adjustments to her machinery. There's one rather large detail to be sorted out yet, and given that uncertainty, one hesitates to say how valuable the discussion may have been. We'll be ready shortly, however. You need to tell your people to prepare. We're leaving for B'yurngrad!"

Those of us who assembled at the way-gate to B'yurngrad included Ferni and Ongamar, all those who had arrived through the gate from Fajnard, plus Caspor and Flek to see us off. Some of us had climbed and some of us had been hoisted; all seemed to have greeted the experience with grim resolution rather than any sense of adventure, except perhaps for Ferni. Ferni was the perennial adventurer, and I could tell that M'urgi was very much on his mind. Ferni, Mar-agern, and I carried armor, knives, and the components of the newly calibrated anti-ghyrm machine, as well as weapons ready for use. The others bore lighter packs of supplies, and Falija rode on Bamber's shoulders.

Caspor said for the sixth time, "You understand, we have no idea where on B'yurngrad the way-gate will come out?"

I gritted my teeth. "Caspor, we know. We intend to use the gate to get on planet, then we'll contact the Siblinghood and have them pick us up."

"If they're reachable," said Ferni in a surly voice. "Which they were not when I left there."

"You can always go back by ship, the way you came," I suggested through still-gritted teeth. There was entirely too much repetition going on. I have never liked repetition.

Ferni growled, "There's a two-day difference. Even if we can't reach the Siblinghood, we ought to be able to . . ."

"Stop arguing," said Flek. "You could emerge in wilderness somewhere, which is why you're all wearing locators, so the ships with the heavier machines will be able to find you."

"Let's get on with it," snapped Margaret. "You're saying the same things over and over, and we've already waited extra time for them to recalibrate this equipment . . ."

I threw her a grateful glance. She winked at me. I thought how odd it was to wink at oneself.

"Keep in mind the machines aren't thoroughly tested," said Flek. "The running time on the prototype is short. With these new settings, it'll burn itself out even sooner . . ."

"Right," I said, almost shouting. "We know, Flek. We know there's a risk, but Margaret's right, we've talked it to death."

Checking our weapons, Ferni and I went first through the gate, while Mar-agern, cradling her weapon somewhat apprehensively, brought up the rear.

We emerged between huge stones into a rock-walled, grass-carpeted corridor that was open to the air above us. A few paces away, the corridor split into two. The right turn brought us to the sister gate, the pale one that would lead, if Caspor was correct, directly to Cantardene.

"Well," said Margaret, "I guess we don't have to use that one. Ongamar's already been rescued."

"Oh, yes, indeed," said Ongamar.

I pointed in the other direction. "That way."

We squeezed through the very narrow opening to the left and

came out between the boles of two huge trees at one edge of a small,
sun-stippled glade. On its far side, a narrow opening showed us grasslands freckled with hide-covered tents, smoke skeining above them
into a calm and cloudless sky. In the opening between glade and
grassland, facing us, a woman sat enthroned, with a considerable
company of armed tribesmen squatting at either side.

"That's M'urgi," said Ferni unnecessarily.

"How did she manage to be right here?" I marveled.

Ferni shifted the weight of his pack. "She probably went night
walking, saw us coming out here, decided to meet us."

"Night walking?" asked Margaret.

"You know. It's an out-of-body thing."

"I don't know, but it doesn't matter." She leaned to one side, de-
positing her pack on the ground. "Naumi should wait, I think, but
Mar-agern, Ongamar, we three should introduce ourselves."

Ongamar chirped, "Might as well."

"No time like the present," said Mar-agern, dropping her load and
weapon.

The three women walked toward the enthroned M'urgi, who was
staring at them in total astonishment. The rest of us followed, getting
just close enough to hear what went on. For a moment M'urgi looked
past the women at me, then at Ferni, then back at them, standing up
and moving toward them as they neared, gaze moving steadily among
them.

"Who?" she asked.

Ongamar said, as we had rehearsed: "We were twelve years old.
The proctor found out I wasn't a two-three-four . . ."

"He said our family was fine," grated M'urgi.

Mar-agern cleared her throat. "We weren't fine, though I didn't
know it until I was twenty-two. We were supposed to be headed to
Omniont space . . ."

"They asked for people who knew Mercan languages," said M'urgi.
"I paid no attention to it."

"I paid attention," said Mar-agern. "I offered my talents, for what
they were worth. I ended up a bondslave on Fajnard."

"Ah," breathed M'urgi, turning to Margaret. "And you?"

"I said yes to Bryan," she said flatly.

After a moment of wide-eyed silence, M'urgi asked, "Where was it he was going? Tercis, wasn't it?"

"Tercis," Margaret agreed. "A Walled-Off called Rueful. I've been there ever since."

M'urgi shifted her weight. "How about him, back there? He looks like . . ."

"Naumi's one of us," said Mar-agern. "He got split off when Ongamar did. He had his sex changed somewhere along the line. He grew up on Thairy. We thought he should wait while we introduced ourselves since he's a little less believable and has gaps in his memory."

"So there's five of us?"

Margaret took a deep breath. "Actually, there have to be two more, seven altogether."

"Seven. How interesting. Lately, I've been dreaming of that number. Those dreams reminded me of one I had years ago of meeting myself here, at this place." She paused, swallowed deeply, managing a casual tone. "I see Ferni's with you."

"He came to Thairy to get help finding you."

M'urgi glanced at the packs the others carried. "What've you brought?"

Mar-agern replied. "Stuff to kill ghyrm. As many knives as we can carry. We have a prototype ghyrm eradicator, and there are bigger ones coming that they can't fit through the way-gate. The Siblinghood should be bringing them by ship."

"I hope it's enough," said M'urgi, with a grim smile. "This morning, a friend of yours arrived to tell us the enemy has declared war."

"Friend?"

"An old guy, Weathereye. He brought a member of the Siblinghood with him, Sister Ella May. She knows Margaret, and he knows Naumi, or so they say. Let's go sit down in my tent and find out where we are."

M'urgi sent two young men running to pick up the packs Margaret and Mar-agern had carried as the others came forward, Falija lying across Bamber's shoulder.

There was a stir among the tribesmen.

"What is that animal?" M'urgi muttered.

"Not an animal. Gibbekot," said Margaret.

Mar-agern said, "Tell them it's . . . it brings good luck."

M'urgi turned and spoke to the tribesmen. Margaret and Mar-agern identified the speech as an intelligible dialect of Earthian with certain consonants blurred or missing: final l's that sounded like w's. R's that disappeared.

"Gibb ah cot," she said. "Come to hep us kill ghyrm."

I saw Mr. Weathereye standing to one side, a woman beside him. I went to meet him. "Mr. Weathereye. And you must be Ella May. You got here ahead of us."

"Ah, well, my boy. Difficult times almost always produce unexpected encounters."

"Turns out there's more to me than meets your eye, Mr. Weathereye. Or less, perhaps. Did you know I wasn't meant to be a man at all?"

"You sound angry about that."

I hesitated. I was angry about that. Anger was sometimes useful, but might not be at the moment. "Yes," I admitted. "Why?"

"Camouflage," said Mr. Weathereye. "If the human race is to survive, we needed seven of you with a broad variety of experiences. Some were enslaved, some were sovereign, some labored, some thought, some were hidden, some were put in unexpected places, some were left out in plain sight to see if anyone showed undue interest. You were camouflaged."

"If the human race is to survive," I said. "All that, dependent on making a man of me?"

"A man of you; a shaman of M'urgi; a spy of Ongamar. You'll have to decide for yourself whether it was worth it." Weathereye sighed. "Since we and the Gentherans have another agenda for humanity, we think it was worth it, yes. We're opposed to your being wiped out. We hope to restore humanity to itself."

"And how we are to do that?"

"You know how, Naumi. The Siblinghood told you how."

"By finding someone who knows everything. Perhaps by walking seven roads that are one road, all at the same time."

"Exactly. And by doing so, regain something humanity lost a long time ago. Something the Gentherans say you once had that was stolen from you."

"By whom?"

"The Gentherans believe it was done by the Quaatar, but they admit they're extrapolating."

Over Mr. Weathereye's shoulder, I saw my companions entering one of the tents. I said, "Later," in a significant tone, and went to the tent where people were seating themselves around the barely smoldering fire with M'urgi. Our small group was surrounded and outnumbered by a silent circle of squatting tribesmen, obviously alert to every word that was being said. Mr. Weathereye and Ella May came to stand inside the tent flap.

M'urgi dipped her hand into an open jar, threw a handful of something onto the fire, and said through the resultant fragrant smoke, "Mr. Weathereye spoke to us before you came. He says that K'Famir, Frossian, and Quaatar ships are about to attempt eradication of the human race, starting here on B'yurngrad. He says it is not a reasonable enmity but merely an old grudge the Quaatar have against humans, one so old they've forgotten the reason for it."

"What are they going to do?" asked Margaret.

"They're going to drop ghyrm all over the planet."

"No," I said flatly. "They must not be allowed to do that. A few days from now, it might not matter, but right now, it's absolutely necessary that they drop the whole load, whatever that amounts to, on top of us, right here!"

"Why?" cried M'urgi, eyes wide with shock.

Ferni answered. "We brought a prototype machine with us, M'urgi: first one out of the factory. They're sending larger ones, but right now, this is all we've got. According to Flek—the armaments person—this one will cover about thirty square jorub, not much compared to the surface of a planet."

"No, but it's still a considerable area," said M'urgi. "Enormously larger than our encampment. You want them to drop the whole load here because we can destroy the whole load if they do?"

"Exactly!"

"How do you propose to get them to do that?"

Stubbornly, I repeated myself. "I don't know how, but somehow it has to happen. We're hoping they bring along many high-ranking members of their societies to watch us being slaughtered. We have to figure out how to make them do that."

Silence. Furtive looks, one to another.

"You mentioned the Quaatar?" Mar-agern murmured, staring at Margaret. "What was it we learned about the Quaatar, Margaret?"

Margaret rubbed her forehead, thinking. "They believe themselves and their language to be sacred. They consider it blasphemy for any non-Quaatar to speak their language. Also, all other races are considered to be food sources."

M'urgi asked, "Who would be doing the actually ghyrm-dropping? Themselves, or would they hire someone?"

Mr. Weathereye said, "There's no way of knowing who they plan to do the actual task of pushing the things out of the ships, but my guess is that most high-ranking Quaatar, Frossians, and K'Famir will want to see it."

"Yes, my friends and I thought that likely," I said. "Torturers like to watch; it's no fun if they can't see and hear what's happening."

"We know where they make the ghyrm," said Ella May. "On Cantardene. Should we ask the armorers to get one of the big machines onto Cantardene? And on Earth, just in case? And on every colony planet?"

"The big machines are later," I said. "I'm talking about now. Within the next few days, right, Weathereye?"

"They have to go to Cantardene, load, and return here. Within the next three or four days, yes."

A silence fell, broken by Falija, who yawned widely, licked her fangs, and said, "If the trick is to get all the high-ups on board, you'll need to insult them."

The tribesmen started, stared at Falija, then shouted, some of them half standing.

"Sit down," barked M'urgi. "Ah say dis is good luck. You heah? Dis is voice of good luck. You heah me!"

"What do you mean, insult them?" asked Margaret, when the tribesmen had subsided into sulky, shoulder-humped silence.

"Say something nasty to them in their own language," said Falija. "Margaret is right. It's blasphemy for another race to use the sacred Quaatar language; the K'Famir have a ritual language as well; and Mar-agern says she suffered the penalty for speaking Frossian to a

Frossian. Insult them in their own languages. It will make them very, very angry."

"She's right," cried Mar-agern. "Remember, Margaret, we studied Quaatar! I—we were almost the only ones who did, but we learned to read it and speak it!"

"I remember," said M'urgi. "Though it seems another life ago. What do we say to them, and how? Does anyone even know where they may be found?"

"On their home planets," offered Ella May.

"Too far, tactically impossible," I said.

No one said anything. I ground my teeth and told myself to be patient. "Think about it. We'll come back to it very soon."

Mar-agern turned to M'urgi. "There's a real mob outside."

M'urgi nodded, tiredly. "One tribe came, two others followed, four followed them. It turned into a horde. They're still arriving. Every group has one or two ghyrm-eaten ones. I've been killing ghyrm for days, but I had only one knife . . ."

"Open the packs," Ferni said. "There are a hundred knives. Give the knives to whoever can best use them."

"Everyone's getting off the subject," Margaret complained loudly. "What blasphemous message could we impart? Falija? Weathereye?"

Mr. Weathereye pursed his lips. "It doesn't need to be subtle. Something along the lines of 'The holy Quaatar people are a crock of shit' would probably do."

Margaret made a face. "I don't remember learning a word for excrement . . ."

Falija said, "*Umfa!,* with a click at the end. That's the Quaatar word for shit. It was in my mother-mind. Gentherans use it all the time, whenever they're talking about the Quaatar."

"While you're deciding that, I'll distribute those knives," said M'urgi, rising and leaving the tent. The tribesmen followed her, and Ferni followed them. I watched through the tent opening as the sheathed knives were distributed, carefully, with many warnings.

Ella May came over to me, saying, "It's possible the Quaatar have some kind of sensors planted here. If not them, then one of the others in the cabal. They've been looking for Margarets. They might have some kind of spy eye around nearby, something they would pick up an insult through . . ."

I turned, alerted by this new possibility. "There's detection gear in the red pack. Use it if you like."

"We two can work on the message," said Mar-agern to Margaret.

"Short, simple, and insulting," said Falija.

"I don't know any way to be useful," Gloriana whispered to Bamber Joy. "Do you?"

"Sure," he grinned. "Keep out of the way, don't whine, and be available if anyone needs a hand. I think we might also eat something, because breakfast was skimpy this morning, and we're growing . . . people."

Gloriana retrieved her pack from outside, and retreated with Falija and Bamber John to a back corner of the tent, where they made themselves comfortable on folded blankets while eating food they'd brought from Thairy. Nearby, Margaret and Mar-agern scribbled and crossed out and once, surprisingly, giggled.

"The blankets smell like hay," Gloriana said half sleepily. "Like the Howkel kitchen. It would be really nice to be finished with this and not have to worry if there's anything you didn't do or haven't done right."

"I think we're all going to be finished very soon," Bamber Joy said. "It feels like everything is coming to a close. It's a kind of sad, autumny feel, like when the last leaves come down, and you know that's it. No more life until spring."

Gloriana started to say something, then caught herself. I knew she had been wondering if spring would come, this time, even though all three of them sounded quite relaxed and sleepy about the whole thing. They were young. They hadn't had that many hard times, but I wasn't at all sure we were ready for the storm that was coming. There were too many ifs: if the machine worked; if the Quaatar people got angry enough; if they dropped the ghyrm only here instead of all over the planet; if the Siblinghood really got the big machines to them in time . . .

Margaret came over and sat down beside me. "Naumi," she said. "I want to thank you."

"For what?" I sat up, astonished.

She frowned, shook her head. "Confession, Naumi. I once let someone do something for me that was against his own best interest. I've spent my life since trying to atone for that. I've been ashamed. Rueful. All my life." She looked up, shook her head. "There've been joyful moments, sure, but in the main, rueful says it.

"And then I met Mar-agern. She's me. She's lived a totally different life, but she's me. And M'urgi, and Ongamar, and you. They're your lives, but they're mine, too. I . . . isn't it weird we all think of as ourselves as me . . . Well, Margaret's identity has not been as unworthy as I always rued it being. And I have you and the others to thank for it."

I took her hand. It was my hand. I knew that hand.

"You're welcome," I said.

I Am Gretamara/on Tercis

On Tercis, the Gardener preceded Wilvia and me, Greta-mara, out of the way-gate and onto a sloping forest floor. Gardener led us slowly downward, stopping momentarily to say, "The outgoing sister to the gate we just used is up there, between those two rocks." She pointed to her left toward another group of stones. "It goes to Fajnard."

"Where are we going?" asked Wilvia.

"Down the hill to the home of Margaret Mackey."

The way was not long. We arrived before a small house, set among the trees, the far side of it looking out across a rocky shelf into great distances of valley and hills. The door of the house was broken.

"Beasts," snarled the Gardener. "Let's see what dam-age they have done!"

I thought it looked even worse than the great house in Bray had looked. Inside, belongings were strewn about, cupboards were open, doors half off their hinges, the bed ripped apart. "What were they looking for?"

"Nothing. They didn't find the woman they were look-ing for, or the Gibbekot they thought would lead them to her. They destroyed out of the spite that was built into them by their designers. It is an old viciousness not un-known to humans: 'If you can't prevail, destroy.'"

"We can set it in order," I said firmly. "Will we be stay-ing here?"

"Only briefly," said the Gardener, looking through the stores in the tiny kitchen. "There is food here enough for several days. Show no light at night. Margaret's daughter lives just down the hill, but the house is empty now, for the families who lived on outlying farms are staying in Crossroads to be safer. The hunters went through the valley like a scythe, and they badly frightened the people here."

Wilvia asked, "Margaret's family? Do they know she is gone?"

"They know she and two children went off into the woods before the happening. They are concerned, but not terribly worried. Perhaps Margaret will be back before they have time to be anxious."

"And we?" I asked.

"For the moment, you stay here. Wilvia, if anyone comes near, take off your diadem. If anyone approaches, say you are Margaret's cousin. You arrived after the damage was done, and you have your daughter staying with you to help. Meantime, I must make sure that several other people arrive here very shortly. The Gentherans expect it of me, and of themselves."

I went outside with her and stood on the rocky shelf that overlooked the valley. Only peace. Far down the road, a buggy. Someone going home to a farm to feed the animals and to be sure they had water. There was no sign that the hunters were still here.

The Gardener read my thoughts. "Likely they are assembling near B'yurngrad, where all the other Margarets are together, making an easy target. Farewell, but only briefly, Gretamara." She walked into the woods, dissolving herself onto a shining road that led to B'yurngrad.

I Am Naumi/on B'yurngrad

After I, Naumi, had done everything possible to help anyone needing help, I lay down in M'urgi's tent and closed
my eyes. The world seemed to be spinning, and I could
not convince myself it wasn't, or that time wouldn't stop,
or that we all wouldn't die . . .

Falija, who had been lying between Bamber Joy and
Gloriana, suddenly sat up and made a loud, spitting noise
of annoyance.

"What?" demanded Gloriana loudly.

I opened my eyes and listened.

"We don't need to insult the Quaatar directly," said
Falija. "We just need to let the Quaatar think they've been
insulted."

Bamber Joy yawned. "Is it any easier to do that than to
actually insult them?"

"Of course," said Falija. "All anyone has to do is go
somewhere frequented by K'Famir or Frossians—or
Quaatar, though that's harder, because they don't usually
associate with other races—and tell someone, loudly, that
he or she was recently on B'yurngrad and there was a great
meeting of Earthians and Gentherans who were insulting
the Quaatar in Quaatarian. We can throw in the Frossians
and the K'Famir at the same time. We need someone who
isn't either Earthian or Quaatarian to do it, of course . . ."

"I'll go get Grandma," said Gloriana.

I sat up, still tired, but interested. Margaret returned with Gloriana and Mr. Weathereye. One might have known!

"Interesting," he murmured. "We need only let them overhear someone saying that Gentherans and Earthians on B'yurngrad are assembled in one place insulting the Quaatar."

"The person saying it can't be human," insisted Falija.

"How about someone like a K'Vasti?" asked Mr. Weathereye, with a peculiar smile. "Who heard it from a Hrass? Thank you, Falija. That is completely doable."

They told me later the place they picked was Gilfras Station, the same nonplanetary transshipment point that Ferni and I had used as a rendezvous not long before. K'Famir and Frossians were numerous there, as were a dozen other races, including the inevitable Hrass, huddled in small groups in corners, trying to be inconspicuous. One of them, however, was accompanied at his table by a loud, drunken K'Vasti, who shouted, "What do you mean, all the Gentherans were talking Quaatar. Nobody talks Quaatar."

The Hrass murmured unintelligibly.

The K'Vasti bellowed, "Called the Quaatar *umfa!* I don't understand that."

The Hrass murmured, gesturing.

The K'Vasti brayed with laughter. "Oh, that's a good one. Gentherans and Earthians, having a contest on B'yurngrad to see who can write the most insulting poems about the Quaatar in Quaatarian!"

The Hrassian leaned forward, saying something urgent.

"Not only the Quaatar? Insults in Frossian and K'Famir as well. Ha. Where's this contest being held?"

The Hrass murmured, swinging its nose in what might be presumed to be laughter.

"At a tribal camp northwest of Black Mountain? Out in the wilderness. Guess they figured nobody would hear them out there . . . Whoops . . ." Abruptly the K'vasti rose to his feet and staggered off toward the toilets. While all eyes followed him, the Hrass, as was customary in his race, quietly slipped away. Seemingly the K'vasti had had far too much to drink, for he, too, did not return.

• • •

M'urgi and I sat wearily at the foot of a tree, looking off across the campgrounds when Mr. Weathereye returned in the company of a Hrass, who promptly took off her nose and emerged as Ongamar. "It's done," he said. "We put on the performance. I played the K'vasti. Ongamar played the Hrass. We were both totally believable in the roles."

"I've recruited bellowers to shout insults, just in case the insulted need convincing," said M'urgi in a weary voice. "What do we do now?"

"We wait," I said. I glared at Weathereye, who from my point of view had a lot to answer for. "You did say the word would travel rapidly?"

"You may rely on it, my boy," said Mr. Weathereye. "It's taken us almost a day to get back, so we did our little playlet that long ago. In half a day, the word was widespread among K'Famir and Frossians, and the first of them to hear of it would have been in touch with at least one Quaatar, if for no other reason than to enjoy Quaatar agitation. The moment even one Quaatar knew, all the Quaatar would know." Weathereye shifted a bit uncomfortably. "I do hope we're ready?"

"The machine's in the center of the camp, and we've checked the new calibrations," said M'urgi. "One of us is always beside it, an hour at a time so we don't risk falling asleep."

"I sent word to the Siblinghood," I said. "Told them we knew the origin of the ghyrm. The K'Famir have been ordering a lot of big weapons from Omniont space, and the Siblings intend to substitute our machines, remotely controlled, for several of theirs."

"How long will it take?"

"Some time. The machine isn't even finished yet," I replied, searching the skies above them. "What do you think they're doing right now?"

"The K'Famir, the Frossians, and the Quaatar? I think they're working themselves up into a killing rage," said Weathereye. "I think they have an interesting synergy going between themselves and their gods. They planned originally to test their ghyrm-drop quietly, without fanfare, hoping nobody much would notice until B'yurngrad was uninhabited, but if they're sufficiently insulted, they won't care who notices."

"It's a pity we have to have all this destruction," said M'urgi.

Weathereye nodded. "Oh, my dear lady, I do agree. From my own personal point of view, however, I'd prefer that humans not go extinct, and I know of no peaceful way to prevent it. That possibility is really a question for races like the Gentherans, who love complex ethical issues. When is it justified to kill or destroy? In self-defense, or never? I, of course, can only think what humans think, and I think we're justified in getting rid of ghyrm along with certain bacteria and viruses."

"Look there," said Naumi, pointing toward the sky. "There, a little east of south, fairly low. That's a ship."

"Go warn Mar-agern," said Mr. Weathereye. "And the tribes."

"There are lookouts," M'urgi said, not moving.

A mournful horn sounded from a nearby rise, a sound echoed almost immediately by dozens of others, from all directions. M'urgi sat up straight and closed her eyes. I knew she was sending herself to the place Mar-agern sat next to the machine, finger on the start button.

M'urgi sighed, relaxed, came back to herself. "Everyone's alert," she reported. "Mar-agern's ready."

M'urgi and I rose. The ship came toward us, four others descending into view behind, followed in turn by four more.

"They're huge," I breathed. "I've never seen anything that size! If they're full of cargo . . . full of ghyrm . . . no way we're going to be able to . . ."

"Nine of their biggest ones," said Mr. Weathereye in a faraway voice. "The ones they use for cargo shipments."

"Our people will need our help," I said, starting away down the hill, M'urgi trailing behind me, only to stop as we saw a red-robed women approaching.

"Naumi," she said. "M'urgi. What have you set up here? A trap?"

I had the very strong impression I had seen her somewhere before. "The dragonfly I dreamed about," I said abruptly to M'urgi. "The dragonfly. She was the pilot!"

"So I was," said the Gardener. "I bring you greetings from Gretamara, and Wilvia. They await you in Tercis. I ask again, what have you here? A trap?"

"We calculated it would be a trap," I confessed, suddenly convinced that I ought to tell her everything that was going on, without reservation. "We have a machine to kill ghyrm, and we thought if we could get them all dumped on top of us, we could wipe them out here. But look at those ships? If they're stuffed full of ghyrm, it will take too long . . . and the power source is limited. If they pour those things out, hour after hour, there won't be time. There's not even time to get word to the Siblinghood."

She looked up at the huge ships, her eyes veiled. "One never foresees everything," she said. "One can only do the best one can, with what one has to work with." She spoke over my shoulder, to Weathereye. "I came to tell you that the Gentherans have found the place on Chottem where a man named d'Lornschilde has been keeping the human children from which the ghyrm are made. They are being transshipped to colony planets as we speak. Also, they have found the ships he used to bring them to Chottem, and those are being destroyed."

M'urgi said, "Yesterday, I would have considered that to be good news! Before I saw that armada overhead . . ."

"Your plan must proceed," Gardener said to me. "I am told you did well as a tactician. I have faith in your plan."

"M'urgi, Naumi," said Mr. Weathereye. "You haven't met the Gardener. She is the one who has kept Wilvia safe, and she is a friend of Earthians and Gentherans. She has been in this business from the beginning."

"Then you know about the seven roads," I said.

"I do," she replied. "Which we'll soon be walking."

"Provided all goes well." M'urgi grimaced.

"Well or ill, still we must walk," said the Gardener. "It took us over a thousand years to find a sevenfold road that would exist for a little while in the now, the here! It took two hundred years to arrange the emergence of the walkers and another lifetime to prepare them. We have only hours to accomplish what it has taken over a millennium to arrange. Even if this world ends, we must walk."

The horns moaned again, more loudly. "Where did they get those horns?" I cried. "They sound like the end of the world."

"They're from old umoxen," M'urgi said. "The tribes find the bones and horns on the prairies, where an umox has died. The older the animal was when it died, the longer the horn and the more mournful the sounds are. Look! They're dropping cargo."

The ships were sowing seeds into the sky, dark specks that drifted downward. At the center of the encampment, something hummed briefly, faded to a drone, then to a hissing sound, like waves on a shore. Out on the prairie, tribesmen danced, waving their spears and insulting the Quaatar at the top of their lungs.

Thousands of the specks were drifting toward them, becoming visible as circles of pale tissue supported by radiating arms, the whole almost transparent, floating downward like tiny parachutes. Looking straight up, we could see the ghyrm dwindling into the distance. As the falling creatures passed an invisible line, the tissue darkened, the arms curled. When they were close enough to be seen in detail, the arms were shriveled, the disks of pale tissue were darkening. The last few dozen feet, the things crumpled and fell, littering the ground around us, unmistakably dead.

Out on the prairie, the tribesmen went on shouting, and I cursed my own stupidity!

"Tell some of them to pretend to die," I shouted. "I didn't think of it until just now. The Quaatar will stop dropping the ghyrm unless they can see some of us dying!"

M'urgi ran down the hill, spoke urgently to one of her messengers, who sped off. I, watching from the hill behind her, saw the message relayed to others who fled away in their turn, a spiderweb of messengers, radiating off into the chaos of the camps. A few men near the hill began to stagger, clutching first their throats, then their bellies, falling and writhing with arched backs and histrionic faces. A few more, not too many, then others, while some of the first played dead.

The ships turned in a wide swoop that brought them lower, and lower still. The sun faded behind the rain of ghyrm. I looked down to find I cast no shadow. Well, if I could not see the sun, likely the creatures in those ships couldn't see what was happening on the ground! I tried to estimate how many ghyrm were being dropped. Millions. Millions. "How many could they have had?" I cried to Mr. Weathereye. "Each of those, a human life?"

"Shipload after shipload of Earthian children, year after year," said the Gardener from behind me. "Plus we understand they've learned to clone them. We can't stay to see the end of this, however. It's time for you and the others to go. Round them up quickly. We go to Cantardene, then to Chottem, swiftly through a gate on Hell, and so to Tercis, where the others are waiting. It will take us less than an hour."

"Who?" I asked. "Who's going?"

"Everyone who came with you from Thairy, plus M'urgi," said Weathereye. "It's time. What we do, we must do now, while the road is open and the enemy fully occupied here."

We were fetched variously: M'urgi, reluctantly, from her station amid the battle, where she had been whispering orders to tribesmen; Mar-agern from her post outside the tent, weapon at the ready; Margaret from her seat by the fire in the tent where Bamber Joy, Falija, and Gloriana lay asleep. I found Ferni in the thick of the shouting, and dragged him away as he protested. Meantime Mr. Weathereye found Ella May and gave her certain instructions.

"No time for you to pack anything," the Gardener told M'urgi, who was reaching for her kit. "Bring weapons only." We joined the others, who were moving quietly through the clearing. One by one, we squeezed between the two big trees and lined up outside the shining gate, all of us keyed up, nervous, frightened, each of us trying desperately not to show it.

"The first stop is Cantardene," said the Gardener. "We may find no one at the Cantardene gate. Their ruling class is in those ships above. In case they've left a guard, Naumi, Ferni, and M'urgi should go first, armed and ready, the rest to follow."

We came out in the mausoleum on Cantardene, empty of any living thing. I heard voices from outside and went to look out over the slanting bulk of the huge door that rested on one corner and one hinge. Outside in the plaza, a few soldiers knelt at a gambling game beside the stone of sacrifice.

The Gardener came up beside me, pointed to the tall stone, and said, "That is empty, too. Whirling Cloud of Darkness-Eater of the Dead is elsewhere. Now the next gate. Cover your faces and walk slowly, for the floor is covered with charbic root."

We waded through the layer of powder, lifting our feet high and holding kerchiefs over our faces. We emerged into darkness. The Gardener said we were in the cellars of Bray, and only the light from the farther gate illuminated our way. Iron grilles were fastened, but the weapon Mar-agern carried broke the locks. The next way-gate took us to a steel room. We walked on a steel floor that rumbled to our footsteps, through the opposite gate and out behind a tangle of vines opening into a forest. Down the slope was a snug little house with smoke coming from its chimney.

"Home," said Margaret, her voice breaking. "Gloriana, Bamber Joy, it's home."

We Margarets Walk

I, Margaret, led the way down the hill, the others in a straggling line behind me. As we approached the house, I saw shattered fragments of my door piled to one side of the porch and a blanket hung where my door should have been. I shivered. The apple tree at the corner of the house was bare. Winter had come while I was away.

Gloriana pushed the blanket aside and called into the house. "It's me, Gloriana."

A glad outcry from inside startled us all. "Gloriana, is Bamber Joy with you?"

Bamber Joy cried, "Mother!" and thrust past Gloriana.

When Gloriana and I entered, we found the boy on his knees beside the couch, his head pressed to the woman's breast. Gloriana shifted from foot to foot nearby as the woman reached a hand toward her.

"Gloriana," she cried. "Oh, sweet, dear girl-child! Oh, poor thing, you haven't any idea who I am, do you? And you both look so much like Joziré, and so tall!" She turned to me, tears covering her face. "Are you the one of us who cared for them?"

"I'm Margaret," I faltered, momentarily witless with surprise. "I . . . I thought Gloriana was my granddaughter . . . adopted, that is . . . Bamber Joy, well, he was left with Abe Johnson . . ." My voice trailed off, and I simply stared. So Wilvia was Gloriana's mother. Which meant that I myself was Gloriana's mother?

"I had to leave them both," she said, tears still flowing down her face. "The Gentherans thought the children would be safer if separated, from one another and from me. The Thongal were paid by the Quaatar to wipe out the royal house, so they had to be hidden . . ."

"Then you're Wilvia," said Gloriana. "And you're my real mother? Which means Bamber Joy is my brother, and my grandmother was my real mother, sort of. And her daughter was my foster mother, sort of . . ." She turned to me. "Grandma, I thought it couldn't get any more confusing!" She stopped, seeing Gretamara for the first time. "Another Margaret?" she croaked. "That's all seven of you, isn't it?"

The new one introduced herself, and I saw Gloriana put on the concentrated expression she wore when she was determined to get something right. She was memorizing them, us. I did as she did, looking at each of us in turn. Gretamara was twentyish, very gentle-looking; Mar-agern and M'urgi looked to be in their early or mid thirties, both brown from the sun and very muscular.

Wilvia couldn't be mistaken for anyone else, not with that diadem, a little older yet. Naumi was about that same age, with wide shoulders and a strong jaw, and a deeply curved mouth. Then Ongamar, smaller and thinner than the others, appearing only slightly younger than I was myself. Some forty years' apparent difference between oldest and youngest (though one really shouldn't count Gretamara), and one of us male . . .

A shadow on the glass caught my eye. Through the window I saw Ferni standing in deep shadow on the porch, unseen by the others and wearing an expression I could not read. His eyes kept going from Wilvia to M'urgi and back again, like an avid cat watching two birds, unable to decide between them.

I turned to the Gardener, and demanded, "How did you do it? You are the one who did it, aren't you?"

She patted me on the shoulder. "The Gentherans did it, Margaret. As to how? Well, I can hypothesize: Say they picked a woman who had twins in the family. Twins in both families, as a matter of fact, father and mother. Suppose they encouraged the original fertilized egg to split, making two, and then again making four, and then again, making eight . . ."

"But there are only seven of her!" Gloriana said.

"One died," I said. "My mother had twins, on Mars. I was one. The other died. What, was she supposed to be a spare?"

The Gardener shook her head at me, and I flushed. "And, I suppose you're saying the other six were taken away, somewhere."

Falija said, "Where they could have grown up just as you did, Grandma, in mirror worlds that reflected everything in your world, each of them thinking she was Margaret, until one was nine, until three more were twelve, until the last three were twenty-two."

"How?" demanded Gloriana.

Gretamara answered. "It may have been in the same way I grew up, Gloriana. In a place that exists but is not real. In a world that may be observed and interacted with, but is not actual. A virtual world, as Earthians would call it, that ended for each of us when we entered a real one. In the end, there were seven real worlds: I was on Chottem; Naumi was on Thairy; Ongamar was on Cantardene; Mar-agern was on Fajnard; M'urgi was on B'yurngrad; and Margaret was on Tercis."

"And Wilvia?" Gloriana asked.

"Here and there," Wilvia herself said. "B'yurngrad first, then Fajnard, then other places, and finally, I was in Hell."

"That is one of the ways it could have happened," the Gardener said. "The how is less important than the why. It was done to save your people."

"Because we owe them a debt," said Falija very solemnly. "From long, long ago. Because humans don't have racial memories, and they need them very badly. And there's only one place in the universe where man's history can be found, and that's with the Keeper."

Mr. Weathereye, who had been leaning in the doorway, said, "We are told the Keeper is an observer, not a creator. It is eternal and omniscient but generally uninvolved; one who hates being bothered but enjoys puzzles and riddles. The last people to bother it were the Pthas, who came to the Keeper with a request. The Keeper honored their request, but then it put itself in a place where no one could bother it again unless one person could walk seven roads at once. It sounds childish in the saying, like a nursery rhyme. Just as nursery rhymes mean far more than the children who chant them know, this meant far more than it said. It was anything but childish in the doing.

"Twice before, the Siblinghood had found seven way-gates that made one road. Stars and their planets move, you know; they don't stay in the same relative positions forever. Consider the movements of billions of stars in a galaxy. Consider how difficult to find seven of them, well in advance, mind you, that will make the one configuration. The First Order of the Siblinghood tried, and most of them died in the attempt. The Second Order tried and was forestalled. Now, this hour, the Third Order of the Siblinghood makes the attempt once more. Here are the seven walkers who are one, and before this hour passes, they must walk the roads, find the Keeper, and ask it to give humans back the racial memory the Quaatar took from them when they were barely human."

"Now?" said Wilvia in weary but dignified disbelief.

"Now, while the vile races are preoccupied elsewhere," said the Gardener. "Before that machine runs out of power and they start thinking again about finding and killing you. We must not take an extra moment. Come now, just you seven and Falija. We must go back up the mountain to the way-gate into Fajnard. Mr. Weathereye is no doubt needed on B'yurngrad, and the rest of you must stay here."

We moved, though unwillingly. Wilvia and I seemed least disposed to go, I imagine for identical reasons. Each of us felt we had just returned home, to those who mattered most to us. As we went, I noticed Ferni still standing at the corner of the house behind us, staring after us as though his whole life were being torn away.

The Gardener walked among us. "I have something to tell you. Some of you may not return from this effort. If a choice were to be made among you, Margaret, how would you feel about that?"

I looked at her with disbelief. "You mean, some of us may end up dead."

"It's possible."

I laughed, shaking my head. "If you had asked me that a week ago, Gardener, I'd have said fine, so long as I don't have to go on ruing all the mistakes I've made."

"And now?"

"When I saw Wilvia's children and realized they weren't cursed, as mine had been, when I saw the others . . . I don't have to rue my life. Together, Margaret has not done badly."

"So you're no longer willing to die, to escape your regrets?"

"If you have to choose one to live, choose someone younger."

"And you, Ongamar?" the Gardener asked.

Ongamar whispered. "Oh, I've looked forward to forgetting what I've seen for such a long time . . . don't choose me to live, Gardener."

"And you, Mar-agern?"

"I have no thoughts on the matter. I've never thought of doing away with myself, but if a choice had to be made, I wouldn't be afraid . . ."

"And you, Naumi?"

He turned to stare at her. "I have wanted only a few things in my life, only one of them greatly. Since that is not to be, further life seems rather barren. There are others here who will live more happily than I."

"And you, Wilvia?"

Wilvia smiled. "My dearest wish . . . one of them, at least, has been granted. My husband and children were, are far more important to me than my own life. If Joziré were still alive, he'd have returned to me! And if he is truly gone, and I can save my children by letting them go, then I will let them go."

The Gardener whispered, "And you, my child, Gretamara?"

She looked up, far up, where the stars reached their light across the universe. "My life has always been in your hands, Gardener. I'm content to leave it there."

"And lastly, you, M'urgi?"

She replied truculently, "Well, don't expect me to march off to battle singing hymns of martyrdom! A few years ago, when life was smoke and dirt and desperate interventions that didn't work a lot of the time, I'd have been more willing. But lately? I have something to live for. I saw Ferni's face back there. He's waiting to see what happens . . ." She stopped, looked up, tears glinting at the corner of her eyes. "Even so, well, even so, if my death helps the human race . . . the shaman taught me to die."

We had arrived at the way-gate and the Gardener lined us up

while glancing at the horizon where the first faint light was showing. "We don't know how the Keeper will respond. It may refuse
us. It may grant your request but take your lives in payment. Nothing of the little we have learned of the Keeper tells us it will do
this, but it is a possibility. It may let all of you live, which is also a
possibility, and if that is so, when this is over, we will have much to
rejoice over."

I, Margaret, heard a sigh from someone, a deep breath from another, the slight shifting of our feet, but nothing more.

"Very well, one at a time: you, Margaret, go seven roads, and stop
just inside the way-gate we just arrived through, up the hill, here on
Tercis." She pointed up the hill, toward the black pool hidden in the
forest. "You, Wilvia: six roads, stopping on the world where we found
you, just inside the gate. You, Gretamara: five roads, stopping at Chottem, and you, Ongamar: four roads to Cantardene . . ."

"The K'Famir . . ." Ongamar said between clenched teeth.

Weathereye patted her shoulder. "The Siblinghood has warriors
between every pair of gates. They will not stand aside for any but you
seven."

Gardener continued. "M'urgi goes three roads to B'yurngrad;
Naumi, two roads to Thairy; Mar-agern, one road to Fajnard, each of
you stopping *inside* the gate. As the Third Order discovered, as Naumi's friend Caspor discovered, when the roads among these gates are
shown in a particular two-dimensional plane, they make a seven-
pointed star with a seven-sided space at its center. On star maps, that
space is light-years in width and empty. We have reason to believe the
interaction of the way-gates around it make the space much smaller
than it looks.

"When you are each in your assigned gate, the center of that space
will be to your left. I have seven timepieces here, to hang around your
necks. When your timepiece says zero, you turn and walk to your left,
through the side of the way-gate."

"And what will happen?" I, Gretamara, asked.

"I don't know," said the Gardener, extending her arms in a gesture
of relinquishment. "Those of us who planned this and brought it to
fruition believe someone will await you there, but this is a blind road
with an unknown end."

Voices murmured a response. The Gardener put the timepieces around our necks. Gretamara reached up to kiss the Gardener's cheek. Ongamar pulled herself erect, and said, "I walk for an end to pain and an end to Cantardene."

M'urgi cried, "If I don't return, give my love to Ferni . . ."

Naumi murmured, "Same message, to the same recipient."

"Enough poignancy," said Mar-agern. "This new brain of mine is equipped with all sorts of hope. Farewell for now."

We went into the pool, I first, since I had the farthest to go. Light and dark, light and dark, counting, being sure I went six gates. Behind me always a quivering surface, shimmering with something that was not light. It might as well have been the sound of dry leaves rubbing together, or the feel of a draft under a door, the smell of old ice, the rasp of a file on the skin of my hand, any sensation or none. At last, the exit to Tercis was ahead of me.

I turned to my left and checked the timepiece the Gardener had hung around my neck. The others would all be in place by now, all of them waiting for zero. I concentrated on breathing quietly until zero came. When it arrived, I stepped through the wall of the way-gate, then stepped again, the scintillating specks that pulsed around me fading with each step: fading, fading, gone. Ahead was nothingness, and I walked into it, wondering desperately if I would be able to keep a straight line.

After what seemed a considerable time, I heard someone calling "Margaret?" into the silence of the place. Naumi's voice, deeper than the others'. "Ongamar?" he called.

A sound, perhaps an answering voice. I started to go toward it, then stopped. Better just go on walking. After a while, he tried again, off to my left. "Margaret?"

"Over here," I called. "Should I come toward you?"

"No!" he said. "Not until we're all within sight of one another."

Calls came from left and right and we walked. The sounds came nearer. The nothing below our feet became something. A surface. I saw Gretamara emerging from a dark fog to my left, and beyond her, M'urgi. On my right, Naumi appeared, then Ongamar. Between M'urgi and Ongamar, two shadows came toward us, emerging as Mar-agern and Wilvia.

"Keep walking until we can touch one another," Naumi called.

We walked for what seemed a very long time. We could see one another, but the distance stayed the same. The floor seemed to roll away beneath us like a treadmill that welled up from some point in the center of their circle and flowed out continuously, keeping us in the same place.

M'urgi called, "Stand still a minute."

We did so, watching her. She stood very straight, concentrating, and a trail of light shot upward from her forehead, high above us all. I thought of her leaning upon the substance that fills the universe, which separates matter and transmits light and knows and remembers everything.

"Shut your eyes," M'urgi called. "Hold out your hands. We're right next to one another."

I reached out my hands, grasping at others I felt on either side, the three of us tugging and sidling as we connected with the rest.

"Now," cried M'urgi. "Open your eyes but hold on tight."

We stood in a circle only a few steps across. In the center, suspended in space, I saw a little creature, legs crossed, a book on its lap. Across the pages words ran endlessly from right to left, left to right, top to bottom, bottom to top, interweaving with one another.

At the same time I saw this, I saw what the others saw, just as I had used to sense as they did when they were part of me. M'urgi saw a pillar of fire, words of smoke pouring up through it. Naumi saw a tree, its roots extending into the depths beneath us, its higher branches beyond his sight above, and every leaf a journal. Wilvia saw a dragon with jeweled scales, each one engraved with a history. Ongamar saw a stone pillar reaching from the beginning to the end of the universe, with little beings swarming all over it, carving words. Mar-agern saw herds of creatures in a meadow, each of them reciting the story of a people. Gretamara saw an anthill, each ant carrying a grain of sand on which was engraved the chronicle of a living race.

I was the eldest. I swallowed deeply, and asked, "Are you the Keeper?"

It looked up from its book, out of the flame, out of the leaves, the dragon's eyes, the words on the stone, the meadow creatures, the anthill. "Think of it!" it said wonderingly. "One road is seven roads, walked simultaneously by one creature. How did you manage that?"

Wilvia smiled at the dragon charmingly. "Only through great sacrifice, Keeper."

"Patience," said M'urgi.

"Labor," said Mar-agern.

"And torment," Ongamar offered.

Naumi shook his head. "Only by doing our duty, but the how is not as important as the why, Keeper—"

"—which is to heal our people," interrupted Gretamara.

The little man hummed, the ants hummed, the tree hummed. "I have not been near creatures in a very long time. The rule is, one must have a bell and a gate, but I thought I'd made both very difficult indeed. Yet here you are. What have I to do with you? Who are you?"

"The human race," I said.

M'urgi added, "You have our history in your smoke."

"Oh, yes," it said, peering at us with myriad eyes. "You're not very old, and you're quite ignorant."

"We are imperfect," said Gretamara to the ants, who had flown together in a swarm before her. "We are lacking. We have no memory of what we were, and thus no reach toward what we may become. We desperately need to know our past, but in all the universe only the Keeper has the racial memory of mankind."

"That is true. I have the histories of every race, every kind, all the move-about, reproduce creatures, and also those of others that have lived without moving or creating. I have the secret lives of stones and the memories of stars. I have the initial impetus, the births of all galaxies, the deaths of a good many. I have millions of years of some races and a few moments of others. Their souls are here."

"Their souls?" faltered Ongamar. "Of every creature?"

"Is each of you a creature?" asked Keeper.

"That's a trick question," Naumi said quickly. "We couldn't have found you if we each were a separate creature. No, all of us are one creature."

"I know that," said Keeper. "All of you are human, and billions more are human, and all humans are one creature, sharing one soul. Yes. And one for birds, and one for the dinosaur . . ."

"One soul for the dinosaur?" asked Mar-agern. "Then one soul for the umoxen, as well?"

"Oh, an enormous, ramified soul for umox, going back to the very beginning of life on its planet. Umox arose from a star race that went before, as the soul of Bird arose from the soul of Dinosaur. The soul of the scurrying lizard inhabits every warm-blooded winged thing, the soul of the brachiating gibberer inhabits the soul of man, and the soul of great singers and sages inhabits the soul of umox and chitter-lain . . . Oh, yes. Keeper has seen this. Keeper has perceived it."

"But no . . . no soul for each of us?" asked Margaret.

The man turned his head, the tree turned a twig toward her, each leaf an eye that seemed to look into her heart.

"Each of you?" the Keeper asked. "One brief life of limited experience, barely informed? Full of false starts, marred by misinformation, rife with regret? Much given to embarrassment and sorrow, lit here and there, if you are lucky, with delight. Do you really want to spend an eternity being only that? What of the lives you've lived within your minds, and what of your other selves in other worlds? Each time you make a choice, your universe splits. One of you does one thing, one of you does the other. One of you goes on to fulfillment and joy, the other is mired in pain and anxiety, each in a separate world, but they are all you . . .

"All the fragments, all the sundered parts come here, melded then into a single me-ness with all possibilities realized, all pains endured, all joys delighted in, one mind containing all that it was and could have been or hoped to be or imagined itself to have been!

"You need not go back to fix it, Margaret. In some world, you did fix it! You need not go back to unsay it, Mar-agern. In some world, it was unsaid. Ongamar, in some life it was untouched. And when you are assembled, you will know it, in that everlasting instant . . ." Keeper paused, stared, as if dreaming.

"An everlasting instant?" whispered Naumi.

"That instant when the whole being that is you is aware of itself as a whole and dances together upon the green meadows of eternity in a dance that seems endless . . ."

"Only that instant?" asked Wilvia longingly.

"Long enough for you to *know*! Once you know, you know. Once you are complete, you are complete forever. And all that, every moment of every day of every lifetime, makes only one leaflet growing on the sprig of humanity. Still, that leaflet is one I keep forever . . ."

Everything became very still. All movement stopped. The Keeper swelled in size: "The Gentherans sent you here, did they not?"

"The Gentherans are our friends," said Gretamara.

"Keeper knows that. You are here because of them, and because my daughter, the Gardener, has espoused your cause. You are here because she and her friends conspired so that nature's laws might be broken without disobeying me. Ah, she is clever, my daughter. Wily, too. And now she sends you here, telling you what?"

"Telling us nothing," said Wilvia in her most queenly voice. "Except that we may die in the attempt. We have agreed to that, even if this plea is fruitless. It is a chance we took to benefit our people."

Keeper seemed to ponder this before replying. "Who is to say the memory of all mankind would work for you as you believe it will? What do other races think? Perhaps they would prefer you fade and die, becoming only a footnote in my journal. Who would speak for you?"

"We would," said someone outside the circle. Margaret looked over her shoulder. "Falija," she murmured.

"Falija," the little person affirmed. "Together with a number of our people, Keeper." She murmured their names as they came into view, a great many of them, gathering into a ring around the seven. "My parents, their Gibbekot and Gentheran friends, their friends of other races who have found humans to be worth the saving."

Naumi tried to see into the fog, but saw only shapes there. He heard a chittering, a birdsong, a bray that was half cow, half horse, the chatter of people.

Falija said, "My people have watched the human struggle for thousands of years. Without the means to be good, still they struggle to be so. Seeing such a struggle, any ethical and powerful race would do what could be done to ease it. Such a powerful race would say, 'Other races have a racial memory, can we not provide man with one of his own?'

"We could try. Still, no matter how much truth it might contain, the whole would be a lie. Should we ask a race to gamble its future on the basis of a lie? Only Keeper records only truth."

"True," said Keeper.

Falija went on, "In the great history of the Pthas we read of the delegation they sent to the Keeper. They found you, they spoke to you, you spoke to them. They asked a boon, you granted it. Will you do as much for Genthera?"

Keeper seemed to look elsewhere, into infinite distances. "Keeper might not will to do it for Humans, who are silly infants, meriting very little. Keeper might not do it for the Gibbekot or their Gentheran kin, for even they are not yet fully grown."

A sigh breathed through the circle, the tiniest moan.

"But," said Keeper, "Keeper would do it for umoxen, whose soul is far older than Genthera." He stared at Mar-agern, and Mar-agern returned the stare, astonished.

Keeper turned to M'urgi. "M'urgi, Keeper would do it for chitterlain, whose ancestors moved among the stars a billion years ago. Ongamar, Keeper might do it for the humble Hrass. Naumi, Keeper might do it for the gammerfree, and Margaret, for the hayfolk Dame. And you, Wilvia and Gretamara, Keeper might do it for a Trajian juggler upon whom one took pity and the other avenged. Yes, all of them are older, and far wiser, than mankind.

"You were kind to their people," said Keeper, focusing on each of us in turn. "There will be a price to pay, of course, but Keeper is fond of their people, and so would be kind to your people."

Into the wordless and shocked silence, Wilvia spoke. "We thank you, Keeper."

The beings who had surrounded us had vanished, drawn backwards into the great wind that came all at once, loosening the grip of our seven pairs of hands and wrenching us apart. I, Margaret, felt them blown away into the howl of a black storm, bodies incapable of movement, wills paralyzed, minds in confusion, scraps of perception driven into an unimaginable otherwhere, each of us holding, only briefly, the same clear, perfectly accepted thought.

Well, this is death, but we have done what was to be done.

And yet I was still somewhere, with the Keeper, now in a shape I have tried since to remember and cannot. It spoke into my ear: "Don't forget what your father told your mother, Margaret. About what he was trying to do on Mars . . ."

"Father never really knew what would happen," I cried.

"No. The Scientist does not know the result until it happens. You are part of its workings. I am the record it keeps of what succeeds and will be used again and what fails and will be excluded forever . . ."

And then, only silence.

On the world called Shore by the people who lived there, and Hell by those who didn't, the people woke one morning with a strangeness in them. None of them rose from their beds. They just lay there very quietly, thinking.

"Did you know we were humans once?" said one to his mate.

"I didn't know it before," she said. "We were humans when we came here on the moon. Except it wasn't a moon. It was a starship, a Quaatar starship."

"Do you think we are human now?" he asked.

"I don't know," she said. "If we're not, why do we remember being? I remember we gave up living in trees . . ."

"I remember we killed Earth," he said.

"I remember we were going up the river soon to cut trees to make a new town and build many boats . . ."

"I remember we have to make room for more . . ."

Outside the house, some of the people were moving about. The town leader came out of her house and sat down on her stool, by the door. Each day the leader did this and the people came with their questions.

They gathered now.

The leader did not wait for questions. "Mika, Dao, Tinka. We have made a nasty at the creek. It smells bad. Nothing grows there. Dig a pit inside the forest, put all the nasty into the pit, and cover it with earth. In time it will feed trees. Choun, Bila, Fet, consult your minds and make a plan so no more nasty happens, then come tell me." The leader fell silent.

"Today we plan to go upriver and make a new town," said one of them. "We will cut trees to make room for more?"

"Not today," said the leader. "Today we count people. Today we count how many trees each person uses every year. Today we count fishes for each person, mollusks for each person, freshwater for drinking. Today we begin to learn how many people can live on this world without ruining it."

"What shall the rest of us do?" someone asked helplessly.

"Today," the leader said, *"you all stop making room for more and take time to remember."*

On Tercis, the Gardener waited, her head bowed. Falija had gone. Time stretched thin, the sound of its tenuity becoming intolerably shrill. No one returned. At last, with a shuddering sigh, the Gardener entered the way-gate before her.

On Fajnard, she found the Siblings guarding the way-gate. "All quiet, ma'am," they reported.

"Come with me," she said.

On Thairy there were other Siblings to join the group, and again on B'yurngrad, Cantardene, and Chottem. They stepped into the last gate but one and emerged into the buried starship on the planet called Hell. A naked woman lay on the metal floor, faceup, hands folded upon her breast. Gardener squatted beside the body, laying her long hands on the woman's face and neck.

"Who is it?" whispered one of the Siblings.

Gardener shook her head. "I don't know. I've never seen her before, but whoever she is, she's alive."

One of the strong Sibling warriors, Sister Ella May Judson, stepped forward to throw her cape across the person before lifting her in her arms. Together they went through the last gate, back to Tercis.

"Will you stay here, Gardener?" Ella May asked. "I was born in this place, and there is a house nearby you can use."

The Gardener said, "We've already been to the house, Ella May, and people are waiting for us there. Carry her for me if you will."

Ella May murmured, "It is Margaret's house, my Grandmother's house. I will stay with you, Gardener. You will need someone to fetch and carry, and I know Rueful."

"That would be a kindness. Thank you, Ella May." She turned to the other Siblings. "The rest of you may return to your own places, with my thanks."

Ella May carried the woman's body down through the woods, and from below them, someone called, "They're coming."

Bamber Joy and Gloriana were awaiting them on the porch, as was

Ferni, sitting on the step, staring at Ella May and her burden, his face
wet with tears.

Gloriana cried, "Is that you, Ella May! Who's that you're carrying?"

The Gardener replied, "Gloriana, we don't know."

Ella May laid the quiet body on the couch.

Bamber looked at the face somberly. "Not our mother, Glory. Not
Grandma, either."

"I think . . . I think it does look a little like Queen Wilvia," Glory
said. "And a little like Grandma, too. From those pictures we have of
her, when she was a lot younger."

Ferni had come in from outside. Now he spoke in a lost, weary
voice. "Is there something of M'urgi there. Something of Naumi?"

"Both, I think," said Glory. "Did the Keeper put her back together?" She turned to the Gardener. "Is that what happened? You
never mentioned that!"

"No," the Gardener confessed, with a low, self-mocking laugh.
"With all our thought, all our planning, we never thought of that. We
recited the old stories, over and over, 'Seven makes one, seven makes
one,' each time thinking of the road, never considering the walkers."

She knelt by the couch, searching the face before her for Gretamara. This woman was older than Gretamara, though much younger
than Margaret. She had lines of pain in her face, as Ongamar had
had, though not as deep. Her hands were hard and strong, as Mar-
agern's had been. The mouth . . . Naumi's mouth, and M'urgi's. The
skin was not as dark as Mar-agern's, but darker than Gretamara's.
The hair was longer than Mar-agern's, shorter than Wilvia's, but she
had Wilvia's eyes . . . which had just opened.

"You're awake," cried Glory.

The woman turned her head. "Gloriana," she whispered. "And
Bamber Joy. My . . . our children."

"Gretamara," said the Gardener.

"Gardener," she said.

"Grandma," said Ella May, with certainty.

"Why . . . Ella May. How strong and well you look, my dear."

"Naumi?" said Ferni. "Naumi?"

"Oh, damn, Ferni. Yes, I'm here!"

"M'urgi? Wilvia?" he whispered.

But her eyelids had closed, and she slept.

"Well," said the Gardener, rising to her feet. "I wonder if Keeper did anything besides reuniting Margaret."

"Oh," cried Glory. "You don't know. Well then, you must not be . . ."

"Not be what, child?"

"Human," said Bamber Joy. "You must not be human, or you would know!"

"Just tell me what it is I should know!"

Bamber Joy said, "Just a few moments ago. Something happened. We all know things now. Things we never really knew before."

"It worked!" the Gardener said, marveling. "It really worked? I hadn't stopped to consult my source." She closed her eyes, after a moment opening them once more to beam at them.

Gloriana smiled at her, a bit tremulously. "It really did, Gardener. And we're all just the way Falija was when she got her mother-mind. We're all itchy and uncomfortable, because our heads are too full, and it's like trying to find our way around a strange house that has too many rooms with too many doors in it."

Ferni said, "Forgive me, Gardener, but is it true? You're not human?"

"Oh, Fernwold, of course not!" she said with some acerbity. "I am not human, and my colleagues are not human. We wonder at ourselves, coalesced, as we are, out of human hope and need and pain. We see, we speak, we are seen, we are heard, yet every thought, sight, word has been created for us by others. We have no creativity; we have no imagination; and yet we seem both creative and imaginative because we have such a vast grab bag of ideas and dreams to draw from. Each thought, plan, idea, notion is like a piece in an enormous jigsaw puzzle. At the end of time, they will all fit together to make a picture of mankind we have no conception of . . ." She stood up.

"In the meantime, we seem to have power, if it is only the power to take an idea from one mind and plant it in another, as a bird takes a fruit from a far, lone tree and lets fall a seed in quite another place. Old gods sometimes do that in their retirement. They become galactic social workers, self-appointed do-gooders."

Falija said from the doorway, "But that's only a lesser part of the truth, Gardener, because you can do things the other gods can't do. They can't move a material thing, but you can and do. You're Pthas, aren't you?"

Gardener looked up, for a moment seeming larger and older than she had ever looked before. "Why, how very perceptive of you, Gibbekotkin! Yes. I am Pthas. As is Weathereye, and Lady Badness, and a few more. The boon we asked of the Keeper just before most of us left this galaxy to go on to another, was that some of us be allowed to stay on, to take a new form and help others who need help. We had long contended against vile races, vile ideas, and we thought our experience would be valuable. The vile races we contended against are long gone. The vile ideas seem to be immortal."

Falija said, "The Keeper called you its daughter. And being Pthas would explain a lot of things, like how you knew about the Keeper. The Gentherans will be interested in that!"

Ferni had been sitting quietly in the corner, his eyes fixed on the woman they had brought from the gate, who was now struggling to sit up, staring wildly at him, and whispering, "Is that you, Joziré?"

"Yes he is," said the Gardener. "Though he still does not know it. Lady Nepenthe has moved in and out of his life several times, but there will be time to talk of that later."

Ferni almost growled, then stood very tall and demanded, "One thing will not wait until later! What's happened on B'yurngrad?"

Gardener was startled. "I don't know. Mr. Weathereye went back to see the end . . ."

"I did see it," said Mr. Weathereye.

They turned to see him leaning in the doorway. "The three races continued dropping ghyrm," he rumbled. "More and more of them at a time. They had unlimited numbers of them aboard, and the persons on the ships were drunk with destruction. It seems Naumi and his talk road had had what Caspor calls 'a hunch.' They had changed the calibration of the instrument so that it covered less surface area but reached much, much higher. The ships came lower and lower, so they could watch the carnage below them, oh, so well acted by the tribesmen, who writhed and twisted and screamed, then crawled away, recovering only to die again. They have a talent for dramatics, those men, born, I should think, from many generations of braggadocio around the campfires . . ."

"What happened?" shouted Ferni.

"We watched the ships drop down, watched the gauge on the fuel cell of the machine, dropping as the ships did, almost reaching zero, and just as the machine approached the end of its power, the ships themselves dropped within range of it, and every ghyrm still on the ships died."

He heaved a great sigh. ". . . and not only the ghyrm."

"Not the tribes? The umoxen," we Margarets cried.

"Quite safe, lady. Not so, however, the K'Famir, the Frossians, the Quaatar on board the ships, for they died as their creatures died. You will remember the size of those ships? They were the ones the trading races use to carry huge cargoes plus huge numbers of crew and their families, and they were full to bursting with Frossians, K'Famir, and Quaatar who wanted to see us die. There might have been a million of them on those ships, the entire ruling class of three starfaring races. We had no idea they would do that . . ."

"We did," said I from my place on the couch. "Naumi did."

The Gardener peered at Weathereye. "But Ongamar thought they made the creatures out of human children!"

"They made them out of human pain," I said. "But it was themselves they put into the making! The tissue, the flesh, was most closely matched to human, in order to be able to attach to it, feed on it, but it wasn't the flesh that mattered! It was the bloodlust that moved them, and whatever will kill the ghyrm will kill those who made them as well." I lay back; my eyes closed; I heard them go on talking.

Gardener asked, "What has the Siblinghood done? They haven't started a war?"

Weathereye shook his head. "They had planned to ship a machine to Cantardene. Then the change happened, you know, the mother-mind thing. Everyone was very confused. When the confusion grew a little less, and when they saw what had happened on B'yurngrad, they decided not to do it. They've put the machines in storage."

The Gardener nodded. "Something in their history has moved them to patience. Wise leaders do not go to war with enemies, not even evil enemies, unless they have thought it through to the end."

Time went by on Tercis.

Gloriana and Bamber Joy went to Maybelle, Jimmy Joe, and Jeff, to tell them, and only them, what had happened. It took more than one telling, over considerable time, and once again Gloriana was accused of telling fairy tales. Despairing, Gloriana took Maybelle to visit the Margarets. Maybelle had tea with them, her, and they talked for hours. When Maybelle left, she still appeared confused and a bit teary, but she looked happier than when she had arrived.

Subsequently, in the Ruehouse in Crossroads, Pastor Grievy held a memorial service for Margaret Mackey, lost in the river while escaping from the bad men during the recent unpleasantness in The Valley. Gloriana and Bamber Joy had been unable to save her; but it gave them solace, they said, to dedicate the stone that was set in the cemetery, next to Dr. Mackey's, in her memory.

"And it's true, sort of," said Gloriana. "Our grandma is really gone."

The Allocation people on Tercis, following the acquisition of mother-mind and after lengthy consultation with the Gentherans, changed many of their assignment procedures. Most of those on Tercis had reacted to the acquisition of mother-memory with significant and positive personality changes, but some had proven to have a mental defect that made them impervious to history. Among the latter were Billy Ray and Mayleen, who together with Benny Paul, Janine Ruth, and Sue Elaine were moved to a new Walled-Off, created especially, as Jimmy Joe put it, "For them as are pigheaded, mule-stubborn, and thick as a post!" Jeff's brother, Til, was assigned to the same Walled-Off, with the understanding that he might receive, from time to time, a chance at reassignment. Trish was moved to a small Walled-Off created especially for people like her, where she could be contented and cared for.

Maybelle and Jimmy Joe agreed to foster Orvie John and little Emmaline while keeping their fingers crossed.

Ferni stayed on Tercis, spending much of his time with Margaret, though he didn't call her that. Or M'urgi. Or anything except you, or lady, or very occasionally, dear one.

Lady Badness dropped by one day and ran her hands over his head while the Margarets looked on.

"Who are you and where did you live your first twelve years?" she asked him in a chuckling voice.

"My name is Prince Joziré. I lived on Fajnard with my mother, the queen. We had to go into hiding. The Gardener took me, and also a girl named Wilvia. We went to B'yurngrad, to school . . ."

"And then where did you go?"

"To the academy, on Thairy. I forgot about Wilvia. Oh, how could I have . . ."

"Don't worry about it. How long were you there?"

"I was there for four years. I met my best friend there. His name was Naumi . . ."

"And then?"

"Then . . . I went to work for the Siblinghood, on B'yurngrad. That's where I met M'urgi . . . But they wouldn't let me stay there, I forgot about M'urgi, I forgot Naumi, I remembered my mother, and I remembered Wilvia, and we were married. We ruled the Ghoss together, for five years. We were expecting our first child, then the Thongal invaded at the behest of the Quaatar . . ."

"And then, after that?"

"I forgot about being the King of the Ghoss. I forgot Wilvia. I was taken into the Siblinghood, I went here and there, I found M'urgi again, and Naumi . . ."

I, Margaret, was crying very quietly while all this went on. After Lady Badness left, Ferni and I spent a great deal of time together.

Time went by on Cantardene.

Though bondslaves were still being imported onto the planet from Earth, the rituals atop Beelshi were no longer conducted, not there, not on any similar site elsewhere on the planet. No one was left alive who knew the procedures, the incantations, the purpose. The standing stones that had existed in all the sacred places began to fall to pieces. Beelshi itself was rumored to be a place of ill fortune, and no one went near the hill . . .

Except, that is, for Mr. Weathereye, who spent some time spying on a few surviving and exceptionally wealthy K'Famir. This surveillance eventually led him to the buried city of the Pthas. A short time later, Gentherans began arriving through the gate in the darkness of moonless nights, traveling to the buried city and taking away everything that could be taken—including all the K'Famir who had known where the place was—and burying the rest beyond finding again by any save themselves. After their final visit, they built an impenetrable wall inside the mausoleum, covering the door and joining the incoming to the outgoing gate for the lengthy time Caspor said this link of the one road would stay in place.

Time went by on B'yurngrad. The Siblinghood moved among the tribes in great numbers, pointing out the historical connections among death-and-honor religions. Those capable of understanding were let alone; those few who could not be reached went to the newly constructed Death-and-Honor Walled-Off on Tercis. Since Death-and-Honor religions were male inventions, almost entirely, so was the population male, almost entirely. So much had been learned from Tercis. For those impervious to history, only sterilization and quarantine are efficacious.

Inevitably, those among the tribes who knew the location of the great treasure hoard talked about it to someone who passed the knowledge on. This great trove, as well, was added to the wealth of the Siblinghood.

Time went by on Chottem.
Sophia summoned the people of Bray to a meeting and told them what d'Lornschilde had done. He was arrested, tried, and sentenced to be deprived of his tongue and sold into bondage in the mines of Cantardene. Saving aside some treasure to implement her own good works, Sophia added the balance of the riches of the House of Lorn to the wealth of the Siblinghood. Subsequently, Sophia met a very likeable young man of nonaristocratic family whose wooing she gently encouraged. When the leading families of Bray and Lorn looked askance, she did not seem to notice.

Time went by on Fajnard.
The Frossian underlings were touched by the same wave of ill

fortune that had taken their leaders. The planet no longer appealed to them. The world was too slow, too uncertain, the umoxen were increasingly reluctant to be herded. One day, as if by prior agreement, the Frossians began leaving Fajnard, waves of them. On the day the last of them departed, the Ghoss returned to the lowlands, and the umox hum could be heard to the outer edges of the atmosphere.

Very soon thereafter, on the heights of Fajnard, a great reception was held for the King and Queen of the Ghoss, long separated from their people, now returned as though from the dead, both somewhat changed, but recognizable. As the couple waited for the fanfare that would summon them to the high dais of the Council Hall, the queen turned to her spouse, rearranged the lace collar that fell in delicate folds at the throat of his velvet jacket, and said, continuing a previous conversation, ". . . I don't think my adoration of you is at all strange. Three-sevenths of me loved you to distraction already."

"True," he said, eyes fixed, for some reason, on the curls of hair around the queen's ears. "Obviously, your very best parts."

The queen smiled and blushed.

Trumpets sounded in the Council Hall. Footsteps clattered far away, down the hallway. Ferni looked into nothingness and the queen followed his eyes, wondering what he was hoping to find there. Answers?

"I was thinking about that fleet of ships above B'yurngrad. When those aboard died, the ships went into automatic orbit, the Gentherans boarded them and sent them into the sun. Everyone on Quaatar, Cantardene, and among the Frossian worlds knew what they had set out to do, but none of them knew what happened. The Gentherans won't tell them. So far as the vile races are concerned, everyone who set out to kill off humanity simply vanished. When asked about it by inquisitive members of other races, those in the Siblinghood merely say, 'Well, of course. What did they expect?'"

The queen smiled. "So, we have become nemesis. Not a bad thing, on the whole. And all Flex's armaments? Where are they now?"

"Stored. Carefully stored. Now we all remember what armaments lead to. As the Gardener said, beginning a war is easy. Any fool could do it and frequently did, but all of us now remember the kind of messes that came after. Instead of going to war, everyone is waiting to see what the vile races will do. Mr. Weathereye says it's possible they'll just dwindle away."

The queen turned to catch a glimpse of herself in the tall, gold-framed mirrors that lined the wall. Light splintered in the jewels of her diadem, swept in glowing rays across her silken robes, became trapped in the incredible cape crafted from cloth of diamond, Sophia's gift from the cellars of Lorn. She was Queen of the Ghoss. "Will we rule perfectly, Joziré? Will our people work together in perfection and joy?"

"Madam," he said, taking my face between his hands, "we will do our damnedest!"

He started the kiss, but I refused to let it end. Holding Joziré wiped out all recollection of old regrets, pains, and sorrows. I could not be grateful enough for several lives' worth of experience cased in one body still capable of this particular delight . . . And even these to be joined at the end, as the Keeper had told me.

The trumpets sounded again. We two stepped away from one another, faces flushed, fingers clinging, as ponderously, ceremoniously, the doors swung open. In the vaulted room beyond were the Gibbekot, the Gentherans, the Ghoss. Near the dais sat Falija, together with the Crown Prince and Crown Princess, Bamber Joy and Gloriana, who looked both determined and slightly embarrassed in their diadems and court dress. In the front row, by special invitation, were Maybelle, Jimmy Joe, Jeff, Ella May, and Sophia, with the young man she had decided to marry. Among the onlookers was a Trajian juggler with his wife; upon the rafters a flutter of chitterlain; in a corner, beside Howkel and his family, a scuttle of gammerfree. Peering through the wide-flung doors of the terrace, ranks of umoxen stood shoulder to shoulder, while upon the dais stood the Gardener, Mr. Weathereye, and Lady Badness.

Everyone present was there for the same reason. We were a cluster of organisms, experimentally working together to bring joy to Fajnard, hoping such joy could be become contagious and infect others beyond Fajnard, and perhaps, someday, spread to the middle of things and the edges of things. If not in this great experiment, then perhaps in the next one, or in the one after that . . .

The wide aisle to the dais was laid in soft, scarlet carpet. Upon the dais were two tall thrones. Smiling at one another and all those assembled, we rested our hand upon the hand of our love, and stepped forward into our lives.